# Banshee Series
# Books 1 - 6

Written by Sara Clancy

ISBN: 9781094784724
Copyright © 2019 by ScareStreet.com

# Thank You and Bonus Novel!

To really show you my appreciation for purchasing this book, **I'd love to send you a full-length novel in 3 formats (MOBI, EPUB and PDF) absolutely free!** This will surely make chills run down your spine!

Download your free novel in 3 formats, get FREE short stories, and receive future discounts by visiting www.ScareStreet.com/SaraClancy

See you in the shadows,
**Sara Clancy**

# Table of Contents

# Midnight Screams
## Banshee Series Book 1

# Chapter 1

Fifteen minutes had passed and Nicole still couldn't bring herself to knock. Her hand remained in the air, an inch from the wooden door, ready for the moment she finally scraped together her remaining shreds of courage. Nervous energy simmered under her skin and she bounced on the balls of her feet to try and work some of it out of her system.

"This is crazy," she said out loud to break the silence. "You can do this. You do it all the time. Knuckles against the wood in a rhythmic fashion."

She strained her breath through her teeth and said with all the casualness she could muster. "It's just Vic."

Hearing it out loud brought home how ridiculous she was being. She shrugged the tension out of her shoulders, put on her best smile, and knocked sharply on the front door. It swung open. The normal gentle squeak sounded like a gasping scream as it echoed through the bowels of the farmhouse. Nicole had never realized how well the drapes blocked out the honeyed light that normally filled the space. Drawn, only a soft glow managed to creep around the edges of the thick cloth, leaving the rest to the shadows. Her picnic basket's wicker handle dug into her palms as she twisted her hands around it.

"Hello?" her voice quivered. "Mrs. Morton?"

The house remained deathly silent. Nicole inched one foot across the threshold and craned her neck to glance around the living room. Nothing moved and her stomach began to twist into a painful lump. Clocks could be set by the Morton family's routine. It was fifteen minutes past midday on a Sunday. They should be in the middle of preparing their lunch right now.

A large amount of her childhood had been spent within these walls and she had never once hesitated to enter. But, as she looked around the familiar surroundings, something deep inside of her told her not to go in. Nicole flicked her eyes around the space, trying to pinpoint some kind of physical change that might be behind the tightening in her chest. Everything was just as she had remembered it, down to the deer statue with a chip in its right antler, and the cups Victor had made in their grade school art class. They had all leaked horribly so were used to decorate empty bookshelves instead. Nothing had changed. Still, she didn't want to go in. She didn't want to admit what was keeping her out.

"I'm just going to leave a note," she called out to no one.

As if in answer, the kettle began to whistle, shrill and sharp. Nicole strained to hear the slightest sound of movement. The kettle was the kind that had to sit on gas burners to work. There was no way any of the Mortons would leave it unattended. But the rest of the house held its silence, holding its breath as the high-pitched squeal continued. She bounced restlessly on her toes. With one hand still clutching the basket handle, she lifted her other to her choker necklace. Thin trails of beads dropped down from it as she twisted them around her digits. No one came. Nothing stirred.

The sound pressed against her skull like a metal weight. She adjusted her grip, feeling her thundering heartbeat as she twisted and untwisted her fingers. Muttering under her breath, she rushed through the house, the heels of her boots clacking against the wood boards. A large pot of meat stew was on the stove next to the kettle and it filled the kitchen with a warm, hearty scent. She placed her basket on the countertop and quickly switched off both burners. The kettle's cry drained away, drifting off until it finally died and returned her to the heavy silence. A cold chill worked its way down her spine and pooled in the pit of her stomach. She snatched up the basket again just to have something to do with her hands.

"Hello?" Nicole put a conscious effort into making her voice as cheerful as possible. "Anyone home?"

A sudden thump made her whip around. Footsteps. They thundered across the patio, the thin shafts of light flickering as someone passed through them. Nicole staggered back as she watched the person run. One moment they seemed to be in the living room, the next, merely a shadow playing across the windows from the outside. She watched the shadowed figure as it passed across the windows. But just before the person reached the front door, she blinked and it was gone.

"Mr. Morton?" she squeaked. It wasn't him, she knew that, but it was a comfort to hear a voice, even if it was her own. "Vic?"

Her legs didn't want to work, but she forced herself to dart back to the door. The sunlight burned her eyes, blinding her momentarily as she stepped out onto the porch. She blinked rapidly as she searched the farm's front yard. Rolling plains stretched out in every direction, offering very few places for anyone to hide, but she couldn't find a single trace of life. Not so much as a stray bird ghosting across the cloudless sky. Her grip tightened against the basket handle until her knuckles ached. Reluctantly, she turned to head back inside.

A startled yelp escaped her. Victor had silently slipped into the doorway. He stood staring at her, his eyes cold and unblinking.

Her words died in her throat as her surprise faded, and she was able to really see him. Only weeks ago, he would have filled the space with his impressive bulk. Now, his paling and blistering skin stretched over his bones like paper. His hair resembled wire as it hung down across his sunken and bloodshot eyes. The cracks in his lips ran deep enough for droplets of blood to seep out as he spoke.

"What are you doing here?"

It took a forced effort to arrange a smile onto her face. "Vic, I didn't hear you. How are you feeling?"

Victor shifted his attention to the spot just to the side of the door. "She doesn't want you here."

Nicole leaned forward slightly, peeking around the corner to catch a glimpse of who he was looking at. No one was there.

"Your girlfriend?" she asked softly.

His eyes snapped back onto her. Nicole straightened instantly, her smile wavering under his unblinking glare. Every instinct told her to run, and it was only her mantra of 'It's Vic' that kept her in place. Her heart throbbed so hard it created a stinging void within her chest, and her voice was far too chipper, even to her own ears.

"You know, you've never actually told me her name."

Victor's only response was to shift his eyes back to that empty spot behind the wall.

"Vic," she rushed to say. "What's going on with you?"

"With me?" he snarled.

She cringed under the outburst. Victor was normally sweet. Gentle. The type of guy that held onto his childlike nature with a sense of pride. All of that had crumbled in just a few weeks. Now he was volatile, unpredictable, and angry. Always angry.

Her words tripped over each other as they tumbled out of her mouth. "I just mean that we haven't spoken in a long time. Catch me up. What's new?"

Victor opened his mouth, but before he could respond, his attention shifted again. For a moment, he did nothing more than stare, as if listening to something she couldn't hear. Nicole could barely contain the restless energy that crackled through her like a lightning storm. She jumped when Victor suddenly reached for the door.

"Go away."

She slammed her hand against the door, keeping him from closing it.

"Wait! Vic, look, I think that your girlfriend and I have gotten off on the wrong foot and I've been wracking my brain to try and figure out why."

Anger flared across his face at the mention of his girlfriend, but he waited as she hurried through her words. She took that as a good sign. Even as she felt his anger like blades of ice.

"And I think that it's my fault."

Caught off guard, he didn't offer any resistance as she pushed the door open a little more. Quickly, she checked the spot he kept glancing at, but still couldn't see what he was looking at.

Victor didn't attempt to keep his skepticism from his voice. "Really?"

"We've all known each other our entire lives. I took that for granted and I think I might have misjudged how daunting it would be for her to come into such a tight knit group. She might even feel unwanted. So, of course you've been pulling away, right?"

She held his eyes, her lungs turning to stone in her chest. It wasn't exactly a lie, just a severely bent and edited truth, but Victor had always been able to read her. As such, it had been years since she had ever tried to put anything past him. Nicole searched the withered edges of his face, trying to pinpoint if he would believe her or not. The world teetered on a razor's edge. She couldn't begin to predict what would happen if he didn't believe her, or if his girlfriend didn't, and it was that uncertainty that made her restless and dizzy. Adrenaline pulsed through her, her body screaming at her to run. Unable to take the silence a moment longer, she continued her rehearsed speech at a rapid pace, thrusting the picnic basket at him with both hands.

"I made muffins. I thought that we might give them to her together. You know, sit down, and really get to know each other. Is she here?"

"She doesn't want you here."

"Are you sure you can't tempt her?" She swung the basket slightly before him. The scent of freshly baked muffins trailed into the air, mixing with creamy white chocolate and fresh mint. They were his favorite. He hadn't been able to resist them since she perfected the recipe. "They're fresh from the oven. The chocolate is still gooey."

Without a word, he let his eyes drift again. It felt like all her insides plummeted at once, leaving only a gaping hole inside that filled her with ice. He wasn't staring at the regular place. His unblinking eyes were locked on a spot just over her right shoulder. Locking her legs, she refused to turn around.

"Can't we just try?" she stammered. "We both love you, Vic, so we already have an ice breaker. And muffins!" She rattled the basket in a way that she hoped was tantalizing.

6

There was no light in his eyes as he watched her. No warmth. Not even the slightest hint of recognition. Nicole shifted as she waited, her arms beginning to cramp from holding the basket on outstretched arms. Then the wind shifted and she heard it. A hushed trail of whispers, words flowing too low and fast for her to make any sense of them. Nicole turned towards it before she could stop herself. There was no one else out on the patio, but the words continued. Heated breath washed against her ear.

Her heart lurched into her throat, swelling until she wheezed around it. She whirled back to face Victor. She began to shake, her knees threatening to drop out from under her. The whole world was reduced to the pair of hands rising up from behind Victor's back. The fingers were unnaturally long, their joints displaced, allowing them to bend and twist in ways that would break human digits. Each nail was a perfect dagger of black opal. The thin, frail arms continued to grow, rising higher and higher until they towered over him. With liquid fluidity, they wrapped around Victor in a tight embrace. But there was no one behind him. All the while, the whispering continued.

She couldn't speak. Couldn't understand what she was seeing. Cold sweat prickled along her spine as Victor's eyes rolled back into his head. When he spoke, his voice was as dead and severed as his gaze.

"Don't come back."

Victor slammed the door shut. The world turned silent. She didn't know how long she stood there, staring at the door, images of the arms burned into her mind. Her body shook as she finally managed to take in a full breath.

"Vic?"

Her whisper barely broke the silence.

\*\*\*

*He opened the eyes that were not his own and walked with legs he had never used. Candlelight flickered. It toyed with the gaps in the stones, creating deep shadows that weaved over the walls like spider webs. The play of shadow and light was a thing of beauty as they draped over the polished wood of the caskets. He weaved through his collection, lovingly running his taloned nails along the edges of each one he passed. It had taken so long to build the collection. To find his pristine specimens amongst the entire firth. To find those worthy to be here. Preparing each had been an* equally painstaking task, but it had all been worth it. They were perfect and, finally, the time was right to add another.

The newest coffin was more of a masterpiece than a vessel for the dead. The craftsmanship was exquisite, carved and polished to a high shine. He ran his fingers over the cool, slick surface as he rounded the foot and peered down at his newest addition. The man lying within the coffin eagerly sought out his gaze. They always did. When they were his, everything they needed could be found in his attention. Fear still lingered in the murky depths of the eyes of his new toy, but it didn't matter. It never did. Their need for him always surpassed their instincts to survive.

"Are you scared?" He spoke the words with a voice that didn't belong to him. It was one he didn't recognize.

"A little," the man stammered.

"It's okay," he assured as he fluttered his fingers over the nearby instruments. "It will all be over soon. And then you'll be with me forever."

The young man was going to make such a fine possession. Trust. Loyalty. Love. He gave it all so freely. He reached out, his borrowed hand like a glove pulled too tight, and then wrapped his fingers around the large needle. His new claw-like nails clacked against its surface, the sound making his newest possession hitch his breath. But he didn't attempt to crawl out of his zinc-lined coffin.

The obedience made pleasure blossom within his chest. He repeatedly shifted his fingers, just to produce the sound again. The limited light danced over the inch long needle and its adjoining glass jar. While he didn't try to escape, his delightful young man didn't immediately move to take the needle when offered. Instead, he eyed it carefully, his growing fear forcing the first few tears out of his eyes.

"I don't want to die."

Unfurling his new long fingers, he cradled the needle in the palm of his hand.

"Do you love me?"

The answer came immediately, dripping with devotion. "Of course."

"Is there anything you would deny me?"

"Nothing. I'll give you anything."

The finely pointed nails left thin red trails along his possession's skin as he trailed his hand over his cheek. Like a loyal dog, the boy nuzzled against his palm.

"All I ask for … is your life."

*Even though the terror never left the boy's water-lined eyes, he still reached out and took the needle. His hesitation came back only after the sharp tip was poised over the soft blue trail of his vein. A fine tremor shook his hand until blood began to well around the tip.*

*"Show me how much you love me."*

*With a choked sob that ended with a pitiful whisper, his precious new toy pushed. Blood quickly swelled and flooded the tube. It created a sweet, gentle gurgling noise as it filled the jar and drained the life out of the man's veins.*

***

Benton's eyes snapped open.

*Just a dream,* he told himself.

It didn't stop his heart ramming against his ribs, or the uncomfortable sensation of his terror sweat cooling against his skin. He fixed his eyes on the sunlit car roof and scraped his fingers over the padded bench seat beneath him. None of it felt real. He was still back in that room, occupying a body that wasn't his own. The needle still felt heavy in his hand. Each time he blinked, he saw the stranger's face. But he wasn't a stranger. *Scott Molson.* The name boiled like lava over his brain, scorching the inside of his skull with a crushing force. A need to tell him. To warn Scott that Death was stalking him.

A shadow swallowed up the light. Instantly, the temperature dropped and he froze under the sudden loss. A sound rattled above him, one he recognized from numerous dreams. It was the sound of bones thumping together. Hesitantly, he rolled his eyes back to look at the open car window above his head. The second he saw the talons, his mind scattered to a stop. As black as wet ink, the three spikes curved for at least an inch before tapering into a needle-like point. They clenched and shifted, easily slicing open the material that covered the door. He was suddenly painfully aware of how exposed he was. How vulnerable the flesh of his eyes and neck were. The sound of clacking bones drew his attention higher.

An owl. A massive, dark owl with feathers that rose like horns from its head. It filled the space of the open window, the sun creating a golden halo around its edges. Never once had Benton given any thought to how sharp an owl's beak was. Now, he was consumed by images of how effortlessly it could slice him apart. He watched it snap its hooked beak again. It sounded just like rattling bones and shivered as it hit his ears. Its large, sickly yellow eyes fixed onto Benton. All he could do was stare back, watching his reflection in the mirror-like surface.

The door at his feet wrenched open and the colossal bird screeched in protest. It turned. The tips of its wings brushed across Benton's forehead, sticking in the blood he hadn't known was there, before it took flight. Despite its size, it moved as silently as a ghost. Benton fought against his seatbelt as he struggled to sit up. The second he was freed, he twisted to watch the owl gliding over the seemingly endless rolling hills of the prairies.

"Benton!"

He whirled back to the sound of his mother's voice and instantly regretted the sharp movement. Pain exploded out across his forehead, bringing reality with it. They weren't moving. The steady strum of the car's engine had been replaced by a feral hiss that struggled to be heard over the colorful string of swear words his father was currently screaming.

"Honey, you're bleeding!"

"I'm okay."

He dabbed the back of his hand against his forehead. The slight touch was enough to provoke a new wave of pain, and he pulled his hand back to find fresh blood smeared on his wrist. It finally clicked and he noticed the strange angle the car was in. He shuffled to the door his mother held open and almost staggered to the side when his feet found the sloping earth. They weren't on the thin road that stretched over the Alberta prairies. Now, the car was nose deep at the bottom of a soggy ditch.

Above them, his father paced back and forth across the road, throwing his arms around as if he were swatting away invisible bugs. At least his screaming had ebbed out into muttered ramblings. Benton helped his mother up the incline, biting down on his question over what had happened until they were all together.

"What happened?" his father snarled, his hands flying with renewed rage as he turned to face them. "You fell asleep in the car, didn't you, Benton?"

"Theodore."

Both of his parents only hurled their full names at each other when a line had been crossed. His father's anger faltered for a moment. Holding Theodore's gaze, his mother continued pronouncing each word carefully.

"They are night terrors. He can't help it."

Instead of calming down, the sharp tone sent Theodore into another tirade. "I know that, Cheyanne. Which is why we have a rule set in place. It's simple but effective." He locked his steel gray eyes onto Benton and snapped. "What's the rule, Benton?"

Benton skirted his eyes to the side. "Don't sleep in the car."

"Sounds pretty simple, doesn't it?" his father fumed.

"I'm sorry," Benton said. "I didn't mean to. I'm just so exhausted."

"You're exhausted," his father laughed, the sound somewhere between bitter and hysterical. "We're all exhausted, Benton! You wake us up every night with your screams! I know you're not the brightest spark, but I never thought you'd be so stupid as to let yourself fall asleep in a moving vehicle!"

"Theodore!"

His parents turned to each other. At that moment, Benton knew that he wasn't part of this conversation anymore, just the topic being discussed. His father ranted on about all the possible outcomes a scenario like this could have ended in. *What if there had been another car? What if the ditch had been deeper? What if the car had rolled?* With the dream still firmly lodged in his brain, Benton wasn't in any position to handle a lecture of hideous ways to die.

It had been close to seven years since his 'night terrors,' as his parents insisted on calling them, had started. That long without a decent night's sleep had a way of grinding people's resistance to dust. Not to mention their tolerance for each other. Mostly him. And as time wore on, they steadily stopped believing that it wasn't his fault. The dreams, they still acknowledged, were beyond his control. The following impulses, and the fall out they created, were placed squarely on him.

His parents had put in place orders that he wasn't to contact any of the people he dreamt of. As if it were that easy. Just something he could put aside, dismiss and ignore like any other ordinary nightmare. He told them it wasn't so simple, but they never listened. Every time he tried to keep his silence, it felt like there was a burning railroad spike being hammered into his head. He could already feel the blistering heat at the base of his skull.

"I'm going to try and figure out if the engine's okay," he said over his shoulder as he scrambled back down the embankment.

Benton wasn't exactly known for his grace, and his recent growth spurt had only made things worse. So, he took it as a win when he managed to keep his gangly legs under him instead of falling on his ass. Reaching the car, he leaned in through the driver's side door and pulled the latch to pop the hood. The sunlight glistened off the screen of his mobile phone, beckoning him.

*Don't,* he told himself as his fingers twitched to pick it up. He dredged up all the memories of what happened when he got involved and hurled them at his impulse. But none of the examples of how his life could implode could compete with the growing sensation that was currently driving deeper into his skin. It still felt like a bite, but now he could almost feel the poison pouring under his skin like acid. He slapped his hand over the nape of his neck, but the contact only made the pain spike. He hissed and clenched his teeth. It wasn't going to get better. Not unless he gave in. Not unless he did what Death wanted.

With a quick glance back up at his parents, who had yet to take a pause in their argument, Benton snatched up his mobile and attached his headphones. They felt heavy in his hand as he scurried to the front of the car. He popped the hood and latched it into place, using it as a shield to hide him from his parents as he fumbled with the buttons. Technology was a wondrous thing. An anonymous email account gave him the needed protection.

For all the people that had dismissed his dreams over the years as simply that, no one had ever been able to explain to him why he knew their names and, more importantly, how to get in touch with them. As quickly as he could, he typed out Scott Molson's personal email address and set up a message that he knew was probably going to be ignored.

*Scott, you don't know me, but something bad is going to happen. Be careful of a woman with long nails, and watch your back.*

He stared at the message. No matter how many times he did this, he could never figure out how to word it in a way that people would take seriously. All he really wanted to type was, 'You're going to die.' But history taught him that blatant honesty only ever led to dismissal, police investigations, or restraining orders. His mental debate came to a sudden stop when he heard his father crunching through the grass towards him.

"Benton? What are you doing?"

The pain in the back of his head flared. He hit the 'send' button with a trembling thumb as he used his other hand to force his earphones into place. There was no need to keep the screen up to know if the message had sent. He felt it. The second it went through, the boiling pain that had seeped into his spine began to ebb away, returning him to the steady throb of a normal headache. His father smacked the side of the car and called for him again. Benton brought up his saved music and cranked the volume until the beat threatened to fracture his skull. He skipped to halfway along a random song just as his father came up behind him.

"Benton!"

He turned around in what was his best impression of a startled person. From the pull of his father's brow, Benton seriously began to question his acting abilities, but he wasn't about to give up the story. It was hard to keep the relief from his face when he pulled out one of his earphones and the song was still clear through the tiny speakers. At least it was convincing that he wouldn't have been able to hear his father coming.

"What's up?" he asked as innocently as he could.

Again, he must have fallen a little flat. His father tried to subtly catch sight of the phone's screen. The move was obvious and Benton took some solace in the fact that he wasn't the only pathetic actor in the family. He was careful to keep his confused expression as his father eyed the device. Seeing that the song had, apparently, been playing for a while, he seemed to ease up and his shoulders lost their tension.

"Just wanted to see how the car's going?"

Benton knew for a fact that he was a far better liar.

"I only just started looking." He squished his sneakers against the layer of weed-mangled muck that oozed around his feet. "But I'm pretty sure some of this got in there."

"Probably," Theodore wrinkled his nose as he examined the slop. "We're not getting it out of here without a tow truck."

"Sorry," Benton mumbled and hunched over the engine.

Theodore placed a hand onto Benton's shoulder and squeezed slightly. "I know you are. But you need to be more careful."

"I will be."

"And remember, you can't control what you dream..."

He let the sentence trail off with an expectant look. Benton swallowed his resentment and completed the last of what had become a makeshift family mantra.

"But I can control who I tell."

"Exactly." His father squeezed his shoulder before patting him in a way that was both comforting and awkward. The list of whom his parents found appropriate to talk to about his dreams consisted of absolutely no one. "We need to make this place work. That's going to take all of us working together. We can't afford to keep moving."

Benton nodded. Personally, he didn't see the need to move this far out into the middle of nowhere. Toronto was a big place, just like all the other cities they had burned through. Shifting neighborhoods seemed like the better option. Quicker, cheaper, completed over a weekend. And able to be repeated numerous times before the majority of the population would catch on. Besides, it hadn't been that bad. Not yet anyway. At least nowhere near as bad as it had been in other places.

But his parents stubbornly clung to the belief that a change in location would make all the difference. As if they just needed to find the right longitude and latitude to shove him in, and whatever was wrong in his head would magically be corrected. Benton didn't know why Death had selected him to be some kind of demented groupie, but he knew that there wasn't a chance things would get better. No one ever won against Death.

"It's going to be different here, son. It has to be."

*Different.* Benton let himself roll the thought around in his head for a moment before deciding to test the theory.

"Dad," he said softly. "This one really got to me. There was this guy and–"

Theodore's hand tightened on his arm before he could even finish the sentence.

"Just forget it, Benton. Everyone has bad dreams."

"But these aren't *just* bad dreams."

"Yes, they are," he said sternly.

"But, then why–"

"Son," Theodore said sharply. "You know this kind of talk scares your mother."

A long sigh pulled from Benton's chest as his eyes drifted to the ground. He nodded. *So much for different,* he thought before chastising himself for letting his hopes rise even that high. *Stupid.*

"There's a car coming," Cheyanne called down from the road.

Theodore shared a slight smirk with Benton. As if the last fifteen minutes had never taken place.

"Who is going to stop for three strangers in the middle of nowhere, huh?" he asked with a chuckle.

Benton shrugged and watched his father awkwardly climb back up to the road. He didn't follow. A broken down motor in a ditch held a lot more appeal then introducing himself to some people who were probably going to hate him in a week anyway. While he turned off the phone and shoved it into his back pocket, he secured the earphone back into place. To perfect the 'please keep away from me' vibe, he pulled the hood of his favorite worn down sweater over his hair. So what if it had taken him close to an hour to spike it up just right? Sacrifices had to be made for the greater good.

As he began to check the cords and cables, the rumbling engine of the new arrival stopped and he heard the sure thump of a door closing.

"Hello," said a voice far younger than Benton expected.

Since there were only a few ways that the following conversation could turn out, Benton let his attention drift. More so after his mother started weaving a story about how a rabbit had darted across the road and avoiding it had sent them into the ditch. But, while he didn't have any interest in what was being said, he couldn't deny a certain degree of curiosity. He leaned to the side just enough to catch sight of the girl his parents were currently lying to.

"Wow."

That one word summed her up. Benton took in her amazing cheekbones, wide blinding smile, and rich brown eyes that somehow still managed to be bright, and he couldn't think up another word to describe her. She talked with her hands. Each movement making the straight edge of her silky hair brush against her hips. The sway was kind of hypnotic. His mother pointed down in his direction and Benton threw himself back under the hood of the car. It occurred to him a heartbeat later that fleeing was probably the creepiest option he could have picked. His stomach dropped when he heard them coming down the hill. *You couldn't just wave?* he snapped at himself. *Even a nod would have been better.*

"Benton!" Cheyanne called. He was really starting to hate his name.

He ducked back out before she could call for him again. A jolt ran through him when he found himself faced with a beaming smile. Now that she was closer, he was pretty sure that she was around his own age.

"Hi," she waved, and he felt an answering smile tug at his lips.

"Hey."

Cheyanne placed a hand on the stranger's back and gestured to Benton with the other. "This is our son, Benton. Benton, this is, I'm sorry, we didn't catch your name."

She turned her bright eyes onto Cheyanne, her smile never diminishing. "I'm Nicole Rider, Mrs. Bertrand."

Theodore seemed just as charmed at her manners as Cheyanne was.

Benton's brow furrowed and he asked, "How do you know our last name?"

Catching onto his line of thinking, his parents quickly exchanged a glance, both clearly worried that their reputation had preceded them. In unison, they turned back to Nicole.

"Oh, no. I just took a guess." She noticed their unease and smiled all the brighter. "We don't get many new people in Fort Wayward. The last time someone moved to town that wasn't related by blood or marriages was." She pursed her lips in thought. "I want to say the 50's. I'm part of the welcoming committee."

"You don't get new people, but you have a welcoming committee?" Benton asked.

His words were instantly met with hissed reprimands from both parents. He didn't care.

"Well, no, not technically," she said with a hint of bashfulness that she quickly recovered from. "When I heard you were coming, I decided to form one. It's just me, actually. But I do have a great welcome basket I was going to drop over tomorrow morning."

Something in the explanation didn't sit right with Benton and he found himself drawing out the word 'right' into three syllables.

"I made muffins," she said with pride.

He nodded. "Great."

"That is very kind of you, Nicole," Cheyanne said before throwing Benton a sharp glare.

"I don't mean to pry," Nicole said, "but are you bleeding?"

"Oh, yeah. It's just a bump." Benton pulled the hoodie firmer onto his head.

"I have first aid training and a full kit in my truck."

*Of course you do*, Benton thought. It was something in the way she spoke, he decided, that just made her seem fake. Every word came out dripping with a bubbly energy that was normally only displayed by pageant contestants, airline stewards, and Stepford wives. No one is ever *that* happy. She had to have some kind of end game in the works, and he didn't want to be blindsided by it.

"It's nothing," Cheyanne quickly assured. "But we do need to get to the local hospital if you could spare the time to take us."

"Of course, Mrs. Bertrand. If you're sure it's nothing pressing, we can move your suitcases from your car to mine. That way, when I drop you home after the hospital, you'll have everything you need."

"We'll be there for at least an hour," Theodore said. "We can't expect you to hang around that long."

"The point of the welcoming committee is to be welcoming," she said with that pristine smile that looked riveted into place.

The trails of her beaded choker necklace rattled as she turned to look at each of them in turn. Its pattern of vibrant orange, yellow, and red brought out the golden hues in her skin tone. It made her seem all the more like a sunbeam personified.

"It won't be any bother at all. And I can pass the time by checking in with Barry for you."

"Barry?" Theodore asked.

"Barry Smoke. He runs the town's garage and tow service. It's only a few streets over."

Benton checked with both his parents and, apparently, he was the only one who thought that the offer was just a little too welcoming.

# Chapter 2

Benton pulled another hunk off of the muffin Nicole had given him. 'Given' wasn't exactly accurate. Insisting that he take it, as if she couldn't stand the sight of it, was more in line. It was quite good. *Of course, it was*, a voice still mumbled in his head. Honestly, two different kinds of chocolate and peppermint in a muffin sounded like a horrible idea, but she made it work. He took another bite. He wasn't hungry. He just needed a way to pass the time that didn't involve picking at the band aid that now covered a rather large part of his forehead.

The plastic chair was uncomfortable and positioned in a busy area of the one level hospital. The remaining floors of the brick building were scattered with other businesses, including his new therapist. His parents had gone up to see him first, which he had expected. After all, it was awkward to ask a stranger to dope up your son when he's standing in the same room.

When the nightmares had begun, Benton had been excited to go to therapy. His childish understanding was that it was someone who was paid to listen to you. That idea had called to him like a siren's song. To be heard. Back then, he had been so sure that if he could just get someone alone for an hour and explain everything that was happening to him, he would be able to make them believe him. Believe that something was wrong, that his nightmares were true. That he was predicting the real deaths of real people. But reality had fallen very far from his ideals. He discovered the vast wasteland that existed between being heard and being *listened* to.

Their main focus was always to discover the roots of his anxiety, and when the insomnia had started, they had prescribed sleeping pills. They didn't stop the dreams, though. All they did was make it harder for him to wake up and prevented him from screaming. At first, his parents had listened to him enough to pressure the doctor to keep looking for a different cocktail. But time had changed their minds. About a year back, they had subtly brought up the pills again. *Would it really be so bad? Would it hurt to take one every so often? Wouldn't it be worth it for a good night's sleep?* After today, he was sure that they weren't going to be taking the time to work it into a conversation anymore. It would no longer be an option for them – merely a plan B in his back pocket if he got desperate enough.

They were desperate enough.

He rubbed a hand through his hair. His carefully arranged spikes were destroyed anyway, and the sensation of fingers carding through the fluffy tufts was always comforting. For all the effort he put into it, Benton wasn't a huge fan of his hair. Like he didn't have enough problems without going gray in his teens. Right now, it was just a hue, a twinge of silver that distorted the dirty blonde in the right light. But the writing was on the wall. At this rate, he would probably be as gray as a storm cloud before he was through his twenties.

He dug his nails into his scalp and enjoyed the tingling trail they left behind. The stress that had clenched his shoulders began to seep away and his eyelids fluttered closed. The memories of his dreams flooded his head. Suddenly, all he could think about was how his scalp would split wide under those fingernails. He snapped his hand away, but the sensation of blood oozing through his hair didn't fade until he opened his eyes.

A solid mass passed through the corner of his eyes, close enough to touch, devouring his sight. He threw himself back with a choked cry. The flimsy chair skidded out from underneath him and he dropped to the floor. He pushed himself back, shuffling a few feet before his brain caught up with the fact that there was nothing looming over him. A half second later, he caught sight of the dark shape again. The center was a solid slap of ebony, but the edges coiled and rolled like drifting smoke. He watched as it disappeared around the corner at the far end of the hall.

*Don't follow it,* something whispered in the back of his head. But even as he resolved not to, a foreign pull twisted around his stomach. He couldn't argue with the sensation. He was impaled on a hook and the attached cord was pulled taut. When there was no slack left, there was nothing for him to do but stand up or be gutted. Getting to his feet, he ignored the strange looks that were cast in his direction and hurried to catch up. The rubber soles of his shoes released a high squeak as he skidded to a stop. Despite its massive head start, he was still able to spot the towering mass. It had waited for him. They stared at each other, and a point of chalky white emerged where a face should be. Silently, it drifted around the next corner, never quite touching the floor.

*Don't go.* Dread turned his stomach into a pit of twisting snakes. Fire blazed out from his bones but was unable to burn off the ice that encrusted his skin. Even out of sight, the image of the shape lingered in his mind. He desperately looked around but couldn't find a single person that seemed to have seen it too. *Don't follow.* The voice echoed in his mind as if everything else had been hollowed out. He wanted to listen. He longed to keep his feet rooted in place. But the unseen cord jerked. A pained groan broke from his chest as a dozen more unseen hooks dug into his flesh. Together, they wrenched forward. He staggered to keep his balance before breaking into a jog.

Slowing at the corner, Benton tilted his head to glance down the new hallway. The shadow loomed in a doorway at the very end of the hall, darker than the shadows behind it. It was facing him. Waiting for him. He reeled back and plastered himself against the solid wall. A few people walked by and he struggled to hold onto at least a pretense of normalcy. Once more, his acting left a lot to be desired, and they passed him with strange glances and shared whispers.

Watching other people casually walk along the halls made it easier to peel himself off the wall. Benton had never *seen* things in real life before. *Maybe I hit my head harder than I thought.* The notion was dismissed as quickly as it had formed. It was real. It *felt* real. Steeling himself, he glanced around the corner. The doorway was empty but his need, the hooks, were still pulling at him with a rising ache. He had only meant to take a tentative step. Go slow. Be cautious. But his body overruled his mind and he found himself sprinting down the narrow hallway. The overhead speaker system crackled as it paged a doctor, the words heard but insignificant. The sound seemed less real than the mist he was pursuing. Reaching the door, he slowed his pace and peered into a dark room.

A single light illuminated the single bed. It was narrow and small, but the woman who lay on it made it look enormous. Her tiny, pale frame was dwarfed by the space. Each breath wracked her chest, the sound rattling within her lungs, melding with the buzz and whirl of the machines that surrounded her like sentinels. Despite the brittleness of her body, and her struggle to keep her eyelids up, her gaze was sharp, her green eyes as piercing as daggers.

"You're younger than I thought." The effort of speaking made the woman cough.

Benton staggered forward a step, sure that the sudden bursts would snap her in two.

"Though I guess you're older than you seem."

His brow furrowed. "Sorry?"

She reached for him. There was no meat to her hands. Merely skin draped over bone. Benton's gaze shifted over the room as he edged closer. The first step was the hardest.

"I think you've mixed me up with someone else."

Whatever she was going to say was lost under another coughing fit. Blood spurted over her lips as she wheezed each breath. *She's dying.* The words drifted into his mind like a beast rising up from the depths of the ocean. He reached across her, hand finding the nurse alarm button without having to look. From somewhere far away, he could hear a warning siren begin to chime. She gasped and turned her eyes onto him. They were weaker now, their strength dulling, as if the color was seeping from her, her life escaping from a thousand points.

He didn't know what to say, so he mumbled a few words about them arriving soon and how everything was going to be okay. There was no way to tell how much of it she actually heard. Though he doubted that she believed any of it. She held his gaze with all of her remaining strength.

"I'm dying, aren't I?"

"Yes," he whispered as he reached her bedside.

Another coughing fit made the woman curl in on herself. A fine mist of blood washed over her sheets but Benton didn't attempt to move. She struggled to breathe. To hold his gaze.

"I don't understand," she finally managed to force out.

"Don't understand what?"

She still reached for his hand, but her eyes were focused on something beyond his shoulder.

"If you're death, who's that?"

Benton spun around. The mass loomed in the corner, a blurred collection of light and darkness that expanded out to cover every inch of the wall. It lunged towards him. Benton staggered back but had nowhere to go. The shape crashed down over him like an icy wave, robbing him of his breath and weakening his knees. He slumped against the bed, shivering and unable to tear his eyes from the now vacant corner before him.

Vaguely, he became aware of the people running into the room. They didn't seem real. Nothing did. Except the woman's hand in his and the droning sound of the heart monitor flat lining.

***

Benton couldn't keep still. Adrenaline coursed through him, making his foot twitch and his hands shake. There had been questions. Of course there had been questions. And he had spotted a familiar expression on more than one face; one that said they expected he had something to do with the woman's death. He hadn't even lasted a day in Fort Wayward without arousing suspicion.

"We can talk about it."

Benton jolted. He had actually forgotten that he was in his new doctor's office. Aspen De Champ was stoic and reserved, but still managed to maintain a calming presence. If first impressions were actually worth anything, Benton might have liked him.

"Nothing to talk about," Benton dismissed.

He didn't want to be here. He didn't want to go through yet another dance with a partner that was trying to trip him up.

Aspen kept his voice light, conversational. "There is the woman."

"Chelsey." Benton said.

"Pardon?"

Benton got to his feet and began to pace the room. "Her name was Chelsey Williams."

"Well, you obviously care about her enough to learn her name."

"I didn't learn it."

"Benton," Aspen smiled. "You just told me her name."

"Just because I know something doesn't mean that I learned it."

His eyes fell on the small, colorful box by the door, filled to the brim with numerous toys. The baseball on top got his attention, and he scooped it up on his next pass.

"Is this one of those things you just know?"

Benton huffed a laugh as he tossed the ball into the air. "Which quack sent over my files?"

"Does it matter?"

"Duh. How else will I know what diagnosis to live up to? Am I delusional? A compulsive liar? A sociopath? Suffering from some deeply suppressed traumatic experience? Help me out here, doc."

"Why don't we come to our own conclusions?"

Benton tossed the ball again, waiting to feel the solid weight back in his palms before he turned to look at the older man.

"You get paid either way right? Whether I talk to you or not?"

"Yes."

"So, why bother?"

"I'm inclined to help people," Aspen smiled as he spread his arms out. "It's kind of why I got into this business."

Benton couldn't help but smirk. "You think you can help me?"

"I'd like to try." At Benton's silence, he ventured again, "Would it hurt to give me a shot?"

Benton turned the ball over in his hands as he sunk back down into his overstuffed chair, his adrenaline finally subsiding. He couldn't help the thin traces of hope that bloomed and swirled within his mind. It was that little voice in the back of his head that whispered over and over that life *could* be different. It was a stupid voice that he wished he could smother.

"Death follows me." The words slipped out before he could stop himself.

"You've had a string of bad luck, admittedly."

"Bad luck? Is that what they chalked it up to?"

"What other explanation is there?"

"What I just said." His tone turned sharp. "What's the point in talking if you're not listening?"

"I am listening. But I'm going to have to ask a few clarifying questions every now and then."

Benton shrugged and hunched forward, resting his forearms onto his knees. For the first time, he met Aspen's eyes.

"Death follows me." He said each word with force.

Aspen smiled. "Death isn't a person."

"Well, not one person. That would be some Santa Clause level bullshit. How could he get around to everyone at once? Maybe that's what I am. A helper, a reaper, or a minion. Pick a name, any name."

"You think you bring death?"

"I touched that woman's hand and her heart stopped. What does that tell you?"

"Bad timing?" Aspen offered.

Benton closed his hands around the ball, tightening his grip until his knuckles were white peaks under his skin. Aspen noticed the shift in him and leaned forward to mirror Benton's posture. It was supposed to make people feel better, more at ease, understood. All it did for Benton was highlight that Aspen was trying to manipulate him.

"I don't want sleeping pills," Benton snapped.

"I never suggested them."

"My parents did." Before Aspen could say anything, he rushed on, "They don't work. I still dream, but I can't wake up. It's torture, and I won't take them."

"Then I won't prescribe them."

Benton didn't know the doctor enough to tell if he was lying or not. But at least it was out there. At least, he knew that it would be a pointless exercise.

"What do you think I am?" Benton asked.

Aspen tilted his head. "Confused."

"Oh, come on," Benton groaned. "You have the files. You have to see that things aren't normal. I know things I couldn't possibly know. I see things I shouldn't be able to see. Something is off. You have to see that. I just want you to tell me, honestly, what you think is going on."

"I think you're very confused."

He felt that small flickering bit of hope die. It hurt. *Stupid,* he hissed at himself. *Stupid.* Leaning back in his seat, he pulled his phone from his pocket and opened up his email. He was two paragraphs into writing up his dream when Aspen tried to regain his attention.

"I told you," Benton said without looking up. "There is no point in talking if you're not listening."

"And I told you I am."

"No, you're not."

Aspen tried again and again to get his attention. One more look. One more word. Benton gave him nothing and was gone the second his time was up.

# Chapter 3

The slight twists of the road did little to keep Nicole's attention. The sun gave a few last gasps before surrendering the sky to the night. The road was almost completely lost in darkness when she remembered to turn on her headlights. Her mind was still with Victor. The arms. She had hoped the Bertrand family would serve as a distraction, but all they had provided so far was tension. They all sat in loaded silence. It had been odd when both parents had decided to sit in the back and she had begun to wonder if she had done something wrong. But then Benton had climbed into the passenger seat without ever acknowledging his parent's presence and she realized it wasn't about her. They had almost completed the long drive to their house and the situation still hadn't improved.

Of all the properties that lined the outskirts of Fort Wayward, the new Bertrand home was by far the finest. And the most isolated. The property was separated from the paved highway by a long gravel road, barely wide enough for one car to use. There were no other houses nearby. Nothing close enough to even be a pinprick of light on the horizon. Without competition, the starry sky curled over them, coming all the way down to reach the earth. Benton sat up straight as the silhouette of the house and barn came into view. It was a tall structure, three stories and sprawling. It was quite impressive during the day. The barn was set a few yards to the side and was remarkable all on its own.

She tried to watch Benton from the corner of her eyes as she pulled her jeep up in front of the property. He looked annoyed. And worried. In the glow of the dashboard console, she watched him lick his lips, a nervous twitch that he didn't seem aware of. She was a little too transfixed on him and almost shot through the front door. Overcompensating, she stomped on the breaks and brought them to a sudden stop.

"Sorry," she said to the people startled from their own thoughts. "Welcome home!"

Benton leaned forward and looked up at the property with hesitation. "This is it?"

"It looks a lot nicer with the lights on," she promised.

"You know who lived here before?" Cheyanne asked from the backseat.

"Yes, ma'am. But then, everyone knows everyone here. It's one of the great things about living in Fort Wayward."

She let her eyes wander back to Benton. He had stopped looking at the house and had now fixed his attention squarely on the barn a few yards away. The growing dark rose to hide the structure, leaving only the faint moonlight to trace its edges. Benton stared at it, his body completely rigid.

"What's that?" he mumbled.

"That must be the barn," Theodore smiled. He nudged Cheyanne with a smile. "We have a barn."

"I never thought I'd see the day," she chuckled.

The joke was lost on Nicole. All farmland properties had barns. It wasn't that uncommon, and not that humorous either. So, as she often did when in doubt, she held onto her smile and didn't say anything. The overhead light clicked on as Benton's parents opened the back door, the dim glow blinding her. Benton's parents slipped out of the car. He didn't move. Unconsciously, he balled his hands into fists on his knees, his eyes never leaving the barn.

She couldn't fathom why it would hold his attention. It was a renovated barn. He would have seen hundreds just like it before he had even gotten near the town. For a moment, she considered shaking him out of it, but it didn't seem right to break his concentration. So she just waited. Watching him as he stared at the barn while his parents began to unpack the truck.

Benton took a sudden, sharp breath. It expanded his lithe frame and brought him back to life. He blinked rapidly and looked around, surprised to see that his parents had gotten out of the jeep.

"Where are they?"

The house lights clicked on and negated any reason for her to answer. He winced at the addition of light and sunk back into his seat.

"Sorry." He sounded meek and confused as he began to fumble with the seatbelt.

They had only known each other for a few hours, but already he seemed like a different person than the one she had met by the roadside ditch. Instead of stark and confrontational, he looked almost shy, scared. That promise of fear wafted out from him, calling her own nerves back to the forefront. He still hadn't managed to work his seatbelt free.

"Here, let me. It's a bit tricky."

Benton snorted a laugh but moved his hands back. "That's a mighty fine face saving tactic you have there."

Nicole smiled slightly. Normally, a snarky comment like that would have her playing through every second of her actions, trying to pinpoint where she had caused offence. But, with Benton, it just struck her as his natural state. The belt clicked open and he pulled it off him as if it were a snake. He took a deep breath and ran his hands through his hair.

"Are you okay?"

He barked a bitter laugh. "That's all relative."

"Didn't you like Aspen?"

Benton froze before he snapped around to face her. "How did you know I was seeing him?"

"There's no such thing as a secret in Wayward. Give it three days and everyone will know your underwear size!"

Shaking his head, he covered his face with both hands and leaned back against the seat. "Great. That's just friggin' great."

"There is no need to be embarrassed," Nicole rushed to say. "Half the town has seen Aspen at one point or another. More than for a little check-up."

"Check-up." He didn't move his hands, but she could hear his smile.

"Yes," she said. "Mental health requires maintenance. Like dental care. Going to Aspen doesn't mean you're different."

"But, I am different."

He didn't say it like it was a burden or even a badge of honor. Instead, Benton just sounded resigned.

"We're all different." Before he could say anything else, she went on to ask, "Why are you so fascinated with the barn?"

"I wouldn't call it fascination."

"What would you call it then?" she asked with a smile.

"Healthy paranoia."

"Of a barn?"

Benton didn't answer. Instead, he slipped out into the night. Most of the work had already been completed by his parents and the house now shone like a boat on a dark ocean. All the windows were ablaze, but the barn stood still just beyond the rim of light the house created.

By the time Nicole was out of the car, Benton was already halfway to the barn. His movements were slow, hesitant, like he was being forced into every step. The sight chilled her. It was echoingly similar to how the arms had moved. She tried to force the thought away as soon as it formed. There was no way she was ready to face that yet. She needed a few more seconds of peace before she could head into the swirling pit of madness that encounter had provoked. Pulling her smile into place like a shield, she darted off across the yard, following after him. Weird company was better than no company.

Falling into step beside him, she pulled out her mobile and turned on the flashlight app. It cut a small ring of light into the shadows and seemed to startle Benton out of his stupor. He quickly joined his own phone's light to the path before them.

"If you're paranoid, why are you going towards it?"

"Just seemed like the thing to do," he mumbled.

Tension simmered in the air around him, growing stronger the closer they got to the barn door. Since they had barely spent more than an hour together, it was hard to know which button to push to break the awkward silence.

"How did you like the muffins?"

Benton's stride stumbled. She didn't need much light to know that the expression he threw her scrunched up his face in almost every conceivable way. Like his face alone couldn't quite get across the sheer bafflement he felt.

"The muffins?"

"Yes."

"They were good."

She smiled as a warm sense of pride flooded through her. "Thank you."

Apparently done with the conversation, he shrugged one shoulder and picked up his pace. "They were a little dry, but nice."

Nicole paused. "A little dry? What do you mean a little dry?"

Her questions fell on deaf ears as Benton lifted his hand. His fingertips hovered just over the latch for the large barn door. It was like a re-enactment of the dilemma Nicole had experienced earlier. Only he didn't linger in that state of indecision. His long, strangely elegant fingers wrapped around the latch and pulled it open with a sense of resigned conviction.

Moonlight poured in from the high set windows, casting a silver glow over the room. The space was mercifully bare. No metal tools or towers of hay for the light to play tricks with. Together, they worked their thin trails of light over the space, seeking out each corner. She didn't know what she was supposed to be looking for. But she followed his lead nonetheless as they crept deeper inside. He shone his light up into the rafters and craned his neck to search the area above, the motion making his hoodie drop from his head. The first thing Nicole noted was that Benton's hair was almost as pale as the moonlight. The second was that he had a rather long neck.

It didn't take half a second for him to notice the attention. He turned to her with a furrowed brow, the question clear on his features even in the pale light. She smiled. The confusion shifted to something that was both unsettling and disapproving, and he turned away.

"You knew the previous owners?"

"The Ackerman's," she nodded. "They're family friends."

Benton took to searching the walls as he spoke to her, "Why did they leave?"

"I'm not sure. The property had been in their family for a few generations. They were using it like a summer home."

He kept his flashlight directed at the wall but turned to face her. "Who the hell would summer here?"

"A lot of people find Fort Wayward to be the perfect holiday location."

"No," he said simply. "They don't."

She bristled at the insult to her home town but figured he was too new to know any better. Once he settled in, he would realize just how wrong he was.

Bit by bit, his attention narrowed down until only the right wall held his interest.

"Why did they put the place up for sale?"

"I don't know."

He glanced at her. The movement was brief and quickly lost out to a few feet worth of wall. "I thought they were your friends."

"They are."

"But you don't know why they left town?" He shook his head. "You know, you have to do more than just nod at someone in the hallway for them to be considered a friend."

"Friends also respect each other's privacy."

He snorted, but didn't say anything as the wall grabbed his attention once more. The second his focus was fixed, the tension began to drain from him. His shoulders went lax, his features slack as he tilted his head forward. The only thing that retained any sign of life was his eyes. They focused and narrowed until he was glaring at the wall with singular determination. For a fleeting moment, Nicole wondered if he was having a seizure. Maybe a stroke.

"Benton?"

Just like in the car, he sucked in a deep breath, haggard and broken, like he had just pulled himself from the earth. She couldn't quite decide if she liked the sound or not. It sounded grotesque, but also signified that he had come back from wherever corner of his mind he had disappeared into. He blinked rapidly.

"Something bad happened here."

She licked her lips and ventured a step closer. "Are you like a psychic or something?"

He chuckled and shook his head slightly. "Not exactly."

"Then what, exactly?"

"Observant." He offered the word as if he had lost all interest in speaking.

Nicole jumped at his sudden burst of energy. He rushed at the wall and clawed his fingers into the slats. In his haste, his phone slipped from his grasp and scattered, forgotten, over the dirt floor.

"Are you sure you want to do that?" she asked, only to be ignored.

The wooden slats cracked and groaned as he yanked them from the wall. Her brow furrowed when she noticed what lay beneath. The planks were just a covering, thin and cheap, hastily put up to distract from the real wall below. She shone her light through the gap he had created. There was something painted on the wall.

With quick glances, she searched the space for somewhere to rest her phone that would still give them light. Benton never stopped scratching. Piling up a mound of dirt, she angled the beam from her phone at just the right angle. He shuffled wordlessly to the side as she moved to help him. They worked together to rip apart the wall, exposing more and more of the paint until the lines joined together to make a pattern.

The sound of their panted breaths filled the barn as they finished and stepped back. The symbol stretched from the floor to the high ceiling, the paint withered and worn, chipped away with age and the splintering boards. She crouched down and gathered her phone. Benton noticed the shift of light and looked over to her, watching her carefully until she had the light shining back on the space.

"How did you know this was here?"

"I have no idea," Benton whispered numbly. "Have you seen something like this before?"

She shook her head. "But I can look it up if you want."

"No," Benton snapped.

She was going to ask *why* but forgot about the question when something shifted behind the wall. It was a soft sound but enough to make them both freeze. Benton finally met her eyes. He was searching, striving to assure himself that she had heard it, too. She nodded.

Something slammed against the wall. They both lurched back, too startled to scream. The light swung around the room as she lifted her hands to fend off an attack that never came.

The silence that followed was stifling. It was hard to keep the beam of light steady as her hand began to shake. Benton took a step forward. The movement was slow but steady, the dirt crunching under his sneakers like cracking twigs. Seeing him move made it easier for Nicole to follow, and she began to trail along behind him, her phone high, and her heart in her throat.

Thump.

Scrap.

Scratch.

The sounds lured them closer to the wall. All the while, the faded symbol lured over them like a dead unseeing eye.

Thump.

Benton pressed his hand against the flat side of the wall, his fingers stretching for purchase.

Scrap.

Nicole stood on the other side of the gap. Their eyes met for the briefest moment before Benton found the courage to glimpse into the abyss.

A sudden scream and a clacking of claws streaked past them. Benton staggered back, his arms covering his face as the bird swooped and climbed up towards the rafters.

Relief and a deep sense of foolishness crushed through Nicole as she lifted the phone and searched the ceiling. It didn't take long to spot the raven. It sat by one of the windows, wings fluttering. Every now and then, it released a cry that Benton seemed to take as a personal affront. He placed his hands on his narrow hips and glared at the animal, his chest heaving with every breath.

"What the hell is with the birds in this place?"

"There must be an opening that leads to the outside," Nicole said as she tipped the light into the gap. "Maybe it was chasing a mouse."

She looked back at him to find that the anger on his face had morphed into something more personal. They lacked the necessary exposure to each other for her to grasp all of the emotions that played across his face, but there was a distinct hint of fear that played around the edges. His eyes never left the bird.

"At least it was just a raven," she offered.

It was as if Benton had forgotten she was there. He jumped and spun towards her voice, his brow knitting.

"Sorry?" he mumbled.

"Oh, right, you're of European decent, right?" She smiled. "You guys have problems with black animals."

His face scrunched up even more. "What?"

"You know, black dogs, black cats, black birds. There is a theme there." She walked closer to him, the gaping hole in the wall no longer daunting. "But around here, ravens are more like tricksters, in general."

"I'm not fond of its pranks," Benton said with one final glare at the bird.

It crowed back at him as if to state its victory. Or as if it were laughing. It took off in a start when Cheyanne's voice cracked through the night. Benton closed his eyes, physically trying to block out the noise. His mother's tone took on a shaper edge as she called for him again. He finally gave in, and called back.

"Where's Nicole?" Cheyanne screamed.

Benton dragged a hand through his hair and let it rest on the back of his neck.

Meeting Nicole's eyes, Benton jerked his head towards the barn door. "You better answer her."

It felt odd to scream at a complete stranger; it went against all the manners that Nicole's parents had hammered into her from a young age. She made sure to keep a happy tone as she assured Cheyanne she was in the barn with Benton. The response came almost instantly, coaxing them back to the main house. Cheyanne spoke with a slight twinge that left Nicole feeling uneasy. The woman sounded afraid. Benton heard it too, and his mouth twisted into a snarl. They moved to the barn doors. It was only when she caught sight of Benton's mother standing on the porch that the pieces clicked together. *She's afraid of you being alone with Benton.*

"Well, come on in, you two," Cheyanne said with a forced smile. "It's getting late."

Nicole's gut twisted as her mind churned. *Why would she be worried?* It occurred to her that she actually didn't know anything about Benton. With the thought lodged in her head, his slight eccentricities suddenly seemed less harmless.

Benton looked in her direction but didn't meet her gaze. "We really should go."

"This whole thing will seem less creepy in the daylight. When we get a proper look at it, it'll probably be a giant smiley face."

"Who would paint a giant smiley face on a barn?" he muttered.

"Mr. Dodger."

He glanced towards her but decided at the last moment that the more appropriate response was to shake his head. She had just stepped through the barn doors when he called her name. A flashlight shone on them and he waved one hand to whichever parent was holding it. Nicole waved too and waited for Benton to continue. He seemed to stumble over how to start what he wanted to ask. With one hand still on his hip, he waved the other one behind him, back in the general direction of the barn.

"Ravens," he got out before falling silent again.

"They're very beautiful birds," Nicole prompted.

"But not omens of death?"

"Not for my people. In some Siksika Nation legends, they're actually helpful and wise, but not above messing with people. I can't speak for every First Nations tribe, but, like I said, linking them with death is more of a European thing." She smiled reassuringly.

Benton's lips twitched with the urge to return the expression, but he ducked his head before she could see if he did or not.

"That's good."

"It's the owls you have to look out for."

Nicole started across the field, only catching the slightest glimpse of his head snapping up before he was lost to the shadows.

# Chapter 4

Nicole didn't have to time to look up as she heard the front door open. The newest batch was due out of the oven and she still needed to clean the mixer for the next recipe. She settled on just calling out a greeting as her mother passed by on her way to the stairs. Her mother returned the greeting and waved one hand around the corner in an exhausted display of affection. It wasn't until she rushed over to the oven that Nicole noticed her mother lingering, leaning back to get a better look into the kitchen.

"Nicole?"

She smiled widely and tried to inconspicuously brush the layers of flour off of her hands. "How was work?"

"Not bad."

Nicole cringed. That was her interrogation voice. The low crime rate of Fort Wayward and Nicole's inability to tell a believable lie without a few days of planning stood as a testament to just how effective Constable Dorothy Rider's interrogation voice was. Nicole plastered a smile on her face and pulled the batch of muffins from the oven like it required the grand total of her focus. It wasn't until she had the hot tray in her oven-gloved hands, that she noticed there wasn't any counter space left. The results of dozens of previous attempts ensured that there wasn't a single flat surface not devoted to tray after tray of cooling muffins.

"When is the bake sale?"

"Oh," Nicole dismissed with a slight chuckle and a wave which, given her grip on the tray, admittedly looked awkward. It wasn't completely abnormal for her to bake hundreds of muffins on a Sunday night. "All this? No, I was just thinking that it might be nice to have some fresh baked muffins."

"Nicole," Dorothy sighed with a mix of annoyance and fatigue. Nicole hated that combination. It was worse than the interrogation tone. "We're not going through this again."

"What do you mean?"

"Your obsessive search for the perfect recipe," Dorothy searched for a gap in the counter big enough to lean against. Eventually, she gave up.

"It's not obsessive."

"How many recipes have you tried out, tonight?"

"Only ten. That's not obsessive. It's due diligence."

"And how many did you go through the last time?"

Nicole shuffled on her feet. "Thirty-three."

"So, forty-three recipes?" she snapped, her face twisting up in horror. "How are you even affording this? Where are you even finding that many recipes for the exact same thing?"

"Internet."

"Pack it up. You're done."

"But, I'm so close," Nicole protested with a whine. "One more tweak and they will be perfect."

Dorothy's brow furrowed. "Didn't you do this years ago?"

"Maybe," Nicole mumbled.

"What changed?"

"Don't you think they're a little *dry*?" She tried her best to sound casual. A bit too much, apparently, because she didn't fool her mother for a second.

Dorothy heaved a sigh, hooked one thumb lazily around her gun belt, and rubbed her forehead with her free hand. "Who said that?"

After numerous attempts to shy away from her mother's attention, she offered a weak smile. "Benton Bertrand."

Instead of the teasing she had expected, Dorothy's attention took on a laser-like focus. "When did you meet the Bertrands?"

"When I was coming back from Vic's place. Their car had broken down so I gave them a lift."

"You went to see Vic? How is he?"

Nicole swallowed thickly as she hurriedly went back to arranging her muffins. "I think he's still sick. And still really into his girlfriend. I didn't see his parents, though," she rushed on before her mother could ask any questions that she wasn't ready to answer. Even just the memory of the hands made her shiver. "Why are you so interested in the Bertrands?"

"I never said I was."

Dorothy might have had the tough cop persona down, but she had schooled her daughter well. Nicole prided herself on her showdown glare. She didn't know if she won out or not, but her mother picked up one of the muffins and began to pull off hunks, eating a few mouthfuls before asking.

"What was your impression of Benton?"

Nicole shrugged, her lips quirking as she finally found a spot for the tray. Now that her hands were free, she found the few loose strands on her apron oddly fascinating. She toyed with them restlessly.

"I don't know," she said. "He's pretty socially awkward and seems to be constantly on edge." Her smile grew a little more and she pushed at a patch of flour. "But he seems nice, although he tries hard not to show it."

A moment later, she noticed that her mother wasn't asking any questions. She lifted her eyes and frowned.

"Why are you looking at me like that?"

Whatever Dorothy was going to say was replaced with a scoffed huff and another bite of the muffin. She hummed pleasantly and, as she chewed, pointed to the muffin and gave her daughter a thumbs up. Nicole made note of which batch it came from.

"Have you heard about Miss Williams?" Dorothy asked after swallowing and before ripping off another bite.

"No, not lately," Nicole said. "How is she feeling?"

Dorothy swallowed, her eyes turning soft. "She passed this afternoon."

"Oh," Nicole said meekly. It wasn't exactly a shock. Poor Miss Williams had been sick for a while now and everyone knew she wasn't going to get better. "I thought she had more time. How is her family taking it?"

"As well as can be expected."

"I'll have to take them a casserole," Nicole didn't know what else to say. "Who was with her when she passed?"

"Benton."

"Say again?"

"Benton was with her when she died. He was actually the only one in the room with her."

"Why? I mean, it was good that someone was with her. I'd hate for her to have been all alone. But Aspen's office isn't anywhere near Miss Williams's room."

Her mother made a noncommittal noise that Nicole knew could mean a thousand things at once.

"You don't actually think that Benton had something to do with it, do you?"

"No, of course not," Dorothy said. "But it is a bit odd."

"He never said anything about it."

That got Dorothy's attention and, once again, Nicole had the sinking feeling that it might be in her best interest to call a lawyer.

"I thought you just gave them a lift to the hospital."

"Well, they still needed to get to their new house," she said as if it were obvious.

"Do you often give complete strangers lifts to isolated properties in the middle of the night?"

"I don't often meet strangers. And it wasn't the middle of the night."

"I'm not comfortable with this," Dorothy said before waving a hand over the array of muffins. "Or any of this. But I am way too exhausted to get into what will undoubtedly be a long and tedious battle on both fronts. We will discuss both of these matters in the morning."

Nicole nodded that she understood and her mother headed for the door. Just before Dorothy slipped out of sight, Nicole called after her.

"Did Benton say why he was in that part of the hospital?"

"He said that he was aimlessly exploring."

"But you don't believe him?"

Dorothy sighed and fixed her with a weary look.

"Oh, come on, mom. Don't make me waste a day figuring it out."

"Some of the nurses had spotted him staggering around the halls. They said it looked like he was following something but they couldn't see what." Dorothy released a jaw-cracking yawn and again waved a hand out to indicate the entirety of the kitchen. "All of this is going to be clean when I come down in the morning, right?"

"Of course."

Nicole held her smile until her mother had disappeared from sight. Then she just stared at the empty doorway, the traces of happiness melted from her features, the silence of the kitchen overpowering, her baking forgotten. Her mind was consumed with shadows and claws and the unmistakable feeling that there was something unseen lurking just behind her spine.

***

Since only the bare basics of their stuff had arrived before them, the Bertrand's new house stood cold and barren. The bare walls, made of raw slate stone that ran the spectrum of charcoal back to snowy white, echoed every sound like the hollow recesses of a tomb. The layout of the house embraced two key concepts. Windows and limited walls. The near entirety of the bottom floor was one massive room, with only what Benton assumed was the laundry, hidden from view. Sliding glass doors opened out onto the wide porch that surrounded the building. In places, the ceiling was high enough to accommodate two huge windows stacked upon each other. The combination meant that anyone could stand just about anywhere, inside or out, and see almost every inch of space. The sense of utter exposure worked on Benton's nerves until they were raw.

It didn't help that the world seemed to drop out of existence a few feet from the house. Benton had only ever known night to be something that clung to the sky but couldn't compete with the constant strum of the city below. He had never realized that it could be so dark. So completely and utterly impenetrable.

Sitting on a rickety chair, he stabbed at the soggy remains of his Kung Pao beef and tried his best not to ask a question he knew he didn't want to hear the answer to. His parents were city people. They hated gardening, detested small talk with strangers, were infuriated with any store that closed before eleven pm, and used the sound of traffic as a lullaby. They didn't pick an isolated house in the middle of oblivion for themselves.

Over the years, they had clung stubbornly to their belief that his nightmares were nothing more than a misfiring of neurons. But they hadn't been able to keep their growing doubt from showing in their eyes, reverberating in their words. This move stood as unrelenting proof that they no longer believed him to be innocent in the growing pile of corpses that followed him. This house, a ship set adrift in a void, wasn't the peaceful refuge, like they claimed. It was a prison. He knew it. And they knew he did. But he doubted that the actual words would ever be spoken aloud. Instead, they clearly expected him to play his part in their little masquerade. To smile and laugh and join in on their fantasy that everything was normal. That he was normal.

Benton snapped out of his thoughts when the motion sensor lights clicked on. The stark white glare of the floodlights poured through the windows and, with no curtains to fight against it, turned the room into a mockery of midday. He winced against the sudden blinding light and poked at his dinner again.

"I do not understand your father's fascination with those damn lights," Cheyanne sighed.

Theodore had spent most of the evening putting up an expensive and elaborate light system around the house. When completed, it would be impossible to set a foot on the porch without alerting everyone inside, no matter what room they were in. Even the growing chill of the night wind wasn't enough to break his father from his task. Benton let the statement pass without comment. He knew exactly why Theodore was so obsessed with them and was too tired to play along with Cheyanne's smokescreen. This didn't sit well with his mother and soon, she tried to start the conversation again.

"Someone tells him that there are coyotes around here and he acts like they're going to break down the door."

The lies were just getting insulting. For once, just one time out of his miserable existence, he wanted to hear her tell the truth.

"Maybe he's more concerned with people sneaking out."

Cheyanne's hand stilled, her fried rice momentarily forgotten, and Benton released a long sigh. He couldn't go through with it. He might be ready to leave the delusion, but she wasn't.

"What? You think I haven't heard about the parties that bored country kids have? Refusing to let me get my driver's license before we left Toronto was subtle, but this..." He spiraled his fork to indicate the light that still burned the room like a personal sun. "It's a little too on the nose."

Neither one of them believed the other's explanations. But pretending to believe them was a whole lot easier than admitting that the security system was designed to keep him locked inside. Suddenly, the chicken tasted stale and sour. He stood and thrust the container towards her. She blinked up at him and slowly raised her hand to take it. "I'm going to bed."

"Okay, honey," she smiled weakly. "You've had such a hard day. Do you feel like taking one of your tablets tonight?"

His attempt at a calming breath was choked off by his rising frustration.

"No." The word came out as a growl and he stormed across the vastly empty room to the stairs. "Why don't we just soundproof my room?" he snapped without looking back.

She steadfastly refused to acknowledge the insult. Instead, she called out in that infuriatingly pleasant tone that his room was the one at the top of the staircase.

Benton was yet to explore the house. After Nicole had left, he had stayed in a corner and written down his dream. It was a habit, a compulsion, not as strong as his urge to warn the people, but a strong one, nonetheless. It had distracted him well enough until the food had arrived. He had yet to venture upstairs.

The insides of the rustic ranch home had been gutted and replaced by a sterile modernized arrangement. The carpet was new and thick. It squished under his feet with every step and made the trek up the long staircase a little easier to bear. His eyelids drooped and his muscles grew lax. It didn't matter that his box spring was still en route. He was going to be asleep the second he hit the mattress. Benton finally reached the top of the stairs. He could see his bed through the open doorway and it was like coming to Valhalla. A moment later, his sleep-deprived brain reminded him what was missing.

"Mom!"

She appeared behind him before he had even made his way through the doorway. She had been following him, waiting for the fallout. Benton surveyed the room as she hovered behind him. His mattress was pressed against the opposite wall, the end turned towards the doorway, making him clearly visible from the hallway as he slept. The room itself was huge, longer than it was wide, with an enclosed fireplace separating the space. Beyond it was a large, modern bathroom. With sandstone tiles, a huge tub, and a shower built for two.

"Amazing, right?" Cheyanne said. "There is no way we could have afforded a place like this in the city. You even have your own bathroom."

"And a distinct lack of doors," Benton snapped.

"It's open plan, honey," she said with exaggerated patience. "Just like downstairs. No unnecessary walls to clutter up the place. Doesn't it just feel liberating? Honestly, I don't know how we didn't feel claustrophobic in our old apartment."

"There isn't even a privacy wall for the toilet."

"Now you're just nit-picking."

Benton turned to her, his jaw clenching tight enough to hurt. "Where is my bedroom door?"

"What do you mean?" She looked behind her and gasped. "Oh, would you look at that. Maybe there isn't supposed to be one."

"You can see the holes where the hinges were!"

"Do not raise your voice at me," Cheyanne snapped. "You should be thankful. Look at the space you have. How many other kids do you think have this?"

"I think they have more privacy than an average prison inmate."

Cheyanne threw her hands up. "There is no pleasing you!"

"I can be easily pleased. With a door."

"I'll talk to your father and we'll see what can be done. But I doubt there is a good carpenter in Fort Wayward. It might take some time."

Benton gnashed his teeth and balled his hands. This was against the rules. The unspoken but long-standing rules that they all had to abide by. They didn't trust him, he didn't trust them, but neither party ever made it blatantly obvious. That's how it worked. How they had coexisted without a civil war.

"Right." He ran a hand over his face. "Until then, I'll just pin up a sheet or something."

"Benton, this house is an investment. I don't want you ruining the paint with tapes and tacks just yet."

He met her eyes and all pretenses faded away from them like a retreating tide, leaving only the raw brutality of the truth lingering between them.

"So, I can't have a door?"

"Of course you can." She smiled, a reflex movement that held no warmth or meaning. "You just have to be patient."

His neck ached as he forced himself to nod. The outside floodlights flicked on and filled the room with a tainted but searing glare. Cheyanne took the silence as a victory and, with that smile still solidly in place, turned to leave the room.

"Out of curiosity," Benton waited until she met his gaze before he continued, never attempting to keep his simmering resentment from his voice, "Do you and dad have a door?"

Cheyanne's eyes widened. For a moment, he reveled in snatching his mother's supposed victory away from her. But the sensation didn't last and, when it faded, all that remained was the crippling knowledge that, on some level, his mother was afraid of him. Shoulders slumped, he moved to brush his teeth. She left without a word, the soft shuffle of her feet across the carpet sounding slightly faster than it had before.

***

The cold seeped into Benton's veins. It numbed his limbs until the throbs of pain pulled him from sleep. He wavered on his feet, barely able to keep upright. Sweat beaded across his skin and drenched the thin material of his Chicago Cubs tee-shirt. Ravaged by the night air, it felt like a layer of sleet. He wrapped his quaking arms around himself, seeking warmth but only adding to the burning chill. Grains of damp earth crumbled from his finger. He stood, alone in the cold, unable to see anything in the surrounding darkness. The frost-covered mud cracking slightly under his bare feet.

Light exploded over him. It hit his eyes like a thousand needles and he reeled back as much as his frozen limbs would allow. It wasn't very far, but it was enough to prove to him that he was in his own skin. His own body. This wasn't a dream. The realization rocked him more than his body's sway.

*Where am I?*

He blinked rapidly but couldn't discern anything around him. With a feeble wince, he attempted to raise his hand to shield his eyes. He could barely move. Blood rushed through his ears. It roared like crashing waves and muffled the voices that rose up from within its depths. He couldn't pinpoint where the sound was coming from. Hands grabbed him. The touch like fire against his raw skin. They tried to pull, to get him to move, the staggered motion clearing his head enough for the waking world to seep in.

"Benton! What have you done?"

He blinked and turned towards the sound. Cheyanne stared at him, eyes wide with fear, her panted breaths turning to mist as they left her mouth.

"Get him out of here!"

The voice belonged to his father. It came from his feet. Benton shifted to look at him but got distracted by the dirt that covered his hands. It took only a moment for his vision to shift beyond his grime covered digits. A corpse lay at his feet. It was still half covered with dirt, its skin mangled and lips shriveled from years of rot. His mother pulled at him, but he continued to stare at the gaping holes that had once been eyes.

"Go!" Theodore ordered as he covered the sight with his coat.

Cheyanne's sobs and repeated question became a constant background noise that he couldn't understand. She yanked on him, hard enough to make him stagger. His head lolled back and he caught a glimpse of the symbol formed in faded paint on the side of the barn. Then the security lights flicked off and he plummeted back into darkness.

# Chapter 5

Benton trudged down the stairs, mumbling to himself as someone continued to pound on the front door. He felt every blow like it was thumping against the inside of his skull. He hadn't been able to get back to sleep after finding the body in the barn and everything that followed. It had taken more than an hour to convince his parents that he had nothing to do with the corpse. Even longer for him to get them to agree to call the police. By that time, the cracks that always existed in the foundation of their relationship, the ones that they painstakingly ignored, had become a gaping gorge.

Despite the fact that it was still pre-dawn, Constable Dorothy Rider had arrived looking clean cut and alert; a picture perfect officer of the Royal Canadian Mounted Police. Benton had felt the lack of sleep. The RCMP officer had asked the same questions his parents had and a few more creative ones. There wasn't much Benton could tell her. She cordoned off the barn with bright yellow tape that reflected light like a mirror. It looked too polished for such a dirty task. Thankfully, it had been a lot easier to convince Constable Rider of his innocence than it had been to convince his parents. But then, without the fuzz of hysteria, it was pretty damn obvious that the body had been in the earth longer than he had been alive.

The working theory became that it was a strange happenstance. A coyote probably came to check out the strange activity happening around a normally silent house. It must have caught the scent of decay. As the Constable reasoned, the sounds of a wild animal scratching about in his yard would have been confusing for a city boy, and he had probably wandered out without fully waking up, scaring it off before it had finished digging up its would-be dinner. She had let him go to bed but, lacking both a door and curtains, Benton had no barrier against the invading light or noise. He hadn't slept; only stared at his eyelids until the relentless knocking had started.

Benton thought that when someone accused their only child of being a murderer and then refused to apologize for their glaringly obvious mistake, that the least they could do was answer the door. Apparently, they thought differently. Because the knocking had continued until he had peeled himself from the minimal comfort of his bed and half tumbled down the staircase. With one hand in his hair and the other on the handle, he wrenched the front door open.

He had intended to snap out a few well-chosen words, but forgot everything the second he was sucker-punched by a billowing pile of helium balloons. They swung back into him each time he swatted them aside, like a school of bobby rainbow piranha. It made him look around for something sharp to pop them with. The split second before his dignity was not worth one more hit to the face, they pulled back and he was left staring at Nicole's smile. It was perfect. Despite the nervous energy she admitted and the fact that she had just parked behind an RCMP cruiser.

"Welcome to Fort Wayward," she said awkwardly.

Benton stared at her. Eventually, she held out the basket again, high enough this time that the balloons wobbled over his head. The basket was huge, wrapped with cellophane, and brimmed with assorted items and food, all statically placed for maximum effect. It was topped with a massive pink envelope that he couldn't stop looking at.

"I didn't know you could do calligraphy with glitter pens."

"You can do anything with glitter. I'm kind of famous for it," she said and rattled the basket slightly.

He didn't move to take it.

"You don't have any questions, Nicole?"

After a moment of thought, she said almost sheepishly, "Can I come in?"

"Not even a little curious about the police cruiser, huh?"

"Oh, I kind of know a bit about that already," she said with diplomatic sensitivity.

"How?"

She tilted her head. "Well, the police officer who interviewed you this morning is my mother."

The second she said it, the obvious last name connection snapped into the forefront of his mind. "How did I not get that?"

"You had a lot on your mind," she dismissed easily.

Her arms had to be hurting by now, but she refused to lower the gift basket. She only adjusted her grip on it to wave at one of the police officers who was still lingering around. He seemed to be in his forties, and had a narrow face that made his smile look wider. Spotting her, the officer jogged up onto the porch, his eyes locked on the gift basket.

"I'm guessing this is the famed welcome basket. It looks great."

Nicole preened under the praise.

"Are those some choc-mint muffins?"

"Yep," she said with glee. "I'm trying out a new recipe."

"I don't suppose you've got a few extra?"

Nicole twisted, putting her shoulder between the officer and the basket. "Not until you get your cholesterol down."

"Geegee sold me out?"

"You can't blame your wife for being concerned."

The officer, whose name Benton had yet to be introduced to, rolled his eyes playfully.

"Fine. But seriously, it all looks great." He acknowledged Benton for the first time. "Doesn't it?"

"Yeah," Benton said with a fake smile. "It's almost enough to forget about the dead body in my backyard."

The officer shifted his attention to Nicole. They seemed to have a silent conversation that finished with Nicole sending him on his way with a slight tip of her head. Benton watched the whole display with confusion and a little resentment. The officer made his apologies, gave Benton a pat on his shoulder that he assumed was meant to be some sign of camaraderie, and trotted back down the stairs to his post.

"Bye, Uncle Chuck."

A surprised laugh choked off in Benton's throat. "So you're just related to all law enforcement in this town?"

"Chuck?" she asked innocently. "Oh, we're not actually related. He's been my dad's best friend since they were in fourth grade."

"Great." He pulled the basket out of her hands and moved to close the door. "Thanks. Bye."

Her hand was instantly on the door, forcing it back open. Benton stared at the door, trying to express just how odd and unwelcome her behavior was with facial expressions alone. She caught on well enough but didn't seem deterred.

"I'm sensing that you're not much of a people person."

"It's a side effect of my overall distaste for the human species," he acknowledged with a nod.

"But you and me," she said. "We're going to get along great."

"No," he said flatly. "We're not."

Her smile only grew wider. "Yes, we are. I'm friends with everyone in this town, and you're not going to ruin my streak."

"But there is that pesky overall distaste," he noted.

"But I'm awesome."

He sucked a breath in through his teeth. "That's a problem for me," he said. "I'm allergic to awesome. And happiness. And the general will to live."

"Do most people get your sense of humor?"

"I'll let you know when I tell a joke." He attempted to close the door again only for her to stop him. "You seriously need to take a hint."

"You need a ride to school," she countered. "Unless you're thinking of going on an hour-long stroll."

He was about to mention that he had an excellent excuse to take the day off when he remembered that both of his parents had recently arranged to telecommute. They were both going to be home. All day. There was something deeply twisted in knowing that he didn't have a problem hanging out with a corpse, but the idea of being in the same house as his parents was too much.

"Fine. I should brush my teeth, though."

He turned from the door, leaving it open, and only hesitating when she mentioned.

"And probably pants."

His fingers clenched the staircase banister. It hadn't even occurred to him that he was still in just a tee-shirt and boxers. He was saved from complete humiliation by the thought that he had at least showered once Rider had sent him up, so he didn't smell like stale sweat. Nothing helped the fact that he was in his boxers, though. Shoving down his blush, he forced himself to continue up the stairs. It was hard to keep himself from thinking of how gross he must have looked. Sleep deprived and haggard. His long bare legs making him look like he was cross-bred with a praying mantis. Bed head. Reaching the top of the stairs, he ran a hand through his hair in a feeble attempt to make it obey.

"What happened to your door?"

Benton let out a yelp he would never admit to and spun around to find that Nicole had followed him all the way up and into his room.

"Why didn't you stay at the front door?"

"You didn't tell me to." She examined the missing chunks of wood where the door's hinges should have been fixed as she continued, "It's just weird to loiter in someone's house."

He flung his arms out, sending the balloons into chaos. "Everything you do is weird."

"That's debatable," she dismissed. "The door? Do you need a carpenter? I know a good one."

Benton opened his mouth, the truth on his tongue, but he couldn't force the words out. Losing all his steam, he mumbled that his parents were taking care of it.

Since she wasn't paying attention to the massive 'go away' expression he was throwing at her, and he was too embarrassed to mention that he was going to get naked, Benton decided that he would just pull on a pair of jeans and be done with it.

He tossed the welcome basket onto the tangled mess of sheets and towels that made up his bedding and dug into his suitcase. Nicole lingered in the doorway. He turned his back on her and tried to ignore that she was there.

"When is your stuff due to arrive? I could get a few friends over to help you move it in. It will be a great way for you to meet people."

"By getting them to do manual labor for me?" Benton asked as he jumped into his jeans.

"Some people actually like doing nice things for each other."

"No, they don't," he muttered. "They like how other people think about them for doing nice things."

"That's a lonely way to go through life."

The actual sympathy that hung in her words made him turn. For the first time, she didn't look ecstatic. There was still a slight smile curling the corners of her mouth, but it looked almost sad. A sliver of guilt made its way across the pit of his stomach. As much as he found her constant Care-Bear levels of happiness annoying, he didn't want to be the one to rob her of it.

"Yeah, well," he stammered for an excuse. "Worse ways to be, I suppose."

*Well, that was pathetic,* said a mocking voice in his head.

"Are you okay?" she asked.

His shoulders hunched at the question. "Why wouldn't I be?"

"Because of Miss Williams," she said. "And last night. Seems like you might be going through some things. And as your friend–"

"We're not friends," he cut in.

"As your *future* friend," she amended, her smile regaining its strength. "I care about how you're handling this."

She sounded so genuine that his readymade snarl died in his throat. He licked his lips and rubbed the back of his neck.

"Ain't anything new," he mumbled.

He instantly regretted the slip. Nicole hadn't missed it. Her brow furrowed, her eyes became sharp, and she looked at him like she was studying a new puzzle. A lot of people had looked at him like that. He hated it. "Nicole," Benton's mother appeared as if she had formed from the air itself. "I thought I heard voices."

"Voices, you investigate. But someone banging on the door for fifteen minutes you let slide," he mumbled.

Cheyanne threw a warning glare at Benton and, for the first time, he didn't instantly shy away. He was still angry and hurt and a petty part of him wanted her to feel just an ounce of it. But he soon lost his nerve and turned his attention back to his suitcase.

"Is that the welcome basket?" Cheyanne continued, her fake happy tone grinding against his nerves. "It's lovely. Thank you. You put far too much effort into it."

"Not at all," Nicole smiled. "A lot of the items were donated by local business. There are even a few maps and some coupons for the Buffalo Jump."

"Buffalo Jump?" Benton heard his mother ask as he sniffed at his gray hoodie.

It didn't smell too bad but he decided to go for his sweater instead. It was as he moved to brush his teeth, that he was hit once again with his distinct lack of privacy. He couldn't even duck behind a wall to escape the conversation happening behind him.

"It's a cliff face that the local First Nation tribes had once used in the buffalo hunts," Nicole explained. "I work part time at the museum there. It's really great if you want to learn more about our history. And it has some of the best views around."

He didn't have to look to know the nervous expression that flittered across his mother's face as she asked, "And you belong to one of these tribes?"

Having been born and raised in large cities, the only distinctions Cheyanne could really get her head around were 'locals' and 'tourists.' It made her nervous around certain people. Like she was hyperaware of saying something that could be culturally insensitive, but completely at a loss over what those things might be. If Nicole noticed the strain, she politely ignored it.

"Siksika Nation, ma'am."

"Oh, I must admit that I haven't heard much about your people."

"You might know us as Blackfoot," Nicole said. "Most of the town actually has some kind of tie to the tribe."

"Well, I look forward to educating myself. Thank you so much for the gift. We really appreciate it," Cheyanne lowered her voice to add. "Especially given the circumstances."

Nicole didn't hesitate to meet her confidential tone, "Circumstances?"

"Dead person buried in the barn," Benton mumbled around a mouthful of toothpaste froth. "Mother's a little worried the locals will think we're responsible."

Nicole actually laughed. "Don't worry, Mrs. Bertrand, no one thinks that. After all, first estimates are that the body is at least sixty years old."

Benton watched with a hint of amusement as his mother's relief mixed with suspicion. "How would you know that?"

"Well," Benton said with glee. "I'm glad I'm not the only unobservant one."

Nicole explained the connection between her and the officer his parents had been so reluctant to call. The fun of watching his mother try and cling to her smile soon lost its charm. His mother honestly feared that he was a killer, or at least feared his potential to be one. The knowledge settled against his chest like a lead weight. He tugged the hood of his sweater up over the disaster of his hair. It wasn't worth staying here for a second longer to try and fix it. Throwing his clothes aside, he found his backpack and shoved his phone and headphones into it.

"We should go," he said to Nicole.

The room felt like the size of a football field. It seemed to take forever for him to cross the space.

Cheyanne struggled to keep her blatantly fake smile in place and the hint of fear out of her voice. "Go? Go where?"

"School," he said as he slung his nearly empty backpack onto his shoulder. "Need to get that education."

"I thought you would stay home for the day."

She threw everything she had into silently telling him that she wanted him to ditch Nicole. Now, by the look of it. Benton met her eyes.

"Why?"

She stumbled, not expecting to have to come up with an answer that would be appropriate for the current company.

He turned his attention to Nicole. "Ready?"

"Always."

Cheyanne finally found her voice. "You haven't even had breakfast yet. Let me make you something, sweetie."

He ripped open the cellophane that was wrapped perfectly around the basket, and grabbed a muffin and a few cookies.

"Taken care of," he said as he waved them in the air. "Come on, Nic."

Nicole gave him an odd look. It only lasted a split second before she turned to his mother with a dazzling smile.

"Don't worry, Mrs. Bertrand. There's a coffee shop right across from school. I'll make sure he gets something a little more substantial and isn't late for his first day."

Benton hid a smile as he thundered down the stairs. He couldn't remember the last time it had felt like someone was actually in his corner. Cheyanne followed close behind him, shifting between babbling excuses and calling for his father. To say goodbye, as she insisted. Benton pulled on his sunglasses and practically jogged to Nicole's jeep. Cheyanne stopped on the porch, constantly sneaking glances back into the house, searching for Theodore. Her urge not to make a scene, especially with a RCMP officer present, won out, and she settled on waving after him. He didn't look back as he hurled himself into the passenger side. Half a second later, Nicole got into the driver's seat.

"Are you okay?"

"Just drive. Please."

She turned the engine on and headed down the gravel road without further comment. Tension clawed at his muscles like insects, the sensation growing until they passed the raw wooden logs of the property fence. The air instantly lightened. He sagged against the door and watched the incredible expanse of green and golden grass, the lofty blades shimmering in the breeze like ripples on an endless ocean.

"So this is the new kid?"

Benton shouted every curse word he knew in a second flat. He whipped around to find two women sitting in the back. They were identical twins, both with their dark hair pulled back, the same fine features, and matching jackets. Nicole made quick introductions.

"This is Meg and Danny."

Each girl raised her hand in turn when their name was called.

"Girls, this is my friend, Benton."

"Still not friends," Benton muttered.

Nicole happily ignored him, but Meg was quick to scoff. "So you're just using her for the ride? Aren't you great at making first impressions?"

Benton narrowed his eyes but there wasn't much he could say in his own defense.

"Be nice," Nicole reprimanded.

Rolling her eyes, Meg leaned back in her seat and crossed her arms over her chest. Benton turned back to face the front.

"You're pretty good at describing people," Danny said.

A quick glance in the rear view mirror was Nicole's only response.

"You described me?"

"People were curious," Nicole said innocently.

Benton snorted and aimlessly shuffled his legs in an attempt to get comfortable. At his silence, Nicole made her own attempt at conversation.

She addressed both girls at once. "Where are your normal jackets?"

Meg was the one to answer, "We always wear these."

"No," Nicole said with growing suspicion. "You don't."

"I don't know what you're talking about," Danny said.

That earned them a scowl. It was an odd look on Nicole and Benton found himself somehow drawn back to the conversation.

"Not again," she groaned.

"There's an Algebra test today," Danny shrugged.

Benton glanced over his shoulder. "What's going on?"

"I'm good at Algebra," Meg said as she jabbed a thumb at her sister. "She's better than me at Biology. We trade."

"So you take tests for each other?" Benton said.

"No," Nicole cut in sharply. "They make very bad jokes about it. Because if they did do such a thing, it would completely–"

"How many times have you given us the morality-must-win speech?" Meg interrupted.

Nicole actually gave thought to the question. "Eight."

"And how many times has it worked?" Danny asked.

"Eight. I hope."

"Oh, sweetie," Meg giggled. "You're going to be very disappointed."

Danny leaned forward and gave Nicole a hug from behind. "You can just pretend that this is the one time that we actually do listen."

"That is exactly what I'm going to do."

"What about you?" Meg said as she kicked the back of his seat. "Are you going to tell on us, Benny-boy?"

Benton tilted his head towards her but didn't bother to look all the way around. "I've gone this long without caring about your existence. No reason to change that now."

"Wow," Meg laughed. "Can you even remember the last friend you had?"

Without conscious thought, Benton slipped a hand under his hoodie and deep into his hair. He traced along a surgical scar that would never quite heal. His mind was trapped in a dark alleyway he hadn't set foot in for years. He shivered.

"Yeah, he was pretty memorable."

Benton turned back to the window. The small brick buildings that made up the town became specks on the horizon. They grew, rising up as Nicole pulled onto an asphalt road. The crystal clear sky hung low. It felt close enough to touch. Opening the window, he ignored the girls' conversation and enjoyed the brisk breeze. His eyelids drooped at the soft scent of fresh grass.

His body turned rigid. His eyes crawled over his bones. Frozen in place, he snapped his eyes open, trying to see what had provoked the reaction. Needle sharp claws slipped out from behind him, growing until he could see the long, disjointed fingers that followed. They twisted and curled, perpetually searching. Benton recognized them instantly. They had remained in the back of his mind since the moment he had seen them in his dream. Since he had been in the field of glorified dead. Been forced to watch a man drain his own life.

The hands silently slithered forward, flanking him, enclosing him. Thin, twitching arms expanded out around him until the claws scratched against the dashboard before him. He darted his gaze to Nicole. She was still talking with the twins, undisturbed by the rough grooves the nails were digging into her car. The hands snapped around to face him, the claws bare and sharp, poised, deadly. They struck.

They destroyed his chest, slashed open his lungs, transforming his emerging scream into a slick whistling whine. He thrashed, unable to move within the limited space as agony seared through him. The tips of the nails traced the edges of his heart, nicking it with every frantic beat. Nicole's voice rose over the chaos and blinding pain. Benton clung to it. Focused on it as the only center of reality.

Then the hand was gone and the strap of the seatbelt was all that was left fixing him into place. A few swift tugs and he was able to double over. He put his head between his knees, coughing and sputtering until he was able to force his lungs to function. He tugged at his sweater, thumped his chest, searching for the gaping hole. There was nothing. His mind whirled but he couldn't grasp onto a single explanation. He hadn't hallucinated before. He wasn't on any medication.

"Should I pull over?"

Ignoring Nicole's question, Benton nearly scrambled out of his seat as he whirled around to glare at the sisters. Each of their hands were normal. No claws or blood or hunks of his flesh clinging to their nails. Nicole called for him again and he shrunk away from the flood of questions the twins were now throwing at him.

Swallowing thickly, he leaned back into his seat, mumbled an apology, and pulled his phone and earphones from his pack. The questions continued and he cranked up the volume, until it drowned them out. Squeezing his eyes closed, he focused on getting his heart to slow down.

# Chapter 6

The second they arrived at the school, Benton threw himself out of the car and practically fled into the building. Nicole had tried to follow, but he was an expert at hiding in small crowds. Even at lunch, she wasn't able to lay eyes on him. The longer she didn't get to talk to him, the more the questions crammed into her mind. She tried to sort everything she had learned over the last few days into something that made any kind of sense. But it was as if she was missing the centerpiece that would hold everything together. The problem was, the longer it didn't make sense, the more her brain refused to make room for anything else.

By the time the last class of the day came around, she was functioning mostly on autopilot. Leaving the locker room, not at all excited for gym class, she drifted out onto the baseball field and instantly searched for the twins. They had adopted their normal styles once again. Meg with her overabundance of eyeliner and aversion to color, and Danny with her hair slightly curled and more feminine. Both of them looked unbearably smug.

"How was your fraud?" Nicole asked.

"Do you really want to know?" Danny asked softly.

She really didn't and let the conversation drop. More students filtered out of the gym and, in the absence of a teacher, formed into different groups and began to chat. It wasn't hard to pick Zack out of the crowd. It never was. He was tall, boisterous, and a massive flirt. He lumbered over to them, winked suggestively at Meg, and slung his arm over Nicole's shoulders.

"How are my favorite girls, today?"

"I'm good," Meg smiled. "How's my least favorite guy?"

"Why hurt me?"

"Have you met Benton, yet?" Nicole asked.

Zack had been looking forward to the new addition for a while, and she was sure that the two could actually be good friends. Her hope dwindled when she saw Zack's brow furrow.

"You mean the weird new kid?"

"He's not weird," Nicole said.

"Yeah, he is," Zack said.

"He did completely freak out this morning," Meg noted.

"He's just under a lot of pressure. If you haven't noticed, he's had it rough the last couple of days. You'd be a little weird, too."

Meg and Zack shared a smirk.

"So," Meg said. "You're admitting he's weird?"

"Don't get her riled up, guys," Danny sighed.

"Oh, look who finally showed up," Meg smiled and glanced over Nicole's shoulder.

She turned and scanned the crowd. Benton tried to melt into the background, but his gray hood was visible against the brick walls. Apparently, he knew his disguise didn't work all that well, since he hid behind his sunglasses and hunched his shoulders like he could somehow get rid of his height. They turned to each other, Nicole waved for him to come over, but he somehow managed to vanish in the sparse crowd. An act like that had to take a great deal of effort.

"Wow," Zack chuckled. "This must be so embarrassing for you, Nicole."

"Want to revisit the whole 'weird' thing?" Meg said with a smile in her voice.

Nicole tried to shrug it off, but the rejection stung more than a little. She had never really had much experience with it and wasn't about to accept it. The conversation continued and Zack's teasing laughter drew her back in, despite herself. Then the air shifted. Within the same instant, everyone fell silent, but no one could place why. A nervous anxiety filled the air as the groups absently shuffled closer, closing their ranks. Nicole's stomach went cold when she spotted Victor stalking across the grass, closing in on them with a ferocious snarl, his body vibrating with restrained energy. He looked to be out for blood, and she instinctively took a step back.

"Hey, man!" Zack greeted.

Despite his happy tone, Zack quickly finished putting his shoulder length raven hair into a ponytail, ensuring his hands were free and his chest protected by the time Victor joined them.

Victor didn't respond. He just silently joined their circle and stood rigid, hands balled.

"Not that it's not great to see you," Danny said hesitantly. "But you look horrible. Maybe you should drop by the hospital."

"Baseball today?" Victor's voice sounded like shattered glass.

Zack cast his eyes around the group, but none of them really knew what to do.

"Yeah," Nicole answered. "But don't you think you should sit this one out?"

Victor locked his bloodshot eyes on Zack. "You pitching?"

Zack once again looked around for help before answering, "Yeah."

Victor twitched uncontrollably. Still, his eyes were an unwavering force as they locked onto Benton. He acknowledged him with a jerk of his chin before speaking to Zack, "Hit him."

"What?" Zack laughed awkwardly. "You want me to hit the new kid with a pitch?"

"As hard as you can."

A grin twisted Victor's face but never reached his eyes. It ripped open the broken flesh of his lips, released beads of fresh blood. Zack was famous for his arm. He could bring in a speedball that rivaled some of the best minor league talents. Nicole's mind instantly summoned the memory of a time when one of his pitches had accidently struck a batter's hand. It had shattered a few bones.

When no one else spoke up, Nicole said, "You can't be serious. Vic, you hate violence, remember? Why would you want to hurt anyone?"

Victor's eyes remained locked on Benton in a venomous, unblinking glare. Blood dripping from his mouth, the smile grew wider.

"Hey," Zack nervously nudged him, trying and failing to get his friend's attention. "What's going on, man?"

"He's messing with my girlfriend." His knuckles popped as he balled his hands.

"Benton?" Meg's eyebrows shot up. "Are you sure you have the right guy?"

Victor growled, the tone feral. Meg edged closer to her sister's side.

"I think you got the wrong guy," Nicole tried again. "He hasn't had time to meet anyone yet."

"She visited him this morning."

Meg's nerve was something hard to lose but easy to retrieve. She didn't hesitate to cut back in, "That sounds more like she's messing with him."

A raw growl rumbled within his ribcage as he lunged at Meg. Zack instantly placed a hand on the center of his chest and pushed. A month ago, Victor would have easily won by weight alone. Now, he staggered back a step and was unable to regain his ground.

"Just calm down," Zack kept his voice low, trying not to draw any attention. "Take a breath."

"Are you going to help me or not?" Victor snapped.

Zack hesitated.

The silence only spurred Victor on into a wild, near hysterical scream that Nicole had never heard before.

"You're picking him over me?"

His voice cracked on the last word and Zack had to put more force into keeping Victor's frail form back.

"Okay, just settle down. I'll do it," Zack muttered under his breath, but it was still enough to satisfy Victor. The wild anger seeped away. By the time the coach arrived, he had such little energy left in him that he just stared vacantly ahead like a zombie. He turned, shuffling towards the bleachers with an exhausted lurch, getting out of the way before Coach Lam made it to their group.

Nicole watched him carefully as he took a seat on the bottom rung of the bleachers. He just sat there. Unmoving. Unblinking. It would have been easy to confuse him with a corpse. But still, his eyes were strong, watching Benton like a hunter stalking a deer. Her stomach twisted into knots as she grabbed Zack's forearm, yanking him close.

"You're not actually going to do it, right?" she whispered.

"You want to see how badly he freaks out if I don't? Besides, he's my friend." Zack pulled his arm away and stepped back. "Don't worry. I'll go easy on the freak."

She opened her mouth but Zack cut her off with a smile and a nod towards Coach Lam. She had just come into earshot, leaving Nicole with only facial expressions and minimal hand gestures to express how much she hated this plan. Zack only found her efforts amusing, and she fought the need to stomp her feet in frustration. Resolved to at least warn Benton, Nicole spun on her heel and almost smacked into the Coach. Nicole wasn't short, but Coach Lam was a towering woman and wasn't above using it to intimidate the more uncooperative teens in her care.

"Oh, excuse me," Nicole smiled and tried to slip past her.

"Not so fast, Rider," Coach Lam said and pointed back over Nicole's shoulder. "Out on the field with your team."

Nicole glanced around, stunned to discover that the class had already been split into teams and were preparing for the game. *Maybe Zack and Benton are on the same side.* For a moment, the thought made her smile. But then she spotted Zack on the mound, kicking at the dirt and stretching out his shoulder while Benton was third in line to bat.

"Can I just quickly tell Benton something?"

At the sharp point to the outfield and a tiresome sigh, Nicole started to think that she may have used up all of her goodwill with Coach Lam. Understandable really, after that rather unpleasant semester of badminton. Feeling defeated, she headed out onto the field, meeting up with Danny in the area designated for people who weren't all that helpful. Danny was a runner, good at sprints and an all-star at cross country, but wasn't exactly great at hand-eye coordination.

"Do you think Benton would understand some hand gestures?"

Danny's lips tilted in a light smile. "I'm sure he's been on the receiving end of a few."

At least she had the decency to look remorseful when Nicole shot her a reproachful glare. The first ball was thrown, hit, and people quickly scurried around to grab it as a student ran for first base. Nicole bobbed on her feet, her eyes darting between the three men, the memory of cracking bone lodged in her head.

"Hey," Danny said as the next pitch hurled towards the new batter. "He's going after Vic's girl. A bruise is him getting off easy."

"Vic's girl?" Nicole groaned and swung her arms wide. "Who the hell is she? Does she have a name? Have you ever seen her? Does no one else see how monumentally strange this is?"

"So they're being discreet."

"Look at him," Nicole said. "He could pass for a junkie. Even if she exists, even if she's human, this relationship is killing him."

"*If* she's human?"

The tone alone was enough to make Nicole snap her mouth shut. For all the times she had churned it over in her head, she had never actually considered that Victor's mystery lover might, in fact, be an 'it' over a 'she.' Hearing it come out of her mouth, it sounded ridiculous. But it lodged in the forefront of her mind and refused to shift.

"Well, how about this, have you *ever* known Vic to be the jealous type?"

Danny was saved from answering by Coach Lam's bellowed 'strike three.' It didn't matter. The unsettled concern that crossed her face spoke loud and clear. Nicole had thought that she might feel some measure of victory. It had taken her weeks to get anyone to even admit that much. But all it did was feed the sick feeling that chocked her until she could taste it.

"Huh."

"What?" Nicole pressed, her stress turning the word sharp.

"Nothing. I just get your fixation a little more."

"I don't have a fixation."

It was an automatic response to the common accusation. A heartbeat later, she realized that she didn't know what Danny was talking about. She followed her line of sight and was caught off guard to see Benton getting ready to head towards the plate. *What had happened to the last guy?* she thought wildly as she glanced around. She had been too preoccupied to notice that the second batter had been easily struck out. Zack gave her a half apologetic shrug which she quickly met with her best 'are you kidding me' arm gesture. Then it clicked what Danny was talking about.

Benton had removed his loose sweater, revealing a tee-shirt that was just a little too tight. It was his shoulders. Everything about him was lithe and strong, but his shoulders were broad and pulled the shirt across his chest like a second skin. He ran a hand through his hair, the motion bringing attention to the slivery streaks, and picked up the bat. With his hood, he looked awkward. Without it, he just looked generally infuriated by everything around him. And completely unaware of what he was walking into.

"Do you think his face would crack if he smiled?" Danny laughed.

"That's what you're thinking about right now?" Broken bones were playing over and over in Nicole's head until she could almost hear them cracking.

"Oh, relax, Zack's not going to hurt him."

Nicole watched as Zack glanced to the stands. Victor was still there, his body vibrating with rage, his fingers clawing at his own hands until they were streaked red with blood. Zack shivered, coiled up, and sent the ball hurdling towards Benton in a blur. Benton dropped.

When the dust settled, she was relieved to find that Benton was okay. He was staring at Zack, his face surging between shock and anger. Behind him, the catcher pulled his hand out of his mitt with a sharp hiss.

"What the hell, Zack!" the catcher snapped over the shrill cry of Coach Lam's whistle.

"That was at his head," Danny muttered in disbelief.

Zack hunched his shoulders at the Coach's reprimand and kicked the dirt.

"It got away from me," he called back.

Benton got to his feet, one hand clenching the bat while the other dusted the dirt off of his jeans. His eyes never left Zack. Nicole couldn't keep still as nervous energy built up inside of her. Once more, Zack looked over to the stands. Like a man possessed, Victor was shredding his skin, his hands sinking under his jacket to find unmarred flesh. Even from this distance, she could see blood trickling out from under the material. Zack threw all his effort into the next pitch.

Benton dropped down onto a knee as the ball sailed over his head. He ran a hand through the tufts of his hair as he got back up. The shock had faded. Now he looked almost as enraged as Victor, if not as crazy. The catcher reeled in pain, Lam screamed about safety, and Zack protested that the batter had been crowding the plate. The next time Zack looked over to the stands, Benton followed his gaze and locked eyes with Victor. They stared at each other with barely matched rage, then, without a word, Benton turned back to Zack and lifted the bat again. Zack was given a final warning, but Nicole knew it was nothing compared to the unspoken promises Victor was making. Her heart clenched in time with the muscles of her legs. She inched forward.

"Don't," Danny whispered.

Nicole turned to find Danny watching Victor, her breathing unsteady and the first traces of actual fear seeping across her features. The ball was thrown. Benton swung. A solid crack cut the air as the ball streaked back to Zack in a blur. It drove into Zack's stomach, forcing him to double over in pain, the air forced from his lungs. The ball bounded down the mound.

"Sorry," Benton smiled as he twirled the bat around his hand. "I guess it got away from me."

Zack snarled and charged for home plate. Coach was faster and within a second, had both by the back of their shirts.

"That's it! Laps. Both of you!" She shoved them hard enough to get them moving. Still glaring at each other, they reluctantly obeyed. "And best break any plans you had for this afternoon. You're both mine!"

As the boys began to trace the edges of the field, the rest of the class erupted in excitement and badly hushed whispers. Nicole didn't hear a word of it. Her attention was focused on the now empty bleacher seat and the trails of blood that slowly seeped from it onto the grass below.

***

Jeans were not built for running laps.

After close to an hour, that point was painfully clear. Sweat dripped from his face and ran in very annoying rivets down his spine. His legs felt useless, but it was a welcomed change from working his shoulder. Coach had watched them like a hawk as Zack had lobbed in pitch after pitch. Apparently, their punishment wasn't over until she was satisfied that they now knew how to 'play nice.' Benton had lost count of how many he had hit, but his shoulders felt like there were razorblades lodged within the joints. Zack didn't seem to be doing any better.

"Is she still looking?" Zack panted as they lumbered along.

"Yeah."

They had to run side by side, and their original contest to outpace each other was, in hindsight, a bad idea.

"This is your fault."

Benton resisted the urge to trip him. "Mine? You were the one taking orders from the ghoul in the stands."

"That ghoul happens to be my best friend," Zack snapped before his voice softened. "And he didn't always look like that."

"So he was alive at one point?"

"How do people stop themselves from hitting you?"

Benton decided that silence was the best response. It also allowed him to catch his breath again.

"And it's still your fault," Zack said out of nowhere. "You just had to mess around with his girlfriend."

He jolted. *Idiot,* the mocking voice in his head laughed. *Of course, Nicole has a guy.* The thought was out before the rest of his mind caught up, throwing out facts. Like that he wasn't interested in Nicole. Also, he had in no way been 'messing' with her or anyone else.

He settled for snarling, "What the hell are you talking about?"

"He said you were messing with his girl."

"Who is his girl?"

Zack looked almost bashful. "I don't actually know."

"Sorry?" he hissed.

"He hasn't introduced us."

"What did he say I did?"

Zack was suddenly paying a lot more attention to his feet.

"He didn't actually–"

Benton latched onto Zack's arm and yanked hard. He was shorter than Zack, but anger had a way of making people seem a lot bigger than their bones.

"You don't know this girl, you don't know me, your friend is obviously deranged, but you're willing to give me a concussion over it?" he screamed into Zack's face.

"You saw him, right?"

"Reanimated corpse. We covered that." The words flew from his mouth as he steadfastly refused to hear Coach Lam behind him.

"Would you have said 'no' to him?"

"Yes!"

His body quaked with the amount of force he put behind the word, and he was sure he popped a blood vessel. But it was worth it. Anger pulsed through him, shaking him like unspent adrenaline as they forced themselves back into a trot.

"No, you wouldn't have," Zack muttered.

Benton fumed, but the need for air was more demanding than correcting him. The loaded silence remained between them as they rounded in front of the building. The further they went, the harder it was for Benton to hold on to his anger. It eroded under the tide of exhaustion, pain, and the nagging feeling that Zack had a point. Benton wasn't exactly a stranger to letting fear trump his better nature.

"I'm sorry." Zack said, keeping his voice so low that Benton almost missed it.

"Sorry," he mumbled back. "How's your stomach?"

"I feel like I got kicked by a horse."

Benton grinned and Zack instantly whacked him.

"You just said sorry."

"Yeah, but I used it in the regrettable sense, not the actually feeling repentant sense."

"God, I want to hit you."

"Alright, boys," Coach Lam hollered from across the field. "What's the lesson here?"

"Play nice," they said in unison.

"And if you do this again, I'm going to be really mad. And I'm vindictive when I'm mad."

They both knew the correct response and wasted their lungs on it. "Yes, ma'am!"

"Good. I'm going home. You guys can do the same, showers are still open."

They staggered to a stop. Benton braced himself on his weak legs and just focused on sucking in deep breaths. Zack folded his arms behind his head and continued to pace in slow circles. His heart was still pounding when footsteps raced towards them. He wanted to ignore them, but survival instinct forced him to straighten up. It wasn't exactly a surprise to see Nicole walking towards them, two bottles of water in her hands. A small smile tipped his lips.

Her smile dropped, her eyes flicking over his shoulder. Brow furrowing and still panting, he turned to see what she was looking at. Victor was right behind him. Before Benton could move, Victor's fist smashed down against his jaw. Pain cracked out under his skin. His vision turned white. He staggered back, blinking wildly as rage boiled under his skin. Saliva flew from Victor's mouth like a rabid animal as he pushed Zack aside and charged.

Benton ran to meet him and ducked just before they collided. His shoulder drove into Victor's shoulder, hard enough to make him grunt. Grabbing his legs, Benton used the momentum to lift Victor off his feet and drop him onto his back. They hit the earth hard, not bothering to detangle themselves before they started to swing. Victor was taller than Benton and had a strength that his frail appearance didn't give him credit for. Benton knew that he couldn't let Victor throw him off.

Benton clenched his aching jaw as he took the pain of the blows. Victor swung savagely as Benton shifted his weight to try and keep him down. With his shoulder still driving his weight down upon Victor, Benton slammed his knee into Victor's side. The taller man released a pained cry, his legs stilling the split second Benton needed to straddle. It was easier to pin him down like this, and it left Benton's arms finally free to attack. He got in two decent punches before arms looped around his chest and pulled him off of a now raving lunatic. Victor thrashed, kicked out, trying to land a blow into Benton's exposed chest.

Zack grabbed Victor's arms, trying to pull him back as he begged him to calm down. It didn't change anything. Victor howled like a wounded beast, frothing at his mouth, lunging at Benton until his joints strained in Zack's hold.

"You can't have her!" Victor screamed. He gnashed his teeth hard enough to crack them, blood spurting out from his possibly broken nose. "She loves me!"

Benton threw himself forward, gaining a few inches before he was dragged back. "Touch me again and I will kill you!"

He lost sight of Victor as Nicole filled his vision. She placed her hands against his shoulders and crowded in until he couldn't swing without the risk of hitting her.

"Benton," she gasped. "Stop!"

"Let me go," Benton shrieked.

More voices joined the static filling his head. The hands continued to shove and pull. Someone kept screaming his name into his ear.

"Get off of me!"

He tore himself free, spun around and shoved the person who had been holding him. His brain staggered to a stop the moment he felt the rough, unforgiving texture of a stab vest under his palms. He gaped up at a very angry Constable, the urge to fight fleeing on a huffed breath.

"Hi, mom," Nicole said with a nervous little wave. "I can explain."

# Chapter 7

Benton flinched at each dab of the alcohol swab against his split lip. He tried to stifle the urge, but it burned and he had lost too much adrenaline not to notice. It was distracting, especially when he was trying to keep up with Constable Rider's questions. Somewhere between Benton pushing a police officer and his mortification at realizing it, Victor had slipped off, leaving Benton to face the consequences alone. He quickly discovered that Rider would make a great poker player. He couldn't get a read on her at all. Nicole blotted his lip again and he hissed.

"I'm a trained first aid administrator," she defended.

"My pain receptors don't care about your qualifications."

She flushed as Zack chuckled.

"I'm good at this," she snapped. "His body's just weird."

Zack snickered into his hand, but Rider managed to stifle her smile before it got too big. She placed a reassuring hand against the back of her daughter's head. Nicole sulked into the touch as she cracked a single use ice pack, shook it to make sure the chemicals mixed, and handed it over to him. The chill grew and felt like heaven as he pressed it against his already swelling jaw. Victor had one hell of a left hook.

"So you have no idea why he would attack you?" Rider clarified.

"And hadn't even seen him before last period," Benton said.

"You're sure? Not even around town? In the hallway?"

"I'm good with names and faces."

Nicole tilted her head, "You didn't remember she was my mom."

"I didn't make the connection," Benton corrected. "There's a difference."

Her only response was to dab him again with the alcohol swipe.

"And you never met his girlfriend?"

"I already gave you the list of everyone I've talked to."

Rider lifted her note pad and read off the list. It was short. Aside from the teachers that he had been forced into communicating with, there were only the two teens present, the twins, and a guy he asked to borrow a pen from. Rider cocked an eyebrow at him.

"A whole day and those were the only people you interacted with? Do you suffer from social anxiety?"

"No," he said. "I just didn't want any trouble."

"How did that work out for you?" Zack smiled.

"Pretty good until a psychopath started putting hits out on me," Benton shot back.

"What was that?" Rider asked.

"Nothing. That got resolved on its own." Benton pulled his free hand through his hair, scratching at his scalp as he released a sigh. "Could this have something to do with Miss Williams?"

"No, I don't believe so. There was very little connection between them."

"What about the body in the barn?" Nicole said.

Less than twenty-four hours in town and he was already connected to two deaths. He groaned. Even scrubbing his scalp couldn't bring a measure of comfort anymore. He buried his face against his hands as Nicole asked if they had found a name yet.

"Oliver Ackerman," he muttered against the palm of his hands.

"Pardon?"

He sucked in a deep breath and lifted his head to make sure his voice was clear.

"His name was Oliver Ackerman."

"How do you know that?" Rider asked.

The stern voice seeped through the fog in his head and he sat up straighter.

"I don't know," he admitted. "I guess I heard it somewhere."

Rider held his eyes even as she poised her pen over her note pad. "But you can't remember where?"

All he could do was shake his head.

"Have you eaten?" Nicole asked abruptly, not so subtly trying to change the subject.

"I had that muffin you gave me."

Zack perked up at that. "She gave you a muffin? Choc-mint?"

"What is everyone's obsession with muffins?" Benton snapped.

"That's how she gets everything she wants. She bribes people with baked goods."

"I have never bribed anyone."

Zack ignored her. "If she pulled out that recipe, she really wanted something from you."

"Sorry to disappoint you, but it was just part of a welcome basket."

"Wait," Rider cut in. "Is that all you've had?"

"I forgot to grab my wallet this morning."

"And gym clothes," the officer noted.

"Yeah," he sighed. "Is there any chance I can go soon?"

"We really should get him something to eat," Nicole said.

Rider considered that for a moment and put her notepad away. "I'll swing by Victor's place and have a talk with him. If you have any more problems or if you see him, notify me immediately."

"Sure," Benton said as he slid off of the picnic table and handed the icepack back to Nicole.

"And I would like you to have a discussion with Aspen before you head home."

He froze, watching the officer carefully, trying to judge if he had any wiggle room in this.

"I reek."

"Oh," Nicole chirped as she happily passed him a bag. "I got you these. I had to guess your size. I hope they're okay."

His brow furrowed as he looked into the plastic bag and found another tee-shirt and a pair of worn jeans.

"You didn't have to," he stammered.

"Truthfully, I got them at the thrift shop. The whole outfit cost me five bucks," she said. "And I didn't want you stinking up my car."

Benton chuckled, his lips aching anew as they stretched. Still, it felt good to smile.

"Thanks."

"Go have your shower and we'll have Aspen around by the time you're out," Rider said.

It took everything he had to keep his back from hunching up.

"Nicole's my ride," he said quickly. "I've already held her up."

His gut clenched when Nicole cut in, still using her overly happy voice.

"I've been meaning to mention. Trish just remembered that today is her anniversary so she needs me to cover her shift at the diner. Good news is that you'll have time for the chat." She held his gaze as she added, "Bad news is I won't be able to get you home until after eight. Maybe even nine."

With everything that had happened, Benton had completely forgotten what was waiting for him at home. The excuse for an out seemed like a lifeline, and he found himself floundering towards it instantly. He was once again blindsided with that warm, sweet, and all too alien feeling that he actually had someone looking out for him.

"Thanks." He cleared his throat before looking away. "I'll let them know I'll be late."

\*\*\*

Nicole was taller than Trish and not quite as well endowed. It made the uniform sit a little awkwardly and, now halfway through her shift, she was more than a little tired of adjusting it. The twin braids of her hair swung as she bustled around the tables. Even as her feet began to throb, her step was light. She liked working at the diner. There were limited restaurant options in Fort Wayward, so each one was the perfect place to catch up with people you hadn't seen in a bit. While everyone referred to it as a diner, the menu pretty much revolved around burgers, which made it a favorite for school kids and families.

The wall opposite the counter was devoted to windows and booths. A small dirt parking lot separated the diner from the highway. Normally, the nearby streetlight filled the area with enough of a glow that they had never put in an independent light source. A few days ago, probably in an act of boredom, someone had broken the light. It left the parking lot completely at the mercy of the night. The only time the parking lot was even visible from inside the restaurant was when a random passing car's headlights flooded the area. For Nicole, it added a bit more excitement to the night. She never knew who was coming in next.

She had tried to keep track of the conversation happening in the booth closest to the door. It was the least popular of the tables, and so the owners didn't mind Benton occupying it for the length of her shift. Benton wasn't exactly shy about showing his annoyance at Aspen's presence. They had spent an hour eating burgers, drinking milkshakes, and making polite but forced chitchat. Just when she thought they were going to finally get to something interesting, the evening rush had hit and she hadn't been able to get into earshot again. By the time she had a second to look over, Benton only had his phone for company.

The rush had continued longer than expected and it was closing in on ten by the time the crowd thinned. She had just rung out Mr. Dodger, the last straggler keeping them from the closing clean-up, when the other waiter came to the counter. Rick was a year younger than her but had hit puberty early and was very proud of the chest hair he had grown. For reasons she couldn't fathom, he seemed to think women were very impressed with his body hair and popped open a few extra buttons whenever the managers weren't looking.

"He's out again," Rick smiled.

She had already set up her tray. "I'll get him."

Before she could round the counter, Rick had blocked her path. "So he's the new guy, huh?"

"Benton," she offered.

"Is it true that he went completely nuts on Vic?"

"He defended himself." She picked up the tray and fixed him with a stern look. "And you shouldn't spread rumors."

Rick leaned his back against the counter, puffing out his chest until the fledgling muscle looked stronger. "He's a bit of a runt to do anything against Vic, ain't he?"

"Button up your shirt," she sighed.

Quickly crossing to the booth, she slid the tray onto the table before crouching down. She now had enough practice in waking him up to know that a gentle approach was best. She softly rested her hand on his arm, ready to catch it if he woke with a start, and called his name in a whisper. After a moment, she repeated it slightly louder. It took longer this way, but the steady approach kept him from freaking out. It also gave her more time to study his features.

It was strange to see him sleeping. The tension that seemed an inseparable part of his features smoothed away, his near constant scowl softened, and the darkness under his eyes was lightened by the pale strands of his eyelashes. She hated to wake him. If anyone ever looked like they needed the rest, it was Benton Bertrand. Still, she forced herself to raise her voice just a little higher and rub his arm. He snapped awake with a staggered gasp and a jolt that ran through his entire body. She tightened her grip, keeping his elbow from flying, and offered him a soft smile.

"Again?" he grumbled as he rubbed a hand over his face. "Sorry."

They had gone over it more than once, but she couldn't help defending her actions. "I would let you sleep."

"No, you don't want that," he quickly assured.

"Why?"

Regret played across his face. She watched as he waged a war within himself, seemingly wanting to answer her and wanting to back away at the same time. Eventually, he croaked out 'nightmares' with a sleep broken voice. He sat up straight, or rather poured himself against the back of the chair, but the result was the same. There was distance between them now, and with it, enough room for him to construct his walls once again. It was in those few moments when he just woke up that he was the most honest, and she was going to figure out a better way of exploiting that.

"Is that what happened this morning?" She knew it wasn't. Every instinct screamed at her that there was more to it. But she wanted to see what he would say.

"Yeah. Sorry. I guess dad's right about me not sleeping in moving vehicles."

She had no logical reason to be ticked off at his evasion, but she was. After a moment's hesitation, she forced herself to nod and stood up.

"I got you coffee."

"I'm not a huge fan of coffee," he said.

"You'll like this one," she said simply as she set it before him. "It's my spicy taco latte."

"That sounds horrible."

"You like spicy."

"Who did you bribe to know that?"

She rolled her eyes. "You use hot sauce like ketchup. I made the Sherlock-like leap. Just drink it."

He eyed her suspiciously but slipped his hands around the steaming mug. It took him forever to raise the cup, and she was about to grumble some words at him when he finally took a sip. He paused, brow furrowed, the tip of his tongue licking the foam off his lips, finally humming noncommittally.

"Is it really that difficult for you to admit that I was right?" she laughed.

"A little, yeah."

She picked up her tray and swatted his arm with her cleaning cloth. "I'm always right. Our friendship will go a lot more smoothly if you just accept that now."

"Still not friends," she heard him mumble as she moved to clear the next table. But since it was followed by a pleased hum and him taking another sip, she didn't put much stock into it.

After packing the dirty dishes onto her tray, she wiped down the table as a car's headlights washed over the parking lot. She looked up to watch the car continue along the highway. Then a shadow caught her attention. The person stood on the far side of the thin highway, the light making them appear like a shadow sculpted into human form.

The car drove on and the darkness rushed back to claim the shape. Nicole straightened, the plates forgotten, and peered into the night that lay beyond the glass. All she could see was her own reflection. Absently, she wrung the cloth around her fingers and edged back to Benton's booth. Another car rounded the corner. Its high beams flashed across the road and she could see the shadow again. It was on this side of the road now. Standing completely still. Staring right at her. Chills encased her heart, strangling until the beats became heavy, sluggish thumps. Light glistened off something metal in the man's hand. But then the car was gone and he vanished back into the night.

"Someone's out there."

Her voice barely rose over a whisper, but Benton immediately looked up from his half drunken coffee.

"Yeah," Rick snorted as he came up behind her. "We're a restaurant. That's supposed to happen."

No car came. It left her blind, but she knew he was still out there. Her skin prickled like a lightning storm was rolling in. The dread that had locked her heart shattered as fear took hold. Her heart thundered into a frantic pace as she felt the man's gaze remain on her. He could see her but, for her, the glass had become a flawless black mirror.

"Where's the boss?" she asked Rick.

"Went home already."

"What?"

He scoffed and leaned against the side of the booth seat. "We're only doing the drinks menu at this hour. I think we can handle it."

Benton wasn't as dismissive as Rick. His spine straightened, his jaw tightened, and he slowly turned his head to study the window beside him. An unstable silence descended upon them. Nicole pulled the cloth tightly around her hands, her knuckles aching in protest. They all jumped when a sharp, shrill squeal cut the night. It repeated, over and over, but she couldn't see what was making the noise.

A car passed, offering them a fleeting glimpse of the parking lot. Victor was plastered against the window, his lips curled back with a sick smile, his hands pressed against the glass. Blood smeared across every inch he touched, oozing around his hands in a sickening halo, swelling to trail down in thin rivers. A butcher's knife was trapped between his left hand and the window. It scraped against the surface each time he twitched, releasing that high-pitched squeal that frosted the marrow of her bones. He locked eyes with Benton. His smile grew. The car drifted away and its light began to fade. Victor didn't move. His smile remained. His eyes never left Benton as the shadows crawled over him, gradually darkening. Then the light was gone and they were left staring at their own horrified expressions.

The fine screech of the knife against the glass trailed slowly across the window. It filled the diner, pouring over the empty chairs, highlighting how alone they were. Just the three of them and the bloodied man outside.

The sound kept moving. Carving a slow path, inch by inch, step by step, towards the door. Nicole burst into a sprint and the knife lifted from the glass. Without it, she had no way to know where he was. She barreled towards the entrance, not certain that she could beat him in this race, knowing that she had to. The door pushed in an inch before she could slam her weight against it. Her feet slipped out from under her and she crashed to the ground.

The blade of his knife slipped inside, slashing wildly, jabbing in an attempt to hit her shoulder. Plastering her feet to the tile floor, she rammed herself back. The door slammed closed but it was a short-lived victory. Her legs were strong but her feet slipped with each of Victor's attacks.

"Lock the back door!" Benton ordered Rick as he lunged free of the booth and ran to help her.

Rick bolted into the kitchen and Benton pushed his weight against the door. With him holding it steady, she focused on getting the lock in place. Each attempt was met by another stab, the blade squirming as it searched for flesh. *He can see you.* The thought repeated in her head, growing more hysterical each time. *He can see you!*

"Rick, get the lights!" she bellowed.

She flicked the lock. The lights snapped off. The mirror that had separated them reverted back into a window and she found herself a few inches from Victor. His eyes were fevered; the pupils grew wide to swallow all color, rendering them black pools that fixated on Benton alone. The grin remained, manic and wild, dripping with blood tainted saliva.

"Vic," she stammered, tears clogging her words. Even as she got to her feet, the lock engaged, she couldn't stop herself from holding her weight against the door. "Why are you doing this? You would never hurt me. You'd never hurt anyone!"

Benton grabbed her arm and tried to pull her back. She held her ground, her eyes on Victor, staring at him as if she could force the real Victor to the surface by will alone.

"This isn't you."

Victor's smile died. He stared straight ahead, unmoving as stone, not even breathing. As if stuck from behind, his head slammed forward. It crashed into the glass with a sickening thud. Fine cracks formed in the glass, his blood seeping into the hairline fracture as he was forced against the door. The glass whined with the strain.

"Victor?"

Benton yanked her back as Victor straightened. He slammed his head forward again. The fractures splintered, expanding into a spider web of cracks.

"I'm calling the police!" Rick yelled from the kitchen.

Victor ploughed forward again. Benton pulled at Nicole's arm, no longer taking care not to hurt her.

"I need to help him," she snapped.

"Crazy guy with knife," Benton hissed back. "Run now, help later."

Crack. The glass shattered enough that blood oozed out onto their side.

"Yeah," she nodded.

They pushed and shoved at each other, both trying to force the other in front as they fled to the kitchen. Rick already had a mobile at his ear, a frying pan clutched in his other hand. He held it up as they stumbled in, but realized it was them just before swinging. Benton grabbed a handful of his shirt as they passed, dragging him along behind them as Nicole led the way to the end of the prep station. There was no real good place to hide, but at least there, they wouldn't be illuminated by the moonlight if Victor was to open the door. Huddled in the dark, she cowered into Benton's warmth, one hand searching the counter for some kind of weapon.

The thumping continued. She hadn't known just how well she could identify the sound of breaking glass. But she could. She could tell in an instant that it began to yield to Victor. Her fingers ghosted over stainless steel, but everything had been packed away for the night. She heard the glass rain down over the floor. His shoes crushed it into the tiles. Victor was inside.

Nicole sunk back down in the resounding silence and placed a hand over her mouth to stifle the sounds of her breathing. They waited. Rick's mobile was still pressed to his ear, its glow like a lighthouse in the shadows. A beacon that would lead Victor straight to them. Silence. A cold chill built against her legs. She peered around the corner to the kitchen door, Benton's hand a steady weight against her back. Her heart stammered as the door slowly opened. In the thick shadows, she couldn't see anything pushing it. Just the door, growing wider. Benton's grip tightened, balling in her uniform, twitching as he fought the urge to drag her back. The door released a soft groan as it opened. Wider. Moving at an excruciatingly slow pace but never showing why.

Suddenly, red and blue lights flashed across the door. Whatever had been forcing it open vanished, allowing it to swing free, back and forth, the slightest whisper it produced lost under the wail of the police sirens.

# Chapter 8

Hours later, Benton trudged wearily through his front door and followed his parents into the kitchen. He didn't question his father when he was instructed to sit on the kitchen counter and wasn't surprised when he was handed a fine china tea cup with a matching saucer. The Bertrands weren't cooks, lacking the time, inclination, and anything resembling taste. But they always had the fixings for a decent cup of tea. His hands always felt too big and clumsy for the delicate little cup, but he appreciated the normalcy. It was what his parents gave him when they wanted to offer comfort but didn't know what to say or do. He'd had a lot of tea over the years.

He took a sip of the steaming liquid and grimaced. It tasted flat and overly sweet. If it was a local brand, he really hoped that it wasn't going to become a constant in the family routine. But, not wanting to offend his father, he forced himself to take another sip, trying to figure out how to whip up a spicy taco latte.

"Drink the whole thing, dear," his mother said before busying herself cleaning nothing in particular.

Theodore stood in front of the sink, his back to Benton, the faucet constantly running as he absently washed the same cup repeatedly. The lingering silence grew thick enough to choke on, but it seemed that no one wanted to be the first to break it. Benton kept his gaze fixed on the cup in his hand, forcing down one sip after another of their peace offering.

His mother abruptly stopped wiping down the counter. "You know you're safe now, right honey?"

Benton eyed her suspiciously as he swallowed another mouthful. She was throwing a lot of endearments his way and he couldn't tell if it was a symptom of concern or some attempt to smooth over the events from this morning. For a while, he contemplated making this as difficult as possible, but the long horrible day had robbed him of his anger.

"Yeah," he forced a smile. "I know."

"It wasn't about you," Theodore said as he roughly turned off the faucet. "The rumor in town is that this Victor character has been struggling with a drug problem of some sort for a while."

"I have half a mind to sue our realtor. She told us this was a nice town."

"One sick boy doesn't make a bad town, Chey."

Benton didn't comment and was quickly losing track of the conversation. There was something homey and comforting in just sitting still with a hot beverage, and he savored the moment, feeling the stress that had been keeping him in knots trickle away, leaving his limbs feeling boneless and heavy.

"But you're safe," Cheyanne said softly. She cupped his jaw with both hands and he let her take the weight, suddenly too tired to lift his head on his own. "The police officer is right outside. He checked the house. You're safe, baby boy."

It was hard to keep track of what she was saying through the rising static in his brain. Every time he tried to focus, the world seemed to lurch and roll, and colors began to blur around the edges. Benton shook his head, or at least he thought he did. The insides of his skull seemed to slosh about, but his mother's fingers remained as a solid, unmoving pressure against his skin.

"We have a chance here, Benton. One we can't let pass us by. We are safe. We can finally get a good night's sleep." Her fingers stroked his hair and her voice turned into a syrupy sweet whisper. "But you can't scream, baby. You can't scream. The whole town would hear about it. After everything that's happened, we can't have these people thinking you're sick."

*That's stupid,* he thought. *Who would question him having a nightmare after someone actively tried to kill him?* He opened his mouth to say as much, but his tongue remained thick and heavy. The teacup slipped from his fingers but it didn't smash against the floor. Benton couldn't understand it until he saw Theodore place the cup gently on the counter next to his thigh. The loose-limbed sensation spread down to his bones and his addled mind finally saw it for what it was.

"You drugged me?"

Theodore pulled at Benton's eyelids, checking to see how his eyes dilated, if the drugs had fully taken hold. He tried to pull away, but his father held him easily in place.

"This is for your own good. You'll feel better once you have a decent sleep," Theodore said. "We all will."

The words lodged into Benton's dulled mind, but he couldn't get any of it to make actual sense. Victor had tried to kill him, twice, in one day. He couldn't fathom why his parents would choose now of all times to render him vulnerable. A heartbeat later, it hit him that it wasn't just Victor he would be helpless against. The narcotics would knock him out and keep him out. He'll dream. Over and over. *You need to throw up,* his mind shrieked. *Now!*

He slipped off the counter and his legs gave out the second he put weight on them. Cheyanne and Theodore instantly moved to help him. With an angry, uncoordinated swipe of his arm, he pushed past them and staggered to the kitchen sink. *Don't sleep,* he clung to the thought like a lifeline. *You can't go to sleep.* He shoved two shaking fingers down his throat, trying to force himself to gag. Theodore appeared by his side and, despite Benton's struggle with every last ounce of strength, he was able to easily pull his hand away. Benton slumped against the counter. The fight only made the drugs work faster.

"He wants to kill me." Benton's snarl dwindled into a sob as he said it.

His parents only shushed him as they steered him towards the staircase.

"I hate the drugs."

"It'll be okay," Cheyanne said.

He wanted to scream that it wouldn't be. Wanted to holler it to the ceiling. Bellow and rage until the officer busted down the door. But all that came out was a staggered, pained groan. The drug was thick within his veins. It melted each of his muscles into useless sludge that sloshed within the shell of his skin. By the time they were dragging him up to the second floor, his eyes were burning and throbbed in unison with his heartbeat. The battle was not just to keep his eyes open but to remember *why* he had to.

Theodore took Benton's weight as Cheyanne ran forward to push aside the tangled sheets and crumpled towels that were piled atop his mattress. The security lights clicked on and exploded through the windows like a supernova. It felt like acid being poured against his quickly drying eyes. *Stay awake,* he repeated like a mantra. He tried once more to shove his fingers down his throat but could barely lift his hand. Everything was garish white as Theodore let him crumble onto the mattress.

"Mom," he groped for her, unable to wrap his fingers around her wrist. "Don't leave. Please."

She easily broke free of his feeble grasp. Before he could try again, she pulled the blanket tightly over his arms and tucked the end of the sheet between the mattress and the floor. It was a loose hold but enough to shackle him as his body melted. She kissed his forehead.

"Just sleep. Everything is okay."

He rolled his head, searching for his father. The motion shattered what remained of his brain and made his vision blur all the more. The ceiling above him was a sheet of blinding white, one that seemed to glow and dim on its own accord. His heartbeat resounded within his chest when patches of darkness seeped out of the light. Black claws tore their way through the ceiling. He could only watch as they grew, unnoticed by his parents, and became curled talons that reached down towards him.

"Dad," he gasped as he began to thrash against his bounds. "Let me up. Please."

His words morphed and shifted within his slack mouth. They made sense in his head but lost all meaning as they shifted past his lips. The noise he created was something his parents ignored easily enough. Benton was barely able to move under the raging current the sedative created. Flat on his back, watching the hand descending towards him, he could do little more than drown in the tide. The nails flashed in the light. Sleep pulled him deeper into his own bones. Adrenaline pulsed into his blood, but it still wasn't enough to combat the toxin. His eyelids drooped.

"Don't leave," he begged them both.

The security lights flashed off. For a second, the whole world was lost as his sluggish eyes strained to adjust. Moonlight washed through the windows to distinguish shapes within the shadows. He could make out his parents once more. They still loomed over him but the features of their faces began to twist and melt. The hand was almost between them now but they still didn't see it. The nails glistened in the dim light. *Just look,* he tried to scream. All that came out was a pitiful squeak. Sweat pooled at the nape of his neck, cold and clammy. His mother gently patted his forehead once more.

"Just relax," she cooed.

"Don't leave. It's here."

Theodore's hand became a solid pressure against Benton's arm as his father lurched back onto his feet.

"You'll feel better in the morning," he assured.

"No. Please."

Benton lost the battle to keep his eyes open. They slid down like sheets of iron, casting him into complete darkness and keeping him there. He could barely hear his parent's retreating footsteps over his whimpered pleas for them to stay. But he could tell that they never hesitated. Clinging to the last shreds of his consciousness, Benton tried to get off the bed, away from the falling hand. His limbs were heavy. Sleep warped around each of his movements, making him slow and heavy against the thin bed sheet that served as his shackles. Finally able to weave one arm free, he tried to roll to the side, the movement an arduous struggle. Flopping it to the side, he scrunched his useless fingers into the carpet, using the loose grip to drag himself forward. Exhaustion weighed him down like an anchor. He couldn't even move from the mattress.

One by one, long taloned fingers curled around his forearm until the entire hand had closed around his skin. He tried to scream. To pull away. To somehow dislodge the creature that was now holding him in place. The tips of the talons pressed against him, a strong pressure threatening to break the skin. A new kind of fear simmered in the pit of his stomach as the mattress below him dipped. He could feel himself falling away from his body, tumbling into the deep pit of his diseased mind. A presence plastered itself to his spine. It held him like a lover, nuzzled against the nape of his neck, and cradled him as his nightmare rose to swallow him whole.

\*\*\*

*His skin wasn't his own. It was too tight. Like a snake that needed to shed. Sobbing broke the silence that hovered around him. It was a helpless, broken sound. A pitiful wail that rolled over the walls to create its own echo. It was insulting. Being chosen was a gift. A position of glory. He was offering it a chance for its life to mean something. His new addition should be groveling in gratitude, not clinging to its former, mediocre existence.*

*He walked with legs that were not his own and came to stand before his new possession. It looked up at him with tear-rimmed eyes. Like a child grasping for its comfort blanket, it wrapped its arms around his legs and burrowed its face against his stomach.*

*"You can't leave me," it whined while shuddering under the weight of its grief.*

*In a gentle caress, he placed his hands over its shoulders and cradled it close. Each desperate plea hit his ears like music. How had he ever questioned his hold? Or its loyalty?*

*"Sweet love," he said with a voice that wasn't his own. "You can stay with me." With one hand under its chin, he lifted its face. "But I need to know that you love me. And only me. Completely."*

*"I do," it rushed to assure him. "Of course, I do."*

*"What would you do to prove it?"*

*"Anything."*

*He smiled and gently traced the tips of his fingers along the curve of its cheeks. A thin trail of blood oozed up to show the path his nails had taken. It didn't attempt to pull away but instead closed its eyes as if to relish the touch.*

*"Will you die for me?"*

*"Yes," he said without hesitation.*

*He smiled and held up his nails, bearing the edges for its appraisal. It eyed them with caution before turning its eyes to meet* his own. After a few moments, it rose its arm. Its frail, narrow forearm rested atop his nails. For a moment, it did little more than watch him. All it needed was a gentle smile to move again. With a final gut wrenching sob, it impaled its forearm onto his nails, cleanly severing the skin.

Hot blood gushed over his fingers and the scent of iron filled the air. Reality filtered in within the edges of the dream. Somewhere in the back corners of his mind, Benton's true nature began to scream and struggle. Trapped within the constricting flesh, enough of his own mind took shape that he could recognize the man before him. Victor. The fingers weren't his own but he could still feel Victor's blood trickling down them and pooling within his palm. It was hot and slick and made him want to gag. Veins twisted around Benton's fingers. Bones scraped across his nails. He tried to pull back, but his hand refused to move. This is where the dream should end. He should be free. But Victor continued to saw his forearm across his borrowed claws and he was forced to watch it unfold. To feel it with every sense while still completely paralyzed.

Victor's eyes dulled as his blood splashed across the floor. He crumbled to his knees at Benton's feet. With the last of his energy, the last traces of his life, Victor continued to shred his arm. Benton was desperate to move, but still his borrowed form wouldn't permit it. He was a spectator. A witness.

A scream he couldn't release filled Benton's mind as a thousand unseen hooks dug into him. He could feel them, scorching hot and solid, gouging into his dream body as if it were real flesh. Hunks of his flesh tore free as the hooks began to pull. Bit by bit, he was ripped apart. Fingers squirmed free through the blood and puss. Like an insect hacking its way out of a chrysalis, a new body clawed free of his current form. His bones crunched and popped. The sickly wet sound of skin separating from muscle filled his ears. His screams of agony lodged in his throat as it was destroyed. The last chunks of his original dream form toppled onto the ground with a heavy plop and with it the dream he had been trapped in.

Benton blinked with eyes that were not his own and glanced around his new surroundings. His own mind evaporated like vapor, and once again another personality took hold. He was a new person now. With a new victim before him.

\*\*\*

78

Nicole's hand still trembled with unspent adrenaline. She watched them shake uncontrollably as she sat in the brightly lit waiting room of the police station. Somehow, Victor had managed to slip away unseen and was still missing. Fort Wayward didn't have a large force. There were only eight of them in total, and a few were far better with paperwork than anything else. They couldn't spare Dorothy for the evening, not when they had their first manhunt in over one hundred years. So, after insuring that her daughter was okay and in the safety of the station, her mother had left.

Every so often, the radio behind the desk would crackle and someone would call in an update. Time had lost any real meaning, but she knew it was getting late. Victor still hadn't been found. Their house was completely abandoned and she couldn't stop herself from thinking over the possibilities of what could have happened to them. She listened to the calls, scrunched her fingers into the aged padding on the seat, and tried to think where Victor could have possibly gone. There were surprisingly few hiding places in Fort Wayward. Mostly because there was a distinct lack of excess. A few houses stood empty as they waited for new tenants but everything else has a purpose and severed it. During the night, he could hide well enough on the planes, but come daylight all of those options would leave him completely exposed.

*Vic's with his girlfriend,* she realized with a sinking sensation. *He's in the same little hole she's been hiding in this whole time.*

The thought jarred Nicole's mind from the circles it had been running in. The image of Victor emerging from the dark with a knife in hand was replaced by a barrage of questions. She could no longer push aside the strange things she had seen. The niggling suspicions that had been haunting her since her slip of the tongue. And if she was honest, long before that. *It.* Not she. Whatever had latched itself onto Victor, whatever was breaking him, body and mind, wasn't human. She had no idea what it could be, but she knew without a doubt that, whatever it was, it intended to kill Victor. And it had apparently already found its next victim in Benton.

Shock loosened Nicole's jaw when she remembered Benton struggling in the car. She had dismissed it as a vivid nightmare, but what if it hadn't been? She had no way of knowing what this thing's abilities were. What if Benton had seen what she had that day on Victor's porch? The arms that stretched beyond reason and ended with deadly claws. Was it also Victor's monster that had lead Benton to the sign in the barn? *What even was that sign?* Nicole thought. Under all of the chaos within her skull, she edged towards a decision. She needed to help him. She had stood on the sidelines for too long and Victor was suffering for it. Nicole couldn't just sit back and watch him die.

The problem was, she would have to cross a lot of lines to find any answers. Lines that would be illegal and immoral to cross. Biting her lips, Nicole tittered on the edge of conviction and uncertainty. She needed guidance and there was really only one person she could turn to.

Nicole glanced over to the officer on duty. When Chuck continued his work undisturbed, she got to her feet, smoothed her hair down with both hands, and crept closer. He glanced up and she fixed a small, timid smile on her lips.

"Hey, Chuck."

She sounded as lost and scared as she felt.

"How are you holding up?"

She hesitated. "I'd like to talk to my dad."

"I know, Nicole," he said softly. "I'm sorry, he's deployed."

Just like her mother, Logan Rider was born with a singular passion, only his wasn't the Royal Canadian Mounted Police. It was the army. Her parents had been friends since childhood and had decided that, since they both needed to pass strict fitness exams, they could train together. Their ruthless competing had led to a deep bond and mutual respect. After that, falling in love had just been the natural next step. Two days after their honeymoon, her mother went to the training depot and her father enlisted. Since they were both highly motivated, independent, and driven, it was an arrangement that set their marriage on sure footing. Nicole had grown used to it.

"He's still at the base. I might be able to get him on Skype. Do you mind if I use mom's office?"

Chuck gave her an indulgent smile. "Go on, then. Good luck."

She tried not to run to the office set in the far back corner of the building, but it was a close call. Lit only by the small desk lamp Dorothy had left on, Nicole booted up the computer and breezed through the few security measures. Chuck was well aware that Nicole knew her mother's password. But he had yet to catch on that she knew everyone else's as well. Even though she tried not to, she couldn't stop her attention from drifting around the room.

Case files were stacked neatly on the far corner of the desk and her fingers itched to just reach over and go through them. Somewhere in the pile of paperwork were the answers that she needed. She was sure of it. But aside from being immoral, she was sure it was also illegal for her to rummage through a cop's office, and she hadn't decided yet if she was ready to do that sort of thing.

"Come on, dad," she mumbled as her foot began to jump with nervous energy. The sound of the call picking up made her jump. The screen filled with her father's face, sleepy but pleased.

"Hi, angel."

His voice was hushed, his face illuminated by the light of his phone while the rest of the room remained in darkness. She never really knew what his sleeping arrangements were at any given point. It seemed to be constantly shifting, so it was almost impossible to judge how many people might be in earshot any time she called.

"Hi, Daddy."

Tears began to well up in her eyes as the distance between them became real and tangible. She felt every foot of it. All she wanted was a hug, and the fact that it was something she couldn't have made an ache grow within her chest. Concern etched into his features and it made her hurt all the more.

"What's wrong?"

She sniffed. "Things are just getting really weird here, and I miss you."

"I miss you, too," he said. "Weird how?"

It was a race to get the words out before she broke into a sob. "Vic did something really stupid, and creepy, and violent, and I happened to get in the way."

Every last trace of sleep vanished from his face instantly. "Did he hurt you?"

"No," she wiped the moisture from her eyes. "No, mom got there in time."

"I'm going to kill him."

"Daddy, no," she chuckled slightly and swallowed past the lump in her throat. "It wasn't really him."

"Wait, what?"

"Can we cover that later? It's not why I'm calling," she quickly said. "I have a different problem that I wanted your advice on."

"Is it that I want to beat the daylights out of your friend?"

"Daddy."

He wiped a hand over his face and muttered an apology. "Sorry, angel. I'm a little out of it. What is it you want to talk about?"

"It's a moral question of sorts."

Her father smiled wide enough that his dimples flashed. "And you're asking me? You know your mom's moral core is a lot more solid than mine. The whole world's black and white to that woman."

She took a deep breath and chewed her lip. "Yeah, I'm thinking about dancing in a gray area."

Logan pressed a hand over his mouth to stifle his chuckle. "Gray area, huh? Now that, I can help with. What have you got for me?"

"I know a few people that I think are in some really bad trouble. I might be able to help them, well, I know I can, because I'm awesome."

"Granted," Logan acknowledged with a nod.

"But to do it, I might have to employ some unconventional methods."

"Are we talking illegal?"

"Maybe." She rushed to add, "But I'm pretty sure I can get away with only a slap-on-the-wrist level of illegal."

"What are the odds you can do it without getting caught?"

She thought about that for a moment. "Fairly high."

"Okay," he nodded again. "I want you to think about the worst case scenario. Everything goes wrong, all your shots at college are destroyed, your mother needs to arrest you, and since I had no part in any of this, you're left as the sole embarrassment of the entire family. You've got that in your head?"

She organized her thoughts and nodded when she had the crippling image set in her mind.

"Would it be worth it?"

She weighed her options. There was something more behind this. She knew it, and if no one did anything soon, Victor and Benton were either going to kill each other or remain as sitting ducks for the evil circling them. Whatever this thing was that was stalking her friend, it was dangerous. What would it do once it was done with Victor? And what does 'being done with Victor' even entail? And how many other people had it done this to? It had to be stopped.

"Yes," she decided. "It would be worth it."

"Then do what you need to do. Be careful, I love you and know that I've always got your back," he said. "Unless your mother finds out. Then this conversation never happened."

"Understood, sir," she smiled despite the pain that radiated out from her chest.

"That the answer you wanted?"

"I didn't just ask you because I thought you'd tell me what I want to hear."

"Of course, angel."

There were very few people that could make her feel calm just by being present. Actually, only her father could do that, and she had forgotten how much she missed it. Tears sprung anew and she wiped them away with a vengeance.

"Be good, angel. And if you can't be good, be lucky."

"I'm going to go and potentially ruin my life now."

"Let me know how it goes," he grinned with a wave.

After an exchanging of endearments and a final warning to be discreet, Nicole ended the call. Running her tongue over her bottom lip, she looked around the office once again. Nothing stirred. The world beyond the door was silent minus the random crackle of the radio. She made sure that the computer's screen wasn't visible from the door, took a deep breath, and then quickly used her mother's password to log into the police database.

"Well, that is one crime down," she mumbled to herself.

She had hoped that the fidgeting nerves under her skin would settle down once she had taken the first step. Like passing the threshold of no return would allow her to commit fully to the insane task she had set herself. It usually worked like that. But the nerves remained. Scampering within her stomach like a swarm of ants. Before her bravado broke altogether, she hurriedly typed Benton's name into the search engine.

"How on earth are there thirty-two Benton Bertrands?" she groaned softly.

She had assumed it would be an uncommon enough name, one that would negate her needing to know any other personal information to pick him out of the masses. While she didn't know his birthday, she could guess at the year, and that knocked a few of them out of consideration. There wasn't time to check them all. The tip of her tongue tracked restlessly over her lips as she glanced to the door, half expecting to see Chuck or her mother suddenly materializing into the room. Nicole upgraded to nipping painfully on her lip as she scanned the names again.

"Benton Bartholomew Bertrand," she read aloud in a whisper. "Your parents do seem the type to like alliteration."

Holding her breath, she clicked on the name, and couldn't resist the fist-pump of victory when Benton's picture was displayed on screen alongside a staggering amount of raw information. After a quick check on the door again, Nicole began to scroll through the decades' worth of police records. It seemed that he had first appeared on the RCMP's radar when he was ten. And he did it with a bit of dramatic flair. Unoccupied, he had walked into an Ottawa police station and confessed to the murder of his friend.

Delving deeper into the records, she speed read through the transcripts of the confession. Despite Benton being able to recite a damning amount of information, there were a few things missing. Like the actual location of the crime scene, a motive of any kind, and an actual victim. Nicole leaned in closer to the screen as she reread the last part. The victim in question, Steve Howell, had been found alive and well only an hour later, sitting at his normal classroom desk, with no idea what Benton was talking about. It had been decided that the whole incident was nothing more than a vivid nightmare by a very sensitive little boy. The file had been amended three days later when Steve had gone missing.

It took a week for them to find the body. When they had, his tiny frame had held the exact wounds Benton had described. Nicole clicked on the links that led her to the crime scene photographs and autopsy report. She wished she hadn't. Even prepared, a single glance was enough to make her stomach roll. The boy looked more like a heap of discarded scraps than a child. She instantly shut the newly opened windows and went back to the safety of the detached words of the reports.

Nicole quickly scrolled through the records, hoping that the bold black lettering would somehow replace the images that were now burnt into her mind. The murder had been part of a horrific series. One child a month, for eight months. None of the victims had reached their teens and they ran through a spectrum of physical descriptions. But there were two similarities that connected all of the children. Every one of them had lived within the same four block radius, and Benton had visited them all, days before their abduction. There were a few notes scattered under these incidences indicating that there had been a few reports of complaints and a few petitions for restraining orders.

In each case, Benton insisted that everything he knew had come from a dream. Nicole could see how scared parents wouldn't accept that as an appropriate explanation. The reports of units responding to disturbances involving Benton and his family steadily increased as suspicions grew. Everyone had come to the conclusion that Benton knew far more than he was letting on. Accusations were made that he himself was the killer and when that didn't pan out, people looked towards his parents. And then any relative or friend or general acquaintance that Benton would feel the need to protect. They all assumed that he knew who the killer was.

Nicole could already understand where this combination of fear and hysteria was likely to lead long before she read the correct passage. Ten year-old Benton had been found beaten behind a bowling alley. She hadn't wanted to read those reports. It was easier to imagine what they had done to him without having to know, or see. But she steeled herself and opened the links. The ice in her stomach grew with every blatant word, every photograph that documented the evidence. Benton had been tiny for his age. His wiry little frame looked far too small to even withstand all the damage that had been inflicted upon him. Internal bleeding, massive blood loss, a concussion so devastating that he needed a metal plate to replace a segment of his skull, the inventory of injuries seemed to have no end. She clasped one hand over her now aching throat as she read about how they had found flakes of yellow embedded into the bone just behind his right ear. For a while, they had thought it had been left by the weapon used in the assault. The forensics team concluded that the substance was actually the outer coating for a pencil he must have had tucked behind his ear when the attack started. Nicole's eyes burned as she stared at the photographs.

"How hard would you have to hit a child to grind a pencil into his bone?" she wondered aloud.

Suddenly drained, she rubbed her hands over her face. No matter how hard she pushed her palm into her eyes, the haunting images remained. With a deep breath and a painful swallow, she forced herself to continue. The injuries had caused massive swelling to his brain and the doctors had no choice but to put him into a medically induced coma. It had taken almost two weeks for Benton to stabilize. His parents had been out for blood, but Benton had refused to cooperate. The investigating officer once again believed that Benton was protecting someone, and this time they might have actually been right. Through the course of the investigation, the substantial list of suspects was narrowed down until only the group of children Benton had been at the bowling alley with, remained. Still, Benton kept his silence. And without him, the general public were all too ready to blame the killer whom they still believed Benton to be entwined with. The officer hadn't been able to press charges. Both the killings and Benton's attack remain unsolved.

What followed from there was a long list of suspicion and death that crisscrossed the country. It didn't matter where the Bertrands moved, it always ended the same. A murderer stalking the streets and Benton in the midst of it. Always speaking of his dreams, but never really believed. Sitting in an office that was filled with hundreds of pleasant memories, Nicole read about things more disgusting and twisted than she could have ever conjured up on her own. The brief and efficient language did its part to ease the blow. But nothing could spare her of the horror that poured from the screen. She felt unclean in every sense of the word by the time she reached the end of the file and an attachment to Oliver Ackerman's case.

Her thought process once again rounded back to the weathered paint that had been hidden within the barn wall. It niggled at her, probing and prodding at her that this meant something. Something important. The decision to move had barely finished crossing her mind when she leaped up and began her search through the files on her mother's desk. Dorothy was still working the Ackerman case. The file should be there, complete with hardcopies of the crime scene photographs and any conclusions they had reached.

Under a file about two farmers having a dispute over the height of a dividing hedge, Nicole found what she was looking for. Rolling her chair back to the other side where the desk lamp waited, she flipped open the file and scanned through the sheets. The symbol had barely warranted a mention. The symbol had been noted as 'graffiti of unknown purpose.' Nicole knew her mother well enough to know that she was intrigued, but not actively trying to make any sense of it. Her focus was on Mr. Ackerman's body, the cause of his death, and tracking down any surviving family members who might be able to shed some light on the event.

Repositioning the light, Nicole got her first real look at the symbol. There was something about the circles and curves, the layout and spacing, which looked vaguely familiar. She couldn't place the where or why of it, but that little voice that told her this was important, was growing louder.

Making sure she logged out of the database, Nicole pulled up a new Skype call and deliberately kept from looking at the time. She was horrible at lying under direct questioning. She knew it. Almost everyone else did too. It made plausible deniability a must in these kinds of situations. The call connected and a very unhappy Professor Lester filled the screen. It looked like he hadn't fully woken up yet as he roughly pushed his slightly long hair from his face. It had just begun to gray around the temple, only noticeable due to how dark the rest of his hair was. He also scrubbed his face vigorously before groaning out an annoyed greeting.

"Hi, Professor."

"Do you have any idea what time it is?"

"Honestly, no," she said.

He groaned again. "If this is about another book report–"

"I got an A+ on the last one," she cut in happily. "Well, the teacher wanted to just give me an A, but once I told her that you were my reference she couldn't argue with the facts. Thanks again for your help."

Pinching the bridge of his nose, he flopped his free hand about. "Well, that's exactly why I completed the long, painful and expensive journey to be a professor at a respectable college. To help high schoolers with their history teachers."

"I wouldn't word it quite like that," she mumbled. "Did you get the 'thank-you' cookies I sent?"

He lost his emerging anger with a reluctant sigh. "Yes. Thank you. So, what do you need this time?"

"Why couldn't I have just called to talk?"

"Far too late for this, Nicole," he warned.

"My friend found this weird symbol hidden in his barn and I was hoping that you would be able to help me identify it."

He blinked owlishly at her. "That's it? That's what couldn't wait for the morning?"

"Well, to be perfectly candid, a dead body was found buried under this symbol and I'm admittedly a little freaked out and worried that my mother might not be giving it the significance it needs, since I'm sure that it has something to do with the corpse that you might remember me mentioning earlier in this very long sentence." She gulped down a need for breath as she waited for his reply.

Professor Lester just stared at her for a long moment. "Why didn't you just lead with 'police investigation'?"

"Because I'm not a police officer and, as such, have nothing people would normally consider to be authority. Besides, I don't really have any evidence that suggests the symbol means anything. It's more of a feeling."

"So," he said slowly, "absolutely no reason to believe that it isn't a bit of random graffiti that just happened to be there?"

"Not really."

"In reality, you woke me up for an unsubstantiated hunch."

"Basically."

"And you couldn't wait a few more hours."

"It was really bothering me."

He muttered a few words that she took great care not to hear.

"Am I right in assuming that, if I don't do this, you're going to engage in your special brand of mild stalking?"

"I will be quite persistent in the matter, yes, sir."

"Fine. Email it through." He lifted a hand to cut her off from thanking him. "And let's keep the calls between office hours in the future."

"Of course. Thank you!"

He grumbled, nodded and ended the call with a sharp jab. Nicole hurriedly scanned the photograph and sent it off using her private email. She replaced the files and took a few extra minutes to ensure they were in the exact same position she had found them in. Her mother had a sharp eye for detail. Freakishly so. Even the slightest change would have her asking questions. Once that was done, and she had made sure her tracks were covered, the first stages of her plan were officially complete.

"Huh, would have thought committing crimes would have been harder," she muttered to herself as her panic began to wane. "Why do people make it look so difficult?"

But her nerves came back with a vengeance when it was time to start stage two. Snooping around her mother's office was one thing. She had done it a few times in the past. All in drastic situations where she had no other choice, of course, but she couldn't deny that her past actions had been more legal-adjacent than entirely-legal in a proper sense. But stage two would be out of her comfort zone.

What she had learned about Benton, so far, had only filled her with more questions. This whole situation felt like a puzzle and she was missing some key pieces. And the next most obvious place to look for them had to be Benton's psychiatric records. His parents had secured him a psychiatry session before they had even set foot into town. That was not something most people would do unless they were used to having that kind of care, so she was pretty sure that his past doctors would have already transferred their files and patient notes to Aspen's office. There would be things in those files that Benton wouldn't have told anyone else. She needed that information. But breaking into Aspen's office was a degree of illegal and wrong that she had never even flirted with before.

"You've never been attacked by a knife-wielding friend before, either," she whispered to herself as she strode towards the window.

There was no way Chuck would ever let her leave on her own, which meant any of the normal exits were out of the question. Her bravado crumbled away when she reached the window. It was still dark enough outside that she had to struggle to see past her own reflection. Streetlamps lined the road with a soft orange glow. There wasn't a single sign of life. No people. No cars. Nothing but a stillness that forced memories of tonight to rush to the forefront of her mind.

"You're being silly," she told herself in her best stern voice. "Vic hadn't even been after you, and the hospital is only two streets away."

It wasn't enough of a pep talk to make her ready to leap out, but it did get her to slide open the window. For the first time, she realized just how little security the police station actually had. It was all too easy to slip out of this window and into the street unnoticed. And it wouldn't be that hard to get back in later. A nagging voice in the back of her mind told her that she should probably remind her mother to lock her office window in the future. But not tonight. Not until she had exploited the opportunity.

Gathering her resolve, Nicole threaded one leg out through the gap. The office was on the ground floor and the bottom of the window was at hip height. It made the crawling out undignified but easy. The cold wind instantly welcomed her and she quickly buttoned up her coat against the chill.

The darkness that had looked intimidating from inside the office became a lot more threatening as it encased her. Each shadow seemed to shift with movement. Each breath of wind sounded like a whispering voice. She felt utterly exposed and turned to climb right back through the still open gap.

"Stop that right now," she snapped at herself. Reluctantly, she stepped away from the window. Her casual stride turned into a jog, then a full out sprint down the block, her heart hammering within her throat.

*I knew Danny and Meg were wrong,* she thought. *That tone really does work.*

# Chapter 9

The staircase to the second floor was halfway down a long and annoyingly exposed hallway, with the gift shop at one end and the nurse's station at the other. A few feet from the bottom stairs was a vending machine that had given Nicole a little bit of cover to creep forward unnoticed. But there was no way she could actually round it to get to the stairs, and consequently Aspen's office, without being seen.

Leaning heavily against the cool metal side of the vending machine, she peeked around it to check if the coast was clear. There were at least four people milling about the nurse's station. Apparently, the skeleton staff didn't have much to occupy their time with tonight because they never seemed all that interested in going anywhere else.

It hadn't occurred to Nicole until after she had entered the hospital that she would stick out. She knew everyone in town. Anyone who saw here would question why she was here so late. Not to mention that, by now, everyone and their mothers would know what had happened at the diner. Even if she had the world's most perfectly constructed lie, and managed to execute it flawlessly, word would get back to Dorothy that she had visited. It was the first time in her life that she had actually wished that she didn't live in a small town.

Minutes dragged on. The nurses chatted, drank their coffee, and while some left to do their rounds, they never left the station unmanned. *Do you have to be so damn dedicated?* The angry thought was quickly chased by the more reasonable part of her mind that mentioned that dedication in the health industry was a good thing. That reasonable voice was really starting to get irritating. Another minute passed and she knew it wasn't going to get any better. Either she took her chance or stayed with the ever-increasing risk that someone would walk down the hall behind her.

She snuck another peek, waiting for the right moment when they would all be distracted by whatever it was they were doing. Finally, the opportunity opened up and she took it before she could second-guess herself. The hardest part was to keep her boots from thumping against the tiled floor. She rushed around the vending machine and threw herself into the stairwell. Her knee smacked against the edges of the stairs. The blow sent out a long throb of protest but it wasn't enough to keep her from scrambling up and pressing herself against the wall. In the shadows of the stairwell,

Nicole held her breath and waited for someone to call her name. Once again, it occurred to her much too late that she really should have worked on an excuse. But no one called. No one came. Their conversations and the steady rhythm of clicking computer keys went on, undisturbed.

Sagging with the force of her relief, Nicole silently pulled her feet back under her and stood up. She crept up the stairs, never taking a full breath until she reached the darkness of the second floor. It didn't take long for the shadows to shift from comforting to confronting. Since none of the businesses ever stayed open past five, the floor was completely deserted. Each one had large windows that looked out onto the street and matching ones that opened onto the hallway she was standing in. The only source of light was the glow of the streetlamps. They filtered in through the vertical blinds and sliced spurs of light across the hallway.

Her feet refused to move. Every time Nicole had seen this place, it had been awash with lights and people. There was something inherently wrong in seeing it so empty. It felt like something was watching her from the shadows, waiting for her to come closer. Her eyes searched every inch of space they could find but there were far too many hiding spots to assure herself that she was alone.

Lingering by the top of the stairs, one hand pressed against the wall, she struggled to resist turning on a light. It would be a comfort but was the exact opposite of being sneaky. The sensation of eyes upon her intensified. She tried to dismiss it, to justify it, to reason with the hair on her arms that were beginning to rise, but nothing worked. Memories of her last hiking trip were worth far more than her own assurances.

She had been hiking for half a day with the cold, constant pressure pressing against her spine. It was only after she had circled back around that she noticed the coyote tracks in the soft earth. Dozens of them. The whole pack must have stalked her for at least a mile and she never saw them. But the most primal part of herself had felt it. Had known the exact moment when she had captured a predator's attention. It was an unmistakable breed of bone-deep dread. And she felt it now.

Aspen's office stood at the very end of the hall, the last in the long row of identical doors. The minimal light shone off the metal handle, taunting her. Controlling her every breath, forcing them to go slower than her racing heart, she took her first tentative step forward. The desire to run was instant and forceful. She chanced a glance over her shoulder at the staircase.

"You came here to do something," she reminded herself. "You're not leaving until you get the job done."

Locking her eyes onto her final destination, she bounced on her toes, working herself up until she could force herself into a sprint. She felt both ridiculous and pursued at the same time. The confliction leaving little room for logic. It was probably why it took getting her hand on the doorknob to realize that it could be locked. She spun, ready to abort the mission and race for the stairs. But the movement twisted the handle slightly and the door popped open with an easy swing.

For a moment, she could only stare at it. "Wow, our town is trusting."

Holding tight to the reminder of where she was, her small, quaint, safe little town, was enough to ease the fear that had built up under her skin. She crept into the dark space and closed the door firmly behind her. Pulling her mobile phone out of her jacket pocket, she clicked on the flashlight app. The weak circle of light it produced wasn't enough to chase off the shadows. It more or less just weakened them, allowing her to see shapes within it but still keeping all colors muted. Still, it was all she needed to get across the room to his desk without stumbling into anything. The charger cord for his laptop coiled across the floor like a sleeping snake but the laptop itself was gone.

"Well, that sucks," she whispered.

She had hoped hearing her voice would be soothing. Unfortunately, the nervous tilt lingering in her words had the opposite of the desired effect. It made her want to talk all the more, to just babble until it was all out. Like an anxiety exorcism. Making any noise that wasn't absolutely necessary was a horrible idea but she wasn't sure how long she could hold out. The more she kept it in, the more nervous she got.

"At least Aspen is taking some steps to protect his client's privacy," she blurted into the darkness. "Of course, it's that privacy that I'm currently trying to violate. I might not be the good guy here. Oh. Am I the bad guy? No. I'm sure a murdering soul-sucker is worse."

She sunk her teeth into her bottom lip, hard, to stop anything more from tumbling out. Savoring the sharp pang, she trailed her light around the office. It only took a few moments to notice the tall filing cabinet that melted into the shadows. It was tucked into a back corner, nestled between a pot plant and a coat rack. Aspen was a man who had reluctantly embraced technology. Odds were, he still didn't trust it enough to completely forgo hard copies of his patient records.

She rushed to the cabinet and tested the handle. The drawer remained solidly in place and gave a rattle that was way too loud for her liking. For a moment, she froze, ready for the door to burst in, her lip starting to protest the abuse she was inflicting upon it. No one came. Her nerves slowly ebbed back to their normal level of controlled chaos. Wiping her sweaty palms on her jacket and tried to think of what to do next.

"Spare key," she decided abruptly.

There had to be one hidden away somewhere. She took one step towards the desk before a better idea struck her. Placing the phone on top of the filing cabinet, she braced her feet and pulled the large hunk of metal a few inches away from the wall. It screeched across the tiled floor. Loud enough that she instinctively dropped down to hide behind the side of the desk. The door remained closed.

"Is there no security in this building?" she whispered with indignation before catching herself. "Wait, why am I complaining?"

On all fours, she crawled over the short distance and slipped between the side of the cabinet and the potted plant. There wasn't enough room or light for her to properly see behind the metal drawers. So she twisted into an uncomfortable angle and slid her hand into the gap she had created. The plant leaves brushed against her face as she strained her shoulder to the point of pain, groping over every inch of cool metal she could touch. Finally, about halfway up, her fingertips brushed against a slip of sticky tape. A little more fumbling and she was able to hook her nails around the sides of the secured key.

A smile curled her lips as she pulled it free. Still celebrating her victory, she popped onto her feet and opened the lock with an unnecessary flourish. Aspen had a lot more clients than she would have guessed. It seemed like almost everyone in town had their own file. But they were all neatly organized and it only took a second to find Benton amongst the others. File in one hand and her phone in the other, she knelt down and opened it, scanning each sheet of paper before snapping a photograph with her phone. There wasn't time to read any of it in detail but some words stood out more than others. Ones like 'sociopath,' 'delusional,' and 'death,' tended to grab her attention.

Taking the last photograph, she scrambled to get the room back into order. It was hard to remember exactly where she had found the key but she doubted that Aspen was as observant as her mother was. She shoved the cabinet back into place with a sharp push of her shoulder. The scraping sound was still an ear-splitting screech but she handled it a lot better than she had before. Probably because everything she had come for now fit into her palm. As the possibility to actually get away with this came closer, her legs began to shake with the desire to run. It was nearly impossible to keep herself still long enough to insure that she hadn't left some telling sign. Cramming her phone back into her jacket pocket, she hurried through the darkness to the door. It opened smoothly but the metal clack seemed far louder than what she remembered. As hard as she tried, she couldn't stop the door from releasing the same sound as she eased it back closed.

The second she turned to the dark hallway, the sensation of being watched hit her like a solid wall. Painfully aware of the sound of her own footsteps, Nicole inched towards the stairs, her eyes darting over each shadow. Her body protested, trying to surge forward instead of taking the slow, measured steps she was forcing it to. The stairwell was in sight when a soft whisper broke the silence.

She froze instantly. Her brain staggering, unable to comprehend what she had just heard. Her lungs seized. Her heart skipped. A sickly sense of dread bubbled up inside her, turning her to stone from the inside out. Her father. That was her father's voice calling to her from behind the closed door beside her.

"Daddy?" she whispered before she could stop herself.

The voice didn't come as it should have. It rolled out like roaming fog, curling around her feet before climbing up to reach her ears. She could almost feel it against her skin. But it was his voice. She was sure of it. Swallowing around the solid lump in her throat, Nicole slowly turned to glance behind her shoulder. The hallway was quiet. Still. Shadows toyed around the thin streaks of light, shifting only when a tree outside forced it to.

She went cold as she heard the now familiar clack of a door handle turning. The sound was quickly lost under her fast, raspy breath. Feeling light headed, she watched the door open, its hinges releasing a soft rasp. Nothing stood in the threshold. There was only the empty office space shrouded with shadows. But the voice came from the space all the same.

"Over here," *it* coaxed, a perfect mockery of her father's voice. "Come closer."

It felt like everything within her skin crashed together at once, creating a roaring swell that prevented her from doing anything. She wanted to scream, wanted to run, wanted more to somehow make sense of the world again but she stood frozen, staring into the empty air.

"Nicole," it extended her name into a death rattle.

Long fingers wrapped around the edge of the door, nails clicking against the wood.

"Come to me, angel."

Nicole bolted before her mind could catch up with her instincts. Her boots slammed against the floor as she barreled down the stairs. She didn't hesitate this time. She ran into the hall, moving as fast as her legs could possibly take her. She didn't care who saw her. All that mattered was the glass doors before her now and the chilled air of escape that lay beyond. She didn't stop until she had hurled herself back through the window of the police station and firmly locked it behind her.

***

The sun had already cracked across the horizon, turning the sky into a flush of muted pink, by the time Benton was able to claw his way out from under the layers of hell he been buried in. He was left shivering atop his sweat-drenched sheets. Cold even, as a fever took hold. He scrunched his fingers in the waterlogged sheets, just to assure himself that they were his own. That he was back in his own body. That he was awake. He blinked and the horrors he had witnessed fell away from his sight. But each of them remained perfectly preserved within his mind.

Blood and flesh clogged under his nails. He swiped them across the sheets over and over but the sensation remained. The dozens of deaths poured across his brain like bubbling lava. It filled him until the pressure cracked his skull, seeking some kind of release, threatening to erupt and burn him alive. The pain was enough to blur his vision. It seized every cell of his being. Every inch of his mind and soul. Quaking under the assault, he reached out, trying to find his phone. He needed to tell them. Needed to warn all of them. Needed to make this stop.

As he fumbled with the buttons, memories of the creature crept into his mind. He remembered an unseen force pressing against him. The weight. The flesh like crocodile skin. The nuzzling press of its face against his neck. For a split second, his pain was forgotten under a spike of fear.

He snapped around, flailing madly, his arm smacking against the mattress. Every sense told him he was alone. But he couldn't bring himself to believe that something unseen was lurking nearby, hunting him, ready to strike. The heat in his head became a firestorm as he clawed his way onto the carpet. He only managed to scramble a foot from the mattress before his shivering limbs gave out and his spine smacked against the floor. On instinct alone, he had kept his tight grip on his phone. Every second that passed pounded like a cathedral bell against his neck, growing until his body rocked with the blows.

There were too many. Too many names and deaths and monsters screaming in his ears. A new wave of agony bore down on him like a tidal wave. It crushed him against the floor, his teeth rattling with the impact as his fingers clutched the phone. It was his lifeline. His only chance for survival. The names rose into a ghastly howl, each one tripping over the other, becoming a snarling beast all of its own. Demanding that he tell their story. Demanding that he speak. He longed to scream. To release some of what was festering within him. But the last traces of the drug still hugged him tight, smothering each attempt to summon his voice into a meek whimper.

With whatever control he had, he furiously clicked his fingers over the keys. An unseen boulder pressed down on him until his bones bent with the force. Each one of them became a branding iron, roasting the flesh and muscle wrapped around it. He could almost feel the smoke pouring into his blistering lungs. Writhing against the onslaught, his thumb made the final tap and the email was sent. Benton knew the very second his mobile had completed the task. It was marked with the sensation of ice thrown upon him, a moment of relief that quickly deteriorated into stifling scorching steam. But it was enough. Just enough that he could keep his thumb moving over the key pad, forming the next warning that his mouth couldn't voice.

\*\*\*

Nicole sat on her bedroom floor, her laptop in front of her. Sheets of papers and odd books covered every other available surface. Her library had proven to be exceedingly lacking in books about mythology. But then, she wasn't even sure it was mythology that she needed to be looking up. Monsters might have been better. Or demons. Or a thousand other things that people around the world have taken to calling the unknown. And that was the problem; she had no idea where to even start researching Victor's 'girlfriend'. And typing in 'monsters with creepy hands' into a web search didn't exactly produce helpful results.

As for the second problem, the 'what on earth is Benton's' problem, his medical records had proven more fruitful. His past therapists mentioned time and again that Benton's problems began when he attempted to contact the people that he saw in his dreams. It didn't matter how many times he was told not to, or even who told him not to, he always found the future victims and told them what was coming. But even as they all mentioned the dreams, no one seemed all that interested in finding out *how* he knew how to contact the victims. Benton always knew their names and at least one contact detail. A number. An address. An email or social media page. That wasn't information that a child should readily know about a stranger.

Nicole had waited anxiously for her mother to go to sleep. The second she was sure that enough time had passed, she snuck downstairs and found her mother's work laptop. She also checked for the hundredth time that all the locks were firmly in place. Back in the safety of her own room, she booted up the laptop and returned to the police files. With them, Benton's records, printouts of Google maps and a lot of coffee, she had set about marking down what she thought was a good representation of their daily routines.

Any place Benton would have gone to, she marked with gold star stickers. Glittery love hearts of different colors marked the victims' home, friends, workplace, and known hangouts. Or at least the ones that the investing officers had made note of. She used smiley faces for Benton's father and unicorns for his mother. The end-result looked inappropriately pretty and made her head hurt more. The points of overlap kept dwindling.

With the first cases, the children from his neighborhood, there had been plenty of common points. Same school, same friends, same hobbies. But the older he got, the less chances there were for him to even learn of the victim's existence, let alone know how to contact them. They were big cities. She had checked the population density from the censor's bureau and had hardly been able to wrap her mind around those kinds of numbers. Staring at the maps until her eyeballs ached hadn't helped to resolve the problem as much as she had hoped it might.

When she couldn't deal with one of the mysteries for another second, she would switch to a different one. Hours passed with her printing, highlighting, and organizing her growing information into two files. The first, dedicated to Victor's love interest, was steadily filling with options but very little answers. A succubus was the first thing to go in there. She didn't know much about mythology but even she had a vague awareness of the sex demon. After that, she found psychic vampires who feed off life force instead of blood and a Hungarian legend about a Liderc, who seemed to like going after both.

She found tales about demons and ghosts that destroy a person through obsession and madness. It had been a little disheartening to learn how inaccurately pixies and fairies had been depicted in her beloved childhood cartoons. Knowing how they were originally thought to be cruel, and sometimes deadly pranksters, left her feeling a little odd about having dressed up to look like them. They went into the file too. Also from Ireland was something called a Leanan Sidhe. Like the psychic vampire, it appears to its victims as a beautiful woman and seduces them while feeding off of their energy. But they differ when it came to what they gave back. According to the legends she found, their victims of choice were normally artists. Victor couldn't draw a stick figure, but it went in anyway. Maybe they had expanded their menus.

Pishacha, a monster that drives people mad while they made them sick, was placed just above stories of ghostly hitchhikers that attach themselves to whoever picks them up. There were even a few stories about witches and medicine' men who enjoyed making people self-destruct. Each segment was organized neatly and clearly defined with color-coded tags.

Benton's file was equally full of possibly useless information. Her first instinct was that he was psychic or maybe a medium, although she was a little shaky on the difference. But, judging by his comments in his therapy sessions, this wasn't an idea that Benton himself subscribed to. Actually, he seemed to get annoyed every time someone threw out the word. She put the research in anyway but continued looking for other possibilities. His newest idea, that he was a grim reaper, or at least stalked by death, was researched next. She couldn't find much to back it up. Although there wasn't a reputable site of people claiming the same. The few that she had found were scary and she read things she wished she could scrub from her brain.

She had also looked into the idea that it wasn't really him. It was something else that was forcing the ideas into him as he slept. There were a staggering amount of creatures that, historically, liked to torture sleeping people. The Russian Nocnitsa would get into bed with people, filling them with nightmares as it smothered them. Maybe one of them had decided to keep its torments grounded in reality, just to add an extra layer of twisted to the whole ordeal.

Then there was the Welsh Gwrach-Y-Rhibyn. It would invisibly stalk people until they crossed somewhere it couldn't follow, which she figured he was sort of doing with his dreams, if you took 'following' in more of an astral projection kind of way. When a Gwrach-Y-Rhibyn could no longer keep up, it would scream as an omen of death, and Benton's files did say that he woke from his night terrors making the most horrific noises. But, more than its method, all of the stories were insistent that the Gwrach-Y-Rhibyn was hideous to a terrifying degree. Frail and crooked but strong, with disgusting matted hair and manic eyes. Benton didn't look in any way intimidating. Still, it was research, and needed to be filed in all the same.

The one that caught her eye the most was again from Irish legend. The Banshee. Everything she found on them said that they were female, but the Gwrach-Y-Rhibyn was instant on that too. And, since those same legends couldn't decide if a banshee was a ghost, fairy, or simply born a banshee, she wasn't about to dismiss a theory because of a gender technicality. Besides, the older legends noted that a banshee was rarely ever seen. Normally, it was just the disembodied shriek that warned people someone was about to die. So who's to say, by otherworldly voice alone, what gender the supernatural creature was. And, Nicole decided, an email or text message could pass as a modern version of a scream in the dark.

It also fit that, according to what she could find, no one knew where a banshee got its information from. They just seem to know. It was possible something unseen was telling him. According to Aspen's notes, Benton had eluded to seeing something the night Miss Williams passed. The nurses had said he moved like he was in pursuit. And Nicole had seen that behavior herself. The night in the barn when he had found the hidden symbol. She had seen his eyes glaze over, the way he had moved without thought. What they had found might have thrown him but he had been certain that there was something to find. Not to mention poor Mr. Ackerman. After studying the police photographs again, she was certain Benton had been standing right on top of him that night. And he had come back to find him later. And all of that had happened after he had been so reluctant to be anywhere near the barn.

There was no doubt in her head that somehow, in some way, Benton was right. He and death were linked. And that was a relationship that would make a lot more sense if Benton was a banshee. Her last bit of evidence was that a lot of the banshee legends were far more forgiving in their descriptions. There were some that spoke of an ugly hag, but a few depicted otherworldly beauty with long pale hair. Again, he wasn't a woman, and she wouldn't exactly describe him as 'otherworldly,' but there was nothing about him that was haggish or scary or even a hardship to look at.

Nicole had just clipped the latest pile of printouts into the 'Benton' binder when her mobile rang. She jumped and whipped around to the sudden sound. It took sending almost every sheet airborne to find which one had covered the device and she answered it without checking the caller ID. Her gut lurched when Victor's voice roared down the line. The words jumbled into an unintelligible mess that was almost lost by the rush of blood through her ears.

"Victor?"

"Have you been listening to me?" he snarled.

"You're talking too fast, I can't understand what you're saying," she continued before he could say anything. "Vic, you have to turn yourself in."

"What?" His laughter was sharp and bitter. "Why should I do anything?"

"You tried to kill us, Vic. Don't you remember that?"

"Of course, I do. I'm not deranged."

She didn't argue but her eyes shifted to her bedroom door. A part of her brain screamed at her to go get her mother but it wasn't enough for her to stand up.

"The police are looking for you."

"You sent the police after me?"

Her jaw dropped at the raw betrayal that rang in his voice.

"You tried to kill us," she spat out each word.

"You keep saying 'us.' I was only after him."

"That's not any better."

Victor snorted. "Of course you defend him."

"Benton hasn't tried to kill you."

"Didn't he tell you? So, what then, he just asked for my email and you gave it to him?"

Nicole braced herself against the side of her bed as her insides disappeared, replaced only by a gaping hole of dread.

"Benton sent you a message?"

"A long story about how he's going to kill me. This is why I have to take him out, Nicole. I can't let an unstable guy like that around my girl."

"Victor, I need you to listen to me carefully. Benton wasn't threatening you. He can predict death. You need to turn yourself in. Now."

"He can what?"

"He's psychic or a banshee, maybe a Gwrach-Y-Rhibyn. I'm still figuring it all out."

Victor's confusion was quickly transforming into anger. "A what?"

"It doesn't matter. What matters is that he dreams about people dying and then they do. The message he sent you was a warning. You're in danger."

Nicole pushed up onto her feet and began a frantic search for her jeep keys.

"From who?"

"Your girlfriend." It was the first thing that popped into her head but there was no doubt in her mind that she was right.

"She loves me!"

"She's not human," Nicole shot out the words with venom that matched his own.

Victor laughed.

"Vic, look at yourself. You're malnourished. You're sick. You're trying to kill people because you believe they flirted with your girlfriend who no one else has seen."

"He did! He was even with her tonight."

"No, he wasn't. Because it was busy stalking me tonight. I know it must be tricking you somehow. It sounded like my dad when it came after me."

"Stop calling her 'it.'"

"Vic, I'm you're oldest friend and I'm asking you, begging you, please tell me where you are. I'll come and get you right now." She finally found the keys in her discarded school bag and raced for the door.

"I'm not going anywhere with you."

"Please, Vic. It will kill you."

"You don't believe me," Victor snarled. "I can't believe you're taking his side."

She barreled down the stairs, her feet missing more than they found, rushing to the front door. "Vic, I love you. I'm on your side. We can talk everything else out after you're safe."

"I'm going to send it through to you. You can see how sick he is, yourself."

"Where are you?" She struggled to open the door, forgetting in her panic that the deadbolt lock had been used for the first time tonight. Engaged for the sole reason to keep Victor out. "I'm coming to get you. Just tell me where you are."

"Leave us alone, Nicole."

"Victor. Please."

She flipped the bolt. It opened with a sharp clack, a mocking imitation of the sound the phone gave as it died.

# Chapter 10

Benton wrapped his arms around his legs, compressing himself in until his thighs crushed his lungs. The pain had faded but the carnage it had created still lingered. The jagged, splintered edges of his own being. The parts of him that had broken when everything else had been shoved inside. It would take days for that ache to fade. He sat with his back plastered against the smooth metal side of the fireplace. It was the only spot in the room where he could get a sliver of privacy.

He had written down his dream of Victor, the violent tremble in his hand reduced the letters into childish scribbles. Through some kind of miracle, the photographs he had taken of the pages had turned out to be legible enough. Hours had passed since he had sent the file to Victor but the need to do something still sparked under his skin. It burned like searing barbed wire coiled within the joints that connected his neck to his skull.

*It's because you know him,* Benton reasoned. It was always worse when he knew them outside of his dreams. Seeing someone walking around when he knew how warm their blood was, the exact sound of their last breaths, made it impossible to dismiss it all as a nightmare. An email just didn't seem like enough.

Burying his head against his knees, his brain struggled with the aftershocks of the killer's emotions rippling through him. Within the throes of the dream, there was no way to separate his mind from the dream persona. He inhabited them. Became them. Two souls bleeding together, different but inseparable. The boundaries were more defined when he was awake. Although sometimes, things still got muddled. Especially after numerous dreams in one night.

This morning he had spent twenty minutes looking for a jacket he didn't own. He could remember it perfectly. The way it fit just a little too tight across his shoulders, the missed stitch in the left pocket that always swallowed up his keys, the way it smelled like coconuts from his perfume. Then he recalled that both the perfume and jacket belonged to the killer in his forth dream.

Later, he had panicked after eating some of the muffin left over from yesterday, convinced that he was a celiac. Only after emptying the entire contents of his stomach did he remember that he, Benton Bertrand, didn't have any food allergies. That was when he curled up in his hiding place, determined to remain still until his mind had time to splinter away from the lingering remains. Music helped. But he had to make sure that he had an eclectic mix, just in case their tastes overrode his own.

The problem was, the more he came back to himself, the guiltier he felt. *Victor tried to kill you,* his mind snapped. But it was a weak argument. Benton had lived as Victor's killer. He knew that the teen wasn't the one in control. *I took everything from him,* Benton thought with a quick, satisfied smile. He caught himself a second later, and pressed his forehead hard against his arms, his eyes squeezed shut, nails digging into his palms as he balled his hands tight. *It wasn't me.* He repeated it until it felt true.

The pages of his notebook crinkled under his clutching fingers. *Victor won't read it,* he knew. *Even if he did, he won't believe it.* A new wave of despair hit him. Benton had seen what grief could do to a large city. He couldn't imagine the damage it would wreak upon such a small town. It would be like a plague, spewed forth from his diseased mind, destroying all that it found. But even if he did try to help, his past failures had proven that he couldn't change the outcome. The person would still die and he would be left under a cloud of suspicion, fear, and parental rage.

His hollow stomach twisted at the thought of his parents as anger struck him like lightning. They had drugged him. Even if they were truly oblivious to what they had just put him through, Benton couldn't let it go. He had lost out to their need to preserve the good opinion of people they didn't even know. It was enough to provoke his petty nature; they had hurt him and he wanted to hurt them back, which was all the flimsy excuse he needed to go against their wishes.

Resolving to warn Victor was easy. Coming up with a way to do it that wouldn't lead to the complete implosion of his life, again, was harder. His fingers twitched around the mobile phone he refused to let go of. For a while, he stared at the screen, watching the little bar move as the song played. He searched every inch of his brain, trying to think of someone, anyone, he could call to ask for advice. Or help. Or just to listen to him. He couldn't come up with a single name. Contemplating just how pathetic he felt was a momentary distraction.

The paper crinkled and slid under his fingertips, drawing his attention. He really had done a horrible job. It didn't even look like his handwriting. Benton sat up a little straighter. Just because he couldn't place the surroundings he had glimpsed in the dream, didn't mean that no one else could. *Constable Rider,* his mind supplied. Nothing about her struck him as someone prone to wild explanations. But she was exactly the type who would follow up on every lead.

*How do I do this with the least potential for blow back?*

He pondered the thought as he got to his feet. The best he could come up with was to leave it on her doorstep. It was still ridiculously early, everyone would be asleep, and he doubted that she would have security cameras. With a new energy, Benton crammed a change of clothes into his backpack. He needed to leave before his parents checked on him, and the school's locker room should be open. He'd have time to shower before class.

This time he remembered to grab his wallet, which would take care of breakfast. He shoved his feet into his sneakers, brushed his teeth, and pulled a comb through his hair at the same time. Luckily, for all of his faults, Benton had great coordination and managed to do all three jobs to some degree of success. As an afterthought, he shoved a towel and a bottle of hair gel into the last remained area of his bag. He yanked off his sweat-drenched top and didn't bother to replace it. Instead, just shoving on a red hooded sweater as he neared his door.

Benton leaned out to check if the hallway was clear. As he glanced over the closed doors that lined the L-shaped hallway, he realized that he didn't know which one was his parent's bedroom. He couldn't judge which one he needed to tip toe past. The carpet absorbed the sound of his footsteps as he crept forward, carefully testing for any creaking floorboards. His process was slow, but effective. He breathed a sigh of relief when he closed the front door behind him.

"You're up early."

Benton whirled around. A police officer whom he had never seen before was sitting against the hood of her patrol car, both hands shooting up in a placating manner.

"Sorry, I didn't mean to startle you."

"I'm a little on edge," Benton mumbled.

He pulled the strap of his backpack onto his shoulder, not sure what to do next. The woman relaxed her arms and offered him a wide, pearly grin.

"I guess you've got reason to be," she said. "I'm Abby."

"Benton."

"Everyone knows," she dismissed.

"Abby?"

"Yeah. That's right."

"Don't you want me to use your rank or last name?"

She laughed, loud and nasal, until she realized that he wasn't joking. "You've never lived in a small town, have ya?"

"No."

Amusement laced her words "It shows."

Nodding once, Benton jogged down the porch steps, and started towards the property gate.

"Where are you going, then?"

Benton glanced back at her as he jammed a thumb over his shoulder, indicating his intended direction. "School."

"A little early, ain't it?"

"I have to run an errand first."

"Do you know how far a walk that is?"

Benton's feet froze. He did know, he had just completely forgotten. Just like he had forgotten that he had no idea where Constable Rider lived. He might be able to get to town before everyone was awake and moving, but if the Riders lived on another distant property, he was screwed. *How do you fit this much stupidity into such a simple plan?* A voice in his head snickered. Abby must have seen him deflate because she stood up.

"What do you have to do, love?"

The sudden endearment caught him off guard. "I've got to drop something off."

"Can it wait until your parents are up? You probably shouldn't be out and about on your own."

"No."

"What's so important?" Abby pressed, her smile wide and eyes hidden behind her sunglasses.

"Just a text book I borrowed from Nicole." *Stupid,* his mind snapped. But he was committed now. "I was supposed to give it back last night."

Abby's eyebrows shot up to her hairline. "Nicole Rider?"

"Yeah."

The word tilted up at the end, as if it were a question, and he winced at hearing it. He was so busy berating himself that he didn't notice Abby leaping towards the driver's side door.

"Trust me, love. If you told Nicole that it would be there, you want it there. That girl never forgets a mess up. She still goes on about that one time I forgot to pick up the ice for the police officer's ball. She was eight when it happened. I love her but that girl is a special level of irritating."

Benton didn't move.

"Well, come on. If we hurry, we can get there before she wakes up."

She slipped into the cruiser and Benton rushed to follow.

It was after he clicked his seatbelt into place that she added, "Don't worry, love. You can pop it on the doorstep and I'll back you up that you put it there last night."

Benton turned off the shower and cast the empty locker room back into silence. He popped his headphones in the second he was dressed. Clean and fully awake, he was finally feeling like himself again. At least enough that he could put on some of his own music. He smiled slightly as a fast, dance-worthy beat pumped into his ears. The trumpet kicked in and there was no other choice but to dance along. His sneakers squeaked across the tiles as he scooted and spun his way to the mirror. It was a small victory, to simply be alone in his own skin, but it was definitely one worth celebrating.

By now, he figured Constable Rider would know everything he did. It made him feel light, purged even. Washed clean in more than just the physical sense. His bruises weren't hurting and his split lip was healing nicely. Even his hair was being uncharacteristically cooperative. As he spiked the last tips, he decided that today, despite all odds, might actually be a good day. Singing along, he shoved everything into his backpack and glanced at his watch. There was still plenty of time for him to duck over to the café before class. If it had decent coffee and donuts, this would officially be the best day ever.

He left the locker room and proceeded down the hall with a shimmy, a shake, and a flurry of footwork. Ending with a slide, he managed to travel a few feet before a hand grabbed him roughly by the hood of his sweater and yanked. Stumbling to keep upright, he was dragged into a janitor's closet, crossing the limited space in a few steps. His back crashed into the shelves hard enough to shake his earphones free. The music still whispered into the room as the door swung shut, sealing him within utter darkness.

Benton didn't hesitate to charge forward the second he felt movement. He pushed the person before him into the now closed door with a solid thud. Aware of his lithe form, he pressed against the body, attempting to pin them before they could throw a swing. Shock turned him rigid when, instead of Victor's bone and muscle, he found himself pressed against a far more yielding form. His limited experience with the sensation didn't stop him from instantly recognizing the feeling of breasts molding to his chest.

"Easy, it's just me," Nicole whispered.

Her hot breath brushed over his neck in a way he enjoyed just a little too much and he lurched back until his spine collided with the shelf wall again.

"Nicole?"

After a shuffle and a soft tinkling sound, she found the pull chain and switched on the weak overhead bulb.

"What is wrong with you?" he snapped.

"Keep your voice down," she whispered.

"Why?"

She rolled her eyes. "I don't want anyone to overhear us, obviously. That's the whole point of meeting in the closet."

"This isn't 'meeting,' it's kidnapping," he hissed back. Every time she shushed him, he rose his voice a little louder. "And if you want to have a private conversation, we could have just talked in the completely empty hallway!"

"Are you always so tense?"

He stared at her for a long moment. She stared back, as if she didn't understand why he would object to being randomly pulled into a storage room a day after being violently attacked. Coming down from his shock, he reached for the door handle.

"I'm leaving."

She slapped his hand away.

"We haven't even talked yet."

"Why ruin a good thing?"

Again, he put his hand out and again she slapped it. Somehow, she was able to get a lot of pain out of such a small movement.

"Could you be serious for one moment?" she asked, her mouth scrunching up into a frown.

"I am. I don't want to talk to you."

"That's not how you should talk to a friend."

"Yeah, still not my friend."

Nicole closed her eyes, lifted her hands, and took deep soothing breaths. When she spoke next, her voice had returned to its peppy hostess tone.

"I apologize, I don't mean to pressure you into saying it. Your actions speak loud enough."

"My actions?"

His eyes widened when she lifted the stack of loose pages he had ripped from his notebook. The dream. She had the printed copy of the dream.

"Why do you have that?"

Casually, she folded the stack in half and neatly slid them back into her bag. "I couldn't leave them at home. Mom might have stumbled across them."

He rocked on his feet as his stomach plummeted into his shoes. "She hasn't seen them?"

There was a slight squeak in his voice but she didn't seem to notice. She actually looked proud.

"Don't worry, I kept it out of sight."

"Why would you do that?" He bent forward with the sheer force of his bellow.

At last, he got a reaction out of her. Unfortunately, she just looked surprised.

"What is wrong with you?" he snapped.

"Keep your voice down."

"You need to give that to your mother! Now!"

"If you wanted her to see it, why did you leave it for me?"

A manic bubble of laughter escaped him as he clutched his hands into his hair. "I didn't."

"It was on my porch."

"Your mother's porch."

"Benton, you need to calm down," she said with practiced control. "You're not making any sense."

"What?" He clenched his jaw to stifle his anger as she shushed him again. "Let me get this straight; you find a story depicting a gruesome death, quite possibly evidence in a crime, on your doorstep. And you decide that it can't be for your mother, a highly trained, law enforcement officer with access to firearms. No, it has to be for you, a neurotic overbearing teenager. Did I get that right?"

"Well, I just naturally assumed."

"When *Hannibal Lecter* comes to town, you tell the Federal Police, not the *Scooby Gang!*" he hissed.

"*Mystery Inc.*" she mumbled sorely. "The company name of the *Scooby Gang* is *Mystery Inc.*"

"It doesn't matter!"

"*Scooby-Doo* is a much loved childhood memory for many people–"

"Oh my God," he muttered as he began restlessly shift around the limited space. "You are deranged. Give that to your mother."

"No."

"Say again."

"No. We're going to find Victor and take care of the *empusa* on our own."

Confusion forced aside his anger. "What the hell is an empusa?"

"It's from Greek mythology. Kind of like a transporting vampire that preys on men."

He stared at her.

"I couldn't figure out what it is. So I'm working the different options into sentences and seeing what sounds correct," she pulled a slip of paper and pen from her pocket and scribbled something out. "Not empusa."

"Nicole," he said slowly. "You do remember that I'm on the outside of your head, right? I'm going to need a little more of an explanation."

"Vic's so called girlfriend. It's not human, right? You've been in its head, you know. I'm trying to figure out what it is so I can kill it."

He stammered, "What?"

"It's going to kill my friend," she said, jutting her chin out defiantly. "It's killed others. We need to take care of this."

"No, your mother needs to take care of this. She's the one with access to guns, remember?"

"I have access to guns."

"Why do you have access to guns?" he snapped with horror. "You should not be allowed to have that."

"That hurt my feelings."

He pressed his fingers to his temples as he tried to regroup. "Nicole, she's trained for this sort of thing. She signed up for it."

"She's trained to handle human felons. Even if we did tell her, she's not going to believe us. She'll be putting herself in unnecessary danger and I can't allow that."

"Yes, you can."

"We'll be just fine on our own."

"Why do you keep using plurals?" Benton asked hesitantly.

"Because you're coming with me."

"No, I'm not."

"Yes, you are."

"I can assure you that you are mistaken," he said as he reached for the door again.

"I need help looking through Victor's house." She slapped his hand again, sharper than before.

Holding her gaze, he stressed every word. "I do not care."

"Well, prepare to care," Nicole said sternly. "Because if you don't help me, I'm going to tell my mother exactly who wrote that story."

"Go ahead."

She jolted. "Huh?"

Feeling like he finally had the upper hand in this conversation, Benton smirked. "It will be your word against mine."

"And why would *my mother*," she stressed the words with a hint of mockery, "not take my word over yours?"

He pointed to her bag. "Maybe because if you're telling the truth, you're admitting to willfully tampering with evidence in a criminal case. You really should have handed that over."

"Oh," she whispered.

"You're horrible at blackmailing people."

She frowned. "I'm just new at it."

"Right," he shook his head. "I'm leaving."

Nicole instantly moved to block his path. She scrunched up her mouth, narrowed her eyes, and balled her fists until her arms shook just a little.

"What is that? What's going on here?" He waved a hand in the air to indicate her face.

"I'm staring you down with my steeling glare."

"I'm not going."

Her confusion was quickly replaced with determination. "Aren't you a little curious as to how I knew you wrote it?"

Benton froze. "How?"

"Victor sent it to me. So I'm guessing there's a file somewhere on his computer which will look pretty incriminating given recent events. Like how you promised to kill him in front of a police officer." Nicole took a step closer, holding his gaze with a challenge of her own. "Now I'm not tech savvy. I have no idea if that file will lead straight back to you, but that doesn't matter. What matters is; are you tech savvy enough to be sure that your butt is covered?"

The truth was, Benton wasn't.

"Damn it," he hissed.

"Exactly. Now, stop fussing and get in the car." She flung open the door and pointed down the hallway like a teacher sending a child to time out.

# Chapter 12

Benton shivered as Nicole edged her jeep deeper into the shadows of the house. It loomed up outside of his window like a gigantic beast made of warm wood and crimson tiles. Nicole didn't stop the jeep. Under the roar of the engine, he could hear the gravel drive crunching under the wheels, the sound putting him on edge. The house was picturesque, set upon the brilliant green of the surrounding property. He couldn't see a single thing that wasn't beautiful and quaint. Not a single reason why he suddenly felt like spiders were crawling under his skin. He didn't want to go in there.

"Are you picking up on something?"

Benton rocked forward with shock as Nicole sharply slammed on the breaks. He turned to find her watching him intensely, expectantly.

"I'm not psychic," he snapped.

"Are you sure? Have you tried?"

His mouth pulled into a snarl. She sighed, pulled out the paper and pen he had seen in the storage closet, and scribbled something on it.

"What was that?" he said.

She snapped her head up to study the house. "What? Where?"

"I meant in your hand."

Instantly, she shoved everything back into her pocket. "Nothing."

"You have a list on me?"

"In my defense, there's obviously something up with you and you're not being forthcoming."

"You're unbelievable," he muttered.

"Thank you."

He closed his eyes. She had to be messing with him and he refused to give her a reaction. When he felt a little more in control, he opened his eyes to look out the window. A scream ripped from him, sharp and short, as he threw himself back. The gear shift dug into his spine, Nicole shot questions at a rapid pace, but he didn't notice either. Everything within him was focused on the dark specter by his side. Separated by a thin layer of glass, its edges blurred as if it were a smear against the air itself. It didn't have a face, just a blob of white bone that tarnished the bottomless pit. Still, he knew it was looking at him.

"What's wrong? What's there?" Nicole asked hurriedly.

It moved like smoke as it lifted another patch of white to the window. A sharp, grinding squeak cut through the car; Nicole heard it. Her fingers dug painfully into his right shoulder as she finally fell silent. Benton recognized the sound. Not from his real life, but from the shattered remains of a dream. It was the sound of bare bone grinding against glass.

He jolted when the being moved. It drifted backwards, gliding over the earth without ever touching it, slipping up the stairs, and disappearing through the front door. The journey took a split second. It never stopped looking at him. It never stopped pointing.

"Go," Benton said numbly. "Now."

Nicole brought the jeep back to life then stopped. "We need to find Vic."

His frustration boiled over and he whirled around to face her. "Death just went into that house, and it was staring at me."

"What?"

Instantly, Nicole fumbled with her seatbelt and was out of the jeep before he could grab her. Hurling every profanity he could think of at her didn't stop her from running towards the house. He jumped out of the car but didn't follow.

"Did you miss the part about Death?" he roared.

Without hesitation, she wrenched the door open and ran inside. "It's after Vic!"

A second later, she was gone, taken from his sight by the shadows of the house. Alone, Benton glanced over his shoulder, his hands tightening around the edge of the door. The jeep was still rumbling, the keys swinging tantalizingly, begging him to just get in and go. With a sharp growl, he ran towards the house, leaving the jeep door wide open.

His conviction vanished when he reached the threshold and saw the deep shadows that drenched the house. None of them seemed real. As if they had no dimension to them, no depth. Unsure what to do, he shouted for Nicole. His voice echoed back to him like a taunt and he shuddered. Awkwardly shifting his weight, he strained to hear over the thunderous roar of his own heart. Racing footsteps slapped across the kitchen floor. He moved towards it before he could stop himself.

The shards of sunlight cutting through the kitchen windows were a comfort. They illuminated the space in a homey glow, lighting up the dust that drifted lazily in the air. He took a single step onto the tiles and the world went black. Blinking rapidly, he turned around, desperately searching for a single trace of the light. There was nothing. Almost tripping over his own feet, he spun around, ready to flee to the front door. There was nothing there. Only complete, unbroken darkness.

At first, he had just thought it was a trick of his eyes. He couldn't breathe as a slow procession of white patches began to litter across the world around him. They began to move, drifting closer without creating a single sound. It was then that he knew. They weren't a trick of the light. Death was before him, around him, so numerous that they blotted out the sun. He screamed.

\*\*\*

The house was empty. Nicole checked every room in rapid succession but couldn't find a single person. There was no trace that anyone had been there in days. Panting, she burst out the back door and glanced around the backyard. The sun twinkled off something metal in the distance. She squinted into the glare and was about to move forward when she heard Benton scream.

Heart lurching into her throat, she barreled back into the house as fast as her legs would allow. She slipped over the kitchen tiles as she tried to bring herself to a sudden stop. Benton stood in the middle of the room, arms thrashing, stumbling around with wide, unseeing eyes.

"Benton?"

He instantly turned to her voice but didn't look at her.

"I can't see," he whimpered as he staggered towards her.

"We're getting out of here."

She reached out to grab his questing hand. Then she saw it. An eye. It watched her from within the gap created by the cupboard doors. Glassy and wild, it belonged to something far too big to fit within the limited space of the cupboard. Impossibly, the clawed hand snapped out through the slip of space. Benton turned within the same second.

Blood splattered across the walls, punctuated by the ripping of clothes and the wet sound of severing flesh. Grasping at his chest, Benton staggered and crumbled onto his back. She was by his side in a second, hands wrapping around his arm, her back aching as she dragged his weight back onto his feet.

"It's me," she told him as he struggled against her.

Teeth clenched against the pain, he scrambled to his feet and allowed her to pull his arm across her shoulders. Together they hobbled towards the door. The eye followed. It appeared in every crack. The gap between the window frame and the wall. The slats of the floorboards. The space between the couch cushions.

Blood soaked Benton's hoodie. His knees buckled, jarring her with his weight and almost bringing them both down onto the living room floor. The floor rug bunched under their feet, making it harder to keep them upright. He clung to her, his fingers leaving trails of blood across her jacket.

"Just a little further," she assured.

Benton was shaking as they ran out the front door, the eye watching them go with an unblinking glare. They staggered down the steps. His feet stopped moving, forcing her to drag him, his shoes cutting groves into the gravel. She didn't dare to look back. Blindly, Benton reached for the car and half fell onto the passenger seat. Sweat dripped from his fevered skin. Heat radiated through the denim of his jeans as she forced his legs up. The second his feet were out of the way, she slammed the door shut and ran to the driver's side.

"I'm so sorry," she sobbed as she locked the door behind her. "It's going to be okay. It will. We're leaving."

She reached across him to lock his door just as he lurched forward. A thick sludge spewed from his mouth. It was stark white and had the appearance of a solid form even as it dripped over the dashboard. Nicole pulled back, watching in horror as Benton hurled again. He slammed back against the chair, body rigid and neck straining. The white substance began to seep through the blood oozing from the open wound on his chest.

"Oh, God," she breathed.

Her hands shook as she clambered back into her seat and reached for the car keys. There was only empty air. She smacked her hand over the ignition and the surrounding area. Nothing.

"Where are the keys?"

Benton's eyes rolled within his skull and he was struggling to keep his head up. The seat below him creaked and groaned as his whole body began to quake.

"Benton," she reached across and cupped his face with both hands. "Where did you put the keys?"

Each breath rattled in his chest, wheezing as it worked its way through the muck bubbling up from his throat. She could see how much focus he needed to just look at her. The storm gray of his eyes was lost to the expanse of his irises. His body cracked against the seat. A gargled cry forced the sludge to bubble from his mouth and slide down his jaw in a putrid trail. His face flushed a brutal red. It took all of her strength but she was able to force him forward. The white muck sloshed across the car floor. With a sputter and a spit, he was able to draw in a wheezed breath.

"I don't know what to do," she babbled. "Just tell me what to do."

He didn't respond. She pushed him back just enough to pat his pockets in search of the keys. The window exploded in. Nicole ducked away, too startled to scream as shards rained down upon her. Shielding her eyes, she looked up to see Victor dragging Benton through the broken window. She lunged forward, her hands scrambling for purchases across Benton's retreating legs. All of her pleas fell on deaf ears. Suddenly, Victor's hand clutched her hair, tightening until it tore hunks out from the roots. She clawed at his fingers, digging into the flesh, but it didn't stop him from smashing her head against the dashboard.

For a brief moment, everything became white. She slumped down against the now empty passenger seat as the world swam and shimmered around her.

"Stay down," Victor whispered. "She only wants him."

The car keys struck her temple and toppled onto the seat before her. Then everything went black.

*** 

The loose earth crumbled under Benton's hands. Shadows danced off the broken hunks of raw earth above him. Benton blinked. The motion took what remained of his energy and he was unable to open them again. Sounds began to shift within the freezing air. A soft, wailing sob hit his ears and he winced, his stomach rolling over itself. He knew that sound. He had heard it in a dream. When he had presented his claws for Victor to die upon. Unable to move, he could do nothing but lay there and listen, waiting for it to inevitably end.

# Chapter 13

Nicole blinked aside her welling tears as she burst into her room. She had pulled into her driveway before her mind had caught up with anything that was happening. Grabbing her stacks of research, she hurled them onto the floor, knelt down, and began to search through it all.

"The answer is here. Just talk it out." Not quite believing her own words, she closed her eyes and took a deep breath. "You can do this Nic. I believe in you."

A layer of calm settled over the raging chaos in her stomach. Opening her yes, she hovered her hands over the scattered papers, as if willing the answer into her through osmosis.

"Why take Benton?" She remembered Benton's written description of a dark room filled with coffins, each one carefully placed like a beloved art exhibit. "It's a collector."

She flipped Benton's binder open to the banshee page and skimmed until she could confirm that she had remembered correctly.

"Banshees are rarely seen. A male one has got to be unique. Something worth collecting. So, we're going with banshee?" she asked herself. Her spine straightened when it hit her. "It hid. After he screamed, it hid. He was blinded, it could have just come up behind him, but it hid."

Despite knowing it was flimsy evidence, her gut told her she was right. Benton was a banshee and he, in some way, could hurt it.

"But why not just seduce him like it did Vic?"

She ripped off her jacket and eyed the pale fluid Benton had vomited onto the sleeve. It had already bleached the suede.

"Leanan Sidhe." She snatched up the sheets. "They take human lovers. Acting as their muses while making them euphoric. But Benton's not human."

Nicole barreled to the hall bathroom. Dorothy had given her some at home drug tests for a science experiment last year. There were some left over. Everything in the cupboard ended up on the floor. Nothing. She flung open the mirrored door of the medicine cabinet and scooped out its contents. Finally, she found the few remaining slips of test paper and, tossing the jacket into the tub, shoved it into the sludge. It took three minutes to get results and she spent every second of it worried that it wouldn't work. Surely, it wasn't built for this. There might be a whole cocktail of things it can't measure. When the time came, there were a few readings. She read and reread the strip in disbelief.

"Cocaine, ecstasy, and oxycodone? Oh, Victor." She felt crushed under a new wave of despair and guilt. Tears dripped free and she wiped them away harshly. "So, either Benton's rejecting the drug or overdosing."

The thought of him being immune wasn't comforting. If the Leanan Sidhe can't drug Benton into compliance, what would it do to break him? She released a startled yelp as a scraping noise crossed the window. Her legs hit the tub as she fell painfully into it. It was the same squeal she had heard in the jeep. The one Benton had attributed to Death personified. The noise came again. This time, it trailed across the mirrored door of the medicine cabinet.

With a flail of limbs, she latched onto the doorframe and hurled herself to her feet. She hesitated in the doorway, heart racing, fear stewing within her until bile rose in her throat.

"Hi," she croaked out to the empty air. "I'm Nicole. And you're Death. According to Benton, anyway. I hope that's not derogatory, I just don't know what else to call you."

The silence was both crippling and charged. She glanced around the bathroom.

"Running theory, Benton is a banshee, which I'm guessing bonds you and him in a way. I'm at least hoping it does."

Only silence met her.

"You were trying to warn him, weren't you? I didn't listen and I'm so sorry. Please help me save him."

Silence.

"Do you know where he is? I know there's probably rules about interfering, but please, even just a hint?"

A long, shrill screech cut through the room. She staggered back a step as the medicine cabinet door began to move. It inched closed, the sound never ending. Catching the light from the window, it shot the glare into her eyes. Nicole winced and lifted her hand.

It hit her. "A car! The glint I saw behind Vic's house was a car."

She barreled back into her room and pulled a map of Fort Wayward from her drawer, one that had been too crumpled to include in the Bertrand's welcome basket. With a sweep of her arm, she cleared her desk and spread out the map. Victor's house, and a number of the connecting ones, were made of dirt. They were rarely used and any new tire marks would be easy enough to follow. She traced the thin lines of the map to an array of different properties. According to town history, there had been eight properties built there when the town was first founded a hundred years ago. They had only stood for a year before a wildfire destroyed them all. Believed cursed, the properties were left abandoned.

"It's hiding in one of the basements."

She grabbed a new coat from her cupboard and she wondered if her mother had locked her office window, or if anyone had changed the code for the station's gun closet.

***

Benton's limbs felt encased in stone. With excruciating effort, he dragged himself across the floor. Colors hit his eyes like flares. Victor's cries and the sound of tearing flesh blended together in his ears and merged with the memories within his head. It was killing him. Benton couldn't move. He tried to speak but the viscous muck rose again, choking him like hardening concrete. It took every muscle straining together to force it out. Exhaustion made him slump against the earth. By the time he was able to draw in a deep breath, the sound had stopped. The dust stirred as Victor's body crumpled.

Tasting the dirt on every breath, Benton closed his eyes. Tears scorched his chilled skin as they rolled from his eyes. In the deafening silence, he heard each drop. Soon, the droplets increased until they were a steady leak. He knew they didn't all belong to him. They weren't all tears. The blood slipping from the monster's hand sounded heavier. Drip by drip, the sound edged closer, until the warm trickling struck his cheek. He flinched with every hit but wasn't able to move away. The tips of claws nicked his skull as it began to pat him. Every stroke left behind a thick trail of blood and the growing stench of copper.

***

Nicole clutched her hair as she looked at the four options before her. The tracks of Vincent's truck had disappeared as it crossed the hard stone of the crossroads and she couldn't find it again. Not knowing what else to do, she had gone to each property in turn. A century of neglect had left the foundations of the settler's homes lost under thick grass as high as her hip, swallowing them as if they had never been there. Now, purple glitter ink criss-crossed her map and she was back at the crossroads, hoping to spot something she had missed. She racked her brain but was sure that all of the text books only spoke of eight.

A scream devastated the air, rattling the stones of the road with its force. Nicole threw her hands over her ears but it was no protection from the unbroken wail. It was human and other, the different sounds bleeding together even as they layered one over the other. A shrill whine of microphone feedback. A hunting screech of an owl. Rolling like thunder. Roaring like a river. And at the heart of it all, a very human voice, raised in terror, quivered at an astonishing pitch.

Then it stopped. Her ears rung as she stared, shell-shocked and enthralled, in the direction the sound had come from. Nicole was certain that, for the first time in her life, she had just heard the scream of a banshee.

***

The world shifted around him like oil in water. A line of burning candles were placed on a table by the far wall, offering just enough light for him to make out the staircase beyond the coffins. Benton couldn't fathom how he had produced such a sound. The monster had left in the wake of it but he knew it was nearby. He felt it. Eyes darting around the room, he lurched and lumbered towards the only way out. Beside him, a coffin on his right creaked open, just a fracture of a slither, and Benton bolted forward.

He didn't see the hand but he felt it. Fingers coiled around his leg, tripping him and sending him crashing into the staircase railing. Riddled by time, the wood shattered under his weight. He kicked wildly at the hand on his ankle as he crumbled onto the floor amongst the fractured pile of kindling. A scream lodged within his throat when he saw it. Death stood at the top of the stairs like solid smoke, watching. His hands scrambled for something to grab onto as the monster dragged him back into the room but found only loose hunks of wood and dirt.

Splinters gouged into his palms as he latched onto one chuck, rolled onto his back, and swung blindly into the shadows behind him. It shattered as it struck something solid and the hand on his ankle released. Benton lurched onto his feet, kicked another chunk of wood into the air, and cracked his makeshift bat into it. Even as his eyes blurred, his arm was solid. The hunk crashed into the side table and toppled the candles. Each one extinguished as it hit the dirt and the room was lost to darkness.

With death above him, Benton threw himself to the side, using the shadows as a shield as he crawled under one of the coffins. They all sat on tables with fine velvet curtains separating them from the rest of the room. In his hiding place, Benton tried to force his mind to work. The raspy scrape of a match-head igniting made his heart stammer. A small patch of light flickered, growing as a candle was lit. Another strike and the glow increased, encroaching around the edges of the velvet. Another, the sound far closer, and he could see the metal bars crossing over the wood above him. The next match burst to life; the sound coming from just beyond the curtain. Shaking uncontrollably, Benton turned his head towards the sound.

The fingers were a vice around his neck before he ever saw the hand. He was wrenched out of his hiding place. His legs slammed into the side of the coffin, making it rock and pop open with a burst of decay. The monster's face hovered before him as sludge rose back up in his throat, unable to get past the tight grip of its fingers. Benton could only stare into the monster's mirror-like eyes. It allowed him to watch as he gasped for air, his face discoloring and swelling with his need for oxygen. It looked human, only mangled and mummified. Its lips shriveled over a disjointed jaw. The top of its skull engorged, bulging out as its face sloped in.

His lungs burned and fluttered, aching to be used. The sludge bubbled as it seeped further up his throat, taking the last of his air with it. Black smoke pooled in the corners of his vision. An arctic chill pressed against his spine. Death was behind him. Surrounding him. Blacking out the light.

A sudden light scorched his eyes as it flooded the room. A resounding crack and the hand around his neck released. Benton sagged against the wall, the flood of slop gushing from his mouth as a series of blurs joined together to reveal Nicole edging across the room, a gun held in both hands.

"Where did it go?" she whispered.

Benton heard the question but couldn't understand the words.

"Benton, do you see it?"

Fear and desperation warred in every syllable. He tried to speak. To turn her away before she saw who was in the open coffin. But it was too late. Her eyes fell upon Victor and she raced to him with a soul-crushing scream. She didn't see the figure rising up behind her, the arms with no end, the razor tipped talons. He called for her but only vomited. The arms wrapped around her wrenched her back from Victor's side. She struggled but couldn't get her hands up, couldn't position the weapon in her hand. Death drew near. Benton forced the last of the liquid clear of his throat as the monster bared its claws. Death reached for Nicole's cheek as the claws drove down to her chest.

Benton screamed. The sound hollowed and filled all at once. It filled the small space, growing like a living thing until it couldn't be contained. Clumps of earth broke free from the ceiling and fell like hail around them. The enormous coffins vibrated as the monster reeled back from Nicole. She didn't hesitate to whirl around. The barrel of her gun cut through Death, scattering the fumes of its body, and fired.

The gun was fired, but his voice swallowed the sound. One bullet hit the shoulder. The next hit the chest. And still it came forward. Nicole aimed, her feet braced, and the monster's twisted skull exploded. A wave of blood coated the wall. It beaded against the refined coffins and forged tiny rivers as they ran to the ground. Benton's scream died and he toppled to his knees. His ears rang but it wasn't enough to smother Nicole's ranting. She raged, paced back and forth like a caged lion, the polished handgun still within her grasp.

"Vic was my friend! He was a good person!" She bellowed the words before snapping her hand up and firing another round into the twisted corpse. Benton flinched and pressed his back against the wall. "You had no right!" The remaining last hunks of its skull burst as she fired again. Again. Again. "This is my town! My home!"

She didn't stop firing until the top pushed back. Still, she fired, clicking the empty gun as if hoping to find one more bullet. With a scream of fury, she raced forward and began to kick savagely at the mangled remains of its skull. The crack of bone gave way to wet squish. Benton found his feet. He wrapped an arm around her waist and tried to pull her back. She fought against him, breaking free more than once to stomp on the remains. A sharp pull sent both of them onto the ground.

"It's dead!" he yelled over her wild screams. "Stop!"

Nicole trembled within his arms, but stopped fighting him. Instead, she twisted just enough to wrap one arm around him in a tight but uncomfortable hug. She sobbed into his neck, each sob breaking him a little more. He held her tight and felt the thick, hard vest hidden under her jacket. The question burned in the back of his mind, hidden under his own helplessness, until she fell silent.

"Are you wearing a bullet-proof vest?"

"Yeah," she sniffed.

"Where did you get a bullet-proof vest?"

"Mom's work." She flopped her hand, the empty gun still tight within her fingers. "I grabbed it when I got the gun."

"That's a police weapon? Won't all those bullets be traceable?"

"We're going to have to get rid of it," she said, her eyes never leaving the bloodied remains of the monster before them. "I know a good spot we can bury it."

"We can't tell anyone."

Nicole didn't reply. Didn't move.

"My DNA is all over this place, Nicole," Benton pressed. "I won't be able to explain that. And we can't just take Vic and the others with us."

"They stay here for now. Not forever."

"Okay."

"We'll have to move it, too," she said, still staring at the twisted remains. "It doesn't get to stay here with Vic. Or the others."

While the dim light glistened over the polished wood of the numerous coffins, it was still too dark get an accurate count of their numbers. Benton almost wrenched again at the thought that one of them were still empty, waiting for him. Nicole turned her head to look at the field of beautifully encased corpses but her eyes didn't seem to focus.

"Do you think these are all of its victims?"

"No," Benton answered with certainty. "It had other nests that it needed to abandon."

Nicole made a soft sound of understanding but didn't question how he knew that. He was grateful for that. Right now, he didn't want to think about how much of this monster would live on, tucked away deep with his brain. He distracted himself by trying to think of something that he could say that would offer some measure of comfort to his friend. But nothing came to mind.

"Benton?" she asked numbly.

"Yes."

"There's brains on my shoe."

***

Sweat plastered the back of her shirt to her skin as she stood up and brushed her hands off on her jeans. For all of their efforts, the pit wasn't that deep. The small collapsible, camping shovel that she kept in her car for emergencies wasn't ideal for digging graves in the solid earth. Her shoulders ached as she lifted her hands over her head. Benton, having scrambled out before her, reached down to help her up. They were both too exhausted and sore for the movement to have any dignity in it. Her boots loosened up clumps of earth as she scraped the walls in an attempt to be helpful.

Eventually, they managed to get her out of the pit and they trudged the short distance to her jeep.

She glanced at him. "You look like hell."

"I just got back." The retort came quickly but his weak smirk took longer.

Spring had to be the worst possible time to try and discreetly bury a body. It was past nine and the sun was only now inching down towards the horizon. The towering grass shone like gold in the dwindling light and offered them a slight amount of cover as they pulled the mangled remains of the monster out from the boot of her jeep. The sudden jerk of weight made her shoulders throb and her fingers clutched to keep her grip on its ankles. Benton had mercifully agreed to take the arms. She wasn't sure if she could stomach being near its crushed skull. Shuffling back to the pit, Benton seemed desperate for some kind of distraction. "When did you decide you were going to come for me?"

Nicole grunted as she adjusted her grip. "It was never a question."

Just when she was sure she couldn't go another step, they reached the pit and let the body drop. A puff of dust drifted up on the impact and they both took a moment to catch their breaths. When they were able to straighten, they kicked the body into the hole.

"Thank you."

"Any time you need a serial killing Leanan Sidhe shot up, I'm your girl."

"A what?"

"I'll explain it later," she dismissed as they slumped down and began to push the pile of loose earth over the corpse. "You're a banshee by the way. I figured that out, too."

He paused to look at her. "I'm going to have follow-up questions."

"I see a lot of research in our futures," she said instead of admitting that she had pretty much revealed the complete extent of her knowledge.

She remembered a heartbeat later that the gun and vest had to go in too. They dropped onto the body with a thick thud. It was a lot quicker to fill it back in than it was to dig it up, but still, the sky was ablaze with the final gasps of the sunset when they finished.

"Are you sure it won't be found here?" Benton said.

They had picked one of the paths that delved deeper into the unmapped area, following it until the road ended.

"Well, this place isn't supposed to be here, so I think so."

"What do you mean?"

"Town history mentioned only eight properties in this area. That basement was of a ninth. There is no record that anything was ever built around here."

"Well, someone built there. Why would people remember all the others but forget that one?"

They slumped against each other, shoulder to shoulder, both the only thing keeping the other upright.

"I'm starting to think that there's a lot more to Fort Wayward than I know," Nicole admitted.

Silence descended over them until, a peace neither was keen to break until Benton mumbled, "You're a good friend."

Too tired to fully celebrate her victory, she let her head fall onto his shoulder and hummed in agreement. Nicole had forgotten about her mobile phone until it began to announce a Skype call. Fishing it out of her pocket, she checked the caller ID and began to battle her hair into some kind of order.

"Just let it ring out," Benton said.

"It's Professor Lester."

"I don't know who that is."

As she pulled his hood up to hide his blood soaked scalp, she explained what he was calling about and how, if she didn't answer, he would contact her mother. When they were somewhat presentable, she answered the call and forced a bright smile. Professor Lester's eyes darted between them, suspicious of their frazzled appearance, but didn't mention it.

"You owe me," Lester growled. "That symbol is from an obscure cult that faded into oblivion around 64 BC. Do you know how hard that is to find?"

"I really appreciate it," Nicole smiled.

Lester rolled his eyes but continued. "I only bothered to get the basics."

She made her voice shine with happiness. "Basics are great."

He sugared his tea as he continued, "So this cult believed that there was a kind of supernatural lay that rested over the world. When something tied to that world died, it marked the spot, which, in theory, would send other supernatural creatures scattering."

"What's this got to do with the painting on my barn?" Benton asked.

Lester glared, his mouth scrunching up until Nicole assured him that they wouldn't interrupt again.

"As I was saying," he accentuated. "The problem was, this death was like a controlled burn. It gets rid of creatures for the present.

But as soon as it grew back, it lures more critters to the area. And then, of course, predators follow the critters."

"They thought that killing a supernatural creature would lure more dangerous supernatural creatures to the area?" Nicole said.

"Essentially." He leisurely sipped at his tea, ignoring the impatience of the teenagers. "In keeping with the analogy, the symbol was designed to salt the earth. To stop anything from growing back. No growth, no monsters."

"Does it work?" Benton blurted.

Lester eyed him for a long moment, his brow furrowed. "Do a lot of squiggles help stop mythological creatures from migrating to an area where an imaginary fog was disturbed?" He rolled his eyes. "Sure. Why not? Look, Nicole, I have a class to teach. Good luck with your research."

"Can you send through the research you already did?" she hurriedly asked.

Professor Lester made a noncommittal noise that she chose to assume was agreement. She had just enough time to thank him before the screen went dark. Beside her, Benton heaved a heavy breath and appeared to deflate upon its release.

"We totally screwed up, didn't we?" he mumbled.

"No," she rushed. "We'll just put the symbol here. And one in the basement. It will be fine. It'll all be fine."

She felt him watching her and slowly turned to meet his gaze.

"Do you really believe that?" he asked.

"Not exactly. But I do believe that we can handle whatever comes our way."

A fleeting smile crossed his face and she turned to watch the wind playing with the long grass.

"The banshee and the neurotic teen," Benton smiled.

She gave him a rueful smile. "Best friends."

"I never agreed to *best*."

* * *

# Whispering Graves
## Banshee Series Book 2

# Chapter 1

The small round dining table made it impossible for Benton to ignore the corpse that sat in the chair across from him. Death had claimed its eyes, hiding both the color and pupil under the milky film, but it didn't weaken the weight of its gaze. Sitting on either side of him, his parents continued their conversation between mouthfuls of the Chinese takeout that had already gone cold and soaked through the paper containers by the time it had arrived. Benton flinched each time their cutlery scraped against their plates. Familiar aromas clung to the warm air of the living room and filled his nose.

And the corpse kept staring at him.

"Benton," his mother said softly.

Benton didn't respond. Instead, he kept his eyes locked on his dinner plate, one of the few places he could look where the corpse wasn't visible. His mother's perfectly manicured hand crept into his field of vision and tapped the edge of his plate.

"It's getting cold, sweetie."

He could feel the weight of his father's gaze as it shifted onto him. And with that, Benton now had the full attention of all three people seated at the round table. Clutching his fork until his fingers lost feeling, Benton forced his eyes up. With his parents sitting on either side of him, there was nothing to disrupt his view from the dead man before him. Sixty years had passed since Oliver Ackerman had been buried in a shallow grave, and only a month since Benton had dug him up.

It hadn't been an intentional thing, at least not consciously. Benton and his parents had moved into the house hoping for a fresh start, and on their first night, while sleepwalking, Benton had found the mangled corpse in their barn. The whole event had seemed to fit right in with the long progression of twisted nightmarish happenings that constituted his life. People liked to tell him that it was just bad luck or a coincidence. He knew it wasn't. He knew that there was something about him that wasn't quite right.

But no one ever really believes a teenager when he says that he feels he's different. It didn't stop him from feeling it; like an alien body under his skin. Something growing. Something that had strengthened the night he had found Oliver, and evolved the day a demonic spirit had tried to kill him.

That attack had forever shifted something within Benton, and Oliver had marked the occasion by making his first appearance. He had begun almost timidly. Standing at the foot of Benton's bed as he slept, or lurking in the shadows only to disappear when Benton turned a light on. He wasn't so timid anymore. Now he liked to be seen, but only by Benton, and always appearing undeniably dead. Oliver was as bloated and festering as a fresh corpse, nothing like the brittle, discolored remains that had been pulled from the earth. Each time he saw him, Benton could smell the lingering stench of decay. As soon as Benton locked eyes with Oliver from across the table, the scent of rotting meat grew until he gagged.

"Are you feeling okay?" his mother pressed.

"Yeah," Benton said after swallowing down his bile. "I'm fine."

His mother talked across him, her attention focused solely on his father. "He looks pale."

Benton jumped when his father pressed a hand against his forehead.

"Relax, Chey, he's not warm."

"Really, I'm fine," Benton assured as he let his eyes drift back down to his plate. The broken eye contact didn't distract him from the ghost's attention. It only intensified it, until Benton could almost taste the putrid smell in the back of his throat. Oliver never took his eyes off of him. "I'm just not that hungry."

"Well, you need to eat something," Cheyanne said. "You can't keep expecting Constable Rider to pay for your meals."

His father scoffed. "Don't be so dramatic. We let the Constable's daughter eat our food when she's over."

"It's hardly the same, Theo," his mother shot back. "He's been having at least one meal a day over there. That adds up. We don't want her thinking that we're taking advantage of her hospitality."

What neither of them was taking into consideration was that Constable Rider's daughter, Nicole, was a force of nature, like a hurricane of bubbly energy and glitter. When she decided that something was going to happen, she didn't give up until she made it happen. Whether it was making Benton agree that they were friends, or hunting down and slaughtering a serial killing demon, she put the same amount of energy into both tasks. While Benton had decided that he needed to get out of the house, somewhere far away from his parents, and Oliver, it was Nicole who had declared that he would spend that free time over at her place. And, somewhere along the line, it just sort of happened.

The stench grew stronger, ripping Benton from the safety of his thoughts and thrusting him back into his meal with the dead. As subtly as he could, he pressed the back of his hand against his nose and breathed through his mouth. He could feel the traces of airborne fat coating his throat and making his eyes water.

With renewed determination to ignore Oliver, Benton stabbed at a hunk of pork. The crimson sweet and sour sauce swelled around the prongs of his fork. It appeared to thicken as he watched it, darkening until it looked like blood oozing out from the slice of meat. His stomach churned and he forced the morsel off his fork. Instead, he quickly shoved down a bite of honey chicken before Oliver could play any mind tricks with it.

The mouthful was enough to satisfy his parents and they resumed their previous conversation, chatting happily, unaware of the corpse only inches from their sides. They didn't see him, didn't feel the weight of his dead eyes upon them, but they did feel the shift in the air. It was a small comfort to see them shiver and watch as his father went to check the thermostat. But it was still a comfort. It was a slither of proof for Benton that he wasn't crazy.

Forcing himself to swallow the mouthful, Benton glanced up at Oliver. He was closer. Sitting perfectly still, his hands on his lap and his spine straight. The specter had drifted forward, entering into the solid wood of the table. Benton's heart hammered as a cold sweat bristled his skin. He blinked and Oliver was an inch closer. Staring. Silent. Benton lowered his gaze and felt the shift, the press of frigid air against his skin as Oliver drew closer. Benton looked up, and Oliver was halfway through the table. This time, Benton didn't take his eyes off of the ghost, but he couldn't quell his need to blink. Each time his eyelids flicked down, Oliver leaped forward until his decomposing face swallowed Benton's vision. His sunken, cloudy eyes held Benton's, while the stench of death gushed from him like a physical force. Benton felt drenched in it. His clothes grew heavy with festering vapor and he could almost feel a thick putrid mucus covering his arms and face. Oliver lurched forward again. Close enough now that the decaying flesh of his nose pressed, wet and weeping, against Benton's own.

"Benton," Theodore said from somewhere now unseen. "Eat your dinner."

***

Nicole shuffled in the driver's seat of her jeep, tucking in one leg and pressing her side against the back of the seat, making it very clear to Benton that he now had her full attention. The night surrounded the jeep with deep shadows that the weak overhead light could barely fight off. It wasn't hard to get out of town in a place like Fort Wayward. All you had to do was drive for fifteen minutes, in any direction a dirt road would allow you, and it was as if civilization ceased to exist.

Benton normally only called her at night when he needed to escape into that kind of oblivion for a bit. His parents were still dead set against him having a driver's license, and since walking blindly into the dark plains surrounding his ranch house wasn't the smartest idea, she was his only ticket out. And she was always happy to help. When Benton had hurled himself into her still moving car, she had expected a long tirade about something. He was a fan of suppressing his emotions until they exploded out of him like some kind of verbal volcanic eruption. But he had remained silent for most of their trip and responded to her attempts to start a conversation with the most minimal word usage possible. At his uneasy silence, Nicole had swung the jeep onto a new path, crossing through the lush Alberta plains before climbing up to the tip of a Buffalo Jump.

There were a few sheer drop-offs scattered around Fort Wayward that had once been used by local First Nations tribes during buffalo hunts. The animals had been coaxed into a stampede and herded over the edge to plummet to their deaths, earning the location the title, 'Buffalo Jumps.'

Nowadays, they were more commonly used for tourist attractions and for their breathtaking views. It was possible to look for miles in each direction and see nothing but untouched beauty. And at night, with nothing to compete against, the stars seemed like a blanket that covered the world, spread so thickly that they even sparkled along the horizon. Nicole liked that. She adored how the view could make her feel both larger than life and absolutely tiny within the same instant. It always helped her to put things into perspective, and she brought Benton here the first time he had begged her to 'just drive.' He hadn't gushed poetically about the sight, but he had smiled and relaxed into the passenger seat. It had taken her a few extra trips to learn that, for Benton, loose easy smiles were pretty much his version of extravagant praise.

As they sat, with Benton constantly skimming across the radio stations, Nicole was partly hoping that he was in the mood to discuss the life altering fact that he was a banshee. It had been almost a month since Nicole had been forced to realize how little she actually knew about the world, or even just her own sleepy little corner of it.

When she had first been told that Santa wasn't real, Nicole had spent days learning everything she could about where the legend had come from and how it had grown to the point that she had believed in flying reindeers. She had the same impulse now. To throw herself into discovering everything there was to know until she could feel certain of the world again. But she was nowhere near ready to begin researching the monster that had murdered her friend. The wounds were still too raw. She needed time to reconcile what had happened before she faced it again. And she could take as much time as she wanted where that particular monster was concerned. After all, she had chosen the spot for its unmarked grave. It was a patch of earth in the middle of nowhere. No one would ever find it. Only she and Benton knew where it was. So it could wait for her, rotting in the earth as she mourned, and she would study what was left.

She was, however, ready to start exploring Benton; a real live male banshee. She had a thousand questions and a million things she wanted to try. The problem was, every time he seemed to be on the verge of agreeing, she got way too excited and ended up bombarding him with too much, too fast. Overwhelmed, he would change the topic and that would be that. But not tonight.

As Benton leaned forward to, once again, search through the radio stations, Nicole took a deep sobering breath and reminded herself of the plan. She had spent some time going through her list and had arrived at a first request that would be simple and non-threatening. She wanted to try and get his banshee wail on tape. She had only ever heard it twice before, and, since they were fighting for their lives on both occasions, she hadn't thought to record it. If she could just stick to that one request tonight, Benton would have his distraction and they would have finally taken their first step into exploring a world beyond their understanding.

She smoothed her hands over her long hair, licked her lips, and forced on her most charming smile. Benton froze instantly, hand still on the radio, and turned to face her. His normally stormy eyes looked almost silver in the dim light as they studied her face closely.

"No."

"I haven't said anything," she said with a whine.

"You're giving me your Lady Frankenstein look and I'm not up for it tonight."

"I do not have a Lady Frankenstein look," she grumbled. "I had a simple request."

"Nope."

"Fine. So we'll talk about you."

He scrunched up his nose. "Are those my only options?"

"What options? You already made your choice. But don't worry, I came prepared," Nicole said.

He jerked back slightly as she flung her torso between the two front seats and began to grope along the dark back seat for her bag.

"You came prepared for a conversation?" he asked, lingering behind her as he tried to see what she was doing.

She had leaned in so far that she almost head-butted him when she swung back into her seat, hefting the bag onto her lap.

"I don't think you realize how taxing you can be," she said.

Ignoring how his eyebrows shot up to his hairline as he mouthed 'me' to himself in disbelief, she unzipped the bag and whipped out two baseball mitts. She victoriously brandished them, holding them closer to the shadows to better display the glow sticks she had taped along their seams. The effect was vaguely reminiscent of a big, cartoonish hand outlined by a multi-colored halo.

Benton blinked owlishly as she pressed one of the mitts against his chest. "What is this?"

"We're going to play catch," Nicole declared as she retrieved a clear ball from the bag. She tapped it against the dashboard and the globe lit up with a flurry of flashing lights that changed color in rapid succession.

"I can talk about my feelings without the crutch of sports," Benton said. The sharp tone he was aiming for faltered as he tried to keep himself from smiling.

"I know," she shrugged. "I just thought that it might be fun. But if you think it's silly we can put them away."

His fingers tightened on the mitt against his chest, the squeak of the leather giving him away. "It is stupid. But you went through so much effort."

"Not that much," she said, only to be ignored.

"And I don't want to hurt your feelings ..."

"Seriously, I just sticky-taped them on."

"You owe me," he barely got the words out before he thrust open the jeep's door and happily fled into the crisp night air.

It was a new moon, with only the stars to see by, leaving a thick layer of darkness clinging to the world. It was possible to make out the outlines of some shapes, but they would always disappear when she tried to focus on them. Through the windows, she watched as Benton, now only a colorful mitt swirling about, shook his hands until the light bled across the air to form an unstable streak.

With a large smile, she switched over the internal light so it would work when the door was ajar and took the keys with her. By the time she had reached the back of the jeep, she had patted her jeans' pocket at least ten times to reassure herself that the keys were still tucked safely within it. She was still a bit anxious every time she left her car unlocked. It wasn't that long ago that she wouldn't have thought twice about it. But, after Victor stole her keys, keeping them trapped so he could hunt Benton down, she had developed a certain amount of paranoia.

"It'll look better with the lights off," Benton noted.

She wished that she could see him. It sounded like he was now wearing her favorite smile. The one that made him look like a giant goof. But it was too dark. She wouldn't even be able to tell where he was if he hadn't been holding his glowing mitt.

"Yeah, but I want to be able to find my jeep later. Plus it'll be a good marker so we don't run off the edge of the cliff."

"Good point." His voice was laced with the beginnings of unease. "How far down is this jump again?"

"Around this area?" She gave it some thought as she watched his mitt follow her further from the jeep, swinging loosely with his stride. "I'd say around thirty-six feet. So, a bit under two and a half floors into solid earth."

They kept walking until the gravel gave way to soft tufts of grass. It wasn't that far from the jeep, but they were already well beyond the reach of the light. She waited until she heard him punch his fist into the soft leather of his glove. When she was sure he was ready, she tapped the plastic ball against her thigh. The sudden burst of flashing color hit her like a strobe light as she tossed the ball to him. It streaked like a comet, leaving a multicolored arch across the ebony until it hit his glove. The light was all but smothered as the ball was passed from his mitt to his hand, but it exploded across the night once again as he sent it back. She made sure to give the ball a good thump every time she had it, ensuring the timer didn't run out as she waited for him to gather his thoughts and break the silence.

"Thanks for picking me up. I couldn't handle Oliver tonight."

"He's still not talking?"

"Nope. Just being creepy and completely disregarding well-established laws of personal space. I'm used to the nightmares, as much as I can be, but I don't know what to do with a ghost."

"How is it that you have never been haunted before?" she asked as she caught the ball again. "Honestly, you're a banshee. You literally see death. I would have thought you'd be ghost-bait."

"Thanks for that image. That's just buddies right there," Benton snipped.

She let the ball pass between them a few times before she tried to approach the conversation again.

"Maybe you're getting stronger." she suggested.

"I have been eating my vegetables."

"I'm serious," she said. "You told me that you had never screamed like that before. You know ... your banshee wail."

"Yeah, well, I had never been cornered by a serial-killer demon before."

"Well, what if the scream wasn't an adrenaline rush kind of situation, but a natural next step?"

"Sorry?"

"Not many multi-celled organisms only have two stages of development, so there has to be other steps as well, right? I'm still looking, but I can't find anything on banshee puberty."

"Banshee puberty?" he said with a note of annoyance.

"You have a better name for it? I'm willing to use your terminology but, until you drop a name, I'm calling it 'banshee puberty.' And the point is, this might be a normal stage of your development. You get hair where there wasn't hair before, your voice deepens, and now you see ghosts."

"I'm getting really uncomfortable having this conversation with you."

"Nonsense. It's all the natural wonders of your growing body."

"Stop."

"I'm still trying to find out why you're not a girl. That sounds a bit discriminatory. What I mean is that I can't find one mention of another male banshee. Even according to legends, you don't exist. Unless it's like what I've heard some fish can do, and you'll grow into a female later on when it's time for breeding."

Benton thumped the ball in the mitt and hurled it again. It deliberately went wide and bounced its way into the darkness.

"You better find that before it goes off," he remarked, his voice adopting that soft lilt it always got when he was embarrassed and annoyed at the same time.

Nicole rolled her eyes. Benton had a petty streak a mile wide, but she enjoyed dealing with it a lot more than him being scared. So she flung her arms out, just so he would see the movement, and jogged after the still flashing light. The grass grew higher every few feet, but the ball never seemed to get any closer.

"How hard did you throw it?" Nicole muttered under her breath as she picked up her pace.

She couldn't remember how long the timer sensor ran for, but it was going to be impossible to find it in the darkness and grass if it ran out. As if on cue, the flashing beacon staggered and died, leaving her eyes to adjust to the impenetrable wall of the night. She was still drawing in her breath to heave the large sigh this situation deserved when the flashing suddenly continued.

"Were you double timed?"

She had the sanity to know that the ball wasn't going to reply, but it didn't stop her from asking. At a slower pace, she edged towards the ball, but it still never got any closer. It took a moment for her brain to work through her growing anxiety and remind her that she was currently on a hill.

"Great, it found a slope," Nicole mumbled and broke into a jog again, hurrying to catch it until she was forced to run down the entire hillside.

A few more feet and the niggling feeling in the back of her brain returned. She couldn't place why but it continued to grow, transforming into a flutter in the pit of her gut, demanding her attention. The grass rustled under her boot as she slowly moved forward. Then it hit her. Every step she took was on flat earth. They weren't near the slope. There was no reason the ball should have travelled this far. And it was still flashing. Nicole stopped moving altogether and glanced back over her shoulder. The dim light of the jeep was a thin dot on the horizon, barely a speck. She couldn't catch sight of Benton. Or the stars above her or the town lights in the horizon. There were only the three patches of existence within the world; the jeep light, the ball before her, and the mitt on her hand. Everything else had been taken by the night.

Her stomach flipped and crushed as she turned to look back at the ball. It wasn't moving. It had stopped when she stopped following. Each flash of shifting color lit up the night around it and she strained to use the flickering glimmer to search the shadows. It didn't work. The sick feeling inside her grew sharper as she realized how silent it was. No insects, no birds, no hint of Benton shuffling somewhere behind her. It was quiet enough that she could actually hear the mechanics of the ball clicking.

Wetting her suddenly too dry lips, Nicole began to shuffle backwards. Her eyes remained trained on the little ball, certain that at some point the colors would illuminate a demonic face. With each uneasy step, a thought clarified within her mind. *The jeep is gone.* She fought back the notion, but it was no use. It just felt like a certainty. She could perfectly imagine herself sprinting for its safety only to find the area vacant. Unable to help herself, she shot a quick glance over her shoulder. The jeep was still there. Benton still wasn't. Then the light of the ball clicked off.

Darkness rushed over her like a tidal wave, too thick for the glow of her glove to compete with. Soft shades of blue and pink barely survived an inch beyond their plastic containers. She lifted the mitt anyway, hoping to use it as a flashlight and wishing that she had brought her phone.

The tiny light source did little good. Her instincts screamed at her to get out of there and she listened, spinning around to hurriedly walk towards the comforting light of the jeep. If something was there, she didn't want to startle it, didn't want to provoke any impulse it might have to attack. A cold chill swept up her spine. She shivered and walked a bit faster. *Not too fast,* the little part of herself that clung to the hope that it was only an animal, whispered. *Don't run. Don't run.* Her mouth became painfully dry when she heard the grass crunch behind her, from somewhere deep out of sight. Something was following her and it sounded heavy. The crunch repeated. One after the other. Closer each time, it sounded like trotting hooves. She glanced around, trying to find the source of the noise, but was only met with a blanket of darkness. The hoof sounds didn't stop edging closer.

Breath catching in her throat, Nicole looked over her shoulder, back towards the ball. With the sharp, snorted grunt, twin floating flames burst into existence. They crackled and sparked with embers as they hovered at least a foot above her head. Ice flooded though Nicole's veins as she watched the flames dance and heard a horse snort and snarl. The flames barreled towards her, bringing with them the thunderous roar of the hooves smashing the earth and shattering stone.

The mitt slipped from her hand as she bolted for her jeep. Her legs strained to move as fast as she urged them to, her lungs burned, the sole of her boots slammed down on the thick layer of grass with a slick squish. She wasn't fast enough. The rhythm of the horse changed, drawing closer, faster, shifting into a steady gallop. Its every breath was a grunt that snapped and hissed like dying flames. The earth shook as it drew closer behind her, making her lose balance, forcing her to go slower as she tried to keep upright. The stench of rot filled her lungs. She heaved it in, desperate for air, and almost gagged. Without breaking stride, she risked a glance behind. Nothing followed her. Nothing but the twin flames that now hovered just an arm's length behind.

"Benton!"

She snapped her face back around to see him standing next to the passenger side door, the weak light turning his blonde hair into a ring of silver.

"Get in!" she screamed.

Benton didn't hesitate to follow her command and flung himself inside. The door slammed shut behind him. A spark of relief twisted up through her core as she heard the tell-tale clack of the trunk being popped open. She hooked her fingers around the edge of the metal and swung it open just enough for her to leap through. The cool metal of the trunk smacked against her stomach as she landed inside. Instantly, she scrambled up and whirled around. In the dim light, she easily found the truck door and slammed it shut with a resounding whack. Her hands fumbling to engage the lock. Seconds later, Benton closed the driver's side door and the overhead light went off, casting them into darkness. The silence was broken only by Benton clicking the locks on the doors, and her panted breaths.

The galloping noise continued and Nicole reached over the back seat, stretching until her hands found Benton's arm. With a few hard yanks, and a couple of painful collisions, she managed to pull him over the back seat and into the open space of the trunk. He didn't fight her. But shock and odd angles made it hard to organize his long limbs with any kind of dignity. He landed hard beside her with a painful gasp. She could feel him rolling onto his stomach as she searched for the picnic blanket that was always kept nicely folded in the corner.

It was near impossible to tell if her hurried jerks of the blanket had managed to cover them both. In such darkness, it was just as likely that they were both still exposed. Or that the creature was already outside, watching them through the thin layer of glass that was the window. She tried not to think about that as she pulled Benton closer. Her stomach plummeted as their tiny makeshift shelter warmed with a soft glow. Benton's mitt was still on his hand, glow sticks perfectly in place, signaling their hiding place like a search beacon.

Shadows clung to Benton's face, stubbornly remaining even as the soft multi-colored light played within the space. Slowly, careful not to make any large movements, he pulled the glove from his hand and tucked it under his chest. It didn't fully smother the glow. In the play of shadows, his eyes became silver disks, almost with a light of their own.

"What is going–"

She shushed him, her hand trembling as she pressed it over his mouth. He fell silent, but his eyes never stopped asking her questions she couldn't answer. The solid thud of the hoof steps made them both freeze. Its breath sounded like a growl as it panted against the windows inches above their heads. There was something inherent within the sound that pushed every nerve in her body on edge; something that made the more primal part of her brain cower.

Beside her, Benton had the same reaction. She could see it in the widening of his eyes. Hear it in his hushed gasp. His hand clamped over her own and he inched it from his mouth. His breath, hot and fast, flushed over her fingertips as they both waited. The creature snorted, loud and savage. Still, it was impossible to tell exactly where the sound had come from. Neither willing to move, they twisted their heads as much as they could, listening for the slightest hint that would give it away.

The massive beast of a horse slowly began to circle the jeep. The vehicle jolted with every step, the suspension squealing as it rocked. Nicole had been around horses her whole life, but she couldn't fathom one ever being large enough to provoke that kind of reaction. Benton's hand tightened around her own with every monstrous thud.

The jeep trembled violently as something unseen landed on top of its metal roof. They both flinched, clenching their jaws to keep down their startled cries. Nicole's teeth ached with the effort. She couldn't help but flinch as thump after thump echoed through the cab. The metal groaned and popped with the heavy footsteps that crossed over the top of them. Cold shock clawed the inside of her ribs when she realized that stride sounded human. Then it stopped.

Silence curled up around them, thick and smothering. Her muscles twitched, unsure if they should be ready for a fight, or slacken with relief. There had been no retreating steps. Either the monstrosity of a horse and its rider were gone, or they were still out there, just above them, beside them, with only a few inches and some steel keeping them away.

Benton met Nicole's gaze, his eyes as wide as her own. She couldn't tell which one of them was trembling as she pressed her lips into a fine line, holding her breath as she struggled to hear what was happening. The crushing silence was broken by a faint, gentle slide. She could hear a few of them, moving as one, making it impossible to tell their actual numbers. It was a familiar sound that she couldn't quite place. Benton recognized it instantly. Her heart stammered within her chest when he helped her eyes and mouthed one word, 'locks.' With a sharp flurry of mechanical clicks, the trunk door flung open.

Cool night air rushed in. They bolted up, limbs tangling in the blanket. Blindly, they both began scrambling back, kicking and thrashing in an attempt to hit whatever was coming in. The side doors burst out, their hinges almost coming apart as they swung wide open. The overhead light turned on. The dim bulb now burned her eyes as she pressed herself into a corner, her hands raised up to protect her head.

There was nothing. Nothing grabbed her. Nothing moved. Her heart was still within her throat as the soft sound of life came back. The call of birds roosting for the night and crickets chirping coaxed her to lower her arms and blink into the darkness. Benton was in the corner opposite her, looking just as rattled. His chest heaved as he hesitantly stretched out his legs. Nicole followed his line of sight and blinked into the darkness. She could just make out the edges of the trunk door but nothing beyond.

Benton rose onto all fours and pushed himself back into a crouch. He looked ready to spring in any direction and his eyes kept flicking back to hers. Slowly, keeping herself close to his side, she crept to the edge of the trunk. She stretched her arm out until her fingers shook with the strain but the handle of the truck door always seemed just beyond her reach. The darkness seemed like a living thing, ready to devour her whole, waiting for her to edge out just a little too far. Carefully, her eyes ever scanning the visible depths, she leaned out a bit further. Benton shifted anxiously. Her fingertips grazed the handle. And the world reeled back into silence.

Lurching forward, Nicole gabbed the handled and threw herself back. The trunk door slammed shut, hard enough to make the back window crack with the strike, as her spine collided with the back of the seats. Benton was already shoving her into motion the second she stopped moving. They both scrambled over the back of the seats and Benton pushed her towards the front of the car. Slipping into the driver's seat, Nicole searched for her keys as Benton yanked the doors shut once more.

She fumbled in her pocket, twisting her fingers into painful angles to wrench the keys free. The metal tip scraped into the ignition as Benton pressed against the back of her seat to pull the last door closed. The light went off once more, but the engine roared to life. The steady, reliable strum kept her from panicking. She clutched the gear stick, but before she could force it into reverse, a blinding, flashing light burst into existence. It radiated out in front of them. The light danced off the hood of her car, washing their stunned faces in a constantly shifting array of color.

Benton leaned down between the two front seats as Nicole reached out with a shaking hand and turned on the driving lights. The ball hovered in mid-air, still flashing, for a moment longer. Then it dropped, plummeting down the deep cliff, tumbling unhindered until the shards of light disappeared from view. Dirt and gravel flew up in a billowing cloud as Nicole forced the jeep into reverse and pounded her foot against the accelerator a second later. She carried them a few feet, not even glancing behind, never taking her eyes off the empty patch of air that had held the ball. With a hard yank, she whirled the jeep around. The gears ground together as she forced them into place. Nicole pushed the aging jeep as fast as it could go. They barreled down the long, twisting road back towards the town, never once daring to glance behind.

# Chapter 2

Benton didn't say anything. He couldn't. Not until they were once again on the paved highway, passing under the spatially placed streetlights and approaching the growing light and life of the small town. Fort Wayward wasn't big enough to warrant a single stoplight, and the buildings were just a light speck of structures along one side of the narrow highway. But, within that moment, it felt as bright and lively as a capital city. A gas station and diner were the first places that met them. With a sudden burst of words that made Nicole jump, Benton insisted that she pull over. Nicole swerved into the gravel drive parking lot that stretched across both buildings and slammed on the brakes. The sudden jolt lurched him hard against the front seats, a reminder that he hadn't moved since they had left the Jump.

Nicole stared straight ahead. She dropped one hand from the wheel but only long enough to turn the engine off. Then she put it back on the steering wheel and continued her staring contest with the diner's front window. The neon sign buzzed as it drenched the car with a rosy red glow. He twisted and slipped through the gap of the front seats, ungracefully dumping himself into the passenger seat. His back ended up against the dashboard and it took a few extra moments to organize his gangly legs over the seat back. Nicole, mercifully, didn't comment. Somehow, he twisted himself around and up enough that his feet hit the roof and he paused.

"It dented your roof."

Nicole turned around to look, one hand pressing against his thigh to hold him still so she could see the damage properly. It left him in an awkward and unflattering angle but he didn't fight it, holding still with his back crammed in the jam of the dashboard and door as she made her appraisal.

"What do paranormal creatures have against my jeep?"

He jolted at her sudden wail.

"Why are you asking me?" he snapped back.

She glared at him, her warm brown eyes narrowed and mouth a firm line. He quickly shifted his attention back to the damage above him. Whatever had come after them had bent the metal enough that it would probably brush the tips of his spiked hair when he sat up.

"It's not that bad," he offered. He quickly rushed to follow up the obvious lie with, "I'm sure you can get it hammered out."

She twisted in her seat to face him straight on. His jeans couldn't stand against her nails as she dug them into the flesh of his thigh. "Do you have any idea how expensive it was to replace the window that stupid Leanan Sidhe broke?"

"Well, Victor broke it."

"While under a drug-high caused by the Leanan Sidhe, so it's still the paranormal's fault," she defended sharply.

"We're not a collective community," he shot back, hoping to move the conversation along before she remembered the mention of Victor.

They hadn't really talked about him yet. It seemed Victor's death was a personal loss for Nicole; something she kept separate from Benton. He didn't want to be the one to broach the subject that she had avoided so long. Especially when he wasn't sure if he could be as supportive as she needed.

He had only had a few limited interactions with the other teenager, and every one of them had been violent. So it hadn't really affected him when the Leanan Sidhe had added Victor to its collection of corpses. If anything, he had actually felt a sense of relief.

But Nicole had grown up with Victor. She had known him before the Leanan Sidhe had gotten under his skin and into his mind. They had been friends, and she had loved him. The loss had destroyed something within her that hadn't quite begun to heal, the damage only growing with the guilt that they couldn't tell anyone where his body was. As far as Fort Wayward knew, as far as his family knew, he was a runaway. Not dead and rotting in a forgotten basement a few miles out of town. Luckily, she was too worked up to linger on the memory of him and quickly carried on with her tirade.

"Not to mention the time it took to clean up all that junk you vomited over my seats."

"I was drugged," he defended. "It's not my fault that my body can't take Leanan Sidhe venom."

"It bleached everything! I lost my favorite jacket."

"I apologized."

"Apologies don't pay the dry cleaning bills."

The back of his neck was starting to cramp from the awkward angle the dashboard was forcing him into. It also made it impossible to pull off the shrug that he wanted to.

"I really don't know what you want me to say about this, Nic."

Finally, she let go of his leg and let him scramble fully into the passenger seat. As predicted, he could feel the roof pressing against the gelled spikes of his hair and gently scraping against his skull. Not enough to hurt. But definitely enough to be noticed. Nicole still hadn't turned off the headlights even though they were safely within the glow wafting from the diner, and it was starting to draw the attention of the staff.

He followed Nicole's example and offered them a wave. He felt like an idiot, especially since he still couldn't get his legs under the dash without slamming his knees against it. But the gesture seemed to appease them and they went back to clearing tables.

"Does Oliver like horses?" she asked.

The abrupt question distracted him from his sense of victory at finally getting his feet under the dash without breaking his kneecaps.

"I've never really discussed it with him," Benton replied.

She whirled around to face him so quickly that her long hair swung up and brushed against his shoulder. "Did you see a horse at the Jump?"

"No. Why are you stuck on horses?"

She jolted. "You did hear the thing circling us, right?"

"That thudding noise. Yeah," he said before he caught on. "That's what a horse sounds like?"

Nicole closed her eyes, her expression softening into one of forced patience. "Yes, Benton. That is what a horse sounds like. Kind of. Whatever that thing was, it sounded way too big to be any breed of horse I know."

"I didn't see a horse. Is that what you think was chasing you?"

She edged closer and her hand clamped down onto his forearm with an iron like grip. "You saw what was chasing me?"

She looked so hopeful that he actually felt guilty to say, "No. Sorry."

"What about the ball?" She leaned towards him a little more, her hand tightening around him until his forearm began to throb. He could almost feel her restless energy simmering under her skin, pushing against him with the heat of a noonday sun. "When it was hovering in mid-air. What did you see? What was holding it?"

"I didn't see anything."

"What?" she snapped.

"All I saw was the ball."

"But you're the one who can see ghosts!"

"Well, I don't know what I'm doing," he shot back.

That got her to simmer down, in a way. Her grip loosened, but he could practically hear her rolling different ideas around in her head.

"Okay, we can figure this out." While she spoke out loud, he was sure that she wasn't addressing him. "Maybe you can only see Oliver when *he* wants to be seen."

"It wasn't Oliver."

Her eyebrows shot to her hairline, a spark of interest sparkling in her eyes.

"How do you know that?"

"I just do." The moment Benton said it, he knew it wasn't nearly enough to satisfy her ravenous curiosity. He sighed, the long breath allowing some of his remaining anxiety to seep out of him. While Nicole wore the perfect expression of patience, the nails digging into his arm told a different story. "It just didn't feel like him. Oliver has a very distinctive feeling. I get it every time he's around and I didn't get that with whatever this was. It felt different."

Her head cocked to the side. "How does Oliver feel?"

Benton took a moment to give the question some real thought, trying to translate something that was never supposed to be put into verbal language.

"Like pins and needles in my bone marrow."

"And what did this feel like?" She jerked her head in the vague direction of the Jump.

Benton didn't have to consider his response, "I felt threatened."

"No kidding," she said with an unimpressed lift of one eyebrow.

"Not like it just wanted to hurt me," he said as his stomach churned. "Like it hated me. Like my very existence offended it."

Nicole's eyes softened and her strong hold was replaced with a soft rub, as if he would actually be offended that the creature that had traumatized them didn't want to be his friend.

"Thanks, Nic," he mumbled, still slightly suspicious that she was messing with him.

But Nicole offered him a sad smile before she started to work her seatbelt open. How she had managed to fasten it, while breaking every speed limit sign, was beyond him. She didn't say anything more and she didn't need to. They both wanted to get into someplace with a bit more light. Someplace where the shadows weren't pressing in on all sides. Someplace that didn't have any attachment to what had just happened.

The second they entered the diner, the tension that had twisted up each knot along his spine began to loosen.

Like a lot of Fort Wayward, the diner was old, but pleasant. Family sized vinyl booths lined the wall of windows, while one long counter with stools separated the room from the kitchen. There were a few small tables speckled around the remaining space, but none of them were able to seat more than four people.

They were too late for the evening rush, but there were still a few people winding down their night on the town. In Fort Wayward, painting the town red never went past eleven PM. But even in their more busy moments, it was pretty standard for the first booth by the door to be left untouched. It was perfectly positioned to receive gusts of air each time the door opened, exposing whoever sat there to freezing chills in the winter and humid breezes in the summer. Nicole quickly scooted into it until her shoulder pressed against the window, her attention constantly jerking back to her jeep. Benton still felt a little awkward every time they sat here. It was where he had been when Victor had attacked him the second time. It was the first time he had come at him with a knife. But at least they had finally replaced the bulb outside so the parking lot was visible. Then they had added a few more, carving out a small patch of light in the darkness. The whole town had been shaken up that night. Violence wasn't a common occurrence for the small town and no one had known quite how to take it.

With her eyes still on her damaged car, she toyed with the beads that draped down from her choker. She seemed to have an endless supply of them and had recently been favoring any that were reminiscent of legends from her Siksika heritage. Nearly the entire population of Fort Wayward was connected in some way to a Native Canadian tribe. Like Nicole, most of them had their roots within the Blackfoot. Additionally, this was the first time he had ever lived outside of a major city. With these two factors working against him, it wasn't uncommon for him to find himself surrounded with references and customs that he didn't understand. But then, he supposed that this sensation would be the norm for anyone entering a small town community that wasn't accustomed to new additions.

So he felt proud when he actually recognized the legend on the choker that she wore now. A black thunderbird stretched out across a bed of red and yellow beads. From what he understood, it was the legend that spoke of a gigantic eagle-like bird that could carry off unsuspecting people. It wasn't exactly a comforting thought at the moment. She restlessly began to brush her hand over her dark, hip length hair.

"How am I going to explain that dent to my mother?"

"We'll think something up," he said as he settled into the other side of the booth, making sure that he had a direct line of sight to the door.

Her eyes skirted to him. "She's an R.C.M.P officer, remember? As in Royal Canadian Mounted Police. She's trained to investigate. She can always tell when I'm lying."

"Everyone can." He quickly continued before she could refute him, "And you can just tell her the truth. It was dark and you have no idea what it was."

Nicole nodded to the side, indicating that Rick was quickly approaching their table, looking bored and staring at the phone he had not so discreetly placed on his notepad. With the time they had left, Nicole leaned across the table and whispered.

"How did I not think of that?"

"Too close to the project," he replied in the same hushed tone.

Rick reached their table and they both sank back in their seats. Despite the fact that Rick was only a year younger than Benton himself, he still hadn't been able to kick the habit of thinking of him as a kid. It didn't matter that Rick had twice as much bulk as Benton did. Or that he had an impressive amount of chest hair for a sixteen year-old, which was once again on proud display.

"Button up your shirt," Nicole groaned.

"You don't really work here," Rick said with a wide, smug grin. "So you don't get a say."

Rick and Nicole had both been with Benton when Victor had attacked him. And they had both been caught up in the mix. At first, Benton had carried some guilt over that. But it was hard to hold onto it when Rick decided that the way to cope with that kind of fright was to be as obnoxious as possible in every available opportunity.

"I can tell the manager," she noted.

"Do they make chest hair nets?" Benton asked.

She glared at him. Her patented, 'you aren't helping' glare, that never had as much effect as she seemed to think it did, was showing.

"Hey," Rick cut in. "I work for tips, and women like it."

Benton turned to Nicole with a smile. "I didn't know that about you."

She strengthened her glare. It still didn't do much good.

"Are you guys ordering or just taking up space?" Rick asked, with no trace of amusement.

"We'll have some coffee and a banana split," Nicole said in her most sugary sweet tone.

Benton waited until Rick had left before he cocked an eyebrow at her.

"What?" she said as she straightened her hair again. "I survived an encounter with a violent paranormal entity, so I get a treat."

Feeling increasingly relaxed, Benton didn't try to fight the smile crossing his face. He rested one arm on the back of the booth seat and stretched out his legs. It was curious how quickly good overhead lighting and the promise of caffeine could make the world seem right again. And the company didn't hurt. Nicole was exhausting at times, but she had a way of making him feel normal. Like being a banshee and all the baggage that went with it was just a personality quirk.

"What?" Nicole said, her lips quickly pulling into an answering smile.

"It's still weird to think of myself as a banshee, you know?"

"Not exactly, but I can imagine." She leaned forward again even though it wasn't likely that many people would be trying to overhear their conversation. "Are you sure neither of your parents are banshees?"

"I haven't asked them."

Her eyes widened with far more surprise than he personally thought warranted.

"Come on, Nic, it's not something that you can easily work into a conversation. And besides, I know they're not. Neither of them can see Oliver. Or have my nightmares. And they're both always so surprised whenever a dead body turns up. Which in itself is weird, since it happens a lot."

"Not that often." She couldn't even get through the whole sentence before she lost complete faith in the statement. "How have your dreams been going? It doesn't look like you've slept much."

Benton rubbed a hand over the slope of his jaw and brushed his knuckles against his slightly pointed chin.

"You haven't been sleeping, have you?" she pressed.

"I haven't felt like killing anyone lately." He raised a hand to cut her off, "I know I'm not. But it doesn't stop it from feeling that way."

The memory of last night's dream broke through into the forefront of his mind and he could almost feel the hot blood on his hands again. He kept rubbing them together until the sensation faded. Nicole didn't know what to say to that, so she sat silently, waiting for him to give her some sign of where he wanted the conversation to venture to. For all of her empathy, he knew she would never really know what it was like to be forced under someone else's skin, have them flood all of her senses, and force you to do the most horrific, bloody things one could ever imagine.

But the silence between them wasn't uncomfortable and he wasn't in any hurry to disrupt it. Sinking back into his seat, Benton looked out of the window and watched as a group of teenagers headed out into the night. He recognized them from his high school classes and, while he had tried his best to ignore just about every living person around him, he could place a name to all of them. It was a natural talent. As soon as he had the connecting name and face, he never forgot it.

They seemed happy, their constant conversations overlapping each other's as they lingered just outside, no one eager to head towards their car. As he watched them, Benton tried to imagine what it would be like to be in that group. But, no matter how attractive the idea of being accepted on a more massive scale was, it seemed like a lot of work. All he really wanted was to be back playing midnight catch with Nicole. It had been fun while it lasted.

Rick came back to the table and dropped the different items on the table, deliberately being as loud as possible and throwing a few elbows. It drew Benton's attention and he had just started to turn when he noticed it. One of the shadows within the group didn't belong. It was deeper than it had any right to be, dark enough to block his view of the others behind it. Benton focused his full attention back onto the cluster of teens, searching once more for the dark shadow that he had seen.

Nicole noticed his shift immediately and looked out the window as well. "What is it?"

"Not again," Rick groaned with loud dramatics. "Who did you piss off this time?"

"Go away, Rick," Benton snapped as something sick but familiar settled within his bones.

Not moving a muscle, Rick began to protest the dismissal with a bit of colorful language, and for once, Nicole didn't seem to have any intention to correct or soothe him. He could feel her watching him as his eyes drifted over the parking lot. No matter how many hiding places he searched, he couldn't find it, but he knew it was there. Death. He had seen it before and it always felt the same, looked the same. Like a shadow, impossibly dark, and solid in the middle, even as its edges evaporated like drifting smoke. Indefinable, bone white smudges replaced its hands or face. They never had definition, but he knew exactly where they were looking nonetheless.

"Benton?" It was a rhetorical question, just a gentle reminder that she was there and waiting for some kind of response. When his only response was to press himself closer to the glass, she said his name again.

His eyes shifted to her, then to Rick, who was still around at the end of the booth. Rick had placed both hands on the table and was leaning in as much as possible, joining their search even though he had no idea what they were searching for.

Meeting her eyes again, Benton spoke calmly, "I thought I saw an old friend."

He willed with every ounce of his mental strength for her to catch on. There was no need for such effort. Nicole was instantly on the same page. How she had sorted it out from all the other things that Benton could have been talking about, he would never know. But she had and forced a fake but brilliant smile on her face.

"Maybe we should go say hi," she said without a hint of concern seeping into her voice. "Who did you see your friend with?"

Benton turned back to the window. The group had started to disperse. It only took a moment to see it again. Death was silently following a trio of girls. They were heading towards their car, completely unaware of the specter drifting behind them, never touching the ground, never moving but still leaving a trail of curling smoke drifting behind it. The flock of girls splintered as they moved towards the doors.

"Kimberly Bear Head," he snapped.

Both of them lunged out of the booth, startling Rick enough to make him yelp, and raced the short distance to the front door. He let Nicole take the lead. She prided herself on being friends with everyone in town. Benton hadn't had any contact with Kimberly, so there wasn't really a non-creepy way for him to coax her into his car.

"Kimmy," Nicole beamed as she jogged out into the parking lot.

The lot was small, making it impossible to grab one person's attention without getting everyone else's as well. Nicole didn't hesitate. Using her positivity like a shield, she headed over to the young woman with a confident stride.

"Hi, can I talk to you for a second?"

Benton remembered a moment later that Nicole was horrible at lying. If she had some wiggle room, she could bend the truth with some degree of success, but all of her straight out lies were accompanied with obvious unease. However, he wasn't in any position to help her now. Trusting that she could figure it out, Benton kept his eyes on Death. It still lingered behind Kimberly's shoulder, close enough to touch, but its attention wasn't upon her any more. Any structure its face might have had was smeared beyond any recognition, and he knew that it was now watching him.

He slowed his pace and moved slightly to the side, but its eyes followed. And, while Benton could sense its presence and his insides twisted up with it, he couldn't feel any threat from it. He had expected it to be frustrated or enraged by the interruption of its harvest. Its curiosity caught him completely off guard and played on his nerves. Swallowing heavily, he chanced a glance to Nicole and froze when he noticed Rick out of the corner of his eyes.

"So where is this guy?"

Nicole hesitated for a moment but, like the pageant girl she undoubtedly was, her smile remained untouched and pristine.

"What guy?" Kimberly said.

She had taken one step closer but was still near enough to the car to get in before anyone could stop her.

"Apparently, Benny-boy thought he saw a friend of his hanging out with you. And, well, come on, I can't pass up a chance to see what kind of weirdo would actually like him."

"I like him," Nicole defended on a knee-jerk reaction before remembering what they were actually doing. She took another few steps towards Kimberly. "Can I talk to you for a second? It's private."

Benton was caught off guard when someone actually addressed him, asking where his friend was. Death crept back, only an inch, its attention still locked onto Benton. Everything seemed to fade back, his world narrowed entirely on the ghostly figure. Then it turned its head as if glancing down the road. Benton looked but couldn't see what it was looking at. He could hear it though.

Thunder rolled in the distance and rushed towards them in a ferocious growl that consumed the sky. It rumbled just above their heads as if the atmosphere itself had shattered, but Benton was the only one to cringe away. Vaguely aware of his audience, he turned back to Death. It had moved back to Kimberly, the dark cloud of its body rising up to slowly encase her. He took a staggered step towards her, remembering a second later that no one else could see what he did. The grim reaper was coiling around her and she'd never realize it. Not until it was too late.

Nicole startled him, as she rested her hand against his arm. He whirled around to her, eyes wide as another clap of thunder swelled towards them. But, before he could think of a single thing to say, a way that he might be able to tell anyone around him what was going on without sounding like a lunatic, a new sound dominated the other noises. The sound of pounding hooves ascended as a monstrous roar. Within moments, it was loud enough to drown out all the other sounds around him and rattle within his chest.

He watched as Nicole spoke. Her mouth moved, but her words were lost under the crashing noise that split painfully within his skull. The resounding clash of the metal horseshoes against stone made him stagger towards the road. There was no real reason for him to bother with a façade. He had already built a decent reputation of doing weird things, and Nicole was more than capable of distracting the others. So he focused his attention on the land that Death was looking at.

The highway stretched out in each direction, a straight narrow path that was swallowed up by the night before it reached the horizon. Across the strip of pavement, there was a groove that ran the length of the town, a small stream nestled at its bottom. Beyond that, there was only the consuming darkness of the untouched grassland. It was from those dark recesses that he first saw it.

His chest heaved as he watched the blanket of nothingness shift like someone had thrown a rock into a lake of ebony ink. As the wave of air rolled out, the complete nothingness was disrupted by a burning patch of flame. Then another. The twin eyes blazed, growing steadily larger. It took him a second to realize they weren't getting bigger, but instead were barreling towards them. The fires sparked and spewed embers into the air. A new blast followed every resounding crash of the invisible horse that was bearing down upon them. Benton staggered back, one hand blindly reaching out for Nicole, his eyes never leaving the patches of fire.

Her slender fingers wrapped around his palm. Warm and solid, they served as his only tether to reality as the veil, separating the real world from the world of his mind, crumbled like broken stone. She squeezed, hard enough to make him turn to her. But her words were still hidden under the whine and grunt of the charging beast. His own fear was mirrored back within her eyes. Too shocked to think of anything to say, Benton turned back to face what was coming for them.

A startled cry escaped him as he dropped to the ground. The massive beast of the horse was closer than he had thought. It leaped over his head, the fire clinging to its hooves scorching his skin as it passed an inch from his face. Rolling onto his stomach, he meant to push himself up instantly, but his limbs froze as he caught his first real look at the animal. The horse was a towering, massive creature with muscles strung over old and tattered bone. Both were exposed as its skin, rotted and frail like parchment paper, pulled taut over its body. Fire crackled within the gaping sockets of its eyes and glowed through the gaps of its exposed teeth. Cages made from human finger bones swung from its saddle and draped from its harness. Each one was filled with a hunk of flesh, all in different states of decay, barely recognizable as internal organs.

But it was the rider that kept Benton frozen in place. Blackened slabs of flesh, sewn together by what appeared to be long tufts of human hair, served as his clothes. The weeping chunks draped from his colossal, towering form. Bones were latched together to create an armored chest plate, while others were latched to his boots. They clacked softly against each other as it moved. A human spinal cord served as his whip and he thrashed it with every step he took. Benton's breath turned into a choked whimper when his gaze lifted enough to see. The rider didn't have a head.

Black mucus of rancid blood bubbled up from the severed remains of its neck and spewed down its body in chunky trails. Bile rose within Benton's throat at the sight, urged on by the repulsive stench of bad blood and decaying flesh. Beyond it, Benton saw that Death had cocooned Kimberly in a thick, shifting pillar of smoke. Benton couldn't see within the shroud but the headless man could. It stalked towards her without a moment of hesitation. Every few steps, as if spurred on by anticipation, it would crack its spinal whip. The resulting sound was ear-splitting, a twisted sound that blended the crack of leather and a shatter of bones.

Benton's feet slipped over the loose gavel under him as he hurriedly tried to get up. Vaguely, he was aware of Nicole casting him an odd look, trying to steal glances while she kept everyone else's attention locked onto her. But it took too much effort to put one foot in front of the other for him to try and calm her. A few people staggered back from his broken lurch. He noticed their odd looks, but if they were speaking to him, he didn't hear a word.

The horseman reached the swirling, black mass that now covered Kimberly. The white disk that served as Death's face rolled up from the depths to meet it. For a moment, the two entities glared at each other, a being with no eyes and a monstrosity with no head. Their clash allowed Benton the time he needed to shake off the crippling layer of shock and finally get his feet firmly under him again. In a staggered lurch, he rushed towards Kimberly, hands outstretched as if he could pluck her from the predators that were posed to sink their teeth in and tear her apart.

He was still a few feet away when the headless man thrust his hand deep into the black mass of Death's form. It splattered back, like traces of oil meeting water. Peeling aside, it revealed Kimberly to the horseman. Benton caught a glimpse of her expression. She had no idea what was swirling around her.

A disembodied voice echoed to him from all around him at once. It rose out of the gusting wind itself, the ghastly whispers combining and bleeding together to create words.

*"Kimberly Bear Head."*

156

Kimberly's back jerked at the sound of her name being spoken by the disembodied voice. Her body became rigid. Her eyes grew wide. And for one alarming moment, Benton knew that she saw the horseman. No one else did. Just them. Benton tottered forward, but the movement was pathetic. Fear swelled his throat shut, while his head started to spin. It didn't seem to matter how many steps he took towards her, or how fast he took them, he was always too far away.

A sudden crack of crimson lightning severed the sky. It crackled down like a living creature and split her in two. Electricity charged the air, forcing it out in a blast of static charge that prickled at Benton's skin. He winced, teeth gnashing against the sensation. When he forced his eyes back open, the world had lost its color. Everything was muted and dulled into shades of black and dirty gray.

But not Kimberly.

Light sparked and clashed around her in vibrant swells, as if her life was gushing from her wound like crackling livewires. The headless man didn't hesitate to reach into the burning cavity of Kimberly's now open torso. One sharp twist of his mammoth wrist was all it took. When the horseman pulled his hand free, Kimberly's heart fluttered within his palm. Exposed to the air, the organ didn't just blaze with color. It vibrated. The sensation slammed against Benton until he could feel each pulse, each squeeze. It poked against his sides, rattled against his ribs, and swept over his skin like heated air. And the pulse was starting to slow.

Benton's useless feet finally brought him within reach of the creature. He didn't know what he could do, but his lungs burned with the violent need to release the sound raging within his chest. He opened his mouth and the horseman spun around. Even without a face, the force of its gaze rattled Benton to his core. It hollowed him out, ripping him apart until only icy fear remained. He knew, without question or hesitation that the headless monster was looking at him. That it *saw* him. That it knew what he was.

With Kimberly's heart still in one hand, the horseman struck out with the other. The bones of the spinal cord rattled together as the whip lashed forward. The hard bones cracked against the side of Benton's skull. His teeth rattled from the sheer impact. An agonizing explosion of pain blurred his vision as he crumbled to the ground. For an instant, he felt the gravel as he hit the turf, but it was soon lost as he stumbled into darkness. Nicole's scream followed him into his dreams.

# Chapter 3

Nicole's hands trembled as she paced around the nurse's station, her footsteps still audible under the dim bustling sounds of the hospital. Her knees ached from her time spent kneeling on the gravel beside Benton's unconscious body. It had felt like hours before the ambulance arrived, although it couldn't have been more than twenty minutes, given that only a few blocks separated any two points in Fort Wayward. She had spent the whole time with one hand pressed against his chest, feeling the steady rise and fall, needing the reassurance that he was still alive.

Kimberly had been declared dead at the scene, leaving a thousand questions with a distinct lack of answers. At first, everyone who had witnessed the death had flooded to the hospital, cramming themselves into the tiny waiting room, their numbers only growing as more people heard about what had happened. But, after the police had interviewed everyone who had been present, and the doctors still hadn't released any information, it became clear that they weren't going to learn anything new. With that, the numbers had begun to dwindle. When it was after midnight, only Nicole and Benton's parents remained.

She turned to continue her pacing anew and almost smacked into her mother. Dorothy Rider was out of uniform and looking more than ready to turn in for the night.

"We're going home, Nicole."

"Did you hear about Benton?" she asked at the same time.

Dorothy sighed. "He's stable but still unconscious, just like the last eight times you have asked me."

"And they haven't sedated him? He hates that. You can't let them do that to him."

Releasing her crossed arms just long enough to rub her forehead, Dorothy suppressed a groan that sounded oddly close to Nicole's name.

"We've been over this. Neither of us have any legal right to determine his medical treatment."

"I know but–"

"His parents will take care of him. And I'm going to take care of you. Get in the car, we're going home."

"Just another hour."

"You have school in the morning."

"I don't want him to wake up alone."

"His parents are here," Dorothy insisted. Her struggle to keep her composure resulted in a viciously sharp tone when she said, "He doesn't need you."

Nicole cringed under the words. Tightening her arms around herself she lowered her eyes to the floor.

"Mom, what happened to Kimberly?"

Her mother instantly huffed out her frustration. "We're not doing this."

"Fine," Nicole said and squeezed herself tighter. "Don't tell me. I'll find out on my own."

With fatigue pressing down against her, Dorothy pinched the bridge of her nose. "You do not have the right to another person's medical file. No one will tell you anything."

"Sure," Nicole said. "But, really, how hard can it be to break into a morgue?"

"That's a crime."

"So just tell me."

They stood frozen, glaring at each other, neither giving in an inch until Nicole flung her arms out with a huff.

"Everyone will know tomorrow anyway. Where's the harm in telling me?"

Dorothy grabbed her daughter's arm and pulled her further away from Benton's parents. Somehow, despite everything happening within a few feet from Benton's room, neither Theodore nor Cheyanne entered into the hallway.

"What aren't you telling me?" Dorothy whispered harshly.

The question caught her off guard and she shrugged a shoulder. "Nothing."

"Nicole, if you know what killed Kimberly, you need to tell me."

"I told Chuck everything I saw, I swear," Nicole said.

"I've read his police report. You have to be holding something back."

"Why?" Nicole said with a matching whisper. "What happened?"

Dorothy took a long breath, caught between her duty as a police officer and her concern for her child. Nicole didn't know which one won out in the end, but didn't question it as she got what she wanted.

"This stays between us."

"Of course."

Dorothy looked at her with an icy gaze. "I mean it, Nicole. No further."

Nicole nodded and watched as her mother quickly glanced around the hallway. When she turned back to her daughter, Dorothy's face had hardened into her police persona.

"Her heart is missing."

"What?!"

Dorothy didn't flinch as she repeated the statement.

"Who loses a heart?" Nicole said, struggling to keep her voice down. She barely managed it as she continued, "It has to be in the morgue somewhere, right? There can't be that many places to look."

Dorothy shook her head. "It wasn't in Kimberly's chest when she came in."

Nicole couldn't wrap her mind around that. "That doesn't make sense. I talked to her, mom. I would have noticed a gaping chest wound. And she had to have been using it, by the way."

"The oddest thing is that there wasn't a single mark on her body."

Nicole blinked at her. "How do you stay alive when someone has removed a very vital organ?"

Dorothy raised her eyebrow.

"You think that someone stole it after she was dead?" Nicole ventured hesitantly.

"Doesn't that make a little more sense?" Dorothy said.

For Nicole, the possibility of a dead person talking was a lot easier to swallow than the idea that someone she knew was stealing organs. But then, her idea of what was possible had changed drastically from what she had once believed.

She tried not to sound defensive when she asked her mother, "What do you think the question is?"

Dorothy didn't miss a beat, "How can you remove an organ without making a single cut?"

***

*He had no eyes but he didn't need them. He could feel. Vibrations rattling against skin that wasn't his own. It trickled and pricked. Waves of sensation that brought the world into sharp focus. Every molecule brushed against his skin, charged with its own energy, each shaking with a unique intensity. One vibration in particular captured his attention and drew him on, the horse below him; charging, racing with the northern wind as it swept across the brewing storm clouds.*

*Below him, the sparks of life he had been searching for called to him with a siren tune. Without a signal from himself, his stallion dipped down. Cool air rushed around him, chilling the meat that was draped over his body, clamoring the cages attached to the saddle against his thighs. The earth moved up to meet him with a bone-rattling thud, but his horse never faltered, never slowed. Bit by bit, his target's vibrations grew and took shape. With a sudden jerk, he brought his horse upright, forcing it to whine and strain, its teeth gnashing against the metal bit within its mouth as it pulled against the reins.*

*Benton felt like his skin was severing, ripped apart by a thousand unseen fingers until he was tossed aside as a heavy slop against the dirt. Sensation bombarded him, ravaging his every sense as each one snapped back into existence. The world shattered and reshaped itself as he looked up to find the horseman looming above him, its non-existent eyes glaring down at him with unbridled rage.*

*Scrambling back over the earth, Benton's eyes widened with fear. This couldn't be happening. It was impossible. Within his dreams, he always melded with his hosts. Their minds entwined, their bodies as one, completely inseparable until the dream shattered and he was flung back into reality. He was never felt, never noticed, never separated by force. This was the first time since he was ten years old that he was simply Benton within a dream, and he didn't know what he should do.*

*The turmoil of his thoughts were cut short when the horseman jumped down from his steed. Each step he took shook the earth, and Benton scrambled to pull himself back faster. Grass twisted around his fingers like vines trying to trap him to the earth. His limbs were heavy and useless. He still couldn't breathe. The world in his dream crushed in around him, tightened by the coils of the horseman's rage. As the last of it fell away, the one thing that remained solid was the charging horseman. It reached for him.*

*Benton screamed.*

\*\*\*

Benton snapped his eyes open as his spine dropped against the thin mattress of the hospital bed. The world swirled around him. Colors locked in a hurricane until they settled back and the world became solid once more. Air rushed deep into his lungs as quickly as it was forced out, and he was panting hard enough that his head spun. He tried to sit up, desperate for the elevation like it could somehow make everything tumble back into some kind of sense.

The separation rushed through his body like a phantom pain. He could almost feel the raw wound where the horseman had ripped himself free. The edges of the laceration wheezed with every breath, releasing the air before the tattered remains of his body could absorb it.

As if slipping from between the threads of reality, his parents materialized by his side. Their hands were cold against his heated skin. He couldn't tell which one was rubbing his back, but he was endlessly grateful when the circular motion turned into a sharp blow against his spine. Each strike increased until the intangible clog in his throat was forced free and his lungs swelled.

"It's okay, sweetie," his mother cooed as she squeezed his hand.

Her attention shifted from him as she talked to the nurse that was pressing an icy disk to his chest. Half a heartbeat later, he realized it was a stethoscope. His father continued to hit against his spine, stopping only when the nurse needed to reposition the disk.

"Your lungs sound clear," the nurse said before appearing into his field of vision. "Do you have any history of asthma attacks?"

Benton shook his head. There wasn't enough air in his lungs to form a word and all that came out was a broken gasp. Bit by bit, as the cold disk repositioned itself seemingly at random, he was able to settle.

"I'm okay," Benton weakly said. Bits of his memory came back as his vision sharpened. His gut twisted up like razor wire and he searched the room with quick glances. "Nicole?"

"It's two in the morning." Theodore's deliberate calmness had the opposite effect. Benton was a second away from screaming with frustration when his father finally continued. "She's at home."

"Is she okay?" The extra words made him lurch forward and he started heaving again.

"She's fine," Cheyanne said. Her chipped tone could fracture like ice.

His mother had long since started to believe that Benton was responsible for all of the deaths that followed him. He doubted that she would ever say it directly, but it would have been impossible not to pick up on her growing suspicion through the years.

She had been subtle when she had first started to suspect him. He just hadn't been allowed over at other kids' houses anymore. Simple enough. But then they weren't allowed to come over, either. After that, he wasn't allowed to interact with anyone unless it was within her direct line of sight. The conditions had grown and grown until her suspicions became blindingly obvious to everyone. They had actually gotten to the point now where there were extra locks on his parents' bedroom door. Which wasn't as insulting as his mother's knee-jerk reaction to assuming his involvement in any and all missing person's cases. She had once gave him a worried look when she heard that a hiker had gone missing in Alaska. They had been in Toronto at the time.

Before they had moved to town, before he had known Nicole, he had been able to endure it all easily enough. Benton never had much of a desire to socialize and, in many ways, he still didn't. Nicole was the exception, not the rule. Neither of them had actually planned on him developing a friendship. And, now that he had, their precarious relationship had been forced onto shaky new ground that neither of them knew how to deal with.

Benton looked between his parents as he spoke, "I want to talk to her."

"She'll be asleep," Theodore said. "It can wait until the morning."

He shook his head. "She won't mind."

It was something that he knew with absolute certainty. Any time he called, she would always answer, without hesitation or resentment. Nicole would answer. His parents tried to soothe him as he painfully pushed himself higher up on his pillows.

"I need a phone."

"In the morning," Cheyanne said sharply.

He met her angry gaze. "Kimberly's dead, isn't she?"

It only took a second for her anger to fade, replaced by a mix of fear and concern. "No one is blaming you for that."

"It wasn't my fault."

"We know," Theodore said as he gave his son a few more firm pats. "We all know."

It didn't matter how many times they reassured him. He knew that tone. Knew what it meant. The town might not be rallying to drive him out, but his parents weren't so ready to believe him innocent in tonight's events. They were scared and were closing ranks fast. At this moment, he didn't have the effort to break free, so he slumped against their hands and surrendered to the pounding pain radiating from his temple.

"What happened?" he asked through clenched teeth.

Cheyanne stooped down to capture his eyes. She spoke in a deliberate manner, more like she was telling him which lie to keep rather than explaining anything. "You fell and hit your head."

"And Kimberly?" He needed to know what everyone was saying.

"They're still looking into it," she said. "But from what I have heard, it sounds like she had a heart attack."

"People are buying that?"

"It's just one of those freak things, sweetie," Cheyanne said. "No one could have done anything."

Benton finally felt settled within his own skin once more, but even that couldn't remove the hollow sensation lingering in the pit of his stomach. Images of the horseman remained lodged behind his eyelids, reappearing with his every blink. He could still feel it, even now, like frost encrusting his skin. His brain was filled with horrors but nothing he had ever seen compared to the figure of the horseman. Half of him resented that no one else had been forced to witness it. The other half burned with jealously because he knew that he'd never be able to forget what he had seen. How it had so effortlessly ripped her apart to retrieve its trophy.

*Is her heart now in a cage?* The thought blistered across his mind and made his brain ache. Kimberly hadn't even been on his radar. He had dreamt of a thousand people dying in excruciatingly gruesome ways, but Kimberly had never been amongst them. For all the times he had woken up screaming, her name had never been in his head.

"I didn't see it coming," he whispered numbly.

Cheyanne brushed her hand over his hair. The comfort of the gesture was tarnished when his parent's both skirted their attention to the nurse entering the room.

His mother crouched lower, kissed his forehead and said, "There was no way anyone could have."

Her words were soft, but still the undercurrent of a warning was clear. *Don't talk about past deaths. Don't speak of your dreams. Don't try and contact the next victim whose name was now lodged within your mind like a railroad spike,* he thought to himself. Interpreting his mother's words drew his attention from the horseman and it hit him; he didn't have a name.

He had rode in the horseman's skin on his hunt, and felt his delight, the thin trails of bloodlust that warmed his very being with a predatory glee. It hadn't been aimless. The horseman had selected its next victim. It knew exactly who it wanted, what part of them it wanted. It was already coming for them, and Benton didn't have a name. He hadn't even been able to see the victim before the connection had been severed. Right now, his banshee need to give warning should have been setting the back of his skull alight with the fires of hell. But there was nothing. Just a bottomless gaping void.

"The doctor will be in shortly," the nurse said as she patted his shoulder. "But you look good. Just try and rest up, okay? You've had a hell of a shock tonight."

"He's a sensitive boy," Cheyanne said as she pulled closer to Benton's side. "Always has been."

The nurse smiled and gave Benton one last lingering pat before she allowed Cheyanne to usher her towards the door. His mother never stopped talking and he was able to hear her long after she had left the room. Benton remained silent as they watched them go. Theodore pulled slightly back from his side and smiled softly. Within that moment, it was tough to tell which one of them felt more awkward.

"Thanks," Benton said awkwardly. "For not letting them drug me."

"There was no need. You just hit your head," Theodore said dismissively.

"Right. Still."

Theodore cupped the back of Benton's head in a motion he was sure was supposed to be one of fatherly affection.

"Just get some sleep, son."

Benton nodded and began to slowly lean back against the pillows. The sheets felt plastic and sterile against his skin, and he was grateful for the warm light that flooded the room. His insides twisted and raged, but without the scorching pain within the back of his skull. There was no way to fend off the fatigue that pressed down against him. With a jaw cracking yawn, he shuffled further down on the bed, which wasn't overly comfortable. But, within that moment, he was tired enough to sleep on a bed of nails.

"Did she leave a message?"

"Who? Nicole?" Theodore asked.

He couldn't suppress his yawn. "Yeah."

"No," Theodore's voice followed him as sleep slowly trickled around him and pulled him down. "Just go to sleep."

# Chapter 4

The endless blue sky looked almost disrespectful to the grief that had broken Fort Wayward like a tsunami, leaving nothing but desolation in its path. It wasn't just Kimberly's sudden death, it was the mystery that surrounded it. Rumors had spread through the night and by the time morning had come, everyone had their own theory of what had happened. They ran the spectrum from believable to complete lunacy, and still more were evolving as everyone searched to make sense of the senseless.

The school had still opened for the day, but it was more for a sense of normalcy than in any belief that the students would pay attention. It had also been the easiest way to gather them for grief counseling. Since Aspen was the only therapist in town, the process was slow, and the teachers had decided to allow the waiting students to either attend their classes or wait out in the school yard. It was a beautiful day, and sitting at her usual picnic table with her two closest friends, it was almost possible for Nicole to think that it was all just a nightmare. Something that she would wake up from. Something that could drift away with time and become a strange memory in the dark corners of her mind.

Despite being identical, there were little similarities in Meg and Danny Yellow Wolf's personalities. Meg's default setting was to abandon all sense of tact, while Danny was gentle and thought through her words a dozen times over before she spoke them aloud. It was a rare occasion when both of them were silent. The novelty left Nicole reeling and at the mercy of her encroaching exhaustion. Hyped up on adrenaline and panic, Nicole had obsessed over the events all night. Her first instinct had been to research what had happened, to find something to fight, but her limited information had led her from one roadblock to the next. Her other coping mechanism had proven far more fruitful.

After decimating her cupboards, Nicole had spent what had remained of the night baking. The result was one cherry pie, good enough to give to the grieving Bear Head family, and two dozen others that she had lugged to school in an attempt to get rid of. The visit with the Bear Head family replayed in her head as she stared down at the smooth paint of the picnic table. They had all been so lost in their grief. Numb to the point that they simply walked around unsteadily, a hollow shell of their normally vibrant selves. Nicole doubted any of them would remember that she had visited moments after she left, and maybe it was better that way. It seemed like a mercy not to remember the day you were told a loved one had died.

Nicole tried to stifle a bone cracking yawn. It turned into a sob. It wasn't an uncommon sound today. She clutched at the purse on her lap, running her fingers endlessly through the buttery soft tufts of coyote fur that created the bag.

"So you got her new bag, huh?" Meg asked weakly before she helplessly waved an iPod for a moment.

The case studded with fake diamonds was instantly recognizable as Kimberly's. They both turned to Danny and she meekly placed Kimberly's school bag on the table.

"I wouldn't have thought they'd be allowed to give away her stuff yet," Meg mumbled as she picked at a random stone in the case with one fingernail.

"It's tradition," Danny said. "Everything she owns ... owned, will be given away."

"Yeah, I know. We have the same heritage, sis," Meg snipped. "I just meant that, well, wasn't she just murdered? You'd think that a police investigation would stall the process a bit?"

"She wasn't murdered," Danny sighed. "She had a stroke."

"Yeah, that's something that healthy teenagers have all the time," Meg said.

"There were witnesses, Danis."

"Saying my full name, Megis," Danny shot back, "doesn't mean that poisons no longer exist."

Nicole drove her fingers deeper into the fur bag, clutching the strands as if it would help her hold tight to her silence. She had promised her mother that she would keep the secret and, while she knew that she was going to tell Benton, she was determined to honor it to some extent. The siblings continued their argument without her. It was the same argument that everyone around them was having, and Nicole tried not to listen to any of it. She had her own internal arguments warring within her. Something had been there with them. Benton had seen it. And she couldn't shake the suspicion that whatever had attacked them at the Jump had followed them down. That led her swirling thoughts to the single question that haunted her; *Would Kimberly be alive if I had just kept driving?*

"How many of those did you make?" Meg asked suddenly.

Nicole turned her head towards Meg, who sat across from her but wasn't looking in her direction. Instead, she was eyeing the neighboring picnic table that was currently hosting the dwindling collection of pies. It wasn't uncommon for her to bring food to share, so no one ventured over to their table to ask permission. Instead, people just grabbed a slice of comfort food, sometimes threw a smile in her direction, and headed back to their own groups.

Nicole chewed on her lower lip until it hurt, only vaguely aware that she had yet to respond to Meg's question. Over the years, the twins and Kimberly had grown further apart until the beginnings of resentment had started to grow between the three women. It was just enough to immunize the Yellow Wolf girls from the sharper edges of the collective grief. It also gave them more time to worry over Nicole.

"I didn't count," Nicole finally forced herself to say.

She barely heard the words over the constant questions that echoed within her mind. Something had hit Benton. There were a few rumors that offered a different take, and they too were becoming more outlandish over time. Some were saying that he had fainted. Others said that he had taken the same mystery drug that had killed Kimberly. But she knew something had struck him. Out of all of the wild speculations clogging her mind over what could and should have been, rose a singular concern; Benton still hadn't called. He should have called by now. *What if he hadn't woken up?* her brain whispered. *What if it found him again? What if this paranormal creature had poisoned him like it did Kimberly? Did his parents change their mind about the sedatives?*

"I'm out of flour," Nicole added numbly.

*Where is Kimberly's heart?* The thought slammed into her and she jumped to her feet, wobbling, as her foot got caught up in the leg of the chair. The sudden movement startled the twins and they reached for her in unison.

"I have to go," Nicole forced out. She was going to be sick. She couldn't breathe. "I have to do something."

Sitting next to her, it was far easier for Danny to grab Nicole's wrist than it was for Meg. With surprising strength, Danny yanked, destroying Nicole's already unstable balance and forcing her to slump back down on the seat.

"There is nothing you can do, Nicole," Meg said.

Danny opted for a far softer tone as she agreed with her sister, "You already paid your condolences. The Bear Heads know that you care. Now you need to give them some privacy to grieve."

*What if it comes back?* Her hands began to shake as she swatted at Danny's hand. *What if it follows me again?* Nicole pushed the thought back into the rising swamp of guilt that bubbled within the pit of her stomach. She refused to believe it. There was always an answer. An option. Something she could do. She just needed to find where to start. She just needed a moment to think.

"I need to see Benton," she decided and quickly tried to get up again.

Danny's grip tightened, keeping Nicole in place. "If he's not here, it's probably because he needs to rest."

Both of them turned to Meg, seeking some kind of back up from the most direct one of the three. Meg never shied away from any uncomfortable topics and once again was quick to answer the challenge presented to her.

"Danny's right," Meg said simply, continuing on as Nicole slumped. "Plus he might not want to see you right now."

Nicole stilled enough that Danny decided to let her go. "Why? What did he tell you? When did you even talk to him?"

"He fainted." Meg's desire to smile at Benton's possible embarrassment couldn't compete with her sadness, yet left the promise of a smile, that never fully formed twitching on her lips. "His ego's probably pretty bruised at the moment."

Nicole opened her mouth to snap about the stupidity of that when a second thought made her hesitate. "You don't really think that Benton's like that, do you? That he would care more about his reputation than Kimberly's death?"

The girls exchanged a glance and for once, Danny was the first one to get enough nerve to reply.

"We don't really know Benton."

"Yes, you do," Nicole insisted. "We hang out all the time."

"Yeah, but he only ever talks to you," Meg said.

"He just tolerates us," Danny agreed.

Any reply was forgotten when Nicole caught her first sight of Benton. His movements were stiff and an angry bruise was claiming half of his face, but he was there. He was okay. Relief poured through her and she leaped free from the table, quickly covering the distance separating them, and embraced him in a tight hug. They staggered back a few feet, neither ready for the additional weight, but he lifted his arms up to wrap them around her, nonetheless. She felt the tension ease out of his shoulders as he threaded the fingers of one hand into the thick hair she had at the base of her skull.

"I'm so sorry, Nicole," he whispered. He readjusted his grip on her, as if he could find the perfect way to hold her that would take all of the pain away. "I didn't know. I didn't dream of her."

His voice cracked with the promise of tears and his arms tightened.

"I would have told you," he said softly. "If I had seen that it was coming for her, I would have told you."

"I know."

Her assurance didn't have much of an effect, not if his broken whimper of a response was anything to judge by.

"I didn't see it."

Nicole pulled back, but only far enough to see his face. Constantly shifting his weight from one foot to the other, he kept his eyes locked onto the patch of ground by their feet, refusing to meet her gaze. As gently as she could, careful to avoid the growing bruise that swelled out from his right temple, she cupped his jaw and forced him to look at her. It was a hard task to keep from hurting him, given that the damage traced a thick line down the side of his face, but he didn't flinch away. When he finally lifted his gray eyes to meet hers, he made no attempt to hide the misery that was etched onto his face. Unshed tears and sleepless nights had combined to rim his eyes with layers of red and black. The bruises highlighted the lines and arches of his face, making him appear sickly, fragile, and far older than his years. But it was his hair that concerned her the most.

Benton didn't have much love for his hair. He hated how, in the right light, the pale color took on an ashen gray tone. So he devoted a great amount of effort into carefully arranging his hair into a halo of spikes using gel. This was the first time she had seen him looking like he had just come out of the shower. It seemed like a simple thing, but it was such a sharp change from his norm that she couldn't help but worry.

"This wasn't your fault," she said.

Instantly, he skirted his gaze away and turned his head. Stilling her hold on his cheeks, she ducked to recapture his retreating gaze. While he looked at her, he didn't allow her to lift his face again.

"What happened to Kimberly wasn't your fault."

She spoke each word carefully and, while she knew that he heard her, she doubted that Benton believed it. His soft nod didn't trick her for a moment. She could see it then. That it didn't matter what she said or if she repeated it until her last breath. Just like her, he was going to keep this weight forever secured on his shoulders. All the motion of his nod did was shatter the last shreds of his restraint, and he rocked forward until his forehead rested against her own.

"I know Kimberly was a friend of yours," he whispered. "Are you okay?"

It was a source of pride for Nicole that everyone within her hometown was her friend. Fort Wayward didn't have the numbers to rival other small towns. But a population of a few thousand was still more than enough to make it difficult to spend a decent amount of time with each person individually. She had been racking her brain for hours, trying to remember the last conversation she had had with Kimberly that wasn't just in passing or involved a class assignment. Nothing was coming to mind, and the guilt of that coated her stomach like tar.

"I'm okay." Her voice cracked with a dozen different emotions and she closed her eyes tight, as if she could prevent herself from facing them. "I wasn't a very good friend to her lately. I should have checked in with her more often. I should have ..."

Her words trailed off as Benton gently hushed her. For a moment, they just stood in silence, struggling to hold their ground in the current of their fear and grief.

Benton broke the silence with a lulled whisper, his voice becoming intense, "I need to talk to you."

Reluctantly, she pulled away from the warmth of his body and nodded. But before Benton could continue, Meg and Danny were behind them, awkwardly shuffling and casting them weak smiles.

"Hey," Meg said, her leather jacket squeaking as she offered Benton a swift wave.

"Hi," Benton said. After sparing a quick glance to Nicole, he forced himself to continue, "How are you holding up?"

Meg shrugged. "I'm fine." She swirled one finger in the air to indicate the side of his face. "That looks painful. You got all that from just hitting the ground?"

In an abrupt motion, Benton let go of the back of Nicole's head and sharply pulled up the hood of his jacket, hiding the damage as best as he could.

"Yeah," he mumbled. "I guess I should learn how to fall properly."

He skirted his storm gray eyes to Nicole, looking at her with a clear edge of need. Whatever he wanted to talk about, he wasn't prepared to wait too long. She nodded her understanding, but it didn't seem to put him at ease. Stepping back, she clutched one hand in his jacket and fixed a small smile onto her face.

"Benton and I just need to have a quick chat," Nicole said.

"Privately," he added in a whisper.

"Privately," she repeated for the twins to hear. Her smile felt fake and hard, but she couldn't stop herself from holding it as she stiffly spread her free hand out to indicate the pie table. "So, just help yourself to a slice, relax, and we'll be right back."

Nicole wouldn't have been worried by one of them giving her an odd look. But seeing the exact same suspicious, dumbfounded expression on both of their faces at once was a bit unnerving. It was even worse to glance over and find that Benton was apparently also questioning her mental state. A few weeks ago, she would have surged on, convinced that she could find some way to dig herself out of their skepticism. But hanging out with Benton and witnessing how easily he could do it, had made her begin to doubt her skills of deceit and misdirection. So, instead of staying to deal with it, she quickly made a few more apologies, grabbed Benton's hand, and dragged him towards the main building of the school. Out of the corner of her eyes, she noticed a few teachers watching them as they separated from the group. But no one tried to stop them.

The clank of the glass door opening echoed down the hallway. The minimal number of classes actually in session didn't make much of a competing noise against her squeaky sneakers. A few people still lingered in the halls, clustered into small groups that leaned against the locker lined walls. They talked softly amongst themselves, their words interrupted by barely heard sobs, and ignored Benton and Nicole as they passed.

The school itself wasn't a huge building, but it had been constructed in segments, added to over time, ending with an odd layout like a capital H. They rounded the first corner and found that, while the crowd had diminished quite a bit in this segment, there were still a few people loitering outside of the classrooms. Not willing to risk being overheard, Nicole slowed her pace, waited until she was sure no one was looking, and shoved Benton into the nearest janitor's closet. It was a tiny space but she did manage to get the door behind them.

"What is your deal with closets?" Benton said as Nicole pulled the small chain that turned on the overhead light. The weak bulb jiggled slightly, casting erratic shadows as it tapped against Benton's forehead. He swatted at it as he continued, "You know, it is possible for us to have private conversations without being in one."

Unable to think up a decent response, she decided to just ignore the comment. "What really hit you?"

He stiffened at that. Losing what had remained of his ease, he became oddly fascinated with the floor. After spending far too long staring at his sneakers, he reluctantly glanced up under his lashes to meet her eyes. "A spinal cord."

She stared at him. A statement like that should have only been uttered with a smirk following close behind. So she waited. He only grew more uneasy in the lingering silence.

"You're not joking," she said at last.

He shook his head and her insides turned to ice.

"Okay," she said slowly. "I'm going to need a little more information."

Benton groaned. "You didn't see the horseman, did you?" He rubbed both hands over his face, having forgotten about the damage to the side of his head until his fingers pressed against it. The spike of pain only made him resentful. "Of course you didn't. You wouldn't have left if you had."

"I didn't want to leave. Mom forced me to. And I was planning to sneak back when she fell asleep, but after seeing my jeep and everything that happened to Kimberly, she watched me like a hawk."

"I wasn't taking a shot at you," Benton said with a softer tone. "I was just kind of hoping that I wasn't the only one. I kind of feel like I'm losing my mind."

"What did it look like?"

Her stomach twisted tighter with each word of his description of the stench, and the horseman, and the creature that it rode. Without thought, she wrapped her arms around her torso, tightening her grip as if the outside pressure could somehow ease the ache forming within. Eventually, his words ran out and they stood in silence once more. Bile rose up in her throat, burning the back of her mouth and splashing a foul taste over her tongue as she contemplated what he was telling her. There had been a headless giant draped in raw flesh three feet from her and she hadn't seen it, hadn't heard it. Her eyes nervously darted to the dimly lit corners of the room as if expecting to find it lurking there now.

"I don't understand." She took in a deep breath. "At the Jump, I could hear it. The horse at least. My jeep is proof that its presence has actual effects. But at the parking lot, I didn't hear anything. How can it be real and not at the same time? How can it be heavy enough to mess up my jeep, but not solid enough for its footsteps to shift gravel? How is any of this possible?"

Benton bristled, a sharp snarl curling his lips into a bitter frown. "Why are you asking me? I don't know *anything*, Nic. Why can't you get that? If I knew how any of this worked, I would tell you, so stop asking."

"I'm just thinking out loud," Nicole defended. "That's how we're going to figure this out. Develop a plan."

"I have a plan. I'm going to grab what I need and get the hell out of town."

Nicole straightened, her brow furrowing. "You don't mean that."

"Like hell I don't."

"Benton, you can't run away from this."

"But isn't it worth giving it a try?" Benton replied with a sharp smile.

"And what about your responsibilities?"

"What responsibilities? I don't owe anyone anything."

"You're the only one who can see this thing."

"When it wants me to," he hissed. Suddenly, the space seemed too small to contain all the things that he wanted to express. His legs twitched with the urge to pace and his hands crashed into the shelves as he tried to throw them about. "Don't you get that? It wanted me to watch. It wanted me to see it rip Kimberly's heart out of her chest and know that I couldn't do a damn thing to stop it. It wanted to make sure that I knew just how weak I am in comparison and, believe me, I got the message."

"Benton, you're a banshee."

"So what? What possible difference does that make? It won't even let me dream about it."

The heat in Nicole's words faded at this. "What?"

Benton flashed his eyes to the side, his chest heaving as testament to the anger that was quickly leaving him. "It ripped me out of its head," he finally confessed. It seemed to pain him to say it. Almost as if shame was slipping in-between his fear and anger. Still, he forced himself to continue. "In my dream last night, the one I had in the hospital, it knew I was there. And it forced me out."

"Out of the dream?"

"Out of its mind. It severed the connection."

"Wait," Nicole grappled with her surprise to form a meaningful sentence. "I thought your dreams were, like, snippets of the future or something."

"Me too," he said.

"So, in the future, the horseman would stop an attack to figuratively deal with you?"

"I don't know!" Benton's hands flung out as a new wave of anger hit him. Loose items scattered off the shelves and toppled down to fill the limited floor space. He didn't seem to notice or care as he snapped, "I have officially lost the few shreds of certainty I have in this world."

"We're not going to get anywhere if we keep letting our emotions get in the way."

Benton laughed, the sound tittering on the edge of hysteria. "The only thing I know for sure right now, Nic, is that this guy terrifies me."

"I'm scared too," Nicole said with a soft tone as she reached for his hand. "We all are. But we can't turn away from this. We have an obligation."

"Obligation? I'm not old enough to rent a car on my own, but I have an obligation to fight a meat man?" Benton roared. "Why? Because of some fluke chance of my DNA? I'm stuck facing off against every random demon that comes into town?"

"Random," Nicole repeated as an idea sparked across her mind.

She was smiling now and the sight was enough to throw Benton off of his rage induced rant.

He scrunched up his face and muttered a confused, "Sorry?"

"What if it's not random?" she said.

"Like," he said slowly, "someone summoned it here?"

Her hands tightened around both of his arms. "Like we did."

She watched him expectantly, her fingers restlessly squeezing his arms as she waited to see realization dawn in his eyes, for him to jump onto her train of thought like he normally did. But he just blinked back at her, confusion etched onto his face.

"We summoned it? Have you been doing some dark magic I'm not aware of?"

"Remember the symbol? The one painted on your barn wall?"

"No, I often forget giant things associated with random graves I find in my backyard."

"No one likes sarcasm, and it was your front yard," she quickly corrected, before getting back on topic. "Do you remember its meaning? The one Professor Lester told us about?"

It took Benton some actual effort to fight his automatic response in favor of an actual answer.

"He said something about it showing up in an ancient cult somewhere in Europe."

She nodded, urging him to go on. He heaved a sigh.

"The cult believed that places where paranormal creatures died will naturally draw in others, possibly stronger beings unless the symbol is put in place, and ... Oh, crap. This might actually be our fault," he hissed out a long breath. "But we put the symbol up. And you're a perfectionist. If it works at all, then it shouldn't matter that we killed the Leanan Sidhe."

"But you haven't gone back to the graves to check on them, have you?"

He shook his head.

"Me neither. What if the symbols got damaged somehow? It might not work if the lines are broken. Maybe that's why whoever put it up for Oliver hid it behind a false wall to protect it. And maybe that's why Oliver's acting out now. He's been trying to warn us."

"No. He's just a jerk."

Her mind was spinning with the possibilities, making her words tumble out faster as she ignored his response. "Okay, this could be good. Maybe all we have to do to get rid of this horseman is a simple paint job? Just a couple of touch ups and he'll move along. We could go do that right now."

He rolled his eyes. "You have paint in your jeep?"

"Mom's on shift. We can swing by my place and pick some up."

"Nic, think this through. You don't honestly think that no one's going to notice us leaving school?"

"We've been in a closet for the past fifteen minutes and no one's cared."

"Yeah," Benton said, "this school has horrible supervision."

She bounced on the balls of her feet and shook him as much as she dared, given his injuries. "So let's go. This whole thing could be over before last period."

"Seriously?"

"Okay, with travel time, it will probably take us a little longer. But we should definitely be back before my shift at the Buffalo Jump Museum starts."

"You're actually working today?"

She propped her hands on her hips but still felt more defensive than righteous. "My co-workers have kids, Benton. I can't just leave them hanging."

He was silent for a long moment, his lips pinched into a tight line as he thought.

"Oh, come on," she whined. "It's not like you have a better idea."

"Yeah, I do. Leave town."

She heaved a sigh. "I don't want you to feel bad, but your plans are stupid and doomed to fail. Let's do my smart thing instead."

"Name one thing wrong with my idea and I'll tag along with you."

"You can't drive and there's no bus service out of town until Wednesday."

"Fine, I'll go with you. But if this doesn't work, come Wednesday, I'm getting the hell out of this town and you're not going to say one word about it. And I mean not one single guilt trip. Agreed?"

"No."

"That's not how bargaining works," Benton snapped.

Nicole shrugged as she swung open the door and ushered him out with a wide sweep of her arm.

"I've never really tried bargaining before. I just go straight to getting my way."

# Chapter 5

Benton slid further down in the passenger seat to try and keep the crown of his head from brushing against the dented roof. The damage was a lot more impressive in the daylight, as if someone had taken a sledge-hammer to the metal. As they left the town, Benton had pulled his feet up onto the dashboard. The position forced his knees tightly against his chest, and the pressure was oddly comforting. Aside from that, he kept his eyes fixed out of the passenger window and spent the trip contemplating his life choices.

Sunlight blazed across the open fields, playing off the lush green and dusted golden colors of the towering grass. The rolling hills stretched under the low sky like a heaving ocean, expanding out to the snow-capped mountain range that lined the horizon. Only the confined road they were on and the Buffalo Jump Museum, perched on the highest point around, disrupted the view.

Everything he knew about the history of Fort Wayward came from Nicole. According to her, when settlers had first started to develop the town, eight properties had been set up on the very outskirts of the town limits. There was nothing really notable about them until a wildfire had swept across the prairies. They had all been destroyed, and given the superstitions of the time, the properties had been abandoned, leaving them as the perfect setting for local urban legends. But, for all her school classes and personal research, Nicole had never been told about a ninth property.

The forgotten basement had served to be the perfect hiding spot for the Leanan Sidhe. It made its nest in a cellar that shouldn't, and historically didn't, exist. It was also why, after they had killed it, neither he nor Nicole had felt any need to hide the den. They had simply closed the basement door. A month had passed with people searching for Victor, and still no one had stumbled across it. Why the ninth had been forgotten, or deliberately omitted from the history books, was a mystery that still annoyed the hell out of Nicole. It never seemed to sit well with her when she was confronted with things about Fort Wayward that she didn't know.

He cringed and sunk deeper into his seat as they passed a slim dirt road. It was barely wide enough to be considered a path, but it was enough to make his spine turn to ice. Weeds and twisted saplings littered the dirt trail. When the wind blew just right, the towering grass on either side of the road bowed and hid the path from view. At the very end of that road, where the grass finally won, sat the basement, a pit carved out of dirt and filled with the Leanan

Sidhe's museum of death. If Nicole hadn't come for him, if she had been just a few seconds late, Benton would have been a part of that collection. He would be rotting in that hole. Forgotten.

A chill crawled over him like spiders made of ice. Benton forced himself to look away. With determination, he managed to keep his eyes focused on the world passing by the windshield. He took in a deep breath, just to prove to himself that he could. It was easy enough to fill his lungs. Keeping his thoughts from dwelling on what could have been was harder.

When they had first started their trip, he had thought that going to the Leanan Sidhe's grave first was the worst option. It was the basement where he had almost died. And the basement that still held Victor's remains. He had wanted to get that pit out of the way, sure that he would lose his nerves if he had to wait. Now, however, he was actually grateful. Having the reminder that the Leanan Sidhe was dead and not lurking in any of the shadows, waiting for him, was going to be helpful.

Nicole turned the jeep onto a new path. The tires bumped and bucked over the uneven road, slowing their progress as they edged towards the dead end. The grass rose higher, swallowing the road and scraping along the sides of the jeep to release ghostly whispers. Neither of them spoke, leaving only the sound of the tires crunching the earth.

There wasn't enough space at the end of the road to turn the jeep around without entering the grass field. The tiny clearing was just big enough to expose a cluster of pebbles and a patch of disrupted earth. Nicole brought the jeep to a stop a few feet from a slight mound, and put it into park. After she killed the engine, she remained where she was. The hard plastic of the steering wheel squeaked slightly as her fingers tightened around it.

"Well," she awkwardly broke the silence. "It looks like we buried it deep enough to discourage scavengers. I can't see any coyote or bear tracks. Can you?"

Benton snapped his head around to face her. "There are bears around here?"

She nodded, looking both confused and oddly proud. "Black bears. I never mentioned that?"

"No, you didn't. I guess it just slipped your mind every time we headed out into the fields."

"Maybe you don't listen." Nicole shrugged as she, apparently emboldened by the idle conversation, slipped out of the jeep.

He was still seething as he watched her cross the front of the vehicle, one hand constantly patting the keys she had shoved into her pocket. But, no matter how much energy he put into his scowl, she never turned around to see any of his efforts. Grumbling under his breath, Benton yanked off his seatbelt and got out of the jeep to follow her. Swallowing thickly, he followed Nicole to the mound. In another ignored sign of protest, he moved as slowly as he could get away with.

Nicole crouched down by the disturbed earth of the grave and dusted off the loose debris from the large flat stone they had painted the symbol onto. It unintentionally served as a marker for the grave and he glared at it, fisting his hands to resist the urge to hurl it into the field. Nature was well on its way to reclaiming the small area they had carved out for the corpse. The soil of the mound had almost returned to the same color as the surrounding area, and tiny sprigs of grass poked out around the thick clumps. Wiping her hand on her jeans, Nicole retrieved her phone from her pocket, fiddled with the device for a moment, and placed it next to the stone. Benton's chest tightened as he watched her. Logically he knew that it was dead and not about to reach out of the grave to grab her. Still, his body tensed in anticipation.

Searching for a distraction, he shifted his attention to the glowing screen of her mobile phone. He could just make out the photograph the phone displayed under the glare of the sun reflecting off the surface. It was a copy of a picture taken for a police report, and he wondered just when she had stolen it from the RCMP files. And if her mother knew that she had it. The sun warmed the side of his face as he mulled over the question while Nicole continued to ignore him. The sum total of her focus was on her detailed inspection of the symbol, tracing her finger over the lines on both stone and screen.

"It seems to be fine." She spoke with the muttered tone that she used only when talking to herself. "Everything's there. There might be a ritual that goes along with it. Like a chant or something. Or maybe it needs to be engraved into the Leanan Sidhe's skin?"

"Can we check out the other one before you jump to defiling a corpse?" Benton asked.

Nicole jumped and blinked up at him owlishly. Apparently, she hadn't been purposefully ignoring him but had legitimately forgotten that he was there. Frowning slightly, she snatched up her phone, brushing the specks of dust off the case, and stood up.

"Yeah, I suppose you're right," she said as she turned to face him. "It's not the smartest idea to dig it up in broad daylight."

"Yeah, that's what I have an issue with." He forced a smile as he backed up towards the jeep.

Nicole had the most remarkable talent for tunnel vision. Sometimes he really envied how she could dedicate every cell of her being to accomplishing whatever task she had deemed worthy. But at times like these, it creeped him out. Craning his neck, he checked the back seat before he swung himself into the jeep. Nicole took her time, carefully using the spray can of glue she had found in her garage to coat the symbol in a protective layer. It only occurred to him then that she might actually want to wait until the glue dried. His relief battled with his growing anxiety when Nicole jogged back and climbed up into the jeep as soon as she was done. Not wanting to disrupt the area any more than necessary, she twisted to look between the seats and reared the jeep back until they were again on the main path.

"Maybe we should burn it."

Benton closed his eyes. "Sorry?"

"You know, cremate it. That way we can seal the remains in a jar and just cover the entire thing with the symbols."

He didn't respond as they drove almost casually down the road, but it didn't seem to bother her. It was possible that she hadn't really been talking to him anyway. The closer they got to the next turn off, the more it seemed that the ice spiders were burrowing into his flesh.

"How long do you think it would take to burn a Leanan Sidhe to ash?" Nicole asked abruptly as she turned onto the side road.

"I don't know."

"The smell might give us away though," her voice trailed off as her thoughts caught up to claim her.

While she still continued to chat, and every once in a while would throw a question at him, it was pretty obvious that she didn't need him for the conversation anymore. By the time they had reached the end of the next path, she was attempting to calculate a proper cooking time for a demonic beast by what she knew about preparing turkeys. She brought the jeep to a stop and Benton happily jumped out of the door, grateful for the excuse to escape the conversation.

But without Nicole or the constant grumble of the engine, the world was completely, unnervingly silent. Anxiety rushed back to fill him like a swarm of ravenous insects. His fingers and shoulders twitched as he felt spiders crawl on the underside of his skin. No matter how hard he searched the world around him, there was no other sign of human life. The grass rose up to the height of his hips. The blades swayed in the wind and smothered any hint of roads they had just travelled. From where he stood now to the lines of the horizons, they seemed entirely alone. It left him with a crippling sense of isolation that he couldn't shake or fathom.

He sought out Nicole's gaze from across the jeep's hood to find that she was already looking at him. The first traces of fear trickled around the edges of her expression, and the instant she realized he was watching, she did everything she could to hide it. A small smile served as her war paint, and she pushed the long strands of her hair back over her shoulder. It slipped back like silk and idly swayed across her hips.

Pulling her phone out of her pocket, she turned on its flashlight and brandished it, as if the weak glow would somehow protect them from whatever was possibly waiting for them. The display of incorruptible confidence was weakened slightly when she couldn't stop her other hand from slipping to her front jeans pocket and patting the bump that the keys had created.

"Ready?" Despite her effort to hide it, her voice still wavered slightly.

"Any chance you'd let me stay in the car?"

"You can stay if you want," she said. However, she quickly continued, "I mean, I would totally do it for you, but apparently I have a different standard for friendship than you do."

"Are you honestly trying to guilt me into this?"

She didn't respond. He was about to spit out that he wasn't her corpse-hunting buddy when he remembered just what was waiting for her down in that pit. It wasn't just a faceless multitude of dead bodies. One of those corpses had been her friend. Someone she had seen every day of her life. Someone who had become like a brother to her. It had devastated her to keep him within the ground, hidden away, deprived of his proper burial rights, but she had done it because anything else would have risked exposing them both. He couldn't let her face that alone.

Apparently, the full force of his survival instincts didn't really add up to all that much because, even as they screamed at him to stay outside, he still pulled his phone out and turned on the flashlight. The brilliant smile she gave him was almost enough to make him forget just how stupid he was being. It was remarkable that for all her willingness to influence people to get her way, she never thought to use the fact that she was stunning. It would make her life a lot easier.

Despite the fact that neither of them would ever forget the first time they were there, it still took them a while to find the trap door. His heart sank when they actually located it under a thick tangle of twisted grass. The bare brittle slabs of wood were nearly the same color as the moist earth that surrounded them. Without a proper handle and the hinges submerged in the dirt, the effect was a near perfect camouflage.

They took longer than necessary to clear it, carefully pushing aside the knotted mess, making sure that they were still usable to hide it again when they left. That was part of the reason. The other was that they were both putting off the actual task they were there to complete. Finally, there was nothing left to do, and the door was exposed. Still, they lingered. It was Nicole who reached for the door first. There was only a slight tremor in her fingers as she hooked them around the planks and yanked the trap door up. The hinges screamed in protest, shedding flakes of rust into the sun-drenched air. They both cringed at the sound and stared into the pit that was now opened before them. Even the midday sun couldn't penetrate the shadows. The scent of wet earth, mildew and rot, wafted out from the depths, carried upon a cold draft that curled out over the rim and drifted into the air.

Nicole swallowed, but her voice still came out strange. "Remind me to bring out some oil for the hinges later."

His eyebrows shot up. "We're doing maintenance now? You want to make the place nice? Maybe get a throw rug? A potted plant?"

For a long moment, she held his gaze. He wasn't quite sure what she was waiting for, but when she didn't get it, she settled for rolling her eyes.

"No one ever accomplishes anything with a negative attitude," she chastised.

He couldn't help himself. The words were out before he thought about it. "I accomplish being negative."

She glared at him, fighting down a weak smile as he smirked in response. With a huff that sounded disapproving, she leaned forward, hovering her arm over the open space, vainly attempting to chase away some of the shadows with her phone light. The darkness didn't budge. That was enough to tell Benton that they really shouldn't go down there. But Nicole took it as a challenge; one she met with a deep breath. He could actually see her inflate with her mounting confidence. She squared her shoulders, straightened her back, and fixed an almost serene smile onto her face.

"Please, for me, remember that reason has to trump impulse," he said.

She ignored the comment. "Don't suppose you want to go first."

*No, thank you, I'm sane.* He hurled the thought out to her but still got to his feet and shrugged his shoulders with as much casualness as he could summon.

"Sure. Why not?"

Her surprise was clear, but she had the decency not to mention it. Instead, she waved her hand out towards the dark hole in the earth, her phone passing a thin ray of light over the shadows. It still didn't help. He still couldn't see the bottom of the wooden stairs. He couldn't see anything that lay beyond the first three steps. The wood looked as rotten and worn as the trapdoor. As Nicole repositioned herself, her fingers pushed a bit of dirt over the rim. It felt like a cloud and he could swear he saw the stairs tremble under the additional weight. So, instead of taking a step and hoping that it would still hold him, he sat down on the edge and swung his legs into the abyss. His fingers tightened painfully around his mobile phone as he lifted it up to the level of his eyes.

He hadn't fully inched his toes onto the first step when it started to groan. He froze, air trapped in his lungs as the soft trickle of dust drifted down into the abyss and scattered against the unseen dirt floor. The wood stilled, the pebbles drifted over the floor, and the world was reduced back into a heavy unbroken silence. Nicole met his worried gaze with one of her own, but didn't stop him when he slowly edged more weight onto the plank. He kept one hand fisted in the tangled grass and dirt, hoping that the hold might be enough to pull him back up when the stair inevitably gave way. To his surprise and resentment, it held. Now he was actually faced with the task of standing up.

Again, Nicole didn't stop him. Instead, she hovered one hand along his arm, like she truly thought she could catch him if things went bad. The wood moaned with renewed force, the thin trail of dust became a downpour, but still the step held. Before he lost his daringness, he hurried down, sinking deeper into the frigid earth with every step. Each one creaked and shuddered in turn. The handrail was eroded and he didn't trust it, but without it, he felt completely exposed.

As he descended, he trailed his dim light over the emerging room. The cellar was carved out of the earth with no care taken for appearance. The walls were rough and uneven and the floor was still layered with a thick coating of soft soil. Roots had grown through the ceiling and dangled down like skeletal fingers. A chill lingered within the depths of the hole. The deeper he went, the more it rose up to meet him. It clung to his clothes and invaded his body with every breath. But it was the silence that made his gut twist sharply.

It was as if all life had been gouged out of the space, leaving only a dank pit of nothingness.

The beam of Nicole's light soon joined his as she followed as close behind him as she dared. Even together, the lights did little against the lurking shadows. The whole staircase rattled with their continued efforts, and despite the sound, he still found himself slowing down. All he wanted to do was run back up into the light and get as far away from here as possible. He forced himself to keep going, Nicole right behind, one hand pressed firmly between his shoulder blades. Before he could give in to his urge to flee, his foot found the earth again. What he had thought would be a relief instead resulted in his heart lurching into his throat, hammering until he could barely breathe around it. The soft dirt under his sneaker was proof that he was actually back here. Back in the room where he had almost died.

The minimal light glanced off the polished surface of the coffins even as they hid within the shadows. It was the Leanan Sidhe's collection. He had come so close to claiming a place amongst the others. It wasn't a new thought, but to be here, to see the others, was something else entirely. The sensation hit home with a crippling force as he took his first real step back into the basement. With Nicole's aid, the glow of their phones beat back more of the shadows and flashed across the polished wood of the coffins that filled the space, each one arranged with care into perfect rows. For the first time, he allowed himself to count them. His lungs nearly squeezed the life out of him as he wondered if they were occupied or if one of them was still empty, waiting for him.

His head spun as his breath became short and shallow. A cold sweat prickled on his palms as he quickly glanced over his shoulder, searching for Nicole amongst the shadows. Her dark hair fanned around her face, surrendering her more to the darkness than was reassuring. Even though she kept her attention focused around the room, her free hand found his and they threaded their fingers together. He squeezed and she answered with a squeeze of her own. The solid warmth of another human being made it easier to venture further into the room.

Nicole didn't release his hand as she took the lead. She cut a beeline across the room, refusing to look anywhere else but the spot on the far wall where she had painted the symbol. He followed without comment, constantly scanning, searching each shadow with his dull light and realizing how little he knew about the space. It was strange that some moments were forever engraved in startling detail within his memory, while others were lost to the fog that the demon's poison had created within his mind. He could remember the mirror-like eyes of the monster in perfect detail. But any actual words that had been exchanged were reduced to vague notions. His ears echoed with the perfect replica of the sound of Victor's ripping flesh. He could remember the exact resonance of Victor's blood as it dripped down from his arm and hit the untreated ground, and the slight slurp of it being absorbed into the dirt. Without his permission, his hand navigated the light over the patch of clumped earth that still clutched the teen's blood. His attempt to force the light aside only exposed the white viscose goo that Benton had choked on as he overdosed on the paranormal poison.

Nicole's hand tightened around his, the insistent squeeze bringing him back to the moment, forcing his head to snap up and meet her gaze. Even the shadows couldn't rob her eyes from the obvious concern that dwelled within them. Guilt flooded him when he realized that he was failing miserably in actually being helpful to her. He forced a reassuring smile, but couldn't keep his thoughts from going back to that night again. It was a jarring loss when she slipped her hand free. Instead of heading to the far wall, she drifted towards the nearest coffin. He watched as her fingers brushed over the polished wood, tracing the same path his fingers had been forced to touch in his nightmares. It was distracting and he didn't see her fingers finding the gap until it was too late.

"Don't," he whispered.

A slave to her curiosity, Nicole forced her fingers around the edge of the top and cracked it open. The scent of decay engulfed them as it crept out from the confines of the coffin. Benton rushed forward to stop her from casting her light into the gap she had created. His hand wrapped around her wrist, but she had already seen the corpse within.

"Nicole, don't look."

"It's not Vic," she mumbled, like that would be his only point of protest. Her brow furrowed as she ducked down, squinting into the space. "We should have brought flowers. When you visit a grave, you're supposed to bring flowers, right? I should have thought of that. Why didn't I think of that?"

"I'm sure they won't mind," Benton said as he inched closer, still not sure if he should stop her.

Nicole didn't look away from the gap as she spoke, "He looks like stone."

Rust hadn't yet ravaged the hinges of the once loved coffins. The lid opened with a sound reminiscent of a sigh and clicked into place, holding upright to let her examine the corpse. Nicole edged closer still, her curiosity winning over her disgust. The dim glow of her phone light trailed over its occupant. While the man might have been settled into a peaceful pose, his malnourished and gaunt form spoke of the horrors he had endured before his murder. Her hand trembled as she reached out. Benton flinched beside her but didn't try to stop her. He wouldn't have been able to anyway. Biting the inside of his cheek, he watched as she traced a fingertip along the smooth marble of the man's skin.

"It's the zinc coffins," Benton explained. It was unnerving to hear his own voice bouncing back to him from the damp walls, and he lowered his voice to a whisper. "When matched with humid conditions like the one in this room, decomposing tissue produces a waxy substance, which in time hardens into what you see here."

Slowly, she turned just enough to look at him and whispered back, "How do you know that?"

Benton tapped his mobile phone against his head with a bit more force than necessary. "Each time I dream, bits get left behind."

The confession made him restless. The need to flee built up within him until his feet began to edge back towards the staircase. Admitting that there was one foreign mind, still flicking through the recesses of his brain, made it easier for all the others to rush to the surface of his thoughts. He knew that all the voices in his head belonged to him alone, and that others were only memories. But when they combined within one moment, the voices created a shriek too loud to ignore.

"Can we just check the symbol and get the hell out of here?" he moaned.

He didn't believe for a moment that he was doing a good job at covering up the mounting stress he was under. It was more that Nicole was far too captivated by her discoveries for her to notice. Rising up onto her tip toes, she lifted her light high above her head like it would somehow increase the source and give her a better look at the rows of coffins.

Memories that weren't his own began to twist around the edge of his awareness, encroaching so softly that Benton didn't question them. After all, it wasn't a completely alien experience. Each time he dreamed, the murderers he inhabited left a stain on his soul and a whisper in his head. Now, standing before the Leanan Sidhe's treasured possessions, the slivers of consciousness it had left burrowed within his brain started to inch to the surface.

He could feel it. Its dedication to the singular task of making its collections as perfect as possible. The unrelenting pride of what it had created within this room. The grotesquely deformed love it had for each of its victims. Those emotions weaved through Benton's own disgust until they flowed into each other.

The polished wood slipped smoothly under his fingertips as he dragged them along the side of the nearest coffin. It was perfect. It was a work of art, chiseled and refined; something fitting of the results of his life's work.

"How can anyone do this?" Nicole whispered on a choking breath.

*She looks like she's admiring the perfection of my work,* Benton thought to himself.

"Time and love," he smiled. He pressed his hand against the top of the coffin and stroked the surface with a lover's caress. "They all loved me so much. Now they can love me forever."

The beam of light tilted and focused on his face. He flinched as the light assaulted his unprepared eyes. That split second of reality was enough to jar the Leanan Sidhe from the forefront of his mind. It left a gaping hole within him and he quickly shook his head, rearranging the contents of his brain back into their rightful positions. Blinking into the glare, he couldn't quite bring himself to meet her gaze.

"Sorry," he mumbled. "Not my thoughts."

"Please tell me you're not possessed," she said with a slight croak in her voice. Her eyes flicked over the room like she was searching for a second exit. "I really don't have the time for that right now."

Benton huffed a laugh. "No. It's more like daydreaming than anything else."

"Does that happen a lot?" she asked, her voice taking on a crisp and all too chipper tone. A happy mask that she believed perfectly hid her concerns.

"It's worse when there are reminders," he mumbled as he rubbed his forehead. Pain sparked across his skin as his finger dug against his bruises. It helped to clear his mind a little more. "Can we please just go?"

She nodded hurriedly but closed the coffin with respectful care. With renewed purpose, she crossed back to the painted symbol and resumed her appraisal. Every so often, her eyes would shift to him. For all the ones that he noticed, he gave her a reassuring nod. It didn't matter what he tried, he could tell that she never truly believed him. Her movements became hurried, the light passing over the clumped earth in short, sharp sweeps.

"Can I do anything to help?" he asked, desperate for some way to convince her that he was in control of himself, or at the very least to be of use.

"I'm almost done." That all too excited voice remained. He was starting to hate that sound. "You can wait outside, if you want."

The offer enticed a relieved sigh out of him, but he couldn't bring himself to leave. Not if it meant leaving her down here by herself, with only the corpses and memories. But he did take to pacing the room, prowling around the edges with a desperate need for a distraction. He moved along the wall, passing his light over the encroaching darkness, making it scatter away from the dim light for the simple reason that he could. Then one shadow refused to move.

He jumped back when a blotch of white emerged from the ebony abyss and reached for him. His startled yelp made Nicole whirl around, and she charged her arm up, adding the beam of her flashlight to his. It was enough to cast off the darker shadows, revealing the looming specter of Death before him. No matter how many times he saw the living embodiment of the grim reaper, it was a sight he never really got used to. Its body seemed to shift between a solid mass and whispering smoke within the same moment. Real but not. There but so much like a figment of his imagination.

"Benton!"

Nicole's sharp snap was enough to make him turn. Idly, he wondered how many times she had called to him before she resorted to that tone.

"What do you see?" she asked.

Benton swallowed thickly and turned back to the figure before him. Death hadn't moved, the featureless white smear that served as its face watching him from mere inches away.

"I see Death."

"You're going to have to be more specific," Nicole said, the startled edge remaining in her voice. "With you, that could mean a lot of things."

"Death like the grim reaper."

"Oh." She moved closer to him, her eyes searching the space even though she wouldn't be able to see it. "Where is it?"

Breathing heavy, Benton lifted one finger and pointed towards the ghostly shape. While he moved, the specter didn't. It simply hovered before him, silently watching. The shape consumed so much of his focus that he hadn't noticed Nicole shuffling closer until she was practically beside it.

"What are you doing?" Benton hissed, his heart suddenly thundering within his chest until his ribs ached. "Get away from it!"

"So I'm close?" she asked, one hand lifting as if to try and locate it.

"What is wrong with you?"

She sighed like the sound could cover her anxiety. "Could you please be helpful?"

"Helpful?" he snapped.

"Well, It wouldn't have come here without a reason," she shot back.

"Its reason is death," he snapped. "It's a fairly simple purpose. Pretty straight forward, really."

"That wasn't when 'It' appeared to you at Vic's house, remember? It wanted to warn you. So there's probably something here that 'It' wants you to know."

"We almost died at Victor's house," he mimicked her chipper tone. "Remember?"

"That wasn't Its fault," she defended.

"And what about Kimberly?"

"It might have been trying to warn us then too. We just didn't know how to interpret it." Turning to the air before her, her unseeing eyes scanned the area as she continued with a soft smile. "I'm sorry about him. He's under a bit of stress lately. It makes him grumpy."

"Don't talk to It!"

The look that she gave him was one of pure rebuke. "Death isn't your enemy, Benton. I wouldn't have been able to find you if it hadn't been for It. If it wasn't for Death, you'd be ... well, dead."

"Wait. What?"

She brushed off his confusion and continued, "It gave me a hint about where to look for you. And I think It's giving you a hint now. So, please, be helpful?"

Benton released a strangled sigh and felt himself being pulled under the weight of her conviction. She was going to find a way to do what she wanted, with or without him, so he might as well get ready for a ride.

"It's about three feet in front of you."

"What is It doing?" she whispered.

"Nothing. Just staring at me."

Nicole squirmed closer to the abyss. Benton's gut twisted into ever tightening knots as she lifted her hand. The black smoke of death wafted from its being like living tendrils. Death continued to stare at him, unconcerned by Nicole's progress, but still the air seemed to fill with tension, like a lurking animal ready to strike.

Nicole's breath came in heavy gasps as she reached a little further, the ghostly tendrils twisting around the tips of her fingers.

"Stop!"

Nicole froze, her eyes wide, her fingers shaking slightly. But her voice remained pleasant. "Did It move?"

"You're touching It."

"Oh," she said. "Does It seem angry about that?"

"I'm not even sure It has noticed you."

Benton staggered back a step, one hand reaching out towards Nicole as the ghostly figure suddenly broke into motion. There was too much distance between the teens for Benton to actually touch Nicole's forearms, but she still followed his lead and took a few retreating steps.

"Benton, I can't see."

Death didn't walk. It drifted, shifting through the air with an unnatural grace until it disappeared behind the lean table pressed against the wall.

"Benton!"

He told her what he saw and instantly regretted it as she rushed forward and began to examine the table.

"What are you doing?"

"He wants us to do *something*," Nicole said with annoyance. "So, I'm doing something."

She pressed her shoulder against the side of the rickety but heavy table and began to push. The dirt that layered the floor piled up around its base, making it harder to move, but she kept going with a strained groan. Swearing under his breath, Benton rushed forward, grabbed the side of the table, and rocked it onto its side. It slammed against the floor with a pathetic crack and splintered into kindling. Nicole released a strange sound and glanced up at him.

"How are we going to fix that?"

"Why would we?" he shot back.

The annoyance that played across her face broke when she realized that they really didn't have anyone to answer to about the destruction. With a shrug that acted as both agreement and dismissal, she crouched down and trailed her light over the newly exposed wall. A large metal dish, tarnished and eroded with time, was embedded within the damp mud of the wall. She dug her fingers into the soft, crumbling earth, burrowing them deeper until she could get a solid grip on the edge of dish and yanked sharply. But it held solid. Sitting down, she braced her feet against the wall and put her body weight behind the next attempt.

"Are we sure we want to do this?" Benton asked.

"I am. I can't speak for you. I'm not a mind reader."

Cautiously eyeing the wall, Benton edged closer and crouched down behind her. With the beat of his heart surging into his throat, he eyed the wall carefully. Death didn't reappear. Nicole gnashed her teeth as she pushed back harder. With a wet, suction sound, large clumps of earth broke away and the metal dish jerked free from the wall. Nicole slumped back into him, striking his chest hard enough to knock the air from his lungs with a grunt of protest.

A rush of heated air pushed against him, scorching his chilled skin like a barrage of needles. As it cleared, they found themselves staring down a long tunnel carved into the earth. A light flickered at the far end but wasn't bright enough for him to be able to get any sense of the distance separating them. The hole was barely large enough to move through, even on all fours, with twisted roots breaking though the surface, ready to snare anyone who attempted to pass.

"Okay, we're leaving," Benton said.

"What? Now?"

"Don't tell me that you actually want to crawl down that thing."

"Death wants us to."

Benton tried to calm down his anger but couldn't stop it from drenching his words. "Who cares? Nic, we came here with the sole purpose of checking on the symbol. We've done that."

"What if the answer we need is down that tunnel?"

"What if it's at the end of a *Google* search?" he snapped back. "Can't we try that before the possible fire tunnel of death?"

She twisted in his grip until she could meet his eyes. "Fire tunnel?"

"The flame at the end," he snapped with annoyance. "And the heat is a pretty big tip off."

Her eyebrows nearly rose up to her hairline before a renewed energy lit up her face. Snatching up his wrist in an iron grip, she lifted his arm to trail the light from his phone to the hole. Even when she added her own light, there wasn't much extra detail to be seen.

The sudden realization made his stomach drop. "You don't see a light, do you?"

"No. Which means that there is something paranormal down there," she said with far more joy than he believed the situation warranted. "I knew I was right."

"Or," he said slowly, "I'm insane. Seriously, you never asked if I've had a cat-scan."

Benton knew he was in trouble when his protests couldn't even distract her long enough to give him an annoyed look. He struggled to keep ahold of her as she surged forward. Despite his efforts, she easily squirmed from his hands and pushed herself onto all fours. Benton blindly swiped his hand along her side, trying to latch onto the waistband of her jeans. Still, she crawled hesitantly forward, studying the tunnel with a renewed fascination.

"I don't think it's that deep," she mumbled softly to herself. "The earth is too soft here for it to hold up that long. Or would that make it easier? Why don't I know more about tunnels?"

"Nicole?"

She acknowledged him with a 'hmm,' but didn't pull her eyes away from her new curiosity.

"Can we go now? *Please,*" he said with emphasis on the last word, ensuring that she heard it, hoping that she couldn't let the polite gesture pass.

It worked to some extent. She did turn to look at him but continued to twist her long hair over and over. Somehow, that actually kept it back off her face.

"We have to see what's at the end."

"We really don't," he retorted with barely controlled panic. "Or we could at least hold off until we plan this properly."

"It's crawling down a hole."

"And what if it caves in?" he countered.

But reasoning didn't usually win out against a determined Nicole Rider.

"It won't," she cut him off before he could respond. "What if the answer for how to get rid of the horseman is down there and someone dies because we didn't go looking for it?"

"People die. It's kind of what we do," he said gently.

"Okay, well, you stay here and make a list of all the people you're willing to let get slaughtered, and I'll go."

"That's not fair," Benton snapped.

"I can't just walk away, Benton. We have to try."

"I have tried! For ten frickin' years I've tried! It never changes anything."

Nicole didn't immediately raise her voice to meet his, and he instantly resented her for it. Instead, she reached out, and covered his hand in her own.

"That's when you were alone," she said sweetly, her eyes somehow beseeching and encouraging at the same time. "You're not alone anymore."

Desperate for something, anything, to break through her denial, he went for a low blow. "And yet Victor's still in a coffin."

He cursed the light coming from the tunnel. Without it, he might have been able to avoid seeing the pain that crossed her face. But the orange glow danced across her face, clearly illuminating every ounce of anguish the words had caused. He tried to hold her eyes, but it was a losing fight. He ducked his head and lowered his eyes to the floor, the motion just weakening his argument.

"We didn't save Vic. But we did save all the people it would have killed after him. And that means something, Benton," she said with certainty. Her fingers squeezed his palm, the gentle reassurance making him hate himself just a little more. "I'll be quick. I promise, I'll be right back. You can stay here."

"You know I can't do that," he mumbled as he took his place on the other side of the tunnel. Finally meeting her eyes again, he jabbed a finger towards her. "When this goes bad, and I'm no record for saying that it will, I don't want to hear any positivity crap. Instead, you're going to tell me horrible, embarrassing, negative things about yourself in penance."

Nicole just shrugged that she was okay with that and began crawling into the tunnel. Benton wasn't quite sure what to do with his mobile phone. After watching her feet slip out of sight, he tucked the phone between his thumb and index finger, and shuffled in behind her. The soft earth bowed under his palms and turned to mush under his knees as he crept deeper into the tunnel. Roots snatched at his hair and jacket as he continued on. Before him, Nicole's body cut off the flickering light as she moved, leaving him with only his phone for guidance. The heat encompassed him, creating sweat beads on his skin before soaking into his shirt. The temperature climbed, the air grew thick and humid, the sensations worsening as they continued at an excruciatingly slow pace until he could barely choke down a breath of the steaming smog. With a high squeal, Nicole jerked down. The heel of her foot crashing against the top of the tunnel, dislodging clumps of earth before she disappeared from his sight completely. The now open gap blinded him with a sudden burst of light and he cringed back, shielding his eyes as they burned.

"Nicole?" he gasped with a hint of panic.

"I'm okay," she replied quickly. "I didn't see the tunnel stop short. Wait a second and I'll help you out."

Benton squinted and blinked, his eyes already adjusting to the brilliance. Her shadow dipped back into view, eclipsing the inferno slightly and sparing his eyes from the burn. She trained her phone back to highlight him, but the soft glow was actually pleasant after the precious glare. She reached for him. He waved her off but she didn't take the hint.

"It's okay, I can see."

Before she slipped out of sight once again, he caught a glimpse of a frown and a muttered, "That's cheating."

Although the opening was only about a foot off the floor, there wasn't enough room for him to actually turn around, so entering the room with any kind of dignity was impossible. He dropped onto his forearms and pulled his legs out awkwardly behind him. The heated mud seared his skin despite the protection of his jacket sleeves. The fire ravaged air blistered against his eyes and made them water. Shielding his eyes, he felt Nicole's hand tracing along his arm and drifting over his fingers.

"Do you mind if I borrow your phone? You don't need it and the light on mine is horrible."

He nodded and let her take the device from his hand. Nicole's body heat naturally ran on the warmer side. It was both startling and disturbing to find that her touch felt like ice compared to the heat radiating within the room. Seeing things while awake was a new development, and he was still grappling to find a way to deal with it properly. He wasn't prepared for all of his senses to combine in promoting a delusion like this. It was hard to believe that it was just a trick of his mind when everything was telling him that it was real.

He opened his eyes, squinting into the light, and instantly threw himself back. The hot mud of the wall burned him as he stared at the blazing inferno before him. Fire spewed from the floor, creating thin sheets that towered over him. The plumes of fire didn't crackle or sputter. Their thin trails tracked patterns that filled the huge room in a blistering intensity of light.

"Benton?"

"You don't see that?" he screamed as he shuffled back to the hole, seeking some kind of refuge from the climbing heat.

Nicole looked around her, one phone in each hand, waving them about like she was trying to land a jumbo jet. She ducked and weaved, searching every corner, obviously straining to catch sight of what he was talking about.

"There seems to be a big room, deeper than I would have thought, but it looks pretty much the same as the other," she replied calmly. "Oh, wait. I think there's something carved into the floor." He lowered his hand as she made an annoyed noise. "There isn't enough to make out the pattern."

She began to edge towards the flames and he forced himself back up to his feet.

"We need to go," he gasped as he surged forward to pull her back.

Losing his nerve at the last moment, he pressed back against the wall. His eyes had adjusted and, now that he could look into the eyes, he couldn't look away.

"Not again," she sighed.

He turned just in time to see her stepping off from the wall, striding towards the flames with renewed purpose. This time, when he lunged for her, he didn't pull back. But he wasn't fast enough. Without a moment of hesitation, Nicole took the final step, disappeared into the erupting pit, her hand vanishing before he could grasp it.

Without her hand to hold onto, Benton edged back as far as the wall would allow, his eyes constantly searching the flames. They were too thick for him to even make out the silhouette of her shadow play against the burning wall. The flames released only a low hiss, but his voice cracked as he called for her. When her reply wasn't instant, his panic drove him to desperation. He took a step forward, felt the flame press against him, and quickly retreated once more.

"Nicole!"

"I'm right in front of you," her disembodied voice replied. "I thought you said you could see."

"You're in the flames," he snapped.

"Really?"

She must have caught sight of the glare he sent her because her next words weren't nearly as excited.

"You really can't see me? It's okay, it's not real. It doesn't hurt."

The sincerity in her voice couldn't compete with the flames that rose as silent pillars reaching the ceiling, or the way the heat burned his eyes and blistered his lungs with every breath. Her hand emerged from the hellish blaze and she coaxed him to take it. Pushing deeper into the agonizing heat of the wall, he shook his head rapidly.

"Okay," she said softly. "Stay right there. I'll take some photographs of this pattern and we'll go."

"Nicole."

"I'm okay," she replied instantly. "Just hang tight."

Balling his fists, he stood as much against the wall as his skin could stand. He bit the inside of his cheeks and tried to endure. The flames never weakened and his head was spinning as the heat continued to consume him. His mouth became a dry pit. His heart pounded until he felt each beat hammering against his spine.

"Nicole!" he croaked as his lips began to crack.

"Almost done," she called back, her tone matching his haste but lacking his need.

An iron grip suddenly crushed into his stomach, creating an icy hold around his intestines and twisting him up until he released an anguished cry.

"We need to go," he nearly begged through his pain as the stench of rot filled the space. "Now!"

She came crashing through the flames, all reassuring smiles and the wave of a phone. She hadn't fully left the flames behind before a shadow blackened the fire just beyond her shoulder. A split second later, the horseman rose up behind her, the spinal whip thrashing as it narrowed the distance between them. He bellowed as he darted forward. Seeing his expression, she whirled around, trying to spot what he was looking at. But she couldn't see the figure charging towards her. It grabbed her shoulder. Wrenched her back. Her feet kicked up as she was yanked once more into the inferno. Benton latched on to her wrist but couldn't stand against the pull. His feet sunk into the mud as he was towed towards the flames.

Agony rushed through him as the flames licked across Benton's skin and welled against his palm. He could feel the blisters forming as he hurled himself back. His back slammed against the wall and his knees buckled in. The scent of burning flesh polluted his nostrils as he writhed, gripping his own wrist until the bone felt like it was about to break. The pain was nothing compared to the sensation of his flesh blistering.

The horrific sound of the horseman's voice cut through all of the pain raging within his body. The ghastly, disembodied voice ripped and curled around the first syllables of Nicole's name.

Benton screamed.

The walls shook as his banshee wail rose to a deafening pitch. The fires flamed and shot higher until they washed over the ceiling like a raging flood. An ear-splitting shrill, wild as flooding rapids, cracking like thunder, the sound drowned out everything else within existence.

Nicole rushed from the flaming pit. She balled her hands into his jacket and yanked him to his feet. The sharp yank shook him from his stunned stupor and the scream died off into a sharp whine. The flames were still blinding as they scrambled back towards the tunnel. For once, Nicole didn't argue when he shoved her before him. He felt every grain of earth as it pressed against the rising boils of his hand. The pain almost brought him down each time he put pressure on it, but fear alone kept him moving, twisting deeper into the consuming darkness. Every inch, every second, he waited to feel the horseman's hand around his ankle.

The shifting light of Nicole's phone scurried out of sight. After the bonfire, his eyes refused to adjust and he was forced to carry on in the impenetrable darkness. He only stopped when Nicole grabbed his arm with both hands, her insistent tugs letting him know that it was time to stand. Grasping each other tight, they thundered up the trembling staircase. Loose dirt drifted down from the mouth of the trapdoor as chunks of wet dirt dropped from the walls. Benton could hear their feet slam against the steps, could feel the wood bend under their weight, but the wood itself didn't make a sound. *It's still here,* a voice in the back of his mind whispered.

He focused on the rectangle of sunlight above them, the patch of salvation they were racing towards. The gentle warmth of the sun welcomed him as the stairs gave way to grassy earth. Fresh air drew deep into his lungs and he found himself reeling with the sensation. Even as his eyes adjusted to the softer light, details still abandoned him. The pain of his burn was no longer contained to only his hand. He could feel his flesh continuing to cook, the burn growing deeper, spreading wider. Sparks of agony flushed along his nerves and veins, charring his bones as it claimed his entire arm. With a broken cry, his legs buckled in and he slumped onto the earth.

Nicole gasped his name breathlessly as she knelt down beside him. He ground his teeth, but he couldn't keep the pain from escaping him in a long string of whimpered sobs. Blinking and shaking, with his vision steadily returning, he let go of her and dragged his throbbing hand into his line of sight. The skin of his hand was ripped raw and molten. Thin trails of puss trickled down his fingers where his skin couldn't pull to the lengths the forming blisters demanded. The seeping liquid carved through the layers of grim that covered his broken skin. Nicole's hand was gentle as it wrapped around his wrist, but even that pressure was enough to make him cry out.

"You need to get up," Nicole struggled to keep her panic out of her voice.

He tried, but his legs were too weak to hold his weight and he crumbled in on himself, pressing his forehead against the slick grass that layered the ground. Nicole kept hold of his wrist, keeping him from cradling the smoldering limb against his chest.

"Benton," Nicole said. He could barely hear her over his barely suppressed sobs. "We need to get you to a hospital. Your hand could become infected."

Benton nodded, smearing his head against the soil. He resisted the urge to curl tighter when she released his wrist. Feeling clammy and weak, he trembled as she passed behind him and looped his good arm over her shoulders. He wasn't a big guy, more lanky than muscled, but it was still a struggle for Nicole to lift his dead weight. His feeble attempts to help made it possible for him to get his feet back under himself. The tips of his sneakers dug grooves through the soft dirt and twisted up in the roots of the grass as he failed to take a proper step. He cradled his hand, palm up to his chest. Each time he lurched a step, his hand struck his chest. The contact sent a fresh burst of blinding pain through him and left a smear of mud and puss across his stained shirt.

The sun-warmed metal of the jeep burned him and thrilled him as Nicole propped him up against it. Barely able to keep his eyes open through the constant surges of pain, it was hard to keep track of everything that was going on around him. It was hard to even keep his head up. As much as he could, he trailed his eyes over the grasslands, searching for any sign of the horseman. Beside him, Nicole began to search through her pockets, muttering a long string of whispered swears as she tried to free her keys from her jeans.

Lost within a fog of panic and fear, neither of them had noticed the car pulled up next to Nicole's jeep. Not until Nicole victoriously pulled the keys out of her pocket. She froze, keys still held high, the slips of metal catching the light. In the same moment, Benton's mind cleared just enough that he was able to attach meaning to what he was seeing; a police cruiser. His stomach plummeted as a figure lunged from the basement door, a sharp bellow of 'freeze' announcing its arrival.

Shaking with the beginning tendrils of shock, Benton could only stare as Constable Rider moved closer to both of them, the sunlight glistening off of the smooth barrel of her gun. There wasn't enough within him to fully understand the emotions that played across the woman's face, or the greater meanings attached to them, the consequences. He slumped heavily against the side of the car as a pained cry rattled his teeth. The fire was spreading. It never appeared on his skin, but he could feel the blisters climbing up the length of his arm.

"Nicole?"

"Mom, I will explain everything," Nicole said in a sudden rush of words, "but we need to get Benton to the hospital."

"There are bodies down there," Constable Rider snapped. Her voice didn't carry any of the uncertainty that lurked within her eyes.

"He's really hurt," Nicole pleaded.

"What are you even doing here?" she stammered and hesitated before she was able to voice, "What was making that scream?"

Nicole's hands trembled as she tried to unlock the passenger side door. The sharp edge of the key scraped across the metal of the door, producing a squeak that was brutal to Benton's ears.

"I can explain everything, I promise," Nicole begged on the verge of tears. "But we need to get out of here. It's not safe."

"Get away from the jeep, Nicole."

"Mom, please! He's going into shock."

Constable Rider's dark eyes flicked between Benton and her daughter for an excruciating moment before she finally holstered her forgotten gun and rushed forward to grab Benton's arm.

"We're taking my car."

"Thank you," Nicole rushed to say, but the words were lost under her mother's angry gaze.

"The second he's checked in, you and I are having a very long conversation."

# Chapter 6

It had taken two members of the hospital staff to pry Benton away from Nicole. She hadn't wanted to let him go, not when he was left so vulnerable. The drive into town had been torture. With every passing second, his pain had only gotten worse until he could barely move any limb without screaming. He had clung to her the entire time. Each breath he took carried a strained whimper and was released with an agonized moan. Nicole could only watch helplessly as he writhed in increasing anguish. The muscles of his neck strained against his skin as he attempted to keep his screams contained. There had been nothing she could do to help him. The closer they got to town, the more it seemed that her attempts to soothe him only made things worse. Finally, the nurses had managed to pry the fingers on Benton's good hand off of Nicole's jacket, and he was led down the hallway. She wasn't allowed to follow.

Her staring contest with the now empty hallway was cut short when her mother grabbed her shoulder and whirled her around.

During the car ride, Nicole had resolved to tell Dorothy everything. The option to be discrete was well and truly gone. She was scared and in deep over her head. She couldn't even trust her judgment. They needed help. So when Dorothy had started with a seemingly endless stream of questions, Nicole hadn't even thought about selecting her words with care.

Everything that she had kept inside for so long, exploded out in an untamed current of raw information. From her first encounter with the demonic force that had latched onto Victor, to discovering the meaning of the symbol over Oliver's grave, to resolving to destroy the creature that had slaughtered everyone who now filled the basement. She hadn't meant to be so honest about Benton, about what he was and all of the possible implications, but it had rambled out with everything else and there was no taking it back.

By the time she got to the end of the story, where Benton had been kidnapped and Nicole had resolved to save him, she knew her mother had stopped listening. But the confession of stealing a firearm from the RCMP lockup, directed her from disinterested frustration to barely contained rage. Dorothy grabbed Nicole's arm, dragged her down the hallway to the nearest empty room, and hurled her inside.

"You better be lying to me right now," Dorothy hissed.

"Mom ..."

"No. You listen to me! What you're talking about is a crime. You're confessing a *crime* to a member of the law enforcement. Do you understand that? I'd have to arrest you."

Nicole stuttered, "You ... you wouldn't do that."

"This is not on me!" Dorothy snapped as she jabbed a finger towards Nicole. "You abused my position to break into a police station. This is all on *you*."

"What was I supposed to do?"

Dorothy threw her hands wide. "Call the police! Tell me what was happening!"

"You never would have believed me. I was on my own and terrified and I did what I had to do." Squaring her shoulders, Nicole met her mother's furious glare and refused to back down. "Benton is alive today because of what I did."

"Stop it!"

"Mom—" Nicole pleaded, only to be cut off.

"Monsters don't exist, Nicole. You should have outgrown these childish notions years ago. And that Bertrand boy," Dorothy continued on in a rush. "He's injured right now and probably scarred for life."

"So am I," Nicole shot back.

"There are bodies down there. This isn't the time for foolishness."

Raking her hands through her hair, Nicole was a second away from screaming when a thought occurred to her.

"The dash cam," she said.

Her mother only furrowed her brow. "What?"

"Your police cruiser is fitted with a dash cam, right? It would have recorded everything."

Dorothy huffed. "It wouldn't have had a view into the basement, Nicole."

"But it would have recorded Benton's scream."

Her mother's voice lost all its hot temper as she asked, "What?"

"You heard it. You asked about it," Nicole insisted. She watched as the anger seemed to escape from her mother's features and she knew that she finally had something not easily denied. She had proof. "You remember it, don't you?"

"I heard something."

Nicole rushed forward a step. "That was Benton. It wasn't exactly how he sounded the first time, but it was him. You heard a banshee wail."

"I don't know what I heard. It could have been anything."

"Are you kidding me?" Nicole said. "Let's go listen to it right now and you tell me what else it could have been."

Dorothy shook her head and Nicole felt her advantage slipping away.

"Mom, none of this matters."

"Yes, it damn well does," Dorothy shot back.

"Not right now," Nicole said. "I know what killed Kimberly."

"*What* killed her?" her mother said with a hint of warning.

"I haven't figured out what it is by name but–"

"Stop," Dorothy demanded as she lifted her hand. After a long pause, she shook her head and motioned her daughter to the door. "Get in the car. I'm taking you home."

"I can't."

"Don't argue," Dorothy spat back. "I don't know what is going on with you and Benton, but it's clear that this relationship is sick and is getting dangerous for that poor boy. You're going home and you're not contacting him again."

Nicole crossed her arms over her chest. "I have a shift tonight. I can't just not go. People will start to talk and as so as they do that they'll start suspecting something's up."

"Something *is* up," Dorothy said, her voice both infuriated and slightly mocking. "You're facing some serious charges."

Nicole toyed with her fingers, wringing them together as she watched her mother carefully.

"Are you going to do that?"

In the longest moment of her life, she could only watch as her mother shifted between parental love, to the obligations of duty, and back again.

"I haven't decided. It is possible that you are merely delirious after ingesting some kind of drug. Not to mention the shock you must have had. I'll need to investigate further. For now, get in the car and I'll give you a lift to the museum."

\*\*\*

The passing hours felt like purgatory. While her mother had allowed her to retrieve her stuff from school, under strict orders that she wasn't to talk to anyone, her phone had remained completely silent. The dwindling strum of tourists offered an ever-decreasing source of distraction, as she worked the gift shop, located on the middle floor of the museum, giving her the perfect view of one of her favorite exhibits. It was a buffalo herd stampeding across the far side of the room, their massive bodies forever frozen within a singular moment as they passed a real sized teepee and headed for the drop off of the makeshift cliff. Their taxidermy was extraordinary and the greatest care was taken in even the finest details. The exhibit even smelt of grass and sun warmed dirt. In a singular charge, the frozen buffalo displayed the moment the herd would have toppled over the edge of the Jump, with some suspended in the air as they tumbled down to the bottom floor.

More than one exhibit was fitted with motion sensors. They were each tripped by anyone who ventured too close. Over the hours, she had heard a thousand thunderstorms from the first floor, traditional songs repeated hundreds of times from the third, and more phantom hooves crushing the earth than she could count. Each time, she found herself sure that she must have missed her ringtone, and reached into Kimberly's purse to check her phone.

Nicole was aware of the annoyed looks she was getting each time she began digging into the small purse, especially when she was supposed to be setting up the display for the newest shipment of gold necklaces. But time went by and still no one had called her on it. They hadn't even asked her to put her bag away. News spread fast in small towns. By now, everyone must have known she had witnessed Kimberly's death, and with Benton in the hospital, it seemed that everyone was willing to let her get away with a lot tonight. The lingering guilt Nicole felt for exploiting the situation wasn't enough to make her willfully give up her only line of communication with Benton. She promised herself that she'd make it up to them later, as she once again stopped what she was doing to check the screen.

By the time the sun had set and the museum was closing, Benton still hadn't called. The radio silence prickled at her nerves and crammed questions into her mind. *What if they had knocked him out?* a voice whispered in the back of her head. *What if the burn had only gotten worse?* Unable to get her laptop and do some actual research, she could only wildly speculate over what had actually injured him, and what was going to happen next. *What if he didn't tell them the truth?* she wondered. *Was there a lie I was supposed to tell? Why hadn't we prepared for this?*

"Nicole?"

"Huh?" She snapped her head up from the book she was supposed to be shelving to meet the annoyed gazes of her coworkers.

"Museum's closed," one of them said, as she waved her hand out in a loose gesture to the rest of the museum.

Nicole glanced over her shoulder to see that even the overhead lights had been turned off already. Beyond the gift shop, the only sources of light was the small runway lights that lined the staircases and the few spotlights that were aimed at the exhibits. It hit home just how slack she had been. They were always gone, long before the cleaning staff mopped the floors. She still had to restock, vacuum, and do a final check around the exhibit for any missed trash.

"Why don't you guys go on ahead," Nicole suggested.

They glanced at each other for a moment. It was clear that they were all eager to leave, but no one wanted to be the first one to agree.

"I insist," Nicole said with a forced smile. "No reason for us all to stay because of me. And someone will be by to pick me up soon."

Since they all had families to get back to, it didn't take much more prompting than that, and soon she was left alone to finish shelving the kids' books. The rough sound of the cutter slicing through the tape of the final box punctuated the stillness that had settled around her. Cardinally, she filled the empty shelf, while her mind stormed and raged. That done, she insured that the jewelry cabinet was locked and stowed the key away in the now empty cash register.

She jumped as her mild ringtone burst to life. Her fingers fumbled over the latch of her bag, delaying her enough that she didn't bother to check the caller ID before she answered.

"Nicole?" Benton's voice whispered down the line.

Relief weakened her knees and she sagged against the counter.

"I've been going out of my mind," Nicole gushed in way of greeting. "Are you okay? What happened? Why didn't you call me earlier?"

"I'm on painkillers, Nic," Benton groaned. "I can hardly remember why I called you right now, so can we do one question at a time?"

"Right. Sorry. Are you okay?"

"I think so. My hand's bandaged up so I can't see it. But they did say that I won't need a skin graft, so, you know. Score," he pulled the last word out like he had forgotten how it ended.

"Are they keeping you in?"

He snorted. "I've shown up with injuries that are unaccounted for, twice in two days. There are some theories floating about that I'm hurting myself. Or that someone's hurting me," he seemed to get confused for a moment before he picked up the conversation again. "Aspen is talking with my parents right now. They don't look happy. He looks tired."

"Has my mom spoken with you?"

"Yep," he chirped. "Quick question; what the hell, Nicole? You told her everything?"

"We need her help."

"Huh, that sounds like something a very wise person said a month ago."

A soft smile tugged at her lips. Of course, even while drugged, Benton was ready to point out that he might have been right.

"Yeah, well," she said weakly. "I'm sorry I told her about you. After I told her, she wasn't ready to listen to me about the horseman."

"I tried explaining, too."

"How did that go?" she asked quickly.

"Not good," Benton said. "She was a lot more focused on the criminal stuff."

"I don't suppose she gave you any hint if she's going to follow through on laying charges."

"Not really. She's kind of hard to read."

Her stomach dropped and she suddenly had a great need to move. With no real destination in mind, she began to wander out into the exhibit.

"Nic," Benton moaned again. She could hear him squirming deeper into his bed. "My hand hurts. Stop worrying so loudly. It'll be okay."

"Thanks," she smiled.

"Worst case scenario, just blame me for everything," Benton said.

"What?" Her steps faltered as her stomach lurched. "Benton, did you miss the part about criminal charges?"

"Nope," he said with a lax sigh. "But better me than you, right?"

"Let's keep it as plan B."

She walked across the small streaks of water left behind by the recent mopping. Her mindless path brought her in the field of sensors. Brilliant floodlights clicked on, reminiscent of the noon day sun. Hidden containers sprayed the scents of grass on earth into the air as the recorded sounds of the rampaging herd boomed throughout the empty building.

"What's that?" Benton asked suddenly, the frantic question followed quickly by the sound of rustling fabric.

"Just a recording," Nicole dismissed.

"Recording?"

"Of one of the museum exhibits. I'm just finishing up my shift."

The speaker of her mobile crackled slightly with his jaw-cracking yawn, "Don't you work at a diner? I remember a diner ..."

"I was filling in at the diner as a favor for Trish. My actual job is at the museum," Nicole explained quickly, eager to lure him back to a more important topic.

"Do I know Trish? I don't know a Trish."

She opened her mouth to respond, her breath halting as Benton began to mutter 'Trish' repeatedly like he just couldn't wrap his head around the word. The hospital staff had definitely given him something for the pain.

"I introduced you. Twice. Never mind that, what's going on over there? You need to keep me up to date."

"No one's keeping me up to date," Benton muttered.

"When we were in the cave, something grabbed me. It was the horseman, wasn't it?" she asked.

"Yeah," Benton said. "I'm guessing by that question that you still didn't see it."

"Everything was so dark."

Benton snorted again, his words turning into a soft mumble. "For you. My eyes are still aching. Well, that's not true. I'm actually pretty buzzed at the moment."

Nicole rolled her eyes. "You are?"

"Yeah," he giggled, the sound loose around the edges. "Burn victims get the good stuff."

Nicole smiled as she switched the mobile phone to her left hand, leaving her right to hold the cool railing as she headed up the stairs. It only took a few steps for guilt to come creeping back in. After all that had happened and with everything that was waiting in the future, it just didn't feel right to smile right now.

The exhibit on the third floor depicted just how important the Buffalo Jump was. Not just for survival but for the overall sense of community, for the different tribes that called the plains home. Unfortunately, there wasn't adequate space to properly display the sheer size and scope of the gatherings that would take place. So instead, they had settled for one depiction of a typical campsite with a detailed mural describing the rest of the scene.

The exhibit was completely interactive and allowed guests to enter into the real sized teepee set up against one wall. This, of course, meant that a few odd items were often found scattered about the place. Most commonly, there were just things that could have slipped from someone's pocket as they sat down to explore or take a photo of a kid's shoe. It fell to whoever was closing to search the place thoroughly.

"What do you think that fire was about?" Benton asked with a sudden rise of interest. "I've been thinking about it, but all I came up with is that it was an elaborate prank. Or it has something to do with that symbol you kept yapping about. But that just brings up a whole lot more questions."

"Do you see fire with any of the other symbols?" Nicole asked.

"Nope. They just looked like paint to me."

"So," Nicole said as she reached the top of the staircase. The recording abruptly turned off, leaving only her footsteps to break the silence. She shivered as a chill swept across the back of her neck. Whirling around, she searched the shadows in an attempt to pinpoint the person she was sure was watching her. All she was met with was the long sweep of the three-floor staircase, and the trail of lights weakening the shadows into a soft gray.

Swallowing hard, she forced herself to pick up her lost line of thought. "Either those symbols are wrong or this one is designed to do something different."

"Huh?" Benton mumbled as if just startled awake. "Um. Yeah. Maybe. Hidden purpose. That makes more sense than what I was thinking."

Nicole took a step away from the stairs and felt her stomach twist into a tight knot. The sensation of being watched settled again onto her shoulders.

"What were you thinking?" she asked for some sense of distraction.

"Supernatural Smores."

Nicole paused, looked at the mobile phone in her hand, and stifled a laugh.

"You're so high," she said as she pressed it back to her ear.

He grunted, "We need to consider all options."

"Okay, well." Nicole shook her shoulders but couldn't dislodge the sensation. Slowly, she walked across the space, checking the usual spots people tended to hide their trash. Each thump of her shoes rolled like distant thunder across the wide expanse of the room. "Maybe the first question to tackle is why he was there? I doubt it was just to grab me."

He mumbled a reply. At the same time the hospital speaker system came to life. It was impossible to make out what was being said on his side, but it was clear by the tone and rhythm that the nurse's station was trying to page someone. Tapping her finger against the mobile on her ear, Nicole waited for the noise to die down. There was no way she would be able to hear Benton with all that was happening in the background. It felt like years had passed before his side of the line fell quiet again.

"Was that about you?" she asked quickly. "Is someone coming in?"

"Huh?" he grunted. "Oh, no. Dr. Youngman's dinner just got delivered. The nurses are threatening to eat it if he doesn't get there soon. I'm still alone."

"Good," she said as she once again switched the phone to her other ear. It wasn't likely that either of their parents would let the call continue if they found out. "I missed what you said before the food announcement."

"Is it normal that they announce that over the hospital speaker system?" Benton asked with way more consideration than the question required. His voice became slow and lax as he continued. "It seems really weird."

"No, Dr. Youngman's always late for dinner."

"How do you know that?"

"Everybody knows that," Nicole replied. She pulled her free hand through her hair, sighed deeply, and placed the mobile phone against her ear. "Benton, please focus. What did you say before the announcement?"

Benton tried to put energy behind his words, but he still sounded on the edge of sleep. "It said your name."

"What?"

"The horseman. It started to say your name. Please tell me you heard that."

"I think I heard something," Nicole said. "But then you screamed and I kind of went deaf for a bit."

"It said Kimberly's name, too. Right before it ripped her heart out." Benton's words sounded sluggish, like he was fighting to keep his thought as he gave voice to it.

"That's it!"

"It is?"

"Well, it's a start," Nicole said with increasing energy. "You can't really do an internet search for 'headless horseman' and get anything useful in response. But 'headless horseman that kills by saying your name' is a lot more specific. There can't be that many legends of something like that. I can find it."

"And old stories will be helpful?" he said slowly.

The dragging pace of his voice made her smile.

"Legends often talk about the paranormal creature's weakness, Benton. It worked for the Leanan Sidhe."

"Right," he said softly. "Right, right, right. Wait, you shot the Sidhe in the head."

"Details. The point is, I'm right." Checking her watch, she quickly continued before he could correct her. "I need to finish up here before mom picks me up. I'll hit the laptop as soon as I can and you get some sleep."

"It pushes me out." The drug haze in his words couldn't conceal the hints of growing fear.

"I know," she said gently. "Be careful, okay? Call me as soon as you wake up."

Benton agreed, but didn't feel thrilled with the plan.

"Okay, I'm going to hang up now," she said.

"Wait," Benton said sharply, startling her into keeping the phone by her ear. "Don't do anything stupid."

"I don't intend to," she smiled with warmth.

"You never intend to," he shot back. "But you always do. And it *always* backfires."

"It does not."

Benton kept talking like she hadn't said anything. "Just, keep a tight hold on your stupid impulses until I'm around to absorb the worst of the fallout, okay? Do that for me?"

A cold lump of remorse pressed heavily against the pit of her stomach.

"I'm sorry you got hurt, Benton."

He hushed her. The silence that followed made her heart ache.

"My parents are coming back. I have to go."

He had hardly finished the sentence before the line went dead and she instantly missed the connection. Without it, the silence crowded in around her like a physical force. Hunching her shoulders against the encroaching cold, Nicole slowly lowered her phone and put it back in her purse. She stroked her hand over the fur, raking her fingers into the soft material and pulling a measure of comfort from the familiar sensation.

A gasp choked her as an unexpected burst of light blazed through the shadows. An instant later, the building was filled with the recorded sound of the charging herd, the phantom hooves crushing the earth as they charged. Nicole's hands tightened around the straps of her purse as she fixated on the golden hue of light spilling down over the level below. Something had tripped the motion sensor.

The sound of her footsteps died under the clash and thump of the recording as she slowly backed away from the mouth of the staircase. She waited, straining to hear her mother calling for her, or maybe the sound of a stray worker she hadn't known was still there. Anything that would prove she wasn't alone. But there was only the buffalo.

Careful not to get too close to the display by her side, Nicole took another step back, staring at the staircase, not daring to blink until her eyes went dry. The track came to its end and was cut off. As quickly as the darkness had been broken, it reformed to consume the museum. Silence rushed back and seemed to blanket the entire earth. Standing in the middle of the wide, empty space, her light-drenched eyes slowly adjusted back to the dimness while she held her breath.

She didn't want to go down there. And, since the museum had been built into the side of the mountain, she didn't have to. One more flight of stairs and she could exit out onto the top of the Buffalo Jump. There were dozens of walking paths that led down both sides. It was a steep walk down to the parking lot at the base, but even attempting it in the dark seemed like the better option than waiting for whatever was down there to come up and meet her.

Keeping to the shadows as best she could, Nicole silently moved towards the final staircase. It too was lined with little guide lights; their faint glow just enough to leave her completely exposed the second she set foot onto it. From the base, she could see the exit, but she still hesitated to run for it. Ice encrusted her veins as the metallic click of a lock rattled down towards her. With a soft clack of the latch, the door swung open.

Her heartbeat throbbed with a strength she didn't know it possessed. She shuddered with every beat of it against her ribs as she nervously edged her feet back. Drums and a chorus of voices broke into existence as light erupted from the exhibit next to her. She whipped around to face the display depicting a scene of family life. A cold sweat broke out on her skin as the lights splashed a shadow across the side of the teepee; a large, broad shouldered, headless man.

Nicole bolted. She almost tripped down the stairs as she pushed herself faster than her feet could move. The gift shop lights were lit brightly before her. The recorded voices filled the space, comforting and terrifying. She had heard the short recording more times than she could ever recall. Still, she couldn't be certain that one of the multitude of voices hitting her ears wasn't the voice of the horseman.

Stumbling to a stop, she searched the middle floor in quick glances for any hint of the horseman. She couldn't hear its movement over the blaring of the stereo system. Couldn't catch sight of it as she vainly searched every trace of light and shadow. The lighting of the gift shop cast a glow over the distance separating her from the next flight of stairs. Still, the distance felt insurmountable. She was gearing herself up to make the final sprint when the timer ran out and the flaring lights clicked off.

Her ears rung in the presence of the bellowing noise. The only thing she could hear over the piercing sound was her own ragged breathing. She grappled with her purse, yanked it open, and snatched her mobile phone back out. Her fingers fumbled as she hit the speed dial button and pressed the device to her ear. The ring tone repeated in her ear as she hurried into the relative safety of the gift shop, restlessly casting her eyes over everything around her. Finally, the call connected.

"Mom, where are you?"

"What's wrong?" Dorothy asked instantly.

"It's here."

"What is?"

"The horseman," she whispered.

She eyed the shelves of the gift shop, caught between her desire to run for the stairs and her gnawing need to find a place to hide.

"There is no horseman," Dorothy said, her voice now carrying a sharp but tired edge.

"Yes, there is," Nicole said in a hushed voice. "Can you come and get me now, please?"

"You need to stop this right now," Dorothy quipped back.

"Mom!"

"You need to start thinking about the consequences of your actions. I won't tolerate you lying to me."

"Mom!" she raised her voice as loud as she dared. "Someone is going to kill me. You can lecture me later but right now, I need you!"

A booming crash slammed against the top stair behind her and Nicole jolted back with a sudden scream. The sound cut through whatever Dorothy's next comment was going to be and her mother shifted to repeating her name with a hint of desperation. But Nicole's attention was focused on the footsteps. They descended towards her, growing ever louder, banging like they should rightfully crack the stone stairs. She didn't bother to disconnect the call before she shoved the phone back into her purse, leaving her mother's voice to create a slight buzz in the air.

The resounding footsteps died and she was left grappling for any indication of where it had gone. And any hint of where it was now. No matter how many times she told herself that she had to think, she couldn't come up with a single idea of what to do next.

Run. Hide. Both seemed like equally damning options. Either way, she'd hear its voice. On a split second decision, she broke into a run and sprinted towards the exhibit.

She ran until the sensors picked up on her movement. Noise shattered the silence as lights poured over the area. Standing on the rim of the exhibit, she couldn't even hear her own panted breath, let alone any whispers. Her momentary sense of safety was destroyed as one of the massive buffalos was flung to the side. The base where it had stood was reduced to splinters as the huge animal hurled across the distance and slammed into the wall.

Protecting her face with both arms, she threw herself back, her feet threatening to slip out from under her with every step. The air itself seemed to hit her, hard enough to shove her cleanly off her feet. The air rushed from her lungs as her back crashed full force against the tiled floor. She managed to curl herself just enough to keep the back of her head from colliding with the floor. With a broken yelp, she instantly forced herself onto her stomach and pushed off like a sprinter.

Even as she fled, the whispering began. The sound crackled along the back of her skull, buzzing in her ears, but unable to compete against the blaring noise from the speakers. No matter how fast she forced her legs to move, she couldn't escape the earth shaking footsteps that followed. It hunted her down. Pain exploded across her back as something solid struck her.

Thrown off of her feet, Nicole's momentum slid her over the floor until it dropped out from under her. The sudden plummet made her stomach lurch. Panic rushed through her, promising a scream that the abrupt collision would spurt out from her throat. She crashed into a suspended buffalo with a bone rattling thud. She clawed at the surface. Hunks of the thick buffalo pelted freely as she continued to fall. Her fingers clutched desperately for some kind of support, but it was her leg that found one. She looped her leg around the crooked angle of the buffalo's right foreleg and jerked to a painful halt.

Her chest wheezing with each breath, she struggled to get her mind to catch up with what had happened. Her fingers burrowed deeper into the buffalo's pelt until the solid surface met them. Then she clenched. Her fingers vibrated with the force she made them exert, her leg pulsed with sharp pain as she wrapped it tighter, but she still didn't feel stable. Pressing herself against the side of the colossal animal, Nicole lifted her eyes to seek out how far she had fallen.

The fall hadn't been as far as her body had suggested, but still, the buffalo she now hung from was fully suspended in the air, leaving the rim of solid ground she had dropped from just out of reach. Nicole steadied herself, bit her lips, and looked down. There was nothing to catch her. There was only a sheer drop to the hard tiles below. Small traces of water marred the surface, making them glisten in the dim display lights below. She instantly squeezed her eyes shut and pressed her face against the soft tufts of the buffalo.

It took an enormous amount of will power to keep herself from looking back down. Instead, she looked up. The wires that held her and the stuffed animal up stretched an insurmountable distance from the ceiling above. She wasn't sure how much weight it could hold. Tears burned her eyes, blurring the edges of her vision before they ran free. *You need to move,* she told herself. She had to repeat the command a dozen more times to summon up the courage to actually move.

Every muscle in her hand screamed as she carefully forced herself to let go. She brushed her hand along the side of the animal. Despite all of her efforts and convictions, she was only able to gain a few inches before she surrendered to the need of clutching the fur again. It wasn't enough. The ledge still seemed a world away. No matter how far she stretched, she couldn't reach the edge. It glistened tauntingly, beckoning her forward. But there was no way she could reach it without releasing the unrelenting grip her legs had on the buffalo. Bit by bit, she shuffled over until it felt like her hip was about to pop from its joint. She stretched out again until her shoulder joint ached and her fingers shook. For all of her efforts, she was just barely able to brush her fingertips over the edge.

The footsteps came again. She scrambled back along the buffalo, abandoning the edge until she could hook her arms around the buffalo's thick neck. Step by step, the invisible horseman drew closer. The buffalo shook with every step. The wires that were keeping her from plunging to her death whined with the strain. Nicole tightened her grip until her arms throbbed, every muscle in her body straining until they felt on the edge of tearing. The horseman's footsteps ended at the rim. All Nicole could do was wait to see what it would do next, but it seemed content to leave her hanging in uncertainty. The sound of the blood rushing through her ears rose to rival even the recorded herd. Still, the familiar sound was clearly distinct. Unmistakable. It was the soft cry of the 'hunters' that was at the end of the tape. It was going to cut off soon and she'd be left to silence. And the whispers of the horseman.

With frantic jerks and sharp yanks, she tried to work the strap of the purse free from her shoulders. The task was made all the more difficult since her survival instinct wouldn't allow her to release her grip. Letting go was a desperate measure. Tossing her purse, phone included, felt like she was willingly ready to sacrifice a limb. She could live without an arm, but she couldn't live with her heart ripped from her chest. Barely able to keep her balance, she clutched the thin chain of the purse and worked it carefully from her shoulders. Tightening her legs and her hand, she steadied herself and forced her hand off of the buffalo. Quickly, she began to swing the purse, building up the momentum. That proved easier than actually letting it go.

She threw the purse at the exhibit and the motion sensor. It should have been a hard enough throw to start it once again and ensure that the recording played again. That the light remained, but more importantly, the noise continued. The bag sailed in a wide smooth arch. Then it stopped.

Caught by its strap, the purse swung wildly in mid-air, as if held up by an unseen hand. It took her a heartbeat of gawking, her gut plummeting to the heels of her feet, before she realized that it wasn't hovering. The horseman had caught it. It was standing on the edge of the precipice, watching her, holding her last hope in its hand. Her mouth dropped, her heart sunk. Helpless, fear drenched tear-blazed paths down her cheeks. Then the bag dropped.

She watched it as it plunged into the waiting shadows, tumbling over and over, the brass buckle glinting with every flip. It hit the stone floor with a soft, timid thud. It was a completely underwhelming sound for something that could very well signal the end of her life.

"Fight or flight," she muttered to herself.

The barely whispered words were hollow to her own ears, but she made her burst forward anyway. The buffalo rattled under her as she clambered over it, forcing herself on top of it until she could make a final leap for the edge. Her upper body landed hard against the unforgiving tiles. There was nothing to hold onto, leaving her body weight to drag her back down. Her feet kicked wildly in the empty air as she slipped. The soles of her shoes squeaked and scraped against the smooth wall, desperately looking for even the slightest nook or cranny that could serve as a foothold. But there was nothing, and her efforts made her slip all the more.

Out of the corner of her eyes, she caught a glimpse of shifting lights, a dancing pattern of red and blue. Hope sprang within the hollow cavity of her chest as her nails cracked against the tiles. She had never been so happy to be derelict in her duties when she heard the front door, the one she should have locked at least an hour ago, fling open.

"Mom!"

Her voice cracked over the last of the recording, containing every trace of terror raging within her. Vaguely, she heard an answering cry, but she couldn't quite believe that it was real and not just a comforting figment of her imagination. Planting her feet against the wall she pushed up again. Every fiber of her body was pushed to its limit, and all it earned her was a single inch. Blood began to ooze from her splintered nails, turning the smooth floor slick.

Her hair created a curtain between her and the world as she lifted her head from where it was pressed desperately against the floor. The recording was reaching its end and the lights began to flicker. Each time the room turned dark, a silhouette was cast onto the air before her. For the first time, she saw it. The horseman. Benton's hurried descriptions hadn't come close to explaining the sheer size of the man. His shadow alone was enough to turn her skin to ice and her racing heart into a lump of stone within her chest. It drew closer, forcing the floor to vibrate under her. Her grip loosened. She slid again and desperately struggled to get back what she had lost.

The recording shut off, leaving only the backdrop lights and the faint glow of the gift shop to see by. The outline of the man remained darker than the rest of the world, like something gouged out of existence rather than living within it. The whispering began once again, rising up within her skull until it seemed like a thousand voices speaking at once. They piled on top of each other until she couldn't drown it out with her own thoughts or screams. A hand, cold and solid as steel, wrapped around her right wrist. It yanked her up, taking all of her weight and lifting her clear from the ledge. She dangled in mid-air, held hostage by something unseen. She thrashed wildly, but despite the grip on her arm, she was completely unable to strike anything solid.

She could barely see past her tears, but the shape of her mother was unmistakable as she emerged from the top of the staircase and sprinted towards her. Nicole shrieked for her to run, but her mother only yelled her name, voice sharp with fear and desperation. Still, the horseman spoke louder, its voice slipping in-between the syllables of every word the women spoke. It had just begun to speak her surname when its grip on her arm jolted, its hold loosening, threatening to drop her. The shadow of the horseman jerked and thrashed, its free hand clawing at the back of his severed neck. It was a moment later that Nicole heard it.

It started so gently, steadily growing like a rising tide rushing towards them from some distant place. The first time she had heard Benton wail, his human voice had been layered upon the screech of an owl and something reminiscent of a microphone feedback. This was different, but inherently Benton. His banshee wail steadily increased like an air raid siren, shrieked like metal streaking against metal and mingled with the shrill cry of an enraged bat. The tidal force of a sound accelerated into an impossible pitch and the horseman was shaken, lashing out wildly, clawing at himself and then the air, as if trying to rip the very sound from within the core of its own being.

When the pitch grew to an ear-splitting volume, the horseman released his grip and began to claw at the shadowed body with both hands. The solid rim of the ledge drove into her stomach as she dropped onto it, forcing out the air from her lungs in a painful whoosh. She scrambled across the surface as she slipped back. The horseman ripped off hunks of his shadowy self, creating gaping holes that allowed her to see right through it. The tiles slipped out from under her, but she only felt an inch before another hand grabbed her tight.

Blinking the fire out of her eyes, Nicole looked up to find her mother lying flat against the rim, reaching over the edge to latch onto her forearm with astonishing strength.

"Mom!" she gasped.

"Just hold on!" Dorothy shouted back as she struggled under the weight she was carrying.

The scream cut off sharply, leaving Nicole's ears echoing at the loss. Benton wasn't in the horseman's head anymore. He had been ripped out, just like the last time he had dreamed, and could no longer serve as a distraction.

"Mom, you have to get out of here. You can't stop it!" she cried in a rush. "Find Benton. It will go after him next."

Dorothy ground her teeth, her arm trembling as she tried to pull herself up. The horseman's shadow loomed over her mother's shoulder.

"Mom! Go! It's right behind you!"

The horseman reached down, the black mass of its hand still intact and solid. The fingers inched closer to Dorothy's own.

"Mom!" Nicole shrieked.

Dorothy glanced over her shoulder but still refused to release her grip. Her eyes widened as she saw the monster creeping over her shoulder; seeing the hand that approached her own. Dorothy's free right hand fumbled with her gun belt, trying to yank it free from its holster as the phantom enclosed her fingers with his own.

Steam fogged the air at the contact. The shadowy hand began to crack like dry clay, clumps toppling down past Nicole before disappearing into smoke. It reared back, evaporating before Nicole could lose sight of it over the rim of the ledge.

"What's going on?!" Nicole was bewildered.

"It's gone," Dorothy said, her chest heaving as she abandoned the search for her gun and instead wrapped her right arm around Nicole's forearm.

"We can't see it. Not if it doesn't want us to," Nicole said. "You have to go."

Dorothy's fingers only tightened around Nicole's forearm. Her teeth gnashed as she fought to pull her back up. "Find your feet, baby."

"But ..."

"I'm not letting go," Dorothy growled. "So find your footing right now!"

Nicole's body shifted instantly and she plastered her feet against the smooth wall. With their combined, relentless efforts they managed to pull her, inch by agonizing inch, back over the rim. Nicole's shoulder joint screamed and her ribs ached, but all of the lingering pain meant nothing compared to the relief she felt being on the flat, solid surface she was now laying on. Both women took only a moment to enjoy their victory before scrambling to their feet.

"Where is it?"

"I told you, it's gone," Dorothy said. "The question is, what was it?"

"I told you!" Nicole snapped despite herself. "At least I tried to. You didn't want to hear about it. But none of that matters now. What does is finding out why it left."

"How would I know that?" As she said that, her thumb aimlessly rubbed over her wedding ring.

The simple gold band shone with a weak glow, the surface looking newly polished and robbed of all the scratches earned by more than a decade of constant wear. Nicole snatched up her mother's hand and yanked it closer. She rubbed her thumb over the band, but the shine remained.

"Gold," she whispered. "It couldn't touch the gold."

Dorothy yanked her hand back and glared at her daughter. "What is wrong with you?"

Nicole ignored the question and sprinted back to the gift shop. Not willing to waste her time to go and retrieve the keys from her bag, she picked up the closest heavy object she could find and hurled it through the glass cabinet. She ignored her mother's screaming as she continued to collect the dozens of golden necklaces that filled the shop.

"We need to hurry," Nicole said in a rush. "We have to get to Benton before it does."

"Stop and talk to me."

With the last chain wrapped tightly around her fingers, Nicole turned, pushed past her mother, and ran down the stairs.

"I tried doing that, you didn't want to listen. And now we don't have time."

Dorothy followed close behind her daughter, grappling for some sense of normalcy. In the end, there was only one thing her chaotic mind was able to grab onto.

"This is theft," she snapped as she jogged down the stairs alongside her daughter.

"It's borrowing," Nicole shot back as her feet hit the bottom floor and she broke into a run. "I'll give them all back. Right after we save Benton's life."

# Chapter 7

Benton bolted upright with an aching cry. The monitors around him buzzed and sparked, the lights overhead flashed wildly as they threatened to shatter. His scream hallowed him out, leaving him to flop back, empty and boneless. The mattress bounced once as it accommodated his weight before his brain began to work again. *Get out,* his mind snapped. He yanked at the tubes that were embedded into his arm. *Go!*

The world lurched and rolled around him like a rushing tide. It made the floor swim under his feet, and he slumped back against the bed until he was able to regain his footing. The sound of horseshoes clashing against the tiles, trotted down the hallway. It was a slow, steady pace, but still enough to have his chest hammering against his ribs, narcotics or not. His knees threatened to buckle with every step. He pressed on, hurrying towards the window in broken, crumbling lurches. The cold night air poured into the room as he slid the window open, assaulting the bare skin of his arm and prickling through the thin material of his shirt.

The Fort Wayward hospital had one very helpful feature when one wanted to escape. Most, if not all, of the rooms were on the bottom floor. He twisted and stumbled, but managed to work his long, drugged, and heavy legs to open space. The hooves echoed from just beyond his door. He flung himself out into the night, his haste making him trip and end up sprawled across the rough concrete alleyway. The sudden movement scrambled his brains and, for a moment, he couldn't tell which direction he was looking at, the ground or the sky. It all came back to him the second he heard the horse now galloping across the room with renewed speed.

The harsh ridges of the concrete scraped against the palms of his hands and the battered skin of his face as he forced himself to move. The thin material of his medical scrubs didn't offer much protection for his knees as he positioned himself on all fours. From there it was easier to get his feet back under him. He pushed off, not sparing a glance behind as he raced to the mouth of the alleyway.

His legs refused to work. Each step felt like he was battling his way through tar, refusing to perform the quick sprints that he knew he was capable of. He rounded the corner and emerged onto the street, the sudden shift in light blinding his sensitive eyes. Swiftly, he glanced, searching for some kind of sign to tell him which way to turn next. Streetlights carved sharp circles of light from the shadows, illuminating patches of the deserted street, and empty parked cars. Benton hurried along the side of the hospital, his helpless stumbles slowing him down. His shoulder crashed against the wall. It bewildered him how he felt no pain from the solid impact even as the burn on his hand begun to swelter.

Benton's lungs struggled to meet his demands on them. His already abused heart kicked up to a faster pace while the air was filled with a metallic clicking noise. Trembling, he pressed against the wall of the hospital, the brick scratching at his scrubs while the chill of one of the basement windows seeped the heel of his left foot. The sound from all around him echoed out like a rolling rumble of thunder. Then the world became silent and he held his breath.

A sharp creak cracked in the night as the sheet of glass lifted from his heel. Within the same instant, something whooshed above his head. Benton ducked and whirled, his knees almost giving out as his mind was flooded with images of the horseman's huge hand reaching for him. But there was no hand. He watched as every window within the hospital wall slid open at once.

The cars that lined the street shook violently as their doors flung open. Alarms blared as car lights flashed, their beams exposing more of the world around him. Benton slumped and swayed to the side. His instincts surging him on even as his brain struggled to understand what he was seeing. Every door and window, from homes to businesses, was opening.

Benton ran, urged on by the chaos around him. The clash of galloping hooves rose over the vehicles' screeching sounds, becoming louder with each passing second. He glanced over his shoulder, the horseman visible, but only as a bottomless black smear, a dark shadow that existed within the light. But it was all too easy to see its whip. The long trail of connecting bones glistened in the ever shifting light, as slick as if it had freshly been pulled from someone's skin. The ground shook under the titanic horse, the thunderous quake growing stronger as the horseman ran him down. Benton swung his head back, catching the glint of the windows that gave natural light to the hospital basement. In a split second decision, he threw himself towards them.

The drugs that still pulsed within him weren't enough to compete with the muscles from the many years of baseball practice. He dropped, hurling himself into a slide, ignoring the pits of his skin that the uneven concrete roughly scraped at, as he slipped through the nearest open window. But his aim was off, his motions sloppy, and he smacked against the sides of the window as he fell through. He was still reeling from the blows as he dropped a short distance and crashed onto a metal surface. The impact sent a snap of pain through him, followed quickly by another as he toppled off and smacked against the unforgiving concrete slab of the floor.

Every molecule of air rushed out of his lungs in a single pained grunt. His limbs flopped uselessly over the floor, as if his primal instinct was physically searching for the air that had left him. Lights danced and swirled before his eyes, burning and blurring his vision. His back arched as his lungs forced themselves to work once again, and he used the momentum to roll onto his side. He clawed at the floor, focusing all of his efforts into getting back on his feet. It was only after that task was accomplished that he bothered to start looking for an exit.

An icy feeling filled him as he took in the stainless steel that made up the room. The walls on either side of him were lined with small, square, freezer-like doors, their polished surface reflecting the light that crept in through the windows behind him, and a silver colored table sat in the middle of the room that made his stomach plummet. He was in the town morgue.

With a soft, raspy gasp, the rows of freezer doors began to open. Layers of thick fog trailed out of them, falling like waterfalls to pool across the floor. The more that was released, the more he could get a glimpse of the bodies that lay in the freezers. Benton stepped forward on wobbly legs but was too late. He could hear the horse closing in. Each sharp clack echoed through the only door, the only exit out of the room. He was trapped.

Benton turned and tried to scramble back up onto the table he had banged against. The sharp crack of the whip made him stop. His knees jerked and his feet toppled back to the floor. Gripping the table edge tightly, he glanced back over his shoulder. The once empty threshold was now filled with the horseman. And it no longer gave him the mercy of not being forced to see it.

With black, rotted blood bubbling out of its severed neck, the stench of rancid meat polluted the air and made bile burn at the back of his throat. The slabs squished as it stalked closer. Each footfall shook the building and jolted the table he was holding on to. Benton couldn't take his eyes off the whip as it curled and twisted. He flinched and its hand snapped out, sending the spinal cord crashing into the freezer doors, leaving deep grooves within the surface. Benton threw himself back but had nowhere to go.

Like a snake striking, the whip snapped towards his head. Benton tossed himself to the side, feeling the breeze the chain of bones created as they streaked past an inch away from his back. The edge of the whip bore down on the table Benton had abandoned, slicing through the space he had just stood in, crumbling the metal.

Benton flung himself to the ground and slid across the floor until he slammed into the table in the middle of the room. The horseman whirled, pulling the whip out of the dent it had created, the bones clanking together as it rose, preparing for the next strike.

A scream ripped from Benton's core. The sound split him in two, carving a wide path from the very depths of his soul and out of his physical form; tangible and incorporeal at the same time. Within the same moment, the scream filled him to his breaking point while emptying him completely. The horseman shuddered under the sound as fractures began to split its body. Light poured through the hairline cracks and the horseman retreated slightly, thrashing as if it had lost all sense of equilibrium.

But the disorientation didn't last long. It lunged forward, the skeletal whip cracking as it raced towards him again. Benton rolled. The air stirred as the bones crashed down into the concrete where he once lay. Hunks of stone exploded, the broken shards cutting into the tender skin of his face and neck. Benton struggled onto all fours and desperately evaded the next strike as he tried to force his banshee wail into existence. He had never been able to force it before, never tried to, and his screams remained simply shrieks of fear; human and pitiful.

He sprinted for the door but the whip was swift to cut him off. Shrinking back, his arms raised to protect himself from the hurdling shrapnel, Benton noticed the first traces of the whispering voices. They came from all around, carried through the air itself, accumulating together to gather strength. The sound boiled against his brain like acid. He clamped his hands over his ears, but he couldn't keep the sound out. It filled him up until it felt like the plates of his skull were beginning to break apart. Benton tried for the door again, but the horseman kept him trapped, its otherworldly voice forming into recognizable sounds, developing into words, slowly merging into the beginnings of his name.

Bending under the sound, he clawed at his ears, his nails raking across the damaged skin around his temples. His fear rushed up to meet the clarifying voice and broke out of his throat in a high-pitched wail. The metal doors violently shook, as fluorescent lights flared and began to strobe. The horsemen took one step back and swung the whip out. Benton snapped his hand up, managing to protect his face. His forearm absorbed the strength of the blow but couldn't break the momentum. The long string of vertebrae went over his arm and wrapped around his neck. With a sharp yank, Benton was pulled off of his feet. His hip collided with the table, but the force didn't relent.

Dragged up onto the surface, the cool steel pressing against his back, Benton clawed at the whip as it tightened around his neck. The pieces twisted tighter at his every touch, squeezing his windpipe until it choked off his scream and his breath. He slipped his fingers under the band and pushed up with all of the strength he had. It stopped the advancement, but that didn't let him regain what he had lost. His feet slipped and smacked against the tabletop, now as useless as his hands, to help him find any escape.

His chest swelled with the scream he couldn't bring to life. It ignited within his ribcage like wildfire, scorching him from the inside out, boiling and blistering the tender flesh of his lungs while it charred his bones. The horseman loomed over him, its dark hand appearing within the corner of Benton's blurring vision. The first touch burned like dry ice, freezing his skin, making it as frail as frost. The whispers came back, battling the fire within him for dominance over his mind.

A beam of blinding light streaked across the body of the horseman. Its hand pulled back and it whirled around, revealing Nicole to Benton's wavering gaze. Her eyes widened and her jaw dropped as she tilted her face up. The terror that surged into her gaze made it clear that the horseman had decided to reveal itself to her. She was, for the first time, seeing it in all of its grotesque glory. But instead of running, Nicole clenched her jaw and struck out towards it with the long gold chain she held tightly in her hands.

The connected gold chains were thin and sliced across the horseman's chest like a blade, releasing a blazing light as the gold itself began to glow. Benton heard Dorothy before he saw her. The constable stormed across the room, gun trained on the horseman, her conviction narrowing, her eyes steady while fear tightened the lines of her face. But she didn't have a clear shot when Nicole struck out again. The whip loosened with the blow, just enough to allow a thin trail of air to slip down his throat.

Benton snapped himself up, yanking the whip loose, coaxing the small hunks of bone out of the ridges they had imprinted into his skin. The horseman turned back instantly. It rushed towards him, needing only one hand to pin Benton down against the cold slab. Unable to fight against the bulk, twice the size of his own, he continued to rip at the whip, keeping the end from the horseman's seeking grasp. Finally, the whip went lax enough that he was able to breathe in heaving gasps of air through his battered, aching throat. The horseman gave up on trying to grab the whip back, and instead clamped his hand around Benton's neck in a crushing grip, making the bones dig into his throat.

Nicole was just as unrelenting in her own attacks, lashing at its back with the golden chain, each strike making the horseman shatter and break apart. Thin trails of damage wrapped around its torso and light poured from the wounds like solar flares. Squinting against the blinding blaze that cut across the horseman's stomach, Benton reached out with trembling fingers, clawing over the raw slabs of meat of the horseman's clothes. His fingertips found the thin chain of gold and he seized it. Nicole pulled at the other end and the chain cut into both his fingers and the horseman.

Dorothy shot twice. The sudden shooting sound rolled and echoed over itself, spurred on by the hollow metal that lined the walls. The horseman flinched back with both of the shots, but it wasn't enough to make it retreat. It used its grip to slam Benton down against the metal slab. Benton's vision blurred. His face grew hot and swollen. The unheard scream ripped apart his insides as the horseman clenched his throat. Benton yanked the chain, forcing it deeper into the horseman's body. Hunks of cold, damp flesh ripped free from the horseman and dropped down onto his skin, slicking a path across over his body as they dripped to the floor.

The small links of the chain wrapped around his hand began to glow with a gilded radiance. It outshone the breaks forming within the horseman and warmed his skin where it touched. With the triple assault, the horseman couldn't keep its stone-like hold on Benton, and he was able to choke down a breath again. He latched his hands on both the whip and the chain, drawing the horseman closer as he opened his mouth. The volcano that had filled his body erupted out in an air cracking shriek.

The metal doors of the morgue's freezers were torn from their hinges, the windows shattered, the overhead lights exploded like a hailstorm of fractured glass and fiery sparks. The horseman rattled. The gold chain cut into him like a pristine blade, slicing him apart, splitting him like wood. Broken hunks of flesh fell apart like wet rubble. With a last shudder, the horseman burst, raining rancid blood and oozing organs over every inch of the room.

Benton gagged and wrenched as the sludge filled his mouth. Rolling onto his side, he spat the substance out onto the already slick table top. The blood soaked into every inch of his thin clothes, creating a chilled, chunky blanket over him as he hurled the contents of his stomach onto the hunks of flesh by his face.

"Benton!" Nicole shrieked, as she rushed to his side.

He could feel her gently untangling the gold chain from his hand. The soft touch combined with her constant calling of his name worked to ease his nerves. As his adrenaline seeped away, the pain of his hand rushed forward to fill the gap. He whimpered and pulled at the spinal whip from around his neck with desperate yanks. She didn't help him, but instead settled for a comforting rub on his arm.

"It's okay. You're okay. I think the Dullahan is dead."

Benton coughed out another mouthful of blood as he finally managed to pull the whip free and toss it weakly across the room.

"What the hell is a Dullahan?" he rasped.

She rubbed his back as he tumbled into a coughing fit, trying to clear his abused windpipe.

"I looked it up on mom's phone on the way over," Nicole said with far more pride than Benton could handle right now. But his laugh only resulted in another series of ragged coughs. "Its intolerance to gold was the last bit I needed to find it, well, as near as I could figure. It's from an Irish legend. They have some screwed up legends when you think about it."

He tried to catch his breath, but all he could smell was the blood that was smoldering the room. A sharp cry came out of him as he pressed his hand against the slab and forced himself up. It would have been near impossible to actually get up if Nicole and Dorothy hadn't come to his aid. With his vision blurred, he winced when he finally caught sight of them both, covered in the slop of entrails and blood.

"Are you okay?" Nicole asked. "I mean, as much as you can be right now. How's your hand? Are you still high?"

"Nicole," his desperate whine came out with a graveled edged, broken and rough and painful to force out. It was quickly met with another fit of coughs.

"Right, we'll talk later. Just focus on breathing," Nicole said, once again rubbing his back in soothing but ineffectual circles.

Not able to meet Dorothy's shell-shocked expression, he glanced around the blood-soaked room. "People would have heard the shots," he whispered carefully. "How are we going to clean this up?"

The women looked at each other before surveying the room themselves.

"What is he talking about?" Dorothy asked.

"He's a creature of Irish mythology, not deaf," Nicole whispered back before she turned to Benton, "but she does have a point, buddy."

Benton sputtered before he could answer, "The blood."

Again, the Riders exchanged a confused glance, hunks of flesh dripping from their hair.

"What blood?" they asked in unison.

\*\*\*

Benton was still marveling at Dorothy's powers of persuasion when the morning began to turn the sky pink. Caught in the moment, the best lie he could think of was that he became disorientated after a nightmare. After all, he had just stumbled across a pit full of dead people and was too traumatized to even remember how he had burnt his hand. It was flimsy at best, but as soon as Constable Dorothy Rider took hold of it, she managed to work it into something that sounded completely reasonable. He didn't know how she managed to explain away the gunshots. That was a conversation held far away from any prying ears and teenagers. For his part, the hardest thing had been trying to keep from vomiting. The entrails had clung to him, dripped from him, and he had stopped himself from begging for a shower.

His parents had just been happy that he wasn't a suspect. Their reaction had been swift and along the lines that Benton had expected. The stream of questions had easily shifted to warnings and then to complete denial. He had nodded along and said what they needed to hear. At first he had resented when they had decided that the waiting room, or their more comfortable home, was now out of the question and had set up camp in his hospital room. But, as midnight had crept closer and he still wasn't able to sleep, the situation was growing on him. They had both fallen asleep, and the steady undertone of their breathing was relaxing. It wasn't uncommon for them to circle the wagon and try to separate him from the outside world. But tonight, for some reason that he couldn't place, their presence didn't feel suffocating. He actually felt protected. Snuggled down under the sheets, with a pillow cradled against his chest and his arms propped up above him, Benton had drifted on a haze of painkillers and contentment. Right up until the moment Nicole popped up in his window.

At first, he had been sure that she was just a figment of his imagination. After all, she had spent a great deal of time waving her arms about, with a really weird amount of energy. He wasn't sure how long he had just stared at her in confusion before he had realized that she was beckoning him over. Sluggish and slow, he tiptoed out of the bed as quietly as possible. The distance between the bed and the window didn't look that far, but it felt like a mile as he slowly edged his way across it. With every step, he was sure that his parents would wake up and start on a new series of questions that he didn't know the answers to now. But they hadn't, much to his bafflement, and he had finally completed his journey without incident. He didn't have time to feel proud of himself as Nicole had practically pulled him outside. From there it had been a short shuffle to Dorothy's waiting car. He had been vaguely aware that it should have felt like a very long trip, but time wasn't exactly moving at a steady, predictable pace anymore.

Sitting in the backseat, he blinked owlishly until he was able to focus. Still, Dorothy's voice sounded weird and distorted, and he was confused as to why he could taste the stench that wafted off the woman. She fell silent, staring at him as the horseman's congealed blood dripped from her chin. After a long silence and a meaningful glare from the Constable, Benton's eyebrows inched up his forehead.

"You said something, didn't you?" he asked. The rough scratch of his voice startled him as the painful scrape of the words made him wince.

Dorothy scowled. "Yes. I did. I asked you a direct question."

He blinked slowly. "Did I answer?"

"He's on painkillers, mom," Nicole cut in.

Benton jerked to the side. While he remembered following Nicole and her climbing in the car behind him, he had honestly forgotten that she was there. Although her blood-drenched presence did explain why the stench was so bad.

Nicole didn't take her eyes off her mother. "Can't this wait until the morning?"

"I've got a basement full of dead bodies, you were almost killed, and I just shot a man who didn't have a head but was still alive. No, this can't wait."

"What was the question?" Benton asked as he struggled to keep his head up.

Dorothy spoke again and he watched her mouth with the sum total of his focus.

"Okay," he said. "One more time, but stop making your voice do that echo thingy."

Dorothy clenched her jaw but finally spoke clearly, "What happened to your attacker?"

Benton pressed his knuckles together before arching his hands in opposite directions, twirling his fingers as he mimicked the sound of an explosion. He thought he was amazingly accurate, but Dorothy didn't look impressed.

"It exploded?" the woman asked.

"That's right, officer. It went boom." After another long string of coughs, he croaked out a request that someone crack a window open.

Nicole did and he shuffled a little further from her.

"Even if it did," Dorothy said. "Why can't we see the remains?"

He shrugged and tried not to get distracted by how weird one of his hands looked. "Don't know. Still trying to figure out why you can't feel it."

"Feel it?" Nicole asked.

He looked her over, his lip curling in disgust as he gagged.

"I'm covered in Dullahan goo?" Nicole whirled to face her mother. "Can we go home? I need a shower."

"This is more important," Dorothy snapped.

"Is it, though?" Benton didn't mean to bark back, but Dorothy's rough voice didn't give him much option. "I'm still going to be a banshee once you're clean. It seems like you're angry enough without having to clean up my vomit. Nicole still goes on about it."

Dorothy narrowed her gaze on him, but he wasn't sure how he had made her angry. If anything, he had been going out of his way to keep her happy.

"Nicole told me that you weren't involved with the bodies in the basement."

"True," Benton winced as he swallowed. "I dreamt about some of them, but I didn't kill 'em. Did I?" He contemplated it for a moment. "No. I didn't. Definitely didn't."

"And the ... what did you call it?"

"Leanan Sidhe," Nicole offered.

"Oh, she killed it," he jabbed a thumb towards Nicole. Rolling his head to lean it against the chair, he blinked at her, his brow furrowing. "Should I not have said that? It feels like I shouldn't have."

Nicole smiled and reached out to pat his knee. "It's fine."

"Good," he mumbled. "Please, don't touch me with those gross, bloody hands."

Nicole whirled to her mother, but Dorothy still wouldn't hear her. Instead, she kept her attention focused on Benton.

"How did you make that noise?"

"Banshee." He tried to click his fingers and instantly regretted it when the pain in his hand blazed again. After hissing in pain, he settled for finger guns that for some reason sounded like lasers. "And, before you ask, that's about all I know."

"Well, I still have more questions."

"So do I. I suggest asking Nicole. She's really into this sort of stuff. Oh, I have a question," Benton met the officer's gaze as he leaned forward. "What are you going to do?"

"I'm still deciding," Dorothy snapped.

Benton shrugged and slumped back. "Better make your choice soon."

"Don't test me, Benton. I'm still not convinced that you two aren't delusional."

"Living dead guy wasn't enough for you?" Benton snorted.

Nicole lifted her hand to silence him as she spoke to her mother, "What do you need?"

"Real, physical, tangible proof," was the instant response.

"You have his scream on tape," Nicole said in a shrill pitch.

"So he made a weird noise."

Benton laughed, the sound breaking into a painful cough that he didn't quite regret.

Nicole huffed almost petulantly. "Fine. How about the remains of a mythical creature?"

"The horseman exploded," Dorothy said.

"The Leanan Sidhe didn't," Nicole said. "I'll take you to its corpse. Just let me get Benton back inside."

"No, he's coming with us."

Benton felt their eyes on him and shrugged. "Sure, why not? Road trip!"

"Fine," Nicole said as she sat back and crossed her arms over her chest. "But you're letting me have a shower first. That's non-negotiable."

***

When Benton came back to his senses, the rising sun was giving the horizon a gilded edge. A blanket of low clouds crossed the sky in soft wisps of purple and pink. He blinked at it as the pain in his hand fought back the remaining haze of the painkillers.

"Why are we at the Leanan Sidhe's grave?" he asked.

He could barely get his tongue to move, and his voice sounded like a deep growl. Each syllable hurt as much as his hand. Blinking again, he realized that he was slumped against the back door of the police cruiser. And he was pretty sure he was drooling. Pushing himself up, he wiped a knuckle over the corner of his mouth and turned his head to Nicole. She quirked her eyebrows.

"We went over this. Twice."

He slummed back against the seat and instantly regretted it. The lingering stench of rotted flesh still lingered over her skin and had long since filled the car. He leaned back towards the open window.

"Can you stop hanging your head out the window like a dog?" she asked.

"You stink."

"I bathed!" Nicole said indigently. "With lavender and rose bath salts and sweet grass scented soap. I smell amazing."

"You smell like road kill on a desert highway in the middle of summer," he mumbled.

"That's very specific," she said before adding nervously, "but I'm not covered in it anymore, right?"

He looked over at her. "Right."

"Good. And we're here because mom wanted to see the Sidhe for herself. She dug it up about two hours ago. She's still staring at it."

Leaning slightly to the side, he looked between the front seats. Dorothy was crouched next to the open grave, staring at the disrupted earth with wide, disbelieving eyes.

"She's not taking it well," Nicole said softly.

"I don't suppose she'll tell us what she's going to do," he croaked.

"I think we're okay," Nicole said. "I mean, she's told everyone about the basement, but also that we found it. So I guess that will explain why our DNA is everywhere. I don't think she's going to tell anyone about this, though. Or about you."

Benton managed to nod once before he slumped back against the seat.

After a moment of silence, Nicole spoke again, "Thank you, Benton." He could hear a small giggle in her voice. "For saving me. I actually heard your scream while you were in the Dullahan."

"What?" Benton's face scrunched up. "How is that possible?"

"I don't know," she said. "And I am far too big of a person to mention that if you had agreed to let me do a few non-invasive tests, we might actually have some answers right now."

He slid his eyes to the side to look at her. "And you would never rub it in like that."

"Of course not," she smiled. "No matter how right I was, and consequently, how wrong you were, I would never tell you I told you so."

The swift laugh that bubbled from him transformed into a coughing fit. Tears lined the corners of his eyes when he was finally able to draw in another breath. Nicole rubbed his shoulders and he relaxed into the touch.

"Okay. Fine. You can do your tests."

"Oh," she said swiftly. "If you think that's for the best."

"Shut up," he smiled.

"Why do you think your scream was different?" she asked idly. "I mean, this time sounded really different from last month."

"The first time I was scared," he mumbled sleepily. "This time, I was a lot angrier than I was afraid."

"Well, next time I'll remember to get you angry," she said.

"Next time?"

"I didn't have time to put the symbol up straight away. I mean, I went back and sketched one under the table with permanent marker, but it's a morgue. It has to get cleaned a lot, right? At some point, someone's going to find it and scrub it off. And that's assuming the symbol does anything, anyway. I'm guessing, sooner or later, something else is going to come our way."

His eyelids began to shut. "Great."

"Hey, we're doing pretty well," she protested. "This time it didn't even take us a week. I'm sure we can take care of whatever comes next in less than a day."

"It's good to have a goal." He tried to smirk, but was too tired and sore to make it work.

Slowly, he sunk down to the side, falling steadily until he was using her thighs as a pillow.

"I thought I stank," she chuckled.

"You do. What is your mom doing?"

"Still struggling to reconcile with the knowledge that the paranormal exists with what she knows about the world," Nicole said, as she began to trail her nails gently along the curve of his ear.

With a contented sigh, he stared at the back of the front seats, watching the shadows disappear as the sun continued to rise. The drugs pumped in his system, masked his pain and worked with his fatigue to draw him closer to sleep.

"That's probably going to take a while," he mumbled.

"Most likely."

He was silent for a long moment. "My hand hurts."

"I know. Try and sleep. I'll wake you if anything good happens."

Benton hummed, enjoying the soft curve of her fingers, the loose airy feeling the drugs gave his limbs. In the silence, he listened to her breathing and relaxed against her warmth.

"You're going to help me, right?" he asked. "With whatever comes next?"

"Of course. That's what best friends are for. And don't argue with me on that. I have earned 'best' friend status."

"Yeah, you have," he smiled.

Unable to fight it anymore, his eyelids shut, and his dreams emerged and swept him away.

\* \* \*

# Shattered Dreams
## Banshee Series Book 3

# Chapter 1

The sound of rattling bones hit his ears in a constant drone that kept Benton Bertrand tittering on the precipice of sleep. For a moment, he floated within the haze, his body desperate for oblivion. But the clash of raw bones grew louder. It filled his head, and in one startling moment, he realized that the sound was real. He snapped his eyes open, not daring to move. He blinked at the ever-shifting light above him. Ashen clouds sailed across the low Alberta sky. Each time they blotted out the sun, the temperature seemed to plummet as the autumn chill crept up from the earth below him. His sleep deprived mind struggled to remember where he was. He couldn't recall why he was flat on his back with thick blades of prairie grass surrounding him.

Just when he resolved to sit up, one of the sources of the ghastly noise came into vision. The great horned owl peered down at him with blazing, unblinking yellow eyes. Benton held his breath watching the colossal bird as it dipped lower, bringing the razor sharp hook of its beak closer to the delicate skin of his face. The brittle sound of grass cracking echoed in his ears and he realized how close its talons were. The very tip of one grazed his outer ear. It wasn't rough, but still enough to slice cleanly through his skin. Benton flinched, and the owl shrieked at his movement, its wings spread wide. It snapped wildly, creating a sound in perfect mimicry of bone striking bone, the needle-like point edging ever closer to his eyes.

A thunderous crack broke over all other sounds. Benton slightly recoiled from the gunshot sound as the bird took flight. The flock that had surrounded him filled the sky with dark shadows against the gathering clouds, each one as silent as a ghost. Releasing a long sigh, Benton sluggishly lurched into a sitting position. He braced his elbows on his bent knees, and gingerly touched a finger to his left ear, flinching as the sting grew sharper upon contact. Blood smeared his fingertip as he placed his hand back on the grass.

"You okay?" Nicole called to him. He offered her a wave of both confirmation and thanks.

He remembered not to use his left hand, to keep her from seeing the blood, but he had completely forgotten about the scars that now covered his right palm. Flicking his eyes up, he was just in time to see Nicole stiffen and shift her attention down to the handgun she was holding. It wasn't her fault that she had brought it along.

The fire that they had stumbled across wasn't anything they could have predicted or prepared for. It existed only because of a symbol etched on the walls of a hidden room in a forgotten basement. She couldn't see it and had passed through the unworldly flames without a problem. For Benton, however, the flames had felt like boiling oil. Something slick that had coated his skin and continued to cook his flesh, long after he had removed his hand from it. The double standard existed because he was a banshee. The result would have been the same if he had touched it for any reason. But he had been reaching for her outstretched hand, so she carried her guilt over it.

"I'm fine," he called out once he found his voice. "Thanks."

She looked at him. Or at least at his hand.

"It doesn't hurt anymore," he promised, his voice growing a little more intense than he would have liked. But at least it provoked a reaction, and she met his gaze.

"Have you got any feeling back in your palm yet?" she asked.

He puffed out his cheeks and drew his legs up closer, dangling his forearms over his knees.

"Nope. Please stop asking."

"I don't ask that often," she protested.

Benton had completely forgotten that Dorothy, Nicole's mother, was only a few steps to the side until she spoke.

"You've asked him that three times this week," Dorothy said. "And that's just the ones that I know of."

It had been almost three months since Dorothy had been let in on the loads of crazy that made up most of Benton's existence, but she still felt like a new addition. Admittedly, it was nice to have her in on it. Ever since he was ten, Benton had been on his own trying to warn the people that he dreamed about. People didn't tend to react well to a random stranger telling them they were about to be brutally murdered. His attempts generally ended in one of three ways: him writhing in pain, him being completely ignored, or him becoming the focus of a police investigation when what he dreamed became a reality.

His 'ability' – as Nicole liked to call it – had ruined his life more than once, and outright destroyed his relationship with his parents. Things went a lot more smoothly when he had a Constable in the Royal Canadian Police on his side. Benton always worked with a name and the sudden knowledge of how to contact them; sometimes through a phone number or address, but more often an email. And Dorothy could do a lot more with that than he could have ever achieved. She could warn the people and protect Benton at the same time, and it felt like things were finally working as they should. They couldn't save everyone, but they saved a few, and that was enough.

A more unexpected perk, however, was that he now had backup when dealing with the force of nature and neurosis, who was, Nicole Rider. The two women's voices became background music, as a weary ache worked its way into his bones. He rubbed his hands over his tired eyes. The smooth scar tissue of his right palm was still an odd sensation, but not an entirely unpleasant one.

"Will you please back me up here?"

It took Benton a few heartbeats to realize that Nicole had shot the question at him. It effectively drew him back into the conversation to which he hadn't been paying the slightest bit of attention.

He jabbed a finger in Nicole's direction. "She's right."

Nicole's victorious smile only lasted a moment before she asked, "You have no idea what we were talking about, do you?"

"Not a clue," he assured.

"But you still picked my side?"

"Your mom doesn't sulk for three hours when I don't pick hers," Benton said as he let his hands drop.

A sour expression twisted up her doll-like features before she turned to face him fully. The sunlight glistened off the barrel of the gun she still held, and it unnerved him a little how she seemed to have forgotten it was there. At least none of her fingers were near the trigger and it was pointed to the ground.

"Did you sleep at all last night?" she asked.

"I never sleep well," he dismissed.

Her lips scrunched up just a little and he knew she wasn't about to let this go. Heaving a sigh, he loosely gestured to nothing in particular.

"Think I got at least three hours," he admitted.

"But you didn't get a name?" Dorothy pressed.

"Oh, no, I did. I just decided to keep it as a surprise," Benton snapped. He instantly regretted it. And not just because Dorothy could make steel melt with the fire, but she sure could pack in a glare. "Sorry. I'm just really tired."

He rubbed his eyes again and tried, for what felt like the hundredth time, to explain the new breed of madness that met him in REM sleep. "It's like a kaleidoscope of static. I know it's there, but I just can't..."

With a frustrated growl, he threw his hands up in the air.

"The whale recordings didn't help at all?" Nicole asked.

Ever since he had told her, Nicole had been systematically subjecting him to every remedy she could find. Medication was out of the question. Not being able to wake up from hideous and violent nightmares was, in his experience, mental torture. It felt like he had tried every home remedy under the sun. None of it worked, and Nicole was beginning to take that as a personal challenge.

"Do you think it has something to do with the Dullahan?" Nicole asked.

The monster that killed by whispering the name of its victim. The one that had harvested people's organs, for the sheer joy of it, had been the second paranormal creature Benton had encountered. It marked the only time in his life that his 'host' body had ever known he was there. Normally, as he slept, he seemed to slip into the bodies of the killers. Becoming them. The Dullahan had physically tossed him out of its mind. Benton hadn't been prepared for that. The memory was still enough to send shivers down his spine.

"The Dullahan is dead," he said.

"We never saw a body," Dorothy noted.

"*You* never saw a body," he corrected. "Trust me. It exploded, and you guys walked around covered in its internal organs. You both smelled like road kill for days."

Nicole scrunched her nose up and mumbled, "Gross."

"Yeah," he said with a near hysterical chuckle. "It was."

"Even if that's true," Dorothy said, patiently ignoring him when he rolled his eyes and lolled his head back with a groan, "your encounter with it might have altered you."

"I dreamed just fine after it," Benton muttered.

"Maybe this is like banshee flu or something," Nicole offered. She swiftly crossed the distance between them, knelt down, and pressed her hand to his forehead. "Do you feel sick? Maybe I should make you some chicken soup."

Benton enjoyed the touch, but eyed the weapon in her hand with a nervous energy. He had been forced to live all over Canada. It never took long before all the things he said and knew led people to the wrong conclusions. After that, it was a quick downward slide into accusations and police investigations. They had learned the hard way to move before the gossip evolved into violence. Normally, they just went to a new major city. This was their first time in farmlands and the first time he was exposed to firearms. And he wasn't too comfortable with it being so close. Nicole, on the other hand, didn't give it a second thought as she shifted her hand to press her knuckles against his cheek.

"And maybe that's why the owls are acting so weird. Like how dogs can sense when someone's sick," she said.

"I'm pretty sure they smell it," Benton said. He jerked his leg out of the way, as the barrel of the gun neared it. "Can you be careful with that thing?"

She looked blankly at him and then at the gun. "The safety's on and it's empty," she declared as she lifted the dull gray handgun in line with her shoulder. "See? The top bit is clicked back."

"Don't care. Still don't trust you with a gun."

A disgruntled scoff escaped her as she sat back on her heels. "I saved your life with a gun, remember?"

"You kicked a monster's head until the skull cracked," he deadpanned.

"Yeah," she snipped. "*After* I shot it."

"Remember our deal," Dorothy snapped as she rushed forward to join them.

Dorothy had agreed to turn a blind eye to the illegal things they got mixed up in while trying to deal with paranormal murders on their own, but on two conditions; first, they had to tell her every detail, and second, never to speak of it in front of her again. A night filled with very awkward conversations had covered the first part. The second condition was proving to be a bit harder as the two teenagers got accustomed to having her around.

"We'll have some answers after we get him to the sleep center at Peace Springs. There's no use in speculating until we have the facts." She waited for her daughter to stand up before she handed over what seemed to be a full clip. "Now, focus. We're not leaving until you get five more."

Nicole glanced to one of the few trees that actually spotted the plains. Dorothy had dangled a few bottles from the bending branches. A slight breeze made the glass bottles tinkle together like chimes. With confident hands, Nicole released the empty clip from the butt of the gun and tossed it to her mother, then slid the full one into place. Benton heard the safety click off and managed to clamp his hands over his ears before she fired. It took her eight shots, but she got the five. Preening in her victory, she clicked the safety back on and passed the gun to her mother. Dorothy looked proud.

"That's my girl," Dorothy grinned.

"I've been meaning to ask," Benton managed to get out before his voice kicked up a pitch. "Why is there a gun? Seriously, we're going to Peace Springs! It's like a four-hour drive."

"Yeah, but we have to go along Highway 43," Nicole noted, feeling her shoulders shudder.

Benton shrugged. "That's bad?"

The two women looked at each other and he just waited. After nearly half a minute of silent deliberation, they both seemed to remember in unison that he didn't grow up in Fort Wayward. The vast population of the town not only grew up together and had the collective knowledge they all knew, but also shared a heritage. The majority of the population had connections to the Siksika Nation, with the few others having their roots with other tribes. So it was common for him to feel completely out of the loop and in need of an explanation for things that everyone else considered general knowledge.

"Wait right here," Nicole said before she darted towards the car.

Benton gave Dorothy a questioning look but only got the soft shake of her head that told him she had no idea what her daughter was up to. They waited in silence until Nicole came back with her favorite picnic basket swinging in her hand. She shooed off a few owls that had come lurking back before she knelt down and opened the basket.

"This is Fort Wayward," she said, as she placed the peppershaker down before Benton, with a flourish.

Benton glanced at Nicole, who had stopped her impromptu presentation for a few seconds.

"I'm with you so far," he said.

"Good," she smiled as she placed down the saltshaker. "This is Peace Springs." Using a rolled up napkin she connected the two points. "The quickest point between the two is Highway 43. It's not to scale. It's actually a bit curvy and goes into a valley."

Benton closed his eyes. "I know the basics of a highway, Nic. But I'm still shaky on what any of this has got to do with guns?"

Nicole narrowed her gaze but it didn't have any heat to it. "Well, if you stop interrupting me, I'll tell you." She swept her hand over the napkin and surrounding grass. "Nothing good has ever happened in this area. Bloody battles, missing bands expanding different tribes, lost settlers, ghost sightings. It's pretty much the definition of a cursed land."

Nicole fell silent, as if she had just explained everything, leaving Dorothy to continue on.

"The disappearances didn't stop after the highway was constructed. The area is isolated with the natural terrain offering dozens of drop offs, blind curves, and thick bushes that makes it nearly impossible for search parties to find anyone. There are no highway lights through most of it. So unless you have a full moon and know the road really well, it's pretty easy to misjudge a sharp turn and drive into a sheer drop."

Benton huffed out his growing impatience. He could feel the urge to yell at them bubbling up inside him and did his best to contain it. *Why would anyone need firearms because of poor road construction?* The thought ran through his mind a split second before the answer followed. *Fear.* They were both trying to keep it from their faces, but the slightest hints were starting to show on both of them. He swallowed his comment and sat quietly as Dorothy continued.

"Peace Springs was established as a mining town. When the mines closed up, the town was financially devastated and never really recovered. The surrounding reservations aren't much better off. Fort Wayward is the closest town with a decent hospital and fully stocked pharmacy, so they're forced to make the trip over here for a lot of their medical needs."

"A lot of our families have common relatives between the two," Nicole added. "Just about everyone, on each side, has a relative on the other side. Plus, they have the only Walmart, government service centers, name brand junk food, and a movie theater. Travelling the road is kind of inevitable."

"Why can't we just go the long way?" Benton asked.

"Because that takes a few extra days," Dorothy explained. "And most people can't afford a car. Not to mention there's still no reliable public transport that goes that route. A lot of people are forced to walk or hitchhike."

Benton pressed the bottom of his palms into his aching eyes and blamed the fatigue on why it had taken him that long to catch onto what they were telling him. He had the carbon copy of hundreds of murderers embossed on his brain. Normally, he didn't need this much information to spot a perfect hunting ground.

"I have this vague memory of Nicole telling me that there hasn't been a murder in Fort Wayward in decades," he said.

"There hasn't," Nicole affirmed quickly. "Highway 43 is way out of town limits. And most of the time, those who go missing are 'officially' filed as missing under suspicious circumstances or considered runaways. And those that are found are 'officially' accidents."

Benton raised his hands. "Why do you keep air quoting officially like that?"

"Because I'm optimistic, not stupid," Nicole replied.

A slight smirk crossed his lips but was quickly lost. "So the gun is for protection? Just in case?"

"The majority of the missing people are women," Dorothy said, casting a quick glance at her daughter. "Teenagers of Native descent."

Benton winced as his stomach suddenly turned into a pit of snakes, his eyes shifting to Nicole. The vague description worked for just about every girl in town, but with Nicole, it had a few other things working against her. She was stunning, stubborn, and had no sense of her own limitations.

She smiled, obviously trying to ease the worry crossing his features. "That is why mom and dad never let me go near the Highway of the Lost without being chaperoned, and armed."

"And you're not allowed to be armed unless you practice," Dorothy noted.

"I just hit the five," Nicole protested.

Dorothy didn't seem all that satisfied, but she still nodded and checked her watch. "We need to get back to town. It's almost time to go." She motioned them to get ready.

Nicole quickly collected the items back into her basket and clicked the lid into place. For just a spit second, Benton could see how nervous she was to actually go. But then she smoothed a hand over her hip-length hair, fixed a sparkling smile onto her face, and surged to her feet. With the handle of the basket hooked over one arm, she reached out to help him up with the other. She must have been distracted, because not a trace of guilt crossed her face when his burned skin pressed against her palm. They ignored the angry, startled shrieks of the owls as they made their way to the car.

"Hypothetically, would you take it as concern or sexism if I suggested you don't come along?" Benton asked, while there was still enough distance between them and Dorothy, hoping that the question wouldn't be overheard.

Nicole hummed thoughtfully. "Mmm, I'm not sure. It would depend on the tone and wording you use. But either way, my response would be to remind you that I've saved your butt from two different monsters. You really don't do well on your own. Also, I'm always right."

"That's debatable," he muttered, unable to fight off a jaw-cracking yawn.

Ignoring his response, she reached into her basket, retrieved a slender thermos, and handed it to him without as much as a fleeting look.

"Spicy taco latte?"

"Of course!" she scoffed.

\*\*\*

The main street was bustling with energy. People hurried about, setting up stalls and draping just about every surface vibrant red, the color that was conveniently dominant in both the Canadian and Siksika Nation flags. Fort Wayward was not a place that let any holiday pass without thoroughly enjoying it. Canada Day was no exception. With her basket in her hand and backpack slung over one shoulder, Nicole slipped through the crowd. Benton was close to her side, a small frown tugging at his lips as he had to sidestep many other people.

"What is with all the people?" he muttered.

"Gee, I wonder if this influx of tourists has anything to do with an upcoming holiday or event," she teased as they passed someone stringing up a large 'Happy Canada Day' sign in their shop window. "What could it possibly be?"

"There's still three days to go," he shot back. "They don't need to be here yet."

"You sound like an old man telling kids to stay off his lawn," she laughed. "And don't worry. I have Canada Day all set."

"Why do I have a feeling you're about to start dictating a schedule I neither asked for nor agreed to?"

Ignoring him, she cleared her throat, "July first kicks off with a parade down Main Street."

"That's only four blocks."

"It turns back around to where it started from," she dismissed. "After that, we'll hit the school fair, which will give us just enough time for a few rides before you need to be at the baseball competition."

"I didn't volunteer for that," he said.

"I signed you up." She paused as they ducked under a string of decorations that was currently being raised. "Don't worry. You'll be on Zack's team."

"I hate Zack," he griped.

She rolled her eyes. "You do not."

"He hates me."

"That's more accurate," she concurred.

Benton did his best to keep his scowl, but failed miserably and ran a hand through his ruffled blonde hair.

His timid smile vanished when he caught sight of where they were headed. Dorothy had gone on ahead and was currently talking to Benton's parents, while teenagers roamed around them with backpacks on their shoulders.

"What didn't you tell me?" Benton asked, shooting her a narrowed gaze.

"Nothing. Have you seen Old Faithful yet?" Nicole asked, ignoring her unsatisfying answer, as she gestured to the old school bus. It only sat twelve passengers and its once vibrant yellow paint was faded with sun and age, but it had earned a place in the town's heart. "I'm sure I mentioned it. That's the bus we all get to use when we're learning to drive because no one cares if it gets another dent."

"Nicole," he said with a warning tone.

"I'm pretty sure that I mentioned that we were taking it," she added in a rushed mutter, "and that everyone there is coming with us."

He stopped in his tracks. "What?"

"I'm positive I mentioned it," she insisted.

"No, you didn't," he said. "I thought it was just going to be the three of us. This is kind of personal, Nic. I'm not really in the mood to put up with a whole bunch of people."

He still wasn't moving, so she reached back, grabbed his hand, and pulled him along. "No one wants their kids travelling the Highway of The Lost on their own. So we do it sort of like supervised trips. It's mom's turn to drive. She already agreed. Everyone would be super suspicious if she suddenly said she wasn't going to do it. Oh, and Meg and Danny are coming too. And your parents."

"I don't know what to respond to first," he stammered as he trudged along behind her. "You want me to sit in a bus for hours with my parents as well as Meg?"

"And Danny."

"I like Danny," Benton said. "Meg is the evil twin. And we're staying overnight, right? I have to put up with them for that long?"

"You'll have a different room," she defended. "And the crowd is part of the plan. Your parents are chaperons and mom has already warned them to keep an eye on Zack. So, when he runs off, because of course he will, we'll have a distraction to slip away and get you to the center and back before they even notice. See? This is all going to pan out nicely, and you should really stop questioning my genius."

She hurriedly moved towards the crowd, waving at the others and ignoring Benton as he called after her.

"Wait, Zack's coming?"

# Chapter 2

*There was too much. Too much to see, too much to feel. Too many bodies he was supposed to inhabit at once. He could feel his senses ripping like a tangible entity, as they stretched to accommodate the crush. There wasn't enough room within his skin for everything that wanted to crawl in. Images flashed across his eyes at a rapid pace. Overlapping. Blurring. Bleeding into an unmanageable mess. A thousand minds crammed into his own even while they hollowed him out. His head rippled and twisted and his focus tried to take in a thousand minds at once. The hurricane of sensation shredded him. He could feel himself lagging behind, torn apart down to his very cells. He opened his mouth and a dozen mouths moved. He tried to release the agony raging within him, but even the sound crumbled as the last parts of his mind were lost to the gaping void.*

***

Benton's spine bowed. There wasn't enough space between the seats for his long, aching legs. His knees slammed against the metal rim of the backseat in front of him as his head was thrown back. Unable to break free, his scream swelled within his ribcage, pulverizing his organs into mush. The unbearable pressure finally found its escape, not as a wail, but as a long, whimpering whine, like the hot steam from the molten core escaping from the earth. He couldn't breathe, couldn't move. Not until he was completely drained and exhausted, he slumped against the window by his side.

Slowly, he became aware of his mother repeatedly calling for him, her voice straining to cover her concern. He blinked but didn't try to respond. It took far too much energy to deal with the vibrations that still rattled around his core and strummed against his skin. The energy that rushed through him and around him numbed his mind into total silence. He didn't have a name.

Right now, his brain should have been on fire with an echoing name and an unbridled need to warn them. But there was nothing; no throbbing pain that kept growing when he took too long to send out the word. Finally, he was able to work down a dry gulp, and he ran his trembling fingers through his sweat-drenched hair.

"I'm okay," he said hoarsely before muttering an apology.

He didn't know who was close enough to hear it, but it was enough to stop his mother from repeating his name. The worn plastic covering of the chair squeaked as he straightened up. Pain zipped up through his nerves from his batted knees, and it took more effort than should be required to readjust his sunglasses on the bridge of his nose. His parents, sitting together in the front row of the bus, turned around to watch him carefully. Still, their attention restlessly flicked around their captivated audience, trying to judge how everyone was reacting to their son's outburst. Benton hunched his shoulders against the sensation of twelve pairs of eyes fixated upon him.

He flinched as Meg leaned forward and rested her arms on the back of his chair, an inch from his skull. "So that's what all the fuss is about, huh? Honestly, I expected something more impressive."

Benton watched as his mother's eyes widened. She glanced to her husband.

"You know about his night terrors?" his father, Theodore, asked.

A girl who Benton recognized from his biology class, sitting with her back pressed against the side of the bus a few seats in front of him, was the first to respond.

"Night terrors? I had a cousin who had those. He grew out of them when he was little, though."

Zack reached across the aisle and dumped his large hand onto Benton's skull. Nicole flattened herself against the seat to avoid Zack's forearm and glared at him. Ignoring her, Zack used his grip on Benton's head to shake him like a rattle.

"Aw, Benny-boy's a late bloomer," he grinned. "Don't shame him."

In unspoken unison, Benton and Nicole both smacked their hands into Zack's forearm, dislodging the huge boy's grip and forcing aside his long limb. Zack only laughed as he flopped back into his seat.

Danny giggled as she poked his cheek with one finger. "You made him blush. Look how red he is."

That was enough to get questions and smartass remarks hurdling around the limited space of the bus. Benton tried his best to ignore them and the apologetic look Nicole was throwing his way, and he focused instead on repairing the damage Zack had done to his hair.

"Benton," his mother's voice swiftly cut through the chatter. "Are you okay, sweetie?" No sooner was the question out, that his mother shifted her gaze to Dorothy. It didn't matter where she was looking, Benton knew the following comment was meant for his ears. "I hope that he didn't distract you. I'm sure he won't fall asleep again."

"It's fine, Cheyanne," Dorothy insisted.

Beside him, Nicole smiled brightly and called down the aisle. "Don't worry Mrs. Bertrand, I have you covered." She reached into the picnic basket on the floor, pulled out another thermos, and rattled it slightly in the air. "I brought some coffee for him."

While both of his parents smiled at her, neither of their expressions had any real warmth to it. Still, they thanked her, cast one more concerned look at Benton, and turned back to the front.

"Why don't your parents like me?" Nicole fumed quickly.

"Who cares?" Benton muttered, instantly reaching for the metal container.

"I'm exceedingly likable," she said, too distracted to release her grip as Benton tugged on the thermos. "Some would even say adorable."

"You tell 'em. Please give me the coffee," Benton rushed in one breath.

"Huh? Oh! Here's my Canada Day Special."

He slowly pried the thermos out of her hand. "What does that mean?"

"It's a red velvet, white chocolate latte."

Before he could ask again, Danny leaned forward once more. "It's red and white, like the flag."

Sitting in the seat in front of them, Meg twisted around and tucked some of her short, dark hair behind her ear. "Nicole makes up something like that every year." Her eyes brightened as she asked, "I don't suppose you brought snacks?"

Nicole's response was opening a floodgate. Benton and all his strange behavior was instantly forgotten, as everyone surged towards them to claim one of the assorted, baked goods that Nicole continued to pull from her picnic basket. He immersed himself deeper into the corner of the window-seat chair, attempting to get out of the way and protect his drink. Sipping the still steaming sweet concoction, he popped in his earphones, selected a song on his phone, and just watched Nicole preen under the attention.

The smile on his lips died, as a wave of frost descended on them like a heavy fog. It seeped into his bones and spread out to infest his flesh, leaving him shivering in its wake. He turned his head to watch the world passing by outside his window, desperately trying to pinpoint what had changed. Why he now felt like he had been swallowed by an arctic wind.

The noonday sun bathed the world in a buttery glow and pressed a layer of heat against the glass. He could feel it. He could tell that the air around him hadn't shifted at all. But still, he couldn't stop shivering. The road twisted out before them, curving down into the valley created by the rolling hills. A scattering of trees rose tall, lined up along the crystal stream that glistened along the very bottom of the pit, their leaves only just beginning to turn golden orange with the coming of autumn.

Shadows danced across him, and he squinted into the glare of the window to spot the large carnivorous birds. They swept past on silent wings and lined the towering branches, the sunlight glimmering off the twin tufts on either side of their heads. His brow furrowed when he noticed that some of the shadows didn't have the tufts that gave the great horned owl their name.

He pressed closer to the glass and craned his neck, trying to get a better look at the creatures that weaved through the dying branches. Their numbers made the branches bow and bounce. Dead leaves shook loose, creating a crimson rain that captured the sunlight as it fell. The debris twisted and turned. The shadowy creatures came with them.

Benton jolted back in his seat. The dark shapes didn't fall. They simply existed in midair, peeking out from behind the leaves to watch him with penetrating eyes. As soon as he spotted them, they were easier to notice. They lurked behind tree trunks, littered the branches high above, and peered through the layers of lush grass. Everywhere the light couldn't reach became a hiding place for the fathomless beings. Their glowing eyes followed the bus as it passed.

Benton's heart throbbed painfully and his body temperature dropped the longer he met the unknown entity's gaze. His fingers grew numb, and he clutched the thermos close to him, attempting to force some of the lingering heat back into his skin. Pain tingled along his feet, the skin becoming raw and tender with an icy feeling in them. Forcing himself to sit back, he squeezed his eyes shut. Warmth still swept through him with every trembling breath, but now more mildly, as a stream instead of a gushing torrent.

The sunlight that played across his face slowly seeped away, taking with it the last traces of heat that loitered in the air. Refusing to open his eyes, Benton hurriedly gulped down his drink. The liquid burned his lips where it made contact and scorched a path to the pit of his stomach. For a brief, incredible moment, he felt it slosh out against the blizzard within his core. But it wasn't enough. Bit by bit, the coffee cooled within him until it was like sleet lining his insides.

He jolted as one of his earphones tugged free, the music replaced by Nicole's worried whisper. "Benton?"

All of the conversations happening around them continued without hesitation, and he figured that everyone must have already gone back to their seats, treats in hand. He didn't know if anyone else was still hanging around near them, but he didn't want to look.

"I'm okay," he mumbled and took another sip.

"Your lips are going blue."

She kept her voice low, relying on the limited space between them to ensure that she wasn't heard by anyone else. It made her breath ghost across his skin like a tropical breeze. Shivering, he hurriedly drank more of the fluid. It felt like ice water had replaced his blood, and the pricking, numb sensation was quickly working its way up his legs. His face began to ache with the effort he took in squeezing his eyelids shut so tightly.

"How long was I asleep?" he asked.

"Not long," she said before catching onto the real meaning of his question.

The plastic covering of the seat squeaked as she slid closer to him, pressing her side against his. Even through the layers of clothing separating them, her body felt like a blazing bonfire, and he leaned in closer for the slight relief. He could feel the inhuman eyes upon him. Watching him. Almost as if the living shadows were right next to him. He longed to look, to assure himself that they weren't that close. But he couldn't shake the feeling that one more glance and he might just die of hypothermia.

"We just got on the highway," she said like an apology. "It'll still be a few hours."

Benton jerked when he felt something touch his arm. Heat radiated from Nicole's hand, burning his skin, a painful salvation. She inched her fingers along his palm, coaxing him to release his grip on the thermos and accept the comfort she offered. He tilted his hand slightly and she threaded her fingers with his own. Instantly, he clenched tightly to the searing warmth and released a shaky sigh as the agonizing throb began to soften.

His skin crawled, as the sensation of being watched intensified. It took every ounce of willpower he had to keep his eyes closed as his paranoid thoughts began to whirl out of control, conjuring up a thousand options of what could be lurking on the other side of the window. Nicole pressed as close to him as she could, without drawing any unwanted attention, and he quickly chugged down the coffee. Its temperature seemed to climb with every swallow until he was sure his throat was blistering. Still, it wasn't enough to keep the chill from returning. Sitting as still as his quivering body would allow, he longed once again for them to be alone. It was better when it was just the two of them, when he could tell her what was happening, what he was seeing and feeling, without worrying about being overheard. Now, all he could do was clench his jaw shut, and endure the concern that he felt drifting from her like waves.

The hours stretched on and he restlessly shifted in his seat with growing discomfort. With time, it wasn't just the cold. Two very large coffees, in a short period of time, kept him awake but weren't very compatible with long car trips. While it served as a good distraction from the hateful gazes and his skin turning to ice, the more he focused on it, the more desperately he needed to pee. Nicole's hand felt like the only point of reality left for him, and he clung to it above all else. A shaky sigh of pure relief left his trembling lips as the bus came to a halt. He had made it.

"Okay, guys," Dorothy called out over the restless crowd. "Same rules as always. Move in groups, only go to the store and back, and you have fifteen minutes max."

Benton's insides churned and his grip tightened on Nicole's hand. "We're not there?"

"No," she whispered. "We're just making a pit stop."

He could barely bring himself to breathe the words, "How long have we got until we get there?"

It didn't matter that she squeezed his hand and sympathetically rubbed his forearm with her free one. Her reply still gutted him.

"We're about halfway."

He snapped around to face her, the moment of dread flinging his eyes open before he remembered why that would be a bad idea. They had been enclosed for so long that the minimal light stung his eyes as they struggled to adjust. Despite his fears, he didn't find himself face to face with a glaring shadow.

Apparently, he wasn't the only one in need of a little relief, since the bus was quickly emptying. No one paid them any attention, but he still kept his voice low anyway.

"I don't want to be here," he said.

She met his soft tone, "Me neither." A warm smile crossed her face. "Here's the plan. You hit the restroom and get back on the bus. I'll see what I can find in the restaurant that can warm you up. Okay?"

He was too cold and uncomfortable to even reply, so he simply nodded, yanked the remaining earpiece free, and tossed it onto the seat. Mercifully, she didn't let go of his hand as they made their way out of the bus.

Blundering down the few stairs, Benton got off the bus and got his first look at the truck stop. Sitting atop a sea of concrete, the structure was relatively new, with only fifteen years of wear at the most. The main parts, behind two rows of gas pumps big enough to accommodate long haul trucks, were covered with fake wood planks to give it the appearance of a log cabin. A blue neon diner sign was placed in the window, the gathering gloom turning the light into a smudged halo. Narrow standalone cabins speckled the clearing on either side of the main building, most of them drenched in the gathering shadows. A sickly hum above them made him lift his gaze, and he noticed the large neon sign marking the place as 'Lost Woods Motel.'

As a bid to distract him, Nicole had been continuously talking. He was vaguely aware of her telling him that the motel had been opened as a way to give people walking the road, a safe place to spend the night. But all of the finer details were lost to the mist in his brain. The rest of what she was saying floated as he looked up to see the owls that swamped the dark sky and filled the surrounding trees like a swarm of insects. Nicole took a few steps. Benton didn't. She noticed quickly and turned to give him a questioning look.

"I thought you said the trip was only a few hours," he mumbled.

She tilted her head in confusion. "It is."

He sucked in a deep breath, the warmth of the air drawing down into his core, as he closed his eyes.

"It's not dusk, is it?" he asked, feeling a lump forming in the back of his throat.

"Benton, it's two PM," she said gently. She edged closer to him and lowered her voice into a whisper. "What do you see?"

As he forced his eyes open, he looked over the swirling darkness that lingered over the area like a living creature. The sudden rush of sheer dread that the sight provoked, made him dizzy. If it weren't for his desperate need to get into a restroom, he would have given into his urge to rush back into the bus and curl into a tight ball. Barely able to bring himself to meet her gaze, he shook his head quickly, his voice cracking as he whispered.

"This isn't a good place."

She quickly came back to his side and recaptured his frozen hand.

"In and out," she promised.

He nodded. Together, they raced across the lot. The door to the diner opened with the tinkle of a bell above the door. Instantly, they were met by the smoky scents of burgers and fries. While there were only ten teenagers in total, they seemed to fill the limited space that served as both a souvenir and a gas station shop. With an impressive amount of noise, they grabbed at bags of junk food, and studied the odds and ends that filled every tourist trap. Meeting Nicole's gaze, he yanked his wallet out of his pockets and pulled out a few bills.

"Coffee, please," he said.

She was already moving towards the annexed diner as she snatched the bills out of his hand. "Don't take this as approval of your addiction."

Benton rolled his eyes, but enjoyed the attempt at lightening the mood. A quick scan of the room and he found the sign for the toilets off in the corner. The bathroom was old but clean, with only two stalls and pale walls. Even though he had to impatiently wait for his turn, there was still a line when he was done. He was washing up when he discovered just how good their hot water system was.

The steaming water sloshing over his frozen hands felt incredible and he wallowed in the luxury of having his blood running into his fingers once again. Once they felt warm and plump, he pulled off his sunglasses and washed his face. The sensation made pins-and-needles crackle across his lips and cheeks. He kept splashing the water over his face until the pain subsided and he was feeling less like a living snowman.

Turning off the tap, he blindly tugged a few paper towels from the dispenser and dried himself off. The rough edges of the paper scraped across his cheek when the sensation of being watched came back with a higher intensity. His now sensitive skin made the shift in temperature instantly noticeable. It was an encroaching warmth, as if someone was standing right behind him, almost draped against his curled spine. A heavy sigh brushed past his ear, the moisture of the breath clinging to his skin.

Benton whirled around, one arm striking out to shove back the person crowded against him. The bathroom was empty. The low drone of the florescent lights broke the silence as the lingering traces of a person's body heat evaporated from his back. Throwing the wadded paper into the sink, he strode towards the door, grabbing the doorknob just as a hand latched around his ankle.

One swift jerk and he was wretched off of his feet. He was barely able to break his fall as he was slammed down painfully against the tiles. Before he could understand what had just happened, he was being dragged back. He clawed at the floor but couldn't find something to grip. Hands grappled their way up his legs, their fingers digging against his tender flesh with an iron grasp. He thrashed out, kicking sharply, but his feet never found anything solid.

The hands reached his hips and easily flipped him onto his back. He bolted upright and saw her. A woman was crawling her way out of the floor, her movements swift but broken as she hurled herself higher up his body. Muddy clumps of earth dripped from her skin and thumped against his stomach. Her hair, matted and reeking of rot, swayed with the jolts of her limbs. Rearing up to level her face with Benton's, the woman opened her mouth and spewed wet earth over his chest.

It hit him like arctic water, startling him out of his stunned state and igniting his survival instinct. He shoved her off and surged to his feet. The soles of his shoes slipped and skidded over the muck covered tiles making him stumble as he tried to flee to the door. Flinging it open, he threw himself out, smacked into someone, and turned around to catch sight of the woman crawling after him just as the door swung shut.

"What the hell, Benny-boy?" Zack snapped, his voice lingering somewhere between annoyed and amused. "It's a door. You've used them before."

Breathing heavily, he swiped his trembling hands over his chest. His jacket was clean. His eyes locked onto the bathroom door.

"What is wrong with you?" Zack asked.

He walked around Benton and opened the door before Benton could do more than grunt in protest. The brightly lit room was empty, the tiled floor clean. Zack glanced over his shoulder. Whatever he was going to say faded along with his smirk.

"Seriously," Zack's voice became concerned. "What's wrong?"

"I tripped," Benton muttered. "Sorry."

He barely took a step forward before Zack's hand grabbed his forearm.

"I know you think I'm an idiot, but I can tell the difference between startled and scared."

Benton pulled his arm free and raced back to the safety of the bus. He didn't turn back even as Zack yelled after him.

# Chapter 3

Cradling the plush toy in her hands, Nicole lifted it until the beak of the loon bird hovered about an inch beside Benton's face. She waited for him to stop shivering to notice that she was watching him, and he turned his head slightly. He jolted the second he saw the toy so close to his face and muttered a curse.

"Loon," she cooed, until the word was longer than it should have been.

He shook his head.

She pushed up the toy's wing. "Wing five."

That was the tipping mark and he sputtered a laugh. Finally, a smile crossed his face, replacing the pinched expression that he had worn ever since he had bolted from the store.

"You're an idiot," he muttered.

While they weren't the most flattering words, they were the first ones he had spoken in a bit over two hours, so she took it as a victory. Bringing the toy back down into his lap, she shrugged.

"I'm just playing to my audience."

He cast her a sharp look before rolling his eyes. Benton couldn't exactly be called tanned, but his skin always had a healthy, pinkish hue that prevented him from being pale. Now he looked like ice. His lips were rimmed blue, and the dark shadows under his eyes were like deep bruises that went down to his bone. There hadn't been many edibles in the shop, so she had bought coffee, and a basket of fries, of which she ended up eating half. She also bought some cheap red mittens that she doubted were doing much good. About an hour ago, people had started to take notice and offered him their jackets to use as blankets. He had several piled onto him, but he was still visibly shaking, looking like he had just come out of a snowstorm.

"Why did you get that?" he asked, eyeing the toy bird with suspicion.

A smile crossed her face. "Tradition. Every time I had to make this trip, my dad would buy me a toy. I'm going to take a picture of myself with it and send it to him when we get cell reception again."

"There's no reception out here?" he asked, his teeth chattering around each word.

Meg twisted around and rested her chin on the back of the seat. "We're going to get it right after we get on that bus route. You look horrible."

Benton arched an eyebrow. "I'm fine, thanks."

"Seriously, it's not even that cold. How are you going to survive the winter?"

"Indoors," he snapped and snuggled deeper under the jackets.

Danny turned around to join the conversation. For a moment, the twins vied for space on the small bench seats, then Danny smiled and gave Nicole a little knowing smile.

"Speaking of traditions," she said, obviously trying to recapture Benton's attention before he fell back into silence, "are we raiding the vending machine again?"

Zack was instantly in on the conversation. He hopped across the slim aisle, pushing and squishing the twins until they made enough room for him to sit.

"Candy and ghost stories. A tradition worth keeping," he grinned.

"Great," Danny chirped. "This is going to be fun! We might actually have new stories."

"How?" Meg barked a laugh.

"Because we have a new addition to the group," Danny said, as she gestured to Benton.

He peeked over the edge of the jackets before scrunching up closer to the window.

"Oh, he seems like he'll be a pile of fun," Meg muttered.

Danny smacked her arm.

"I'm sure he knows something scary," Zack said, easily reaching over the back of the chair and swatting Benton's leg. "Come on, Benny-boy. Tell me something scary."

Nicole pushed his arm away before he could whack Benton again. No one actually expected him to answer. He was still hidden, pressed to the side of the bus, his voice a vacant mutter.

"Allison Conway."

Nicole's chest squeezed with a painful clench as she flicked her eyes across the others. They all shared the same look. She didn't know what to say until Benton continued, "Someone said her name in the store. They said it weird. Anyone ever heard of her?"

Nicole was quick to answer. "She's one of the missing girls I was telling you about."

The moment the words left her mouth, she realized the importance of the question. He had seen her. And there had been something in the encounter that had truly terrified him.

\*\*\*

Leaving that stretch of the highway was like stepping out of a freezer. The air within his little fortress of jackets instantly became humid and stale. He gulped down the warm air until he could feel it thawing the ice that had gathered around his bones. Timidly, he sat up straighter, poked his head out of the layers of jackets and glanced out the window. Life flooded the valley below them with massive buildings and a large scattering of homes. Cars sped around them, while dark, heavy clouds rolled in to cover the sky. It released a menacing rumble of thunder as the bus jerked to a stop. It was the first time in months that he had seen a stop light.

Next to Fort Wayward, the small town of Peace Springs looked like a sprawling metropolis, even if a noticeable few buildings were standing vacant.

The lights changed and Dorothy drove the bus around the corner, passing by a brightly lit Tim Horton and entering into the vast parking lot of a hotel. She pulled up in one of the lots in front of the door and instantly stood up. It took her a few attempts to get the attention of the suddenly restless crowd.

"Remember," she said, each word brimming with authority. "This hotel is under no obligation to give us such a great discount. If they change their minds, we will be stuck using the hotel on the far side of town."

Benton had no idea what was wrong with that other place, but everyone made it clear with grumbles and groans that it was a horrible option.

"We are not to abuse their hospitality. Act like adults."

With a chorus of agreement, everyone started to gather their things at a more relaxed pace. People collected their jackets as they passed. Benton thanked them, grateful to get rid of the stifling heat, and smiled when they commented that he was looking a lot better. Nicole practically beamed at him as they waited for everyone else to clear out. He cringed at the looks Zack and the twins shot him as they headed off.

"They're not going to let this go," Benton muttered as they followed.

It was hard to put as much venom into the words as he had wanted to. After the last few hours, he felt near ecstatic just to be able to move his fingers properly. He hopped off the bus with a bit more enthusiasm and took a deep breath of the fresh air. It filled his nostrils, laced with the energy of the approaching storms and the scent of coffee and donuts.

He smiled at her. "Think they'll believe I have a medical condition?"

"You kind of do," she teased as they rounded the bus. "Has that ever happened before?"

Benton shook his head.

"Maybe it's like one of those compensation things," Nicole said. "Like when someone goes blind and their hearing gets better. You're not dreaming so you're becoming more sensitive to other things."

It was impossible to keep from smirking just a little. "Now, that's a scientific statement, Rider."

She spun around to face him, walking backwards and jabbing him in the chest with the loon. "You just don't like admitting you have feelings. Or that I'm right."

"I have plenty of feelings. Annoyance is one that comes to mind." His words trailed off when he noticed something out of the corner of his eyes.

A green sedan was parked on the far side of the lot, the beginnings of rust cutting along the edges of the metal, a slight dent creating a thin crack along one of the taillights. Nicole walked beside him and followed his gaze.

"What is it?"

He shook his head. "I don't know."

"Communication, Benton," she reminded in a sing-song tone.

"The green car," he said, no longer sure if he should be scowling or smiling. "Something about it." At a loss for how else to explain it, he just shrugged.

She pressed the loon bird plushy against his chest. "Hold Bartholomew for a second."

He numbly took hold of it as she rummaged in her backpack. Retrieving her mobile phone, she clicked a photograph. That done, she shoved the phone into the pocket of her skirt and plucked the loon from his grip. "We better catch up."

He caught up to her. "You can't name that thing *Bartholomew*."

"Too late."

"That's my middle name," he grumbled as she picked up her pace.

"So? You don't *own* that name."

With one last fleeting glance back at the car, Benton picked up his pace and followed her into the hotel lobby.

\*\*\*

The rooms weren't quite ready, so Dorothy had decided that they would all head across the street to a pizza parlor for an early dinner. Their group took up a few booths and most of the other tables had been filled with families also looking to get fed and go home before the storm hit. The constant clatter had been oddly comforting and Benton had relaxed into the flow of it. A few slices of pizza, and he actually got through a full conversation with Zack, the only insults being thrown around relatively harmless.

Thunder cracked across the sky, loud enough to almost make the building rumble. The rain fell in heavy sheets and they had stayed a few more hours to see if it would let up, but it only showered harder. Eventually, the rooms were ready and they couldn't put off heading back any longer. The short walk was enough to soak them all to the bone, and it was only when they were collecting their keys that Benton realized the hotel itself was actually divided into three separate buildings to allow people to pull their cars up to their rooms. It also meant that they would take another walk in the icy rain.

A few were lucky enough to have rooms in the main building and headed up only after they had systematically mocked every person who had to head back outside. Naturally, Nicole was to share a room with her mother in one of the outside buildings. Since Benton's parents were the other chaperones, they had a room in the building on the opposite side of the parking lot. The thought of leaving Nicole to dart into the rain alone hadn't sat well with him. A ball of dread had formed within him and grew with every second. She reminded him that she was well protected and promised that they would meet up back at the vending machines in the main building after a warm shower and, hopefully, after the rain had died down.

Ducking into the downpour, Benton had given up on preventing it from seeping into his eyes and instead turned his attention to trying to keep his bag relatively dry. He hadn't succeeded, and almost everything he had brought was damp by the time he reached the far-ended room. His parents had been caught up making sure that everyone else got to their correct rooms, and he had entered the small room alone.

Water dripped from him in rivets and soaked into the carpet as he dropped his backpack onto the small round table against the wall. Once again frozen to his core, his fingers fumbled over the zipper, the soaked material of his bag not helping the process of opening it. He tipped the contents out, searching for what had been left relatively dry. He found a pair of sweatpants and a T-shirt that would at least be better than what he was currently wearing.

A flash of lightening rattled around the edges of the drawn curtains, chasing off the dull gray shadows for only a moment before allowing their return. With his items in hand, he padded across the room and into the condensed bathroom. It was only as he turned the shower on that he remembered it would have probably been smarter if he had taken off his shoes before entering the room. He quickly glanced at the carpet and found that he was able to trace each step he had taken by the soggy trail of footsteps looking like ink in the lingering dim light. But there wasn't any mud, so he figured it wouldn't be too big of a fallout for his absentmindedness.

More thunder broke as he turned the shower on, loud enough to shake the florescent tube of the bathroom light against its case. He stared at it. The wind was picking up, turning into a raging howl and condensing the storm clouds now occupying the last rays of sunlight. It was going to get dark fast and he had to decide what was worse; the shadows or the memories that sound could dredge up. He remembered the weight of the woman on top of him and instead decided that the flashlight on his mobile would suffice for tonight.

His fingers felt numb and useless as he pulled the device from his waterlogged jeans and set it up on the counter. Lightening severed the shadows, the thunder that followed strong enough to ricochet within his chest. By now, the wind howled across the walls and squeezed into every gap it found, like a gasped scream. He ducked out of the bathroom just long enough to snatch up one of the chairs and wedge it against the bathroom door. Modesty be damned, he wasn't planning on getting stuck in there.

Steam formed over the top of the shower curtain, the warmth it offered reminding him how cold he was. He pulled the wet clothes from his body, tossed them into a slush pile in one of the corners, and finally stepped under the wondrous spray. His skin flushed and he quickly set to work lathering the hotel shampoo into his hair.

There was a faint noise.

He froze, the suds streaming down his face as he strained to hear anything beyond the noise of the shower and the rampaging storm. Nothing. *Maybe the wind just threw something against the window,* he reasoned. At the same time, deep in the back of his mind, his brain identified the sound. Someone had opened the room door. With a few quick swipes, he washed his face clean. His stomach flipped as he pulled the curtain back just enough to slip his head through.

Steam streamed out from the gap, curling in the cool air of the room. It played with the light from the phone, transforming it into a haze that dispersed and dulled the light at the same time. Goose bumps broke out across his skin as he leaned a little further out of the warmth of the shower, stretching and craning his neck to get a peek around the corner of the doorway.

A bolt of lightning lit the sky, turning the driving rain into droplets of silver as the wind whipped them across the now empty threshold and into the room. The open door swung slightly from the gusts of wind, as the rain soaked into the carpet.

"M...Mom?" Benton stuttered. He couldn't hear any reply over the shower and quickly turned the taps off with one hand as the other clenched the shower curtain in an attempt to cover himself. "Dad?"

Thunder broke across the silence that filled the darkened room. On shaky legs, he stepped out of the shower, now wishing that he hadn't propped the bathroom door open. The frozen air, that now assailed the room, only highlighted how exposed he was as it played against his bare skin. He had to lean across the open space to reach the towel rack on the far-ended wall. He stretched as far as he could but he had to take another step out.

His fingertips snatched at the towel as his foot hit something slick and cold. His hip slammed against the tiles and he flopped onto his back, the soft towel scrunching up on his face as it dropped from the rack. Instantly, he jolted upright, using the towel to cover himself as he tried to see what he had fallen in.

It was slick against his palm and he lifted his hand to his eyes, staring at the black gunk but unable to identify it. For an instant, a lightning strike turned the night into day and he could see the entire room in vivid detail. Mud. He was sitting in a thick trail of mud. From the corner of his eyes, he could see the front door, where the trail began. The lurching, splotched, drag mark stained the carpet, working its way across the room. Into the bathroom. The light dulled again but the glow of his phone was enough to see that the trail didn't end where he sat. It slithered into the tub.

The shower curtain shifted and bunched, the scanty material moving aside as the tips of fingers rose up from under it. His eyes bulged and he scrambled further back against the wall as the fingers slithered and jerked into sight. They clutched at the rim of the tub, broken nails clawing for perches, clumps of sodden earth dripping from its skin. The second arm flung out over the rim and slapped against the floor just an inch from his foot.

Benton bolted upright, bringing the towel with him less for modesty and more because fear kept his fingers from releasing their death grip on the fabric. He barreled out the door, across the room, into the ferocious storm without a single glance behind. The wind lashed his bare skin, driving the icy rain into him like stones as the torrents of water rushed over his feet.

Two panted breaths were all it took for him to lose every ounce of warmth he had garnished. He whirled around, looking back to his room as he shivered from more than just the cold. A clap of thunder shook the ground under his feet as glacial water streamed over his face, blurring his vision and choking his every gasp for air. His hands were shaking as he worked the drenched piece of cloth around his waist. His hands clutched tight to the fabric, holding it just to have something to hold onto.

A streak of movement caught his eye. He looked up to the ledge just above his door. Black, shadowy masses of owls lined the entire building, the pointed feathers looking demonic in the pouring rain. Like grotesque gargoyles, the birds lined every roof top, their eyes reflecting the lightning bolts like plates of polished silver. They swooped overheard, their massive shadows silhouetted by the sky. There was something familiar about the sight that made his heart stagger. A fear he had never known engulfed him, filling every inch of his skin like a sickening virus.

The sky broke again in anger, and with the glow of the bolt, he saw the woman once more, crawling across the floor, her winding hand reaching for him as she vomited an endless trail of dirt and rot.

He ran faster than the bolts of lightning in the dark sky above.

Steam lingered, fogging up Nicole's bathroom mirror as she finished brushing her hair. The storm had rolled in so rapidly that she was sure it would have moved on by the time she had gotten out of the shower. But now, she was showered, dressed, and almost ready to go meet the others, and it seemed like the storm was only getting stronger. The biting wind worked its way under her room door, filling the air and making her shiver.

The long shower hadn't helped her figure out just what had happened to Benton. She had known that it might not be an easy trip for him, given the history of the road and his new skill of seeing ghosts. But she had never seen him react like that. The true extent of his abilities was still a mystery to them both. Just when they thought they had everything sorted out, they discovered something new, or something changed.

That level of uncertainty made it hard to know just how he would react, but she had seen him interacting with Oliver, seen how the ghost scared him, unnerved him, annoyed him. None of the ghost's antics had ever caused a physical response, not a sight, sound, or even smell. And she had been prepared for all of that. She brought a portable charger for his phone to make sure his music kept playing. She also had several perfumed handkerchiefs in her bag, small enough to hide in the palm of his hand if he was feeling self-conscious about it. She had thought she was prepared to help him endure it.

Gathering her long, straight hair over one shoulder, she placed her brush down on top of the toilet tank, the clatter of wood against porcelain was lost under the crack of a lightning bolt sizzling across the sky.

"What did Allison do to him?" she thought aloud, her voice barely over a whisper. Straightening her back, she forced herself to meet her own eyes in the mirror. "Trip one was a failure," she admitted to herself sternly. "That much is clear. So now you'll just have to make sure that everything is ready for trip two. First step, force Benton to talk to you. Second step." She hesitated, uncertainty creeping back in around the corners of her mind. Before it could take hold, she forced a smile and declared with confidence, "Do something about it."

It wasn't much of a plan, but it was a plan, and having one helped her feel like she was on solid ground again. Keeping her smile firmly fixed in place, she blindly reached for the jewelry that she had placed on the counter. She had fallen in love with the matching choker and bracelet set she had bought at the Sundance Festival a few months ago; it had quickly become her favorite. It fixed around her throat in a splash of red and black, while the thick trails of beaded chains created a large orange disk at the base of her neck. The bracelet had the same pattern set in a band of dullish metal. Her fingertips swiped over the chilled porcelain sink, unable to find the large mass of beads that should have been there.

Nicole glanced down and frowned at the now empty spot behind the tap. A sickly feeling crept into her stomach and she quickly spun around. A thunderclap crashed overhead, shattering the silence as the basin rim became a solid press against her spine. The small bathroom was empty. Thin steam created a drifting cloud and the harsh light left little room for shadows. She couldn't see anything, but that didn't mean nothing was there.

Reaching back, she clutched at the sink and tried to slow down her breaths, concentrating on that instead of the lurking fear that the Dullahan had come back for her. It was dead, Benton promised that it was and she trusted that. Still, after almost getting thrown to her death seemingly by thin air, it was hard to trust silence.

Her body jerked with the next booming clap of thunder, her grip on the sink keeping her from falling on the tiles in a protective position. The sound rolled out, leaving behind a soft clatter of metal rattling against tiles. Turning again, she stooped down to glance around the chilled bathroom floor. In the far corner, propped up against the wall, was her bracelet. She crouched down, picked it up, and searched the room once more. No necklace. Just her bracelet, too far away from the sink and on too sharp of an angle to have simply fallen. Her stomach churned.

"Dullahan?" she asked. The rain pattered against the ground outside. The wind howled as it toyed with the cracks in the building. But the room remained silent. Her tongue slipped out to wet her dry lips before she whispered, "Allison?"

A startled squeal escaped her throat as someone began to pound against her room door. She stood up, fingers tightening around the metal in her hands, and watched the door shake with every strike.

"Hello?"

If there was a reply, the torrential rain covered it. The furious knocking grew louder, the blow hammering against the slab of wood, making it buck against its frame and forcing the chain lock to rattle. It and the deadbolt were both in place and she was certain that the twin locks would keep out any human intruder. But there were things other than human that no lock could stand against. That knowledge left her shivering as she edged to the bathroom door and called again. Still no response. Dread made her feet heavy but she forced herself to step out onto the carpet, closer to the door. *It could be Zack,* she reminded herself. *He's not good at being subtle.* The comforting thought diminished with every step she took. Her eyes never left the rattling wood.

"Who's there?"

Beside the now desperate assault against the door, there was no reply. Her head became a swamp of all the things that could be waiting for her on the other side. Monsters both paranormal and human. She couldn't stop herself from remembering just where she was and what happened in places like this. It was quite possible that opening the door was a mistake that some of the missing girls had made before her. Nipping her teeth on her bottom lip, Nicole shook herself out of her stupor. She shoved the bracelet on her wrist and rushed for her backpack which was on the small table halfway between her and the door, her gun still stowed in one of the zipper pockets.

The pounding on the door and continuous storm covered the soft scrape of her working the zipper open. Eyes fixated on the door, she slipped her hand inside her soaked backpack and pulled out her gun. Only the slightest hint of water covered the metal; far too little for it to affect the workings of the weapon. The heavy weight, solid in her grasp made her feel a little sturdier. With practiced confidence, she checked the gun the way her parents had taught her, making sure that everything was as it should be.

Holding it in one hand, she crossed the remaining distance to the door quickly. This time, she didn't call out. There was no need to try and keep her footsteps silent. The rain, wind, and carpet worked together to smother any traces of her movements. Pressing one hand against the door, she stood on tiptoes, bit her lip, and glanced through the peephole.

The patch of blonde hair removed her fear in a sudden rush as she slumped against the door.

"Benton, you scared the hell out of me!" she yelled with a nervous laugh.

Even though she was sure he would have heard her this time, he didn't stop his frenzied onslaught. She fumbled the chain lock off with her free hand and flipped the deadbolt, half expecting him to rush in the first second he could. He only stopped slamming his fists against the door when she pulled the door wide open. He just stood there.

Water plastered his hair to his scalp and trailed down his body in puddles, leaving him pale and shivering. His mouth hung open but he didn't make a sound. He only heaved his breaths and stared at her with wide eyes. A drenched towel was wrapped around his hips but was steadily slipping, dragged down under its own weight. He didn't make a move to stop it. Both of his hands remained in the air, as if he didn't know what to do with them now that he couldn't pound at her door anymore. He looked terrified.

"Benton?"

He only stared at her, water trickling from his lips each time he heaved a breath. Trying not to startle him, she slowly lifted her free hand to gently cup his wrist. She almost flinched away when the deathly chill that clung to his skin brushed against her own.

"Benton, come in, okay?" she eased.

Slowly, and with a lot more coaxing, he took his first step across the threshold. Water poured from him and soaked into the carpet, marking each of his steps with a noticeable squish. His eyes were locked somewhere over her shoulder but she was too focused on getting him out of the storm to pay it any attention.

"What's going on?" she asked.

Still, he remained silent. He didn't turn to look at her as she pushed the door closed, but he flinched at the sound. She reached for the deadbolt and he whispered his first word.

"Don't."

"I can't just leave the door unlocked," she said, before she caught onto what his request meant.

He wanted to make sure that if he had to flee, he could do it easily, which meant that he wasn't just worried about whatever was out there – whatever had made him run naked through a storm. He was also worried that there might be something in here.

"Okay." Her voice was gentle, but her fingers were like stone around the gun handle. "Just until we get you warmed up, okay?"

Silent, Benton stood in the middle of the room, the puddle at his feet creating an ever-increasing mark on the carpet. In the brighter light of the room, she could see his normally pink complexion turning into a hint of blue. She noticed the mild quiver of his body, and the protective hunch in his shoulders. He didn't say anything. He just stood there, staring at the bathroom door.

"Let me get some towels," Nicole said, as she slipped past him.

His hand shot out and latched onto her. His grip tightened, forcing the bracelet to grind painfully against the bones of her wrist. With a sharp wince, she tried to pull away. He wouldn't let go. She put her hand over his and pried at his unmoving fingers.

"Benton, you're hurting me."

His eyes shifted back to her, but he could only meet her gaze for a moment before the bathroom dragged his attention back.

"Don't go in there," he said in a broken whimper, as if worried they were being overheard.

She didn't hesitate. "Okay."

Instantly, his grip loosened until he was only gently holding her wrist, with a limp handgrip that she could easily pull herself free from. She didn't move. As much as Benton shied away from human contact, the sense of touch calmed him, and he needed that now.

"But we still need to get you dry." The words weren't enough to make him look at her, as his eyes remained steadfast on the threshold to the bathroom. "Should I close the door?"

He nodded as if there wasn't a single muscle in his neck. He still didn't let her go. Careful not to make any sudden movements, she twisted her wrist and worked herself free from his icy grip. It was hard to make her steps as confident as he needed, and as cautious as he wanted, but she found a pace that seemed to keep him from going into an outright panic.

She couldn't fight off the slight tremble that claimed her hands. As subtly as she could, she flicked the gun's safety off. The storm overpowered the sound of the sharp clack, and it didn't draw his attention. Slowly, she lifted her free hand and inched her fingers towards the door handle. No matter how hard she focused, she couldn't see what was keeping Benton so transfixed.

The bathroom door was open with plenty of space for something to lurk behind it, unseen. Steam still lingered against the ceiling, catching the glow of the florescent light. The room was bright. Clean. A normal bathroom in a normal room. Whatever had captured Benton's attention, she couldn't see it. Her stomach knotted up painfully and each heartbeat slammed against her ribs.

Her hand lingered over the door, still not touching it, but close enough to feel the slight chill that clung to the metal. She couldn't get her hand to close around it. Glancing over her shoulder, she captured Benton's gaze. The storm raged just beyond the room, filling the air with a clash of clouds and sparks of electricity with the rain thundering against the roof like a charging stampede. Droplets shook loose as his trembling increased. She couldn't tell if it was from the cold or from fear. The blue flush had seeped into his lips. He needed to get dry. She took half a step into the bathroom and his response was instantaneous.

"Don't."

The word was barely audible over the onslaught outside, but it made her freeze. Swallowing hard, one hand still hovering in the air, the gun heavy and solid in the other, she could barely bring herself to ask the question that screamed within her head.

"Benton," she whispered. "What's in the bathroom?"

"Collin Page."

Her stomach plummeted and her lungs tightened. "What is he doing?"

"Staring," Benton's voice was numb.

"At who?"

Benton remained silent until she was sure she was about to crawl out of her skin. "Close the door."

Nicole gripped the handle and slammed it shut. She staggered back a few steps before she remembered that she was supposed to be the calm one in the room, and forced herself to stand steady again. She drew in a deep breath and fixed a smile onto her face.

"Okay," she said in a light tone that oozed with manufactured happiness. "Collin obviously wants some privacy and we're going to give it to him. I don't need that brush and we can just use the bathroom in the hotel lobby. He'll stay in there and we'll stay out here."

A sharp clatter was heard from behind the closed door, as she looked down to see her necklace slip out from under the bathroom door. The beads became a tangled mess as it tumbled over the carpet and came to a stop just an inch from her bare toes. She stared down at the glistening beads, her jaw slack, and her stomach turning to ice. Benton's words barely hit her ears.

"He likes that idea."

Her muscles felt numb and strained as she crouched down and retrieved her necklace. The tangling strands tinkled against each other like chimes, and it seemed like the storm itself paused so she could hear the soft sound. The cool beads rolled against her fingers, solid and real. Behind her, Benton drew in a shallow breath. Like a light flicking on, she remembered the more pressing matters and twisted around to see Benton still standing in the same place, shaking, arms heavy at his sides. But now, his gaze wandered restlessly as if he didn't quite know what to look at since the ghost was no longer in his line of sight.

"We need to get you warmed up," Nicole said.

She rushed to the sliding door of the wardrobe and pulled the closest door open, searching for any extra bedding.

"I didn't know they felt different," Benton mumbled, as a crack of thunder made the overhead lights flicker.

It was clear from the first glance that there were no blankets on the few shelves, but she still searched along through them with trails of hope before moving on to the next side.

"What feels different?" she asked, with a light tone, desperate for something to serve as a distraction for both of them.

A fine tremor had claimed her hands and she couldn't seem to make it stop, not when her mind was whirling, trying to figure out just how long Collin had been there, and if he had been planning to hurt her. The lessons that her parents taught her took over her mind, just long enough for her to click the gun's safety switch back on.

"Suicides," he uttered, almost absently. "They feel different from murder victims."

A cold chill swept down her spine and she pulled at the mirrored doors, sliding open the other side of the closet. The relief she felt at seeing a pile of folded blankets worked to erode the tension that twisted up her insides. Bundling the bedding into her arms until she could barely hold the mounds of thick fabric, she whirled around, walking back towards the first bed before she noticed it.

Benton stood by the second bed, the one closest to the door, looking shell-shocked and rigid. Still, he had slightly moved just enough to keep facing her, and as she headed towards the bed, he adjusted his stance again, his back facing the bed, not seeing the sudden movement that was happening on it. It was so slow that, at first, she wasn't quite sure that she had seen it herself. The bed cover began to bunch.

As if caught in an invisible grip, the sheet twisted and rose. Then, slowly at first but with increasing speed, the cover began to slide, dropping off the bed and disappearing in the space between the bed frame and the wall. The sound of the plummeting rain covered the rasp of the material as she watched the bedding being ripped to the side by an unseen force.

Nicole's shout of warning caught in her throat, becoming a grunt gasp as she rushed towards him. His face went pale before he was flung to the ground. The wet carpet squelched as his chest slammed down onto it and, before she could wrap her mind around what was happening, Benton was yanked back with a startling force. He clawed at the carpet but couldn't prevent his thrashing legs from being devoured by the dark shadows that were now under the bed.

Nicole tossed the blankets aside and dropped to her knees, barely quick enough to latch onto his arms. He clawed at the carpet and she tried pulling him back with all of her strength, but it wasn't enough to counter the force dragging him under. She flopped back against the floor as his arms slipped from her grip. It only took a split second to sit up, but it was enough to lose sight of him completely.

Screaming his name, she shoved at the bed. Its wheels caught and locked, keeping it in place, no matter how hard she pushed. Scrambling to the side of the bed, she flatted her back against the frame, planted her feet on the ground, and forced her full weight and strength against the bed. The stillness that covered the room terrified her, driving her closer to mindless panic as her feet scraped over the carpet. There was barely enough room for an adult to fit under the bed. If Benton was able to move at all, the mattress should budge with his every attempt for freedom. But the bed didn't move. And Benton didn't scream.

With a frustrated cry, Nicole jerked around and shoved her hands between the bed frame and the mattress. There was a moment of resistance before the mattress peeled away like dead skin. She hurled it up, letting it topple and slide down the far side of the frame. There was a sharp crash as the mattress collided against the bedside table, shattering the lamp that stood between it and the floor. The mattress wedged against the wall, leaving the other side to jut down and whack her on the back of her head, as she clawed at the bed's wooden frame.

She could see Benton through the gaps. His fingers gouged out chunks of the carpet as his wrists flattened against the floor. His legs thrashed but he couldn't move his feet. The muscles of his jaw tightened despite struggling to open his mouth. He fought with everything he had, but he couldn't break free of the force that pinned him down.

Bruises began to appear on Benton's ankles, weakening his already diminished strength to break loose. She could only watch the damage spread as she helplessly pulled at the bed slats. With a cheek pressed against the carpet, Benton released a pained moan as he thrashed. The damaged skin went from tinges of gray and blue to a rotted black as his blood swelled. She still couldn't see what was doing all this to him, but he could. That was clear by the horror that twisted his features, and the strangled sobs that worked their way out of his throat.

His legs ceased to function as a new bruise began to emerge. Before her eyes, the injury spread until a perfect handprint had formed on his left calf. He gasped again, a pained, pitiful noise as a new mark began to take shape, this one just above his knee on his right leg. Every last trace of air escaped Nicole's lungs when she realized that the creature was crawling up him.

Releasing her grip on the slats, she quickly darted her eyes around the room. There didn't seem to be anything that was sturdy enough to break through the wooden bed frame. Her eyes fell on the small table and she rushed to it. The single, metal stand of the base was heavy enough that she had to use both hands to carry it, but it would work.

Standing on the side of the bed, she lifted it as high as she could and tried to decide the best place to strike. If she could break a couple of the slats, she might be in a better position to use her body weight on the others. But if she missed, if she accidentally struck the wrong board, she wouldn't be able to stop both the splintered wood and the thick table leg from driving into Benton's exposed back. Images of the damage she could cause filled her mind's eye, and she hesitated.

Lightning struck, its glow blazing through the curtains as the sky released a thunderous roar. The stark white light turned Benton almost silver, highlighting the bruises that now covered his hip, his side, and his shoulder blade. She swung down, driving the end of the table leg into the last wooden plank with all of her strength. It split in two instantly, and she stumbled as she pulled the weight back up. The second blow broke the next plank, creating enough space for her to stand in. Just enough for her to reach down and touch Benton's hand.

Letting the table drop wherever it would, Nicole jumped into the space she had created. The jagged edge of the broken wood sliced at her bare feet and knees, scraping at her skin. She reached with one hand, the awkward angle making her shoulder ache, but she managed to grab his wrist. She still couldn't pull him up. A dark bruise began to surface around his neck. His frantic breathing turned into a splutter then stopped, his eyes growing impossibly wide. With both hands, Nicole shoved at the next plank. It slid in its run only a fraction of an inch before it locked into place. She screamed for him again as she reached for him, this time with both hands, grabbing him under his forearms.

A rush of arctic air slammed into her. Hard enough to slide her back until the end of the bed frame smacked against her spine. Benton came with her, the tension that had been holding him down snapping like a rubber band. Both caught off guard, they were unable to stop his skull form colliding painfully with her knee. The blow stunned Benton. For a moment, his body lay still, then began to quiver as it remembered how to breathe.

"It's okay," Nicole sobbed. She tried to force more confidence and control into her words, but it wouldn't work. "You're okay. Come on, let's get you up."

Pain zipped along her nerves as she straightened up, radiating out from where Benton's body had struck her. Each time she tried to put weight on her seriously injured leg, the knee would threaten to buckle. It made it harder to pull both herself, and the still gasping Benton, from the ruins of the bed frame. It wasn't until he mustered enough strength to offer some help that they managed to escape and tumble onto the floor.

He seemed content to just lay there and panted through his aching throat, but she couldn't believe that it was over. She tried to be gentle, but her movements were hurried, propelled on by a consuming need to know that he was there, that he was okay, that he was safe. He grunted at her manhandling, but helped her pull him into a tight hug.

"What happened?" she asked, even as her mind screamed at her that he needed time to recover. "What was that? Is it gone?"

"She followed me," he managed to say between gasps.

He was gaining some strength and placed one hand on the floor, taking on some of his weight but not holding himself up entirely. She wasn't ready to let him go, but pulled back just enough to check his neck. The mark was there, but not as prominent as the others. With trembling fingers, she reached out to trace the faint lines, as if touching it would somehow make all of this seem real. She was gentle, barely making contact, but he still winced.

"Sorry," she gasped.

Before she could pull back, he reached up and grabbed her wrist. He didn't say anything. He just stared. And it took her a lot longer than it should have to realize that he wasn't looking at her arm. His gaze was solely focused on her bracelet.

"She only let go when this touched her." His bewilderment was clear in his voice, making it useless to ask why. It was clear that he didn't know.

"Is she gone?" she asked, instead.

It took a lot out of him to lift his head and glance around the room. "Yeah."

"Okay. Good," Nicole muttered, mostly to herself.

Benton moved with her when he thought that she was trying to get him on his feet. That cooperation changed the moment he realized that she was instead removing the bracelet from her wrist and attempting to fasten it to his. Between exhaustion, exposure, and near suffocation, Benton didn't stand much of a chance of putting up a decent resistance. As soon as she latched the bracelet on his wrist, Nicole cupped his face and forced him to meet her gaze.

"I've got the gun. You've got the bracelet. We'll protect each other."

A moment passed. The rain fell, and he surrendered with a weak nod. That settled, her adrenaline began to fade, bringing into sharp focus just how cold his skin was. He felt like an ice sculpture pressed against her side. Droplets of water still clung to him even as they soaked into her clothes, making her shiver while her fingers numbed.

"We need to get you warm," she said as she gently released his jaw.

He still needed her help to stand, and with much stumbling she managed to direct him to the unmarred bed. The mattress sagged as he sat on the edge. He swayed slightly but managed to keep upright as she ran back to the pile of discarded blankets. She grabbed the first one she could reach and dragged it back to Benton. A soft clatter reminded her that the gun was nestled under the layers of material. She tossed them all aside until she found the weapon and tucked it into the back of her waistband. The cold pressure against her spine was uncomfortable, although she did find a certain degree of comfort in the constant reminder that it was there. Snatching up the blanket once more, she shook it out and looped it around Benton's bare shoulders.

"Dry off with this, while I put the kettle on," she instructed. "I'll make you some tea."

Mostly recovered from his shock and breathing normally, he begrudgingly obeyed, albeit with sluggish movements and a few pained grunts. Leaving him to absently wipe the rather unabsorbent material over his limbs. Nicole crossed the room to the array of items that sat atop the mini fridge. It was only when she had the electric kettle handle in her hand that she remembered the bathroom was effectively off limits and there was no sink out here to fill it up. Her injured knee throbbed as she crouched down to check the contents of the mini fridge. There were two bottles of water. She used one to fill the kettle and, setting it to boil, then took the other over to Benton.

He took it from her with a smile of gratitude and finished it off in the time it took her to retrieve another blanket from the pile. She was about to protest the way he lazily tossed the bottle across the room when she noticed that it hit the broken remains of the bed she had just destroyed. So instead, she shook out the new blanket, held it up before him, and said.

"Come on. You can't stay in the wet one."

The words weren't necessary since he wasn't offering the slightest protest. They were more for breaking the silence and covering the now unnerving rumble of thunder. Benton made the exchange effortlessly since his shock had mostly worn off.

It was tough to not notice that he was naked. During the attack, modesty had been the last thing either of them had cared about. Now however, it seemed like something in short supply.

He tossed the damp blanket onto the floor as she draped the dry one over his shoulders. There was plenty of fabric left over and Benton awkwardly piled the excess across his lap before wrapping his arms tightly around himself. She tried to keep her eyes averted and found herself noticing how red and splotchy his feet were. And that they were still damp since he hadn't bothered to dry them.

Sighing softly, she knelt down before him, grabbed the corner of the discarded blanket, and began to wipe the stray droplets from his toes. He flinched at each touch, a short snorted breath gushing from his mouth.

"Are you ticklish?" she asked.

"You sound surprised," he mumbled.

"I guess I am," she said. "I never really thought that banshees would be ticklish."

The short, barely smothered laughs quieted as she began to clean the blackened skin that covered his ankles. They were perfect handprints. She could almost see where the nails had dug in. Neither one of them knew what to say, so they let the room lapse into stillness as she worked to get Benton comfortable. It didn't take long for the self-imposed silence to scramble Nicole's nerves.

"You said she followed you." Her natural reflex was to try and cover her fear with layers of cheerfulness, to pretend that nothing was wrong until she could believe it, and normally Benton would tolerate it. Tonight was different and she focused on keeping her words calm and placid. "Did you mean from your room or from the truck stop?"

Benton pulled the edge of the blanket higher around his neck. It looked like he wanted to crawl under it and hide.

"Both."

"Has she ever hurt you like this before?"

Benton nodded, the movement almost lost within the blanket now bunched around his ears.

She cringed. "You didn't tell me that."

"It wasn't really appropriate bus conversation," he said softly.

"And what about after? There were a hundred times you could have pulled me aside at dinner. If something's threatening you, you have to let me know."

"I didn't know she was."

"Benton—"

"It's not like someone gave me the cheat sheet for this," Benton snapped. "The only ghost I've ever dealt with before this is Oliver, and he can't leave the house. I didn't know she could follow me. I thought that she was there and I was here, so there was no point bringing it up."

"No point? Benton, she *hurt* you. That's significant. You can't just ignore it."

"I don't do ghosts!" Benton cut in with a burst of raw anger. "I dream. That's the deal. That's *always* been the deal!" He pulled his hands free and ran them through his damp hair. But the nervous habit didn't help him this time. "I endure whatever messed up crap they shove into my skull, but when I'm awake, I'm safe. I've had ten years to get used to that. Ten years and then they changed the rules."

He slapped his hands down, screaming more at the world around him than at her in particular, his blatant rage deflating into something petulant and scared. "Now monsters get to be a thing. Oh, and I no longer get to be human. Nope. I'm a banshee. What does that even mean?" His exaggerated shrug turned into a violent, halfway flail of arms. "I have no clue. I haven't got the slightest idea if any of this is even normal for my kind. For all I know, not sleeping might be the first sign that I'm losing my friggin' mind. And now, apparently, I have to deal with ghosts, too? No! Just no! I don't do ghosts!"

The last of his energy fled him on the final word and he rocked forward, hunching in on himself as he again ran his hands through his hair. This time the strands locked between his fisted fingers. His grip tightened until his knuckles turned white. He was too tightly compressed for her to pull him into a hug, so she edged closer and rubbed his back in a way she hoped was soothing. It took some time, but the muscles in his back eventually began to relax, and he let out a trembling sigh.

"I'm sorry," he mumbled against his palms. "I didn't mean to yell."

"It's okay," she said.

"It's not. I shouldn't talk to you like that." Drawing in a deep breath, he lifted his head to look at her, keeping his movements minimal enough so that she could still massage carefully along his spine. "She's different than Oliver," he said before hesitating.

"Being around her is like being in my dreams. I feel more like her than I do myself."

"Like she's possessing you?"

"Yes. And no. I don't know how to explain it. It's as if we're blending together and I can handle it when it happens in my dreams, because there's this last, dying bit of my consciousness that knows that there's a time limit. Eventually, I'll wake up. It can take a while, but things will get left behind, and I'll be me again. I don't know if there's a time limit with her, here."

He clamped his mouth shut, desperately trying to keep in something else he had yet to say. As gently as she could, she coaxed him to tell her. For a while, he struggled against it, the toll it was taking on him becoming more visible with each passing second. Finally, he forced it out. "She wants to kill. And she wants to use me to do that."

"That's not going to happen," Nicole promised.

The look he gave her was one of both fondness and sorrow. "How can I stop it?"

"*We*," she corrected. "It's us against her and need I remind you, team banshee is undefeated."

A small smile curled his lips. There wasn't much behind it, but it was a good start.

"You have a plan?" he asked, with the slightest bit of humor.

"Of course, I do."

His eyes narrowed suspiciously. "A good one?"

She bit her lip and then smiled brightly. "So, here's the plan. While you get warm, I'll search the internet for ways to get rid of ghosts. And then we do them all."

His smile grew slightly wider, and finally the helpless look in his eyes began to fade.

# Chapter 5

"I really don't see why you're being so strange."

Benton tipped his head up to Nicole's words, realizing a heartbeat later that the comment wasn't directed at him but at her mother. The two women stood on the far side of the study's small examination room and neither of them seemed to understand that whispering in an echo chamber wasn't really whispering.

"Really," Dorothy replied, her voice low, but completely audible to Benton. "You can't see where I might have a hard time believing you?"

"I told you the truth," Nicole whined.

"I'm sure you did. But when a mother walks into a trashed hotel room to see her daughter rolling a raw egg over a naked boy, she is gonna have questions."

"That's an ancient and very reputable way of casting out evil spirits."

"Says who?"

"Exorcism.com." Somehow, Nicole managed to keep her voice firm and authoritative, without the slightest hint of embarrassment. Personally, Benton wanted to disappear into the hospital-grade bed at just the reminder of it. Of all the things they had tried, it hadn't exactly been the craziest, but it was definitely the most embarrassing for someone to walk in on. He really regretted not letting Nicole put on the chain lock. "If you don't believe me, mom, I can show you the web page."

"Now I'm more concerned about how you determine 'reputable' sources," Dorothy shot back.

"You're making this weird."

"It *is* weird," Dorothy rebutted. "This whole thing is almost the definition of weird."

"Well, it might have worked," Nicole said triumphantly. "Allison didn't come back the whole night."

Benton squeezed his eyes shut, willing himself to fall asleep so he wouldn't have to hear this same argument carried out for the eighth time.

"That might have just been because of the bracelet," Dorothy said. "Iron repels malicious ghosts. Didn't you get that from one of your web pages?"

"I did. Just like I got the stuff about salt, white sage, and avoiding mirrors. We don't know which one worked."

"Well, then. By all means, let me step out so you can roll another egg over him again," Dorothy smirked.

"When are you going to let that go," Nicole muttered.

"Not today," Dorothy countered immediately. "And in the future, I would appreciate it if you call me. Do you know how long it took for me to calm Benton's parents down?"

"They overreacted."

"Benton was missing, the door was wide open, and his stuff was thrown everywhere," Dorothy reminded her.

"Well," Nicole stammered. "They should know by now that if he's not with them, then he's with me. They could have just given me a call and the whole thing would have been cleared up."

"Yes. It's very annoying when people don't make simple yet important phone calls."

Benton didn't need to open his eyes to know that Dorothy was glaring at Nicole, or that Nicole was cringing under the weight of it. In actuality, it was probably better that Dorothy had been the one to handle the situation. If Nicole were forced to tell a lie on the spot, his parents would have been banging on the front door in five minutes. Since Dorothy had been allowed to work her magic, all Nicole had to do was keep a straight face, and explain how there was a research paper due next week which they needed to work on. Oh, and that Benton sucks at securely closing doors during a storm.

"I'm sorry," Nicole finally said. "I got distracted. It was a weird night."

"And you are going to pay me back for all the damages," another instruction Dorothy laid down.

"Of course," Nicole said. "I'm really sorry. Was the front desk mad?"

"You trashed a room. They were a bit upset."

"I'm sorry," Nicole's voice turned weak.

Benton flinched and was about to open his eyes when Dorothy replied in a kind tone, "It's okay. You did the right thing. I'm proud of you."

"Thanks, mom. And thank you for handling Benton so well. I don't think he's used to supportive, authority figures."

And just like that, the conversation had gone from embarrassing to mortifying. He opened his eyes and scrambled up from the examination table.

"You both know that I can hear you, right," he mumbled.

"We're having a private conversation," Nicole said, a smile curling at the corners of her lips. "You hush."

Benton smirked but still swung his legs over the edge. Sleep had been illusive, and after Allison's visit, it always seemed close, but never within reach. He had spent most of his time scrolling through the internet on Nicole's phone. After a certain point, all of the sites were just repeating the same cluster of suggestions. By the time midnight had rolled around, he had given up on both sleep and his study. Nicole had tried to stay up with him but the long hours and adrenaline crash had worked against her. She had ended up drifting off more than once, waking up only when a particularly loud thunderclap shattered the silence.

Getting dressed in the morning had been a lot less painful than what Benton had expected. Dorothy had offered to walk his parents to the nearby Tim Horton's for breakfast, at the same time, Nicole mentioned that she needed to grab a book from Benton's backpack. His parents had gone with Dorothy and had even given Nicole one of the spare keys so Benton could get back in later. The thunderstorm still hadn't passed so the clothes had arrived damp, but he didn't complain. It was good to have pants on again.

He rested his elbows on his thighs and winced, aching from the bruises on his back that hadn't faded away yet. Instead, the pain had sunk deeper into his bones as the night had progressed. Benton had snuck peeks at the injury, never wanting to linger on it for too long. It was harder to ignore his ankles. Against the battered skin, his socks felt like metal shackles, solid and unforgiving. The bruise had darkened enough to resemble frostbite.

Nicole noticed his discomfort and was about to go to him when the doctor came in. He wasn't dressed in the standard white lab coat, instead favoring jeans and a plaid shirt. It was that kind of casualness that kept his near seven foot height from being intimidating.

"Sorry to keep you waiting." He checked his chart and frowned. "Benton? Huh, you don't really hear that name much anymore. Do you prefer Ben? Benny?"

"I don't really care," Benton shrugged.

"Well, I just go by Kyle. Nice to meet you." The second Benton took his hand to shake it, the smile dropped from the doctor's face. "Wow, you're cold. I can get them to turn up the heat."

"Thanks."

Kyle kept up the idol conversation that Benton knew was designed to ease patients into the, sometimes, personal matter of sleep. It wasn't the first time the teenager had been assessed. He knew just how delicate a matter can get as soon as people wanted to explore what could be going on in your subconscious. Eventually, after assuring the doctor that he didn't mind Nicole being present, Kyle pulled up a chair, sat down, and clicked the top of his pen.

"So, you're not sleeping. What specifically are you experiencing?"

"I normally suffer from night terrors," Benton began, trying to find the right way to word things so that they would be helpful but not get him referred to a psychologist. "I've had them since I was little, but can function pretty well around them. I still get a few good hours of sleep."

"But that's changed," Kyle prodded.

"About two weeks ago," Benton nodded. "My dreams have become more ... I guess you would call it, static. It's just a giant mess that wakes me up. I'm only getting a few minutes of sleep at a time, and can't get back to sleep for hours afterwards."

Kyle nodded and glanced down at his sheet. "I've just got a few questions. Just standard stuff." He waited until Benton shrugged before going down his list. "Any allergies?"

"No."

"Well, there is something," Nicole cut in. "We just don't know what it is."

"Right," Kyle said slowly.

Benton rubbed a hand over his burning eyes and struggled to come to terms with the fact that Nicole was bringing this up here and now. It just didn't seem possible that she would honestly try and produce a reaction from the doctor, on Leanan Sidhe venom, in a medical dialogue. *There isn't a box for paranormal allergies,* he threw all of this mental might into the thought, but it didn't seem to register.

"When he was new to town, we went out into the fields and he got really sick," she said. "We don't know exactly what set him off, but it hasn't happened again."

"I'll put down a note," Kyle said, before scribbling something and turning back to Benton. "But nothing else?"

Benton shook his head.

"Are you on any sleeping medication?" Kyle asked.

"He can't go on that," Nicole said before Benton opened his mouth. "He has very bad reactions to them. Psychologically, not physically."

Kyle glanced over his shoulder at Nicole, smiled politely, and then scooted his eyes back to Benton.

"They just make the night terrors longer."

"Okay," Kyle said. "Nutrition. Are you eating right? No late night snacking?"

Benton nodded and barked a laugh when Nicole rushed forward, waving a sheet of paper at Kyle. With his eyebrows slowly creeping up to his hairline, the doctor took the sheet and read over it in a quick glance.

"You've documented his eating," he stated.

"Just from memory. He tends to skips meals if I don't watch him so this should cover most of what he's eaten the last three weeks. Of course, it won't be a complete record and he probably has a lot more caffeine when I'm not looking."

"Who are you again?"

"Nicole Rider. I'm Benton's best friend!"

"Okay, well, thank you for this, Nicole." Slipping the sheet under his paperwork, he continued down his checklist. "No recent trauma? Emotional or physical?"

"Nothing out of the ordinary," Benton said.

Kyle's eyes shifted to Nicole and she quickly became very interested in the far-ended wall.

"Are you sure?"

"Yep."

Benton said before Nicole could answer.

It didn't matter how they tried to word it. There was no way to explain recent events without sounding insane. By his thinking, there was nothing to be gained by mentioning weird owls, monsters, and ghost stalkers. He only prayed that Nicole had the same opinion or this was going to get awkward, fast. She seemed to be struggling under Kyle's suspicious gaze, so Benton shrugged.

"Just the normal adolescent stuff, really."

"Speaking of–" Kyle began to say, but Benton cut him off before he could try and get into some of the more personal questions.

"I'm not sexually active. And I'm healthy."

"Right. And you're not just saying that because we have company?"

"I've had this questionnaire before," Benton reminded him. "I knew it was coming."

"Okay," Kyle said.

Benton didn't know what the doctor was scribbling down but it took him a while, long enough that Nicole began to strain her neck, attempting to read over Kyle's shoulder. It took him a few moments to notice. When he finally did, he flipped over his clipboard and glared at her.

"Now, personally, I would like to keep you overnight. To really get a sense of what is happening in that skull of yours. But I know time is a factor. Especially when you have to go back to Fort Wayward. So let's see what we can do in the time that we have."

He motioned for Benton to lie back down on the examining table. The sheets were comfortable and soft, but the mattress itself was like a strip of cardboard. Staring at the ceiling, Benton tried to relax as Kyle began to attach electrodes to different points around Benton's temples.

"So that will tell you what he's dreaming?" Nicole asked.

"Not exactly," Kyle said as he began to turn on the machines. "When we sleep, we cycle through four stages of sleep. The first two are light stages while the second two are known as the REM stages. That just stands for 'rapid eye movement' and it is at that time that certain parts of our brain light up, our amygdala gets pumping, and the more rational parts of our brain go dormant. That's why dreams are pictures and emotions instead of a series of logical events. Generally, nightmares and dreams happen during REM. These will help me measure Benton's brain activity during these stages and how long he stays in each one."

"But how will you know if something's wrong?" she asked.

"You mean like a tumor?" he asked. "These can't measure for a tumor. That's a completely different machine."

"I don't have a tumor," Benton said sharply. "I had a brain scan six months ago. My brain is healthy."

Nicole rubbed his shoulder in a way that was both reassuring and condescending. He knew he should feel one or the other, but it just made him smile and he bit back a chuckle.

"The most likely problem is that Benton isn't transitioning from one sleep stage to the next like he should."

"And it won't hurt him, right?"

Benton lifted his hand, the iron bracelet slipping along his forearm, and he blindly reached back until he could find her. Her hand wrapped around his, a blazing fire to the chill that still encased him.

"It's just a monitoring system," Benton assured. "I'll be fine." Her only response was to squeeze his hand before she continued her conversation with the doctor.

"Why do you think he gets nightmares, anyway?" she asked. "I mean, more than anyone else?" It didn't matter how much casualness she tried to force into her words, it still sounded completely forced and fake, at least to Benton's ears. Maybe it was the sleep deprivation, but he wasn't quite sure what Nicole was fishing for. It wasn't as if Kyle was going to turn around and declare his belief that Benton was a creature from an Irish folklore.

"The same reason most people get nightmares," Kyle replied. "His subconscious is working through some things. Although, there have been some studies that suggest some people are naturally more emotional, and more prone to nightmares. Is he the sensitive type?"

"He can be very empathetic," Nicole answered.

"I can still hear you," Benton said, only to be shushed quickly by Nicole.

"Okay, Ben, you're just about set."

From somewhere behind him, Benton heard Kyle pull a metal tray closer. It was a common, scraping clatter. That didn't stop the sound from instantly flooding his mind with dark memories. It wasn't that rare for serial killers to like to think of themselves just as skilled as surgeons were. His dreams had made him a witness, a participant, to their games of 'doctor.' He hated that noise and instantly balled his hands on the sheet under him.

"Some people have been having trouble with the storm," Kyle said, now standing to Benton's right. "So we've brought in a sound machine to help you relax."

The lights flicked off, casting the room into murky gray shadows that shifted with every flash of lightning. Benton kept his eyes on the ceiling, kept his focus on breathing slowly, as Kyle plugged up the final device. Ever since this had begun, Benton had been fighting to keep his questions sealed in the darkest corners of his mind. Now, with the possibility of answers lurking closer, it was getting harder to keep them contained. His fingers tightened around the sheet until his knuckles ached, as if he could keep ahold of his stray thoughts if he just held on tight enough.

A sharp click made him jolt, and almost instantly, a music box began to play. The tune was simple, rising and falling down along the scales, almost like a nursery rhyme put to a waltz. Colors splashed across the ceiling. They were pale, given the competing light, but he was still able to just make out the silhouettes of different animals as they drifted around the room.

"Is this a kid's night light?" Benton asked.

"Ours broke and we don't have the budget to replace it until the next fiscal year," Kyle admitted.

The curtains rasped as he pulled them down and drove the room into darkness. The silhouettes grew stronger. Blue horses in full gallop. Pink seahorses. A green bird with its wings spread out in flight.

"Besides," Kyle continued. "Soothing techniques are relatively the same for all ages. What works on us as a child works just as well on us as adults; we just tweak it a little."

Benton longed to tell him that he had definitely outgrown the need for a lullaby and pretty pictures. But his eyelids were already feeling heavy and his bones began to melt into the bed. Someone touched his hand. Benton was surprised when he moved his gaze from a golden lion to discover that it was Kyle, not Nicole. The doctor fixed a heart monitor over one of his fingers, the cuff fitting snugly, before his brow furrowed and he slowly turned Benton's hand.

"That's a nasty burn," Kyle whispered. As if he didn't want the others to overhear. "How did you get that?"

Even in his drifting state, the lie was easy. "I'd never been to a bonfire before and I seriously underestimated how hot a smoldering log can be."

The glow of the nightlight painted Kyle in constantly shifting shades of color, making it nearly impossible to read him.

"You need to be more careful."

Benton forced a weak smile as Kyle drifted away. He didn't see the doctor again, but someone draped a thick blanket over him and he was grateful for that. Already, the soft tune and relative calm was working to lull his weary mind. His eyelids drifted down, remaining just open enough that he could watch the parade of shapes. The tune filled his mind, and he drifted on a haze.

The door clicked shut. He expected to hear only the music after that. Instead, footsteps came closer to his bed. Snapping his eyes open, he jolted back to reality, only to find Nicole standing at the side of his bed.

"Scoot over," she commanded.

The bed was narrow and forced them both onto their sides if they were going to fit. She carefully placed herself around the cords that were littered across the expanse and settled down in front of him.

"Wow," she whispered as she squirmed for a better position. "You'd think that a sleep center would have more comfortable beds."

"There's a child's toy behind you."

"That, I like."

The tune continued to play on a loop, covering their whispers from any prying ears.

"I'm supposed to be sleeping, you know," he said.

"I know. But we're running out of time and you still haven't."

His brow furrowed. "I just lied down now."

"That was two hours ago."

Benton blinked at her, watching the glow of the ghostly animals create a multicolored halo around her. "Two hours? It barely felt like a minute."

"Well, it was two hours and I've already fielded like five calls from your parents. There are only so many times they'll believe me when I say we're on the other side of the store. You need to sleep."

"I'm trying."

"We only have an hour left before we have to go," Nicole insisted.

"If I could, don't you think I would?" Benton said.

She paused for a moment. "Maybe not. I mean, if it were me, I wouldn't be too keen to start dreaming about killing people again."

"Well, I'm not exactly looking forward to it," Benton muttered. Since they were separated by only a few inches at most, it was hard to avoid her gaze. "Do you think I'll dream about them all at once? All the people that died because I didn't dream in time to warn them?"

"That's not your fault, Benton," she whispered.

"Do you think they'll see it that way? Maybe that's why Allison and Oliver hate me. I didn't help them."

"That's silly," she dismissed gently.

"Is it? Collin seemed pretty chill and he was the only one that I wouldn't have dreamt about."

Her hand slid into his. He felt the warmth of her body, both pleasant and excruciating, against his bitterly, cold fingers. "You help who you can and mourn with the rest. That's called the human condition."

"I don't think that's the exact definition," Benton mumbled.

"Hush," Nicole said with a slight smile.

Benton didn't return it. "Nic, have you ever thought that maybe I'm the reason these things happen?"

"What are you talking about?"

"Last night, I stumbled across a site talking about a *tulpa*. It's when people can create something from nothing by sheer focus and mystical energy. They were talking about how, when a group of people have the same fear, and they focus all their energy into that fear, they can literally bring to life whatever they were worried about."

"You should not be allowed on the internet without my supervision," Nicole joked.

"I'm serious."

"You think that all of these murders never existed until you dreamed about them?"

"No. But I'm not so sure that any of these monsters did. You said it yourself, this was a quiet place. I haven't been here a year and things have gone to hell."

"You didn't dream about the Dullahan until after he attacked us and killed..." her voice trailed off. Closing her eyes, she licked her lips and forced herself to continue. "Until after it killed Kimberly. You didn't create it."

"What if I had drawn them in? What if my dreams are like blood in water to them? Maybe that's what the symbol is really for."

"We've been over this. Professor Lester says that the symbol was used by an ancient cult to keep the death of paranormal creatures from luring others in," Nicole explained again.

"Why would a symbol, from a cult that was a dead religion before Rome was even a thing, be in my barn?" Benton asked. "Maybe Oliver was like me. Maybe his presence drew things into the town and that's why they killed him."

"Or maybe the cult isn't dead," Nicole countered. "Maybe it's just obscure. And sure, Oliver had to be something. That's why they put the symbol there, but that doesn't mean that he, or you, were affecting anything. All it means was that they thought his death *might* lure in other paranormal creatures."

"When someone dies of natural causes, they don't end up buried in a barn. And what about the fire? The one that only burns me. It could be to keep me out."

"You're forgetting that it didn't affect the Dullahan," she said.

"So? Maybe I was the bigger threat. When a dam is breaking, you seal the crack, you don't put down a bucket."

"If you're the crack in that scenario, what exactly is the dam, then?" she asked.

"You're not listening to me."

"No, I'm not. Do you know why? Because no one should listen to the wild, fear-induced speculations of someone who hasn't slept in two weeks. You're not the cause of any of this."

His voice was weak as he challenged her. "Are you really so sure?"

"I am. And I'm always right. So close your eyes."

Benton's body instantly began to obey when he caught sight of a figure lingering within the corner. He jolted and would have sat if it weren't for the tightening of Nicole's grip.

"I'm right here," she whispered. "Just tell me what you see."

The consuming darkness congealed and formed into a mass of shadow and smoke. The edges of the figure trailed off and bled into the air while the stark, white disk of its face emerged. There was no definition to its features, but that didn't stop Benton from feeling the now familiar presence of Death's gaze.

"It's here," Benton's voice sounding low and solemn. He knew he didn't need to specify. There was only one *It* that appeared with such regularity in his life that it no longer needed any real explanation. Even as Benton locked his gaze onto Nicole's, the specter of Death lingered in the edges of his vision.

"You know, manners don't cost you anything," Nicole chastised.

"What do you want me to do? Say 'hi' and offer him a drink?"

Nicole shrugged one shoulder. "It's a start."

"It's Death!" Benton retorted.

"And you're a banshee," she said. "You two have a bond. And you would be dead right now, if *It* hadn't helped me out. At the very least, you can you tell it I say 'hello!'"

Benton rolled his eyes, any motion making his head spin. She squeezed his hand again, the grip acting as an anchor that he clung to as the rest of his mind reeled and rocked. When the earth settled again, Death had drifted closer. Benton's heartbeat quickened until his blood rushed through his ears. Nicole's thumb rubbed over his marred palm, tracing an endless pattern of figure eights.

"It's coming closer," he said.

Nicole told him again to close his eyes and, with a broken sigh, he obeyed. Even while his insides raged and boiled, he couldn't keep the lead weight of his eyelids up. Still, he could feel Death lurking closer. It made it impossible to keep his breath from turning into short, sharp pants.

"You're safe," Nicole whispered. "It's just here to help."

Benton scoffed, but the sound didn't come out of his throat. His attempt to tell her that there was no possible way that she could know what was being thwarted by his body's exhausted rebellion. Her voice mingled with the music, almost becoming the words to a tune without lyrics. Each soothing whisper eased the ache inside of him. Every promise sounded to him like a siren's call, drawing him deeper into himself. Death touched him. It wasn't like the touch of a hand. It was like tar pouring over his skin, rising up from under him, encasing him, cradling him. Leaving him floating.

Nicole's words began to echo, as if her voice had extended downwards to reach him, as he began to sink into the shell of his skin. Tar poured down his throat, but he could still breathe.

Temperature lost all meaning, as the thick sludge filled him, holding him gently as he plummeted down into unfathomable depths. Nicole's words drifted away, spreading into oblivion. The music played some sweet notes and then, they too, were lost.

\*\*\*

*He dreamed. A dream of an endless black void. A wasteland of sheer nothingness. He didn't have a stranger's hand, nor skin, nor eyes. His mind was his own and it too seemed to evaporate into the eternal. So he drifted, unable to move or speak. Unable to be certain that he even had a body of his own anymore.*

*From somewhere that was both far beyond and right above him, a light began to shine and the darkness receded. It bubbled and dripped. It bled away to reveal a place he had never been. A place of land and sky and yet was still nothing. Nowhere. Wind began to blow, rushing across and through his shapeless form, howling in his ears like an enraged beast. It would have been impossible to withstand the onslaught if his body was intact.*

*The hurricane gales grew and shattered, becoming shards of glass against his mind, sweeping the land that was something and nothing, dragging a looming wall of white smoke behind it. The clouds rose up like a tidal wave and rushed towards him, its surface swelling, and crawling as if a swarm of deformed creatures was contained within the cloud. Then he heard the laughter.*

*A thousand voices were conversing over each other. Each distinct. Each part of the whole. They all dripped with an unhinged, unbridled malice. The air howled. It cackled and shrieked. It giggled with frenzied bloodlust that, for all the horrors his mind had absorbed, he couldn't begin to fathom.*

*The wall of madness was now only a few yards before him. It consumed his vision. Writhing as it hunted him down. Fear kept his disbelieving eyes open as the smoke stretched into gigantic faces. Their eyes burned as points of crimson red within their gaping sockets. The bones bulged and twisted under their milky, transparent skin. Their mouths were their dominating feature. As each one opened its jaws to join in on their depraved laughter of the chorus, he could see rows of needlelike teeth filling the space.*

*The storm hit and each one of the horde spiraled down upon him to consume his soul.*

# Chapter 6

Nicole felt it the second he finally drifted off to sleep. His body went limp on the thin mattress and his hand became a dead weight within her own. Still, she waited a few extra moments, just to make sure that her movements wouldn't wake him. When his breathing became even and deep, she slowly slipped her hand from his own and crept off of the bed. It was hard not to get tangled up in the wires, especially with a shifting colored light being the only ray to see by. But eventually she was free and able to tiptoe back out of the room.

A two-way mirror allowed for anyone in the control room to monitor the sleeper without disrupting them. It was a tiny room, barely able to fit Kyle along with the equipment, so the door had to remain open to accommodate the addition of Dorothy. As Nicole gently closed the examination room door behind her, she only needed to glance down the hall to meet her mother's smile.

"Good job," Dorothy said, leaning back against the doorframe of the control room.

"I think exhaustion did most of the work," Nicole replied. "He just needed to calm down for second."

She jogged the remaining steps that separated them, anxious to see what was happening on the wall of monitors. There wasn't enough space in the room for a chair, so Kyle was forced to hunch and rest his hands on the tabletop. His attention was fixed on one monitor. Little lines fluttered across the screen, mapping out things Nicole wasn't able to decipher.

"What stage is he in?" Nicole asked as she crammed herself into the minimal patch of space still vacant in the room.

While Kyle's face clearly showed his annoyance, he didn't comment on it. "He's just left stage one." He tapped a long, tapered finger against the screen at a particular patch of squiggles that seemed to be no different from the other patches. "And he's well on his way through stage two."

"So, one more stage and he should be dreaming?" she asked.

"That's right," he said absently as he checked everything once more with fleeting glances. "Everything looks normal so far."

Nicole sucked her lips between her teeth and bit down. Energy strummed under her skin, growing stronger and sharper the longer she struggled to gather even the slightest meaning from the monitors. On the other side of the glass, Benton shifted in his sleep, snuggled down on his back and absently pulled up the blanket higher. He was still cold. It was nothing compared to the way his body heat had plummeted while he traveled the Highway of The Lost, but she couldn't help the twist she felt in her gut every time he shivered. In her mind, the movement had come to mean that there might be a ghost hanging nearby. She had seen what they could do. She never wanted to see it again.

Wrapping one arm around her waist, she began to toy with her other hand with the trails of beads dangling from her choker. She could swear that time itself was slowing just to spite her, and she bounced on the balls of her feet.

"Here we go," Kyle said as he sunk down further, resting one forearm on the counter as he tapped at the screen again. "He's slipping into stage three now."

"So he's dreaming?" Dorothy asked.

"He should be any second now." Kyle jolted up. The easy calm drained from his face as his spine became a straight bar. His jaw dropped slightly, but he didn't say anything. In rushing movements, he began to turn, trying to see every monitor at once.

"What is it?" Nicole asked.

He turned back to the first monitor and she quickly followed his gaze. The squiggly lines were now as flat as the horizon.

"What does that mean?" Nicole said, alarmed.

Dorothy pushed off from the doorframe. "Doctor?"

"The machines must be malfunctioning," Kyle said in a rush, his words tumbling out of his mouth as he struggled to remain calm. "It's probably the storm. Just let me check a few things."

Nicole peered through the mirror, squinting at the one machine she recognized. A heart monitor. There were three bars and one jumped at a steady, strong rhythm. With the reassurance that he still at least had a pulse, she watched Benton carefully as Kyle continued checking the machines. Oblivious to the flurry of activity, Benton's breathing was deep and even, his body still.

"What is going on, doctor?" Dorothy asked with a distraught voice.

Kyle put a hand up as if to fend off that very question. "It's not possible."

"Is Benton in any danger?" Dorothy asked, beginning to feel a touch of panic.

"No. All of his base vitals are fine. It has to be the machine. It just can't happen like that."

Dorothy's patience had met its end and she growled in an imposing voice, "What is?"

Kyle stood still, took a steadying breath, and seemed to piece himself back together. When he had a resemblance of calm again, he turned to the two women.

"These monitors, that I'm sure are broken," he stressed, "are registering Benton as being in a PVS. That's just, I mean, he's..." Shaking his head, he looked back at the monitors. "It's saying he's in a persistent vegetative state."

"What?" Nicole whirled around to him. "He's brain dead?"

"No. They're two very different things," Kyle assured her quickly. "All of his basic functions are still working. But these monitors are saying that his higher brain functions have all stopped."

"The lights are on, but he's not home?" Nicole questioned, metaphorically.

"If that helps you understand," Kyle said. He shook his head and went back to fussing with the monitor. "Of course, that's impossible. It has to be the machine. We should probably wake him up. None of this data is going to be useful."

Nicole turned to find her mother who was already looking at her. Benton had always described the sensation as being absorbed by another person. She had never given much thought to how much the description could be accurate. It couldn't be. Benton dreamed of the future.

In unison, every monitor within the room began to emit a static buzz, the glow of the monitors increasing until it hurt to look at them. Kyle pulled back and bumped into the two women who were blocking the exit. Their bodies knocked into each other as they stumbled out into the hall. The overhead lights began to strobe, flicking on and off, faster and faster as the bulbs strained. They all ducked, covering their heads as the monitors began to pop, sending the thick glass scattering onto the floor.

"Wake up Benton!" Dorothy commanded over the noise.

Nicole was already racing to the door. She flung it open. The rotating night light spun wildly, turning the dancing shapes into streaks of color over the shadows. Something smacked sharply against the outside of the window and she leaped back at the sound. The second sharp blow came with the pained cry of an owl and the thick creak of cracking glass. Then there was another. And another. Glass savagely slashed through the curtain as the next owl burst into the area.

It shrieked as it hurdled around the room, a blizzard of white feathers and murderous talons. A terrified scream escaped her as it swooped past her, its claws finding the arm she had thrown up to protect her face. Blood oozed from her slashed skin and dripped on the floor. The once steady rhythm of the heart monitor became the sound of a loud, shrilled drone that combated against the howling wind and manic animal that now filled the space.

Benton thrashed against the bed. He twisted and kicked in the air. The wires attached to him couldn't withstand his violent movements and were being ripped out from both the monitors and his skin. His motions made the bed shake and shift over the floor. His spine ached, his neck strained, and his hands pawed across the thin mattress.

Nicole tried to step into the room once more but the owl had been joined by at least five more, their true numbers lost amidst the spinning lights, wind, and the rainwater streaming into the room. Standing in the doorway, her fingers uselessly trying to lessen the flow of blood, Nicole screamed for Benton. The wind fiercely blew at her long hair and tossed it across her face, blocking her vision momentarily. Still, she knew he hadn't heard her. That her desperate cry hadn't changed anything.

"Benton!"

Lightning streaked across the sky and for one, glaring moment, the room was filled to the brim with a stark light. Benton bolted upright. His eyes wide. Horror twisted up every muscle of his face and turned his body to stone. Nicole barely had time to cover her ears before Benton's wail exploded through the room. The colossal sound was layered; a human scream, beneath a high-pitched shriek that emulated microphone feedback. The sound vibrated and pulsed, reaching notes no human vocal cord could reach.

The heavy monitors rattled across the floor as the room shook. Never pausing, Benton's banshee wail rose to a pitch that the two-way mirror, the nightlight, and shards of the window couldn't weather. Dorothy grabbed Nicole by the back of her shirt and yanked her off her feet as everything glass in the room detonated, like a bomb, all at once. Then there was silence.

Safe in her mother's arms, Nicole tried to catch her breath as a piercing whine rang in her ears. Dorothy touched her shoulder and Nicole nodded that she was okay. The cuts on her arm weren't too deep and the adrenaline that pulsed through her system dulled the sting. As Dorothy turned to soothe the rattled doctor, Nicole made her way back to the doorway. She had expected to see Benton heaving and confused. Or perhaps hurriedly covering himself with the blanket to protect himself from the still swirling owls. She hadn't expected him to be already on his feet.

With complete disregard for the deadly talons swooshing past him at the height of his eyes, Benton crossed the debris barefoot, found his socks, and yanked them on.

"Benton?"

"We need to go," he said as he put on his jacket. "Now!"

She ducked under a few of the birds as she moved to his side. "It's okay. This wasn't your fault."

Benton laughed and her stomach dropped. She knew that laugh. It was the kind of manic, delirious, bellow laughter he gave when he knew something she didn't; when he had something horrific captured within the cage of his ribs. The sound cleared the panic clashing within her just enough for her to remember what kind of wail he had just produced. It wasn't the one she had heard him give as a furious warning. It was fear. Whatever he had seen was enough to terrify him to the core of his soul.

"Benton?"

He stormed to the door, only hesitating at her side long enough to whisper.

"Something is headed to Fort Wayward. And it's going to kill everyone it finds."

# Chapter 7

Lightning stretched across the sky like skeletal fingers, its electric glow spreading across the world, subduing it in a sterile haze. Thunder trembled the earth as the wind clobbered into Benton's wiry form. He staggered across the narrow parking lot, slumping against the few parked cars as he searched through the sheeting rain for any sign of the bus. The task was made all the harder by the obsidian clouds that choked off the sunlight. They left the day in a perpetual state of nightfall, and with the growing shadows and unrelenting rain, anything beyond a few feet was reduced to splotches on unsharpened color.

He was barely beyond the clinic's doors and already his clothes were heavy from the downpour. Water streamed over his skin in thick rivulets and trickled off of his nose, his ears, and each of his fingertips. The icy deluge had only needed a few seconds to rob him of the warmth that his clothes had kept. Now, as he worked his way deeper into the chaos, the cold had seeped down into his bones.

His fingers trembled as he finally found the bus. From somewhere hidden within the fury of the monsoon, Benton picked up on the faintest cries of the great horned owl. It was impossible to hear their movements and he didn't attempt to get them in sight. His sole focus was on getting the electronic, folding door of the bus to open. With wavering fingers, he clawed at the hinges, pushing and pulling. But the sheets of metal held in place.

Each time his attempts failed, the panic within him surged to a new height. He had dreamed again. And while so much of it had been unlike anything he'd ever known, he instantly recognized the slow, surfacing burn at the back of his neck. His most basic instinct was surging to the surface knowing he needed to raise the warning. He needed those about to die, to hear and listen to him. But he didn't have a name to warn them about, not even a cluster of names. The only thing screaming in the back of his mind, repeating over and over in a frantic mantra, was 'Fort Wayward.'

His fingers slipped over the slick metal again. A bellow ripped from him as he began to pound against the door. The sound didn't emerge from him, from the paranormal part of himself. It was him. His voice, his foreboding, his terror, and dread poured out in a single cry. With every step, every heartbeat, his dream replayed within his mind. He had never been the victim before. For years, he had slipped under the skin of killers and sociopaths, parasitically feeling their euphoria of the destruction and pain they caused, awakening, back into his own mind, the repulsion with himself. He had never been the prey before. He had never been the one being hunted.

A hand fell onto his shoulder and he shuddered from the touch. His feet tripped up around themselves as he whirled around. The bruises on his back flared with pain when he banged against the bus door, but he pressed against it, forcing the wall of metal to keep him upright as he blinked into the rain.

Nicole had pulled her hand back but still kept it in the air. Her long hair, darkened by the rain and shadows, draped over her tawny skin like a sooty cloak. In that instant, she closely resembled the specters that he spotted standing motionless in the downpour. The grim reapers hid too well within the shadows of the storm for him to truly see their numbers but he knew they were there. Each one of them watching. Each one waiting.

"Benton!"

He snapped his eyes back to Nicole, a steady burn filled his lungs, telling him that he had yet to take a decent breath. She inched closer and he flattened his back to the door.

"It's just me," Nicole comforted him. "It's okay."

"We need to get on the bus," he insisted.

"Okay, we will. But breathe for me first, okay."

She walked him through it, exaggerating the motion so even his frazzled mind could understand and mimic. The rampaging energy that ravished his chest began to ease. Then Death drifted closer. Latching onto Nicole's shoulder, Benton flung her around as he lunged forward, effectively putting himself between her and the ghostly figure. He stared into the hollowness of its eyes and Death stared back. Still waiting.

Out of the corner of his eyes, Benton spotted Dorothy emerging from the fog of the rain. Having grabbed their forgotten umbrellas, she stood as the only dry human in their group, a hint of sanity poking in through the clashing thoughts that filled his skull.

Before she could ask, Benton yelled over the storm. "Open the bus. Get inside!" His voice must have come out with a lot more authority than he heard it because she didn't argue. With a quick flick of the key and a mechanical whoosh, the doors folded and they all huddled inside, Benton never taking his eyes off of the nearest grim reaper. It didn't try to follow. It remained where it was, untouched by the rain, watching as he closed the door between them.

"What are you looking at?" Dorothy asked.

Benton didn't look at her as he spoke, "Death is out there."

"Right. A thin metal door should take care of that."

It was clear that the older woman had thought her words would be lost under the rain pelting against the metal roof. Since Benton wasn't particularly keen to think through the legitimacy of his plan, he didn't comment. Finally, ripping his gaze from the foggy glass, he looked around the bus. Wind howled along the sides of the bus, creating the illusion that the bus was filled with hundreds of people. Shadows clung tightly to every crevice they could find and a thick chill spilled across the floor.

Dorothy closed her umbrella and sunk down unto the driver's seat, twisting around enough to keep Benton and Nicole in sight. Nicole pulled her backpack out from under the first row and hurriedly opened one of the pockets.

"How's the doctor?" she asked.

"Shaken," Dorothy said. "But very rational. He thinks that the storm blew out the windows and a power surge destroyed his equipment. He's sending his staff home and was very comforted when I assured him that we're not going to sue."

"Well, that's a win. Right? Go team banshee!"

The light quiver in Nicole's voice drew Benton's attention. He looked over just as she flipped open the lid to the small first-aid kit she constantly carried with her. Blood drooled from three gashes that ran across her forearm. The crimson liquid mixed with the water pouring from her made her entire arm look ripped and raw.

"It's just a scratch," Nicole assured, when she spotted them both watching her. "I got a bit too close to an owl. They have really sharp talons."

For all the cheer she forced on her words, she couldn't suppress her whimper of pain as she began to clean the wound. Benton was faster than Dorothy and had less space to travel. He sat on the seat across the aisle from Nicole and, with gentle insistence, took over the task.

"We should get you to the hospital," Dorothy said.

"I'm a registered first-aider," Nicole said, with no small amount of pride. "And in my professional opinion, I don't need stitches. Just a stable bandage and a couple of pain killers will do."

"You're not a professional," Dorothy argued.

Her angry tone vanished when Benton, being a little too enthusiastic with the antiseptic cream, pushed against the wound. Nicole winced with a pained moan and it took a few minutes to reassure them both that she was okay. Benton was still mumbling apologies as he began to wrap a clean bandage around her arm.

"Almost done," he promised.

Nicole smiled. An expression she refused to lose even as pain flickered across her face.

"I guess this means that you're dreaming again," Nicole said with overenthusiastic glee. "That's great. I told you Death was there to help."

"I'm sorry," Dorothy cut in. "*Death* helped you?"

Her question was left unanswered and Benton concentrated on making sure each wrap of the bandage was perfectly in place.

"I never stopped dreaming," he said. "I just wasn't strong enough to handle it. We need to get back to Fort Wayward."

"Why? What did you see?" Dorothy pressed, with obvious frustration. She scowled as Benton remained silent. "I'll start you off. When you closed your eyes you saw..."

"A horde," Benton said.

"A horde of what?" Dorothy snapped.

Benton couldn't stop himself from matching the tone. "I don't know. These dreams don't actually come with an encyclopedia entry. There are gaping blind spots to my knowledge, and no amount of yelling is going to fix that."

Drawing in a steadying breath, Benton carefully worked the tip of a safety pin through the layers of fabric, cautious to not poke the soft skin underneath. He could feel Dorothy's gaze burning against the side of his head, but it was nothing compared to the fire raging at the base of his skull.

"Please start the bus," he said, with all the calmness he had left. "I need to get to Fort Wayward."

Nicole was quick to rush in before her mother could respond. "Benton, we can't be prepared unless you tell us everything. I know it's hard. But can you please try?"

"Death kept me on the outside. I don't know how it pulled it off but I wasn't contained to one body. That was the problem. I couldn't settle into any one particular skin. There were too many."

After helping Nicole, Benton rested his forearms on his knees, clasped his hands together until they ached, and told them the details of what he had seen. He spoke about the coming storm. The faces within. The manic laughter. Having never experienced his dreams like this before, there was a lingering doubt within his mind of how much of it was literal. Perhaps, if they were lucky, some of it might just be figments of his imagination.

Dorothy's voice shifted into professional calm mode when she asked, "How many of these faces did you see?"

"Hundreds," he shrugged. "Thousands. They're a throng. It's kind of impossible to tell."

"And they hide in the storm?" Nicole asked.

He nodded, only looking up at her as she moved to her seat.

"Well, that's good," she stated optimistically. "When the storm ends, they'll go away or die or something. So, we send out a storm warning, get everyone off the streets, and wait them out."

"Would that work?" Dorothy asked.

"Your guess is as good as mine," Benton murmured.

"If you don't know anything, how are you so sure that this swarm or throng is going to Fort Wayward?" Dorothy asked.

"Because a huge chunk of being a banshee is warning the people that are about to kick it," Benton blurted, his fear fueling the rage that flared within him. "And all my instincts are screaming at me that Fort Wayward is in its path."

"Okay, so," Nicole nervously flicked her eyes between her mother and Benton, "storm warning is still our best bet? Mom can call into the station and tell them that a tornado or something is on the way. Everyone hunkers down and the swarm passes over. That would work, right?"

"Except that things like weather reports exist," Benton said.

Nicole swept one hand up to indicate the storm barreling around them.

"Yeah, okay. But it's possible to check the severity of a storm online. As soon as they know it's just a thunderstorm, I don't think they're going to board up their doors."

Nicole slumped a little, absently covering her wound with her hand as she thought. "But if mom says it, that will have more force, right?"

"They'll trust a meteorologist over me," Dorothy said. "Especially with all the Canada Day preparations."

Nicole bounced on her seat. "Canada Day!" she declared with a smile.

"Yes," Dorothy said slowly. "People will be trying to pack up what they can and—"

"No, but Canada Day!" Nicole cut in.

"We're on the outside of your head," Benton reminded her with a slight smile.

The glare she shot him had no heat behind it. "Oh, I'm sorry. Is it irritating when someone withholds information?"

"Exceedingly," Dorothy cut in. "Get to the point."

Nicole couldn't stop moving as a restless energy filled her.

"The speaker system set up around the Fort. Like the actual Fort. Every year they use it to announce the activities and you can hear it clear across town. It should be set up by now," Nicole explained.

"I guess if people hear me on a loud speaker, they'll take it more seriously," Dorothy mumbled. Benton only shrugged.

"Not you," Nicole said. "Benton. You've heard his banshee wail, mom. We all saw what it did to the Dullahan. Imagine if we could amplify it."

"His scream did kill that horseman thing," Dorothy mumbled in contemplation.

"The Dullahan," Nicole said quickly. "And that was a huge learning curve. The first time I heard it, he was only strong enough to scare the Leanan Sidhe. He's getting stronger."

Benton's stomach lurched and a quake of panic flooded his words, "Or maybe they were just two different species that reacted in two different ways. There is no guarantee that my scream will do anything. It's a stupid plan."

"Hey," Nicole crossed her arms defensively before remembering her wound. "So far, your plan has only been to get to town. I think we need to hash out a stage two."

"How about one that doesn't rely on me doing something that I can't do on command?"

"You've done it before," Nicole pointed out.

"Yeah. But only when something was trying to kill me."

"I'm sure we can get one of them to try and kill you."

Benton gaped at her for a moment before he buried his face into his palms.

"Your scream is really weird. Horrendous even," Dorothy said, thoughtfully.

"Thank you," Benton said without lifting his head. "I was wondering how I was going to get rid of that pesky self-esteem."

Between his fingers, he caught sight of Dorothy rolling her eyes. "What I mean is it's bloodcurdling and not easily identifiable. It's not a sound that makes you want to rush out and see what it is. Even if it doesn't stop the swarm, it will keep people indoors."

"Okay, fine," Benton huffed as he slapped his hands down against his thighs, the impact squishing out another trail of water. "Just to recap. Our plan is to get into town. Hope that we can break into the Fort. Cross our fingers that the speaker system is working and undamaged by the rain. Hand me the mic and pray for the best. That's it. That's our plan?"

"Plan B is to scare you," Nicole reminded him.

Benton clicked his fingers and pointed at her. "Emotional scaring, let's not forget that. Here's an idea. Can we maybe have a backup plan that doesn't rely solely on me?"

"Well, we do have your recording," Nicole said. She glanced around the two and exhaled a long sigh. "Remember? When mom found us after the Dullahan attacked us?"

Benton lifted his hand to display the mass amount of scar tissue across his palm. He had tried hard to forget that day but didn't think that was ever going to happen. Nicole flinched.

"Right. Sorry. My point was that mom had been driving a police cruiser that day. The scream was caught on the dash cam. If you can't scream, maybe playing that in will work."

Benton slowly turned to face Dorothy. "I don't suppose there's any chance you deleted that tape?"

"No. It was evidence. I found more than just the two of you that day," Dorothy said.

Benton cringed. It seemed like his relationship with Dorothy was constantly swinging between gratitude and self-preservation. The Constable wasn't the first person to ever stumble across him with a few unexplained dead bodies. And, by previous experience, things only ever got worse after the police became involved. It was kind of impossible not to look suspicious when you constantly knew a murder was about to happen. He wanted to trust Dorothy. But it was never clear how much she covered his back because he was useful, and how much had only happened because she was protecting her child.

"Oh, calm down," Dorothy said. "It's not like someone would hear it and leap to the conclusion that you're a banshee. And even if they did, I'm pretty sure there is no law against being an Irish folktale."

"I'm still not comfortable knowing that it's in police files."

"Right now, we should be excited that it is," Nicole cut in. "I can get a copy of the tape and if Benton can't scream, we'll play it into the speaker."

"Will that work?" Dorothy asked.

Nicole shrugged and turned to Benton. No matter how much she researched, she was really no wiser about Benton's abilities than he was.

"I'm not ecstatic about this plan," Benton admitted. "But if you are, let's give it a go."

"I am certain this will work. Generally speaking," Nicole said with conviction.

Benton bit back his smile. "Well, that's comforting. Generally speaking."

"We can think up something else on the way."

"You're not going," Dorothy cut in.

Both teens snapped around to face her and gasped a befuddled 'what' in unison.

"I'm not taking my daughter into a paranormal battlefield. Besides, you're injured."

Nicole looked about a second from launching out of her seat. "So is he."

"Yes, but we need him," Dorothy said.

While she did her best to hide it, Benton could clearly see the pain that burnt across Nicole's feature's at that comment. Not knowing what to say, Benton could only ball his hands into fists and watch as Nicole lifted her chin, the muscles around her mouth twitched as she fought to keep her expression calm.

"You need me, too," she insisted. "You couldn't even get Benton to close his eyes in there and he was a willing participant. How are you going to handle him when a demonic swarm is closing in? Not to mention just getting him through the trip back. He'll get hypothermia before you get a mile from Peace Springs."

"Hypothermia?"

"See? You don't even know that about him! This is a three person job, minimum."

Dorothy's eyes flared with anger as she growled her daughter's name.

"Do I get a say?" Benton cut in.

"Well?" Dorothy hissed.

"I don't want Nicole to get hurt," he said weakly, his words almost covered by the storm. "But I'm not sure I can do this without her."

"There," Nicole said triumphantly. "It's settled."

"Can't do it without her?" Dorothy repeated. "How exactly could she help? All you have to do is scream."

"See, right there, that is why I need her. I need someone who has my back. We're a team. We started with just the two of us and we were doing pretty well."

"People died," Dorothy countered.

"To be fair, most of them were dead before we got there."

The Constable's eyes narrowed. "Impertinence isn't your best option right now."

"Well, it doesn't seem like I have many good ones, so I'm just going to roll with it," Benton shrugged as his hackles rose. "And for the record, just because I dream it, doesn't mean I'm beholden to anyone. And it sure as hell doesn't make me responsible."

"She didn't mean it like that," Nicole soothed.

"Yeah, she did. They always do. But that's not the point right now. The point is, when push comes to shove, I'd take Nicole with me over you."

Dorothy held his eyes but the heat was leaving her glare, covered by a lingering silence of dread. "She's my little girl."

"And you raised me well," Nicole said as she rushed over to her mother. Pulling her into a tight hug she added, "So let me show you what I can do."

For a moment, it seemed like all they could do was hold each other tightly. Benton remained in his seat and stared only at the floor, feeling like he had encroached on something not meant for him. The fire in the back of his neck was getting worse. Slowly, but steadily. He honestly didn't know how much time he had left before he would be rendered useless by the pain.

"So," Dorothy said as the two finally parted, "we still have to decide what to do with the others."

"Others?" Benton asked a heartbeat before he remembered everyone was waiting for them at the Walmart across town.

# Chapter 8

A low rumble filled the Walmart as the constant rain struck the metal roof. On occasion, the roaring wind would still just for a moment, as if the storm was holding its breath, and the soft tune could be heard once again streaming out from the speakers. Standing by the wall, not too far away from the electronic doors, Nicole tried to arrange their items into something manageable. It had been crazy trying to snatch up the few extra blankets and self-heating pads they would need to get Benton across the highway in better condition. It had taken a chunk out of her savings, while she had also grabbed some salt and a few flashlights. She had seen enough horror movies to make her paranoid about their efficiency, so she had bought some that ran on battery as well as a camping one that was crack operated. In the end, it hadn't mattered what she bought, she still felt woefully unprepared.

Water still dripped from her as she zipped her bag back up and propped it up against the wall, careful that her shirt didn't roll up to expose the gun tucked into the back of her waistband. All the while, she could feel Benton's parents watching her from where they tried to wrangle the small cluster of teenagers. Arriving soaked had made it obvious she had lied about them being in the store the whole time. Still, no matter how long she waited, they never came over to speak to her. After a short conversation with Dorothy, and an extremely tense moment with Benton, they had simply gone back to the group, intent on keeping an eye on her, but never actually asking her questions. Benton had pointed out that behavioral quirk more than once and explained it away by insisting that it was because they were preserving their ignorance. They could believe Benton was normal if they just didn't ask any questions. Personally, Nicole thought they knew a lot more than they allowed Benton to believe. They knew something. And they were scared.

Benton rushed up to her, bags of new clothes swaying in his hands, and held out a few dollars. A contribution to the coffees she had still yet to buy in the annexed McDonald's.

"I still don't like this," Nicole admitted, pushing the bags aside with her foot.

"I know," he whispered back. "But it's the best plan we've got."

"It's a sucky plan," she replied instantly.

They had been over it a dozen times already but the repetition helped her to believe it wouldn't be a complete disaster.

"They'll be safer at the Lost Woods Motel than here," Benton said. His voice didn't carry a hint of frustration to, once again, be tracing over the same ground. Maybe he needed the reassurance too. "We were supposed to stay there tonight. No point in raising suspicions before we have to."

She nodded, her teeth sinking into her bottom lip. "But those woods, Benton."

"None of them seemed to be affected like me."

"You know that's not the only danger," she said.

He held her eyes as he spoke again. "I do. And so do they."

And that was what they were counting on. If the swarm came across the forest too, it was better for everyone to be somewhere that they were already paranoid about. In groups. Behind locked doors.

"It's the best we can do," Benton said. "Best case scenario; they won't even notice we're gone until it's all over. At most, they'll be alone for a few hours."

"They won't be alone. Your parents will be with them."

Benton shrugged at her comment, his eyes sneaking a glance to his parents. She followed his gaze and found that neither of them looked very happy to see their son talking to her right now.

"It'll be okay." She put every ounce of conviction she had into those words. For a moment, it actually sounded like the truth.

"It will be," Benton promised.

Flipping her hair over one shoulder, she pulled on her new raincoat. The change of clothes and her backpack that she had tried to protect from the rain, were already slightly damp from her skin.

"Go get changed. I'll get someone to mind these and grab the coffee," she said.

They had formed their plan and they would see it through. There was nothing to be gained by wallowing on it. He nodded, squeezed her shoulder, and hurried off to get changed, with his waterlogged socks squishing loudly. Already his fingers were like ice. It was easy enough to find someone to take care of the bags in exchange for some fries and she rushed off to join the lines.

At first, she didn't notice that things hadn't changed. But when she did, she started to glance around. By entering McDonald's, she had removed herself from Benton's parent's line of sight, but she could still feel someone watching her. It was an intense sensation that made her skin prickle and her insides chill. She spun around, looking towards the back of the restaurant, and almost yelped when she found a man right behind her.

"Sorry," he said with a hint of amusement. "Are you okay?"

The man was a bit taller than she was, with broad shoulders covered in a fur lined denim coat. He gave her a bright smile that made his eyes sparkle. It was kind of hard to judge his proper age, but he definitely had at least seven years on her.

She offered an apology and refocused on the front of the line. The man didn't stop looking at her. At first, it was slightly flattering to have the handsome man's attention, but the novelty very quickly wore off. The sensation of being watched continued to smolder against her back and she found herself looking around again.

"Do I know you from somewhere?" the man asked abruptly.

She turned back to him and shook her head. He continued to trail his eyes over the side of her face and she squirmed under his appraisal.

"That's it," he said with a gentle laugh. "I think you went to the same high school as my girlfriend."

Nicole glanced to him. "Really? What's her name?"

His response was immediate. "You wouldn't know her. She would have been a few grades above you. But I remember seeing you when I was picking her up a few times. Man, that was bothering me."

With his broad smile and his gentle ease, Nicole could feel her tension slowly ease off her shoulders. But then his girlfriend came up beside her, and her insides froze within a second. Nicole didn't know the woman's face. She prided herself on knowing everyone in her little hometown, and that woman's face didn't ring a single bell. The arctic blaze within her ribcage didn't dull when the woman didn't move to her boyfriend's side. They were within arm's reach of each other but kept enough distance between them that they were effectively on either side of her, lingering just outside of her peripheral vision. She couldn't keep an eye on both of them at the same time.

The room was full of people and still she felt trapped, caged in by walls of flesh and bone. A voice in the back of her mind told her that she was just being paranoid, and that her nerves were shot and she was just reading too much into the couple's actions. But that little voice wouldn't stop reminding her of the one simple fact that she was barely a mile away from the Highway of The Lost.

Nicole almost leaped with joy as the person before her moved aside and she could rush forward to the counter. Just putting in the few feet between them would help her feel slightly more at ease. She ordered two large coffees and some fries. Then the couple was right behind her again; still, on either side of her. Still perfectly positioned in her blind spots.

"Is that for your boyfriend?" the girl asked.

"My mother," Nicole was quick to reply.

She figured that would sound more imposing, especially if they had seen her with Benton. By physical appearance alone, Benton just wasn't an intimidating guy.

"Is she waiting in the parking lot?" the man asked.

"You know, it is still pouring out there. I was so lucky to get a spot close to the door," his girlfriend said. Her voice went up, becoming soft and sweet, but the words still made Nicole's stomach drop into her shoes. "You know, we can give you a lift to your car."

As quickly and politely as she could, Nicole rejected the offer. Her order arrived and she began to gather the items.

"Are you sure? I'd hate for you to catch a cold," the woman said as she put her hand on Nicole's shoulder.

Nicole didn't have time to flinch away from that touch when, as she reached for one of the coffee cups, a hand shot up from under the counter. Slick with mud and muck, the grip was as firm as steel. The hand around her wrist clenched, until she could feel each rough grain of dirt grind against her skin. Nicole released a startled, pained cry and pulled back with all of her strength. Within an instant, the hand vanished, and she was sent toppling back.

The man caught her and tried to hold on, but Nicole hurled herself around like a wild cat. She pulled herself from their grip. The crowd within the store had begun to take notice. Nicole didn't dare risk reaching for the coffee again. She just turned and ran for the door, her wrist throbbing in pace with her racing heartbeat.

\*\*\*

All three stalls of the bathroom were occupied. Benton didn't mind. He would endure the embarrassment of changing in public if it meant that he wasn't alone in a bathroom again. Dumping his few plastic bags onto the counter, he hurriedly set about stripping off the layers of saturated fabric that covered him like sheets of ice. Water sprayed from his shoes as he dropped them onto the tiles. When he peeled off his socks, he found that his toes had already begun to wrinkle. Suppressing a spike of bashfulness, he opened his zipper and peeled his jeans from his damp legs. Bruises littered his skin. They had darkened with the course of the day, until each one looked like they were made from wet ink.

His new sweatpants were the cheapest pair the store had offered and they felt incredibly decadent against his legs. A sharp crack of thunder shook the walls as he pulled his shirt over his head.

Water dripped out of it with the slightest bit of pressure and trickled onto the tiled floor. He discarded it onto the growing pile of clothes and it landed with a loud squish. As he struggled into his jumper, he caught the soft sound of the door being scraped upon.

Already on edge, Benton glanced over his shoulder. It wasn't exactly a comfort to find Zack standing in the threshold, but still, it was better than another visit from Allison, of course. But the expression on Zack's face was dark and ripe with the promise of violence. Benton had seen the expression too many times, and had endured the fallout not to be instantly on guard. Seemingly intent on reminding Benton of their vast size difference, Zack crossed his arms over his broad chest and flexed. The silent threat was heard loud and clear. Benton felt as small and vulnerable as a child.

Keeping Zack in the corner of his eyes, Benton focused on pulling the cheap, thin sweater over his head. The sharp spikes of pain reminded him too late of the damage that criss-crossed along his spine. He tugged and pulled but it was too late to keep Zack from noticing the bruises. In the seconds that it took to get the material over his head, Zack burst forward. His wide hand gripped Benton's shoulder and shoved him deep into the corner, forcing him to spin so he could get another glimpse of Benton's back before it was hidden.

Rage burst within Benton, filling him until his hands shook from it. He whirled around and smacked Zack's hands away.

"What the hell is your problem?" Benton spat.

Zack recovered quickly from his moment of shock and narrowed his eyes. "We need to talk."

Benton scoffed and moved to walk around him. With one hand flattened against Benton's chest, Zack shoved him back into the corner. The edge of the counter felt like knives as they drove against the bruises that plagued his hips and he couldn't keep in his pained gasp.

"You're not leaving until you answer some questions," Zack said in a low whisper.

Still, no one seemed ready to come out from the stalls and intervene. For some reason, Zack was under the delusion that Benton would play along. Instead, Benton made sure that his laugh was loud and abrupt, hoping to draw some attention.

"That's not a weird thing to say to a half-naked guy in a public restroom."

"I'm not kidding, Benton. You can start with how you got those bruises. They're messed up. People don't bruise like that."

With a dismissive snort, Benton tugged down the end of his sweater and turned back to the counter. It was hard to keep himself looking casual as he searched through the plastic bag for his socks.

"Aw, I didn't know that you cared."

Zack slammed his hand against the counter, but the heavy thump was lost under another crack of thunder.

He kept a tight hold on his casual air. "What do you want from me, Zack?"

Zack's response was immediate, and he grabbed for Benton's shoulder. While he was ready for Benton to smack his hand off him, he wasn't ready for the thin boy to rush at him. It took both hands and a full assault of his weight, but Benton managed to make the towering teen stagger back a few steps. Huffing each breath, Benton shoved a finger into Zack's face.

"Don't ever touch me again," Benton hissed.

"Or what?" Zack challenged, his rage keeping him from remembering that they were possibly being overheard. "You're going to do to me what you did to Victor?"

Benton couldn't contain his surprised laughter. "What are you talking about? Victor committed suicide. It's tragic, but it wasn't my fault."

"Suicide? You found in him in hole with a dozen other bodies and you want me to believe that's suicide?"

"I found him, but that doesn't mean I know anything more than you do."

"What I know," Zack said in a threatening whisper, "is that he was never violent until you came along."

"That's correlation, not causation."

"You're the only person he attacked and you just happen to find his body? Yeah, nothing strange about that."

Benton balled his hands until his knuckles strained. The muscles along his shoulders twitched as they readied for a fight.

"He attacked Nicole, too," Benton said. "She was also with me when we stumbled across the mass grave. Are you going to corner her as well? And, while we're remembering facts, and not just things that fit your theory, according to the cops, most of those people were dead before I was even in Alberta. So, unless you think my parent's overlooked the heap of corpses piled into the moving vans next to the sofa, you can't pin this on me."

The slew of facts didn't deter Zack at all. "And it was just coincidence that you were also there when Kimberly died?"

"Who told you that?" Benton challenged. "What about all the other people that happened to be there, too? You know, the ones that can attest that I never even got near her? Fun fact of the law and logic, I'm not guilty just because you don't like me."

"And yesterday? What was that in the bathroom?"

"Maybe a creepy guy cornered me and started yammering on about insane theories of me being a – I don't even know what to call this – Psychic killer?"

Zack's jaw twitched as he tried to keep his temper in check. "And what about the trip here?"

"To the bathroom?" Benton tried to deflect.

But, as if he could smell blood in the water, Zack pressed forward. "What happened to you on the bus?"

"I got cold."

"You looked close to death. I have eyes, Benton. Something is really wrong with you."

Feeling cornered in more ways than one, Benton pushed forward. "I'm sick of this!" Benton proclaimed with every bit of rage he could muster.

Zack tried to grab him again and this time he raised his voice into a major bellow, one that would be impossible for the people in the stalls not to hear. Or the people outside.

"Don't touch me!"

One of the toilets flushed and Benton wasn't about to let that kind of distraction slip by. With his socks in hand, he snatched his shoes off the floor and bolted for the door. He left everything else behind without so much as a glance. Not even when he heard the door open again allowing Zack to follow him.

"Okay, guys!" Dorothy yelled from the front of the store, her authoritative voice gaining the attention of almost everyone in the store.

"This storm is getting worse and we need to get back on the road. We're not going to be stopping, so if you have to use the bathroom, do it now. You have three minutes left until I want everyone around me for a headcount. Once we're all together, we'll be heading straight out to the bus. Understand?"

"Yes, Constable Rider," the small group chanted in near unison.

A few people passed by Benton before he could catch sight of Nicole standing with the twins. She lifted her hand to pass him a cup of coffee before she noticed the expression on his face. Within a second, her smile vanished and she was raking her eyes over him with open concern, looking for any trace of physical damage.

"What happened?" she asked.

He saw Meg open her mouth, but didn't wait to hear whatever she had planned to say.

"If Zack puts his hands on me again, I'm going to kick him in the head." He knew that he had bellowed the words but he didn't care. It was obvious that Nicole wasn't sure how to respond. She didn't have time to figure it out before Zack came hurling toward them.

"I'm not done with you, yet!" he roared, also giving up on any hope for subtlety.

It made his skin crawl and his muscles tense. Forcing people to own up to their theories in public was a good way to get them to back down. No one wanted to look like a ranting lunatic around their friends. The few times people stepped up to that kind of challenge from Benton, it had ended as a mob. Passing by Nicole, just enough to keep her out of the line of fire, he pointed back at her and then Zack.

"Keep him away from me."

She was already jumping between the two of them, arms outstretched, like she could physically keep them separated.

"One of you needs to start making sense right now," she said with so much authority that Benton almost mistook her for her mother.

"He attacked me!" Benton spat the words out with the solid push of his anger and fear.

"What? Zack?" Nicole didn't seem to know which one of them to look at, quickly turning her head side to side between them before settling her gaze onto Zack. "Well?"

"I just asked him a few questions," Zack said. "He's freaking out because he doesn't want to answer them."

"What questions?" Danny asked.

"He accused me of being a serial killer who also has some kind of time- twisting abilities!" Benton had hoped that the offense attack would leave any of Zack's coming accusations sounding like a tone of madness.

But he still didn't back down.

"There is something wrong with him," Zack accused, looking from Nicole to Danny to Meg, searching each pair of eyes for an ally.

"Zack," Nicole said in a warning tone. "You've been acting weird ever since he showed up. You're skittish and secretive. Hell, you skipped out on us last night. You've never done that."

"Benton got sick," Danny said.

"Yeah. Like on the bus. Did that look in any way normal to you?" Locking his eyes back onto Benton, he spoke loud enough for them all to hear. "I know you had something to do with Victor's death."

"What is going on here?" Cheyanne snapped as she hurried over.

Benton recognized the fear that lurked in his mother's eyes and quickly looked away. "Nothing," he mumbled. "Just a misunderstanding."

"Okay, both of you, apologize to the other, right now!"

Zack hesitated. But, for all his certainty, he apparently wasn't ready to voice his suspicions to an adult. With a stern look and a firm hold on Benton's shoulder, his mother forced the apology out of him. Zack mumbled something that might have been mistaken for words, but Benton didn't care. The matter was apparently settled since Dorothy bellowed over the crowd again and began to encourage them to get closer. Zack shoved past Benton, his elbow easily finding one of the bruises that littered Benton's body. The spike of pain forced a grunt out of him but he refused to double over. Nicole lingered on, waiting for Benton to catch up. He only managed to take one step towards her when Cheyanne caught him by the arm.

"Go on ahead," she dismissed Nicole easily as her fingers tightened around his arm.

"It wasn't my fault," Benton said the moment that they were relatively alone. "He attacked me."

"You're to stay away from Nicole," Cheyanne said without looking at him.

"She's my best friend," Benton defended.

Still, she refused to look down to meet his gaze, but her words were clear. "People like you can't have friends, Benton."

And with that, she released his arm and walked away agitated, leaving Benton to wonder once more if she thought him a freak or a madman.

# Chapter 9

The night came early under the influence of the coming storm. Shadows had gathered across the thick grass and between the tree trunks, churning through the mist until it was nearly impossible to see farther than a yard beyond the side of the road in any given direction.

At first, the bus ride was tense. The rain struck the roof and sides of the bus like hale, muffling the whispering conversations. News of Benton and Zack's confrontation made a quick round, allowing Nicole to pick up the bits and pieces of a dozen conversations. From what she could tell, not many of them seemed to take Zack's accusations seriously, but it had been enough to make them recall some of the odd things they had noticed about Benton over the last few months. Nicole had waited it out, and soon the conversation had naturally drifted to other topics.

It felt weird to not have Benton next to her. She wanted to tell him about the strange couple and, more importantly, her encounter with Allison. She could practically feel the words on her tongue. But he wasn't on the seat beside her. The second they had set foot back onto the bus, Cheyanne and Theodore had kept a secure eye on their son. It had been a tight squeeze, but they had forced him to sit between them on the narrow seat of the front row. At first, it had been an annoyance. But as time passed, her frustration had grown into deep resentment.

They were now entering the Highway of The Lost and Benton was struggling.

Slight shivers had turned into near violent quakes, his color going pale. She had only managed to catch a few glances of his face as he shifted to find a more comfortable position. When they had only been about half an hour in, his lips had shown the bluish tinge, she had seen before. Soon after, the dark circles under his eyes looked like sooty smears. His parents had noticed. It would have been impossible not to. Their son, squished between them, was deteriorating into a living block of ice.

When Nicole couldn't take it anymore, she gathered up the blankets she had bought and hesitantly approached them. Her hope had been that the gesture would break whatever strange tension that had come between them. It hadn't actually worked that way, but at least Theodore and Cheyanne accepted the blankets. With a forced smile and a reluctant attitude, they had insisted she head back to her seat. Benton looked miserable, with sheets wrapped around him, but at least he had his headphones on. He always handled the weirder things better when he had a decent song to listen to.

On the way back to her seat, her eyes had met Zack's. He wasn't joking along with the others around him. His usual smile was gone. Instead, he was seething, his mouth turned down into a deep scowl. She tried to give an apologetic look, yet it wasn't clear if he understood her or not. Either way, he wasn't ready to accept it. Danny and Meg weren't in any mood to talk either. So she sunk into her seat, against the bus wall and focused on the pouring rain that sprayed down the window.

She had been so lost within her thoughts and concern that it took her a moment to realize just how bad the storm was getting. As the bus had climbed up from the depths of the valley, the rainwater had gathered into a near waterfall that rushed back down the slope. The bus's engine groaned as Dorothy forced it to go faster around the slick, twisting roads.

Time dragged on and the shadows became thicker, transforming the encroaching fog from a dull slate gray into an impenetrable darkness. It consumed everything around them until only the bus's headlights could gouge a path through it. The deluge limited even that feeble visibility. It steamed the windshield faster than the windshield wipers could force it aside. Nicole watched, with rising dread, as the night took a firm hold, swallowing up the world, allowing it only to reemerge when bursts of lightning lashed out at the sky.

They had to be nearing the motel, but Nicole wasn't sure how much more she could take; or, more precisely, how much Benton could. Hunched under the layers of his blankets, his interval moments of discomfort had become a state of constant squirming. It seemed no matter how he tried to position himself, in the limited space between his parents, he couldn't get comfortable. Having to sit there and not help was steadily driving Nicole nuts. Her fingers ached from gripping the back of the seat in front of her and her forearm began to steadily throb. If her painkillers wore off causing her pain, she couldn't even begin to imagine what was happening within Benton's skull.

The engine groaned in protest as Dorothy proceeded to force it through a flooded road. It looked as if they were passing through a boggy lake, one that was quickly rising as the water trailed down the slope to pool into it. Muddy waters sloshed around the wheels as the lake pooled around the bus, making it buoyant for moments at a time before the tires could find the ground again. Her mother increased the speed, surging the bus fast through the stream, desperate to get out before they were stranded completely.

Then Benton snapped up, his attention focused on the windshield as he lunged towards Dorothy. In that split second, Nicole could see the woman. Encrusted in filth from head to toe, standing knee deep in the churning water. The woman didn't move a muscle as the bus barreled down upon her. Dorothy slammed on the breaks. Hysterical screams rang in Nicole's ears as she was thrown forward. She whammed into the seat before her, her wounded arm trapped between her coming body and the unmovable slab. Hot pain blinded her, and water sloshed around the locked wheels of the bus, making it skid forward. It fishtailed well past the point where the woman had been standing and jolted violently as it found traction again. Nicole was shoved back into her seat as the bus climbed up the hill a few feet and lurched to a stop.

Panting heavily, Nicole glanced around. The dim light within the bus brightened as person after person pulled out their mobile phones. When they first switched their flashlights on, the stark glow only brightened their look of shock and horror. Then, one by one, the lights were plastered against the windows of the bus. In the turmoil, Nicole could only pick up on shards of conversations. It was enough to know that they were looking for the woman. The woman they had just run down. *They saw her too,* the thought hit Nicole like a branding iron, and she spun around to face Benton.

He wasn't looking back at her. His eyes were locked on her mother as he purposefully shook his head; short, decisive movements that could be mistaken for tremors of shock. But Dorothy saw it, and a moment of recognition crossed her face before she popped open an overhead compartment and pulled out a flashlight. *She's going out there.* Nicole was on her feet before the realization had fully formed in her mind.

"Mom!" she yelled as she scrambled out over Danny's lap. "Mom!"

Theodore and Cheyanne were already trying to calm everyone down. The aisle was narrow and it wasn't hard for the two adults to effectively block her path.

"Everyone, settle down," Dorothy said with calm authority. "Now, I'm sure it was just a trick of the light. I'm going to check it out, but I need everyone to remain where they are."

Benton was still shaking his head. He tried to get to his feet more than once, but each time he slumped back into his chair, shivering and drained. It made a new spark of fear flicker through

Nicole and she pushed forward again. This time, Theodore grabbed her arm.

"You need to listen to your mother and go sit down," Theodore said. "We'll take care of this."

"I'll sit next to Benton," she replied quickly.

Cheyanne narrowed her eyes with annoyance. "For once, just be cooperative."

"For once, look what you're doing to your son."

In a small miracle, her voice came out strong, devoid of the jittering nerves that often hid under her skin. But it took a lot more fortitude to hold the woman's gaze. Eventually, after what had felt like a small eternity, Cheyanne said in a dark hushed voice.

"You don't know what you're talking about."

The doors folded open with a whoosh. Icy wind raced inside, bringing with it a near solid stream of rain. Between the two adults, Nicole spotted her mother heading down the small steps, her flashlight doing little against the shadows. Nicole nearly pushed Theodore into a seat as she forced her way passed and outright ran to her mother.

"Mom!"

Dorothy looked up to see her daughter at the very front of the bus. Nicole gripped the back of the front seat and forced herself to a stop.

"Don't go out there," she pleaded through panted breaths.

"I have to," Dorothy said, with obvious reluctance.

"This is a situation where you listen to Benton," Nicole whispered, in a hush, and loosely gestured to the boy by her side. He was still shaking his head as if this was the only warning he could offer. "It's Allison."

"But what if it's not?" Dorothy asked. "I can't just drive away when someone could need medical help."

"Then let me come with you," Nicole begged.

Dorothy rejected the idea and, before Nicole could protest, held up her hand and whispered, "Have you got it?"

Nicole knew exactly what she meant and shifted just a little to feel the solid push of the handgun against her spine.

"Yes."

"Close the door and don't open it for anyone but me." Her eyes flickered across the still, stunned crowed before she added. "Keep Benton safe."

And with that, Nicole watched her mother walk out into the raging night. The thin beam of her flashlight danced across the windows as she headed to the back of the bus. It was almost a physical pain to obey her mother's order, but Nicole forced herself to scramble back up to the driver's seat and pull the lever.

The doors snapped shut, closing off the encroaching wind and her mother's main escape route. She wanted to rush back to the stairs, and plaster herself against the glass and search for any trace of her mother. Instead, she remained where she was, sitting in the driver's seat with her fingers clasped around the lever handle. Across the aisle, Benton shifted closer to the window and strained his neck trying to look. His whole body was shaking and she was sure she could hear his teeth rattling amid the bedlam.

"Can you see her?" Nicole asked.

Benton shook his head but didn't stop looking. A rolling tide of thunder crossed over them. It shook the windows and pressed on already frail nerves. Nicole had been so fixated on the door that she hadn't noticed Meg approaching, until she slid into the space beside Benton. He seemed just as surprised, but after sparing her a passing glare, continued his search of the world beyond the bus.

"What did you see?" Meg asked. She kept her voice low and Nicole could barely hear her over the pounding rain and worried chatter.

Benton's only response was to pull the blankets around himself a little tighter.

"Come on, you would have had an unobstructed view," Meg pressed. "Did you see a woman? I swear I saw this woman standing right in the middle of the road. She didn't even try to get out of the way."

"Why did my parents let you up here?" Benton asked, with a stuttering whisper.

Meg looked startled. The expression mystified Nicole. That kind of dismissive remark littered most of their conversations. But then she realized; that was the exact moment that her friend noticed just how badly Benton was fairing.

Before Meg could decide which line of questioning to pursue, a noise weaved its way through the wind. The chatter on the bus instantly died down as people strained to hear it again. It wasn't that the sound was loud or commanding that it drew attention, but it was how out of place it was.

Giggling. Someone was laughing. Not a happy, carefree kind of laugh. This was a cackle. High and fast, and echoing in on itself like a metal chamber. Malicious. Deranged.

Nicole nearly stopped breathing, and it didn't seem like she was the only one. Within seconds, the bus had fallen into an apprehensive silence. They waited. The wind rushed over the sides of the bus and whistled through the few trees that surrounded them. Water babbled and bucked as it ran down the incline creating more puddles. Nicole's skin crawled. Thunder snapped somewhere in the distance and Nicole turned back to Benton to see recognition fueling his eyes. Slowly, carefully, she stood up to remove her jacket. Discursion be damned. She didn't want anything between her and the handle of her gun.

A deathly scream broke the silence as something came crashing down on top of the bus. The metal dented under the assault, and the teens parted as they threw themselves down. All other sound died amid the cackling roar. It streaked past the window, passing from one side to the next in a second. Everyone lurched to get away from it, but it always beat them to the other side of the bus. The demented sound chased them down until it seemed to come from all sides at once.

In a sudden burst of energy, Benton sprang up from his seat and hurdled over Meg to get into the aisle.

"Open the door!" he commanded, but Nicole was already rushing to do so.

"No!" Theodore's bellow was soon joined by a chorus of others.

"My mom is out there!" Nicole blared out as she grabbed the lever.

With a speed Nicole would never have guessed, Cheyanne lurched forward. Her hand closed over Nicole's on the lever and kept it solidly in place.

"You can close it after I get out there!" Nicole said, in an outcry, as she forced her weight against the lever.

The folding door creaked open just a little, just enough for a burst of frigid air to slip through the gap. Some had begun to pound on the glass, trying to draw Dorothy's attention. Nicole could only see the movement of her flashlight shifting aimlessly across the darkness.

"Mom!" Nicole screamed as loud as she could. "Get in here!"

"She's around the back!" Zack yelled, in response as he smacked his fist against the glass again.

The laughter grew louder as it rushed towards them. Nicole realized, an instant too late, that it was racing towards the front of the bus. The impact made the bus slope backwards a few feet. The breaks strained. Even while being braced, Nicole couldn't keep herself from toppling, grasping for the dash to keep herself on her feet. Hysteria rampaged through the bus like wildfire. The noise was deafening and Nicole almost missed Zack's frantic bellow.

"She's under the bus!"

Caught in a state of shock, Cheyanne didn't put up resistance as Nicole cranked the lever. The door hurled open and Nicole leaped into the pouring rain before anyone could stop her. She didn't need to look back to know that Benton was half a step behind, followed by a few others. Those that remained on the bus plastered their phones to the glass once more, creating tiny shafts of light that lit out in all directions. Nicole focused on the beam of her mother's flashlight. It broke free of the murky pool of water that now grounded the back wheel of the mini bus.

Even in his near broken state, Benton was fast. Spurred on by adrenaline, he easily overtook her and rushed into the floodwater without hesitation. He was already blindly groping the obsidian depths before anyone could catch up. With a bellow that was more sound than words, he dropped to his knees and dragged Dorothy back to the surface. It was an awkward angle and her mother didn't seem to have the strength to keep her head up on her own. Benton slipped deeper into the icy water, positioning himself behind her so he could keep her afloat. Water careened down the road and against their heads making the puddle swell high and the tires slide. The bus rolled a little back, and Dorothy screamed in agony.

"The wheel's on my leg!"

Nicole could see Benton's strength was draining fast as she waded through the puddle. The water was only as high as her knees, but by the time Nicole was behind the bus, the water lapped against her thighs and her body shook. Joined by the others, Nicole pressed her shoulder against the flat end of the bus and shoved. They could force it up a little before the breaks engaged. She didn't see who spoke, but someone reached up and slapped their hand against the glass, yelling for whoever was inside to release the brake.

Having already taken the weight, the bus didn't rock back far. But the slight movement was enough to force a horrific, bone-crunching scream from her mother. The cluster of people around her continued to push and slowly the bus began to inch up. That was when the giggling returned.

It swirled around them, drawing nearer with every loop. People struck the glass above them in rapid bursts, trying to warn the others of what instinct alone would tell. Rain poured down the side of the bus, drenching the metal and making it slippery. The laughter came from all around, until it echoed within her head. Nicole's body trembled in strain and fear. Inch by excruciating inch, the mini bus was pushed up the hill.

"She's free!" Benton's words were almost lost under Nicole's mother's sharp cry, and the demonic laughter.

A boy next to her reached up and slammed a hand against the window. The body of the bus jerked and rocked as the breaks were reengaged. Some had already begun to scatter back to the bus, while the vehicle lurched again. Nicole glanced up. Heavy rains impacted her vision and she blinked against the water to see the shape perched upon the very edge of the bus roof. It was only a few inches above her head yet was still shrouded by the ebony clouds. But its eyes weren't. Twin pinpricks of glowing red burned like embers within the darkness. She stared at it and it stared back. Rows of milky white fangs glistened with blood in the weak light as it opened its mouth and laughed.

Spinning on her heels, Nicole sprinted through the water as fast as she could. Out of the corner of her eyes, she could see two of the bigger boys lunging up onto the bus, Dorothy holding on to both of them. Most were back on board with the others cramming their way inside. But Benton was slower, his body failing under the strain. His knees buckled and the cackling creature swooped. Without thought, Nicole pulled her weapon, aimed it a good foot over Benton's back, and fired.

The sharp crack brought new screams that smothered any sound the demon might have made. She couldn't tell if she had hit it. But it had soared back up into the blackened sky. She lost sight of it within the clouds as she raced to Benton's side. He blindly reached for her and didn't protest as she yanked him roughly onto his feet.

His skin was as cold as an arctic wind as he pressed against her side and he swayed more than once. But he kept pace with her, forcing his body to respond to her demands. Nicole's fingers tightened around the handle of her gun as she kept one eye on the sky and one on the small opening of light they were headed towards. Hands reached out from the depths of the bus. They latched onto both her and Benton the second they were within reach and hurled them inside. The door swung shut just as the cackling materialized once more.

Slumped against the small staircase, Nicole and Benton struggled to catch their breaths. Every heartbeat throbbed within her throat and she could practically feel her body heat being sucked into Benton, where he lay beside her. She didn't check to see who pulled her up onto her feet. She was just glad that they did. Clutching onto one of the chairs for support, she called for someone to grab her backpack and the first-aid kit within. Dozens of questions circulated around as the group crammed together, each voice turning into a shriek as something unseen slammed into the bus.

With the shifting light of the mobile phones, Nicole saw her mother's leg. It was swollen and raw, the skin scraped away with part of a protruding bone visible.

"It's okay, mom," Nicole said as she snatched up the first-aid kit. "I'll get you fixed up."

"No, let someone else do it," Dorothy grunted. Nicole's words died on her tongue when she saw the sheer terror in her mother's diluted pupils. "Get us the hell out of here!"

# Chapter 10

Benton hunched his shoulders from the cold and jogged the few last steps to Nicole's motel room door. His feet were heavy and drawing air was near painful, but the shower had helped him regain a little of his warmth. Of course, his new clothes were soaking wet and with his previous outfit, now in a Walmart bathroom, he had been forced back into the clothes he had worn on the trip here. They were still damp and a deathly chill clung to them, even as the thick layer of his raincoat trapped in a rising humidity.

A mild quiver overtook him as he pulled himself up onto the small deck outside of Nicole's room. Something inside him shifted and his skin prickled with the sensation of being watched. Slowly, he turned and swept his gaze across the parking lot. It was easy to see the rooms that housed their groups. Every possible light at their disposal was turned on and a luminous glow glistened on the growing puddles. The wind bent the treetops into sharp angles, and the whole place just felt soggy.

A shiver rushed in the pit of his stomach as a car turned off the highway and made its way across the lot. He used the light of its high beams to check the darker shadows, but still couldn't see anything. The car inched down to a crawl as it passed him and his brow furrowed. *That's the same car*, his mind whispered. The one he had seen in the hotel parking lot last week. The simple sedan that made something rise and hiss in the back of his mind. It was too dark inside to see anyone.

Benton was startled out of his trance from the door behind him flinging open. With an annoyed huff, Nicole reached out, grabbed him by the back of his raincoat, and yanked him inside. The room's thermostat had been cranked up and the air now carried a near tropical heat. Just like his shower, it felt great on his skin, but did little to warm his bones.

"You're going to catch your death of cold out there," Nicole chastised before adding in a secretive tone. "How are you parents?"

"Rattled. They *really* don't like you."

"I saved your life!"

"You did. And I am very grateful," he said as he flopped down on the end of her bed. "But they can't really acknowledge that without admitting that I was attacked by a flying monster. It's easier to just focus on you having a gun."

"This is getting ridiculous," Nicole complained as she locked and relocked the door. "Maybe I should make them a punt cake."

There was a lot about Nicole that, given time and exposure, Benton could understand. But her obsession for getting everyone to like her would forever be lost to him.

Confident that the locks were in place, she crossed the room and sat down next to him. "So how did you get out?"

"Turns out that a dozen terrified teenagers is a really good distraction," Benton shrugged as he toyed with the iron bracelet Nicole had given him. It was too small to spin around his wrist, so he had taken to flicking it along his arm instead. "Especially since my parents are now their sole caregivers for the night. How is your mom?"

Nicole shifted her eyes to the bathroom door before looking back at him. "Rattled."

He smiled at her attempted joke but it didn't seem to help.

"If her leg's not broken, there is definitely a few fractures," Nicole said. "I've done all I can but I think she's in a lot of pain. And she's going to be in a lot more when the shock wears off."

Benton couldn't look up from the bracelet as he spoke. "I'm really sorry, Nic. I should have done more to make sure she didn't go out there."

"It wasn't your fault."

His attention flicked to the new, clean bandage that was wrapped on her forearm. "Yeah, it never seems to be my fault."

"Hey, at least this isn't going to scar," she said before rushing on. "I keep going over it but I can't understand why Allison would do this."

"I think it was just bad timing when she showed up."

"Other people saw her, you know."

"Yeah," Benton nodded. "I felt her more, too. That girl's got a lot of rage."

"Well, if she wasn't so horrible to you, I'd be a bit more sympathetic."

The bathroom door opened and they both jumped to their feet. Since the front desk's well prepared emergency kit had included crutches, Dorothy was somewhat mobile. Still, they kept a close eye on her as she crossed to the nearest bed and eased herself down. She sat with her back against the wall and Nicole helped her to raise her leg up onto the mound of pillows. The rulers that were used for a makeshift splint gave the bandages around her leg an uneven shape. Only her toes were visible and they had become discolored and swollen. He tried not to stare as he sat down on the opposite bed with a pained grunt. Instantly, he felt stupid for being so delicate when the woman before him was under a bus an hour ago.

It felt like all the fluid in his joints was freezing into place and he couldn't stop wincing at almost every movement.

"We should call you an ambulance," Nicole said.

"I'm not putting anyone else on that road," Dorothy shot back.

Benton got the distinct feeling that this was a conversation the two women had been having for a while and resolved to stay out of it.

"And besides," Dorothy said, "they can't get here. We barely did. That road would be completely swamped by now."

"Okay, so we keep going forward." Even as Nicole said it, the words morphed from a statement into a question and back again.

Benton flicked the bracelet on his wrist as the room fell silent. It felt like they were both waiting for him to say what they all knew.

"We can't bring her in this state," he said softly.

Nicole shot him a dirty look and he rubbed his face so he wouldn't have to see it.

"Come on, Nic. I'm already slowing you down. If you try and look after both of us at the same time, we're all going to get killed."

"I'm not leaving my mom here," Nicole said.

"I'll be safer in here than I will be out there." Dorothy spat out the words as if they tasted foul in her mouth. "You two need to leave. And soon. More roads are going to flood and you need to beat these things back to Fort Wayward."

"Mom."

"Honey," Dorothy stammered. She closed her eyes and took a deep breath. It didn't remove the tremble in her voice. "I saw it. Really saw it. After it rolled the bus onto me, it landed on my chest. It's nothing but teeth, eyes and claws."

"Claws?" Benton asked.

"You can't see them when it flies. Just when it lands. I felt them cutting me as it forced me under the water." Her words trailed off, broken by a gasped breath. "It smiled at me. It laughed as I was drowning. That laugh…"

Quickly but carefully, Nicole bundled her mother into a tight hug. The older woman clung back, her hands balling into the sleeves on Nicole's sweater. She looked pale, worn, but no matter how many times she closed her eyes, they always snapped back open. Benton sat silently. He had seen them, heard them, felt their teeth sink into his skin, and knew there wasn't much that could be said to make that memory better. So he flicked at the iron piece on his wrist to keep his fingers from freezing into place and waited.

Eventually, Dorothy let go of Nicole's arms and sat up straight once more. "You said there are hundreds of those creatures?"

"At least," he nodded.

"It's okay," Nicole said with a tremble in her voice. "I'm not going to let them get in here."

"You can't let them get into town. Folks won't be ready. It'll be a slaughter," Dorothy countered. She looked from Benton to Nicole and back before adding, "I will probably rot in hell for this, but you were right, this isn't a two person job. You're going to have to get some help."

"Benton's parents will never listen to us," Nicole said a second before she caught onto what Dorothy was actually suggesting. "Do you have any suggestions?"

"Well, I know two people who have been eager to get in on the secret," Benton said.

Stunned, Nicole turned to him. "Meg and Zack? You really want to trust them?"

"Zack is strong and Meg is resilient," Dorothy muttered as she mulled the choices over.

"We'll have to get Danny, too," Nicole said.

"Nope."

"Benton, Meg isn't going to go without her sister."

"Yes, but I'll be upset if Danny dies."

*** 

The rain pelted against the bus windows, accentuating the lingering silence. Nicole nervously flicked her gaze from one friend to the next, but couldn't figure out how any of them were reacting to the information she and Benton had just laid out before them. It was a lot to ask a person to accept. Time dragged on until Nicole could feel every second of it consuming her. Benton wasn't faring much better. While he tried to be patient, she could see the stress on his face. The cold in his bones was warring with the fire within his skull, and he was quickly losing his ability to simply sit back and give them the time they needed.

"A banshee?" Meg said slowly. "You think we're going to believe that?"

"It would be impossible to accurately describe how little I care about what you think or believe," Benton said as he rubbed his temples again. "Just help me get into town."

"Yeah, that's the way to ask for a favor," Zack scoffed.

"I'm sorry," he said as he pushed his fingers harder into his pressure points. "Am I not being polite enough offering to save the lives of an entire town? Not living up to your standards?"

"Zack, he's just trying to help," Nicole commented.

Zack bolted up straighter. "Help? I'll help as soon as he starts telling me the truth."

"I just did," Benton said. "Thanks for paying attention, by the way."

"The whole truth. Not just the bits you want to tell us."

Benton was practically grinding his fists against his skull now and Nicole quickly tried to take up the conversation to give him some time to regroup his thoughts.

"Zack, that was everything, I promise."

"Come on, Nicole. You think I can't do a Google search? Everywhere this guy goes, people die."

"That's what people do!" Benton bellowed in exasperation. "It's like a third of our existence; we're born, we live, we die."

"There are way too many bodies for it to be coincidence."

Spreading his arms wide, Benton leaned forward and yelled with every ounce of strength he had left in him, "Banshee!"

"This isn't getting us anywhere," Nicole cut in. "So let's find common ground. Hands up if you saw Allison."

Meg shot her a sideways look. "Well, we only really have Benton's word that it's Allison."

Nicole twitched and Benton looked to the ceiling as if praying for salvation. "Fine. Hands up if you saw the woman in the middle of the road."

She thrust her own hand into the air and looked expectantly at Benton until he lifted his too. Meg, Danny, and after a moment of hesitation, Zack, all put their hands up.

"I'm not disputing ghosts. Or whatever that flying thing was," Zack grumbled. "I'm disputing that this guy has a magical scream. Because if he doesn't, this is pretty much a suicide mission. Anyway, banshees are females, everyone knows that."

"I'm done," Benton mumbled. Nicole tried to soothe him but he just rubbed his hand over his face before snapping, "In or out? And I don't just mean that abstractly. If you're not coming along, get off the bus so we can go."

"He's in a lot of pain," Nicole offered as Benton burrowed his hands in the blanket on his lap.

"I'm in." Danny didn't flinch as both Zack and Meg twisted around to face her.

"Seriously," Meg whispered.

"Yes," Danny affirmed.

"You really think he's a banshee?" Zack asked.

"It doesn't matter," Danny challenged. "That demon is heading to our home, our families, and they're the only ones trying to stop it. I don't care if he's a unicorn, I'm going to help."

Nicole reached across the space separating them and squeezed Danny's hand. "Thank you."

"And you wonder why I like her better," Benton mumbled, now holding the blanket to his chin and trembling. He seemed to be having a hard time keeping his eyes open.

"Well, you're not going without me," Meg cut in before she turned to Benton. "For the record, I'm following Nicole, not you."

Benton didn't give any indication that he had heard her or cared.

Zack shook his head and pushed further back into his seat. "Let's get going."

# Chapter 11

The rising water was quickly swallowing the road, and Nicole was losing track of it. The bus's steering wheel rattled within Nicole's grasp. Her fingers ached as she struggled to keep the bus from fishtailing every time the wheels found a mass of water and forced them to shift. With only the dim headlights to judge by, Nicole was never quite sure if she was about to drive them off a cliff. She wanted to slow down but Benton's low, agonized groans forced her to go faster.

Benton had pulled himself into a tight ball, but not even all the sheets could help him maintain any of his body heat. Danny had taken pity on him and sat close enough that her warmth might transfer to him. It wasn't helping. He was visibly growing worse and was no longer able to silence his moans of pain.

"He's really not looking so good," Zack expressed as he came up beside her.

"I know," she said breathlessly, sneaking another glance at him in the rearview mirror.

Meg had come up behind her and leaned against the back of the driver's seat.

"What is wrong with him?" she whispered.

"I think it's this land," Nicole whispered back. "Or maybe all the dead people. But we're almost there."

Yanking hard on the wheel, she rounded a blind turn. The high beams swung around, illuminating the falling rain like crystals as the windshield wipers struggled to force the water aside. A white mass suddenly came into view. It filled the road as they hurdled towards it. Nicole slammed on the breaks. The back wheels hit a watery patch and the bus started to swerve, shifting further to the opposite side each time she tried to compensate. For a moment, the earth dropped out from under them and they lurched down. With an intense crack and a bone-rattling jolt, they finally came to a stop.

Mud and muck covered the mini bus. The lights were off. The engine was dead. Surrounded on all sides by near complete darkness, Nicole lifted her head from the steering wheel. Rain pinged against the windows and streamed over the back of the bus. Slowly, the sounds of rustling, of strangled grunts and shifting material, drifted to her ears.

"Is everyone all right?" she called.

Benton growled in answer, sounding more bothered than anything else. One by one, the others announced themselves. Small patches of light flicked into existence and she struggled to see what was happening by their glow. The mini bus was propped up onto a forty-five degree angle, nose deep in a pit. They were sinking. She could tell that much when water began to pull and lap around the cracked windshield.

There was some more rustling and a bright light carved a vivid narrow tube out of the night. Benton had found Nicole's bag and retrieved one of the flashlights. He wavered as he tossed it to her without a word. She caught it with fumbling fingers.

"Okay, well," she said, trying to stay calm as she drifted the light around the bus, "the important thing is that no one's hurt."

"Right," Zack grumbled. "And the fact that we can't get this out of here without a tow truck is coincidental?"

Danny clicked on the second flashlight Nicole had brought and, after flashing it around for a moment, set it on the windshield.

"That water's rising. We need to get out of here," she warned.

Zack paused for a moment as he looked at them all in turn. "Do you think it was a ghost that ran us off the road, again?"

Using the chairs on either side of the aisle as a handhold, Meg pushed herself up towards the rear window. She shone her light through, but couldn't compete with the rain and reflection.

"Nicole had been speeding in the rain around tight corners," Meg pointed out before looking back and adding. "No offense."

"There was a car in the middle of the road," Nicole defended.

Benton perked his head up at that but didn't comment. He already looked exhausted, and every breath was a struggle.

"Make sure your raincoat is buttoned up tight. We need to get you out of here," Nicole told him.

With a staggered nod, Benton detangled himself from the blankets and pulled the hood of his coat higher. His silence set off a thousand warning signs in the back of her head. Benton was many things, but silent wasn't one of them. With everyone's help it took a far shorter time than Nicole had thought to gather them all just below the rear hatch.

Zack put his hand on the lever and his shoulder to the door before he hesitated. "What if those things are out there?"

A scream ripped from them as something smacked against the door. It was met with a sudden light and a high voice.

"Hello? Is everyone okay?"

Zack ducked lower as if to keep himself from being seen. "Can these monsters talk?"

The sweet voice called again from beyond the glass and the outside emergency latch was wrenched open. The door yanked open, allowing in a flood of water and a howling wind. Nicole's long hair whipped across her face. With one arm looped around Benton's and clinging to the flashlight, and the other holding tight onto the back of the nearest chair, she couldn't clear her face of her hair or the water. She aimed the beam of her flashlight onto the stranger's face. A second later, she realized that it wasn't a stranger. Not completely. It was the woman from the McDonald's line.

"Oh, thank God," the woman smiled before turning back to call over her shoulder. "They're okay. We're coming up."

"Who are you?" Zack asked, cautiously pulling himself out.

The question remained unanswered as they worked to pull the others up from inside the bus. When Nicole and Benton were the last two remaining, she gently coaxed him before her, careful not to hurt him as the woman reached down to grab his hand. With her hands on his waist, she felt the jolt that ran through him when they made contact. She snapped her head up to see him frozen in place, his eyes wide even as the rain drizzled into them. The woman stared back with a faint smile, urging him to let her help him out. Benton didn't move.

At his hesitation, Zack mumbled something about him being sick and reached back in to yank Benton up himself. Nicole could only watch as Benton was pulled from her hands and out into the night. Rain washed over her face, a cold chill that made her cringe back at them. The woman stretched out a hand towards her, but Nicole was looking past it. Benton was staring at her, fear lacing his eyes as he slowly shook his head.

"Come on, Nicole," Zack urged. "We have to go."

Benton shook his head all the harder but the pace seemed to drain him. She couldn't refuse, but his warning turned her guts into a trembling mass. Slowly, she reached up. The woman snatched up her hand the second it was within reach. The sensation only grew worse as she was hurled from the bus.

"Oh, hi again," the woman smiled.

Nicole mumbled a hello and tried to pull her hand back. The woman's fingers tightened and locked her in place. Benton pushed past Zack and latched onto Nicole's wrist. It made the flashlight in her hand sway and the beam skittered across the area. The glare from his eyes that Benton narrowed on the woman, didn't hold a hint of the sickness that was pressing down on him. But it startled the woman enough that he could yank Nicole out of her grasp.

The tension was broken by Zack's insistence that they move back up to the road. It was a much slower process as water gushed down the steep incline. Nicole deliberately went slower, letting the others move on ahead. Before she could say anything, Benton whispered into her ear.

"Have you got your gun?"

"Back of my waistband. What are you seeing?" she asked.

"Death. It's following her," he whispered. "How do you know her?"

"She's the one I told you about. The one who was around when Allison grabbed me."

After what felt like an eternity, Benton met her gaze. All of her anxieties were mirrored back in his gray eyes and she felt her guts twist.

"Keep close."

She couldn't tell if it was a warning or a plea, but she nodded all the same. They scrambled over the last hump and Benton slumped down over the road. Tremors rippled through him as he clawed at the ground. Nicole instantly dropped down beside him and tried to pull him back up onto his knees. He slumped against her as his chest heaved.

"Is he okay?"

Nicole snapped her head up to see the man from McDonald's standing beside the white sedan that was blocking the road.

"He's sick," Nicole said. "We need to get him back into town."

The couple looked at each other and a cold chill swept up Nicole's spine. There was just something about the exchange that put her on edge.

"Why don't we give you a lift?" the woman offered with a sickly, sweet voice.

It didn't matter how kindly she said it, the question naturally put each one of them on edge. They all exchanged quick glances, weighing out their options, before Zack answered.

"That would be good."

"Well, we can't fit all of you," the man laughed heartedly. It was a pleasant sound, but Benton's hands still tightened in Nicole's jacket in response. "It's not that far into town, though. Why don't we give Nicole and her friend a lift first, seeing he's so sick, and then we'll come back for the rest of you?"

Meg was quick to answer, "This isn't the kind of highway you split up on."

"I've heard some rumors about this road, too," the man acknowledged, "which is why I'm not all that comfortable giving four of you a ride at the same time; especially, when it's just me and my girlfriend."

The woman opened the car's back door. "Nicole, isn't it? Your boy isn't looking so good. We should hurry up."

Benton shook his head as the pit in Nicole's stomach became a gaping hole.

"Something's really wrong with him, Nicki." The man spoke it like a general comment, but there was no mistaking the edge that lurked within his words.

Zack stepped in between them, using his bulk to try and cut off the man's view of Nicole.

"Hey, man," Zack spoke with that same forced casualness. "Why is your car parked like this anyway?"

Meg and Danny began to edge back, closing ranks with Nicole. The air became a thick swamp of tension as the smiles faded from the couple. Even as the man scowled at her, his voice retrained that warm, all too friendly tone. The disconnection made Nicole's insides squirm and the twins became less subtle about going back to the safety of the group.

"I'm just trying to be friendly and help you out. It doesn't seem like you kids have many options right now."

The man took a step closer. The simple action had provoked immediate reactions. Zack balled his fists. Meg squared off, making sure to keep both strangers in sight. Danny shifted so she blocked the path to the weakened member of their group. And Benton laughed.

It was the strange, strangled sound that always seemed to brew up within him when the seemingly crazy pieces of his life fell into place. Hunched against Nicole with his head hung low and water dripping from his hood, Benton's barked laughter caught everyone off guard. The couple hesitated, but only for a moment.

"What's the joke?" the woman asked.

"The white sedan," Benton disclosed before he summoned the strength to lift his head. "I've seen it each time we stopped. Don't you get it? Allison wants to use me, but she isn't following me. She's following them."

Realization dawned within Nicole like a razor edged wind. "They killed her!"

Her words barely conquered the sounds of the storm, but they instantly grabbed everyone's attention. Heavy silence claimed each of them as they grappled with all the implications. It was their own silence that allowed them to hear it.

The cackling.

It drifted along the air like rolling thunder. But it wasn't just one voice. Dozens crowded in the air, mingling with each other, blending in a wild frenzy that made Nicole nearly drown in her paralyzing fear. Holding Benton close, she glanced over her shoulder, the threat before incomparable to what was rushing up from behind.

Midnight darkness held the world tight, refusing to release it to their flashlights. The maniacal, frenzied laughter grew louder. Rushing towards them. Over them.

"Get in the car!" Zack bellowed.

Chaos broke out at the call. Zack charged for the open back door, but the man swiftly cut him off. Meg and Danny burst forth in the same instant, Meg trying to shove the woman aside while Danny scrambled into the car. A moment later, the high beams flicked on, severing the darkness and illuminating a dozen, ghostly pale faces a few feet down the road. Blinking back into the light, the faces smiled at them, their mouths stretching into impossible lengths, revealing row upon row of twisted fangs.

Someone screamed but Nicole couldn't tell whom through the crushing laughter. The demons scattered into the darkness, their yowling cackles testifying that they didn't have a face. Nicole pulled Benton onto his feet with shaking hands. He moved with all the speed his adrenaline rush would allow, and they lumbered towards the car. The wind whipped at them, pushing them back from the safety of the vehicle. The car now seemed an impossible distance away.

The woman was still grappling with Meg. Clawing her hands into Meg's short hair, the woman tossed her to the side, propelling the teenager out across the road. In the light pouring from the open car door, Nicole caught a glimpse of metal in the woman's hand. And then she was gone. Shock slowed Nicole's movements but Benton kept urging her on. The woman was gone. The space she had once occupied, suddenly empty.

Meg picked herself up to race across the now vacant space and dive in through the open front passenger door. She twisted around instantly and reached back outside, screaming at Nicole to hurry up. The man roared as he lunged at Zack. He was strong, but Zack was stronger and refused to yield an inch. Nicole dragged Benton past them and had just flopped him onto the back seat when an earsplitting crash shook the car. The rear window became a spider web of cracks as the metal of the roof buckled. Nicole threw herself back, shielding her face from debris with both arms as she dropped to the pavement.

A limp hand flopped down over the side of the car. Bloody, rainwater drizzled from the fingertips as the air became deafening with the sound of panic and laughter and the ever present thunder. Forcing herself back onto her feet, Nicole aimed the beam of her flashlight to the roof of the car. The woman stared back at her with lifeless eyes. At the sight, the man's fury grew and he pushed past Zack, his fueled rage apparently focused on Benton. The car shook as the man hurled himself onto Benton and flattened him against the back seat.

Nicole sprinted for the car. Even through her raincoat, she could feel the cold rush of air grazing across her back as something swooped at her. Zack had already gone around the far side and slipped in behind Benton. With the closed door to his back, he was trying to shove the man off of Benton and out of the still open back passenger door. But there wasn't time. She could feel claws slashing through the plastic of her jacket as she reached the car. With one hand, she slammed the back passenger door shut, trapping the man in with them, but keeping the ghostly demons out. With the other hand, she grabbed Meg's waiting hand.

Meg's grip was as solid as stone as she leaned back, throwing her weight behind the task of dragging Nicole into the car. Nicole's shin hit the door a second before a different hand had grabbed her leg. It pulled hard, and if it weren't for Meg's firm grip, Nicole would have been flung back out. Danny reached across her sister and grabbed Nicole's sleeve. Together, they tried to pull her back in while the grip on her ankle dragged her violently into the air.

The car was filled with a frenzy of screams. The twins shouted for help, while Zack was torn between wanting to rescue Nicole and trying to pry the man's hands from around Benton's throat. Nicole could feel the claws shredding her jeans, slashing at the skin underneath. It wrenched her up until her back slammed against the top of the car. The twin's grip was failing. The rain that covered her jacket was making the material too slippery to hold onto properly. Her attempts to hit the creature that was on her leg only made it harder. Over the tops of the seat, she could see the man's knuckles turn white as they tightened around Benton's neck. It didn't matter what Zack did, the man refused to release his grip. Benton had one forearm pressed across the man's chest, trying to force him back, while the other reached for Nicole.

The flashlight fell into the car seat as Nicole slipped her hand under her coat. She found the handle of the gun easily, flicked the safety off with her thumb, and whipped it free. In her heightened position, the angle was easy enough. A thunderous crack rocked the car and the man's head erupted in a splatter of brain and skull fragments. Shock made the twin's grip falter. Nicole was yanked back an inch before Benton latched onto her outstretched arm, the move saving her from being pulled free, but also stopping her from re-aiming the gun.

His hand was weak. His scream wasn't.

The windows exploded into shards in the wake of the shrilled wail. The sound hovered on a point that made her ears ring as the deeper tones penetrated within her chest. Through it all, weaved within the tapestry of impossible sounds, was the hint of a human's fearful scream. The laughing creatures scattered back into the darkness. Only the one on her leg remained. She could feel it trembling as the pain in her ears intensified. She could feel it melt. Its skin dribbled over her own, rotting away until she was dropped with a sudden jerk.

Benton's grip failed as Nicole fell. Her knees collided with the pavement as the edge of the seat drove into her stomach. She was vaguely aware that the gun had slipped from her grasp, but the notion was lost as Meg and Danny scrambled to pull her inside. The windows were gone, but Danny still reached over her and pulled the door shut, locking it instantly.

Rain showered in through the empty space, where the window once was, drenching the back of her legs. It was that pattering sound that she first heard when the ringing in her ears subsided. In the jumbled position she was in, Nicole could see between the two front seats into the back. Panting heavily, Benton propped himself against the corpse on his lap to keep himself upright. Behind him sat Zack, with his mouth open, his eyes wide and unblinking. She could feel the twins shaking as they held her tightly. No one said anything. It was in that silence that Nicole truly realized what she had done.

Benton was the first to recover, at least from his shock. With a weak turn of his head, he sought out Nicole's gaze.

"Are you okay?" he asked with a slight gravel to his voice.

Nicole nodded although she wasn't quite sure. Physically, mentally, she was still too stunned to know how deep the wounds went.

"Thanks," Benton said with a weary smile. He waited for her to nod again before continuing. "We should go. This car isn't going to keep them out if they come back."

"What the hell just happened?" Zack burst into motion and rage. "We were almost killed. Nicole shot that guy. And you're some kind of..."

"You can say it," Benton said as he shifted uncomfortably under the dead weight. "It's not a derogatory word."

"How are you so calm?" Meg weakly asked.

"I've been around a lot of dead people," Benton shrugged.

"In your dreams!" Zack snapped. "That's kind of different."

Benton rolled his eyes and the gesture made him waver. The others broke into a thousand words, but Nicole couldn't understand them. All she could see was Benton quickly fading, and the corpse she had created. A patch of blood stained the seat just to the side of his face and her gut wrenched at the sight of it. Still, even as her internal organs seemed to melt into a boiling tar, she didn't feel a blinding despair crumbling down on her.

Benton lifted his gaze to meet hers and his body went rigid. It took Nicole a second to realize that he wasn't looking at her. His eyes were focused out on the shattered windshield. The same expression soon covered everyone else's face. They were all focused on the windshield. Feeling the aches in her body, Nicole pushed herself up to follow their gazes. Allison stood before them. The edge of the high beams only just illuminated her feet. Mud bled out from her, mixing with the rain and pooling around her. Lightning sparked the sky and, within that moment, she could see a dozen other spirits hidden within the shadows. As one, they all began to edge closer.

Nicole scrambled back from the door as Allison stalked past. She jerked and jolted. Even the storm couldn't drown out the way her flesh squelched with every step. She stopped at Benton's door and turned. Lightning cracked again and they were suddenly surrounded by the rotting woman. The back door popped open and Nicole snapped around to see Benton nudging the door open with his foot. Zack balled his hands in Benton's shirt, but it didn't stop Benton from nudging the door again.

Slowly, Allison crouched down. Sludge dripped from her matted hair and smeared across her face. The darkened smears turned her eyes into luminous milky pools. Allison's hand twitched as she reached out and closed her hand around the man's leg. She began to drag the corpse out of the car, all the while keeping her eyes locked with Benton's. She slipped the man out onto the road with a whack. The other spirits closed in around them and the car began to shake. The suspension squealed and the rain poured in from every angle. Nicole's hands reached out as she searched for something to hold onto. With one last tremor, the woman's body was dragged from the roof. Then the spirits retreated back into the darkness, taking the corpses with them, and leaving the stunned teens alone to the driving rain.

When Benton broke the silence, his voice was numb. "Please tell me someone has the car keys."

# Chapter 12

The air had shifted the moment Danny had driven the car, careening off of the highway and back onto the main road. Hurricane winds still slammed into the sides of the vehicle and the rain still drove down like hail, but Benton felt the change. His spine arched and his lungs gulped down air as if he had been drowning. The chill that encased him remained, but no longer dug into him like daggers of ice.

Lights flickered across the horizon, barely concealed by the typhoon and the swirling masses of darkness that surrounded it. Danny didn't hesitate to push the car to its limits. How she managed to keep the battered vehicle on the road in such conditions was beyond him. But she never wavered as she veered around the slippery patches that were quickly coming up to flood the roads. The tires created walls of water as they cut through the unavoidable patches.

As they drew closer to the town, streetlights became a common sight. Shadows raced through the patches of light that polluted the air. A howling trail of malignant laughter rushed towards them and slammed against the side of the car. The metal dented under the assault and the tires squealed, forcing the car into the other lane. Danny hardly had the time to right the car before another strike sent them careening back.

Thrown around in the back seat, Benton tried to keep from getting too close to any of the gaping places where the glass had once been. The demonic laughter rose, and into it rivaled the roar of a hurricane. Claws reached in towards him, grasping and slashing. Covering their heads, Benton and Zack vied for safe space, trying to get out of the way of the demonic talons and Nicole's shots. It didn't take long for the onslaught to tax her remaining bullets, leaving them with no protection beyond Danny's driving.

As if sensing this, the demons centered their attacks on ripping their way towards the car's engine. Chunks of metal were torn from the hood, left to bounce and slash their way through the empty space of the windshield and into the car. Without looking up, Benton knew that the water was rising. The engine roared and strained as the water pushed back. It wasn't enough to bring them to a stop but enough to be felt.

Knowing exactly where they were going, Danny ripped through the few streets of Fort Wayward. The water caught the wheels and drove them into a sideways slide. The car diverted and swung wildly as Danny yanked the wheel and slammed her foot down onto the gas pedal. Benton was prepared for the crunch of splintering wood and the jarring jolt that brought them to a jerk. Already huddled, Benton slacked against the door as the car's engine sputtered and died with a hiss. The wind and laughter became distant but without the deluge striking the roof, the world seemed suddenly quiet.

"You just drove through a historical monument," Nicole gasped weakly.

Danny's voice echoed the shell-shocked tone. "We're in a hurry."

Benton had only just begun to straighten when he heard the front passenger door open. A second later, the door behind him yanked open and Nicole began to gently remove his hands off of his head.

"Benton," she eased, "you have to move now. Can you get up?"

"I'm okay," Benton promised. He was still frozen and his every movement felt like he was about to crack, but thinking had become clearer and he felt like he could move again. "Are you okay?"

Nicole nodded and helped him out of the car and over the surrounding rubble. It was his first time within the actual fort that had given the town its name. The streetlights washed in through the rain and windows, casting a honeyed glow over the long room. Taking it in, it seemed that the building had a square design with a courtyard sheltered within the middle. The hysterical creatures circled like vultures, casting shadows over the illuminated space and smacking against the sides of the building as if they were trying to find their way in. They seemed to be within a rustic gift shop, with rows of low aisles dividing the spacious room, and the actual museum beginning at the corner ahead of them.

"Where's the speaker system?" Zack asked.

"The tower," Nicole instantly replied as she pointed out across the courtyard. Grabbing Benton's hand, as if unsure that he could make the distance, she began to drag him forward. "We can get to it through the museum."

"How do you know this?" Meg asked as she followed.

Nicole didn't stop looking at the room as she hurried them through the gift shop. "They let me watch the parade from the control room a few times."

"Of course they did," Benton smirked.

They rounded the corner and entered into the museum just as the screeching horde found the now gaping hole in the wall. Sprinting quicker into the displays of antiques, they barreled towards the back door. Despite the glass shards lodged within his joints, Benton took the lead, and using his shoulder, barged his way through the emergency exit.

Cold air rushed to meet him. Nicole didn't pause. Gripping his hand, she slipped past him and rushed out to the water slick concrete that ran the length to the tower. His sneakers were slippery as he tried to pick up his pace. The flood of monsters streamed out of the door to follow him, their gales of laughter drawing the attention off the others. His lungs burned. His muscles felt like grinding stone, and the doorway always seemed too far away.

A sudden whack against his spine spun him off of his feet. He hit the ground hard, his grip on Nicole bringing her down with him. Their momentum dragged them a few feet before they finally stopped. Zack jumped over them, wrenched the door open, and reached back to snatch them up. Between him and the twins, Nicole and Benton were hurled into the space. The door slammed shut and muted the mocking cackles of the creatures. On all fours, Benton struggled to catch his breath and adjust his eyes to the darkened space. It was only then that the pain, streaking across his back, inched into his awareness. The gashes weren't deep but stung like fire. He blinked rapidly but there was only the impenetrable darkness.

"Nicole?" he gasped.

"I'm okay," came the instant reply.

"We're good too," Zack huffed, his voice coming out breathing and needy, like he was desperate for anything to lighten the mood.

"I was just about to ask," Benton smiled. "Can anyone find a light switch?"

"Why?" Meg asked.

Nicole didn't hesitate. "Benton, what do you see?"

His stomach plummeted. "Nothing."

Ignoring the questions that began to churn, he rocked back onto his knees and glanced around. The desperate sensation within his chest only grew worse when he saw that it wasn't complete darkness. Splotches of white circled him. The grim reapers towered over him, closing in around him until they filled his vision.

"Benton," Nicole gasped as the sound of tearing wood and breaking stone filled his ears. "Benton, we have to move. There are a lot of stairs."

Solid thuds bore down around him. He could feel the splintered chunks of wood crash down, but he couldn't see what was causing the damage. He pushed himself up onto his feet. The reapers didn't pull back but pressed closer still. Benton hesitated to reach through the rising smoke of their bodies in a blind search for Nicole.

"Benton!" Nicole yelled over the laughter and the crashing of stone against stone.

The ebony specters pushed in until the curling trails of their bodies brushed over his skin. Screams bounced off the small confines of the room, blurring with the cackles of the coming creatures. *They're coming through the roof*, Benton realized. The sounds grew louder and he forced his face up until he met the gaping, bottomless holes of Death's face.

"Okay," he said.

He didn't know what he was agreeing to, but they had helped once before. He clung to that hope as the reapers pressed against him, flooded into him, clawing and scraping his flesh. They forced themselves into his skin and slipped from his sight. Ghostly faces swept down towards him. Their eyes burned. Their smiles stretched wide. Their laughter rattled the cells of his being and he felt something inside rush up to meet it.

Benton's mouth dropped open to release a scream, like the world was drawing in a deep breath as wind scurried forcefully towards him. It was strong enough to snap the door open and strong enough to draw the others off of their feet and drag them towards him. The gale force never touched his skin. The pressure grew, pressing against his body, taking up every inch of space within him. Rushing wind covered every other sound the world held. For one agonizing moment, there was only silence and the crushing vacuum that held him.

Then Benton shrieked.

The sound rushed from him as a physical force that shattered the walls and sent the others flying. The creatures above him melted and burst, droplets of their bodies thrown aside by the sheer force of the sound. Stones shattered, wood splintered, and the concrete cracked open beneath him as the pressure was released upon the banshee wail. He screamed until he was empty and collapsed into oblivion.

*** 

Colors played across the metal inner doors of the ambulance, copying the sunset that turned clear sky into shades of pink and purple. Benton sat towards the open back of door of the ambulance and watched the display. It seemed like an eternity had passed since he had actually seen a blue sky. He hadn't realized how suffocating the clouds had been.

The scratches on his back hadn't been that bad. Nicole had given him a few swipes of an antibacterial wipe and a clean dressing, ensuring that he wouldn't have to show his back to any of the emergency medical workers that were now working their way through the streets. He only knew that because she had told him so, once he regained consciousness. To be more accurate, she had screamed it. It seemed that quite a few people were currently experiencing some hearing problems. That gave him a perfect opportunity to call Dorothy before Nicole could.

He slumped against the ambulance and repositioned the phone to his ear, waiting for Dorothy to absorb the information. Telling her the whole story had been harder than he had expected. There wasn't exactly a nice way to inform a police officer that their daughter had killed someone, but waiting for a response was excruciating.

"And you're sure the bodies are gone?" Dorothy asked slowly. "They won't be showing up anytime soon?"

"I think so. I can't imagine that Allison or the others will be willing to give them up. It felt like they had been waiting quite a while to get their hands on them," Benton said.

"And the car?" Dorothy pressed.

"It's pretty banged up. But there are a lot of displaced cars and even more injured people. No one really cares at the moment."

"Displaced and driven through a wall are slightly different," Dorothy said. It seemed to pain Dorothy to add, "When you can, go make sure that the bullet isn't lodged in the seat."

There was a long moment of silence before she asked, "How is she holding up?"

"Good so far," he said as he watched Nicole running around. She had offered to help with the general first-aid. Given how overrun they currently were, they had accepted. "But you know her. She's not going to dwell on it as long as someone needs her."

"Don't suppose you can keep her busy until I get back?"

"I'm a walking disaster. I can keep her busy until the second coming," Benton said with a slight smile. It was harder to keep it. "How are my parents?"

"Annoyed. And worried."

Benton shuffled into a more comfortable position. "Can you tell them I'm okay? And sorry. And, you know, that I love them."

"I will," Dorothy said. "And you're a hero now. I'm sure they'll overlook this."

"A hero?"

"Our story is that you all went because you knew the storm was coming and wanted to raise the alarm. So as long as we're using that, your actions are heroic, so don't mess it up."

"Right," Benton said.

"I still don't know what we're going to tell everyone here."

"Nothing. You're only going to run into trouble trying to explain it. Just keep your silence and it'll be an urban legend in a week." Benton rubbed a hand over his face, feeling the now familiar shift of the iron bracelet over his forearm.

"You sound very sure about that."

"Done this dance a few times," he said. "Oh, they said that a bus will be heading up to you guys soon. It's just going to take a little longer than expected. There's a bit of damage."

He shifted his eyes over the destruction. The tower hadn't been the only thing damaged during the storm. Streets were swamped with water and debris. Hunks of roofs were broken and twisted, and he couldn't spot one window that was still intact.

Dorothy sucked in a pained breath but only replied, "We can wait it out."

Through the crowd, he spotted Nicole coming his way. Quickly, he said goodbye and ended the call. He made sure to tuck the device securely into the shelf the EMT had asked him to leave it in. Benton honestly had no idea where he had lost his phone and he made a mental note to check the car.

Nicole pulled herself up into the ambulance and sat down on the seat next to him.

"Hi," she practically shouted. "They say my hearing will come back in a day or two, but I think I'm already better."

"Obviously," he laughed.

Her brow furrowed. "What did you say?"

Shaking his head, Benton wasn't exactly surprised when Nicole pulled out her mobile phone. Of course she had managed to keep ahold of it and still have it in working order. She opened up its notebook, fluttered her thumbs over the keys and passed it to him.

'Are you in any pain?' he read. Meeting her eyes, he shook his head and then pointed to her to shoot the question back her way. She shook her head but took the phone.

'Sluagh.'

Benton's brow furrowed and typed back, 'What did you just call me?'

'Not you. The faces. They made me take a lunch break and I did some research. I think they're called Sluaghs.'

Reading the message, his first instinct was to ask her if she had at least eaten. But that was a question for later. She loved to cook and she loved to protest his bad eating habits, so, if he played it right, he could wrangle her into cooking dinner, effectively giving her two things to keep her mind busy.

'Awesome,' he typed back. 'Will you let me get up and help soon?'

'I'm not the boss of you,' she replied before snatching the phone out of his hand, clicking off a few keys, and handing it back. 'But no.'

He laughed and let himself lean against her a little more. Heat had risen back up into his body, but she was still so delightfully warm that he felt himself relaxing into it. He knew he shouldn't, but he couldn't stop himself from typing out the question.

'You know, if there is any truth behind the theory that the death of a paranormal creature will draw more in, we could have a problem.'

She read it. But instead of the hesitation he had expected, her fingers were instantly in motion.

'Maybe. But we have a bigger team now. We can take care of it.'

Benton looked at it for a moment before he scanned the crowd. Zack was still helping to clear some rubble from the street. At the far corner, he spotted Meg passing out hot drinks and Danny trying to simultaneously entertain a group of children, while keeping them from running into the mess. He wasn't exactly in a position to call any of them a *friend*. But he couldn't deny that, to some extent, he really did trust them. And that was an odd sensation.

With Nicole a constant weight by his side, he tapped the phone against his wrist, listening to it click against his bracelet, and watched the sun set across the Alberta sky.

* * *

# Rotting Souls
## Banshee Series Book 4

# Chapter 1

*He's close.*

An icy chill came along with that thought. It clawed up Benton's spine and burrowed deep into his bones. He balled his hands against his knees, pushing his knuckles painfully down into his kneecaps. *Keep still. Wait.* Allow the lurking ghost to gather its nerve. A surge of adrenaline sharpened his senses, allowing him to track the soft sounds of the ghost as it crawled over the walls. It moved with a slickly tearing sound. Something between the sharp break of bone and the snap of sapling trees.

Benton knew he shouldn't look. He had enough trouble sleeping without observing the twisted monstrosity that Oliver Ackerman had become.

Being riddled with rot and covered with grave dirt now seemed pleasant. But, as the ripping sound crept around to his left, he couldn't stop himself from glancing over. The old man's spine was forced into an almost perfect arch, forcing him to walk on his hands and feet. The bones of his fingers broke free of his skin like gnarled tree roots. They weaved through everything it touched. Constantly growing. Forcing him to snap his bones for every jerk forward. Ackerman met Benton's eyes.

The fury within his eyes was a sight Benton was used to seeing. The fear wasn't.

"Is he back?" Zack called to him, careful not to cross the threshold of the open barn doors.

"He never left," Benton replied absently.

Zack's eyes grew wide, flicking wildly around like a startled deer. "Then where did he go? He didn't come out here with us, did he?"

"Nah." Benton didn't take his eyes off of Ackerman as he waved a hand above her head. "He likes to hang out in the rafters. I think he feels safer off the ground."

"Safer from what?" Meg asked, her voice somehow both meek and demanding at once.

It took a vast amount of effort to keep his eyes from rolling. An effort he only made because he knew Nicole was watching him carefully. "How would I know?"

"Ask him," Meg said as if he were mentally slow.

"You ask him," Benton shot back.

Zack pried one hand off of his camera to gesture wildly. Apparently, that was necessary to get his point across. "You're the medium."

"Banshee," Benton and Nicole corrected in unison.

"What's the difference?" Zack asked.

"I just warn you when you're going to kick the bucket. I don't chat."

"But you can talk to him," Meg pressed.

Benton took his eyes off of Ackerman just long enough to throw Meg an exasperated look. "So can you."

She gnashed her teeth in frustration. "I can't hear what he says back."

"He never *says* anything back," Benton countered.

In his peripheral vision, Benton watched the tag-you're-it game play out for the hundredth time that night. Zack was normally the one who started it. The teen was desperate to get proof of the supernatural. Unfortunately, his patience had the lifespan of a fruit fly. Every time he was annoyed with Benton, he'd wave to Meg, silently telling her to do something about it. Meg instantly handed the task off to her identical twin, Danny. Out of the three, Benton liked Danny the most. Because she had enough sense to know that he wasn't exactly excited about her existence. The downside of that was that she would go to Nicole for help.

"We all know by now that Mr. Ackerman isn't exactly in a chatty mood," Nicole said carefully, obviously looking for middle ground. Meeting Benton's gaze, she smiled sweetly. "Maybe you could tell us what he's doing?"

"He's circling like a shark, and you're having me sit here like chum."

Nicole's smile instantly faded. She began to bounce, shifting her weight between her feet with nervous energy. A small slither of guilt wormed its way through the pit of Benton's stomach. Death had decided that they were besties when he was ten. It had messed with his perception of 'normal.' He sometimes forgot how hard all of this could be for someone on the outside.

"He doesn't make any vocal noises," Benton said in a gentler tone. "But he only seems interested with people inside the barn. He hasn't even looked at you guys."

It didn't stop Nicole from bouncing around like a trapped rabbit, but she seemed pleased that he was making an effort with her friends.

It had been quite a month since the Slaughs had swept across the Alberta plains, hidden within a storm that did just as much damage as the monsters themselves, and Nicole's friends were still hanging around. Necessity had drawn them together. They needed the twins and Zack if they were ever going to make it back. And somewhere along the line, everyone had just sort of assumed that it was the new status quo. Nights like these proved why this was a stupid idea. Nicole's little experiments with the unknown had consisted of blood pressure cuffs and EMF readers. Zack and the twins leaned towards poking the unseen monsters and watching Benton get his butt kicked.

*See, this is why I hate people.*

A sudden burst of frost encased every cell of his being, crashing his body temperature, making him shiver violently. Benton snapped back around, searching for Ackerman, finding the spirit barely an inch away from him. Rage flared in the dead man's eyes. It crashed over him in a frozen wave. Dust billowed up around Benton as he hurriedly scrambled over the dirt floor, desperately increasing the distance between them. Ackerman's decayed lips twisted into a snarl as he retreated, climbing back up the wall to disappear into the shadows around the rafters. Zack's camera flash broke the night like lightning. Benton winced, lifting one hand to shield his eyes.

"Benton," Nicole gasped. "Are you okay?"

"What happened?" Meg snapped.

At the same time, Zack demanded, "Where is he?"

Benton lifted a shaking hand to point into the exposed rafters.

"You scared him off?" Zack said. "What the hell? We're trying to get him on camera."

Benton glared in Zack's general direction, still blinking away the stars in his eyes.

"Yeah, I know your dumbass plan. He startled me."

Zack bristled, his broad shoulders hunching up like an angry cat. "No one will believe us without proof."

"*You.* Not *us.* I'm not putting my fingerprints on this train wreck."

Zack bared his teeth in frustration. "You have something to say?"

"Only the blatantly obvious," Benton shot back. "You can't convince someone of something they don't want to believe."

"I was convinced." His chest damn near swelled up with pride.

"You were attacked by a hundred monsters and witnessed a banshee scream destroying them," Benton countered. "Yeah, that's the exact same as being shown a photo or two by some jerk online."

A string of barbed wire coiled tightly within the pit of his stomach, the sensation making his skin crawl and forcing him to snap around on instinct. Ackerman had started to circle him again, bleeding in and out of the shadows. His progress was marked by the snap and crackle of his twig limbs. While he could hide from Benton's sight, Ackerman couldn't smother the sensation that he provoked. The pain in Benton's stomach. The pressure at the base of his neck. The sleet that worked through his veins. A sudden light made him jump. A cry clogging his throat, he whipped around to find Nicole leveling the beam of her mobile's torch onto him.

"Your lips are turning blue." Concern laced through her words.

Meg made a fascinated grunt and clicked off a few more photographs. It seemed that she never got tired of seeing him in ghost induced hypothermia.

"Maybe we should take a break," Nicole said.

"But we haven't gotten the photo yet," Zack protested. "You can hold on a little longer, right Benny-boy?"

Benton remained silent. He had been ten when Death decided to let him in on the game, filling his dreams with brutal murders. The thing that made that special brand of torture endurable was that it all stopped, or at least eased up considerably, when he woke up. That had changed after coming to Fort Wayward. Now he had to deal with the supernatural insanity while awake, too. So far, he wasn't all that impressed. Not that he wanted Zack to know that. He might be pathetic, but he had some measure of pride.

"He's been doing this for two hours," Nicole pressed, her sweet tone hardening around the edges. "It's about time for a break."

"He's fine," Zack sighed.

"His teeth are chattering. And look at his fingertips. That's the start of frostbite."

"Nicole," Zack swung his arms out as he twisted his torso towards her. "Do you maybe want to leave him with a shred of masculinity?"

*Strike one*, Benton thought with a smirk. He watched with growing amusement as Meg and Nicole turned in unison to fix Zack with a sharp glare. Even Danny returned from her position as a lookout to let Zack know he had messed up.

"I'm confused, Zack," Meg said, crossing her arms around her chest. "Explain to me what exactly is demeaning to a man about a woman showing concern."

"You know what I mean," Zack dismissed with a snort.

*Strike two.* Benton bit his lips to hide his grin.

"No, I don't," Danny replied. "Come on. Explain it to me."

Even Zack was able to pick up on the clear and present danger in Danny's voice. For the first time, he seemed to notice that the girls were annoyed with him. His mouth opened, but no words came out. Benton could watch him flounder all day. It never got old.

A blast of frigid air slammed into Benton's spine, shoving him forward. He hit the ground hard. His thrashing kicked up the dust, letting it line his throat as he twisted around. Tight hands gripped his neck before he could get up, fingers of iron and ice squeezing tight as they slid around his throat. Looping. Squeezing. His lungs swelled, but he couldn't feel any of the air. He choked as he breathed.

Ackerman flung him to the ground, straddling Benton to pin him into place. The ghost was a crushing, icy weight. It felt as if it were enough to freeze Benton's bones as it bent them. His temperature plummeted at the contact, encasing him in agony.

Benton's vision blurred and his body trembled violently. Ackerman loomed over him, bringing his distorted face inches from Benton's own. A feral snarl rippled past dead lips. Benton scratched at his throat but couldn't dislodge the ethereal fingers. Forcing his mouth open, he tried to scream. Ackerman squeezed his vice-like fingers, choking the sound off in Benton's throat, making his body rattle with the residue.

Suddenly, Ackerman's body swirled, dispersing like oil in water. Nicole lunged through the hovering remains, grabbing Benton by the front of his hoodie. The iron fire poker in her hand smacked against his chest as she yanked him up. Benton helped as best he could, which wasn't much. Ragged coughing fits kept doubling him over, and his limbs felt like stone. Together, they managed to drag one of his arms across her shoulders, allowing her to take on some of his weight. His feet carved paths through the dirt floor as she pulled him towards the barn door.

Behind them, Ackerman quickly reformed himself, his limbs now longer and more twisted than they had been before. A furious, animalistic scream ripped through the barn, a brutal sound that pierced Benton's ears like daggers and made his knees buckle. The air became ice upon his skin, locking his joints. Freezing until he was sure the next movement would shatter him like glass. The snapping and cracking sound followed them, closing in fast as they barreled to the door. Sensing the coming blow, Benton threw himself forward, bringing Nicole down with him. Neither could brace for the impact, and they landed in a painful tangle of limbs. Gravel and dust scattered around him as he sat up and twisted around.

Oliver Ackerman paced the threshold of the barn. One swipe of his elongated arms could have claimed either of the teens sprawled upon the dirt. Ackerman didn't even flinch towards them. *He won't leave the barn*, Benton thought with a creeping sense of dread. Until recently, the ghost had refused to leave the sprawling three-story farmhouse. Whatever had forced him into the barn wasn't something Benton wanted to meet.

Snarling and spitting, his limbs cracking and reforming at a constant pace, Ackerman threw himself to the side and scurried up the wall, disappearing into the shadows lingering amongst the rafters. Relief washed over Benton as he lost sight of the ghost. He sagged under its swell and rolled to brace himself on his forearms, head drooping low.

"Benton?" Nicole panted.

Benton forced the words out through a wheeze. "He's gone."

Nicole rolled to face him, flipping her hair out of the way. It was rather impressive. Her hair was a sheet of hip-length silk that by all rights should have always been in the way. Or picked up every speck of dust and twigs it came into contact with. On his good days, he'd admit that he was a little jealous; going gray before he was even twenty would do that.

Still panting for air, he watched as she slipped her bracelet off and fixed it around his wrist. It was a dull metal band embedded with a beaded pattern of turquoise and ebony and trimmed with sunshine yellow. Honestly, he didn't think he could pull off the cheery colors, but that didn't matter. It was the metal he needed. Iron. Natural angry ghost repellent.

"This is new," Benton said, eyeing the pattern.

"Grandma gave me the set this morning." Despite everything, she beamed with pride, running one hand over the dangling strands attached to the bottom edge of her choker. "Isn't it pretty? They're already sold out on the website."

Nicole's mother was part of a group that sold their jewelry at the buffalo jump museum's gift shop. They were doing pretty well. Even the modern pieces got snatched up quickly. Some boasted it was because they were beautiful, the more cynical saying that tourists loved buying items made by an authentic Siksika. Of course, it didn't hurt that they got Nicole to model the items every so often.

"Thanks," he mumbled and twisted his wrist back and forth, making the bright beads glimmer in the house's floodlights. "For everything."

Nicole shrugged it off. As if she honestly thought running into a haunted building and facing off a murderous ghost was just a normal part of day-to-day friendship.

"Did he go back to the rafters again?"

Benton nodded, still struggling to clear his throat. On the next twist, his hand bumped against her fingertips.

"You're freezing." She was instantly sliding over the minimal distance separating them and dragging him into her arms.

Her body heat was heavenly. Benton melted into it, ducking his broad shoulders under her as best he could, burying his face into the crook of her neck. The resumed blood flow was both wonderful and painful.

"You didn't get the shot," Zack snapped.

Benton wasn't sure how long he had been looming over them, and he really didn't care.

"Think you can jump back in there again?"

"Zack," Nicole snapped, voice bordering on sharp. "We're done for the night."

"Oliver didn't show up on camera," Zack protested.

"Then he's not going to," she countered.

Danny was stalking around them, constantly shifting back and forth as she stared up at the barn.

"Oh, God. Look at his neck," she whispered a little too loudly.

Benton didn't need a mirror. He could already feel the bruises beginning to bloom across his throat. Light flashed across Benton's eyelids. He battled against the visual bombardment to glare angrily at Zack.

"Look over there," Zack instructed. "I want to get a good shot."

"Give him a second to catch his breath," Nicole said.

"Guys," Meg hissed the word as she waved her arms about. "Keep it down. Benton's parents will hear you."

In her panic, Meg's voice got a little louder with every word.

"Everything will be okay," Nicole soothed, her voice shifting from cold stone into something sweeter than honey. "Can you do me a favor and grab my duffle bag?"

It was one of her father's old deployment bags. Frayed with use and stained with gun oil. Nicole had the kind of preparation skills that would make boy scouts envious. Really, as a daughter of a Mountie and a soldier, it wasn't all that surprising. Tonight, she had outdone herself now. A fur-lined hat, gloves, and slippers were all pulled out of the camo bag and shoved onto Benton. The minimal addition to his warmth left him reeling.

"How are you feeling?" Nicole asked.

"Like I just ran naked through the Arctic." Benton's teeth rattled as hard as his body. "Ackerman, you suck."

One graceful swish and Nicole cocooned him in a thick wool blanket. She pressed a flask between his shaking hands.

"Spicy taco latte?" he asked.

"Of course." Nicole almost sounded insulted by the question.

There was an almost physical need to taunt her, but he settled for sipping at the sweet, spicy liquid instead. The first mouthful made him choke, and he cupped a hand around his aching throat.

"Move your hand," Zack grumbled.

Benton grunted as Zack jerked the edge of the blanket down, trying to position himself for a decent shot.

"Zack," Nicole hissed. "Give him a second."

"No one is going to believe this happened if we don't document it properly."

"Zack."

Nicole's reproachful glare was enough to make Zack back up a step, but he didn't stop clicking off photographs. Benton was too busy fighting for air to care what Zack did. He cared even less when Nicole settled onto the dirt beside him, wrapping one arm protectively around his shoulders. She was so damn warm; a tropical heat in a world of ice.

"This has to be a trick." Zack almost chuckled as he flicked through his photographs, the small screen of the camera illuminating his face. He laughed a little harder. "Nicole, it looks like you're beating the hell out of Benton in these. What did it look like to you, Benton?"

He explained as best he could while keeping his word count low. Coffee was far more important than dealing with Zack's zeal.

"Aw, man! Why can't we get that on camera?" Zack bellowed.

"Keep your voice down," Meg hissed.

"Hey, I got some orbs on film," Danny cut in.

It was a minor thing ghosts did with cameras. Little glowing balls that showed up for no real reason. They weren't all that impressive, but enough to have the twins and Zack crowding around her camera screen.

"I'm just telling you now," he mumbled to Nicole. "If anyone asks me to go back in there, I'm going to have a very colorful response. Complete with hand gestures."

"That sounds fair," she replied, rubbing his arm to work some warmth into it. "What do you think is going on with Mr. Ackerman? He wasn't like this before."

"Well, it's not like he wasn't always a creeper with no sense of personal space."

Nicole shot him a disapproving look. They didn't work at the best of times. Now, still defrosting and with a mug of coffee, there was little she could do to make him feel guilty.

"You didn't have to deal with him in your face all the time," Benton countered. "He never watched you sleep."

"Admittedly, that's a bit odd."

"Amazingly disturbing," he corrected.

Again, another glare that withered away quickly. "He wasn't aggressive before."

Benton sipped at his coffee and countered with, "He wasn't scared before."

"Scared of what?" she asked instantly, a small spike of fear weaving into her voice. "The Slaughs? Does he think they're coming back?"

"You know, I keep forgetting to ask him," Benton grunted. "We just get so caught up in politics and world events."

"Any chance you can be a little less sarcastic for the rest of this conversation?" There was no heat in her words; just an affectionate exasperation.

Benton felt like smiling, but his exhausted body couldn't pull it off. "Nope, sorry. I have a medical condition."

"That forces you to be a jerk?" she asked with a smirk.

He nodded solemnly. "Scientists are hoping for a breakthrough. Until then, the only recommended treatment is to let me do what I want."

She giggled, shook her head, and seemingly decided that the conversation had to get back on track.

"Do you think he's protecting his grave?" she asked. "No, that can't be it. He has a nice new one now. A real one."

"One that doesn't have a creepy cult symbol," he mumbled before taking another mouthful of coffee.

"Professor Lester said that it was only supposed to disperse negative energy," Nicole mused.

Benton didn't bother to reply. They had already said everything there was to say about the damn thing. It was from a cult that historians only vaguely, remembered. As far as anyone could tell, it worked with the theory that there existed a kind of paranormal fog. It blanketed the world. Killing something that belonged in that realm stirred it up and lured in bigger and worse things. Putting the seal at the location of death was supposed to keep that ripple effect from happening. The problem that hung over their heads like a razor-sharp knife was that the Slaughs had been a swarm. A flying one. It was impossible to put them all up. Even if they could, plastering the whole town in the signals would draw some unwanted attention.

"Do you think the Slaughs count as one death or hundreds?" Nicole asked abruptly.

The night replayed in Benton's head. Monsters swirling within the fury of a storm, seeking out souls to take. A scream unlike any he had produced before. Something that cracked him open, coming from a part of his soul that he hadn't known existed. His throat ached as he recalled the last hands that had wrapped around it. Living, human hands. A killer that would have killed him, too, if Nicole hadn't been there. He flinched as a phantom gunshot rang in his ears. Somehow, it seemed sharper, more real, not like it was in the past.

"Benton?" Nicole asked.

He cleared his throat, ignored the spike of pain, and offered her a smile. "They must not count for much. It's been pretty quiet."

"Apart from Mr. Ackerman," she reminded. "Are there any other ghosts in town? Have they been acting weird?"

Benton summoned enough strength to slit his eyes towards her. "I don't exactly go around looking for them."

"Has anyone come looking for you?"

"You mean since three A.M this morning?"

Despite his best efforts not to get drawn into this whole 'friendship' thing, Nicole had weaseled her way into just about every aspect of his life. She'd found out all of his secrets and, she didn't give him time to make any new ones before checking in on him again. She was a one-woman Viking raid, smashing all resistance in her path and claiming whatever she wanted as her own. It was a personality type that should rightfully drive him mad. But, somehow, Nicole had managed to make her knowing every insignificant detail of his existence oddly comforting. She knew him. She heard him. She *listened*. All he needed was a taste of one to be completely hooked on this whole 'friendship' idea. And it was probably why he really didn't want or need the others around.

"Maybe the ghosts are feeding off of the negative energy of the Slaughs' deaths." Nicole mused.

"I can't really express how little I care."

"You probably should care a little," she chastised with a small pout. "Mr. Ackerman wasn't able to touch you before. Now he can and is obviously willing to do so. That's not a good situation, Benton."

He released the hot cup just long enough to gesture to his throat. "Oddly enough, I did figure that out for myself."

Her eyes narrowed playfully. "I hate when you do that."

"Do what?"

"Argue with me while proving my point," she said.

He grinned. "Makes it hard for you to keep arguing, huh?"

"Exceedingly so."

A strange sense of pride washed through him. Nicole lived like a Miss America contestant mid-interview, hiding everything behind a bright smile and sunny disposition. It made it hard to know when he actually got to her.

Benton glanced back at the barn. "I want to move him on."

"I'll look into it," Nicole replied instantly.

"What?" Zack cut in. "You can't do that. Not yet. We don't have him on tape."

Benton was in mid-sip, so Nicole was the one to answer, "So?"

"So, no one will believe us. They'll just think that Benton threw himself around."

"Who do you intend to show this to?" Nicole asked.

Zack shrugged as if it were obvious, pulling his shoulder-length hair into a ponytail. "I'm putting this on YouTube."

Benton swallowed hard. Wincing in pain, he glared at Zack. "I'm sorry, dumbass. What was that?"

"Where do you want me to post it?" Zack shot back.

"Nowhere," Benton said. "Obviously."

Zack paused, looking to each girl in turn before meeting Benton's gaze again. "Then why are we even doing this?"

"Because you're an idiot!" Benton declared. He continued in a rush before Nicole could tell him to play nice. "You saw ghosts. You saw Slaughs. Hell, you even saw me kill them with a scream. What more do you need to convince you?"

"That's not proof."

"Screw off!" Benton snarled. "No one has to prove to you that they exist. You're not that important."

A sudden burst of light washed over them, making all of the teenagers whip around to face the house a few yards off. The variety of spotlights created a noonday glare. It was painful to look at and almost impossible to spot Benton's mother standing at the front door, screen door opened halfway.

"Benton! Honey, is that you?"

Benton cringed at the forced endearment. It just sounded awkward coming from Cheyanne Bertrand. But nowhere near as bad as when his dad tried. Lately, he was attempting to call him 'sport' and make it sound normal. He hadn't succeeded once.

"Yeah, mom," Benton called out.

"Who's that with you?" she asked, her voice overly sweet. "Is that Zack I see?"

The motion lights renewed their time as Zack waved an arm in greeting.

"Hi, Mrs. Bertrand," Nicole chirped happily.

There was a moment's pause before Cheyanne replied, "Nicole, you're back again."

The tension was thick enough that even Nicole couldn't dismiss it. Her smile didn't waver, but her eyes did flick over to Benton.

"Yeah, she's not a fan of yours," Benton whispered.

"What? Why? Since when?" The questions left Nicole's mouth at a rapid pace. "I'm delightful."

"Yes, you are," Benton placated with a smirk.

"What are all of you up to out there?" Cheyanne broke into the conversation again. She still hadn't left the doorway.

"We're working on a film for a class assignment," Nicole blurted out.

"Smooth," Benton mumbled, scrubbing his face.

"I told you we needed to practice," she hissed out of the corner of her beaming smile.

"We did." Even he thought he sounded a bit too smug. "For thirty minutes."

Nicole was steadily getting better at lying, which wasn't that hard given where she had started.

"What subject is it for?" his mother called from the porch a few yards off.

"English," Benton said. Nicole nodded rapidly until he nudged her with his elbow. "We have to do a short movie."

"Well, it's late. You can finish up in the morning."

He might not have been able to make out his mother's facial features, given the floodlights that refused to turn off, but he was sure his mother could see him. And the deadpan glare he was tossing her way.

Cheyanne and Theodore Bertrand were proud city dwellers. For the vast majority of his life, they had displayed nothing but resentment for anything that closed before midnight at the earliest. Staying up to six p.m. on a Saturday night wasn't something they would have ever called him on before.

But Fort Wayward was different. Benton's warnings of death tended to draw unwanted attention. And accusations of being a serial killer. Because of this, the Bertrands had exhausted every large Canadian city. Fort Wayward, a tiny town hidden way in the Alberta prairies, was their last hope. A quiet place to squirrel away their troublesome son. They had prepared themselves to be maximum-security correctional officers. It must have thrown them off script when Benton started showing signs of becoming a well-adjusted teen.

Begrudgingly, Benton struggled to his feet. Zack and the twins hurriedly packed up their stuff, and Nicole swept into action. They were getting pretty good at looking casual while fighting to keep Benton upright. She pressed against his side, hugging his waist while avoiding his most current cluster of bruises. In turn, he slung an arm over her shoulders, letting her take his weight. There was a certain sense of pride that came with being able to pull the move off without snagging her hair. To complete the 'everything is normal' facade, Nicole lazily swung her duffle bag as they walked.

Avoiding all eye-contact with Cheyanne, and with little more than a wave of acknowledgment, the trio fled to Zack's car. Spinning tires kicked up the gravel and dust before they shot past Nicole's jeep and barreled down the long driveway. Benton and Nicole watched the taillights fade into the darkness that surrounded the isolated house.

"Subtle," Benton muttered.

"Come on, guys," Nicole beseeched at the same time.

Sharing a glance, they finished their journey to the front porch. Cheyanne hadn't left the threshold. One hand gripped the sturdy wooden door while the other clutched the fly screen, keeping it halfway open. Her smile was so forced it looked painful. Benton cringed. *This isn't going to be a fun night.* Nicole's skill at concealing her emotions behind a smile made Cheyanne look like an amateur. She beamed like a soldier coming home.

"Hi, Mrs. Bertrand. You look lovely tonight." Before his mother could reply, Nicole continued, "My mother's still eager to have you and Mr. Bertrand over for dinner."

Cheyanne barely hid her flinch. While the Bertrands were on good terms with Royal Canadian Mounted Police Constable Nicole Rider, they weren't exactly friends. At this point, Cheyanne was nervous around law enforcement officials. As if she was waiting for them to start throwing accusations around.

"We've just been so busy," Cheyanne said. "We'll get around to it shortly, I'm sure."

"Great. I'm really excited. I've already decided that I'm going to make my special Saskatoon Berry Bannock for dessert. It's an old family recipe."

"Oh." Cheyanne dragged the word out as she struggled with how to respond to that.

That was one of the things Benton's parents hadn't considered when they decided to move to Fort Wayward. Here, they were the only people who weren't linked to the Siksika tribe by marriage or blood. It left his parents, who had never put any thought into heritage, family connections, or history, in this awkward limbo. They were determined not to cause offense but completely ignorant about how to go about that.

Nicole's smile grew. "Think of scone-cake hybrid with blueberries in it. You'll like it. It's delicious."

"That sounds lovely dear," Cheyanne said swiftly. "But it's getting late. Benton needs his sleep."

"You really do," Nicole agreed with a nod.

What followed was an awkward silence.

Cheyanne licked her lips. "I'm sure you have a busy day tomorrow, Nicole, sweetie."

Nicole pursed her lips and hummed. "No, not really. I mean, I do have to babysit five kids tomorrow. Their parents are still helping with the town clean up. But I'm not complaining. The little ones are going to be a big help. We're going to bake cookies for the blood drive I'm running in the afternoon. I hope to see you there, Mrs. Bertrand. The turnouts have been incredible. We're sending any excess to Peace Springs this time. I'm not driving it over, of course. I've got to help catalog the items in the Fort. We have to get all of the antiques out of it before they can start restoration efforts. I probably shouldn't let the kids help with that."

Benton took advantage of her first pause for breath. "Hold up. You're doing all of that in one day?"

"It's no bigger workload than what I've had before."

"That's the point, Nic."

"I like to keep busy," she dismissed with a shrug.

*She's not dealing with what happened.* It wasn't the first time this had occurred to Benton, but it still made his stomach churn.

"Are you alright?" Nicole asked when she noticed him staring at her. Hooking the straps of her duffle bag into the crook of her arm, she pressed a hand against his forehead, checking for a fever. "Maybe you should rest for a bit."

"I think she's right," Cheyanne agreed quickly.

Once again, silence settled upon them, deep enough that Benton could pick up on the distinctive click of owl talons against the roof slats. When it became unbearably awkward, he leaned over and whispered to Nicole.

"She's waiting for you to leave."

"Oh." Nicole started, toppling into nervous chuckles. "Right. I don't live here."

"You're around enough to make that mistake," Cheyanne said with a bittersweetness.

Nicole's sudden burst of energy caught both Bertrands off guard. Neither were prepared for her to dart off the porch and half crawl into her jeep. A split second later, she was back, bouncing on her toes as she presented Benton with a present. The small box was perfectly wrapped with silver paper that reflected the light like a polished mirror. A tiny string of fairy lights served as a ribbon, accentuating the pristine paper. Benton arched a quizzical eyebrow.

"It's not my birthday."

"I know."

Benton's brow furrowed. "You know when my birthday is?"

"December 26th is kind of memorable," she dismissed with an indulgent smile.

His first instinct was to demand how she knew that. Then he recalled that he was talking to a girl who had stolen both his medical and police reports on more than one occasion.

He hesitantly took the box. "You wrap a random gift like this?"

She nodded, looking confused, as if it were completely normal to put this much effort into spontaneous presents.

"Of course, you do," Benton smiled. "Thanks, Nic."

Unraveling it all was an intelligence test. A sharp yank took off the fairy lights. Not knowing what else to do with them, he dumped them on Nicole's head, giving her a battery-powered halo. She didn't bother to take them off, and instead, watched with barely contained excitement as Benton pulled a small ring of tangled willows out of the box. It was filled with a spider web of sinew and trimmed with three feathers that twisted in the slight breeze.

"It's a dream catcher!" Nicole declared.

"I didn't know they were a Blackfoot tradition." Cheyanne stumbled to add in a whisper, "Is that okay to say?"

Nicole's brow furrowed. "I'm sorry?"

"She wants to know if you prefer to be called Blackfoot or Siksika," Benton explained.

Working at the Buffalo Jump Education Center had perfected Nicole's 'museum tour guide' tone.

"While I can't speak for everyone in my tribe, Mrs. Bertrand, I personally like Siksika. Although either is fine. Regarding the dream catcher, there's a bit of debate over the exact origin, since trade and intermarriages tend to spread traditions. That said, it's generally accepted that they originated with the Ojibwe."

"I learned something new today," Benton said, watching as his dream catcher slowly rotated.

The moment Nicole turned back to him, her smile turned into something real and warm.

"A friend I made at last year's powwow made it for you." Before Cheyanne could ask, she hurriedly added, "It's a week-long cultural festival celebrating numerous tribes. It's open to the public. You and Mr. Bertrand should come." That over with, she fixed her attention onto Benton. "Do you like it?"

"It's cool," he said, transfixed by the motion of the feathers. There was something familiar about them. A rich cameral with darker stripes. "I don't know what a dream catcher is, though."

Nicole giggled until she realized he was serious. "Oh. Wow. Okay. Well, the air is full of dreams, both good and bad. You hang the dream catcher over your head as you sleep. Good dreams, being lighter, can slip right through these gaps and trickle down the feathers." It was a simple idea, but she demonstrated with her fingers anyway.

"And the bad ones?" Benton asked.

"They're too heavy to make it through," she said. "They stay trapped and are destroyed with the first rays of dawn."

Benton marveled at the small ring. *Could it be that easy?* "No bad dreams."

"I'm not saying you should use it all the time. Just when you need a break."

Cheyanne shifted uncomfortably, caught between insisting that Benton's condition could be regulated with medication and denying that he had a problem, to begin with.

"As Grace explained it to me, the custom was that girls got owl feathers, for wisdom. And boys got eagles, for courage. Well, gender restrictions aren't what they used to be. Besides, owls suit you better."

*Great horned owls,* he realized with a chuckle. By Siksika tradition, owls were omens of death, and they sure loved him. Cheyanne looked between the teens.

"What am I missing?"

"Just a bad private joke," Nicole chirped.

Benton's gaze focused through the gaps within the spider web, turning the barn from a blur into a solid looming structure. Ackerman scuttled across the roof, a dark, misshaped figure that the floodlight glare couldn't touch.

"Benton?" Nicole asked.

He swallowed thickly, feeling a slight pang. "We really should call it a night."

# Chapter 2

Nicole stifled a yawn. Her picnic basket swung from her arm, rattling the assortment of cookies that filled it as she moved about the bustling room. Everything had a silver lining. For the Slaughs, it was that everyone had embraced the concept of generosity. Every blood drive was an exercise in organized chaos. It was her job to control the flow of people. For reasons she couldn't fathom, the nurses refused to let her do the stabbing part.

"Make yourself comfortable, Ms. Long Fisher," she beamed to the middle-aged woman. "The nurses will be with you soon." A quick glance and she was on her way to Mr. Smoke. "Ready for your cookie?"

The old mechanic was peering hungrily into her picnic basket before she could finish the sentence.

"What have you got for us this time?"

She plucked out a key lime pie cookie with a flourish. "Don't worry. I remembered your favorite."

The man took it with a grin. He patted her on the head as he moved towards the door. A flush of pride swept through her, helping to fight off her fatigue for just a little longer. Turning around, she was about to call the next donor over when there was a sudden crash.

The single level hospital didn't have an excess of space. The emergency room entrance was just down the hall. And the corridor devoted to it ran the length of the room, visible through a series of windows. Staff rushed past. A blur of white coats and pink scrubs crowded around a trembling gurney.

A gargled scream tracked the progression. Frantic. Panicked. A roar that made terror roll through Nicole's veins. She moved without thought, sprinting across the room to catch a glimpse of what was coming. Through the crush of bodies, she caught a glimpse of the patient. *Amy Black Bear.* Horror distorted the young girl's features. But that wasn't what stopped Nicole in her tracks.

Nicole's stomach dropped. She barely heard the cries and whispers that swept through the crowd like wildfire. The medical workers swept the sobbing girl down the hall and out of sight. But the image of her remained, burned into Nicole's mind.

*Someone took her eyes.*

\*\*\*

"Benton," Dr. Aspen sighed. "Are you sure that this is what you want to spend your hour on?"

Tossing a baseball between his hands, Benton sunk back into the therapist's over-padded patient chair.

"Why not? You get paid either way."

Aspen carefully kept all the frustration he must have been feeling out of his voice. It was an impressive skill. "One of these days, you might want to try talking about yourself."

"Why? They don't matter all that much."

"But Nicole does?"

Benton caught the ball in his right hand, feeling the scars that marred his palm squish against the smooth surface.

"Well, yeah. It's Nicole." *Why do shrinks always ask dumb questions?*

"Nicole is a–" Aspen searched for a way to describe the neurotic teenager completely devoid of personal boundaries. "Unique girl."

"Understatement," Benton noted with a smirk. Leaning forward, he braced his elbows on his knees. "Look, we all know she's been through a lot. Everyone in this town has. But there was this other thing, and I don't think she's dealing with it well."

"What thing?"

*She shot a serial killer point blank between the eyes to save me.* "It's complicated."

Aspen straightened slightly. "Benton, are you suggesting that Nicole has been a victim of an assault?"

"No."

The lie came out with well-practiced ease. It was what they had all agreed on. *Zack, Meg, Danny, and Nicole*, Benton listed them, still unable to believe that there were so many people in on one of his secrets. *Oh, and Dorothy.* Benton hadn't gotten around to telling Zack and the twins that the constable knew what had happened on the road. But he had been expecting Nicole to suffer a complete breakdown and wasn't about to risk her mother not being there to show support.

"Then what?" Aspen pressed, his question pulling Benton from his thoughts.

"You know, stuff. She's had two friends die under strange circumstances within a year. That can't be good for her." He struggled to grasp the proper line of thought but soon gave up on it. "Look, the point is that we need to help her. She's filling every second of her day. I mean, sure, that's kind of normal for her. But this is getting extreme. I don't think she sleeps anymore."

"A situation you can relate to."

Benton arched an eyebrow and started tossing the ball again, not bothering to straighten up. "Can we focus, please?"

"We'll never get to the root of your problems if you refuse to discuss them," Aspen said for the thousandth time.

"What problems?"

"Off the top of my head," Aspen said as he lazily twirled a pen beside his notepad. "Your night terrors, sleep deprivation, and the increasing resentment you hold towards your parents."

"I have prophetic dreams about brutal murders. I'm secure enough in my masculinity to admit that it scares the hell out of me. So, oddly enough, I'm not all that eager to fall asleep." Benton continued before Aspen could respond, "My parents would rather think I'm a murderer than believe me. Have they told you that they think I'm going to kill Nicole? Because I can't have a friend unless death is involved." He ignored how accurate that statement was. "Would you look at that? We've covered all my issues. Today was a good day."

Aspen tried to hide his smile but didn't quite succeed. "Your parents have been expressing some concerns over the intensity of your relationship with Nicole."

Benton sputtered a laugh. "My *what*?"

"They think that you may be becoming co-dependent."

"They wanted me to make a friend. I made a friend," Benton flung his arms out in indignation.

"Have you ever thought of perhaps making a second friend?"

"That sounds like a lot of work."

"It's important for your social development."

Benton huffed. "I joined the baseball team. Isn't that enough human interaction?"

A small sigh slipped past Aspen's lips. The sound indicated he was about to get serious.

"Co-dependence isn't something that you should dismiss out of hand, Benton. It can be damaging for both you and Nicole."

"Did it occur to you that my parents might be exaggerating?"

The office door suddenly jerked open, just far enough that Mike, Aspen's assistant, was able to poke his head inside.

"Are you busy?"

"You ask a man obviously in the middle of conducting a therapy session," Benton mumbled. All things considered, he liked Mike. The guy always had the coffee pot full and never tried to force Benton into small talk. That didn't mean he wouldn't give the guy a hard time every now and then.

Mike leveled Benton with his standard 'I'm completely done with your shit' look. "I was actually talking to you." Shifting his glance to Aspen, he continued, "I normally wouldn't interrupt, but she was very insistent. And irritating."

Before Aspen could reply, Nicole's head popped in under Mike's.

"Hey guys," she smiled, her voice locked into her super cheery Miss America tone. "Sorry to interrupt. Benton, can I borrow you for a second?"

"Sure thing," he hopped up and tossed the baseball back into the toy chest by the door.

"Benton," Aspen spoke sharply as he got to his feet.

"It's been forty-five minutes. I think we made good headway," Benton replied as he slipped under Mike and out of the room.

Aspen drew in a deep breath. "Okay, the two of you—"

"I'm really sorry to be rude, but we have to get going, and I'll listen to everything you have to say later, and I left you cookies as an apology, bye!" Nicole rambled in one rushed breath, latching onto Benton's hand and dragging him out of the reception area.

Benton had to jog down the long corridor to keep up with the pace she set. Without missing a beat, she took him down a flight of stairs to the hospital.

"Um, Nic, remember how these situations go better when you tell me what we're up to?"

"That's debatable," she dismissed as she jumped the last couple of steps.

His sneakers had barely hit the tiles before she was pushing him back against the wall. Pinning him in place with one hand on his sternum, she swooped over to peak around the corner. The tips of her hair brushed across the tiles, creating a dark shiny waterfall that was bound to draw attention. With a sigh, Benton gathered it back for her.

"Why are you attempting to be stealthy?"

She shushed him, paused, then shot him a look over her shoulder. "I *am* stealthy."

"In a Godzilla-in-Tokyo kind of way, sure."

Straightening up, she looked on the verge of an argument before recalling the supposed importance of whatever it was that they were doing. One more glance and she reclaimed his hand, pulling him past the empty nurse's station to the cluster of patient rooms beyond.

"Why are we sneaking around?" he asked.

"So we don't get caught."

"There's barely any staff, and you're still wearing your candy-striped uniform."

The red and white striped apron looked a little odd with her ever-present boots. Recently, she had taken to wearing that. They were Mountie standard issue, something stolen or inherited from her mother. He wasn't sure which. While he never asked, he was sure the soft leather was a deliberate choice. Hopefully, they would survive longer than her other pairs. They had a short shelf life in dealing with the paranormal. Her jeep sustained damaged, but at least it kept running.

Without warning, she backtracked and pushed him into a room they had just passed. Benton stumbled, suddenly aware of every lanky inch of his legs, but managed to keep upright. To his surprise, they weren't in a janitor's closet. For reasons he couldn't guess at, Nicole had an odd fascination with having important discussions in them. He blinked into the dim light filtering in through the closed curtains, taking in the sparse dimensions of the space. He wasn't entirely surprised to see that there was someone in the single bed.

He jerked a thumb in the girl's direction. "You know she's here, right?"

"Of course, she's the reason why we're here," Nicole said as she closed the door quietly. "Don't worry, she's been sedated."

"Are you trying to make me feel like a creeper?" Benton asked.

Nicole dismissed him with a wave of her hand, already perusing the doctor's chart.

"Amy, right?" Benton asked.

Nicole blinked in surprise. Her head finally popped up. "I didn't know you two were friends."

"We're not," Benton said with a half shrug. "I just got that thing for names and faces, remember. I think we have History together. What happened to her?"

"According to her mother, she completed her shift at the fort, did her homework and went to bed."

"And according to her?"

"Well—"

Benton groaned.

"I haven't said anything yet."

"Yeah, but that's your warning tone," Benton said.

"She's in a hospital. That really should have been your first indicator."

"True, but when you use that tone, I normally end up being attacked by monsters."

"Oh, you get attacked all the time. Don't start drama," Nicole dismissed. Drawing him closer, she handed him the charts.

"I can't read these. Just tell me what's wrong."

Nicole huffed with frustration, her body strumming with energy. Eventually, she rounded the end of the bed and waved him closer to Amy's sleeping form.

"Nic," Benton whispered in warning.

"She'll sleep right through it," Nicole promised. "Just look at this."

He reached across the bed and snatched up her hands before she could touch Amy.

"Stop."

The command broke through the haze of anxiety and brought her to a sudden halt. As if waking from a dream, she looked down at the sleeping girl, then back up to Benton.

"I haven't washed my hands," she said numbly.

"What?"

"I was about to touch her wounds, and I haven't washed my hands." Horror twisted up her face, and her chest began to heave with every breath. "How can I treat Amy like this? What was I thinking?"

"Hey, you were just too focused on the big picture."

Nicole looked at him with tear rimmed eyes. "I'm a horrible person."

"If you're horrible, then I'm heading straight to hell," Benton replied. "Now, just tell me what is going on."

"Something took her eyes."

The words came out in a sudden rush, so fast that he was sure he hadn't heard it correctly.

"What?"

Nicole repeated herself, careful to keep to a normal pace.

"You mean, something attacked her, and her eyes got injured?"

"I mean, according to the medical report, her eyes have been completely removed. The muscles were surgically cut."

Benton studied Amy's tawny complexion. His dreams had educated him in just how much eye-wounds bled, and what that kind of volume loss did to a body.

"She hasn't lost any blood."

"There were none on her sheets, either," Nicole blurted out. "Okay, yes, I read the police report, don't tell mom."

"None on her sheets?"

"Not a drop. Her blood tests are all clear, no sign of a struggle, and her mother didn't hear anything strange."

Benton looked between the women once more, his eyes lingering on the small stitches keeping Amy's eyelids secured.

"Something like that takes a lot of skill."

"Creepy way to put it, but yes."

"I'm just saying, whoever did this has some serious game."

"That's not any better," Nicole replied. "And you know that a human can't do this."

"Actually, I know at least seven that can."

Silence lingered between them for a long moment.

"That disturbs me," she said.

"Yeah, well, they're serial killers. So they probably should," Benton replied.

She ignored that and quickly got back on track.

"Did you dream about her?"

"You'd know if I had," he replied.

"Are you sure?"

He wanted to roll his eyes, but it seemed too disrespectful in the present situation.

"I tell you and your mom every dream I have."

Nicole bit her bottom lip almost petulantly as she thought. "I don't think a human did this. It just feels like it's something more. Something," she glanced around like she suspected they were being overheard before leaning in and whispering. "Other."

"Is that why you couldn't wait fifteen minutes to talk to me?"

An angry flush crept into her cheeks as she stared him down. Nicole didn't have a death glare. She was more like an angry chipmunk. Not much of a physical threat and just too adorable to take seriously. That said, the girl could wield guilt like a deadly weapon. She did that now, curling her lips and eyebrows just so to make Benton feel uneasy.

"It's Amy. You know her."

"I'm not saying that this isn't important. Obviously, it is. I'm just saying that your mother might be the more logical choice here." That seemed to appease her somewhat. At least enough for her eyes to stop doing that 'kicked puppy' thing. Giving up the fight, he huffed and swept his arms out. "Just tell me what I can do."

"Use your banshee senses."

"Can we think up a better way to refer to them?" he grumbled, only to be ignored.

"Just look around for me." There was that damn look again. "Look at her. Tell me if you see anything weird. Please?"

"It's not like I can turn it on and off. I see what I see."

His argument dried out on his tongue as she intensified the 'why are you doing this to me?' expression.

"Fine," he grumbled. Not entirely sure what she expected of him, he took a deep breath and let it out slowly.

Releasing Nicole's hands, he examined Amy closely and checking her neck, along her hairline, the length of her arms. When not sure what to do, he always found it best to look busy.

"There's nothing."

"Try closing your eyes," Nicole instructed. "Maybe you can sense something."

"Again, we need to think of a better way to describe this," Benton mumbled as he obeyed. "I feel like a dial-up psychic."

Everything felt normal right up to the second that it didn't.

It wasn't that he had stumbled across something that he had ignored. The timing just worked out. He closed his eyes and Death arrived. He recognized the sensation instantly. The static heat that crept across the back of his neck. The tingle in his fingers. The absolute certainty that he wasn't alone. Opening his eyes, he twisted around to find the black mass standing by the door. An inky smear across reality, marked only with bone white patches that served as its face and hands. There was no detail. Nothing that could be classified as eyes. And yet the unnerving sensation of being watched slammed into his chest like a pulsing wave.

Being in the same room as Death didn't bring with it the horror that it once had. He supposed it was because he knew, with an unwavering clarity he couldn't explain, that it wasn't there for him. Like cage diving with great white sharks. Safe within a feeding frenzy. A perfect viewing spot to watch a colossal force of nature do what it did best. Benton waited for the rush, for the smoke-like body to lunge forth and claim its prey. But Death didn't move. It simply stood there. Quiet. Still. The drifting ends of its body coiling into the air.

"Benton."

He heard the voice like it was coming down a long corridor. Carrying a little echo and easily ignored.

"Benton."

He stared at the unmoving specter, the silence making his heart throb painfully against his ribs.

"Benton."

The voice hit him all of a sudden, and he snapped around. Nicole forced her polite smile. He sucked in a deep breath. While he didn't recall doing anything different, he was suddenly panting hard.

"I'm sorry to break your concentration," Nicole said. "But you were zoning out, so I figured something was going on. How worried should I be, exactly?"

"I don't zone out," he protested half-heartedly.

"I waited sixty seconds to disturb you."

There wasn't a shadow of a doubt that she meant that time period. Probably counted every second. Blinking rapidly, Benton looked back to the door. Death was still there, having grown big enough to cover the door with its body completely, but no further. The last time he had seen Death in the hospital, it had spread out over an entire wall before claiming the soul it had come for.

"Benton."

He had to wonder how many times she repeated his name this round before he noticed.

"Death's here," he murmured.

Nicole tensed. "It's come for Amy?"

He shook his head slowly. Being unable to pinpoint how he knew the Grim Reaper's intentions was frustrating. There was no denying, however, that he knew.

"Yeah. But not yet."

"I'm sorry?" Nicole asked.

Benton had to drag his attention way. It was like breaking the surface of a placid lake. Serene but still desperate for air.

"It's waiting," he said.

"For?" She said it less like a question and more like a challenge to correct her own conclusions.

Benton licked his lip and tilted his head to Amy's unconscious body. "For whatever attacked her to come back."

# Chapter 3

The glow of the computer monitor illuminated the small police office. Dozens of open windows cluttered the screen. It was both amazing and terrifying how many creatures there were that had a preference for human eyes. Nicole stared unblinkingly into the glare, sucking absently on what remained of her large root beer. The burger and fries that served as her dinner were long gone, leaving only oily paper that was somehow always in her way.

Perfect rows of open files covered the desk. It was a lot of paper with very little relevance. Fort Wayward didn't have much of a crime rate to speak of. The crimes tended to lean more towards shoplifting and tractor joy rides. In recent months, there had been a few shocking events. They still hadn't named all of the victims of the *Leanan Sidhe*. Her museum of death had started shortly before Benton had arrived. Those were the first documented cases of murder the town had known in decades. At least the other creatures had the decency to make the deaths look somewhat like natural causes. That didn't stop her from collecting every police file that could be considered vaguely relevant.

The ever-increasing weight of her binder shifted upon her lap, making a collection of glitter pens clink together. Disgusting things were easier to stomach when written with pretty ink. Every demon, monster, legend, and beast she had come across in her searches were neatly filed away. Color-coded and cross-referenced. The binder was actually becoming a point of pride for her. Benton's banshee binder was pitiful in comparison.

Slurping up the last of dregs of her drink, she leaned closer, engrossed in a passage about a Japanese creature called a kamaitachi. The sheer amount of blood in the artist representations drenched the room in a red hue. She leaned closer still, seeking out the details, feeling a cold lump growing in the pit of her stomach. A sudden, shrill cry shattered the silence. Choking on a mouthful of root beer, she jumped, the rolling chair flying the minimal distance to crack against the wall. It took three more screams for her to realize it was just the monotone tune of her ringtone. An awkward crab walk got the chair back to the desk and her blaring phone.

"Have you ever heard about the kamaitachi?" Nipping her straw slurred her words slightly.

It was hard to tell if the pause was for dramatic effect or if Benton was still half-asleep. He was always a bit groggy after his dreams. Proof that fear really couldn't trump fatigue.

"Sorry?" he said at last.

"They're these weasels. Three of them, actually. They work together to mutilate people. One trips you, the second cuts off your legs, and the third stitches you up. And they get it all done within the blink of an eye! That's horrifically impressive."

"Huh?"

"Well, I don't agree with what they're doing but you have to admire the teamwork."

There was a soft groan that was easy enough to ignore.

"You haven't been to bed, have you, Nic?"

"How creepy is that?" Nicole declared, flinging her free hand out for emphasis as she slumped back in her mother's chair, remembering a second later to dig in her heels to keep from rolling. "Just – BAM – no legs!"

"That's a 'no' for sleep." He swallowed thickly, the sound almost lost under the shuffle of bed sheets. "So, you think it's these kama–"

"Kamaitachi."

"Right. You think one of those attacked Amy?"

"No, of course not." She restlessly chewed her straw. "Victims of the weasels don't know what hit them but they are definitely aware that they got hit in real time. Amy slept through her assault. Or she doesn't remember it. I wish I knew how much time she lost. I got a general idea from her mom and dad but I can't narrow it down."

"You talked to her parents?"

"They were happy to hear from me," she protested. Freezing in place, she frowned. "I forgot what my point was."

"The difference between the murder weasels and Amy's stalker."

"Oh, right, thanks. Whatever's coming after her is stealthy."

"How much coffee have you had?"

"None."

"Really?"

"I wouldn't lie to you," she stated firmly, quickly adding in a rushed whisper. "I had caffeine tablets."

"Oh, my God," Benton grunted.

"I have a lot to do today."

Benton made a non-committal grunt.

"Is that judgment I hear?" she snipped.

"No. It's only judgment adjacent."

She smiled lightly and went back to gnawing on her straw. "I suppose that's acceptable. So, what happened with your dream tonight? Was it a bad one?"

"None of them are pleasant."

There was a pause. A moment of hesitation where he tried to keep it inside. It didn't last. The dam broke and the words poured from him. The lines blurred as Benton spoke of a lake somewhere warm and quiet, where people feel safe to swim at night. He described the senses as if they had all been his own. The way the plastic mouthpiece of the scuba gear had made the air taste weird. Forgot that it was someone else that waited in the murky depths for someone to stray too close. He described how light the newest one had been.

"They did the hard part themselves," he said, voice shifting between utter disgust and malicious glee. "All that thrashing didn't do nothin' more than twist the seaweed around their feet. I shoulda thanked them for that. Easier for me. All I had to do was float and watch."

Ice coated his words. She shivered in the wake of it.

"Benton." Her voice was a weak squeak. She cleared her throat and tried again, talking louder to be heard over Benton's chuckle. "Benton."

He cleared his throat. A sharp, almost brutal sound.

"Sorry."

"It's okay."

"It wasn't me."

Desperation made his voice a whimper. A plea. I made something shatter within her chest.

"I know you didn't kill anyone, Benton," Nicole assured.

"I wouldn't do that," he pressed. The rest was muffled by the sound of him wiping his face. "It just gets jumbled up sometimes."

"Benton, it's okay."

"It's really not." His bitter laugh ended with a sniff. "To be completely honest, I'm a little worried that, one day, I'm not going to be able to sort the pieces out."

Nicole straightened her spine and fixed a smile on her face. "That's why you have me. I know exactly who you are, Benton. If you get confused, just ask."

He scoffed. A strange mix between a sob and a laugh.

"You're my cheat sheet, huh?" he asked.

"Ask me anything."

Benton paused for a moment. "Nicole, you're researching banshees, right?"

"Of course."

"So, you'd have like a file or something?"

She glanced to the folder sitting on the desk with a bit of pride. "I sure do."

"But I'm the only banshee you know. Essentially, it's just a folder about me, right?"

"Well …"

"It's basically a stalker file," he said. "I'm going to need you to let me read that."

"Oh," her hand smacked down on the file as if he could come through the phone and grab it. "Well. Um. You've told my mom about your dream, right?"

"I always call her before you," he said. "But just circling back to our original topic."

"It sounds like this sicko has a particular hunting ground," she rushed on. "That'll make it easier to catch him. With any luck, they'll get there before your dream comes true."

"Hopefully."

They both let the conversation drop. Legends spoke of banshees being omens of death. Their role wasn't to save the lives they came into contact with; they merely gave warnings, time to prepare, and mourned the dead. Their combined efforts had saved a few people and helped to catch illusive murders in the act. But they were far from saving their world.

"You did a great thing, Benton."

His laugh was back to normal. Self-deprecating and sarcastic in turn. It loosened the knot that had formed in her chest.

"Yeah, that's me. Just a great guy."

"Better than you give yourself credit for," she said.

"Okay, now I'm getting uncomfortable."

"Oh, have we reached your tolerance level for positive reinforcement?"

Nicole bit her lips until she heard a soft chuckle. His standards for humor really went down when he was groggy.

"We passed it a while back actually," Benton said around a yawn.

She switched her phone over to speaker and propped it up against the base of the lamp.

"So," she said with forced cheer. "No swimming for a while."

"I'm not even getting into a bathtub anytime soon."

She could hear him rubbing a hand through his hair. Scratching at his scalp in a way he always found comforting.

"Can we talk about something else?" he asked.

Nicole's mind picked a topic and hurled it out of her mouth without further consultation. "Can you believe that mom wouldn't let me stay at the hospital? It's not like this is my first encounter with murder happy paranormal creatures. We were dealing with these things before she was."

"We were almost killed. Twice."

She gnawed on her straw. "Semantics."

"It's really not."

"The point is that I'm a responsible young adult, thank you very much."

"A responsible young adult that broke into a police station and illegally rummaged through private files."

Nicole's spine snapped straight. The straw slipped from her mouth as her jaw dropped. "How did you know that?"

"I've been developing psychic powers. Didn't I mention? Thought I did."

"No, you didn't!" Instantly, she was scrambling for a piece of paper and a pen, knocking over items in her rush. "When did this first start? Are they feelings or actual visions? What can you see?" She snapped a hand up. "Can you see how many fingers I'm holding up?"

"Three."

"Oh, my God. This is equal parts amazing and terrifying. Can you read my mind?"

"I don't think I'm ready for that," Benton chuckled.

"We'll start slow. I'm thinking of a number between one and ten."

"Nic, you switched me over to video call."

She froze. With a flush creeping into her cheeks, she glanced over at her phone. Benton waved back, the movement sluggish and sleep-heavy. His normal spikes had been worn down, turning his white-blonde hair into a fluffy halo, the tips of which clung to his sweat-drenched brow.

"Hey," he mumbled, pushing a pillow more securely under his chin.

"Hey," Nicole smiled. "Well, I feel like an idiot."

"Sleep deprivation will do that to you. Trust me, I'm an expert."

"I'm going to sleep. Right after I do this one thing."

It was a little disconcerting that Benton managed to parrot the last sentence along with her.

"You've been saying that a lot lately," Benton noted. "Maybe it's time you actually go and do it."

"You're not my mom," Nicole teased.

"No. She's the one that's going to be your arresting officer someday."

"I'm not going to get arrested."

He made a sound that clearly meant he didn't believe her. That sound got a little bit more annoying each time she heard it.

"How was she when you talked to her?" Nicole asked.

His brow furrowed as he squirmed to get more comfortable on his stomach. "Who?"

"My mom. When you called her, did she sound okay? Anything going on at the hospital?"

"Ah. No, everything's quiet."

Frustration rolled out of her in a growl. "It's almost three in the morning! What is it waiting for?"

"You do remember that we don't want this thing to come back," Benton said with a smirk.

"Yeah, I know," she simmered down somewhat. "I'm just saying that it wouldn't hurt these paranormal creatures to stick to some standard operating hours. Just because you're evil doesn't mean that you have to be rude, too."

Benton flopped his head forward, burying his chuckle into the pillow as he scratched the back of his head with one hand.

"What?" she asked.

"Nothing," he smirked. "Maybe it's full."

Her nose scrunched up. "Ew. That's disturbing."

"What did you think it was doing with the eyes?"

"I'm trying not to skip too far down that particular road of thought."

Again, he made that little non-committal noise. He snuggled deeper into his bed, jostling the phone about as he struggled to get comfortable. A hard task, given that the majority of his bedding was now sweat soaked and filled with tangled towels.

"You're sure it will come back for her?" Nicole asked. "Maybe Death got it wrong."

Lacking the will to keep his heavy eyelids open, he slumped into his pillow and mumbled, "He didn't exactly put a time limit on it."

"So this could take days? Months? We don't have the resources for a 24-hour guard on her for that long."

"And by 'we' you mean the Fort Wayward RCMP," he mumbled.

"Yeah, I'm not a big fan of the attitude."

Her protest only made him chuckle slightly. Not exactly the reaction she was looking for. As they lapsed into silence, Nicole's leg began to jiggle with unleashed energy; a mounting need to do *something*. Although, it could also have been the copious amounts of caffeine she had just ingested. Putting the cup down, she glanced around, seeking a distraction. There wasn't one. Absently, she snatched up her take away cup again and started to hurriedly chew on the straw.

"I can't believe that neither of us is with her," she mumbled.

"Your mom is."

"Yeah, but it should be *us*."

"Of course. What were we thinking, leaving an emergency in the hands of law enforcement professionals?"

"And there's that attitude again," she huffed, flopping her head back to stare at the ceiling.

"We have to respect our parents' rules," Benton said. "No pitting ourselves against demonic forces of evil when we have school tomorrow."

"Because you're all about following your parents' rules, right?" she scoffed.

His sleepy face twisted up, but he didn't bother to open his eyes. "Let's not talk about them right now. Or ever."

Nicole stared at her phone, willing him to pick up the frustration that was simmering in her veins like static electricity. Completely oblivious, he settled down, his breath evening out as he drifted on the edge of sleep.

"Can you just freak out!" she blurted.

Seeing Benton jerk awake as though he had just heard an explosion left her feeling a little guilty. She clamped her mouth around the straw and sunk back in her chair as Benton grabbed the sides of his mattress and pushed his torso up, searching the room for what had woken him.

"What's going on?" he swallowed thickly. "Did you hear that?"

She tightened her grip on her drink and slowly shook her head. Somehow, he saw right through her display of complete innocence. He heaved a sigh.

"Something on your mind, Nicole?"

The straw cracked between her teeth as she tried to keep her silence.

"Really? Nothing you want to get out?"

She shook her head.

"Nothing pushing at the edges of your mind? Itching to get free? Like a beetle crawling over your brain?"

"Doesn't this bother you at all?" her words came out in a rush. Clenching her teeth, she sucked in a deep breath and huffed. "I hate when you do that."

"I know," he said. "And for the record, yes, murder bothers me."

"I'm sorry, you just seem so comfy, and I'm losing my mind."

"You're losing your mind because you're trying to survive on five hours of sleep a night."

"You do the same thing," she protested.

"I handle it better." The reprimand in his tone made her cringe. "Look, I like Amy. She seems nice and I don't want anything bad to happen to her. But I've also got Amir to look out for."

"Sorry," she mumbled. "Wait? Who's Amir?"

The storm in his gray eyes dissipated within a second. He heaved a deep sigh, dragged a hand through his hair, and dropped back down onto the mattress. After which, he continued to squirm and mutter under his breath. *He really should change his shirt.* Benton always woke up in a cold sweat. Right now, his blue Chicago Cubs t-shirt was a few shades darker than it ought to be. *It can't be comfortable.* Eventually, he punched a pillow under his chin again and picked up their conversation.

"Amir Sharma was tonight's victim."

"The killer knew that?"

"No," he chuckled. "The random ones are always the worst. This guy, he didn't even stick around to see the damage. It didn't matter to him *who* he killed. Only that someone was dead because of him. It scares me when I understand that logic. Then again, I never want to understand this kind of logic."

His smirk was easy to return, despite the cold feeling in the pit of her stomach. No matter how hard she tried, she'd never really understand what life was like for him. The things he saw. His dreams. She'd never be able to experience them herself. She'd forever be on the outside, sneaking glances of a world she could never be a part of.

"But at least you're doing something constructive," she found herself saying. "When we're sent home like this, you're still useful. I'm just sitting here."

"You're helping me," he said. "Seriously, Nic. Before you, there was no way I'd be able to get to sleep again. That means a lot. At least to me."

She felt her cheeks flush. "Thank you, Benton."

He smiled at her. "You know, I've come to a conclusion."

"Oh, sounds philosophical. Do tell."

"The central goal of my existence is to have a pizza and a nap. It's not a big goal, granted. But I'm setting my sights on it."

She hummed, "That actually sounds incredible right now."

"You can jump in on this if you want," he said. "Although, I guess you'll be busy fleeing from your mother right about now."

Nicole frowned. "Sorry?"

Benton smirked as he settled his head against the pillow. "I suggest heading out now if you don't want to get caught."

"Mom's at the hospital," she reminded him with a smile.

"With Constable Abby, right?"

"Yep."

"And I just told your mom about my dream. So she'll ..."

Nicole's skin went cold as her brain completed his sentence. *She'll be heading to the office to check it all out.* "Why am I being so thick today?"

"I've told you a dozen times already. Get some sleep!"

She ignored Benton's belligerent grumble, instead dedicating her efforts to cleaning away the mess that cluttered every flat surface. *Stupid. Stupid. Stupid.* From a research standpoint, spreading out had made sense. Now, it was clear that it was the worst thing she could have done. Especially given her mother's sharp, right on the point of neurotic, eye for detail. *If the keyboard's a half inch out of place, she'll know I've been here. She'll know something's up.* Clenching her jaw, she tried to stifle the voice in her head. *You prepared for this, Nicole.*

"Benton, I'm going to have to flick over to my photos for a bit to remember where everything goes."

"Sure thing." He emitted a jaw-popping yawn.

"I'll keep the call connected though," she added.

It had become their routine that they kept the call going until Benton nodded off again. They wouldn't chat for most of it. He just liked hearing someone else around him.

"Pitter patter, let's get at her."

Nicole's body jerked to a stop before her brain caught up with what he had said.

"Did you really just say that?"

"Don't pretend that you're too cool for the phrase," he said without opening his eyes.

Benton nuzzled down before the phone flopped onto a pillow and the screen went dark. From somewhere in the darkness, she heard his breathing even out.

"Have a good sleep Benton."

She smiled softly and clicked over to her photos. Taking them upon entering the office was, single-handedly, the best decision she had ever made. With their help, she managed to get Dorothy's office back the way it was. She checked everything down to the finest detail, shoved her binders into her backpack, and then checked again.

When everything was in order, she was confronted with the question of how she was going to get out without running the risk of her mother spotting her. It was moments like these that she deeply regretted mentioning how easy it was to crawl in and out of the office window. The bars Dorothy put up made it harder to sneak around the station.

Organizing the straps of her backpack onto her shoulders, she cautiously approached the door. She had lost track of time while fixing up the office. It now left her with the growing paranoia that she was too late. That now only seconds separated her from being caught. *Don't panic. Just think.* Forcing herself to take a deep breath, she patted the pockets of her candy striper uniform. *Got the keys in one. Mobile in the other. You're good to go, girl.* All of her bravado evaporated the moment she grabbed the office door handle. Her head was flooded with a thousand options of what her mother might do if she was found here. With a growing sense of dread, she pressed her ear to the door, straining to hear any sounds on the other side. Nothing. Summoning her courage, she wrenched the door open and sprinted down the hallway past the storage room and armory to the fire exit at the back.

There wasn't a large police force in Fort Wayward. Six officers, to be specific. After what happened to Amy, half of the force was at the hospital. Those that remained were patrolling the town, trying to soothe the anxious citizens with a clear police presence. That was the reason why she had parked her jeep in the depths of the alley that ran alongside the building. It was a great hiding place. Just outside of the glow of the streetlights. The moment she burst out into the dark, dank alley, she began to reconsider her choices. *Why am I so dumb today?*

The door smacked against her back as it closed, cutting off her only exit. She lingered in the small archway, hands twisting tight around the bag straps and stomach churning. The shadows pushed in on her, deep and foreboding, making her skin crawl. The skin on the back of her neck began to prickle. Fur crossed the inside of her skull, brushing against her brain; a now familiar sensation that she had come to take seriously. She was being watched.

An earlier burst of rain had completely escaped her attention. Already, the clouds had begun to dissipate, but the thin layer of water that remained gave the glow of the streetlights something to dance off of. Puddles scattered the concrete floor. She figured that they would work as some kind of early warning sign if anything approached her. There was a little bit of comfort in that. Enough that she was able to lift her jaw and take a step forward. Leaving the door behind made her stomach drop and she quickly broke into a jog. The splash of her boots made tension twist around her lungs. Squeezing like a boa constrictor.

Sucking in a sobering breath, she locked her eyes on her jeep, taking a moment to appreciate the new paint job. There wasn't enough peppermint green to cover the whole body of the jeep, so the roof had been covered with snow white. It still looked good and did an impressive job at concealing most of the dents and damage. Supernatural creatures had no respect for her jeep. Her fledging smile faded when a new sound broke the uneven silence.

Jerking to a stop, she held her breath, stretching her senses to pick up on the slightest sound. A car engine rumbled by. It was a few streets over but sounded deceptively close in the stillness. The silence that followed was thick and oppressive. Trapped within it, the sensation of being watched increased, to the point that she looked over her shoulder, expecting to find something lurking merely inches from her spine. She freed her hands slowly, breathed deeply, and bolted forward. The backpack bounced against her as she snaked the keys out of her pocket. She threaded the slip of metal between her fingers, balling her fist to keep them upright. It wouldn't be much of a weapon. But she felt better having it.

Without pausing, she pulled off her backpack. The heavy weight tugged at her arm, dragging her down. Another pathetic weapon, but one that she wasn't willing to give up. She reached the door and jabbed her key in the hole. The tip scraped across the new paint, creating a series of grooves as she struggled to force it into the lock. Finally, she succeeded.

The sensation of being watched crashed down upon her like a wave, nearly causing her knees to buckle and forced her to turn around. The alleyway was shrouded in shadows. The opening of the alley stood a far distance off, painted yellow by the nearby street lamp. Nothing stirred. Tension coiled in the pit of her stomach like agitated snakes. She could feel them slithering along her limbs, spreading her gathering anxiety until she was trembling with it. Swallowing past the lump in her throat, she turned back and unlocked the door. Then she heard it. A soft thud and splash of water. *Footsteps.*

They rushed towards her. Nicole fumbled to yank her key free and open the door at the same time. Her backpack smacked against the steering wheel and, in her hurry to get it, became trapped between the plastic ring and her legs. The footsteps were upon her. Not waiting to get her foot out of the way, she slammed the door shut. A blinding spike of pain didn't stop her from smacking the lock back into place. The instant it engaged, the approaching patter stopped. Breathing heavily, she searched outside her window, all the while struggling to free her foot from where it was lodged between the door and the seat.

An invisible force struck the window inches from her head. She screamed, throwing herself back, half-toppling onto the passenger seat. A split second later, the window shattered. Broken shards rained over the driver's seat. The downpour sounded like chimes, striking her like hail. *Broken from the outside.* The thought clashed with the realization that the first thump had been made on the inside of the glass. *Something's out there. Something's in here with me.* She didn't know which should scare her more. But a Survival instinct kicked in, making the decision for her.

Gripping the steering wheel, she hurled herself up and shoved the key into the ignition. The engine came to life with a thunderous roar. The best sound she had ever heard in her life. Just as she shoved the jeep into gear, a new sound struck her ears like the tip of a pickax. A shrill scrape that streaked across the windshield before her face. She pushed back into her seat with a wince. In the same instant, the air stirred. The unmistakable sensation of something solid barreling past, narrowly avoiding contact. Allowing her to feel the motion but not the touch. The passenger window exploded.

In her panic, she tried to work the gears again. The engine grunted as the jeep protested. She slammed her foot on the gas. Water caught the tires. With a ferocious lurch, the jeep spun out, fishtailing as she tried to bring it back under her control. The rear bumper skimmed the alley wall. The right side collided with a garbage can, tossing it aside and spewing its contents all over the drenched ground. Nicole pulled frantically on the wheel, fighting against the momentum pushing her against the door to force the jeep into the right direction. Instead of hitting the breaks, she pressed the gas pedal down to the floor. Sparks burned like bonfires in the night as she sideswiped the brick wall.

Then, with a final surge, she burst onto the street. And she didn't look back as she tore off into the night.

Benton was well accustomed to fear.

None of it had prepared him for the particular brand of terror of waking up to Nicole's screams. Suddenly snapping back to reality with that sound lingering in his ears had him on his feet before the haze had cleared. It had chilled him to the bone and delayed rational thought. It took an embarrassingly long time to realize that the sound wasn't coming from inside his room but from his phone.

Once that clicked, he ripped apart his bedding. His bed frame had been damaged in the move and it wasn't a top priority for anyone in the Bertrand household to replace it. This left his bed a twisted nest of sheets and towels piled up on a bare mattress. He ripped through all in search of his mobile, heart hammering against his ribs the entire time. His hand was shaking by the time he was finally able to snatch up the device. The sensation only grew worse when his pleas for Nicole went unanswered. Finally, when he felt like he was about to crawl out of his own skin, she replied. Her voice was broken with suppressed sobs; but it proved she was alive.

He couldn't remember the beginning of the conversation. It was lost under a haze of relief and fear. Logically, he knew it had to have been a rather hurried discussion. After all, they had been done by the time he managed to shove his feet into a pair of sneakers. Getting to the front door had taken longer.

His parents had specifically chosen this place to limit his ability to go anywhere unnoticed. The house itself had a distinct lack of walls and doors. The whole lower floor was one large, open space, with towering windows lining most of the outer walls. What little furniture they had was built low to the floor, so as not to obstruct the view. And the upper levels had the same design, with the hallways and rooms pushed to the edges, essentially hollowing up the center of the building. It allowed someone to stand on the third floor and, with only a slight lean over a railing, to see the front door. The finishing touch to their pretty cage was the motion lights. They were all connected. Tripping once set them all off, flooding the house and surrounding area with a blinding light. Since there were no curtains, no matter where his parents were in the house, they would know he had crossed a threshold. So he had to time this right.

Upon hearing the first possible rumble of a motor, Benton grabbed the door handle and held his breath. Listening intensely for its approach. Given that his parents were born and raised city folk, it wasn't likely that the engine alone would be enough to wake them.

After two false alarms, he was finally sure that Nicole had arrived. Waiting until he heard the crunch of gravel, Benton hurled the door open. Light instantly burned his eyes. It didn't matter. He knew the way now by heart. Five strides to cross the porch. An easy jump down the small flight of stairs to the gravel driveway. Then he sprinted, pushing himself as fast as his legs would carry him.

Nicole had already circled around. She leaned over to push the passenger door open, haphazardly tossing her coat over the seat as she pulled back. As gangly as he was, Benton was a fast sprinter. A skill that had only increased after he joined the baseball team. So it was possible for her to keep a good speed as he came alongside. Grabbing the frame with one hand and the back of the seat with the other, he leaped inside. The instant his butt hit the seat, Nicole stomped on the gas, which threw him back and slammed the door shut in the same motion.

"Are you okay?" Benton asked instantly, reaching across the gearshift to cup the side of her neck. "Are you hurt?"

She had so much hair. The long dark strands covered her neck, shoulders, upper arms. He brushed it aside as he tried to check for injuries. Nicole stared straight ahead, her chest jerking with uneven breaths.

"Nicole, talk to me!"

"I'm okay." The nod of her head was a lot stronger than her voice.

"You're sure?"

"Yeah. Honestly, I don't know why I'm acting like this. It was nothing." Swallowing thickly, she nodded again, almost as if agreeing with herself. "I just feel like I need to keep moving right now. I mean, I know it's late. Or early. And I have no idea where I'm going. This was stupid. You need your sleep." She heaved a sigh. A broken whimper of a sound. "I can drop you off somewhere."

"I just got here," he protested.

"I know. I'm just overreacting and–"

"You're stuck with me," Benton cut in. "So, drive."

A small smile played on her lips, but there wasn't a chance it would stay. After a moment of silence, she chimed in.

"Seatbelt."

"I'm sitting on glass."

"Will that stop your head from bouncing off of the dashboard like a beach ball?"

"It's creepy that you say that with a smile," he said while reaching back for the strap. Twisting to click it into place gave him a glimpse of the back seat. He hadn't been prepared to see the black, smoky mass clustered there. He jerked back so hard the seatbelt engaged and cut into his ribs. "Damn it, Oblong! Give a guy some warning!"

"What?" Nicole snapped, the car lurching to the side as she tried to look into the back.

"It's just a Death." He realized after he had said it just how disturbing it sounded. "Don't worry, he's not here to collect. Oblong just likes to hang around you."

*That's even worse.*

"What!" Nicole shrieked.

"Not in a creepy way."

"What exactly would be the non-creepy version of that?"

"I just get the feeling that he finds you amusing. Like watching a puppy."

Releasing a choked-off gasp, she shook her head. "I honestly don't know how to respond to that. Oh, wait, I've got one. Why didn't you tell me this earlier?"

"Because it sounds really creepy."

"Ya think?"

Her eyes widened as a thought hit her. Suddenly, she was twisting around again, only remembering to keep the jeep on the road when Benton screamed about the fence post they were careening towards.

"It was them!"

"What was?"

"Them! It had to be them! Don't you see?"

"No, I live on the outside of your head, remember?"

"The sounds!" She still looked at him expectantly before acknowledging that he needed more information. "Each time, just before whatever smashed my windows attacked me, I was startled by a noise. The fright got me out of the way just in time!"

"Death scared you and made you jump out of the way?" Benton clarified.

"Exactly!"

"So, Death saved your life?"

"I think so." she added, "Ask them."

"There's just the one here. And it's not exactly chatty."

"Please."

Benton licked his lips in frustration. It wouldn't be the first time a grim reaper had interfered. Just in little ways. Hints to move things along. For the most part, they were strictly spectators. Silent. Motionless. He had never heard them speak a word. Craning his neck, he looked back, half hoping that the rear of the jeep would be empty. The haunting figure remained, the bulk of its body still as the wispy edges of its form twisted and coiled in the air like oil in water.

"Did–" he cut himself off, feeling like a complete idiot. "Did you help her?"

It didn't move. Didn't make a sound. But he *knew*. As if the knowledge had been shoved into the deepest recesses of his mind, becoming more of an ingrained instinct than a thought.

"Okay," the word left his lips as he slowly settled back in his seat. "I'm actually impressed. You made friends with Death."

"Really?"

"Yeah. It likes you."

Nicole beamed, the fear that had twisted up her features relaxing for a second. "Aw, thank you so much. That's really sweet. Wait. Benton, why do you call it Oblong?"

"They all look like black mist," he explained. "The only way to tell them apart is the white smear of their skulls. Each one's shaped a little differently. This one's kind of oblong."

"So you call it Oblong?" Her tone said that she wasn't too impressed.

It got his defenses up. "What else would you call it?"

"An actual name. Death are people, too."

"No. They're really not."

The strangeness of the conversation struck him like a physical blow. Not that they were talking about death. That had been a given since he hit puberty. But discussing death, while a grim reaper sat in the back seat, was something altogether new and baffling. It hadn't even been a year since he had seen his first. Since death had stopped being a general concept and had become a real, physical presence in his life. One that he could see and interact with. Before Fort Wayward, they had always been hidden from his senses. He knew now that he had felt them, sensed them. But they had always been only a feeling. Now, he saw them so often that he didn't think it was worth mentioning half the time. He could always tell when they were on the clock and when they were just hanging out. They hung around a lot more. He was starting to think that they just liked the farm.

*Maybe ghosts attract them,* he thought. *Or are we just on cursed ground or something?* Either way, it seemed like it should have taken longer for him to adjust to a complete disruption to his world order.

"Mic," Nicole said abruptly.

Her voice was upbeat and sweet, but her hands were white-knuckled around the steering wheel. She didn't even let go to push her hair out of her face as the wind through the smashed window ravaged it.

"Sorry?" Benton asked.

"Oblong is a horrible name. I think we can both agree on that. And, since she just saved my life, I think we can put a bit more thought into what we call her."

"*She?*"

Nicole glared at him, "What? Death can't be a girl?"

He lifted his hands in surrender and studied the phantom in the back seat. It showed no sign of hearing them. It more or less just sat here. Staring straight ahead. The fog-like tendrils of its body expanding out beyond the confines of the jeep.

"Mic?" Trying out the name didn't make it sound any less odd.

"Yep."

"For a girl?"

"It's short for Mictecacihuatl, the Aztec goddess of the otherworld."

His brow furrowed. "Oh, of course."

With an indulgent look, she adopted her museum hostess voice. *At least she doesn't look scared anymore.*

"You pronounce it meek-tay-cah-SEE-wah-tl. She's also known as the Lady of Death, and was the consort of **Mictecacihuatl**, king of the otherworld."

"Right."

"It's really rather interesting. In mythology, **Mictecacihuatl's** role was to guard the bones of those who had passed and govern over the festivals honoring them. Eventually, some of the traditions were added to what we now call the Day of the Dead."

"And you're choosing this name because?"

She grinned. "Because then it's **Nic and Mic.**"

"Oh my God."

She finally let go of the wheel, reaching back as if expecting to receive a high-five from the Grim Reaper. Benton twisted again, watching the specter intensely. It was somehow both shocking and completely expected when a small cloud of smoke stretched out to cloud over Nicole's palm.

"Oh my God," he muttered again.

"What happened?" she whispered. "Did I get the high-five?"

Benton smirked and settled back in his seat, feeling the pebbles of glass shift under him, but protected by the material of her jacket.

"Well?"

"Only you can make friends with Death," he said.

"Benton?"

"Yes, you got your high-five."

With a sound of victory, she presented him with her hand, refusing to move it until he, too, gave her the requested slap. His hopes that her mood had finally settled for the better was lost when Nicole instantly resumed her grip on the steering wheel. For all of her smiles and laughter, she held on tight enough to dislocate her joints.

"Have you told your mom?" Benton asked.

"I wasn't attacked near the hospital. She and Amy will be okay."

"I meant so she can take care of you," Benton snapped, already fishing in his pocket for his mobile phone.

"Why are you angry with me?"

"You need to tell her this stuff." *Damn Rider women.* Dorothy and Nicole were always so busy protecting the other one that they never thought to actually communicate the important things until it was too late.

"You never tell your parents anything," Nicole noted.

"My parents suck. Your mom is awesome. There's a key difference there."

She looked at him from the corner of her eyes. "Why are you two so chummy these days?"

"I'm allowed to have friends beyond you," he dismissed as he dialed.

Nicole squirmed in her seat, eyeing the phone like it was a rattlesnake. "Just see if she's okay. Don't bother her."

"The whole point of bringing her in on this sort of stuff was so that she would know what's going on."

"Fine. Just don't lead with the danger part. I mean, really, we don't even know that this ... whatever it is, meant to hurt me."

"You have Death in your backseat."

"You said she always hangs around."

He rolled his eyes as the phone rang in his ear.

"We haven't even figured out what happened," Nicole said. "Don't make her worry until you have to, that's all I'm asking."

He hummed.

"Benton?"

"I know how to edit information," he said.

Pressing the phone harder against his ear, he shuffled in his seat and waited for the Constable to answer. It didn't take more than a few rings.

"You had another dream?" Dorothy asked instantly.

"No. Just letting you know that I'm with Nic right now. Some weird stuff happened and we're just taking a breather before catching you up."

"Are you two safe?"

"Yeah. We're just driving around."

"I want contact every fifteen minutes with a location update."

Benton didn't argue. Searching what he could see around him was a bigger challenge. After a certain point, all the back roads looked the same. Gravel and dirt framed by waist-high grass.

"We're heading down towards the Buffalo Jump and I'm setting my timer now."

Dorothy didn't seem satisfied, but since she had set the terms, she wasn't about to mention it. "Tell my girl I love her."

"Will do."

"And be careful. Don't go too far out."

"I'll let her know," Benton assured. "Watch your back."

The moment he hung up, he felt the shift. Not a chill. But heat. A burning pulse that washed out over the back of his neck and crept up over his scalp. It made him turn, searching to see if Mic had felt it too. Before his eyes, the dark shape melted. Pouring down the seats to pool over the car mats.

The heat rolled through his bones as he caught sight of the rear window. Of the creature that was sprinting down the middle of the street. Not fast enough to catch them. But at a steady pace. Something metal glinted in the darkness.

"Get down!"

They dropped just as the windshield shattered. Benton pressed his cheek against the dashboard, trying to hide from the glass that rained down upon him, small pebbles that bounced and scattered, rendering him afraid to move. Something streaked over Nicole's head, passing through her hair before embedding itself in the dashboard.

"Do you see it?" she asked.

"Drive!" he bellowed, flabbergasted by her priorities.

The wild pull on the wheel threw him against the passenger door. In that moment, he was determined to find out who made safety glass and thank them profusely. What few sharp edges the pebbles had weren't enough to cut through his jeans or jacket.

Nicole yanked hard on the steering wheel without looking up. The jeep bounced over the uneven ground. Neither of them was prepared for the sudden drop. The car crashed down the trenches that ran alongside the rural highway. In the back of his mind, a voice whispered that this was pretty close to where his parents had bogged their car on the very first day in town. Nicole's jeep, luckily, was far more suited to handle the boggy ditch. Stagnate water and mud gushed in through the broken windows. With a roar of the engine, the jeep lurched and barreled out into the grass plans.

"Benton, what is it?" Nicole asked.

"How would I know?"

She spared him a sideways glance. "You could try looking."

"Right."

While he agreed, he wasn't looking forward to actually doing it. He braced a hand on the dashboard, ready to use it as leverage to twist around and look between the front seats. Panic kept him from noticing that the arrow dug into the plastic until his fingers brushed against the shaft. Energy pooled against the pads of his fingers. He couldn't figure out another way to explain it. It was pure, primal, crackling static energy.

"Benton?" Nicole's voice hovered somewhere between fear and annoyance. A combination that made him snap his head up.

"You can't see that?"

"What?"

He gestured wildly to the arrow. To him, it looked as real and solid as every other part of the jeep.

"See what?" she asked, glancing back and forth between him and the field of towering grass. The stalks glowed gold in the headlights, smacking around the windshield and covering the view of everything else. "I need some descriptive words."

"An arrow. Like, a bow and arrow kind of arrow."

He wrapped his hand around it, feeling the power tingle against his palm. One solid yank and a well-timed lurch of the jeep helped him dislodge it. Mic's hand reached through the gap. A swirling black mass tipped with bone white. Death's grip didn't touch him, instead coiling to point at the arrow. *A warning.*

He realized it too late. He should have seen it coming. Nicole instantly reached for whatever he was holding, already too captivated to show any caution. The tip of the arrowhead brushed across her index finger. Barely a touch. Nothing that should have cut the skin. But it sliced her flesh open. Before the droplet of blood had time to fall, her eyes rolled back in her head and she slumped against the seat.

"Nicole!"

Dropping the arrow, he lurched forward, grabbing the side of her neck to shake her slightly. The jeep careened onward. Completely limp, the weight of her foot pressed down on the accelerator, urging the jeep faster until they were driving wildly over the flat earth. In a state of panic, it didn't even occur to Benton to take the wheel.

Not until the front of the jeep crushed down a hunk of grass to reveal the side of the barn.

He lurched for the wheel a second before impact.

# Chapter 5

"Where is she?" Dorothy didn't bother to close the door of her patrol car as she bolted towards the remains of the barn.

"She's okay. Mic is looking after her," Benton assured. They fell into step as they hustled back towards the barn. Early morning had turned the sky a rich purple, allowing them to see shapes and figures if not colors. He held up the arrow, carefully holding it by its shaft. "Quick question, can you see this?"

"Who is Mic and what are you talking about?" Dorothy asked.

He explained the arrow and the new nickname for the grim reaper in the space of a few steps. Dorothy's eyelids fluttered as she drew in a sobering breath.

"We are going to have conversations later," was her only verbal response.

They were jogging as they entered the barn. It was a rickety structure. Broken with time and neglect, currently held up by the lime green jeep burrowed into its side. Benton had turned off the lights but hadn't attempted to move the jeep itself. Grass had broken apart the floorboards to cover the floor like a carpet. It had made it easy to stretch Nicole out and keep her hidden from sight at the same time. Dorothy sprinted to her daughter, cooing softly under her breath as she kneeled down and checked her child for injury.

"It's okay, sweetheart. I'm here now. You're safe." Her voice turned into something harder as she looked over her shoulder. "Did she hit her head?"

"No. I don't think anything's broken and she's been breathing normally the whole time."

Dorothy kept Nicole's head stable with one hand on her cheek and shook her shoulder.

"Nicole, honey, can you hear me? Open your eyes."

There was no response. Dorothy pulled out her flashlight, first checking Nicole's coloring before looking for her eye dilation. The glare made her pupils contract like normal. *No concussion,* Benton thought with relief. He only looked away from the examination as Mic drifted closer to his side. The small blob of white was fixed upon Nicole. He couldn't decide if this was terrifying or reassuring. Dorothy took Nicole's hand, still studying her with her flashlight.

"Okay, sweet girl. Squeeze my hand. Nicole, if you can hear me, just squeeze my fingers."

Nothing. Dorothy twisted around to glare at Benton.

"She hasn't woken up?"

Benton shook his head.

"Is there a reason that you didn't take her to the hospital?"

"That's a stick shift," Benton said. "And I can't drive anything."

"Right."

"Plus, I don't think they'll be able to help," he continued. When the woman's brow furrowed, he wiggled the arrow in the air. It took a second for it to click.

"Is it okay for you to be touching that thing?" she asked.

"Nicole was cut by the tip. The shaft seems fine."

"Maybe you should give it to me."

Before Benton could give a response, Mic moved. All he did was turn to look at him, floating soundlessly over the barn floor, not disturbing a blade of grass as it passed, but the meaning was clear enough.

"Mic doesn't think that's a great idea."

"Death?"

"Yeah. I'm going to have to side with her."

Dorothy was still checking her daughter but paused to a glimpse over her shoulder. "Her?"

"What?" Benton said with a weak smile. "Death can't be a girl?"

Dorothy quickly turned her attention back to her daughter.

"She seems to be unharmed. Just asleep."

"Like I said." Benton caught his tone the instant that Dorothy shot him a scowl. "I didn't say anything."

Once again, he was dismissed in favor of her daughter. Crouching low, she pushed some stray hair from Nicole's forehead.

"Come on, let's get you home."

"I can help," Benton said.

"Get the car door for me," Dorothy said without a glance in his direction.

He turned as Dorothy bundled Nicole into her arms, barely catching the words she whispered.

"You were a lot smaller last time I did this."

Pure, undiluted love drenched every word. Tender and warm. Instantly, he felt like he had intruded onto a moment where he wasn't welcome. He jogged out of the barn, clutching the arrow in one hand and keeping it away from his body. The sky was quickly shifting, warming with the morning. He was now able to see for miles around. Towering grass swayed in the morning breeze, catching the light and rustling like a thousand whispers. Pushing aside his unease, he opened the back of the police car. They were all high-set SUV's in Fort Wayward; there were just too many places a car couldn't go. He scrambled up into the high-set cab and turned, ready to help get Nicole in without jarring her too much. He had just enough time to slip the arrow safely under the front passenger seat before Dorothy arrived. Together, they drew Nicole's limp body inside, resting her head on his lap. She shuffled, snoring softly in her sleep before settling back down.

"That's a good sign, right?" Dorothy asked. "At least it's not a dead sleep."

"Maybe."

Dorothy got into the front seat and gave one last look to the barn. "Nicole is not going to be happy about that when she comes around."

His head was already spinning with the freak out that was coming their way. "Yeah."

"One of us is going to have to tell her," Dorothy said softly, almost as an afterthought.

"Not it!"

They rushed the words, trying to get the phrase out before the other. Benton was a little quicker on the draw and he beamed. Dorothy sat up straighter in her seat, transforming herself into the unshakeable Constable Rider.

"I'm an adult."

"You're an adult that's stuck telling your daughter about her jeep," Benton said.

"This is ridiculous." By the time they were heading down the road, Benton was sure she had left the conversation behind. So, he was a little startled when she suddenly started right where they had left off. It was something so akin to what Nicole would do that he had to smile. "And besides, you're the one that didn't think to hit the brakes."

"Nicole was passed out," he said defensively.

"All the more reason not to let her drive."

"I was caught off guard! I'm the one that's always getting hurt, not her. I don't know how to deal with that."

The truth of that struck both of them, rendering them silent. These encounters had quickly developed a status quo. Nicole would charge in, all fire and righteous fury, and Benton would follow. But he was the one that got the brunt of the injuries. Not her. *Waking up to screams. Watching her drop like a rag doll. It's as if our roles are reversed tonight.* Honestly, he wasn't a fan. And obviously not that great at filling her shoes, either.

"Is Death, I mean, Mic, with us?" Dorothy asked tensely.

Benton didn't have to look hard to find the black mass keeping pace with them a half a dozen miles out in the field.

"She's around."

"But not too close?" Dorothy said, gripping the steering wheel until her arms shook.

"She's off the clock," Benton promised.

That seemed to settle Dorothy somewhat. "Good. Oh, while I remember, your mother called. The cover story is that Nicole is having some personal family issues and called you for moral support. That's why you snuck out."

Benton made a grunt of agreement. "That should work."

"What did you plan to tell them?"

"Honestly? Never occurred to me that I'd have to tell them anything."

She met his gaze in the rear-view mirror. "You really need to sit down and have a discussion with your family. Have you even told them that you're a banshee yet?"

"Have you told Nicole you know, yet?" he shot back.

"We're not talking about me, right now," Dorothy said with just as much defensiveness. "Besides, mine's a little more complicated."

"Hey, honey. Heard you killed a serial murderer. Just wanted to reassure you that it was self-defense, no court will ever convict you, and I love you no matter what," Benton said. "You can cut that down to two sentences even. Why do adults keep insisting that these things are so time-consuming?"

"Hey, mom and dad. Just letting you know I'm a banshee. Any idea on which side of the family I got that from?" Dorothy retorted.

Benton narrowed his eyes. "It's emotionally scarring to be mocked by parental figures, you know."

Dorothy met his eyes in the mirror again. There was a second of tense silence filled with him trying to figure out what he had said wrong.

Then she asked somewhat meekly, "You really see me as a parental figure?"

"Well," Benton shrugged, fighting back the heat in his cheeks. "You're a parent. And you've been good to me. And, you know, neglected children seek out – you know, what? I'm gonna stop talking now."

"Don't be shy. I'm touched. Really."

Benton scrunched his mouth up and avoided all eye contact. "Yeah, well, you're welcome."

Mercifully, she did let it slide and moved the conversation along with little more than a sweet smile. "Did you get a glimpse at what did this to her?"

"Just shadows. I was mostly focused on the metal hurdling at my head, to be honest."

"Nothing else you can think of?"

"Why do people always ask that question? What, like I'm just going to recall all these details I didn't mention before because you pushed?"

"You're getting very close to an attitude I'll take offense at," Dorothy warned.

"Sorry," Benton mumbled. A thought struck him, making him curse under his breath.

"What?" Dorothy asked instantly, eyes quickly scanning the horizon for any threats.

Forcing the words out was almost painful. He rushed them, half hoping that she would hear.

"I remembered something."

"Oh," Dorothy asked. "Really?"

"You sound exactly like your daughter when you do that," he deadpanned.

"You mean correct?"

"This is why she is the way she is."

"My girl has a few faults, I'll be the first to admit it," Dorothy said, each word beaming with pride. "But I'm damn proud of how she's turning out. So, stop avoiding the issue and spit out what you remember."

Benton didn't know if he was annoyed or amused. Either way, he instinctively glanced down at Nicole. It just seemed like she should be joining forces with her mother to mock him. That was how it normally went. One of them was always allied with Dorothy against the other. But she was still sleeping soundly. Eyelids twitching as she dreamed. The sight eased the tension on his chest. Rapid eye movement came with dreaming. Dreaming generally meant that she'd wake up soon. At least he hoped that was what it all meant.

"Benton?"

His head jerked up at Dorothy's snappy tone.

"Sorry?"

"At some point in the future, we're going to work on your little habit of tuning out all the time. It's a little creepy. Right now, however, I'm going to need to follow up on what you were saying earlier. About recalling something new."

"It's nothing solid. Just a feeling. It *felt* like a ghost. A murdered one."

Dorothy twisted around to face him, only remembering she was driving when the car veered. Between Benton's shouts and Dorothy's cursing, they managed to right the car again.

"You taught Nicole to drive, didn't you?" Benton snapped.

"You can tell the difference between methods of death?"

"Only in the vaguest way." Benton was more concerned about latching his seatbelt than keeping up the conversation. Only after he made sure that Nicole was also strapped in as best as her position allowed did he bother to keep talking. "I'm pretty sure we went over this at some point. I can feel the difference between murder and suicide. I haven't met anyone that died from natural causes, so I don't know what they might be like."

"And this one was murder? You're sure?"

"Yeah. And there was something else I couldn't put a name to."

"Try describing it."

"That won't help."

Dorothy switched to her stern motherly voice to stress the word, 'try'. Which wasn't fair. Given that she was also a cop, she was good at being intimidating.

"Fine." He glanced back down at Nicole. She was still amazingly unhelpful. Although it did somewhat defuse the situation to hear her snort in her sleep. "It's like an echo of a sound with no beginning."

"That's literally impossible."

"Gee, if only you had some warning that you wouldn't be able to understand."

"This is your second warning about tone, Benton. Don't make me give you a third."

"Sorry," he mumbled. "But, seriously, how did you think any of this would make sense to you? Have you ever even seen a ghost?"

"I've seen more than I care to."

"Of monsters," he laughed. "That's different. They're flesh and blood. Something separate to your own. Ghosts don't have those kinds of boundaries. It's more like energy. No way to stop them from slipping under your skin."

Dorothy glanced at him again. "You can't go a single day being normal, can you?"

Benton shrugged one shoulder. Sometimes, it really seemed like Constable Rider was wasted on a small town. Her interrogation techniques were second to none. She could intimidate someone twice her size and then, with a little smile and some light teasing, get anyone to feel completely at ease around her. Regardless of how much greater good she could do elsewhere, Benton was endlessly grateful to have her here. History had proven to him that the vast majority of law enforcement weren't exactly open to evidence obtained through supernatural means. Let alone killers of that caliber. It was both strange and incredibly awesome to have someone with a badge and a gun willing to hear him out.

Nicole's brow scrunched up. Her mouth twisted down into a scowl and, after releasing an annoyed groan, she began to squirm. Dorothy twisted in her seat again, careful this time, making sure that the car never veered.

"Is she awake?" Dorothy asked.

"Nic?" Benton whispered, not wanting to scare her. After a moment of hesitation, he pushed some of her hair back, cupping her head to stop her from falling off the seat as she wiggled. "Nic? Are you alright? Can you open your eyes for me?"

Her hand lifted. It hovered in place, trembling slightly with the strain, her fingers curling and stretching even as she failed to open her eyes.

"Nicole?" Benton whispered more insistently. "Can you-."

His sentence cut off as she lightly smacked her hand against his mouth.

"Nicole–"

Again, she slightly tapped him. "Five more minutes."

"I'm not an alarm."

Tap.

"Shh, five more minutes."

"You can't put me on snooze." Benton managed to get the words out before she blindly patted his mouth again.

Barely stifling his annoyance, he gently grabbed her wrist and pulled her hand back from his face.

"Stop."

"No talking," she grumbled and, once realizing she couldn't smack him again, she squirmed once more.

"I almost had a heart attack," Dorothy muttered to herself. There was a hint of annoyance in her tone, but it was hard to find under the waves of relief. "I was going out of my mind with worry."

Nicole pressed her face into his stomach and smacked the side of his head.

"I wasn't even the one talking," he snapped.

"Shh."

"Okay, I'm done with this. Come on, get up. Wakey-wakey!"

A grunt of pure annoyance escaped her as he pushed her up. In a purely passive-aggressive move, she went limp, leaving Benton with the choice of either letting her return to her sleeping position or taking on her entire weight. It took a solid shove to get her to sit up. The jolt finally got her to open her eyes, and she blinked around owlishly.

"What's going on?" she mumbled through a yawn.

Dorothy opened up the floodgates on her questions, letting them all fling from her mouth. Even half-asleep, Nicole obediently answered every question. They swiftly established that Nicole was fine, apart from a slight stinging in her hand, and had absolutely no recollection of the last few hours. The last thing she remembered was abducting Benton from his therapy session. All the while, Nicole was searching for a way to get back to sleep. Benton wouldn't let her lay back down, and leaning against the door seemed too uncomfortable. Eventually, she curled up beside him, resting her head against his shoulder. He didn't have the heart to push her off again.

"Where's my jeep?" she asked.

Dorothy pretended not to hear the question and Benton bit his lips.

"Guys?" Nicole pressed.

"We left it in a field," Benton said. "You know, because I can't drive."

"When are you going to get your license?" Dorothy asked.

"My parents don't want to encourage independence."

Dorothy didn't miss a beat. "Well, that's stupid, so I'm going to ignore it. I'm giving you your first lesson Wednesday after your baseball practice."

"Yes, ma'am," Benton said.

Nicole groaned, steadily opening her eyes and looking very annoyed at being awake. He wondered if she was normally this hard to wake up.

"Wait, what happened?" Nicole asked.

Catching her up highlighted just how little they actually knew. Still, it was more than enough time for her to shake off the last tendrils of sleep and return to her energetic norm.

"Do you still have the arrow?" she asked.

"Under the seat," Benton said.

Her eyes roamed as she shuffled again. Her hands twitched with her need to grasp a pen and notepad.

"Okay, okay. We only have one so we have to be careful with it. Organize the tests so we don't ruin it too soon. Where's my backpack?"

"You want to test the arrow?" Benton asked.

He shrunk back in the seat as she whirled around to face him. "Duh! Duh a thousand times over. How could you not want to study it?"

"A healthy self-preservation instinct?" he offered.

"Benton, you told me that it cut my hand *and* it's invisible."

"To *you*," he added. "I can see it just fine."

"That just brings up more questions," she declared. "How can something be invisible and not? How can it be incorporeal and cut me at the same time? It goes against everything. What is science?"

"Honey," Dorothy warned.

Even while frustration crossed her face, Nicole paused and sucked down a deep breath. It was a well-established routine between the two and Benton knew well enough not to interfere. Nicole didn't really calm down. It was more an exercise in bottling her particular brand of crazy. Shifting it from rapid speech to fidgeting. She was all but squirming by the time she was able to speak at a slower pace.

"I'm just saying that this is the only lead we have and we should exploit it for all it's worth."

"We all agree with you," Dorothy said. "I'll take care of it."

Nicole perked up like a meerkat. "You?"

"Yes, me."

"But we'll get to be there, right?"

"You have school."

"I was just poisoned by an unknown creature of mystery and we have an arrow that laughs at logic, and I have to go to school?"

"It's Monday," Dorothy replied simply.

"But ... arrow!"

"I'll tell you what I find out after school."

"I was attacked," Nicole protested, barely able to keep her voice from becoming a whine. "Shouldn't you keep me close? Get into protective mama bear mode?"

"You and Amy were both attacked at night."

"Okay, maybe—"

"And you were both alone. No offense, Benton. It just seems that the paranormal don't really care if you're there or not."

Benton didn't have time to respond before the constable continued.

"I can't keep a constant eye on you without neglecting my duties. If anyone notices me following you around and neglecting my duties, they're going to try and get involved. We still don't know how this ... *thing* picks its victims, so I'm not going to do anything that might draw innocent people into the line of fire."

"Okay," Nicole said. "I hear you. Just a few counterpoints."

"No, Nicole. You're going to school where you will be constantly surrounded with at least a dozen other people. I'll pick you up after."

"And you'll tell me everything then?" Nicole pressed.

"I'll tell you what you need to know," Dorothy said.

Nicole rolled her eyes. "Mom, come on. Don't make me find out on my own."

Dorothy's dark eyes darted to the rearview mirror. "The only way you could do that is to commit at least three misdemeanors."

Nicole cringed. "Well, hypothetically of course, I would say that it was possible to do it more in the felonies kind of area."

"Nicole," Dorothy said slowly. "Where were you last night?"

"I honestly don't remember." The utter relief in Nicole's voice betrayed her, making it clear that even she didn't think she was completely innocent.

"Nicole Ipiso-Waahsa Rider."

"I'm sorry," Benton cut in. "What was that?"

"Ipiso-Waahsa." Nicole waved a hand at him. "It's my middle name."

"And you teased me for Bartholomew?"

That got her to whip around. "I never teased you. I only pointed out that there is a lot of alliteration surrounding your name."

"Alliteration?" Dorothy asked, obviously happy to switch the conversation.

"Benton Bartholomew Bertrand," Benton mumbled.

"The banshee," she added. "You have to admit, that's a lot of B's."

"I want to get back to what your middle name is and why I'm only hearing about this now."

"Well, I want to get back to my mother agreeing to let me stay home today," Nicole said.

"And yet, all either of you are going to get is a meal at the diner," Dorothy noted.

Her tone made it clear, even to an overzealous Nicole, that she wasn't going to budge. With a dramatic huff, Nicole slumped down against the seat, crossing her arms and pouting. Benton wasn't sure what she thought this behavior would get her. Whatever it was, she was very bitter not to get it. Without warning, she hit Benton's arms a few times, like a cat trying to tenderize a sleeping spot. She still didn't say anything as she slumped down against him, tugging his arm into a tight hug, and allowed herself to doze.

# Chapter 6

"Ipiso-Waahsa," Nicole said slowly, stressing the syllables.

Benton parroted it back, his hands spreading out, as if he could only get his tongue to get it right if he was in motion. It actually worked.

"Hey, you got it," Nicole beamed. She nudged her shoulder into his. "And it only took you two periods."

"We didn't have either of them together. So it only counts as three minutes at the most."

That was one of the unexpected benefits of Fort Wayward High. Even when they had classes on opposite sides of the campus, they were never too far apart to not be able to have rapid fire catch-up sessions.

"It means 'morning star'," she said.

"It's nice."

"Thanks. And now that you've mastered it, you can stop using it as a distraction to keep from telling me what's going on."

"You know that there's a difference between avoidance and ignorance, right?"

Nicole jumped in front of him, pushing one finger into the center of his chest. After a moment, she pushed up onto her toes and scrubbed a hand through his hair, cooing about how fluffy it was. He had been lucky enough to wear sweatpants to sleep, giving him something somewhat presentable to wear to school. Everything needed to bring his hair into artfully arranged spikes, however, was at home. It was the first time she had really seen him without them, and she seemed endlessly fascinated.

"Was that arrow dipped with catnip or something?" he asked as he swatted her hand away.

She opened her mouth, frowned, and tipped her head to the side. "Sorry?"

"You're very energetic."

"I know, right? I feel fantastic. Remind me to keep that arrow around for finals week."

"Or, I could hide it away along with all the pixie-stixs."

"I knew you stole them!"

"There should be a law that prohibits you from sugar rushes."

"Why?" she whined, honestly offended.

"Do you remember what you did to our science project?" It was the last time she had decided that a sugar rush would help her get everything done.

"It wasn't so bad."

"I got attacked by beavers while trying to save a replica of the solar system from seven feet of water."

"Don't be dramatic," she said. "It was only six feet. And beavers are cute."

"They're huge up close."

Neither of them could keep a straight face. Nicole shook her head, trying to organize her racing thoughts. Ever since she had fully woken up, she had been unable to sit still, shifting from one conversation to the next midsentence. *Wonder if Amy's having the same side effects.* Nicole bounced on her toes before poking him in the chest.

"Don't think you can distract me," she said, trying to look intimidating but far too hyper to hold onto the expression for long. "I know that you're keeping secrets from me. You and mom. What? You think that I haven't noticed you two are becoming real buddies these days."

"Dr. Aspin says I should make friends," he commented, slipping around her to continue down the hallway, rejoining the stream of students rambling towards their next class.

Nicole spun on her heel, following him with a very bunny-like bounce in her step.

"You two are keeping something from me," she insisted.

Benton schooled his features, trying to keep his expression blank. His mind whirled as he tried to pinpoint when she had first become suspicious. Thinking on it now, it was naive to believe that she wouldn't pick up on it. He always forgot that, while she acted like a beauty queen, she could root out information like a Soviet spy.

"What?" Nicole asked.

"What, what?"

"You were contemplating something. Tell me. Tell-me-tell-me-tell-me."

They reached the large double doors that lead to the gym. He held one side open and she slipped in before him, spinning through the threshold and walking backward so she didn't have to take her eyes off of him.

"Would you watch a movie about a spy that enters the Miss Universe pageant?" he asked.

Her hand absently lifted to touch his hair again. He pushed it aside.

"Are we talking action or comedy?"

"Action," he said.

"Glittery dresses and explosions? Yeah, I'd watch that."

Thinking that he had avoided the awkward conversation was another mistake. The moment he relaxed, she gave a shout to the ceiling and bounced around to face him again.

"You distracted me."

"It's not my fault you can't focus," he defended.

Her hands dropped heavily onto his shoulders. Locking her elbows, she kept him in place as she stared at him. Even now, she couldn't keep completely still and she ended up swaying a bit. Like she was about to break into a dance number.

"You shouldn't hide things from me. Buddies don't do that to each other."

The combination of eye contact and touch made it hard to lie to her. He heaved a sigh and grabbed her shoulders in return.

"Two days," he decided. "Give me two more days. If your mom doesn't fess up, I'll tell you everything."

"I'm not good with delayed gratification."

"No, but you are really good at doing favors for friends." He turned his gaze beseeching. "Please."

"I know what you're trying to do. You're manipulating me. You ... Manipulator."

"Wow, that's some very creative name calling," he said. "Come on, Nic. For me. Just two more days with no questions."

Her mouth scrunched up. Her eyes narrowed. She stomped her feet as if she were on the verge of a full tantrum. It all ended with a high-pitched whine and a begrudging nod of her head.

"Fine. Wednesday morning. You better be chatty."

Not wanting to risk another turnaround, he quickly replied, "Wednesday morning? You're cheating me out a few hours."

"You want forty-eight hours from now? This very second?"

"That's what you agreed to."

She checked her watch then snatched up his wrist, fiddling around with his own.

"What are you doing?"

"Syncing our watches."

He pulled his wrist back but she clung on tightly.

"You're going to break it," he protested.

"I'm good with technology."

"No, you're not. And watches aren't what people mean when they say 'technology'."

Just for his own amusement, he tried to pull away again. Nicole responded as he had thought she would. The extent was a bit of a shock. Instead of complaining and pulling his arm back towards her, she latched onto his arm and tried to run off with it, all the while fiddling with the few buttons on his cheap watch. Digging in his heels only slowed them down. The soles of his shoes squeaked loudly, drawing the attention of the few other students that had made their way in before them. If it wasn't for Nicole's utter, completely insane, level of dedication to the task, he would have been embarrassed.

He yanked his arm back. "What level of crazy are you on right now?"

Again, her response proved to be way more than he had anticipated. Like splashing a feral cat. She twisted around sharply, clutching his arm tightly as they bumped and tangled. Any attempt to calm her down did the exact opposite. Her motions took them both off their feet and they toppled painfully onto the gym floor, still fighting for dominance over his watch. Her knee drove into his ribs, pushing the air from his lungs and making him incredibly grateful that Zack chose that moment to arrive.

The towering teen looped his arms under Nicole's and wrenched her to her feet. "What are you doing?"

The second her feet left the ground, all good nature left her. A feral scream, one of pure, feral frustration left her. She whipped around, trying to free herself from his grip. Zack held on, now desperate to keep his grip on the girl that looked ready to kill him. Stunned, Benton could only watch was Zack helplessly pleaded with Nicole. None of it helped. Nicole's fury worked her into a fury pitch, until her wild screams crackled as they came out of her throat.

Meg sprinted over, her sister a step behind. Their introduction only made things worse. Zack was losing his grip. Benton regained his senses just as Nicole burst free. He lurched to his feet, managing to catch her around her waist as she turned to attack Zack. Unfortunately, he didn't have Zack's height to help him. They swung around, lost their footing, and dropped back down onto the floor.

"Nic, it's me," Benton pleaded as she bucked and screamed. "Stop it. You're going to hurt yourself."

Only once she was exhausted and completely trapped by Benton's limbs did she stop. Like she was waking up. Coming out of a daze to blink at him in confusion. Mortified and shaking, she looked amongst her friends.

"I'm sorry," she whispered. "I – I didn't. I'm so sorry."

"What the hell?" Zack snapped.

Benton's anger at the outburst dwindled when he saw the fear in Zack's eyes. The twins kept their distance. Nicole noticed and trembled harder, mumbling constantly about how sorry she was.

"What happened to her?" Zack whispered.

"She needs some fresh air," Benton said. He held Zack's gaze, willing him to understand what he was trying to convey. "Help me get her outside."

Zack opened his mouth to argue. In a small act of mercy, the twins were a lot better at picking up on vibes. They were quick to rush around them and cut off the number of people that were charging forth to intervene. That was the downside of Nicole's lifelong mission of making friends with every soul in Fort Wayward. No one wanted to stay out of it.

While the girls worked on crowd control, Benton hurried Nicole outside. The whole thing would have gone a lot faster if Nicole had let Zack lift her up. Every time he tried, her inner switch would flip again. It took Benton grabbing at her wrists to calm her down somewhat. They barely got a few feet out onto the grass before she decided that Zack was too close. She spun on her heel and launched herself at him. Benton crash-tackled her to the ground, holding her there as she thrashed and snarled, steadily working herself into exhaustion.

"What the hell did you do to her?" Zack demanded.

"Nothing," Benton said. "I think she's having a bad reaction."

"Reaction to what?"

*Just had to open that door.*

By the time he had explained it all to Zack, the twins had come outside, and Nicole's growls of protest had turned into weak little whimpers. So he left Zack to catch them up and devoted his time to Nicole. She was sitting under her own power now, head against her knees, hands clutching the sides of her head like she was sure her skull was about to explode.

"What happened?" she groaned.

"You apparently like Benton more than me," Zack snipped. "Not that I'm taking that personally."

"Obviously not," Benton cut in.

Nicole made a sound of confusion. She went to lift her head, but a spike of pain had her quickly returning to her original position.

"I don't think it's anything personal," Benton said for her.

Zack scoffed. "She wasn't trying to kill you."

"I'm not human," he remarked without thought.

The truth of his comment brought the group to silence. No one really knew how to respond to it. Benton himself tried very hard not to linger too long on the thought.

*I'm not human.*

If anyone had asked him years ago, he would have thought it would be easy to accept that idea. He had always known he was different. Finally acknowledging that should have been liberating. But there was a ripple effect. A silent undercurrent of doubt that seeped into every aspect of his life. *What will I grow into? How long will it take? Do male banshees have shorter lifespans than humans? Do banshees die at all?*

A spike of panic curled in the pit of his stomach as the thought lingered in his mind. He had developed a deep respect for Nicole's intuition. And the thought that her instincts were now telling her that he didn't count as human enough to bother with shook him to his core. *Do I even count as alive?*

The whole conversation became a buzz in his ears. There but meaningless. Nothing of value until Nicole's voice broke through the haze. He snapped his head down to look at her, unsure how many times she had repeated his name to try and gain his attention. She had barely lifted her head. Just enough to look up at him with wide, beseeching eyes. There was true fear lingering in the deep brown depths, and it made his stomach twist sharply.

"Sorry," he said softly, not wanting to interrupt the conversation happening a few feet away. "What was that?"

"Did I hurt anyone?"

"No," he reassured with a light laugh. "You might have a lot to explain a little later on, though. And I think Zack's going to need an apology."

"I couldn't stop."

Her voice was just a whisper but it suddenly drew the attention of the others. Zack knelt down, careful to keep some distance between them, and hesitantly reached out towards her. Almost as if he was trying to pet a dog he wasn't certain would accept the touch.

"Hey, there, buddy," Zack said, voice as sweet as sugar. "How ya doing?"

"Why are you talking so weird?" Benton asked.

Zack glared at him, "Hey, you weren't the one that just got attacked."

"Yeah, and talking down to her is really going to mellow her out," Benton replied.

"I'm not doing that."

The sudden increase in volume made Nicole whimper. She clutched her hands over her ears, curling in on herself like she could physically block out the sound. Zack quickly dropped his voice down to a whisper again. Meg came forward, putting herself between Benton and Nicole so she could wrap her arm around Nicole's shoulders.

"It's okay," she cooed. "Just breathe. Danny, do you have your water bottle with you?"

Danny nodded and started to rummage through her bag. Just as she pulled the bottle out and handed it over, a few people wandered out of the gym doors, calling out across the distance to check on Nicole.

Rallying her senses, Nicole managed to raise her head and force a smile. "I'm okay. I'm so sorry for the fuss."

Of course, the questions of what happened followed. No one in their group really knew what to say. Benton and Zack both tried to subtly tell Nicole that her adding to this conversation was a bad idea, but she didn't listen.

"I haven't slept a lot lately," she called out. "I was given a sleeping tablet and I think that I'm having a bad reaction to it. I'm really sorry, guys."

And just like that, Nicole had found a loophole for her inability to lie. Technically, everything she said was true. Benton was oddly impressed. He hid his smile as the others reassured Nicole that she wasn't a bother. That everything will be okay. Then, of course, the conversation turned to offers to get a teacher.

"I'm just going to go over to the doctor's now," Nicole said.

"We'll help," Danny said swiftly. "Can you let the coach know that we'll be a bit late for class?"

It took a bit more reassurance to get them back into the gym. Everyone appeared honestly concerned about Nicole, and Benton found himself both amazed and perplexed by the display. It shouldn't have been a surprise. She worked hard to develop and keep her relationships. He was happy that at least some of her efforts would be reciprocated.

Eventually, there came a small window of opportunity for them to slip away. They didn't hesitate to take it, with Meg and Danny helping Nicole to her feet. They started across the grass, reassuring them that they would take care of her. Zack and Benton exchanged a look. Neither knew what else to do, so they followed behind the girls, just waiting to be of use. They all bundled into Zack's car, the twins careful to keep Nicole comfortable between the two of them in the backseat. Benton twisted around in the front passenger seat, having to jerk back at the last moment to make room for Zack completing the same maneuver.

"Okay, recap," Zack said. "Invisible hunter shoots an arrow at you. The tip is poisoned and knocks you out. You come to school."

"Yes," Nicole said, still rubbing her temples.

"That's a horrible idea," Zack said.

"Hey, I wanted to go to the hospital and check on Amy," Nicole protested.

"That's an even worse idea!" Zack shouted.

"Well, not the seeking medical attention part," Meg said.

"Okay, yeah, not that part," Zack replied.

"I think he's more opposed to the visiting a girl attacked by a ghost, while said killer ghost is stalking the person doing the visiting," Benton said.

"Yes!" Zack gestured wildly to Benton. "Thank you."

"But we have to go to her now," Nicole said.

Meg and Danny exchanged a look. "No," they said in unison. "You don't."

Nicole took in a deep breath, lifting her hands like she could somehow pull all her thoughts together.

"Amy could be having the same reaction to this drug, or whatever it is, as I am."

"Yeah," Meg said with a little smile. "But they can just sedate her."

Benton cringed back, the thought sloshing bile against the back of his throat. He had been on the receiving end of that scenario more than once. When you woke up every night screaming, the first suggestion everyone came up with was sleeping tablets. Something that would knock him out and keep him out. It worked for everyone else. He, on the other hand, was trapped in hell. With one murderer after another flooding into his mind. Tearing down the walls between his minds and theirs. All blurring them together until he could barely claw his way through the mess. Logically, he knew that it wasn't likely Amy was going through that kind of thing. But just the idea that she was had him feeling physically ill.

"I'll go check on her," he mumbled.

"And I'll go with you," Nicole said instantly.

"Again, I feel like we should mention just how bad an idea this is," Meg said.

"What else can I do?" Nicole asked. "I know why I'm suddenly incapable of self-control."

"Honestly, you were never that great at it," Danny noted.

Nicole continued as if she hadn't heard.

"She doesn't know what's happening to her. That's got to be terrifying."

"Okay, just a little question," Zack said. "What are you going to tell her? Hey, did you know ghosts are real? Also, head's up, it could be coming back for you. Good luck with that."

"I'll think of something when I get there," Nicole said.

"Yeah, you're not feeling impulsive at all," Zack retorted.

"I'm okay. I promise."

"You just attacked me."

Nicole shrunk back, hunching in her shoulders as she did. She looked small and utterly guilty. "I did say I was sorry, didn't I?"

"Repeatedly," Benton answered.

Zack glared at him.

"What? Quit making her feel guilty. It's in the past."

"It was five minutes ago!"

"Which is the past," Benton pressed, mostly out of a need to get Nicole to stop making that face. Being able to annoy Zack was admittedly a sweet little extra.

"I just need to know that she's doing okay," Nicole cut in.

Zack's eyes darted between Meg and Danny, silently pleading for one of them to come up with something that would knock Nicole off of this line of thought. *Good luck,* Benton thought. He knew that tone well by now. She was about ten seconds away from doing something impulsive. Suddenly, and at least eight seconds too early, Nicole lunged across Danny, scrambling for the door.

Chaos broke out for a few moments as they tried to wrangle her back in. It was as if everything that had been suppressed came rushing out in those few moments. The monsters with the storm. Ghosts. Meeting a serial killer couple. Watching the paranormal murder the woman and, only moments later, witnessing Nicole kill the man. Everything they had buried under mindless tasks and random obsession. The car rocked as the girls struggled. Screams rose to a deafening pitch. Amongst the shrill cries began a tirade of accusations and rants.

Benton tried to tolerate it. To let them all release what they had been holding in. But it all crushed in on him. When it got to the point he couldn't take anymore, he sucked in a deep breath and released a scream. His only thought was to break through the noise happening around him. There was no intention of making it ear-splitting. But it came out like radio feedback meeting nails on a chalkboard. Loud and shrill. The windows rattled, birds burst into the air, fleeing in a swarm that covered the sky. Everyone in the car dropped, covering their ears and bellowing in protest.

"Benton!" Zack thumped him in the chest. "What the hell?"

"My ears have only just stopped ringing from the last time you did that," Danny whined, wiggling a finger in her ear as if that could make a difference.

"You ever do that again, I swear to God, I will kill you!" Meg tried to pop her ears. "Am I shouting? I feel like I'm shouting!"

"What?" Danny asked. "I can't hear you."

"Enough!" Benton's voice cut through the group.

Everyone instantly fell silent. Clamping their mouths shut to avoid Benton opening his again.

"Nicole, I'll come with you to check on Amy, but you need to try and curb your impulses."

"I heard the part where you agreed with me," she replied, her voice a little louder than it needed to be. "So okay."

He shook his head but didn't push the issue. It was probably the best he was going to get. So he turned his attention to the others.

"You guys, no one asked you to come along. If you don't want to deal with this stuff, just step back. Nic and I can handle it."

There was a long paused.

"What?" Danny asked.

"I literally can't hear what you're saying," Meg added.

Zack waved at his ears. "All I hear is a constant ringing, man."

"Whatever," Benton muttered, wiping his hand over his face. He looked back at Nicole to see if she wanted to just walk over. It was only a few blocks, after all.

She was already halfway out of the car.

# Chapter 7

Nicole could feel her hair.

It was the weirdest sensation to be so completely aware of her body. Her nails buzzed, her eyes felt furry, and she could swear that her teeth were ringing. Energy surged through her body, turning her mind into a raging torrent of thoughts. She felt like her skull had been replaced by a pinball machine. Just bouncing her mind about from one thought to another. It left her restless. And no matter how much she bounced on her toes, shook her arms, or chewed on her lips, she couldn't work the energy out of her system. With Benton keeping pace beside her, she made her way through the hospital corridor.

Suddenly, Benton grabbed her hand and yanked her back. Her boots skittered over the tiles and she almost fell over several times. Eventually, once she felt stable again, she looked up at him.

"What is it? What's going on? Do you see something? Is it Mic? Is she here?"

Benton only pointed over her shoulder. She twisted her torso to see Constable Dorothy Rider crossing the other end of the corridor.

"Hey, mom's here." She had barely finished the sentence before Benton's hand grabbed her shoulder.

"What's going on?" she asked as he pulled her backwards. It only clicked once they were safely behind a rack of medical pamphlets. "Oh, right. *We're* not supposed to be here. Hiding. Good call. Solid. Sound decision making."

"I'm going to need you to relax," Benton said tensely.

"I am relaxed. I'm the most relaxed. If there was a contest for being the most relaxed, I'd win by default."

His brow furrowed. "I don't think that came out the way you intended."

"Yeah, it did," she insisted. "Because everyone would know that they can't win against me so they wouldn't even sign up. Ergo, I win by default."

"Did you really just used the word 'ergo'?"

"I just won an argument with the word 'ergo'," she countered.

"Right," he said slowly.

He was looking over her head as he settled his hands on her shoulders and pushed down. Her heels hit the floor and stayed here. *How long have I been doing that?*

"Thanks," she mumbled.

"Any time." Benton was barely paying any attention.

His long neck allowed him to glance around the display without inching out into view. She had every intention of turning around and looking too. But his hair was super fluffy. Like a puffed-up baby owl. Without all the products, his hair was a few shades lighter, especially at the tip, bringing the color to an almost snowy white. All of her research said that banshees were haunting. Although there was some debate over if it was breathtakingly beautiful or stomach-churningly ugly. What they did agree on, however, was that their hair was gray. She wondered if all of the others had this exact same shade.

Reaching up, she poked at a bit that had flopped onto his forehead. He jerked his head away, making her reach further to regain the contact. With a huff, he smacked at her hand. Logically, she knew that she was irritating him and she resolved to stop. So it really surprised her when she found herself poking at his hair again. Another slap.

"Stop," he whispered.

"Will do," she replied with a salute.

And she meant it. Right up until the overhead lights turned some of his strands silver and she just needed to poke it again. This time, after smacking it away, he grabbed her hand to keep it down.

"Stop."

"I totally did."

"You do realize that you're still doing it now, right?"

She stared at her free hand, only then noticing that she was, in fact, still poking his hair.

"Huh. Weird."

Benton huffed a sigh before something caught his attention. "Okay. She's gone, let's go."

Nicole was already heading down the hall before he had finished the sentence. He squeezed his fingers around one of her palms. It meant that one hand was free while the other was practically a leash tethering her to him. While it hurt her shoulder, it really did keep her from spiriting off before him. They hurried around the corner. Amy's door came into view and Nicole picked up her pace. Only a few feet were left separating them when the door opened.

Their sneakers squeaked against the tiles as they tried to duck somewhere out of sight. There was nowhere to go. After a moment of scrambling, they gave up and turned to face the music.

"Uncle Chuck," Nicole beamed.

For a moment, she was relieved to see her father's childhood friend before her. Then she recalled that he was also a member of the RCMP. Panic surged back through her, heightened by whatever drug was still in her system. She spun to check on Benton. Without missing a beat, he lifted his arm up, allowing her momentum to spin her around. She ended up back where she started, staring at Chuck, who, for some reason, was now looking at her strangely.

"Nicole," Chuck said slowly.

"Any hope you haven't seen us?" Nicole asked, working hard to keep her smile in place.

His brow furrowed. Crossing his arms, he glanced between her and Benton. "No."

"You sound confused. Maybe you're not quite sure."

Benton squeezed her hand and she clamped her mouth shut.

"Hi, officer."

Benton sounded so impressively casual that she started turning to gawk at him. He dropped his free hand on top of her head and jerked her head back to the front.

"How are you doing today?" he said without releasing her head.

"Fine," Chuck said slowly. "What are you two doing here?"

"I honestly don't know how to respond to that," Nicole said.

Benton squeezed her hand again. *Oh, right. Shouldn't say that.*

"Take your time," Chuck said.

"Thanks." Benton clicked his tongue as he struggled to come up with something. "So, were you on your way to get a coffee?"

"I know you're both supposed to be at school right now," Chuck cut in.

"Free period," Nicole spouted.

*That actually sounded believable.* She turned to see if Benton was just as proud as she was. He pushed her back around again.

"We just thought we'd check in on Amy," Benton added.

"Yes! Totally." She jerked her thumb over her shoulder. "That."

Chuck gestured past them. "And that's why they're here, too?"

Meg and Danny came running up on her left, Zack on her right. Seeing them brought a wave of ecstasy. *They made it. They came. They're here.* Giggles spilled from her mouth as she started to jump. She would have clapped if Benton didn't jerk her back down. It didn't quell the excitement that was simmering through her.

"Aw, you guys made it! You're the best! I love you guys."

"Nic," Benton hissed.

"Oh, right, sorry." She stopped bouncing, schooled her features, and turned her attention back to Chuck.

Chuck's jaw dropped. "I still saw that you did that."

"Any chance you're willing to pretend that you didn't?" she asked with a toothy grin.

"No!"

"Oh," Nicole said sadly.

"What are you on?" Chuck's mouth became a tense, thin line as he looked to Benton. "What did she take?"

"Just a sleeping tablet," Nicole assured. It was easier now that she had the lie all set up. "Weird side effects, I guess."

"Okay, I don't know what all this is," he waved a hand about to indicate the entire group of teenagers. "But it stops now. Get back to school and I won't tell your mother."

"But ... Amy!"

"Go," Chuck demanded, pointing down the hallway.

"I understand," Nicole said. And she meant it. Right up until she saw the door again.

Before she knew it, she was at the door, pushing her way inside with Benton at her heels. He slammed into her back when she cut short.

Amy wasn't alone in the room.

A creature stood on her bed, crouched down to straddle the unconscious girl. Each muscle was exposed. Dry and brittle. Shortened with rot. Its bones clicked and popped as it swiveled its shoulders, the soft noise mingling under the crackle of the parchment-thin skin. It had no eyes. Only deep, cavernous voids where they should have been located.

Nicole's stomached churned. Her blood became ice in her veins when she found out that she knew that face. It was barely more than a skull. Crushed with skin and lips peeled back to expose its teeth. But she knew. With the same unwavering certainty that she knew it was smiling at her. A toothy, smirk full of malice and twisted delights. Just like that, she was back on the storm-drenched road, watching as the life drained from the man as she put a bullet between his eyes.

The creature was gone before she could summon a scream.

*** 

Shock threw Benton out of his skin, separating him from reality, reducing the world to separate moments in time rather than a constant stream. It only took his brain a split second to recognize the man the monster had been. A phantom pain crushed his throat as he looked upon the man's mangled face, which had almost killed him. This can't be happening. The grotesque being smiled. It ripped the air from Benton's lungs.

Nicole burst forward and reality caught up with him. In an instant, he was aware that Zack and Meg had rushed to the door at the same time, clogging up the entrance and effectively cutting it off as an escape route. The mummified man went for the open window. So did Nicole. She grabbed hold of the sliding glass and shoved it closed, attempting to block off his exit. But the dead man was swift. He passed through a split second before the glass closed with a cracking force.

Chuck's demand for attention was nothing compared to Nicole's bellow of fury. She slammed her fists against the cracked window, shattering it, already climbing out before all the pieces had followed.

"Nicole!" She didn't even look back at him. All of her focus was on hunting down the monster. "Damn it, Nic."

A series of shouts followed him as he jumped from the window, grateful that the hospital itself was on the ground floor. A quick glance and he spotted the flying trails of her hair passing around the corner of the alleyway. He was quick to close the distance. Following her out into the street, down the mercifully empty walkway, heading towards the outskirts of town.

Nestled within the grass planes, Fort Wayward was a handful of buildings clustered on one side of a highway and surrounded by grasslands. There was nowhere for her to go and yet he was terrified of losing sight of her. Or leaving her alone with whatever had crawled out of its own grave. Her sights were set on the mummified man. Following as he ran along the sides of the buildings, leaping from one to the next. Swinging up to perch on streetlamps before sailing down to run along the street again.

He's playing her.

The thought turned his burning chest to ice. With whatever he had given her leaving her blindly impulsive, it wasn't a hard task. One last flip, and the living mummy stopped. It turned around, facing Nicole straight on, shoulders hunched for a fight but still smiling. *It's luring her.*

Benton's head filled with images of it luring her out into the grasslands, where the vegetation served as a hiding place. Where they could be separated by a few feet and never know it. All of that shattered when a big-rig's airhorn broke the stillness. The massive truck was barreling down the lonely highway. Too fast to stop. Nowhere for it to turn. And Nicole was running out in front of it.

"Nicole!"

She didn't hear him, or the desperate attempts of the driver to raise a warning. Her attention was focused on the skinned man alone.

Benton pushed himself harder. Until his legs ached and his lungs felt filled by burning coals. The skinned man cackled with glee as Nicole lunged for him, leaping in front of the speeding mac truck. Horns blared as Benton crashed into her, meaning to push her out of the way but clumsily taking them both down. Rough pavement ground against his skin as he struggled to hold onto the struggling girl. The horn sounded again, the sound filling his head as he looked up to see the metal front of the truck glistening within the sunlight. Its front bar soared towards them. Benton flattened himself against the ground, but metal still consumed his vision. The horn blasted all thoughts from his mind.

He screamed.

It happened in an instant. The steel before his face buckled. Glass rained down and the horn sputtered and died as the massive vehicle bucked, thrown to the side as if hit by a solid force. The scent of burning tires filled the air as the driver tried to compensate. With an earth-rattling crunch, it toppled onto its side, sliding for a few yards before the front end dipped into the trench that ran the length of the road.

Benton's scream cut off, but he didn't close his mouth. Panting hard, he stared at the truck. At the patch of mangled metal that looked as if it had been struck with a wrecking ball. Nicole squirmed in his arms, reminding him of the greater threat.

The skinned man still stood in the middle of the road. He wasn't smiling anymore. The empty pits of his eyes slowly turned from the truck to meet Benton's gaze. That alone was enough to bring forth the sensation of being hunted. The undeniable knowledge that he had grabbed the attention of a predator. What was worse, however, was that he felt known. Crimson red sparked within the skinned man's skull. Just a second. A crackle of pure electricity. And then it was gone. Vanished. In the stunned silence, Benton could hear the soft click and rattle of its bones, but he couldn't tell where it was coming from. Soon enough, it fell away.

"Are you okay?" Nicole asked, snapping him out of his daze.

"Uhm, yeah. Are y–"

"The driver!" She ripped herself from his arms without a moment of hesitation.

She was scrambling down the embankment by the time help started to arrive. Helpful hands brought Benton back to his feet. A dozen questions were thrown at him but he barely heard any of them. His attention was fixed on the endless expanse of nothingness that surrounds Fort Wayward. A gentle breeze turned it all into a shifting sea, whispering a thousand secrets, but showing nothing.

# Chapter 8

The instant Doctor Young Eagle closed the door behind him, Dorothy burst forward to engulf her daughter in a crushing hug once again. Nicole sighed, the sound a mixture of contentment and pain, and hugged her back. "I'm okay, mom."

"You could have been killed."

Until now, the Constable had shouted the words. Lowering her volume had to be a good sign. At the very least, Nicole was determined to convince herself it was.

"What were you thinking?" Dorothy said with a particularly tight squeeze.

"I was trying to catch the ... dang it, I still don't know what it is. I need my files! They're in my backpack."

"The backpack that's currently at school?" Dorothy asked.

Nicole pulled back slightly to look her mother in the eyes.

"I feel like this is a trick question. But, yes."

"I'm just wondering why exactly you aren't with your backpack. At school. Where I told you to stay."

Nicole cringed. "I knew it was a trap."

"Nicole," Dorothy said with a warning.

"But it's actually really good that I took a temporary hiatus from obediently following your suggestions."

"We're going to circle back around to discuss how it was an order, not a suggestion. Right now, however, I'm interested in where you're going with this."

"Right. Well, if I had been at school, I never would have seen ... whatever that was. Now that I have, I'm sure that I can identify it."

"Also, Amy might not have survived this second encounter," Benton added from his position beside the closed door.

Nicole jumped and clapped her hands together. "Yes. Good point. Solid point that backs up my theory. Love it. Thank you, Benton."

"Nicole, settle down. Benton, stay out of it," Dorothy commanded.

Benton hunched his shoulders and leaned harder against the wall, as if he were trying to blend into it. The small examination room didn't offer any places to hide. Nicole was sure that Dr. Esther Young Eagle was getting suspicious of them. It seemed that she was always on duty when they needed a post monster encounter check-up. It had reached a point that the doctor no longer tried to separate Nicole and Benton, instead seeing them both at once with little more than a resigned sigh. It had helped that both of them had escaped with little worse than road-chafed skin and hard bruising. Dorothy obviously wanted to have this conversation in private but wasn't willing to kick Benton out just yet. So, instead, she stared at him until she was sure that he wasn't about to speak again, then turned back to Nicole.

"I told you to stay at school to keep you safe. You didn't listen and you almost died. If you can't bring yourself to care about that, how about the poor driver?"

Nicole instantly deflated. "They said he's going to be fine."

"His arm is broken in two places and he has three fractured ribs. I don't even know where to begin with the property damage."

"That was Benton," Nicole blurted.

Benton's jaw dropped. "What the hell?"

"Sorry. I'm just feeling really cornered right now. I needed a distraction."

"So you throw me under the bus?"

"At least it's not a truck." Her smile vanished as both Dorothy and Benton glared at her. "Too soon?"

"Maybe wait at least a day before joking about it," Benton said.

Dorothy's sharp sigh severed their conversation and instantly put the teens back on the defensive. Benton pressed hard against the wall as Dorothy studied him from head to foot and back. Nicole felt bad that he had once again taken the brunt of the damage. Hitting the road hard scraped some of their skin off. Most of the damage had come from the recoil of the banshee wail. It had ground them against the road, and Benton's gym gear had offered little protection. From knee to ankle, his outer right leg looked almost skinned. It was pretty much the same for his right arm. Constable Chuck's training gear hung loosely off of Benton's leaner frame, covering the stark white bandages that now covered his limbs.

"You moved the truck? It wasn't this newest creature?"

"I think so," he said.

"*Think*?" she pressed.

Benton glanced to Nicole before he swallowed. "I think it was me. I have no idea how I did it and am not entirely sure if I could do it again."

Dorothy's eyes narrowed in scrutiny as she looked him over. Benton squirmed under the weight of her focused gaze and threw a nervous glance at Nicole. She shrugged one shoulder. *I don't know what she's looking for, either.*

"That truck has to be at least 40 tons of metal," Dorothy said slowly.

Nicole couldn't keep in her low whistle. "That's a lot of tons."

Dorothy looked at her, blinked, and then continued, "So, what are we saying here? That you can create sonic booms now? With just your voice? In a split second?"

"Psst," Nicole hissed between her teeth. "Hey, mom. He doesn't like those kinds of questions."

"I don't know the answer to those kinds of questions," Benton corrected with an edge of annoyance.

"Psst, mom." Nicole leaned forward and waved her hand to draw her mother's attention. "I think he can hear us."

"Yeah, I can."

Nicole pouted. "Why don't your ears ever hurt after these screams?"

"There's a slight ringing," he offered.

"Can we please focus back on the fact that you can knock over a moving 40-ton vehicle with just your voice?" Dorothy snapped.

"Do we really know that I did?" Benton countered. "Seriously, the driver was trying to avoid us. We had that rain last night and there's that ditch. I'm not that great at physics, but I'm pretty sure there's a way to explain it all without drawing me into it."

Nicole couldn't help but join her mother in staring at Benton in disbelief. Confronted with the combined incredulous looks, he skirted his gaze to the side. Nicole could see by the lock of his jaw that he was clinging desperately to his conviction. She understood why. Everything was changing so fast. She couldn't imagine how hard it was for him to keep up, to deal with the knowledge that the list of things he knew about himself to be true was quickly dwindling. At the moment, she was only dealing with one major identity crisis and she wasn't handling it well. *He needs some time.*

Unfortunately, Dorothy wasn't of a like mind. Absently placing one arm protectively around her daughter, she pulled her mobile phone out of her pocket.

"Janett was filming her grandchild at the time of the accident," she started.

"Oh, how's the baby doing? Have they settled on a name yet?" Nicole looked to Benton before continuing. "He's super cute. He has knee-dimples."

"Sweetie," Dorothy said. "I know it's hard for you right now, but I'm going to need you to focus."

"Right."

"And not talk."

Nicole popped her lips. "That's going to be harder."

Dorothy decided to continue as if Nicole hadn't spoken. "She sent me the video."

Starting the video, she turned the screen to let Benton watch. Nicole slowly edged closer to him so she could watch as well. She realized her attempts weren't as subtle as she thought they had been when she ended up with both Benton and Dorothy watching her. Still, she continued until she was pressed against Benton's good side. He shifted to give her some room, sparing a moment to brush aside her hair and check on the ravaged skin of her jawline. The scream brought his attention back to the mobile screen.

It didn't sound human. A mangled hybrid of an animalistic roar and the wails of a cyclone. The phone's speaker crackled with strain, threatening to break as the pitch swiftly rose. There wasn't much else to see because, by this time, Janett had realized what was happening and was racing forward to help. Nicole caught glimpses of the main event. The truck rocketing off the ground, toppling to the side with a bone-rattling crunch before sliding in a hail of sparks and screeching metal.

Benton's eyes widened slightly, his jaw dropping. "Huh."

Nicole reached out and poked at the phone to replay the video. After it was done, she repeated Benton's 'huh' and followed with, "That's both terrifying and impressive. I won't even be mad that you let Janett have a recording of your scream even though I've asked you repetitively."

"I didn't let her," he said. "And even if I did, you don't have any right to my screams."

"Well, if you want to be all logical about the situation."

"There is an upside to this," Dorothy cut in.

"Yeah," Nicole grinned up at Benton, "your hair looks great on film."

"What is with you and my hair today?" Benton blurted. "And what is wrong with *you*?"

Nicole shrugged a shoulder and was in the process of reaching up to poke his hair again when Dorothy sharply cleared his throat.

"As I was saying, the upside is that no one has actual footage of Benton in action. People either didn't get their phones out fast enough or the wheels obscured their line of sight. Whatever it was you were chasing, no one else saw it. We do have the scream to deal with, of course. I don't think most people will jump to the conclusion that Benton made it. There's going to be a lot of people with a lot of questions."

Benton nodded, swallowing down the bile that was working its way up his throat.

"Great. Just as my 'new kid' status was wearing off."

Nicole giggled. "You'll always be the new kid. Everyone else was born here."

"Yeah, but I finally got them to the point where all decided I was boring and were starting to leave me alone."

"You get invited places."

"No, you do. I get an afterthought invitation because they realize I'm standing next to you."

Completely unknown to her, Nicole had reached for his hair again. He smacked her hand away.

"Are you two done?" Dorothy snapped. "This isn't a game. We actually have some important things we need to discuss. People could die. You both almost died. Can you give me the dignity of keeping your focus for five seconds?"

"Sorry, mom."

"Sorry," Benton mumbled at the same time.

Dorothy waited a moment to ensure that neither of them was about to go on another tangent before she continued. Then she purposefully pulled out her note pen and notebook.

"This thing you saw. Give me a description."

Nicole clamped her mouth shut and fixed Benton with wide, pleading eyes. Dorothy noticed it instantly and leveled Benton with a demanding stare. Confronted with both women, Benton wavered on who to respond to first. Eventually, he gave Nicole a small, reassuring smile. She was so relieved that he was going to handle it that she almost missed the look he threw her mother.

*What's going on?* she screamed in her head. Normally, Benton was good at picking up on her vibes. So she could only assume that he was deliberately avoiding eye contact with her. A moment later, Dorothy did the same. *Are they actually hiding something from me?* The idea threw her off enough that she struggled to keep up with the conversation.

Benton's voice remained flat and emotionless as he described the monster. Sticking only to the facts. Refusing to elaborate. It made it easy to pinpoint the exact moment tension entered his voice. Even the mysterious drug in her veins wasn't enough to blind her to the shift. With a stunned blink, she looked over to find Benton and Dorothy having a silent conversation. *Okay, something is definitely going on here.* She barely managed to keep the words from coming out of her mouth.

Dorothy crossed her arms over her chest and schooled her features. It was the only reaction the constable allowed herself as she listened to Benton's tale. The only thing he left out was *who* the man was. Or, more precisely, how they knew him. Nicole almost wept with relief when he came to an end and she knew for sure he wasn't about to reveal that bit of information. A heartbeat after he fell silent, Dorothy sucked in a deep breath and nodded absently to herself.

"What are we dealing with here?"

"Yeah, Benton," Nicole said.

He jerked with surprise and looked between the two women. "I don't know! No matter how many different ways you ask me, the answer's not going to change."

"We don't mean anything by it," Nicole said. "It's just that he's one of your people."

"I don't have people," Benton snapped. "Quit trying to put my fingerprints on this train wreck."

"It was a truck," Nicole said with a slight frown. "Oh, I get it now. Never mind."

"Unbelievable," Dorothy hissed under her breath.

Nicole turned to her mother with a flick of her long hair. "If you want to change the subject, can we talk about Amy? Is she okay? What happened to her? What was it doing to her?"

Dorothy shifted her weight from one foot to the other and licked her lips. *Uh oh.* Those were two tells that the constable only showed when she was about to have a very uncomfortable conversation.

Dorothy regained her composure and looked Nicole in the eyes. "She hasn't regained consciousness."

"And?" Benton pressed.

The constable looked to the side then forced out, "Her kidney had been removed."

"Say again?" Nicole instantly shot back.

"You heard me."

"There's wasn't any blood," Benton said.

"Did they find the kidney?" Nicole asked at the same moment. The looked to each other and she shrugged. "They're both legitimate questions. You can pick the order you answer in."

Dorothy let the comment slide. "No, they didn't find it. And yes, there was no blood."

"Okay, I can't express how much effort it's taking me to keep calm right now," Nicole said slowly. "I'm going to need *way* more information than you're currently giving me. And I'm going to need it soon."

"The wound was clean." Dorothy's eyes grew troubled, her voice distant. "I've never seen anything like it. None of the doctors have. It cut her open like a jack-o-lantern. No blood. No redness. No hesitation or struggling cuts. Just this hole in her stomach."

Recognition shot through Nicole like a bolt of lightning. *I know this! I've heard of this!* Her hand latched onto Benton's, squeezing until he let out a sharp hiss. Of course, Dorothy was instantly suspicious. She threw a quizzical look at her daughter. Then at their joined hands. Then Benton.

"What am I missing?"

*Play it cool. Don't let her know,* Nicole told herself. Dorothy was one small push away from trying to cut Nicole out of this altogether. There was no way she was about to let her run down any leads.

"Nicole," Dorothy warned. "I'm waiting for an answer."

*Play it cool.*

"Nothing, mom." Nicole snorted, before falling into a little giggle. "What a question."

*Nailed it.*

Dorothy sighed heavily, pressing her lips tight before leveling a cool look at Benton. "What isn't she telling me?"

"Mom, I'm hurt and offended that you'd think I wouldn't answer you truthfully."

"You're jerking his hand around and eyeing the door like you're about to make a run for it."

"What?" Nicole droned out slowly, stretching the word out as she began to bounce with contained energy. "That's crazy."

Annoyance flashed across Dorothy's face. Her mouth opened but, before she could say anything, there was a sharp tap on the door. An instant later, Chuck poked his head inside.

"Hey, guys. Glad to see you're okay. Dorothy, we kind of need you out here," he said.

"I'm with my daughter."

"I know. But now we've got traffic control duty on top of everything else. We need all hands on deck."

"I'm not leaving my girl again." There was no anger in Dorothy's voice. It was a simple, indisputable fact.

"We can keep her at the hospital."

"Because we've kept this place so safe," Dorothy said.

Chuck's eyebrows knitted. "She ran out in front of a truck, Dorothy."

*Really? No one else saw it?* In the fuzzy recesses of her short-term memory, Nicole could recall her mother saying so. But she hadn't really believed it. Honestly, she just assumed people had gone into denial. With a little more thought, she remembered that

Zack and Meg had become jammed in the doorframe. *Did they block Chuck's view? Did they see anything?* Doctor Young Eagle had refused to let them come into the small room as well. The only other option she could think of right now was that only Benton and herself could see it. But that was too complicated to dwell on right now when every cell in her body was screaming at her to get back to her files.

"I know you're rattled, Dorothy. I get it. I am, too," Chuck continued. "But there's no one to blame except her and her stupid decision making. No offense, Nicole. But if you don't want to be called an idiot, don't do idiotic things."

"Chuck," Dorothy snapped.

"No, it's fair," Nicole said.

"Dorothy, there are people out here who need you. So, come on already and get back to work."

"My daughter needs me," Dorothy said.

"I'll be okay," Nicole assured.

"I'm not leaving you unsupervised."

Benton visibly steeled himself for what he was about to say. "I'll call my parents."

Even Chuck was stunned by the decision, and he had only spent a few hours around the Bertrand family.

"Really?" Dorothy asked, clearly not believing him.

"They both work from home," he grumbled. "One of them can come out and get us. We'll stay at my house until you come and pick her up after your shift."

"You snuck out before," Dorothy noted.

"Yeah, when they weren't expecting it. I doubt they'll let me out of their sight for a while after this."

She contemplated this for a moment, clearly remembering that letting Nicole out of her sight was quickly proving itself a bad idea.

"Dorothy," Chuck said. "I'm not telling the boss 'no' for you."

"Go, mom," Nicole assured. "Benton won't let anything happen to me."

Unhooking one arm from its folded position, she jabbed a finger towards her daughter.

"You go anywhere other than his house and I will destroy your entire existence. Got it? Your punishment will reach into every single aspect of your life and destroy everything you love. Do you understand me?"

"I understand and am appropriately afraid," Nicole said solemnly.

Benton should have been ready for the Constable to lock her eyes onto him. He still jumped, though.

"If anything happens to my girl—"

"Please don't say anything," Benton cut in. "I already have a healthy fear of you."

"Take care of her. Keep her in the house."

Benton nodded. After Dorothy turned to handle her obligations, Benton leaned over to whisper into Nicole's ear.

"What is the likelihood that you'll let me keep that promise?"

"Slim to none," Nicole confessed.

"Oh, God."

"We need to go," Nicole whispered. "I need my files."

Benton sighed. Finally, she released his hand to cup his face, forcing him to meet her gaze.

"I think I know what this is."

# Chapter 9

While waiting in the hospital reception, it became unavoidably clear that Nicole didn't actually have a plan to get around his parents. She had just started to spit ball with him when the electric doors opened and his father stormed into the room. Theodore barreled into his son, drawing him into a crushing hug that almost knocked them both off their feet. They had barely regained their footing when Cheyanne joined the embrace. Benton clenched his teeth as his parents unintentionally squeezed his wounds.

Looking around Theodore's shoulder, Benton caught sight of Nicole watching them as if they were an after-school special. She was beaming brightly, with hands clasped before her and tears in her eyes. *When is that stuff going to wear off?* Even as he rolled his eyes, he couldn't deny that the situation was getting to him, too. His parents weren't the physically affectionate type. If he was ever brave enough, he'd admit to himself that this is why he was touch starved but utterly against seeking out contact. With everything that happened since his childhood, they had become even more standoffish. Sometimes, it was easy to believe they didn't care about him at all.

It was nice to have the reminder.

Theodore cupped the back of Benton's head as he finally pulled away. "Are you okay? Are you hurt?"

"I'm fine. It's just a few scratches."

Cheyanne pushed her hand through his hair, the touch making the dried blood crackle and sending little shots of pain along his scalp.

"It's nothing," Benton insisted. "It just looks like a lot in the blonde hair."

He grew to miss his hoodie with a burning passion as his mother continued to check every inch of his scalp.

"Mom, stop."

"You have a metal plate in your skull," she said. "Head injuries are not a good thing for you."

"The metal plate would help him," Theodore said.

Cheyanne drew in a sharp breath and glared at her husband. "That's not how it works."

"Chey, he's standing, he's breathing, and the doctor's letting him go home. Our boy's okay." That said, he turned back to his son, his fingers tightening at the base of Benton's neck. "Why would you run out into traffic? Should we go talk to Dr. Aspen?"

"I wasn't trying to hurt myself, dad."

"Then what were you trying to do?"

"Let me guess," Cheyanne said, the muscles of her neck growing taut. "All of this has to do with the Rider girl."

"She's right over there, mom," Benton said.

Nicole awkwardly waved when the Bertrands turned as one to face her. Her smile was tense, as if she was physically trying to hold back the flood of words that wanted to spill free.

"Hi," she settled on at last. "Thanks for letting me come home with you."

"Yes, well, Constable Rider didn't leave us with many options," Cheyanne replied, her stone smile still in place.

"Mom," Benton sighed.

"I'm just curious," she continued as if he hadn't spoken. "What exactly were you trying to achieve?"

"A dog," she blurted out.

Her eyes widened and she looked to him for help.

"There was a dog," he agreed. "We thought we saw a dog run out into the road."

"And you ran out in front of a truck for it?" Theodore asked.

"I like dogs." It was clear from her wince that she heard how robotic she sounded.

*This conversation is going downhill fast,* Benton thought. "Can we just go home, please? Mom, dad, I'm exhausted."

"Then perhaps you should have stayed home," Cheyanne said. Casting a quick glance at Nicole, she lowered her voice to a whisper. "We will discuss that matter later."

"I thought Dorothy cleared that up," Benton said.

"Yes, she did," Cheyanne said sourly.

"You're still grounded, though," Theodore added. "We have rules and you willfully broke them."

"Yeah, that sounds about as good as I could have expected," Benton acknowledged. "Can I just go to sleep now?"

Cheyanne mumbled a few words of agreement and quickly began to usher her family to the exit. Nicole was an after-thought. The passive-aggressive insult wasn't enough to take the smile off of Nicole's face.

"What are you smiling about?" Cheyanne asked over her shoulder.

"It's just nice to see Benton getting fussed over," Nicole said before realizing that she probably should have kept that to herself.

Both Cheyanne and Theodore chose to ignore the comment. Benton was grateful for it. There was nowhere that conversation could go that wouldn't be extremely awkward. They stepped outside and the afternoon sunlight burned his eyes, temporally blinding him and almost making him miss the car entirely. Nicole was clearly bursting to start talking again.

"What is wrong with her?" Theodore asked. "She seems weirder than normal."

The answer came out on reflex. "Painkillers. She gets goofy on them. They'll wear off soon. Hopefully."

The highway was the only way in and out of town. Unfortunately, their turn off was on the other side of the accident site. Tension radiated from his parents as they joined the traffic. By the time they passed it and were moving at a normal speed, Benton was choking on it. Unable to bear the stifling silence for a moment longer, he pulled his headphones from his backpack, attached them to his phone, and turned up his music. He let the trumpets and brass band flood his ears. All the while, he kept sneaking glances at Nicole. She was too busy flipping through her binder to notice.

Dread crashed in his stomach as he stared out of the window. The seemingly endless fields of grass. Gathering rain clouds hung as a low blanket over the sky. A few hills rose up in the distance, creating the buffalo jumps that had first drawn people to the area. All the while, he couldn't shake the notion that it was out there. Watching them. Waiting. He constantly scanned the area, anxiously expecting the next attack. A deep sigh of relief left him when they finally pulled up in front of their farmhouse.

"Nic, we're here," he said, pulling out one of his ear-buds.

She didn't look up from her binder, now flicking through the sheets with bitter resentment.

"I know that I know this," she hissed through her teeth.

"Know what?" Cheyanne unclicked her seatbelt but didn't turn, instead eyeing Nicole in the rearview mirror.

Nicole's head snapped up, her eyes becoming as wide as dishes again. "A lot of things," she blurted. "I know a lot of things."

Cheyanne eyed her for a moment but, luckily, didn't care enough to ask any follow-up questions. A low rumble of thunder announced the first raindrops. Cheyanne lingered long enough to order Benton into the house, then ducked out to beat the rain. He followed her without complaint and was halfway to the porch before he noticed that Nicole wasn't following him.

"Benton?" Theodore asked with an edge of concern as he watched Benton turn.

"I'll be right there."

The temperature dropped as the storm rushed towards them. Both of his parents waited under the cover of the porch, watching him carefully, as if they thought he would just sprint off without warning. Nicole lifted her chin to the sound of the door opening but didn't take her eyes off the open binder.

"You need to come in, too," he told her.

"Uh huh."

"Now, Nic."

She flicked through a few more pages. "I'm almost done."

"Come on. It's going to rain."

"Uh huh."

"Nicole!" Cheyanne snapped from the porch.

Instantly, Nicole snapped the book shut and inched over the back seat to push past Benton.

"Seriously?" Benton asked. "What is with you and parental figures?"

"I want your mom to like me."

"She never will," Benton said.

For a split second, he was worried that he had gone too far and hurt her feelings. He should have known that she would just dismiss it with a snort.

"I remember you saying you'll never be my friend. Now you love me. She'll love me, too."

Even as he grumbled, he helped her collect her things, wincing each time the backpacks bumped against his raw side.

Nicole paused. "Does it hurt? Do you want me to carry something?" The now steady patter of rain left them damp by the time they jogged up the stairs.

"Get inside now, talk later," he replied.

It only took them a few steps to get to the porch. A swift dump of rain was nipping at their heels as they hurried up.

"I'm sorry," she said, once they got up.

"You probably should be," Cheyanne said under her breath.

Nicole clutched the binder to her chest and was curling in on herself, shying away from his mother's words as if they were a physical threat. Benton looped his good arm over Nicole's shoulders with an exhausted sigh and let her take his weight.

"Don't worry about it," he said.

"Oh, I think I still will," Nicole said.

"Good," Cheyanne said.

Theodore had unlocked the front door and they all hurried inside. The high roof dulled the sound of the rain, turning it into a low but constant hum. Water ran down the windows, the stream playing with the afternoon light.

"I never get over how large your house is," Nicole said.

It was both the largest and most isolated property in Fort Wayward. Not grand by any means. But while it was basic, it was huge. She tipped her head back as she walked, looking up at the hollow center. He never could figure out what she found so entertaining about it.

"You mother and I are going to put on the alarm," Theodore said casually. "If any door opens, we'll know about it. You might have your friend over, but you're still grounded."

Benton nodded.

"I hope you understand how serious this is," Cheyanne added.

All signs said she was gearing up for a rant. Something Benton wasn't in any condition to deal with now.

"I do. Thanks for coming to get us," he called over his shoulder. "We'll be in my room."

Nicole didn't bother to try and make the transition less awkward. She just hurried behind him, thundering up the staircase without a word.

"Leave your door open!" Theodore called after them.

"You still haven't put one up," Benton shot back.

His parents didn't respond. In all likelihood, they didn't want to open up that particular Pandora's Box. It was yet another one of their safety measures for their potentially dangerous son. A means of making sure that he wasn't torturing small animals in his bedroom. He had no door, which they still hadn't admitted to taking, while they had a few extra locks on theirs.

Halfway up the stairs, he began to feel the aches of his blossoming bruises. Nicole gave him room but wasn't exactly subtle about her preparations to catch him. He deliberately ignored his mother as she trailed along behind them. That was their status quo. Benton could never figure out why she was so concerned with the stairs. *Does she think I'm going to push Nicole over the railing?* They reached the landing and he headed straight for his room.

"Thanks, mom," Benton muttered without looking back. It was half sarcasm, half honest.

"Benton."

His head snapped around, a confused frown curling his lips. He hadn't been expecting a reply. Cheyanne stood at the top of the stairs, clutching the banister with both hands, looking almost close to tears. Silence lingered between them, neither Bertrand willing to speak first. Something about that moment brought whispers of his childhood. Unexpected and gut-wrenching. Looking at her, he found himself recalling an alleyway. The cold and the dank. Pain easing away as death crept closer. And his mother, stroking his hair, telling him that everything will be okay.

*Only she wasn't in the alley,* he reminded himself. *I was there alone.* The plate in his head began to throb and he rubbed at the scar through his hair. The motion snapped the moment. Cheyanne took in a sharp breath and cleared her throat.

"I'll bring you some painkillers. How do you feel about Chinese food for dinner?"

Benton didn't say anything. The disgusted look on his face said enough. *I remember the last time you gave me tablets. At least you're telling me about it this time.*

"It's only aspirin," Cheyanne said.

Benton quickly escaped to his room. It had the same overall grandeur as the rest of the house and was even less decorated. Longer than it was wide, with a fireplace marking the middle and a full bathroom at the very end. Here, too, ran the overall theme of 'no doors'. There wasn't even a privacy wall. In the beginning, Benton's parents had put his mattress into the corner opposite the open threshold, so they could check on him just by walking past the door. As the winter chill encroached into the barren space, he had steadily pushed his bed closer to the fireplace. Beyond the mattress, topped with a tangled mess of towels and sheets, there wasn't much he had done with the space. No decorations. No curtains. Just a small pile of clothes, baseball gear atop ignored moving boxes, and a few books scattered within arms-reach of the mattress.

Dumping the backpacks, he collapsed onto the mattress, instantly regretting it when he felt the impact. Hissing out a few curse words, he squirmed to take the pressure off of his side. Nicole came breezing into the room. He had just enough time to pull his knees up before she claimed the end of the bed as her own. All the bouncing aggravated his wounds again.

"Does it really hurt?" she asked as she gently placed a hand on his ankle.

The brief contact made him smile.

"Don't worry about it. It's just the bruise on my hip that's acting up." Squirming again, he pulled a hand through his hair, aborting the motion halfway through with a grimace. Dirt, sweat, dried blood, and rain weren't the most appealing mix.

"Do you want to help?" she asked as she opened her binder. "I know I've heard of this thing before, but I can't really recall where from."

Benton looked at her for a long moment before he shrugged and struggled to sit up. He took up the other binder and studied its cover. *Banshee* was written in curly, glittery lettering.

"Have you ever heard of the bunyip?" she asked absently. "They're Australia swamp monsters. They look pretty weird."

"Is that what you think this is?"

"No, I just thought it was a fun word to say."

"Right." Benton said slowly. He held up his binder. "So, this is all on me? It's pretty light."

"I'm doing my best," she snapped defensively.

Almost instantly, she lost interest in the conversation and began to mumble rapidly under her breath, "I know him. I know him. I *know* that I know him."

Benton tried to ignore it as he flipped through the binder. Cascading tabs broke the handful of sheets into sections. *Banshee; the wailing woman,* he read to himself. *A creature from Irish folklore considered an omen of death.* The pictures that followed either depicted banshees as decrepit crones or ethereally beautiful young women. There was no in-between. It seemed that the only thing everyone could all agree on was the hair. It was always a stark white. He turned to a new section and frowned.

"You have my school records?"

Nicole flapped a hand at him, the motion a mixture of annoyance and dismissal. "You can't be surprised at this point."

"Are these the scores from my peewee baseball games?"

"Benton, I'm a little busy right now. Is there any chance we can talk about your horrible shortstop record later?"

"I was eight."

"And you sucked."

"I'm a batter," he snapped defensively.

She hummed and flipped over another page.

Her body suddenly went rigid. The abrupt loss of movement scared Benton more than if she had started screaming. Slowly, they each turned their heads to look at each other.

"I know him," she said in a haunted whisper. "The mummy man."

Benton had been preparing himself for this conversation. He knew that they would be forced to have it the moment they were alone and without the looming threat of imminent death. But now that it was here, he wanted to run. There was nothing he could say that wasn't going to gut her.

"Yeah, I recognized him, too," he whispered.

"The man from the road," she said.

"I know."

"I never learned his name."

*You can find my pee wee records but not his name?* He pushed the question aside and offered a sad smile.

"I never bothered," he said.

Nicole began to tremble as she struggled to keep her next sentence behind closed lips. She was vibrating by the time she lost the fight.

"We did this." A sob broke her. "*I* did this."

It physically hurt him to see the sheer amount of guilt displayed across her face. His shoulders hunched and his head dropped.

"This isn't on you," he told her.

"I shot him. Now he's this. That's a pretty straightforward cause and effect," she said.

"I'm pretty sure it's more complicated than that."

Nicole's mouth screwed up in misplaced determination. "If I'm not to blame, then who is?"

"Him!" Benton declared. "The serial killer, Nicole. When you're trying to decide who is morally worse, it's always the serial killer. I shouldn't have to explain that."

"I killed him," she insisted, remembering a heartbeat too late to keep her voice down. "I did that. And somehow turned him into this."

"Or, and hear me out here, he turned himself into it."

"How?"

"I don't know."

"So, it's not that likely."

"Alright," he said. "How did you turn him into a murderous, undead mummy?"

She answered instantly, "I don't know. Yet."

"So it might not be your fault," he concluded.

Instead of acknowledging his point, Nicole started from the beginning, walking him through each step of her faulty reasoning. Any attempt to correct her only resulted in an extended, and increasingly passionate, lecture. The longer she went, the more absurd it sounded. Benton closed his eyes and took a deep, sobering breath. One of them needed to keep their head, and it wasn't going to be Nicole. Not with that stuff still in her system.

"Nic," he cut into her ramblings. "I know it's hard for you to focus right now, but I need you to try. Okay?"

She sucked in a deep breath, held it, and nodded.

"Good. Now listen to me very carefully. This guy is to blame."

She lifted her chin to protest but managed to keep the words inside.

"Death doesn't change people," he continued. "There's no magical metamorphosis that purifies the soul. A jerk in life is going to be a jerk in death."

When he was sure that she had heard him, he told her that it was okay to respond now.

"You've only met a few ghosts, Benton. How can you be so sure?"

"Because I've lived inside the minds of a million killers. And I can promise you, not one of them was compelled to kill because of their heartbeat."

Determination filled her eyes. "What about The Telltale Heart?"

"Where do I begin?" he scoffed. "That's just a story. The main character was already insane. And it was the victim's heartbeat that was the focus of the story. Not the killer's. What else you got?"

"Honestly, I didn't think you were paying attention when we learned that in class. I'm not prepared for follow up questions."

Leaning until his shoulder pressed against hers, he held her gaze and said, "This isn't your fault. But we'll fix it."

A sob tore out of her chest as she buried her face against his shoulder. It didn't take long for her tears to seep into his still damp shirt.

"Every time I try to help, I only make things worse. People keep dying. My mother's in an impossible position. You keep getting hurt. And now I've dragged Zack, Meg, and Danny into all of this. I'm not blind to what's happening to them. They're not coping. How can I tell them he's back?"

"We'll find a way. We always do."

"I can't do this to them."

"Hey, if they're not willing to fight alongside you against the forces of darkness, are they really your friends?"

Benton had only meant to provoke a small smile. Something to break up her string of sobs and whimpers. He was prepared for her to suddenly lurch to the side.

Falling off the bed and becoming tangled in the sheets didn't stop her from declaring, "That's it! I know what he is!"

"What?"

She flipped her hip-length hair out of her face and beamed at him. "He's a Baykok."

# Chapter 10

Nicole heaved herself up onto her knees and flung her arms wide. Benton blinked at her.

"I was expecting a bit more in the praise department," she admitted.

"I don't know what a Baykok is."

"Right. Sorry. Okay, where to start?" She rubbed her hands together as she tried to organize her wild thoughts. "Remember the friend I told you about? The one that made you the dream catcher? Side note; it doesn't really work when you hang it over the bedside lamp."

"I didn't have a wall hook," he cut in.

"I put one in the box."

"Of course you did," he muttered to himself before saying in a louder voice. "Focus, Nicole."

"Right. Good plan." She didn't get any further before the rush of excitement stole her thoughts. "My friend, Kane. Well, her name is actually Biskane, but everyone calls her Kane—"

"Is this important to the story?" Benton cut in.

Nicole shook her head. Her thoughts were like fog. They filled her skull while remaining completely beyond her reach.

"She's Ojibwe."

"I know—"

"This bit's important, Benton," she snipped. His interruptions weren't helping. "At the pow wow, we were all sharing campfire stories. This was before I met you, so I didn't have a monster binder and didn't think to write it down. It was just supposed to be a story. But I remember her talking about the legend of the Baykok." A new thought hit her. Her brain instantly latched onto the new course and she began sifting through the mess of items in search of Benton's laptop.

"Nicole?"

"She commissioned some artwork of a Baykok. I'm sure she's got it on her Instagram page."

Retrieving the laptop, she placed it on her lap and hurriedly typed in his password.

"What is a Baykok? Nicole?"

"I'll need just a second, Benton," she said with as much sweetness as she could fit into the words. "If you need something to do, I'd love a soda."

"I'll get you a beverage with absolutely no caffeine," he replied.

She didn't look up from her typing. "Admittedly, that's probably a better idea."

By the time he came back from the sink with a glass of water, she had found what she was looking for. A picture of the grotesque spirit filled the left side of the screen. The right was consumed with a half dozen open windows which she proudly displayed. It was a near impossible task to find a reliable paranormal message board. A lot of people had no idea what they were talking about. Benton stiffly sat down, passed her the water, and began to study the screen.

"Any chance you can just give me the cliff notes?" he asked.

"The Baykok is an ancient Ojibwe legend. The general description matches our monster. Only ..."

"It's very disconcerting to end a sentence like that," Benton noted with dread.

Nicole swallowed thickly. "Some stories say that they're giants."

Benton's head jerked up at that. "Our boy could be growing?"

"Maybe," she shrugged. "It's possible that it gets bigger the more it eats."

"What does it eat?"

She could see the exact moment it clicked in his head.

"Her eyes. Her kidney. He's taking the juicy bits." He pulled a hand through his hair, squeezing out a few stray raindrops. "He's eating her alive."

Nicole didn't want to think too long on that. Already she was feeling ill.

Sipping her water in an attempt to settle her stomach, she continued, "According to legend, Baykoks can turn invisible."

Benton made a disgusted sound. "I hate when they can do that."

"But it can't hide its sounds," Nicole said. "The crackle of its skin. The pop and rattle of its bones."

His face twisted up in disgust. "Yeah, I remember the sound."

"But I didn't hear it before. When it first attacked me. On the road with you."

Benton tipped his head to the side. "It hunts with bow and arrows, right? Long distance weaponry."

"At least those you can see. Which, yay for us, I guess. It could give us an advantage."

"Hold up," he said. "No one else can see the arrows?"

"According to legends."

"Then how do they know that Baykoks use them?"

Her mouth opened but her brain didn't supply an answer. "How am I supposed to know that?"

"Oh, I'm sorry. Is it annoying when people assume that you know everything about something?"

Her lips pressed into a thin line as she stared at him. He smiled back.

"This attitude thing," she asked. "Does it make you feel good?"

"It doesn't make me feel bad," he said.

Tapping the screen, he coaxed her to continue. She was hoping that she wouldn't have to explain this bit and choked down another mouthful of water.

"As we've learned from experience, the Baykok's arrows are special. I mean, apart from the whole invisibility thing. They render their victims unconscious, allowing the Baykok to take what it wants without a struggle. What gets me is that they're only supposed to take the liver. That's it. That's the deal. Knock them out, switch the liver with a stone, stitch them back up with a thread that completely heals the skin, and leave them to die with no knowledge of what happened to them. They're not supposed to keep picking off pieces."

"I guess our guy decided to up the game," Benton said. "So, how are these things made?"

"According to the stories–"

"You know you don't have to keep saying that," he cut in. "We've only got stories, so it goes without saying."

Frustration ripped through her like a wildfire. Before she could argue, however, he noted, "Your hair looks great today."

"My hair always looks great," she clipped. "I know you're trying to distract me."

"Is it working?"

"Shut up." Turning back to the laptop, she pulled one of the pages to the forefront. "According to the stories," she stressed for the sole purpose of irritating him, "Baykoks are created when a hunter is separated from his tribe and dies alone in the wilderness. As he dies, he's so consumed with anger at his tribesmen for failing him that his soul can't pass on."

The silence that followed caught her off guard. She had expected at least one snide comment. Looking over, she found the anger she felt written upon his face.

"Let me get this straight," he said through clenched teeth. "This dirtbag and his girlfriend specifically targeted First Nations women. Teenage girls. They kidnapped, raped, and murdered them. Then, when one of his intended victims kills him, he's not only angry about it, but feels *betrayed* enough that he can give a middle finger to the natural order of things and come back. That about cover it?"

Nicole didn't trust herself to do more than nod. If she started to rant now, she wasn't sure she'd be able to stop. Rage boiled her blood, heating her face and making her tremble. But she kept her mouth closed. It offered her a little slither of hope that the potion was wearing off.

"I really want to kill this guy," Benton hissed.

"Any chance Mic might want to, too?"

"Mic?"

"What? She's *Death*, Benton. It seems like this should fall under her jurisdiction."

"I don't think it does," Benton said. "Besides, you're working under the assumption that humans have the right of way here."

"Why wouldn't they?"

"Maybe they see all this as the natural order of things. A food chain. Not something to mess around with."

"He's a monster, Benton."

"So am I."

All the things Nicole intended to say suddenly vanished from her head. Without them, she deflated, lowering her gaze to stare at the floor.

"She helped me once before," Nicole whispered.

"No, she hinted at ways for you to help yourself. From your own accounts, she never went after the Baykok. We don't even know if she could."

"She's death. No one escapes death."

"This loser did."

Again, Nicole felt like all of her words had been stolen. Nothing made sense anymore and she didn't know how to regain her bearings. Benton ripped a hand through his hair and sighed.

"Look, we both agree that we want this thing dead and gone, right?"

"Right."

"So," he smirked lightly, "according to the stories, how do we kill it?"

She huffed but couldn't keep herself from smiling slightly.

"Well?" he pressed.

"We have to give him a proper burial."

"Does his actual body need to be there?"

"Of course."

"That's a problem."

"It's time-consuming but doable," she corrected.

"We are remembering that night very differently," Benton said, his brow furrowing. "I recall the ghosts of his victims showing up and taking their bodies."

She rolled her eyes. "I recall that, too."

"So the body we need is most likely hidden in some uncharted corner of a haunted forest. Also, they're a whole month into decay. You don't see a problem?"

"Follow me here," she said. "Plan A; you explain everything and either ask a ghost to show us where they put it. Or do that mind meld thing to get a sense of the location."

"Okay, Plan A sucks. What's Plan B?"

"You can't move a body through a forest that thick without breaking a few branches. We can just follow the path."

"You want to track them?"

"Yes."

"A month after they went through?"

"I never said it would be easy," she countered. "But my dad taught me well. He's really good at it."

Benton opened his mouth but seemed to switch from his intended statement to a question, "Why did he teach you how to track? Is that just an army thing?"

"No, it's a hunting thing."

His eyes widened slightly with surprise. "You hunt?"

"Yes."

"You?"

"Yes."

"What do you hunt?"

"Deer, mostly."

"You, little miss sunshine and rainbows, goes out into the forest and shoots *Bambi* in the face?"

"My father and I help supply sustenance for my family and friends," she countered. "I partake in an activity that connects me to the earth and has served my people well for over thirteen thousand years."

"I'm not judging. I'm just saying that it's hard to imagine *you* killing a deer. They're so cute, and you're essentially a real-life *Care Bear*."

"Yeah, well, what do you think Lionheart ate?"

He frowned. "I never thought about it."

"Lions and bears, Benton. They're not herbivores."

Licking his lips, he seemed to mull it all over. "I have three more questions for Plan B."

"Hit me."

"What do you intend to do about the other serial killers and assorted predators that use that forest as a combination hunting and dumping ground?"

"I'll bring my rifle. You know I'm a good shot."

"I know that you keep stealing guns from the police lock up."

She rolled her eyes. "That was when I needed a smaller handgun. You know, so I don't draw attention. This time, we can just tell everyone we're going camping and are bringing the weapon in case we run into a cougar or bear. Simple. Next question."

"Where do we even begin looking for the track?"

"You don't remember?"

"I'm not saying that it wasn't a memorable evening. It's just that every inch of that place looks the same."

"You're such a city boy."

With a flurry of typing, she pulled up Google Maps and brought up the curve in the road she recalled being a few yards away. From there, it was just a matter of getting into street view and panning for a few moments.

"There," she said once everything was perfectly arranged. "They went right up that incline with the woman. The man they took a few more yards north before turning off at that old Jack Pine."

Benton leaned closer to the screen to study the image closely. "I'm impressed but not surprised."

The praise made a huge smile cross her face. With a rush of confidence, she asked about the third and final question.

"No car. House on lockdown." He looked far too pleased with himself as he asked. "What's your plan to get out?"

*Damn.*

# Chapter 11

"This is a horrible idea," Benton said. The steady flow of rain made the roof tiles slick under his sneakers and brought an early twilight to the sky. "It has to be one of your worst."

"It's not that far of a drop," Nicole replied.

"We're jumping off the roof—"

"The *patio* roof," she interrupted. "Don't start drama."

He continued as if she hadn't spoken. "Into a blanket that Zack and Danny are holding between them. What part of this is good?"

"We don't have to open a door. Your parents really should account for windows in their home security. Now, come on. Meg can't distract your parents forever."

"Yeah, we should get out of here before they look left and see the bright red pickup truck," he said bitterly.

"Exactly."

Benton watched as Nicole tossed her school bag down into the center of the waterlogged blanket. It landed with a splash.

"This is how you get a broken ankle," he said.

"Come on, Benton. This isn't even the hardest thing we have to do tonight."

He begrudgingly shrugged. "You've got me there."

She offered him a dazzling laugh before, without a single attempt to check with the others, she jumped. Danny choked on a flood of swear words and Zack almost lost the sheet. But, between them, they managed to keep Nicole from cracking her head on the ground. Benton's heart remained lodged in his throat until he saw her standing safe and sound, and not gushing blood. Still beaming, she took her portion of the sheet and waved for him to follow.

'I hate you', he mouthed.

She let go of the blanket just long enough to make a heart out of her hands. It wasn't the reaction he had been aiming for. Summoning what little belief he had left in humanity, Benton prepared for the worst, squeezed his eyes shut, and jumped. His stomach lurched. Hitting the sheet made pain spark across his raw skin. They managed to hold his weight just long enough to break his fall before dumping him on the gravel. Nicole was next to him when he opened his eyes.

"See?" she whispered. "Everything's fine."

"Are you checking on me or gloating?"

"I can do both."

The red Chevy pickup belonged to Zack's older brother. Benton didn't have time to ask why he had chosen this one. The vehicle only had a front bench seat. He grabbed the tailgate and scrambled into the flatbed, turning to help Nicole follow. Once they were both lying flat on the uncomfortable metal, there was nothing for them to do but wait. Either get caught by his parents or leave and go on a corpse hunt.

*Why can't I have nice options?*

The truck shook as Zack, Danny, and Meg jumped into the front bench seat of the old truck. Then the engine roared to life, painfully vibrating the metal body, and they were off, creating a cloud of dust that billowed into the dwindling daylight.

*We're actually doing this.*

Benton had to repeat it to himself a few times before he believed it. After the hell he had endured on that stretch of highway, it was madness to go back. It took five minutes to reach the edge of his property. Nicole sprung up the second they passed the boundary and joined the public roads, instantly scrambling for the large bag pushed up against the truck cab. Benton followed. He had been curious about the bag ever since she had called her friends. She had very specially and repeatedly told them that they needed to bring the bag 'with the purple tab'. *How many bags did she have lined up in her basement?*

It was one of those large bags people used to go camping for days on end. Unzipping the top, she collected the first couple of items and thrust them towards him. With the wind whipping the long tendrils of her hair into her face, she didn't bother to say a word. He unraveled the items. A huge parka designed for arctic expeditions and heavy, thick-soled boots. Relief flooded through him.

Each ghost carried a chill. A drop in temperature that signaled their presence even when he couldn't see them. Generations of murder had filled the forest with bodies. Enough that they corrupted the earth and air. Benton felt it with arctic savagery. One that crept into his bones and brought him to the brink of hypothermia. A real physical sensation. Last time, he had almost lost three toes to frostbite. Everyone else had been fine. *And now I'm going in winter. And it's raining again. These are good signs.*

Traveling east to the Highway of the Lost meant that they avoided the town entirely. Here, there wasn't much in the way of speed limits, and Zack took full advantage of that, pushing the truck until it trembled in a desperate race against the sun. Nicole had refused to listen to reason and wait until morning, worried that the

Baykok would kill Amy on his next attack, arguing that the ghosts were just as strong during the day and it was easier to hide from killers in the dark. Benton clutched his snow gear to his chest as he leaned against the side of the truck, dread growing within him as the hours passed and the sun crept ever closer to the horizon.

Trees rose up from the sea of grass. A mixture of hills, deep valleys, and gushing streams had created a dense forest. The highway was the only path carved through the wilderness. A strip of civilization shrouded by towering pines that blocked the light. Shadows clung to the trucks, rolling over the forest floor like fog. Peace Springs was on the other side of the gloomy vegetation. Nothing but a single roadside diner stood within it.

Benton felt the edge of the cursed land before they crossed onto it. Terror scuttled under his skin like insects. He hurriedly shed his damp hoodie before heaving the heavy parka on. The hood muffled the light rain and growl of the engine. Nicole's gesturing let him find two pairs of thick wool socks in the parka pockets before he shoved the boots on. Protected somewhat from the elements, his body heat quickly filled the parka, becoming stiflingly humid. Then they passed over the borderline.

Frozen air slammed into Benton with a crushing force. Doubling over, he gasped, unwittingly drawing the air into his lungs, letting the cold in. Frost filled his lungs until he could feel ice crack with every breath. Pins drove into every inch of exposed skin. He couldn't stop trembling. Nicole scooted over to his side, pressing in close to share her body heat while she rummaged in one of the numerous pockets. *Of course, she packed gloves,* Benton thought with a smile. The rain had left his hands damp, which admittedly ensured that the gloves didn't work as well as they should have. It was still bliss to pull them on.

Benton pressed his back to the wall of the truck bed, trembling as he squeezed his eyes shut. Already the world was pressing in on him. He could hear them screaming while they never made a sound. Could feel their touch while miles separated them. Confusion mixed with his fear and he curled himself into a ball, letting the rain patter against his arched spine. *Maybe if I stay still enough, they won't know I'm here.*

It took a focused effort to keep his breathing slow and even. Everything else faded away into an oblivion of cold and rain and the sense of horror that had taken on a life of its own. Suddenly, the engine died and he snapped his head up.

"It's okay," Nicole said, giving his shoulders a reassuring squeeze. "We're just stopping for a break."

Confusion lingered until he spotted the neon sign of the roadside diner. The night had gathered strength, swelling upon the ground and fighting back the few rays of sunset that played across the treetops. Zack had parked beside one of the two only other cars in the parking lot. Benton stood, but before he could climb down, something caught his attention. He couldn't pinpoint exactly what it was. What shift or sound had made his heart lurch into his throat. It left him scanning the area for nothing in particular.

"Hurry up, I want to get out of the rain," Zack said.

Benton didn't stop staring at the woods on the other side of the road. Droplets of rain struck the leaves, making them shift and giving the illusion of hidden creatures. Nicole gently touched his hand.

"Benton?"

"I'm okay," he murmured on reflex.

"What do you see?"

Turning towards her, he noticed something out of the corner of his eyes. Not a full body apparition. Just a small lump in the middle of the rain-slick road, about the distance of a football field away. A distorted orb surrounded by tendrils of ebony. In the gloom, it took a moment for him to realize what it was.

"A head."

"You mean, 'ahead', right?" Meg asked.

Danny quizzed her sister. "What would that even mean?"

"Hopefully something better than a severed head."

Benton lifted one hand to point at the head. "No one else sees that?"

"I can't," Nicole confessed before checking with the others. "Is it looking at us?"

"No. It's facing back towards Fort Wayward."

"Well," she said with forced cheer, "let's not bother it. Come on, I'll get you some coffee."

Benton gave the silent phantom one last glance before he followed the others into the diner. One front corner was dedicated as the gas station. Nicole hurried them past that and the few stands of trinkets to find a small table.

"We're closing up," a waitress called out from somewhere unseen.

"That's okay," Nicole said. "We just want the table."

There was no response. Just the random clatter of the kitchen being cleaned. Once she had Benton seated, she ducked away to get some coffee from the old vending machine set on the gas station counter. She returned with a few cups and a couple bags of chips.

Benton pulled off his gloves to wrap them desperately around the warmth of the paper cup. Nicole pulled a map out of her pocket, along with a pen, and spread it out over the table. It said something that not one person at the table was surprised to find her so prepared. She talked carefully, precisely, outlining exactly where she thought they went. With a few swipes of her highlighter, she also marked where she thought they might be hiding.

"Because of the terrain," she concluded.

Benton watched as the three other people at the table nodded in understanding. Vastly outnumbered, he decided not to admit that he had no idea what she meant by that.

"Thanks again for all of this," she told the trio. "Really, it's above and beyond the call of friendship."

Zack waved the comment off and claimed the salt and vinegar chips.

"It's not a problem," Meg said.

"Only a mild inconvenience," Danny added with a nod.

Nicole never lost her smile. "We really appreciate it. Not to sound ungrateful but, Zack, why did you bring your brother's truck? Your car would have fit all of us."

Zack laughed. "I've seen what this thing did to your jeep."

Almost knocking over his cup in his haste, Benton jerked his hand back and forth in front of his neck. The universal *please, for the love of God, don't talk about that,* gesture.

"What happened to my jeep?" Nicole asked. She whirled to Benton and he snapped his hand down. "You said that you just couldn't drive it."

"I can't drive," he defended.

She looked at each of her friends in turn. "What happened to my jeep?"

"Nothing," they all said at once.

*Subtle,* Benton sighed.

"So, what's the game plan here?" Zack cut in.

It was an obvious ploy to distract her, but it worked.

"I explained it all to you when I called for help," Nicole said.

"Oh," Meg said softly. "I just thought there would be more to it."

"The beauty is in its simplicity. We go in, retrieve the body, and bury it. And we're done." Nicole looked honestly proud of herself as she finished.

"And the angry ghosts?" Danny pressed.

"I have a half dozen iron bracelets in my go bag," she said. "Along with first aid kit, camping supplies, headlamps, cleaning supplies, and a few body bags."

Danny's brow furrowed. "Why did you bring cleaning supplies?"

"In case we run into a little bit of human trouble and need to cover our tracks."

It was hard to tell which one of the twins looked more disturbed at the prospect of cleaning up a crime scene.

"I'm not saying that we're going to need it," Nicole rushed. "I'm just sick of not being prepared for these situations."

"Which is why you brought body bags. That's comforting," Zack said before choking down a gulp of the milky coffee.

"What did you want me to do? Throw him in my school bag? He'll be in stage five decomposition. I don't want to touch that," Nicole said.

Meg leaned slightly forward, lowering her voice even though there was no one close enough to hear.

"What's stage five?"

"Maggots have almost finished all of the soft flesh and beetles are moving in to eat the tougher stuff," Benton said.

Zack scrunched up his nose, a hand full of chips at his lips. "Dude, I'm eating. Couldn't think up a nicer way to say that?"

"That is the nice way." Benton waited for Zack to crunch down on the chips before adding, "I didn't mention the mold."

Zack was caught between gagging and glaring at him.

"Benton, be nice." Before he could protest, Nicole continued, "Zack, you don't need to know any of this. Like I said earlier, I'm not asking you guys to come with us."

"What? Why not?" Meg asked.

"Yeah, what's wrong with us?" Danny added.

"You've made it clear that you don't want to come," Nicole said.

"Doesn't mean that I don't want to be asked," Danny said.

Zack snorted. "Rude, Nicole Just rude."

"Fine," she huffed a sigh then put a smile on her face. "Guys, would you like to go on a body hunt with us?"

Benton didn't know why Nicole was surprised that they agreed.

Shock dropped her mouth. "You all want to come?"

"I wouldn't use the word *want*," Zack said.

"I didn't bring my hunting rifle for nothing," Danny added.

Meg reached across the table to take Nicole's hand. "We're just as involved in this as you are."

The color drained from Nicole's cheeks. "No, don't say that. This isn't on anyone but me."

"We were all there," Meg protested. "Each one of us. We all have our share of the blame."

"I pulled the trigger," Nicole said.

Zack's voice softened. "None of us were trying to stop you."

"So," she blurted out. "We're all agreed? We're holding hands and jumping onto this crazy train together?"

"How did we get here?" Zack muttered.

"Don't know, don't care," Benton said. "Can you come to the bathroom with me?"

Zack's brow furrowed. "Why?"

"Why does anyone use the bathroom?"

"I meant, why don't you go on your own?" Zack said with a roll of his eyes.

"The last time I was here, a ghost crawled out of the drain and attacked me."

A heartbeat of silence passed between them. In a sudden burst of movement, Zack took another gulp of his coffee and stood up.

"Your life is twisted and pathetic and it makes me sad."

"That's accurate," Benton said as he followed.

# Chapter 12

The soft drone of the radio behind the gas station counter filled the nearly empty diner. Nicole scanned the area, unable to stop her knee from jerking as she studied each face. It was here that the killers had first caught her scent. She hadn't noticed at the time. Hadn't realized that the couple only a few feet away from her were plotting her abduction, deciding how to kill her. And fantasizing about what they would to her during the time in between.

Skin crawling over her bones, she looked around again, trying to determine if anyone had noticed her. A few people hurriedly shoveled down the last of their meals, racing the setting sun, desperate to get home before darkness claimed the world. Others took their time, looking resigned if not relaxed. It made her wonder just why they weren't afraid. *Maybe they don't know they should be,* Nicole reasoned. The more sinister side of her mind whispered; *or maybe they think they're the most dangerous thing out there.* Fur dragged across her brain as she felt the weight of eyes upon her. Launching onto her feet, she spun around, unable to spot who was watching her.

"Nicole?" Meg asked.

"Do you feel that?"

Meg looked to her twin.

"Feel what?" Danny asked.

Nicole didn't bother to clarify. If they felt it, they'd say. *Get a grip,* she told herself as she sunk back down into her chair.

"Never mind," she mumbled, busying herself with folding up the map and handing it over to Meg, the best navigator out of all of them.

She jumped up again when she spotted Benton and Zack heading back to the table. Zack tipped his head to the side like a confused puppy as they approached.

"But – if no one can *see* the arrow, how do they know it exists? Or that they're, you know, arrows?" Zack asked.

"I don't know. Ask Nicole, I'm sure she has a theory," Benton replied.

The boys fell silent as they approached the table.

"Anything interesting happen?" Nicole asked. "Sorry, probably could have found a more tactful was of asking that."

"No paranormal activity," Benton said.

"Good. Great. Awesome."

Benton's brow furrowed. "Why are you so nervous?"

"I'm not." The blurted words sounded pathetic to her own ears and she heaved a sigh. "I'm just being paranoid, I suppose. I thought someone was watching me."

Benton patted her shoulder as he passed. "Nic, you're gorgeous. Someone's always watching you."

"Aw, that's sweetly disturbing."

Benton smiled, his lips blue and shivering. He looked so miserable that it was nearly impossible to keep from fussing over him. Her success was proof that the Baykok's drug was wearing off. *Please don't crash.* It seemed like a deathwish to fall asleep now. Before she had time to smile, the sensation returned, stronger than it had been before. She turned before she could stop herself, checking and rechecking every corner of the room and finding nothing. Just the same bored faces she had studied before.

"Nicole?" Zack asked, concern leaking into his words.

"It's nothing." Even as she said it, she checked with Benton, just in case he sensed something different.

He was more preoccupied with staying warm. Which, she assumed, was a good sign.

"Okay," she said with a warm grin. "Everyone ready to go and fight some undead evil?"

"Would it make a difference if I said 'no'?" Benton asked.

"No."

"Well, it doesn't really matter, does it?"

His weak smile dulled the sharp edge of his words.

"That's the spirit," she giggled, quickly taking his arm and tugging him towards the door.

Desperate for warmth, Benton didn't fight the contact. Only pulled his hood up as they headed for the door. She stopped short before they left as a few items caught her eyes.

"I'll meet you at the truck. I just want to pick up a few things," she said.

Benton hesitated.

"We'll be able to see her the whole time," Danny said, gesturing to the large front window of the store.

The truck was clearly visible through the thin mist of rain. Still, Benton wasn't convinced.

"I don't want to wait in the rain," he said. "I'll wait at the front door."

Nicole made quick work of gathering the items that had captured her notice. A few extra bottles of water. Some jerky snacks. Baby power and earplugs. Jogging back to her waiting friends, she distributed the earplugs.

"Good idea," Meg said. She spared Benton a glance. "You're very loud."

"I'm aware," Benton said.

"I'm not judging," Meg added.

Danny didn't miss a beat. "I am. I'm developing tinnitus. Do you know how annoying it is to have a constant ringing in your ears?"

"I'm terribly sorry I caused you minor inconvenience while *killing monsters.*"

Danny rolled her eyes and shoved her earplugs into her pocket.

"Danny, be nice," Nicole sighed. "Although, she does have a point. Maybe keep that in mind next time."

Her smile did nothing to lessen Benton's glare. He snatched up the earplugs she had bought him so he wouldn't feel left out, his thick gloves fumbling with the small package. After everyone had organized their jackets to best prepare for the rain, they ducked out of the door. They were halfway across the parking lot when Zack jerked to a stop. His jaw dropped, eyes going wide as his chest began to heave with rapid breaths.

"Zack?" Meg asked.

Lifting his hand took a few attempts. As if he thought better about it every time he tried. They all turned to look in the general direction he was motioning towards. The twins gasped and Nicole felt her stomach drop. In the middle of the road, washed in the blue glow of the diner's neon sign, was a severed head. Long dark hair pooled like oil around it, the face ashen and bloated with rot.

"You guys can see it now?" Benton asked.

"*That's* what you saw?" Zack demanded.

Danny threw him a skittish look. "A severed head. Sitting in the middle of the road. That's what you saw? Then casually walked inside and had a cup of coffee?"

Benton didn't reply. Staring into the rain and gloom, fine lines worked their way across his forehead.

"What is it?" Nicole asked gently.

"It's closer."

"What?" Meg squeaked.

"That's not where I saw it before." He was already moving towards the truck. "We should go. Now. Why aren't you people moving?"

"It's a head," Danny said, trying to keep a strong hold on her courage. "What can it really do?"

Meg waved a hand at her sister in exasperation. "Do you really want to stick around and see?"

They bolted for the truck. Zack and the twins climbed back into the cab, leaving Benton and Nicole to sit in the back again. Her first instinct was to insist that Benton have the front seat, needing the protection and heater system more than the others. But, in an impressive feat of agility given the condition of his hips, he grabbed the tailgate and hurled himself up. She had to use the back bumper as a boost to follow him. As she hooked her legs over, she caught a glimpse over her shoulder. A scream escaped her lips as she scrambled away.

"Nic?" Zack demanded.

"It's right behind the trunk. Go!" The first lurch forward threw her onto the metal flatbed. It also reminded her of her manners. "Thanks."

Benton crouched down beside her and together they watched the lights of the diner fade away, taking with it the last glimpses of the severed head.

"I really don't like this place," she mumbled.

"And I was just about to suggest that we build a summer home here."

"Are you trying to make me laugh so I'm not terrified?"

"How am I doing?" he asked with a weak smile.

She took his hand and squeezed it. "The important thing is that you tried."

Huffing a chuckle, Benton flopped down and curled into her side for warmth, pressing his face into her shoulder to block his line of sight. *What else does he see?*

Despite her best efforts, she couldn't stop the thought from taking root in her mind. Paranoia crackled along her senses, made all the worse as the sunset and the last traces of light vanished from the sky. The clustering trees blocked out the moonlight. And there were no streetlamps to break up the darkness. Within moments, the only source of light came from the truck's high beams. Their glow barely reached into the back, leaving Nicole and Benton huddled within the living shadows.

She could feel the woods coming alive around her. Its heartbeat ricocheted within her chest. The rain shifted to come down in rhythmic bursts. *Like a pulse.* Consumed by the thought, she was caught off guard by the shifting darkness. It curled around them. A near physical presence. She could feel them watching her. Creeping closer. Touching her.

Nicole couldn't stand it. Lurching forward, she scrambled for her bag. Ripping it open, she found two headlamps, placing one on her head and passing the second to Benton. He fumbled with the straps and ended up shoving them onto his head with force. Turning it on created a small patch of light. A hazed red glow rather than a direct beam.

"Why is it red?" Benton said through chattering teeth.

"Red doesn't mess with your night vision," she replied.

Slowly, she turned in a circle, barely able to keep herself in her crouch as the truck bounced and lurched under her. Rain pelted her face and the wind whipped her damp hair. Still, the forest held all of its secrets, keeping her from seeing everything that lurked within it. Settling back down next to Benton, she never stopped looking around. Every so often, she caught a glimpse of grass along the sides of the road, soaking wet and dinted as if something heavy stood upon it.

"Do you see anything?" she asked Benton.

He barely lifted his head before responding. "No. But we've got their interest. I can feel it."

Adrenaline made her heart race. She could feel every pulse in her throat, choking off her breath. Instinct made her hands open and close, grasping for the rifle that was in the front cab with the others. Having nothing to hold onto left her feeling weak. A powerless lamb in a sea of wolves.

She curled up next to Benton. Offering warmth and taking comfort in return.

The truck barreled into the smothering darkness, following the twists and turns of the serpentine road. Small curves became blind corners. Every so often, they would round one to be ambushed by the glare of another vehicle's headlights. Nicole flinched each time. Half of her expected that the passing vehicle would make a sharp turn and start to follow them. What remained was preparing for whatever horrors the woods could conjure. Needing something to do with her hands, she began to braid her hair. Because she had so much of it, she needed three separate braids, and then used them to create one colossal braid. Fighting against the wind and rain to complete the mindless task helped to keep her nerves at a manageable level.

Anticipation made each passing encounter all the worse until she was sure that she couldn't bear it another second. It wasn't a relief when Zack finally pulled the truck over onto the thin, moist patch of grass that separated the road from a sudden drop. Numerous camping trips had perfected this part.

It didn't take more than half a minute for them to be ready to go, truck unpacked and weapons checked. Nicole breathed a sigh of relief as she loaded her hunting rifle, shoving a handful of extra bullets into her jacket pocket. Their weight was oddly reassuring. Even if she couldn't fight off a Baykok, she stood a chance against any human threat, and that would have to be enough.

Suddenly, there was nothing left to keep them on the road, and the actuality of her plan settled in. The forest loomed around them. No longer a cluster of trees and ferns but a living, malicious beast longing for them to venture too close. She shivered.

"Are you guys sure this is a good idea?" Meg asked.

"That fully depends on how you define *good*," Benton answered for her.

Without a word, they lined up along the edge of the road, staring at Nicole's marker and all that lay beyond. Not one of them set foot on the grass.

Zack was the first to break the silence, readjusting the straps of the hiking bag he had claimed as his own. Looking at Nicole, he said, "Do you really want to do this? We can still turn back."

"Do you see my hair?" Nicole asked. "Do you know how long it takes to do this? No girl will go to that much effort unless her mind's made up."

Zack turned to the twins as if searching for confirmation. Since neither one of them allowed their hair to grow past their shoulders, Nicole wasn't sure what he was hoping to achieve. The conversation ebbed into silence and they were left to stare once more into the dark abyss.

"We're not going to get anything done standing here," Nicole said, trying to sound as confident as possible.

Swallowing thickly, she settled her rifle strap across her chest and grabbed Benton's hand. The contact did little to reassure him.

"Last minute detail," he told her softly. "If anything bad happens, I'm jumping behind you."

"Aw, I was just about to suggest the same thing," she beamed, lifting her free hand for a high-five.

Rolling his eyes for good measure, he gave her hand a quick slap.

"Unless you feel like screaming, of course," she noted.

"Right," he said.

"I don't mean to backseat a banshee."

"No, no. I could use some constructive criticism."

"And possibly, if you have the time, let us know beforehand. So we can put the earplugs in."

"Got it."

"You know, I'm really starting to worry about lasting hearing loss."

"You mentioned that." He continued before Nicole could respond, "Are you using this conversation to put off heading in?"

"No," she dismissed with a snort, adding in a far softer voice, "Only in the literal sense."

It struck her as a victory to see a soft smirk flutter across Benton's lips. He gave her hand a little reassuring squeeze, sucked in a deep breath, and stepped off of the road. Despite the rain, the squish of the soggy earth under his heavy boot was audible. She cringed at the sound, unintentionally clutching Benton's hand a fraction tighter. Hard enough that she was able to feel the ice of his skin through the thick layers of the ski gloves.

"It's alright," he promised. "Let's get moving before they get the courage to come out and play."

Nicole's hand instantly went for the butt of her rifle. Zack and the twins did the same.

"Who's 'they'?" Meg asked.

Danny added, "And where are they now?"

"More importantly, what are they doing?" Zack added.

The red glow of Benton's headlight washed over the trees and ferns, glistening off of the droplets that clung to the leaves. None of them missed how he paused more than once. Staring intently at nothing at all. He swallowed thickly.

"Don't worry about it," Benton said at last.

He squared his broad shoulders and headed down the slippery slope.

# Chapter 13

The thin rain fought to get through the canopy. Water welled against the leaves before being dumped sporadically to the forest floor. It took a vast amount of effort to keep himself from flinching at every strike. The heavy layers of winter gear made it hard to walk and did little to keep his warmth. His heavy boots randomly became stuck in the mud, forcing him to jerk his legs, and leaving him feeling like a staggering newborn giraffe. Each teen had a headlight, creating five beams of red that glided over the area around them. He wished it wasn't red. It made the sight of the dead hands all the worse.

The others didn't see them, he knew. It would be obvious if they did. The flesh was sloppy with rot and reeked of overly sweet meat. Benton did his best to hide his gag but Nicole caught it instantly. Holding up his free hand to protect his eyes from the beam of her headlight reminded him that he was still clutching desperately to her hand.

"What is it?" she demanded. "And don't say nothing. We need to be on the same page here."

Biting his lips, Benton kept his silence. He couldn't stop his eyes from straying back to the clawing hands, though. They squirmed out from behind trunks and twigs. Scraping and grasping at the plant life. Tearing their nails free with a sickening wet sound. More hands pushed free of the shadows, joining the others, growing in numbers until they looked like maggots battling for position on a corpse.

"You don't want to know," he stressed.

"Why would I ask if I didn't want to know?" Nicole shot back.

Zack leaned between them, partially obscuring his view of Nicole. "Are we in danger?"

"They're not coming towards us," Benton offered, unsure of what else he could say.

"Then I don't want to know," Zack said.

Nicole shoved him aside. "Then use your earplugs."

Waiting a heartbeat for those who wanted to block their ears to do so, Benton heaved a sigh and opened his mouth. Before he could say anything, however, Danny released a startled, terrified scream.

"Oh, you can see them." The words passed Benton's numb lips as he watched the teens twist and turn.

They aimed their lights from one tree to the next, their panic mounting as they realized they were completely surrounded.

Benton watched it all unfold with a certain degree of delight. *They can see it, too.* The notion that he wasn't alone in confronting this brought such relief that he didn't care what lasting effect it would have on them. *Misery likes company.*

"How is this possible?" Meg asked as she drew closer to her sister.

"It must be the woods," Nicole answered.

Zack jerked around to glare at her but didn't dare take his eyes off the ghostly hands for long. "We've been in the woods before. I never saw severed body parts."

"Were you looking for them?" Benton asked.

"Maybe it's you," Zack snarled. "Ever think of that? Maybe you're contagious or something."

"If that were true, I'd probably have a way better relationship with my parents," Benton scoffed.

Zack stormed towards him, fear bringing him to the brink of snapping. Nicole jumped between them before Zack could through a punch.

"Stop it! We clearly have other things to worry about," she said.

"This isn't normal," Zack snarled. "None of this stuff happened before he came to town."

There was no way Nicole could keep Zack back if he truly wanted to push his way past her. This didn't seem to occur to her.

"You're scared. Hitting him isn't going to change that."

"It'll make me feel better."

Benton shrugged. "Yeah, I get that reaction a lot. Normally from children."

It occurred to him a second later that provoking a terrified, towering teen that had a few pounds of muscle on him wasn't the smartest idea. Zack surged forward but stopped himself midstride. Within a split second, the hands disappeared, slipping as one behind the trees. Dread thickened the air until it coated his throat. Experience had helped him to tell the difference between his own feelings and those that were driven into him from an unknown source. *They're hiding.*

Heart ramming against his rib cage, he ducked to the side. "We need to get in the trees."

"What?" Zack asked.

"You want to go where the hands just were?" Danny added in disbelief.

Arguing with them would be a fruitless exercise. So he turned to Nicole.

"We have to get off the forest floor."

He could almost hear her brain clicking into gear, working through all of their options and quickly coming to a conclusion.

"Danny, Zack, hide the bags in that log."

The two of them moved without comment, shoving the bags deep into the moss-covered hollow as Nicole raced to a nearby tree. It was one of the thicker ones, with gnarled branches that started a few feet off the ground. She didn't move her gun as she pressed her back against it, braced her legs, and made a cup with her hands. Benton didn't hesitate to take the boost. Heavy winter gear and a complete lack of experience would make him the slowest. Stretching out, he managed to hook his arm over the damp branch. Pulling himself up was harder. Rather than waiting for him, Nicole shuffled a few feet to the side. Meg and Danny quickly scrambled up past him. Zack followed them, having paused long enough to pull Nicole up.

"Put your foot here," Zack instructed, tapping a small stump left after a branch had broken off.

Benton did as he was told and found the next few feet a lot easier to scale.

"Good. Hand over there. No, the other branch, that one won't hold your weight."

True to his word, the bug-infested wood crumbled under Benton's fingers, spilling crawling insects along his sleeve. Benton ignored them as he followed Zack's cues. The muscles of his back screamed and twitched as he worked his way up. Icy air froze his lungs as he began to pant. Sweat cooled against his skin, numbing his fingers and feet. Zack had to pull him up the final bit to bring him onto the same branch as Meg. She gripped him tight to keep him from falling.

"Thanks," he said between gulped breaths.

Zack nodded, patted his shoulder, and squeezed in between Nicole and the trunk. Danny had a third branch to herself. One that hung over the path and swayed slightly in the breeze. Each one turned their headlamps off, and then there was nothing left to do but wait. They sat within the dank cold, eyes straining against the darkness. Soft breezes came without warning, trembling the leaves, allowing small gaps of moonlight to penetrate the canopy. Each time the wind died, they were thrust back into the oppressive darkness, left to jump at every slight snap of twigs.

Benton's eyes widened when a new sound joined the patter of rain. A rustle and scrape. It was a noise he recognized from a hundred dreams. When, living in another's skin, he had dragged a corpse through the undergrowth. In the stillness of the forest, it was easy to track the sound as it drew closer. The wind blew again, pushing at the leaves and casting aside the shadows.

Benton clenched his jaw until the teeth threatened to crack. Even then, he barely managed to keep in his scream. A gigantic, gnarled monstrosity dragged itself below their hiding place. At least seven feet tall, it had the torso of a naked woman, with long sinewy arms tipped with claw-like fingernails. Its lower body was a trunk. Thick and sturdy, the base gathering the dead leaves at it moved. Its head was topped with a mangled mess of vines, each one as black and charred as its hands. Mold stained bark replaced its skin.

Its upper body was in constant motion at it glided under them. Arms and head swaying gracefully before, without warning, it jerked and twitched, a violent spasm that brimmed with murderous rage. A few times its head snapped backward. Roots burrowed in and out of its skull – a horde of twisted snakes that destroyed all but the shattered fragments of its teeth. It continued without noticing them, the dragging sound dwindling until Benton couldn't hear it at all. They all remained as they were, clutching to the tree and desperately trying to smother their petrified sobs.

He didn't know how long they were staring at him before he noticed. When he did, he squeezed his eyes shut, searching everything within him for a trace of something that wasn't his own, trying desperately to tap into the emotions of the dead around him and learn if the beast was gone.

It never occurred to him that it would work.

Suddenly the floodgates opened. A torrent of emotions, memories, and sensations crushed down upon him, rushed through him, swept him away until he could barely keep a grasp of his own consciousness. A hard thump brought him back. The air rushed from his lungs, leaving him gasping as he tried to make sense of the sudden pain.

"Benton," Nicole whispered as she clambered down the tree.

It was only when she was kneeling by his side that it clicked.

"I fell."

"Yeah, you did." She was already patting him down, sure hands searching for broken bones. "Are you in any pain?"

There was pain. Countless lifetimes of it, echoing through his mind and rolling within his skin. But none of it belonged to him.

"A little sore," he almost mouthed.

"Is it gone?" Meg asked from the shadows. "Benton, is it gone?"

"This is all moss," Danny came out of nowhere to say. "I think it broke his fall."

"Guys," Zack hissed.

Benton wavered as he pulled himself back onto his feet. "It's gone."

Even in their panic, no one dared to raise their voice above a whisper.

"What the hell was that thing?" Zack demanded.

"Do you think it could see us?" Danny added.

Nicole's jaw dropped. "Oh, God. Is that what Mr. Ackerman is turning into?"

The twins and Zack paused long enough to look confused.

"The ghost in Benton's barn," Nicole almost snapped. When she continued, she focused on Benton. "You said that he's becoming almost plant-like. Could that be what he's turning into?"

Benton didn't know where the answer came from, but there wasn't a shadow of doubt in his mind. "Yeah."

"Can that thing kill?" Nicole asked softly.

While he racked his brain, he couldn't find an answer for her. Whatever door he had opened within himself was closed again. And with it, all that had forced its way inside was draining back into oblivion. He could only shrug.

Determination set her jaw. "Let's not wait around to find out."

The others went to collect the bags while Nicole slipped under Benton's arm, taking on some of his weight. Even that was enough to make his head spin. He clung to her as they started to move. The hands returned in greater numbers than before, clawing at the trees until the sound of crunching bark drowned out all other sounds. The hands reached for them as they passed, twisting up in their jackets, trying to tug them closer. Benton yanked his arm away and rotten skin peeled from brittle bones. Rancid blood bubbled free, slicking his clothes and aiding the next escape.

Meg held the map so tightly that she almost tore it in two, refusing to loosen her grip even as the hands ripped her hair from her scalp and left streaks of blood over her jacket. She led the way up an incline, surging forward all the harder as the ghosts tried to keep her back. The others kept on her heels, barely a step behind. She reached the peak of the hill and checked her map once more. A sudden crack resounded over the noise around them and Meg vanished.

Danny screamed for her sister an instant before she, too, disappeared. Benton trained his light on the ground, realizing a moment too late that it wasn't solid earth. A tangled mass of vines and branches had covered the hole. It snapped under his weight and he dropped. His battered back smacked against the wall of the hole. The raw earth turned into a muddy slide by the constant rain.

Flying, he drove his hands into the wall and dug in his feet, trying to slow his descent.

Hitting the bottom came with a loud splash and a wave of filthy water. Momentum took him under the frigid water. He thrashed wildly, barely able to think as the cold ravaged him. Getting his feet under him, he stood, only to have his boots sink a few inches into the muck. His headlamp flickered as the wires fried and died with a hiss. The water frothed and Zack plummeted down to join them, narrowly missing hitting Meg in the head. While barely a few feet separated them, without their lights he couldn't make out their faces.

"I'm stuck," Meg said. "Can anyone move?"

Every attempt to move sucked at his feet, drawing him a half inch deeper. When the water was lapping under his arms, he gave up.

"No."

Danny growled as she failed to pull her feet from the muddy bottom. Zack had tried to climb the wall only to fall back.

"Hold on," Benton squinted into the gloom. Panic suddenly burned like coals in the pit of his gut. "Where's Nic?"

They all came to the same sudden conclusion. *She's trapped underneath.*

The water bubbled and frothed as they frantically searched under the surface. Benton stretched until his joints threatened to pop. For all the strain, he couldn't find her. His pulse quickened in his veins until his head was spinning. Only when the lack of air threatened to knock him out did he give up the search and resurface. Gasping for air, he wiped the mud from his face and was about to duck back down when he heard Meg scream.

"I found her! She's not moving!"

His heart missed a beat as a red light washed down on them from above. Jerking his face up, he peered into the glare.

"Are you guys okay?" Nicole called down.

In confusion, they all turned to see what had confused Meg. By the soft light, he found the teenaged girl tightly embracing a decaying corpse. Her scream broke the stunned stillness. Still shrieking, she tossed it aside, driven mad with the need to get as far away from it as possible.

"Don't lose it!" Benton declared.

His hip spiked with agony as he lunched forward, half drowning himself before he managed to latch onto the corpse and drag it back to the surface. Its arm popped off in his haste and he scrambled to find it in the dirty water. In the end, he had to keep it pressed against his chest, its bloated skin bursting in his hands. He didn't have time to dwell on that when, upon straightening, he found that his struggle had made him sink. He now had to tip his head back to keep his face above the water.

"Nicole?" he called, desperation tinging his voice. He sunk an inch deeper. "Nicole!"

"I'm right here," she said, her voice marked with a small flurry of droplets. It was all distorted to him, given the water sloshing into his ears. "Don't worry; I'm going to get you guys out."

"How did you not fall in?" Danny demanded.

"I jumped," she replied. "Why didn't any of you try and get out of the way?"

"Nicole!" Benton bellowed, choking on a mouthful of foul water that trickled past his lips. "I'm sinking!"

"Is that a dead body?"

"Drowning!"

"Right. Sorry. I'm on it. Zack, can you take off your bag? There's some rope in the outer pocket."

Zack hurried to comply. "You packed rope?"

"Who on earth would go into the woods without a rope?" her reply came as she ducked out of sight.

Heavy thuds rattled the unstable walls of the pit. Nicole came and went, collecting heavy branches and arranging them across the gap, building an uneven but hopefully reliable platform. When she was satisfied with her work, her headlamp peeked over the edge, casting the pit in a crimson glow.

"Toss me the rope," she called down.

Zack had managed to retrieve the rope, but actually getting one end up to Nicole proved to be harder. Benton watched him try and fail a few times as he continued to slip down.

"The end's too light," he grumbled with mounting frustration.

Not willing to risk opening his mouth and let the water in, Benton thrust the broken limb at him.

"What the hell, man?" he roared.

"Tie the rope around it," Nicole explained.

The added weight helped Zack to reclaim his title as the best pitcher in southern Alberta. In one smooth motion, he hurled the limb with strength and procession. It sailed past Nicole's waiting hands. The rope snagged on a protruding hunk of wood, forcing the arm to loop around it over and over. In the end, it needed very little intervention from Nicole to properly secure it.

"Come on, Benny-boy," Zack said.

Benton pushed the corpse out first, much to Zack's horror. But he understood quickly enough. If this was the remains of one of the killers, they couldn't afford to lose it.

"At least pull your feet out," Zack hissed between his teeth.

He thrust the end of the rope at him and returned to rummaging through the hiking bag again, looking for the body bags that Nicole had promised were in there. Benton wrapped one arm around the body's torso and coiled the rope around his other forearm, remembering his injury a moment too late. Clenching his teeth, he yanked, pulling up with all his might and constantly squirming his feet. Slowly, then all at once, the muck released his boots. A pained cry cracked out of his throat. Relief flashed through him as he let the rope unravel and flopped back, floating as best he could.

"Meg, Danny," Zack noted, still shoving his way through his bag. "You guys get up there while we sort this out."

Annoyance and hope fought for dominance on Danny's face. "I can help. I'm not squeamish."

"But you're short. We'll last longer than you," Zack replied. "Not to mention that Nicole's going to need help to get these packages up."

Danny still hesitated.

"She's alone up there," Benton said, spitting out the water that worked its way into his mouth.

The possibility of diseases played across his mind, but he forgot about it in the wake of Danny's reluctant agreement. Benton watched as the sisters quickly and efficiently climbed their way up.

"I never thought gym class would come in handy," Benton noted between controlled breaths.

Zack snorted, then crowed in victory as he produced the body bags. Between the two of them, they gathered the corpse, tucked it safely inside the zip-up plastic, secured the rope around it, and sent it up. A scream followed an instant later. The boys snapped their faces up, instantly calling for the girls. The red glow of Nicole's headlamp flickered rapidly. In the last gasps of light, Benton spotted the severed edge of the rope toppling limply into the pit.

# Chapter 14

Nicole spun, the twigs of her makeshift platform crunching under her back as she fell upon it. With both hands and locked elbows, she held her rifle as a bar above her. It was barely enough to keep the monster's wooden fangs from slashing open her flesh.

The forest had claimed this lost soul as it had the other. Infesting it. Turning the incorporeal flesh into solid wood. Planting her feet against the half-man's chest, she pushed up with all of her limbs, trying to keep the snapping jaws from her throat. Unlike the other they had seen before, this one was tiny. An inch shorter than herself. But its weight was crushing. Her legs trembled and her arms threatened to buckle.

"Nicole!" Meg shouted.

Primal instinct had spared Nicole once again, allowing her to turn just as the monster lunged from the darkness. Meg and Danny had stumbled back but quickly regained their footing.

"Help her," Danny ordered her sister while shoving the body bag a few inches from the mouth of the pit. "I'll get the boys."

Out of the corner of her eyes, Nicole saw Danny loom over the rim while her sister snapped her rifle up. With one last solid shove, Nicole flattened herself against the twigs. A shot rang out. Bark hit Nicole's face like shrapnel, but the monster didn't relent. Snarling in fury, it threw its weight down, buckling Nicole's legs and bringing its jaws an inch from her face.

Suddenly, the monster's head cracked in two, splitting down the center until only its lower jaw kept the pieces together. The sides of its head clattered together as it twitched and swayed, the noise almost covering the sound of the second arrow. The mental tipped shaft exploded through the monster's right shoulder, stopping just before it would have buried into her flesh. Hissing in rage, it turned to glare with unseeing eyes into the forest. High amongst the trees, illuminated by the shifting moonlight, crouched the Baykok. The tip of his arrow glistened as he took aim. Nicole screamed, allowing her left arm to go slack while she threw herself to the right. The monster stumbled, the quick lurch bringing its body between her and the arrow.

The Baykok leaped from the tree as Meg took aim. Racing amongst the trees, it narrowly avoided all four of Meg's shots as it circled the pit, working its way behind Danny. Flat on her stomach and arms full of the second body bag, Danny couldn't even twist enough to keep the Baykok in sight. Meg dropped her now empty rifle and sprinted to her sister, collapsing onto the mud beside her. Danny's rifle was still strapped to her back. It made it impossible to get a decent shot, but the attempt had the Baykok increasing his arch, pushing back a few feet to hide amongst the ferns.

Then it vanished.

With a grunted hiss, the monster of wood and flesh surged forward, slithering rapidly across the muddy earth on its belly to crash into the undergrowth. Towering trees cracked and swayed, trembling violently as the two demonic forces collided. Nicole rolled up onto her feet and jumped from her improvised platform, swooping down to retrieve Danny's discarded rifle as she hurried to join the group. Two body bags were stacked beside the sisters, each one containing a lump that seemed far too small to be the hellish couple she remembered. Benton and Zack weren't with them.

"They're too heavy," Meg said before Nicole could ask the question. "They keep snapping the branches."

"All three of us can hold it," Nicole said.

Savage screams followed the Baykok as it was tossed from the foliage. Flipping in the air, it landed on its feet, mud and grass gathering at its heels as it slid to a stop. The wooden monster followed in a blur, moving on its stomach like a crocodile over the flooded earth. The monsters clashed and tumbled back out of the reach of the moonlight.

"Hurry," Nicole gasped.

Benton's voice had her leaning over the edge.

"What?" she asked.

"Earplugs!" Both boys bellowed in unison.

Her eyes widened as she hurled herself up. "Run!"

The three girls fled from the rickety platform, seeking shelter in the trees as the banshee's wail demolished the night.

It was unlike anything she had ever heard. An almost physical force that threw her to the ground. The shrill scream rose in pitch as it grew louder, climbing the scales until it reached a crimpling note. Falling to the ground, she clawed at her ears, caught between two primal instincts. Block her ears and rip them from her skull to make it stop. The air itself vibrated. Raindrops shattered in midair. A fine tremble shook the loose earth. It crumbled into the pit, widening the hole, sucking in trees and forcing the girls to crawl further away or follow them.

Blinding light filled Nicole's vision. Her body separated from her mind. The two occupying the same space but never touching the other. She blinked sluggishly and rolled aimlessly with every attempt to move. A muffled sound approached. Somewhere, with haze, she was sure the Baykok had come to claim her. But the stunned haze of her mind kept her from caring.

Steadily, a sharp ringing filled her ears. Painful but endurable, allowing her mind to steadily drip back into her incapacitated body. A shadow loomed over her and she was jerked back onto her feet. The sudden motion cleared her head just enough for her to focus. A gigantic crater had gouged a hole into the forest floor, stopping barely a few inches from her feet. The canopy had been shredded by the toppled trees, allowing both the rain and weak moonlight to fall unopposed. A figure of muck and blood grasped her shoulders and shook her hard. She scrambled for her rifle before it clicked.

"Benton?" She couldn't hear her voice over the whine in her ears.

His mouth moved but there was no sound. Only the harsh, unmerciful drone. Finally, he pushed her, forcing her to move around the pit towards the others. Zack and the twins were just as stunned. Benton worked to get them in order, collecting the body bags and supplies and urging them into a run. Nicole moved without thought. Driven on by both Benton's shoves and pure survival instinct. They sprinted until their lungs refused to let them keep the pace. Slowing, they continued as a herd until they dropped. She slumped against a rock, her hearing returning as they panted for breath. Not in full, but enough for her catch the majority of his words.

"Here. Drink." He passed her a bottle of water from the hiking bag.

"What the hell was that?" Zack declared.

Nicole wondered how many times he had asked that before now. *Probably the whole time.*

"It was the first time I consciously did it," Benton defended. "Cut me some slack."

"Where did they go?" Meg demanded, contorting her exhausted body to search the woods around them.

Nicole didn't know the answer so offered the only statement she knew to be true. "There's a pecking order."

"I got that, too," Benton noted.

Meg pushed her filthy hair from her forehead. "And you're not the top."

The muscles in Benton's jaw jumped. "Yeah, I figured that out."

"You can't kill these things," Meg continued.

"I don't need to," Benton said. "We just have to bury them. Can we do that now before they catch up?"

The air ripped from Nicole's lungs. "Not here."

"Say again," Benton replied bitterly.

"What's wrong with here?" Zack demanded, fear crackling within his voice. "Here is good. Now is good. Nic, those things are going to catch up."

"This is our land," Nicole snapped.

Zack threw his arms wide. "So what?!"

"So, it's spreading," she shot back. "We've always known that this patch of earth is cursed land. It's too blood-soaked to be anything else. But its influence was contained. Now it's extending into town."

"Ackerman," Benton mumbled.

"You said it yourself, Benton. Mr. Ackerman's afraid. Whatever's poisoned the land is claiming his soul. It's spreading! What if burying this kind of evil here only makes it worse?"

"We can't stop him without burying him," Danny said.

Nicole's mind whirled. "The map. Meg, do you still have the map?"

After some fumbling, Meg produced the map, ripped and soggy with water, the highlighter bleeding out into large patches.

"Where are we?" Nicole asked.

Meg gave her a disbelieving look before studying the area around them and the map in turn.

"Here-ish," she said, using her fingertip to make a circle a few miles wide on the paper.

A rush of relief made Nicole smile. "That's close enough. We can make it."

"To where?" Danny asked slowly.

Preparing herself for the backlash, Nicole pointed to a spot almost completely off the edge of the map. Tradition dictated that it was never shown in entirety. Chaos broke out amongst their small group, their combined voices like daggers in her abused ears.

"Hey!" Benton's outburst drew their attention. "What's the big deal?"

"Are you kidding?" Danny demanded. "That's the ghostlands."

"I don't know what that means," Benton shot back.

"Oh, God," Zack huffed. "Look, this is all extremely complicated. To get it, you'll need a deep understanding of Siksika lore, history, religion, and our views of the afterlife."

"Not to mention the adjustments made by the local tribe and all that entails," Danny added.

"Explain it to me like I'm an idiot." Benton snapped up his hand, mud flying from his fingertips. and he motioned for Zack to stay silent.

Meg was the first to organize her thoughts. "Basically, our traditional view of the afterlife didn't have it completely severed from the living world. It was a real, physical place that anyone could accidentally walk into. Our small little group believed it was right there."

"*Basically*," Zack mocked, "Nic's suggesting that we literally go to the land of the dead to bury these guys."

"The land literally holds onto the dead," she defended.

"And we're alive," Benton said. "If living people can go in, I'm guessing they can get out."

"Yeah. After being cursed," Zack said.

Benton's brow furrowed. "What does that mean? What curse?"

They went silent for a few seconds before Zack finally answered. "The legends never went into detail. Only that those who passed the boundary line were forever tainted by the dead."

Emboldened by having an ally, Nicole continued, "We only need to go a few feet across the border. You'll be able to keep a foot in the living realm."

"You don't know what's in there," Meg said.

Danny leaned forward, knocked off balance by her rapidly moving arms. "You just learned that all of the stories are true. These things are real. And you want to do the one thing we're told since birth never to do?"

"What's our other option?" she argued. "The paranormal equivalent of poisoning the water supply?"

Zack slammed a hand onto the map and growled. "For once in your life, can you just consider the consequences of your actions?"

An icy calm settled over Nicole even as she vibrated with anger. "Fort Wayward is my home. The home of my ancestors. Their final resting place. Every person in that town is my family." She looked to each of them in turn. "These things are invading our land. Our *home*. Attacking our tribe. I don't care what I have to do, where I have to go, or what they do to me. I'm not giving them a single inch."

Yanking the map out from under Zack's hand, she got to her feet. "None of you have to come with me. But if you want to, just hold these things off while I cross over and bury them."

Benton had stood up before she finished.

"What?" he asked. "I'm already cursed."

Zack looked to the twins. After muttering a few swear words, they each rose and gathered their belongings.

"If we keep up a steady pace, we'll get there before dawn." There was no enthusiasm in Meg's voice as she stuck out her hand. "Give me the map."

# Chapter 15

Benton had never thought that his body was capable of running for so long. Meg set the slow but steady pace, pausing only when she needed to get her bearings. His bones remained frozen under the growing layer of heated sweat. No matter how far they ran, the forest was still alive around them. Hands squirmed out from the shadows to grasp at anything within their reach. Thick blood began to ooze from the leaves, black as tar in the moonlight and tainting the air with a copper stench. Rain and mud made his jeans damp, chafing his skin and running into his eyes as they ran.

Trudging their way up a valley wall almost broke him. The soft earth broke apart under his feet, dragging them all back down as they fought on, surging ever closer to the rising sun. Just when he thought he couldn't endure another step, Meg stopped. Benton dropped to his knees, bracing himself on all fours as he panted for breath.

"It should be around here somewhere," Meg said after greedily gulping down a few mouthfuls of water.

"Where?" Nicole asked.

"It's not exactly well defined on the map," Meg shot back.

Benton reared back on his knees to look around. A small attempt to help the search. Awe claimed him, squeezing his heart and dropping his jaw. *That's not the sun.*

He barely noticed himself. Hardly felt the humid heat pushing against his skin. All he saw was the burning inferno that he had mistaken for the sunrise. Pushing a branch aside, he entered a clearing and got his first true look at the sight before him. A thousand-foot wall of dancing flames. Exploding from the earth like a volcanic geyser. Moving as waves along the swirling patterns mapped out upon the rocky ground.

"How did I never see this from town?"

"Benny-boy?" Zack asked cautiously.

He jerked around. "None of you see this?"

They didn't need to answer. The looks on their faces said enough.

"Your borderline's right there," he noted, pointing towards the flames. "So you know, you're not going to be able to keep one foot out. It's probably two yards thick."

Nicole inched closer to him. "What do you see?"

"Do you remember that weird room we found in the Leanan Sidhe's collection room?"

"The one with all symbols of unknown origins?"

He arched an eyebrow at her.

"And that has the invisible fire that burned your hand, leaving you permanently scarred," she added. "That's totally what I remember first."

Benton decided to give a quick description rather than continue the conversation.

"Are you kidding me?" Zack said.

"What's on the other side?" Meg asked.

Benton tried to look, but staring into the heat for too long made his eyes water and burn. The sudden hoot of an owl made him jump. Looking up, he found the sky littered with the huge birds, circling above them with silent beats of their wings.

"I can't. Be quick," Benton said.

"You're not coming now?" Zack asked.

Wiping his palm on his pants to properly clear the mud off of his scars, he displayed his hand to the boy, remembering a heartbeat later that they didn't have the blazing firelight to see by. It must have been close enough to dawn, because it only took a moment of squinting for Zack to understand.

"Oh, right. You'll die horribly."

Benton shrugged before an owl swooped at his head. Its talons slipped over the hood of his parka as he crouched. Following it with his eyes, his attention was drawn back to the edge of the meadow. People stood within the shadows. Arms at their sides. Rage radiating from them in crashing waves.

"Their victims are here," Benton said. The sheer number was staggering.

"To help?" Nicole asked.

"Go," was Benton's reply. "Now!"

Nicole tightened her grip on the body bags and sprinted, barely getting a few feet before a ghost appeared before her. Skull visible through rotten flesh. Dark eyes burning. Benton rushed forward, pushing her out of the way as he opened his mouth to scream. The ghost flickered and vanished. Only to reappear at his side with a dozen of the others. Hands like dry ice reached for him, pulling back only when he brought his iron bracelet close. There were too many of them. Dozens turned to hundreds, each ensuring that he screamed in agony, rendering him incapable of summoning a banshee wail.

A flash of feathers and glistening talons streaked across his visor, entering one of the ghosts that held him and shattering it like crystal. Another and another. A swarm that carved him an escape route.

He took it, slicing another specter with his iron bracelet to reach an open area. Prepared for a fight, he spun around, only to find that the ghosts had resumed their sentinel posts. Unmoving. Staring.

The arrow pierced his torso a second later.

Pain exploded along his veins as his head flopped forward. His blood made the metal tip glisten in the firelight. *Don't fall asleep.* Wrapping trembling fingers around the protruding shaft, he yanked it free. His scream of agony shook the earth and brought him to his knees. Hot blood rushed from the wound, washing the muck away and seeping into the grass around him. He pressed his fingers to it, ignoring the pain as he tried to stop the flow. Footsteps crept up behind him. A dark shadow settled over him. Panting hard, he lifted his gaze, finding a grim reaper standing before him. Grass squished behind him, the Baykok ready to claim its prize as soon as the venom took hold.

*Banshee.*

The word flickered through his head, imploding the dull haze that had consumed him. He thrust himself up, twisting and bringing the arrow in his hand down like a dagger. It dug through the empty socket of the Baykok's eyes. With a sickening crunch, the tip broke through the mummified hard palate, snapping teeth as it drove out of the Baykok's mouth. Before he could think, Benton yanked the impaled monster closer and released a furious scream.

The Baykok vibrated violently. Fine cracks formed over the skull, gathering until, in one final burst, its head exploded.

Benton staggered back as the Baykok did the same. Thrashing wildly, it blindly searched for him, no closer to death than it had been before. *But we have time,* Benton thought, his free hand raising up to touch his still bleeding wound. *They have time.*

The first tremble took him by surprise, almost throwing him off balance. He had his feet braced to endure the next. The one after that. Three more grim reapers rose noiselessly from the ground as the trees swayed, each one staring in the same direction. Benton turned in time to see the colossal body rise up above the tree line. The jaws of the mummified skull clattered as its bones popped and skin crackled. *They grow each time they eat,* Benton recalled as he watched the twenty-foot-tall Baykok straighten its spine.

*He became obsessed with getting revenge on Nicole,* a voice whispered through Benton's shock-riddled mind. *What has she been doing?*

"Nicole!" Benton bellowed. "His girlfriend's here!"

Horrified cries came through the flames as the giant Baykok stalked closer.

"Bury her first!" he commanded.

A fist larger than a car crashed down towards him. Benton sprinted to the side but couldn't outpace the massive limb. At the last second, he dropped into a skid, sliding on his hip and allowing the hand to pass over him. Planting his foot, he rose up onto one knee and screamed. Forced, the sound came out as a high-pitched squeal, shattering a few trees but doing very little to the beast before him. The flock of owls attacked, clawing for the hollow pits of its eyes. The Baykok threw its arm out but didn't have the speed to catch the swooping birds.

Benton waited for an opening, for the creature to open its jaws. Gathering his strength, he screamed again. The papery skin ripped from its face, but the bones remained intact. A low grumble escaped it as it slammed its hand down, trying to crush him. He jumped out of the way, stumbling into a reaper and falling through it.

He couldn't see the headless Baykok he collided into. The flames surged and lapped at them as they fell, never making contact but drawing close enough to burn. An owl swooped, digging its talons into its spine and refusing to let go. A wild gesture caught the bird on the head and sent it to the ground. Benton scurried away as the ghosts of their victims charged into the fight, each one trying to claim their pound of flesh from the giant. Each one determined to keep their revenge.

"Nicole!"

"It's done!"

No sooner had the words left her mouth that the reapers began to melt. Bleeding into the air like oil in water. Staining each molecule until Benton was breathing it in. Moving as a fog, the deaths coiled around the Baykoks like a snake, tightening their hold as the monstrous figures fought for freedom. Nothing could stop the black mass from growing. It took everything, devouring the world until nothing remained.

Benton grabbed his side as his knees buckled. He slumped to sit on the muddy earth beside the injured owl. Blood pulsed between his fingers as he pressed a hand over his wound.

"Benton!" Nicole shrieked.

She sprinted across the grass towards him.

"I never thought I'd say it," he muttered. "But I want to go home."

\*\*\*

Benton didn't have to open his eyes to know that it was Nicole who settled down beside him. It had become their routine over the past week of mutual grounding. The only time they were allowed to see each other was at school and, still feeling the chill from the cursed ground, Benton used every lunch break to lay on the baseball field and soak in as much sun as he could.

"How's Bird?" she asked. "And I once again insist you come up with a better name for the owl. It saved your life. It deserves better."

"Bird likes his name," he mumbled sleepily. "The vet says his wing will heal up fine."

"I still can't believe your parents let you keep him."

"Dr. Aspen says that pets help kids grow compassion and responsibility."

"Are they still agreeing to family therapy?"

"We have another appointment after school," he said.

"Well, there's a silver lining."

He opened one eye when he heard her sit up.

"Can I see it again?" she asked sweetly.

Benton sighed and hiked up the right side of his shirt. Before they had even left the highway, his wound had closed, flesh knitting together to leave a thin pink scar. It wasn't ever going away.

"I have devoted my free time—"

"You're grounded, Nic," he corrected. "Dorothy threatened to keep you in a holding cell if you ducked out again."

Her mouth tightened. "Which gives me a lot of free time."

"Whatever you say."

"I can't figure out how you survived it."

"Banshee perk, I suppose."

"How does it not bother you?"

"Because it's not the first time it's happened."

She jolted. "Say again."

Benton heaved another sigh as he struggled to sit up. The wound might have healed, but it still hurt like hell.

"You've read my files, right?"

Nicole nodded.

"So you know about that night." Licking his lips, he forced himself to continue. "When I was ten."

"Your friends betrayed you," she said meekly.

*Beat me. Left me to bleed to death in a back alley.* He shoved down all the emotions that threatened to choke him.

"I think I died a little in that alley."

"Of course."

"No, I mean actually died. Or came pretty close to it. I didn't know it at the time, but that's when I first saw death." He pulled his hands through his hair and hunched forward. "It didn't look like they do now, so I just thought that my brain was playing tricks on me. It had a few shards of bone embedded in it at the time."

His joke fell flat.

"What did it look like?"

Benton smile despite himself. "My mom." A sharp cough forced away the tears that threatened to fall. "Who knows? Maybe that's why things are so tense with her. That's the last time I remember her being maternal and it wasn't even her. You know what? I don't want to talk about this today. Some other time maybe?"

Looking at her, Benton found she was close to tears. "Hey, it's okay," he assured.

"I'm a horrible person," Nicole blurted.

"No, you're not."

Now that she had started her confession, there was nothing to keep back the rest. "I haven't told mom about what happened on the highway. Either time."

*I have.* Benton knew better than to speak it aloud. With everything that had happened, he had agreed to giving Nicole a two-week extension on the deadline. The constable still had three days before her deadline.

"That doesn't make you horrible," Benton assured.

Nicole lifted her chin even as tears dripped down. "I haven't told her because I couldn't stand for her to know."

"It was self-defense."

"I don't feel guilty," she said in a rush. The words seemed to physically hurt her. "I put a bullet between his eyes. I *killed* a human being. And I haven't experienced a second of guilt." She wiped away her tears and tried to gather herself. "I always thought I didn't feel bad after killing the monsters because they're monsters. But now ... I'm a psychopath."

Benton barked a laugh. "You are the furthest thing from a psychopath. Trust me, I have some experience in the matter."

"Don't you hate me?"

"Why would I?"

"Because I'm just like the people you dream about," she spouted.

"You obviously haven't been paying attention."

"And you're not listening to me. I murdered someone and slept like a baby. I felt righteous. I–"

"You saved my life," Benton said. "And right now, I'm feeling relieved."

"Relieved?"

He shrugged. "You worry that Zack and the twins can't take all of this. I don't need them around. I just need *you*. And, ever since the highway, I've been living with this fear that I'd have to let you go. That it was unfair for me to put you through all this just because I want some company." Another bubble of uncalled-for laughter slipped out of his mouth. "This is actually a huge relief for me. So, if you're trying to take my crown for 'biggest jackass', you're going to have to up your game."

Nicole smacked into him, the sudden addition of her weight toppling them both over. Still, she didn't release him from her crushing hug for a long time. He endured, patting her back in a way he hoped was reassuring.

"You're okay, Nic. You're a good person," he repeated at random.

Finally, she sniffed and replied, "But we can't tell mom," she insisted. "She won't understand."

Benton cringed, squeezing his eyes shut as he anticipated the sheer amount of screaming and vengeance two enraged Rider woman could bring upon him.

"Yeah," he said, resigned to his fate. "About that..."

\* \* \*

# Weeping Moon
## Banshee Series Book 5

# Chapter 1

Soft light flickered across the canvas covered walls, creating more shadows than it defeated. At the center of the teepee, Nicole hunched over the only light source, her hands raised, and her fingers twisted into claws.

"It was then, as he looked over the rim of the dirt-filled box, that he realized–"

"The guy was a vampire," Benton cut in.

Nicole's face twisted up in frustration. When Benton only smirked in response, she snatched up a marshmallow and tossed it at his head. It bounced off his temple and disappeared into the darkness that clustered around the edges of the room.

"Did you have to spoil it?" she asked.

"Everyone knows that Dracula is a vampire, Nic," Benton defended. "Why are you even telling that as a campfire story?"

"Because we have a test on it after the break, and I know for a fact that you haven't even cracked the spine of that book."

He shook his head. Only in Fort Wayward would the whole town take a week-long hiatus so everyone could go to a powwow.

"I'll listen to the audiobook," he dismissed.

"How is that any different from what I'm offering you right now?"

He shrugged. "Fewer eatable projectiles?"

"Fine." Huffing out her annoyance, Nicole swept her hip-length hair over one shoulder and set about platting it. It was a nightly ritual to prevent it from becoming one massive knot while she slept. "You tell a campfire story then."

"We don't even have a campfire."

He jabbed a finger at the glowing plastic flames. The whole 'campfire' moved a few inches. Nicole used her toes to push it back into place.

"There were only child-friendly teepees left when I booked," she protested.

"You don't trust me with an open flame, do you."

"I do not," she admitted quickly. "In my defense, you're really accident prone."

His fingertips began to rub at the tough, scarred skin of his right palm. The consequences of touching a flame that no one else could see or feel. Months had passed without the scars fading or complete sensation returning, and he'd given up hope that either would happen.

*I've got another ghost scar to go with it now*, he thought.

Thoughtlessly, he shifted, pressing two fingertips against his side. The thin material of his threadbare Chicago Cubs shirt did little to hide the raised scar tissue. Baykoks were ghostly hunters and had pretty good aim. Nicole hadn't been able to see the arrow itself, only the damage it had left behind, but she had insisted she knew the damage it should have caused. The memory came with such clarity that he could hear her voice ringing in his ears. *The arrow would have hit your lungs. Ripped open your liver. Benton, you should be dead right now.*

Benton pressed a little harder against the small ridge marring his torso. It had only taken a few days for it to heal beyond the point of pain. Now, just like with his hand, he couldn't feel the touch at all.

*I should be dead right now.* The thought made the other scar begin to throb. The one that curled around his skull, created by a crushing blow and a surgeon's craftsmanship to save his life. He didn't dare touch it. A part of him was sure he would still feel the blood.

*I should have died a long time ago. But now I have Nicole.*

She was a hurricane contained in human skin. Vibrant and unpredictable and impossible to stand up against. He still didn't know why she had decided that she would put up with him. *A stupid decision, really.* One he was happy she had made. They hadn't known each other for a full year yet, and she had already saved his life more than once.

"Benton?"

He jerked, looking up to see Nicole watching him expectantly. Obviously, it wasn't the first time she had called his name.

"Sorry?" he asked.

"Are you okay?"

"Yeah, just–" He shook his head and forced a smile. "Just thinking. It's nothing important. Let's get back to making fun of you."

"Oh, yay," she groaned playfully.

He chuckled and flopped onto his back.

"This sleeping on the ground thing is horrible for my spine."

"Actually, a lot of doctors say that it's pretty good for you." Nicole's hands never paused as they worked their way to the tips of her hair. "And you might want to actually spend a night camping before you complain."

"I love that your need to correct me won out over your impulse to chastise me," Benton noted.

She scolded. "Are you calling me a nag?"

"Yes."

"Why do people keep saying that?"

"Probably because of the constant nagging," Benton said.

Without thinking, he reached back and pressed his palms against the earth. Planting his feet, he pushed himself up, forcing his spine into a near perfect arch. A few joints popped, and he felt the tension slowly release.

"So, do you have a plan for tonight?" he asked.

The remark was a little passive-aggressive, but he wasn't about to change it. When Nicole first came to him with the idea of coming to the week-long powwow, he had reminded her that he was a Banshee. An omen of death. Forced to live in the skin of a killer every night and wake with the name of a victim filling his head. That, and an inhuman, blood-chilling, wall-shaking wail. It made cohabitation difficult. A more vindictive side of him was waiting with anticipation for the moment Nicole realized that what she had so easily dismissed was actually a massive obstacle. Her silence made him glance over. Half obstructed by his own arm, he got an upside-down view of her face.

"Why are you looking at me like that?" he asked with mounting dread.

"How are you getting your spine to do that?" she countered.

It was hard to shrug while in his position, but he considered it worth the effort.

"I like to dance. It's made me flexible. Can we get to the other topic?"

Nicole blinked at him, a small smile curling the corners of her mouth. *Oh no.* Benton knew that look. *Her rattlesnake smile.* It was the only warning sign she offered before striking, latching onto whatever subject, question, or task that had taken her fancy and refused to let go. She was capable of terrifying levels of fixation. *If she becomes a serial killer, we're all screwed.* Not sure what had grabbed her attention, he flopped back down and let his long, lithe limbs fall where they pleased.

"You asked for the tent furthest from the group, didn't you?" he asked. "You know that they'll still hear me screaming, right?"

She snapped out of her daze and beamed. *Just in time*, he reasoned.

"Way ahead of you."

She lunged for her backpack, half squirming out from under her fur bedding to grab it. Stretching to her tips, she finally found what she was looking for. She tossed the small parcel his way, and he caught it with the same amount of attention. There was a short poem attached to the front of the tiny mesh bag. Holding it high above his head, Benton read it aloud.

*"Night terrors wake me up at night,*
*I'd hate for that to happen to you.*
*So here's a pair of earplugs,*
*And hopefully, you'll sleep through."*

"I put one in every teepee," Nicole said proudly. "And left a basket of them by the entrance for the campsite. I know they won't do much to block out a Banshee wail, but it'll give us an excuse."

*How do you afford these things?!* Out loud, he said, "Thanks, Nic."

He heaved the bag back her way.

"You're going to be a lot closer, though. Not worried about hearing loss?"

"I'm ready for that, too," she declared, brandishing a pair of noise-canceling headphones, the big, bulky kind that people wore when using jackhammers. "One of these days, you'll stop underestimating me."

A smirk stretched his lips as he lay sprawled out across the floor, staring up at where the poles of the teepee met. He hadn't known there was an actual gap there. It made sense, he supposed. Somewhere for the smoke to go and all that. Situated a good distance away from the rest of the campers, they were on the outskirts of the floodlights. He had never been anywhere that had a night sky like Fort Wayward. A full moon had started to rise. It was as bright as a beacon but still didn't wash out the stars.

"It would be a whole lot smarter to just keep me out of this situation," he said.

"You worry way too much," Nicole said. "It's not good for your health."

"I even it out with vast amounts of spite," he dismissed with a loose wave of his hand.

There was a shuffle and a drag, and suddenly some of the blankets were dumped onto his stomach. Before he had time to protest, Nicole settled down beside him, shuffling closer to share his view of the stars.

"Do you want to come jogging tomorrow?" she asked. "Mom and I are going out early."

"Nah, I'm going to tap out of that. Does your mom still have it out for me?"

"She's still a little annoyed," Nicole admitted. "You were supposed to wait a few more days, after all."

Benton leveled a glare at her. In one of their lowest points, Nicole had been forced to kill a man to protect him. Murder, even in self-defense, wasn't something that Nicole wanted to admit to her police officer mother. Unfortunately, Constable Dorothy Rider was very good at her job and had quickly put the pieces together. Both of them knew. Neither wanted to approach the subject, and the weight of it all was slowly eating away at their relationship.

At the time, Benton was on pretty good terms with Dorothy. They had a good thing going. He'd dream about killers and pass the information onto her so she could actually do something about it. Apparently, that was his role in this world. Not to save anyone, but warn them, announce to strangers that death was coming for them. Because of this, he felt he had the right to tell Dorothy to talk to her daughter. And that if she didn't, he would. Watching his only friend spiral down to a pit of self-hatred was more than he could stand.

But then the Baykoks started hunting people down, and everything had been put off. In the end, Benton had told Nicole early, and Dorothy was still a little sour about that. *Or was it because we disobeyed her to run off into a killer-infested haunted forest?* He gave it a little more thought. *Yeah, that's probably it.*

Whatever the case, he had enough on his hands without getting involved with the Rider girl drama.

His own relationship with his parents had started rapidly going downhill a few months before his tenth birthday. That was when the dreams had started. Trying to help had only led to accusations, suspicions, threats, violence, and more than one therapist insisting that he needed to be institutionalized or medicated. Or the police insisting that he must have some kind of connection to the real killers. For years he told everyone who would listen that something else was happening. His parents fled to every major city in Canada before coming to Fort Wayward as a last resort.

And that was where he had met Nicole. *Funny how no one heard me until I gave up.* He snuck a glance at his friend.

It only took her a second to feel it. "What's up?"

"Nothing. Just thinking."

"You're doing that a lot tonight."

"There's nothing else going on to entertain me," he teased.

As predicted, she instantly took offense. She thumped him in in the stomach. Hard.

"Hey, I was shot recently," he protested.

"I know you're already healed."

"That's not the point."

She thumped him again.

"Use your words, Nic," he chuckled.

Suddenly, the air shifted around them. It was barely noticeable. Something that played on the edges of his awareness. Solid but not. A fog that rolled into his bones and robbed him of his breath.

"Oh, no. You're doing that thing with your face," Nicole said as she waved a hand in his general direction. "What's wrong?"

*I don't know. Just picturing how well that would go over*, he thought, but instead, he said, "Firstly, I don't do a *thing* with my face."

"Yes, you do," Nicole cut in.

He ignored her. "Secondly, I'm thinking the same thing I have been for the last week. This is a bad idea."

"Do you know how much effort went into getting your parents to agree to this?"

"Your mom convinced them," Benton corrected.

"I didn't say that it was my effort," Nicole dismissed. "Come on, Benton. We haven't had a chance to hang out together in ages."

"Because we were both grounded for running off repeatedly."

"We were fighting an evil that had escaped the grave!"

"Yeah," he said slowly. "My parents still won't admit that exists."

"Well, we were still in the right. Heroes, one could even say."

"Really?" he smiled.

"I'd, of course, never ask anyone to call us that." She added with a smile, "But we are."

"Right."

"And I think that we deserve a break. This can be our holiday."

"And you're not in any way annoyed that my parents don't like you?"

Her cheeks puffed out as her face flushed red. "I'm winning them over."

"Nope. You're back to square one. They don't like you at all. They say you're a horrible influence on me."

Frustration and righteous indignation rolled off her in waves. Something he shouldn't have found amusing but always ended up chuckling over.

"Just, give them time. They'll come around."

Still smiling, he slipped deeper under the blankets, burrowing down for protection against the cold night air. "Whatever you say, Nic. Turn off the campfire, will you?"

She rolled her eyes and fumbled with the small device.

"Goodnight to you too, Benton," she teased.

"Night," he mumbled. "And remember to put your ear protection on."

"I'll do it once you fall asleep," she assured him.

There was a soft click, and the light died.

It didn't do much of anything since the moonlight was bright enough on its own. It poured through the gap in the ceiling while the artificial light pressed around the edges of the entrance flaps. Muffled sounds drifted in from the few people that were still awake. The steady background noise life was almost nostalgic.

Silence had been the hardest thing to get used to when he had moved to Fort Wayward. From the moment he was born, he had never even set foot in the suburbs. City centers were the only thing his parents could stand. This small town, hidden away from the world in the Albertian grasslands, was as different as it could get. No nightlife, no business that stayed open past five p.m., and only two restaurants, both family style. That was all irritating in its own way.

But it had been damn near impossible to get to sleep without the constant lullaby of traffic, loud neighbors, and police sirens. The random owl screech or howling coyote were of little compensation.

Almost as if conjured by his thoughts, an owl swept across the gap above him, massive wings flapping silently. A small smile curled his lips at the sight of the colossal bird. They were becoming a familiar sight. Releasing a contented sigh, he tucked an arm under his head and relaxed. Sleeping on the ground was a new experience. He had never been camping before, not that the teepee counted in his mind. Laying in the dark, he listened to Nicole's breathing steadily slow.

No matter how he thought about it, he couldn't figure out how Dorothy had managed to convince his parents to let him come to this, let alone share a teepee with only Nicole. Their logic was sound, of course. Benton knew far too much about upcoming murders not to have something to do with it. That didn't stop him from being hurt that his parents would more readily believe that he was the world's most prolific serial killer rather than think he might have some ability beyond their understanding.

Shoving the thoughts aside he closed his eyes. The strange sensation bloomed once more within his chest. Stronger this time. Enough that it made his eyes snap open.

"Benton?" Nicole asked sleepily.

"It's nothing," he whispered, rolling onto his side. "Go back to sleep."

# Chapter 2

Nicole jerked awake with a gasp.

Sleep hung like a fog over her mind, making any proper thought impossible. Blinking rapidly, it took her a moment to understand why the world sounded muffled. It was a bit difficult to get the noise canceling headphones off without waking up Benton.

Cheyanne and Theodore Bertrand weren't physically affectionate people. It wasn't anything personal. Just their way. Benton naturally followed their lead, adding to it until he avoided human contact like the plague. At least, he did when he was awake. The moment he fell asleep, his suppressed touch-starved nature came out in force, and he clutched onto anything and everything like a kid with their teddy-bear. She'd seen it a lot since he had recently taken to having naps whenever possible.

Right now, he had managed to sling one arm over her around her neck, essentially keeping her in a headlock that tightened with every attempt to escape. It took some squirming, but she managed to weasel her way out from under his arm and to freedom. Sitting up, she groggily wiped a hand over her face and glanced around in search of what had woken her.

The air was filled with the musical chirp of crickets, the distant hoot of owls, and the rustling of grass as stray animals scrambled through the undergrowth. All commonplace sounds that put her at ease.

Benton didn't have the same reaction. Frowning in his sleep, he balled the blankets to his chest and rolled to face the back of the teepee, effectively taking all the sheets with him and leaving her to the cool air. She scowled at him and reached for the ends. Her fingertips had just brushed against the soft fur when a shadow passed across the fabric of the teepee.

It was just a flicker of movement—there and gone within the blink of an eye.

It made her freeze all the same.

Straightening her spine, she held her breath and strained to hear the slightest sound. Nothing beyond the common nightlife chatter. Glancing up to the peak of the teepee, she caught a glimpse of the deep purple sky through the gap. The blanket of stars was still visible, but the moonlight was coming from a far sharper angle. *Around two a.m.,* she reasoned. If Benton kept true to form, he'd be waking up in about an hour or so.

Despite the stillness, she had a nagging feeling that there was something *off*. It wasn't an overwhelming sensation. More like a splinter in the back of her mind that she couldn't shake. It brought on a mental debate of whether or not she should get up to properly investigate.

The minutes passed slowly. Benton randomly growled in his sleep. A deep feral sound of real anger. *What is he dreaming about?* It took barely a second for her to decide that she didn't want to know. She'd listen to it all, of course. That's what Benton needed most. For someone to truly listen, even if they couldn't understand. Either way, she couldn't deny that it would be nice to have one day without hearing about the depths of depravity human beings were capable of.

Tugging sharply on the blankets neither woke him up nor got her any of the sheets. With a disgruntled huff, she settled down. Almost instantly, he rolled over and caught her in an iron grip, pressing his face hard between her shoulder blades. The childlike desperation for comfort made it really hard to be annoyed. *At least I get some blankets out of it.*

Fumbling with the noise canceling headphones, she didn't have time to put them on before she heard it.

The soft wail of an infant.

It wasn't a completely foreign sound, given where they were. The powwow was always a big draw with families. For some, it was their best chance to catch up with family members that didn't live in town. With all the planes' tribes coming together for a week, it was basically a giant family reunion. On top of that, there was an endless stream of tourists that came and went at all hours. Kids and newborns were a common sight and, over the years, their fussing had become an easily dismissed background noise.

*So why is it bothering you now?* The thought made her put the headphones aside. Prying herself from Benton's grasp, she sat up again.

The rhythm of the newborn's cry was a steady pulse. She examined it carefully, trying to pick up on anything out of the ordinary. There was nothing. It just sounded like an infant that was too cold or hungry to stand it. But a chill still trickled down her spine. As the last tendrils of sleep slipped from her, she realized what was off.

*It's behind the teepee.*

The campsite was at the base of a buffalo jump. A thin stream snaked along the base, collecting seeds from a distant forest to disperse them along a river bend and create a small woodland. At her request, they had set up their teepee as far back from the others as possible, essentially nestling them amongst the smallest trees. Nothing was done with the area. No light had been set up, and no paths were ever cleared. There was no reason why anyone should be wandering around there at night. Especially with a child. It left an uneasy feeling in the pit of her stomach.

"Benton?"

She regretted the whisper the moment she spoke. Benton was only just starting to raise his standards on self-care. He was forcing himself to eat full meals and increase his napping routine. It had to be in short bursts. The dreams crept up quickly. While it was possible to wake him from them, he found it hard to live with himself. He needed to stay until the end to learn the victim's name. The peaceful beginning was a precious commodity that she didn't want to rob him of.

Benton protested as she moved out of his grasp. She tried not to take it personally that he was able to replace her once again with a blanket. A heavy grunt made her pause. The rage and bitterness contained within the sound turned her skin to ice. Pushing the sensation aside, she continued up onto her feet. *I don't know how he does it,* she thought. She couldn't fathom taking those monsters into her head, knowing that he'd never truly be rid of them.

The baby was still crying.

*It's probably just a lost tourist. I can handle that on my own.*

As quietly as she could, she pulled an oversized sweater over her pajamas and tiptoed around the 'campfire.' Silver moonlight flooded through the gap, giving her enough light to find her newly bought moccasins. The fur lining protected her feet from the frigid wind as she slipped outside. Why the organizers insisted on holding the powwow in winter was beyond her. Granted, the cold snap had come earlier than anticipated. A few more weeks and the snow would start to fall.

Wrapping her arms around her stomach, Nicole stomped her feet to keep her blood flowing, and she took in as much of the campground before her as she could. Thin trails of campfire smoke snaked above the glow of the fairy lights strung around the area. They weren't exactly a traditional decoration, but a necessity for meeting health and safety regulations. They kept the shadows from clinging to the center of the campsite but didn't reach much further beyond. The river was to her right and, beyond that, the sheer cliff face of the buffalo jump. To her left was the campsite for those who brought their own tents. And that seemed to mark the edge of the world. There were no other lights or signs of civilization. Only an endless sea of towering grass that churned in the near constant wind.

Tourists were always surprised by how luminous the moon could be. When every other light source was gone, and their eyes had time to adjust, the night could actually be quite bright. Even as the full moon crept down towards the horizon, it held enough strength to paint the world in bright silver. It allowed her to see all the way to the parking lot beyond the tents, although it was hard to make out any great detail.

The crying continued. Same as it had ever been; a breathless, repetitive bawling.

Pulling the sleeves of her sweater down over her fingertips, Nicole walked around the circumference of the teepee, tracking down the sound. The forest was quick to rise up before her. Moonlight battled to pass through the clustered leaves, but it was no use. Thick shadows made it was impossible to see anything beyond a few feet.

She hesitated.

The crying didn't. Soft but steady. Barely louder than a whisper. At times, she doubted that it wasn't just a trick of the wind.

She glanced back over her shoulder, torn between going further and sinking back into the relative warmth of the teepee. *Don't start something that you're not going to finish*, she told herself. Ducking back inside only long enough to snatch up her flashlight, she inched towards the crouching darkness.

The torch had been a gift from her father and featured a red light that helped preserve night vision, although, having everything bathed in crimson could be a little unnerving. The grass softened her footsteps, turning them into a low muffle as she approached the blanket of dead leaves. A breeze howled as it swept through the trees. Something swooped at her head, brushing against her scalp while never making a sound. Nicole dropped onto one knee, twisting around to weave her flashlight back and forth.

"Really?" Nicole muttered as she settled the beam onto a familiar owl.

It was easy to identify Bird, as Benton insisted on calling him, from the other great horned owls that were now constantly flocking to Benton's side. He had a dark line of fathers connecting his two 'horns,' leaving him constantly looking annoyed at everything around him. Benton insisted that was why they got along. Similar viewpoints. Really, the owl had risked its life to save Benton's, which was a surefire way to get on his good side. She knew that from personal experience. While Bird had healed up quickly and been released back into the wild, he refused to go far. It wasn't exactly a surprise to see him. The swooping was new though.

"Was that really necessary?" she hissed at the bird.

Perched upon a branch, Bird fluttered his wings and snapped his beak. Even though she had seen them for most of her life, Nicole had never really appreciated just how sharp their beaks were. Now they were always so close that it was kind of impossible to ignore it. Swallowing hard, she inched a little further away, slightly worried that Bird was about to swoop again. Catching the motion, Bird expelled another harsh squall. A shrill screech that by all rights should have woken half of the camp. Nicole's stomach almost plummeted into her shoes.

As a Banshee, a living omen of coming death, Benton had a close link with Death itself. The exact nature of it was beyond her, but the obvious connection was there. One that Benton seemed to willingly ignore. Whether he was willing to acknowledge it or not, it was a relationship that was quickly becoming symbiotic.

The Grim Reapers drew closer to him, visible to only *his* eyes, guiding him. And Benton always followed, willingly or not. He was important to death. Meaningful in some sense. As his closest friend, she had been in the position to help him survive the paranormal and human beings that threatened him. And that had, apparently, brought her into a very select group. One that warranted an early warning when danger was near.

She wasn't about to waste it.

"Okay, I get it," she told Bird and hurried to retrace her steps.

The soft crying grew dimmer as she rushed. A sickly-sweet smell filled her nose, coating her throat and thickening until she almost choked. Within a second, the cry became a mere breath again, but the smell thickened and turned rancid, almost making her gag as she pushed herself into a sprint.

The child's cry rang louder in her ears, growing until it was so desperate that it gripped her heart. She leaped through the last of the underbrush and spun around. Chest heaving and sweat starting to glisten on her forehead, she searched the trees with the crimson beam of her flashlight.

A gentle breeze stirred the leaves, the slight rustle making her jump and pushing her heartbeat back into a rapid pace. Bird's screech broke the night. Nicole took the hint and ran the rest of the way to her teepee.

# Chapter 3

Benton had decided that he wasn't going to leave the teepee.

The whole process had gone as well as could be expected. Come three a.m., he woke up screaming. It was a little disconcerting to open his eyes and see the teepee rattling violently around him. But it had held strong, and Dorothy had called a few moments later. She took in all the information he had to give. This time, there wasn't much to go on. A name, a Twitter account, and the knowledge that they'd die screaming in a wildlife park.

Being able to pass on the information instantly was a mercy that he never thought would be given to him. Before they had this arrangement, his attempts to share the warning had only led to trouble. No one reacted well to a complete stranger randomly telling them that they were going to die horribly. His parents had never understood that he couldn't keep it to himself. Holding it brought a blistering, bone-deep pain. It was torture.

Dorothy saved him from that.

After the call, he had curled in on himself and tried to hold onto the last shreds of his dignity. Nicole never teased him about his broken sobs or uncontrollable trembling, but he hated it anyway. Hated how he broke every time his real mind collided with the residue of what was left. It wasn't him. Logically, he knew that he hadn't done the things within his dreams. But he remembered it. The feeling of warm blood on his hands. The twisted delight of violence. Lust and rage and ecstasy all rattled inside him. They weren't just monsters in the dark, villains from a movie, who could really walk amongst the general population. They were real. Flesh and blood and utterly mundane. It had come to the point that he understood their reasoning far more than he did anyone else's. It terrified him that, one day, he might start agreeing with them.

Each dream chipped away at his mind, and he wasn't sure how much of him was left.

He had spent the rest of the night hating himself for not keeping it together. Nicole hadn't pressed him to talk. She just curled up against his spine and held him until he fell back asleep. It must have been a short nap because he didn't have time to dream again. Nicole had already headed out for her run, and he was alone with the voices in his head. It left him with the jittery need to get up and start moving. Since there was no way in hell he was going to show his face out there, he snatched up his phone, shoved in his earbuds, turned his music up until it hurt, and tried to stretch some of the tension from his muscles.

Having a flood of personalities constantly filling his head had given him eclectic tastes in music. He didn't know if it was the cellist that enjoyed killing her children or his own sway, but he had been on a classical music kick for about a week. *Cello Suite No. 2 in D Minor* filled his head as he pushed his legs out a little further and fell forward onto his elbows. His fingers drummed against the floor in time to the notes. While his skin hit the fur blanket, he felt the strings of the cello. He groaned and dropped his forehead onto the ground. *Just don't think,* he commanded himself.

Focusing on the music itself let everything else fall away, hollowing out his body until only the melody remained. He floated in that abyss until the flap suddenly drew back. The sound violently jerked him back into reality. He lifted his head to find Nicole stepping inside, her hip-length hair still dripping from a shower, and running gear balled in her hand. Benton went back to scrolling through his phone until he noticed that she had yet to move.

"Hey," he said as he tugged out one earbud.

"Hey," she chirped back. "Did you hear anything weird last night?"

Benton shook his head. "Why?"

"No reason."

He watched as she carefully hid whatever she was thinking behind a brilliant smile. *That's going to come back to bite me,* Benton thought, but decided to let it go for now.

"How was the run?"

"Mom and I were lazy today. We just did a three mile."

"That's lazy?"

She shrugged one shoulder as she crossed the room. Going back to his phone, he noticed her continued stare out of the corner of his eyes.

"We normally do a four mile. Six if we've been treating ourselves," she said.

"Huh."

While he was yet to meet Logan Rider, spending time with his wife and daughter had given Benton an insight into the family dynamics. The couple had known each other since birth, as most people in Fort Wayward do, but had only fallen in love once they had chosen their career paths. Dorothy had her eyes on the Royal Canadian Mounted Police. Logan wanted to get into the army. The elite Special Operations Forces Command, to be more specific. Both needed a workout partner who would push them. And both, apparently, were insanely competitive perfectionists. A trait they gave to their daughter in abundance. Needless to say, Benton and Nicole had very different definitions of 'lazy.' The earbud was almost back in his ear when he noticed that Nicole was still staring.

"Oh, great," he mumbled, pulling out both buds and turning off his phone.

"Sorry?" she asked.

"What are you obsessing over this time?"

She puffed out her cheeks in indignation. "Nothing."

"Your obsession face says otherwise. I'm gonna have to trust the face."

Shrugging again, she gestured to him loosely. "It's nothing. I just didn't expect to come in and find you casually sitting around in a full side split."

"It's called a straddle split," he corrected.

"Whatever," she said. "I think I have the right to be both impressed and surprised."

Benton rolled his eyes. Reaching forward, he shoved his phone back into his bag, noticing too late that he had once again grabbed Nicole's attention.

"How do you do that?"

"How is this surprising?" he grumbled. "I dance."

"You told me that you *like* to dance. There's a difference between getting your groove on and being able to do . . . that. You look like a ballerina."

Benton sucked in a deep breath and prepared himself for impact.

"You were! Like, with rehearsals and dedication and stuff? How long did you do it? How old were you? Oh, did you wear the tights and everything?" Her eyes grew wider. "Did your parents film your performances? I need to see those videos. Why didn't you tell me this?"

"Is that a serious question? Doesn't this" –he waved a hand in her direction– "cover exactly why I didn't tell you?"

"Huh?"

"You get way too into these sorts of things."

"I do not."

"In the space of three seconds, you had five follow-up questions."

"Okay," she said. "Well, I can reign it in. You can feel free to tell me anything."

He arched an eyebrow. "Really?"

"Of course."

"And you'll just take the information without saying anything? No questions."

"Not a one," she nodded.

A smile crept across his face. Logically, he knew that the nice thing to do would be to let this drop. But the opening was just too tempting. Pulling his legs together, he coaxed her closer. He waited until she knelt down to say.

"Yeah, there are tapes. I was really good. Only problem was I couldn't do the lifts."

Despite the eagerness on her face, she restricted her response to, "Oh. That's nice."

"You know how my teacher got around that?"

"If that is information you'd like to share, I'll listen. Of course, I'm not going to pry."

*Don't be cruel,* he told himself even while he knew he was going to. "I did the girl parts."

She held her breath until her face went red, her gaze locked on the far wall. It was as if she were afraid to move. Like she would break, and all the questions would come tumbling out. It was endlessly amusing to watch her fight her true nature.

"Nicole?" He grinned. "You don't have any follow-up questions for me?"

She shook her head, lips pressed into a tight line.

"Nothing you might want me to elaborate on?"

Again, a rapid shake.

"Oh, good. Well, in that case, let's never discuss this again. I'll get mom to destroy the tapes."

In about ten seconds, she looked ready to burst. She was vibrating with the need to learn every little aspect of what was happening around her.

"Nic? Are you breathing?"

"You're evil!"

Benton didn't even try to stifle his laughter.

She thumped him playfully on the shoulder. "What is wrong with you?"

"You really have issues," he said between gasped breaths. "I'm starting to worry that you're legitimately stalking me."

"What I do in my free time is my business."

"That's not reassuring."

Each attempt to get him to stop chuckling only made him laugh harder. His sides hurt by the time the teepee flap pulled back and Dorothy stuck her head in.

"Do you two always have to be so loud?" she asked.

Nicole and Benton shared a glance, each clearly recalling Benton's banshee screams. A sound that could knock aside a Mac truck like it was nothing and rise louder than the noise of a storm. They both started giggling again.

Dorothy rolled her eyes. "Hurry up. The Elders are waiting."

Chirping a 'right,' Nicole burst into action, swiftly primping herself into something 'presentable.' Not that she ever wasn't. High cheekbones, rich brown eyes, and a pretty face made up for a lot. He'd even seen her covered in Leana Sidhe's brain matter, and she was still kind of stunning. Benton, on the other hand, always took a while to get ready. At seventeen, he wasn't all too keen that his blonde hair was already starting to gray. It took a while for him to spike it up just right.

"Who are the 'elders'?" he asked as he pulled a jar of hair jell out of his backpack.

"The Tribal elders." Nicole said it like he should have known from the start. "The leaders from the local tribes gathered together for the powwow."

There were only three people in all of Fort Wayward that weren't tied to the Siksika tribe by blood or marriage; Benton and his parents. It meant that a lot of things went over his head. And, most of the time, people forgot that.

"So, they're important people?" he asked.

Nicole paused for a moment, brush halfway through her hip-long hair, and shot him a confused look. "Duh."

"Why would anyone important want to see me?"

"Wow. Humble," Nicole teased.

"You know what I mean."

"We've told them a bit about you," Dorothy said.

He snapped his head around to face her. "Like my love for the Chicago Cubs?"

"Obviously not," Dorothy deadpanned.

Rage flashed through him. "You told them I was a banshee? I never said you could do that."

"I never used that word," Dorothy said.

"Oh, good. Because definitions were the problem!"

Dorothy's eyes narrowed. "Keep your voice down."

"I told you about this," Nicole said.

"No, you didn't."

"I did. I said that we've organized for you to have some traditional healing sessions."

"What's that got to do with elders?"

"Obviously they wanted to know why an Irish boy was doing this."

He cocked his head to the side, still twisting peaks into his hair. "Irish boy?"

"Banshees are an Irish legend. I just assumed that you must have some Irish lineage somewhere in your family tree." A thought made her brush pause again. "Huh. I actually don't know much about your family. You never talk about your grandparents or cousins."

A small frown formed on his face. "I don't think I have any."

"Biology dictates that you have to have grandparents," Nicole pressed.

"Mom and dad never mention them. It's always just been the three of us."

"They're waiting," Dorothy cut in, holding up her watch to emphasize the time.

It worked far more on Nicole then it did on him. But, just to be respectful, he did hurry himself along. Keeping his sweatpants, he pulled a hoodie over his t-shirt and shoved his feet into well-worn sneakers. *Not the best outfit for first impressions,* he thought to himself. But there weren't any other options, so it would have to do. *It's not like I expected to meet anyone.* His social skills had narrowed over the months to the point that he just stood behind Nicole and let her Care-Bear levels of cheery energy handle things. If he stood still long enough, people often forgot he was there. It was the perfect set up.

"How do I look?" Nicole asked while smoothing down her skirt.

It was one she had picked up the day before. Bright red with traditional patterns. She kept her RCMP boots, however. That had quickly become her trademark.

"You look great, sweetie." The sweetness that filled Dorothy's voice died when she turned to Benton. "Are you ready?"

He flopped his hands to the side, the baggy sleeves of his hoodie feeling like wings.

"Yeah."

# Chapter 4

The sun was already rising up over the long sea of grass. Its glow turned the swaying strands a brilliant gold. A few people were bustling around, chatting happily in ever increasing groups as children raced around their legs. Most of them were new to the area; tourists or family members. He had forgotten what it was like to be surrounded by unfamiliar faces. Small town living had that going for it at least.

Hunching his shoulders against the chill, he followed behind the Riders as they waved through the crowd. No one paid him much attention.

The number of people thinned at last, and he looked up. Honestly, he had thought they'd be headed towards the larger, more beautifully decorated campsite. Not to a cluster of recreational vehicles. He supposed it made more sense since people would be coming from quite a distance around. They headed to one that had an array of wind chimes dangling from the small pull-out porch hanging. The array of metal and stained glass tinkled together in the cool breeze. Drawing his attention, he glanced up to notice the horned owl that fluttered down to sit upon the roof.

"What are you doing up at this hour?" Nicole cooed sweetly at it. Pushing up onto her toes, she craned her neck to get a better look at its coloring. "Is that Bird?" Benton shook his head. "Nah. Too big."

"You need to get some sleep, young lady," Nicole said with a jab of her finger.

A smirk crossed his face as he watched his best friend try and chastise a bird. It took a little bit of the awkwardness out of the situation, an edge that became razor sharp again the moment Dorothy knocked on the metal door. He wasn't the only one to feel it. Nicole practically snapped to attention. Her brightest, cheeriest smile locked into place on her face.

*This means a lot to her. Damn it. I'm gonna screw this up.*

He was already anticipating the lectures that were going to take place in his future. The air stirred. He thought it was the wind until he heard the loud squawk. One owl had turned into dozens. Talon tips scraped across the metal top as they restlessly fluttered and settled. Nicole looked at him from the corner of her eyes.

"Nervous?" she teased.

"I'm not doing this," he hissed under his breath.

Both Dorothy and Nicole looked at him, their silent judgment making the air as thick as tar.

"I'll just keep my mouth shut and let you guys do the talking," he said.

It was a little offensive that both women gave a long sigh of relief. He shoved his hands deep into the front pockets of his hoodie and clenched his jaw. The RV's door opened, revealing a woman who had only just begun to hunch over with age. Large circular glasses took up much of her face, balancing more on her high cheekbones than the bridge of her nose. Her hair was a wispy sheet of snow white that made her tawny skin seem darker. Her gaze cut him open as she slowly looked him up and down. Every inch of the journey was almost painful, and he squirmed under the scrutiny.

"Hi, Great-Auntie," Dorothy said.

Nicole waved. "Hi, Great-Great-Auntie. This is Benton."

*Of course, they're bloody related,* Benton thought. The Elder adjusted her glasses and continued to shred him with her gaze.

"Benton, this is Wapun Rider." Nicole swept her hand out to gesture between them, like they might have been confused who she was introducing to whom.

Benton forced a smile and nodded in greeting. The awkward silence was broken only by the distant chatter and the far nearer cry of the flock covering the RV.

"So you're the one Nicole keeps talking about," Wapun said, her voice a rough whisper, but still somehow warm.

"Yeah. Probably," Benton said.

Wapun chuckled, the sound dying quickly, and she leaned out again, this time tipping her face up to watch the birds.

"Owls during the day. Well, doesn't that seem like a bad omen?"

"They're just here because of Benton," Nicole rushed to soothe.

Benton glared at her.

"What? They are," she whispered to him. Turning back to her Auntie, she continued. "They tend to flock around him when he's sick or anxious."

"I haven't been sick since I got to Fort Wayward."

"Because every time you get the sniffles, I make you chicken soup and herbal tea. You're welcome."

Benton rolled his eyes. He wasn't prepared for the elderly woman to grab him by his chin and jerk his face back around to her.

"Yeah, I'm not a fan of being touched," Benton noted.

Wapun ignored the comment. "My, what a pretty boy you are."

The grip on his jaw kept him from shooting Nicole a 'what the hell' look. "Not particularly."

"I'm not saying you're attractive," Wapun dismissed.

His brow furrowed. "Okay."

"But pretty." She jerked his head around to view him from different angles. "I don't know how to describe it."

Benton heaved a sigh. Really, he'd had a good run. It hadn't come up in months. "I have androgynous features."

In the corner of his eyes, he noticed Nicole instantly twist around to face him.

"It's why I keep my hair short and wear tighter shirts. People get really annoyed when they confuse me for a girl."

Wapun seemed delighted to find the answer and continued to study him, holding him in place as Nicole and Dorothy inched in for a closer look.

"Huh," Nicole said. "How did I never notice that?"

"I can't un-see it," Dorothy noted.

Benton smacked Wapun's hand aside with a bit more force than necessary. Staring her down, he ignored Dorothy's hissed warning. Wapun smiled softly and nodded once.

"Well, let's get you inside. We have a few things to discuss."

She headed in first. After sharing a few glares at each other, the others followed. It was easier to endure Dorothy's glare than Nicole's analytical stare. She didn't even let up as they sat down on the little table set against the wall. There was hardly enough room for all of them to fit two aside, and Nicole was quick to push in beside him. She had yet to give up the staring. *This is going to be a long day.*

"Hot chocolate?" Wapun asked with a grandmotherly smile.

Benton shook his head. Wapun poured him one anyway and placed it before him. Wanting the warmth, he pulled his hands out of his pockets and wrapped them around the mug.

"The hoodie," Wapun began. "Is that to make yourself look bigger?"

*What is your obsession with my appearance?* "I just like baggy sweaters."

"Are you malnourished?"

"Sorry?"

"Your legs are almost as thin as your wrists," she almost chuckled. "Not to mention that slender neck of yours."

Benton returned his hands to his pockets.

"He is under his body mass index," Nicole said. "But only a little bit. I'm fattening him up."

"So many questions," Benton snapped.

"I think my math is right." Pulling out her phone, she brought up a BMI calculator. "You're five-foot-seven and 115.5 pounds, right?"

"When did you weigh me?"

"That puts you at 18.1," she continued. "You're supposed to be 18.5 for your height. So, you're underweight by 2.62 pounds."

"We have to repeat our talk about personal boundaries," Benton said.

"Are you anorexic?" Wapun asked.

Quickly losing his patience, he narrowed his eyes at the woman. "No. I just don't have an appetite."

"He likes spicy food," Nicole said.

"Will you stop it?" Benton snapped. "Wapun, if you've got a damn point, get to it."

The outburst had no effect on the woman. She watched him patiently, sipping from her mug before responding.

"I need to know your physical and mental state before we begin."

He arched his eyebrow skeptically. "For a spiritual cleanse?"

Wapun smirked. "Are you under the impression that this is going to be painless for you?"

That caught him off guard. Before he could think of anything to say, she continued, "we have to break you down physically to get to your mind. And that's where the real work begins. There is no greater torture in this world than confronting yourself."

"I know a few things that might be worse," Benton scoffed.

Her smile didn't fade. "The spirit world doesn't care about your feelings or self-esteem. Like nature, it's not always rainbows and sunshine. There is a cold, brutal side. It will break you down. Force you to become intimately aware of the darkest parts of yourself, reveal to you the raw truth, whether you can take it or not. How well do you truly know yourself, Benton?"

"Well enough. I'm not all that interesting."

"Do you always act like a jackass to keep from answering questions?"

"No. That's just the raw truth of my personality."

"Benton," Nicole whispered sharply. "Sorry, Auntie. He had a rough night and tends to be a bit grouchy in the mornings."

"It's alright, dear. I'm trying to push his buttons."

"You're succeeding," Benton muttered.

"One last question, little pixie." She smiled in the face of his growing anger. "What's your greatest fear?"

Benton kept his mouth closed.

Wapun sighed heavily. "If you can't even answer that, I'm not sure what I can do to help you."

Nicole sputtered as she grappled for a response. It was enough to spur Benton into answering.

"That I'll forget who I am."

Holding the cup between both hands, she hummed softly. "Interesting. Elaborate for me."

"You need me to elaborate on why I don't want to be a homicidal maniac? If you don't find it self-explanatory, I'm worried about you."

A smirk crossed the older woman's face. She hid it by taking a long sip of her drink. "Do you think this will happen?"

Benton could only shrug and swallow down the bile rising up his throat. The idea that he couldn't stand against the monsters in his head chilled his bones. Wapun took a moment to contemplate his response. At last, after another sip of the hot chocolate, she came to her conclusion.

"I'll help you."

"Thank you, Auntie," Nicole just about squealed in delight.

Whatever Wapun was going to say next, the words were lost under the wild cry of the owls. Within an instant, the air was filled with the scraping of their nails slashing across the metal roof. They all jumped at the sudden onslaught. Nicole leaned across him to peek out the window. Birds whirled around the RV, their numbers growing as the seconds passed.

"So, are you sick or anxious?" Wapun asked.

Benton pressed in near Nicole to catch a glimpse outside. A single figure stood amongst the chaos, the majority of its body frozen in time while its lower body curled and faded into the air. Somehow like both oil in water and fading smoke at the same time. The deep ebony figure watched them with a bone white face.

Benton nudged Nicole with his elbow.

"Death's here."

# Chapter 5

"I still can't believe you said that," Nicole mumbled, her arms folded tightly over her chest.

It hadn't taken long for the birds to calm down once more and scatter off into the clear Alberta sky. The impression had remained. Wapun hadn't given Benton her back ever since, and it seemed that most people in the camp were on edge.

"What? She is. Mic, your biggest fan." He gestured to a vacant space off to their left.

She knew she wouldn't see anything but couldn't stop herself from looking.

"Hey, Mic," she said, because annoyance was no reason to be rude. "Anyway, my point remains."

"I must have missed it."

Crossing his arms in what might have been a mockery of her, he shifted to stand shoulder to shoulder. The slight nudge made them both realize how much she had grown since he had arrived in town. She was almost matching him in height.

"You can't just blurt out that Death is here," she said.

"Aren't you the one who keeps saying I should be more open with the things I'm experiencing?"

"Yeah, but . . ." she huffed, not sure how she could regain higher ground in the conversation. "Just read the room."

He shrugged one shoulder. "Wapun said she needed to know the reality of my situation to help me. If she can't handle your favorite Grim Reaper coming over for a visit, then how's she going to deal with everything else?"

"You just wanted to freak her out."

"Do my motives change the facts?"

Nicole thought about that for a moment before releasing her anger with a bitter huff. "I hate when you win arguments."

"I know. That's why I love it so much."

He repeatedly nudged her with his elbow until she broke and shoved him back.

"God, you're annoying," she chuckled despite herself.

"I know."

One more nudge and she turned to shove him. Unfortunately, Wapun picked that same moment to emerge from the sweat lodge. Nicole cringed back in embarrassment. She always felt like a child around her Great Auntie, and this wasn't helping assert herself as a full-fledged adult.

"Everything's prepared," Wapun said.

Nicole nodded hurriedly and avoided eye contact with her snickering best friend. He truly loved to push her buttons.

"Thank you, Auntie," Nicole mumbled as her cheeks flamed.

Wapun's piercing gaze fixed straight onto Nicole. "He'll take this seriously."

Not a question. A statement and a warning.

"Yes, he will," Nicole hurried to assure.

It only took a split second to get her eyes on Benton, but she found his mouth already open in preparation for a snide comment. He caught her pleading look. The words died in his throat as a broken crackle, and he heaved a sigh.

"Yes, I will," he said solemnly. "Thank you so much for this opportunity."

Wapun nodded once, seemingly satisfied, and moved back into the sweat lodge. "Come in when you feel mentally prepared for it."

The moment the curtain closed, Nicole beamed up at him.

"Thank you," she said.

"Yeah, well, this really means a lot to you. So . . ."

"I'm going to have to hug you now."

While Benton heaved a long-suffering sigh, he did lift one arm to invite her in. She took advantage of it to quickly squeeze his neck.

"Are you ready?" she asked as she pulled back.

"I have no idea what I'm preparing for, but, yeah, let's say I am."

"Everything will be okay. I promise."

"Comforting. But completely lacking any further information."

"It's as good as you're going to get," she said. "Get inside."

Putting up little fuss, he slipped into the darkness, Nicole quick on his heels. Stepping into the steam was like jumping into a lake, leaving her instantly damp with sweat. They had all changed to prepare for the heat, but it still wasn't anywhere near enough to compensate. Sage was scattered across the ground, producing an earthy scent that went straight to her head. The combination was like breathing fire.

Benton clearly reeled from it at first. Wiping a hand over his face, he endured and slumped onto the patch of earth that Wapun motioned towards. Nicole moved to sit next to him.

"On the other side of the stones," Wapun said.

Obediently, she followed directions. The scorching stones made the air ripple, distorting her vision of Benton. He had a talent for saying a lot in a single expression. Right now, he was telling her that he was a little creeped out and not too happy that they had been separated. *I don't like this. I feel like a freak.*

She nodded at him. *It's going to be okay.* The silent reassurance was enough to have him remain in place.

Wapun dashed the stones with medicine water, making them glow red and spew steam like an angry dragon. Benton's pale face turned a dangerous shade of red, and he hunched forward, bracing his elbows on his knees to try and keep his balance. The sizzling hiss and babble of the nearby stream was the only sound for quite a while.

"I'm guessing that the heat's necessary," he said in barely more than a whisper.

"Of course. The sweat lodge is a gift from the Creator. It cleanses your spirit just as water cleanses your skin. The traditions are important. We're already changing it enough to accommodate you."

Benton actually looked bashful and hunched his shoulders like a turtle retreating into its shell.

"The sweat lodge is the womb of Mother Earth. You are safe here Benton," Wapun continued. "Nicole and I are here to guide you. We'll bring you back from wherever the spirits lead you."

Nervous energy started to show in the tight press of his lips. He gripped his hands tightly, soon releasing the hold again when the heat grew too uncomfortable.

"Breathe the steam in deeply," Wapun instructed.

His first attempt to suck it in left him coughing. Wapun hid her smile.

"Keep trying. Focus on your breath. Clear your mind and open yourself up to the spirits around you."

"That seems like a horrible idea."

He jolted at Wapun's scoff.

"White folks," she whispered to her niece.

Nicole giggled before she noticed Benton's questioning frown.

"Siksika don't really have the same perception of the paranormal as other cultures do," she hurried to explain. "We just accept it as another part of nature. There's no real need to rationalize it."

Something clicked inside his brain. "That's why you're always so keen to jump on the crazy train?"

"How is it crazy if I'm right?"

Wapun cleared her throat, and they both fell silent. When she was satisfied, she settled her focus onto Benton alone. "I'll admit that there are evil spirits. But you have to acknowledge that there are good ones, too. Invite the good ones to come to you now. Approach them humbly, and they will hear you."

It was clear that Benton wasn't ready to believe that. *He hasn't had much contact with things that weren't terrifying,* Nicole acknowledged to herself. Still, he drew in as deep a breath as he could, given the scented steam, and closed his eyes. Wapun began the ceremony. Although Nicole didn't come to the sweat lodge every year, she knew the prayers and songs enough to notice the parts that Wapun had altered. It was still the same overall request; guidance and protection. Nicole swept her plaited hair over one shoulder and tried to relax. Wapun's words stuttered to a stop when the temperature of the room suddenly dipped.

The stones continued to sizzle, spewing a continuous stream of heat into the air. Wapun dropped another ladle of the medicine water onto the stones. Still, the chill remained, a growing wall of ice that drifted across Nicole's back. Wapun shivered a second later. *It's going around the circle,* Nicole realized with a start.

"Benton." It came out like a broken whisper.

He didn't open his eyes, instead choosing to hum in acknowledgment.

"What's behind me?"

His eyes snapped open, growing wide as he quickly glanced around, never focusing on anything for more than a few seconds.

"Benton?"

\*\*\*

*Thump. Thump. Thump.*

The heavy rhythm was the only sound that remained in the world, each one a thick squelch that came from near and far at the same time.

"Nic-" He didn't get through the full word before he noticed what was off.

While the rhythm remained stable, the rest of the world had slowed down, reducing to a slow creep that stretched the seconds out into minutes. The muscles of Nicole's face gradually bunched. It took him a long moment to realize that she was speaking.

The sudden screech of an owl made him jump. The flaps of the tent rattled as the bird beat its body against it. A rapid, wild fluttering that didn't match the slowed down world. He looked helplessly to Wapun and Nicole, looking for some form of guidance. Neither of them could shake off the effects that had settled upon them. Heart slamming against his rib cage, he got to his feet and hesitantly approached the exit. His fingers trembled as they wrapped around the edge of the flaps. All the while, the sound continued.

*Thump. Thump. Thump.*

"Trust in the good spirits," he muttered to himself.

One final glance back and he gripped the curtain tight. Before he could stop himself, he ripped it back and stepped out into the blinding light. Icy air bombarded his overheated flesh, freezing his sweat, making him shiver violently.

*Thump. Thump. Thump.*

Hands balled into fists, he stepped forward, his legs threatening to drop him. The camp was set far from the sweat lodge to give its users some privacy. He could still spot people in the distance, each one of them suffering the same state as Nicole and Wapun. Whatever the cause, the influence went far beyond the sweat lodge. Crows hung high overhead, the flock moving far too slow to stay aloft. Trees looked more like seaweed swaying with the soft motion of placid water. The grass swayed and rippled.

*Thump. Thump. Thump.*

He glanced around to find the bird, the only other creature he knew of that wasn't trapped in the elongated time. Its caw came in a burst from behind him, and he whirled around to see it.

"Bird?"

His somewhat pet flapped its colossal wings, the feathers moving soundlessly through the air. Mind whirling, he could only come up with one answer.

"I don't know anything about this," he babbled nervously. "Is this what they mean by a 'spirit animal'? Like, you're here to help me?"

Bird made a weird rattling, clicking noise, almost a purr. Benton took that as confirmation. *So mine's the omen of death? Great. Isn't that a refreshing change?*

*Thump. Thump. Thump.*

The noise sent dread pulsing through his veins. His bravado shattered like glass, and he couldn't gather up the pieces again. Trembling slightly, he turned his head towards the sound. *It's by the river.*

"We don't have to go over there, do we?" he asked Bird.

The horned owl beat its wings once and took flight. Looking serene and majestic, it swooped low to the earth before climbing higher, all the while heading off behind the sweat lodge. His dread turned to fear as he realized Bird was carving a path towards the one place he didn't want to go.

*Don't go,* a voice whispered in the back of his head, even though he knew he didn't have a choice. Whatever was going on, it was for a purpose. And he doubted that the creature in control would allow him to leave until the purpose was complete.

*Thump. Thump. Thump.*

His heartbeat fell into step with the slick beat. Grass crunched under his feet and brushed against his hands as he made his way to the stream. At first, the walk seemed to take hours. A constant trudge forward. Endless. Terrifying. Then the grass parted, and the river came into view. The banks were lined with figures, hunched down so that their bone-thin legs were folded on either side of their torsos. The skin of their back was stretched so tight, it showed off every contour of their arched spines. There wasn't a single stitch of clothing on their haggard forms, leaving only their long, matted hair to cover themselves. In perfect unison, arms that looked barely strong enough to lift a feather flipped soaked clothing over their heads, slamming them back down onto blood-soaked stones.

*Thump. Thump. Thump.*

Bloody water oozed from the fabric with every strike. There were dozens of the withered women, the combined efforts staining the river red. Whispers hit his ear. A thousand people speaking at once.

*Names.*

It hit him like a solid blow. Just like waking from his dreams, knowledge that wasn't his own became lodged in the forefront of his mind like a burning spike. *Prophesies. They're all speaking the names of people who are going to die.* Throwing himself back made his knees buckle. The moment he hit the ground, the distorted women snapped their heads around, locking their tiny eyes upon him. Panic swelled within his chest until his ribs threatened to shatter. He gulped for breath but still felt like he was drowning.

The women didn't make a move towards him. They didn't do anything but stare at him as their voices grew louder in his head. Harsh, hissed, voices that chipped away at his skull. There were too many names. All of it coming too fast. He couldn't make any of it out.

*Thump. Thump. Thump.*

Benton clamped his hands over his ears, trying to dull the onslaught. It was useless. The sounds only continued to grow until it rivaled the wail of a hurricane.

*Thump. Thump. Thump.*

Bloody clothes hit the stones, spewing fresh torrents of crimson out into the water. A coppery stench filled the air, gathering until he almost gagged. Motion drew his attention back to the grotesque figures. Unseen hands rose up from the river, latching onto the women at random and dragging them down into the depths. It didn't matter how many they took. The whispering never stopped.

A cry lodged in his throat as the strip of red began to bulge and writhe. Patches of ebony broke through the surface, rising up and forging themselves in the towering figures of the Grim Reapers. Benton scrambled further away, stopping only as his back hit a sheet of ice.

His breath lodged in his throat, choking off his scream. It was small comfort to find Mic, the particular Grim Reaper that had befriended Nicole, looming above him. Over the months, Mic had become a near-constant presence, and Benton latched onto that familiarity now. Like all the others, its body was a bottomless abyss gouged into reality, broken only by bone-white smears that served as its hands and face. Mic rippled under Benton's pleading gaze, her body stretching out like living smoke, shrouding him, cocooning him, shielding him tight against the ever-increasing noise of the others.

*Thump. Thump.*

The silence shook him to his core. There was peace in it. An unstable serenity that left him panting hard. He didn't recall gripping his head in his hands, and they shook violently as he peeled them off. The darkness was gone, replaced by the stark, almost blinding, white. *Don't look up,* he told himself. *Don't react.* This, like following Bird, wasn't really an option. On his knees, he gathered his courage and glanced up, searching for another glimpse of Mic's familiar oblong face.

The last tendrils of black smoke fell away from the glistening body of a young woman. Barely ten years older than Benton himself, the woman consisted of only two colors. A polished mother of pearl gray claimed the long, flowing tendrils of her hair and delicate skin. The dress she wore was of the same shade, making it hard to tell flesh from material. Her lips and eyes kept the Grim Reaper's polished onyx. Slowly, she extended a hand, offering to bring him up to his feet. After a moment's hesitation, he took it.

It wasn't the human pliability of the skin that surprised him. Instead, it was the warmth. He was literally holding the hand of death. *Shouldn't it be cold?*

She wrapped her fingers delicately around his. The gentle touch made him jerk his gaze up to hers. There was something haunting about Mic's face. The lines and curves whispered something on the edges of his mind. Niggling at him until it clicked. *She looks like me.*

A little rounder in places. Thinner in others. But nevertheless sharing the overall aesthetic.

"Mic?" he asked.

A small, wistful smile curved the corners of her lips as her eyes softened.

Logically, he knew that the Grim Reaper had chosen the image in some attempt to put him at ease. He was grateful for that. But there was no suppressing his eerie shudder. It was like looking into a funhouse mirror. He flinched away when Mic rose a hand. Her delicate fingertip hovered a few inches from the side of his face, testing to see if he moved again. When he held his ground, she closed the distance separating them and cupped his cheek. The tenderness in the touch almost burned him. He longed to move away but was terrified to leave the only slither of protection that had been offered to him. He locked his knees and held his ground, enduring the contact as best he could.

Eventually, Mic's hand moved. Instead of falling away, it rose towards his hairline and sunk into his sweat-drenched hair. There was no hesitation in the motion. Her fingertips went straight for the scar hidden beneath his pale hair. The long, curved gash that marked where the doctors had repaired his shattered skull. He could almost feel the metal plate embedded in his skin warm at the contact. A fine tingle raced across his nerve endings, surged inside him until he felt like his skin contained the churning ocean. He tried to pull away and found that he couldn't. The sensation increased, crackling within his lungs and sparking over his brain in fireworks.

*Thump. Thump. Thump.*

The sounds of the blood-soaked washing came sloshing back into his ears. Each pulse accentuated his thundering heartbeat.

*Thump. Thump. Thump.*

The whispering came along with the noise. Within seconds, it was back to its unbearable level, driving down onto him until his legs buckled under the weight. He dropped hard to the ground and found himself sinking deep into blood-stained muck. The noise grew louder still, echoing within the marrow of his bones, grinding him into the earth, burying him into the mud. Stray bones clattered against his limbs. The soaked soil was filled with rotting bodies and bare bones.

"Mic," he gasped.

He looked up, desperate to find any form of help. What met him was a look full of sorrow. Slowly, she turned away from him. Through the searing pain in his skull, he followed her gaze, looking on in horror as monsters began to claw their way from the earth. An army of thousands. Millions. Watching the horde surge towards him turned his flesh to ice. The ground rattled with their approach. Strong vibrations that drove him deeper into the mud. Twisted reeds crept over his shoulders like living creatures, wrapped around him, and dragged him down.

The sudden jerk whipped him back, and he caught a quick glimpse of the woman hovering before him. Her skin like milk and her hair a flowing stream of black ink. Sick delight danced within her eyes as she watched Benton struggle against the tightening grass. The next hard pull dragged him completely under the surface and into his own grave.

# Chapter 6

Nicole sat on the far side of their fake fire, close enough to keep a constant visual. But far enough that Benton had, for hours now, completely ignored her presence.

Most of the time, it was easy to forget that Benton wasn't human. Not entirely. He was a Banshee, and that made things unpredictable, especially when anything supernatural was concerned. She'd seen it herself more than once. Fire that she couldn't see or feel left him permanently scarred. He immediately overdosed on the venom of the *Leanan Sidhe* instead of getting high. A *Baykok's* arrow, which sent anyone else into a deep sleep, did not affect him at all.

Going in, she knew that he could have a bad reaction to the cleansing ritual. Nicole had spent hours preparing for anything she could think of. She had convinced herself that she was ready. It was devastating to realize just how wrong she had been. All of her plans had hinged on one certainty; that he would talk to her.

The process sent him into a deep trance. A bit worrisome but not completely out of the ordinary. She watched him carefully as the hour stretched on, her stomach knotting up as his ever-present expression of irritation melted into placid neutrality. There hadn't been any warning. Like he'd been struck by a lightning bolt; his whole body jerked, and he crumbled. The epileptic fit took full hold before he hit the ground. Every muscle clenched and twitched. Tendons bulged under the slender column of his throat. Each vein pushed against his rapidly discoloring skin, and froth seeped from his mouth.

Her years of first aid training kicked in automatically. Without thought, she rushed to his side, moving him farther away from the heated stones so that his long limbs wouldn't touch them, and kept Wapun from putting anything in his mouth. In time, he settled. But his eyes remained closed. Even now, the memory of that cold, crippling silence haunted her.

She completely lost count of how long it took for him to come back to her. His storm-gray eyes didn't hold their usual tendency and wouldn't focus on her. Still, she almost sobbed with relief to see them.

The seizure left him as weak as a kitten. If he hadn't leaned against her, he wouldn't have been able to sit up at all. Sweat that was cold to the touch trickled down his skin in rivulets, and he rattled with the aftershocks. None of her words of encouragement seemed to reach him. When he started speaking, it was more like he was muttering to himself, recalling the bare basics of his experience in a whispered breath. All the details he kept to himself.

Wapun hadn't listened to Nicole's pleas to keep from pressing too hard. She knew it was too soon. But Wapun sharpened her voice and demanded answers. In response, Benton had struggled to his feet and worked his way back to the teepee with a wobbling stride. There, he had collapsed onto his blankets, curled up onto his side, and stopped responding altogether. The most he did was shiver violently when the air cooled the sweat against his skin. The morning crept into the late afternoon, and he hadn't spoken another word.

Winter air chilled his skin, leaving him trembling aggressively. Draping her blankets over him succeeded in stopping the trembling, but nothing more. So she started her ritual; waiting patiently for him to come around in his own time.

Night had fallen about an hour ago, and all of her hope turned into dread. However, even fear wasn't enough to keep hunger at bay. She pressed a hand against her stomach, trying to dull the ache. It wasn't all that effective. An answering growl echoed from Benton's stomach.

"Are you hungry?" Nicole asked.

Benton didn't so much as blink in response.

"How about some of the stew I've been talking about?" she pressed. "You know, it's the only place you can get it. Mrs. Milton only makes it for the festivals."

Again, there was only silence. Nicole remained where she was until the gnawing feeling in the pit of her stomach became too much to ignore.

"Benton," she whispered, trying not to startle him. He didn't even flinch. "It's almost six o'clock. I'm going to quickly go get us some dinner, okay? And I'll get you some water, too. You have to be dehydrated."

Still nothing.

"I'll be back before you know it," she promised as she rose to her feet.

Sitting for hours left every muscle in her legs as dense as rocks. She staggered the first few steps to the flaps, barely remembering to grab her wallet and phone on the way out. *Not that he's going to call me,* Nicole told herself. Still, she shoved it into the pocket of her yoga pants. *I probably should have a shower, too.* Even while she thought it, she knew there wasn't a chance in hell that she was going to leave Benton alone for long. *I should get Zack or one of the twins to sit with Benton while I'm gone.* Her phone was in her hand before she realized that might not be the best idea.

It wasn't that they weren't on good terms. Most of the time, it seemed like they could get along. As much as Benton got along with anyone, that was. Things changed when they recalled that he wasn't quite human. When they remembered what he could do with his voice alone. She wasn't quite sure why it bothered them so much. All three of them were still enthralled by ghosts.

*Benton's way more interesting than any ghost.* Deciding not to put any of her friends into that awkward situation, she put her phone back and pushed her way out of the tent.

One step and she was struck with the knowledge of just how out of control the situation was. Owls now covered the campsite like a swarm of locusts. The colossal birds perched on every surface and covered the ground like a living blanket. They fluttered around the sky like drifting leaves in autumn. Razor sharp talons glistened like polished onyx in the last rays of sunlight.

Her sudden presence stirred the birds closest to their teepee. Feathers toppled down like snow as they fled from the overhead branches. The ones at her feet furiously squawked and clicked their beaks. The sound produced was eerily similar to bones rattling. Suddenly very aware of her bare feet, she shuffled back slightly, disturbing the owls that had resettled in the minimal space between her and the teepee opening. Swallowing thickly, she couldn't help but stare at the array of beaks around her. Until they were this close, it was easy to ignore how sharp they were. Small but perfectly curved to cleave flesh from bone.

The gathering flock had thinned the crowds. Without moving forward, she could see that a mass number of tourists had fled, taking down tents and clearing the parking lot. Those that remained stayed close to their homes or huddled in the food and souvenir area. It was the only place where the sheer number of people had kept the birds from taking hold.

A handful of people were trying to move the birds along; banging fry pans, whipping shirts around their heads, and working in teams to heave large blankets. It went about as well as trying to hold back the rising tide. Newly arriving owls quickly filled any pathway they managed to create. Eyes wide, she surveyed the scene before her.

*Where are they all coming from?*

Mind-reeling, she unintentionally caught sight of a few Elders. Three of them stood on the edges of the eating area, talking amongst themselves while they stared in horror at the still increasing numbers. Superstitious or not, it was going to be hard for anyone to dismiss a mass gathering of the living omen of death. The pit of her stomach went cold when she saw Wapun join the group. *She knows about Benton*, a voice whispered in the back of her head. She'll blame him.

Instantly, she tried to chastise herself for even having such a thought, stubbornly keeping hold of her righteous indignation even as she reminded herself that this was kind of his fault. Glancing over her shoulder, she contemplated heading back in to keep close to him in the off chance that anyone had the sudden urge to demand answers. That option was gone when she checked on the group of Elders again and accidentally caught their eyes.

*Don't arouse suspicion.*

Nicole's back stiffened at the internal demand. Forcing her cheeriest smile, she waved at the group. They looked at her like she was an idiot. Not the intended reaction. Hurriedly, she surged forward, ignoring the angry birds shifting out of the way of her bare feet. She was halfway to the food tent when it struck her that casually strolling amongst harbingers of doom probably wasn't the best way to look nonchalant.

With everyone concerned with the sudden infestation, she was able to get to the front of the line pretty quickly. The aroma of steaming buffalo stew and fresh mint balm tea made her mouth water. It was a source of injured pride that she could never get the recipe right on her own. Distracted by the gnawing ache in her stomach and the promise of a warm meal, she almost ran straight into the person who suddenly cut into her path.

"Mrs. Bertrand," she gasped. *Oh, not now.* "How are you? I hope you and Mr. Bertrand are enjoying yourselves."

"Where's Benton?"

Reluctantly, Nicole came to the conclusion that Benton's mother really didn't like her. It wasn't that the woman tried to hide it. Her animosity seeped into every chipped word she shot Nicole's way. Also, they'd almost known each other for a full year and she still insisted on calling her *Miss Rider*. That was a pretty big hint. Despite Nicole's attempt to win her over, Mrs. Bertrand had only grown more dismissive.

"He's resting," Nicole said as sweetly as she could.

"At this hour?"

"The sweat lodge is a lot more physically grueling than people give it credit for."

This didn't appease the older woman. With a sharp twist of her mouth, she snapped. "Please tell him to get his stuff together. We're going home."

"Home? Why?"

Mrs. Bertrand gestured to the birds.

"They'll head off soon," Nicole assured.

"This obviously isn't normal. Something is very wrong."

*Are you kidding me?!* Nicole had to bite her cheeks to keep from laughing in Mrs. Bertrand's face. Or scream. Or both. *This is where you draw the line? Your son having prophetic dreams for a decade is just luck, but a few birds get together and suddenly you're open to supernatural explanations?*

Schooling her features, Nicole fought to keep her smile. "Wild animals can be unpredictable. I know it can seem very intimidating for someone not used to having them around."

"I don't know why you're arguing this," Mrs. Bertrand snapped. "You don't have a say."

"It's just that Benton's been having so much fun. And it's great to see him being social."

"Why are you so obsessed with my son?!"

The sudden outburst caught Nicole off guard. She flinched back, her heels knocking into a few owls and sending them scurrying away.

"I'm his best friend," she stammered.

Mrs. Bertrand's eyes narrowed into deadly slits. "I don't know how you fooled my son, but I assure you Miss Rider, I see right through you."

"I just want what's best for him."

"Funny. That's exactly what his other stalker said."

Nicole choked on her breath. *Benton was stalked? By a human?*

"Oh, I'm sorry. Did you think you were the first?" Mrs. Bertrand continued.

"I'm not-"

"Cheyanne!" Nicole sagged with relief to hear her mother's voice. A moment later, Dorothy Rider came charging to the rescue. "There you are. Ready for dinner?"

Cheyanne's shoulder's stiffened. *Still not comfortable around my mom, huh?* Later on, Nicole would chastise herself for finding some malicious glee in that thought, but right now, she was just going to enjoy having the backup.

"Constable–"

"Come on," Dorothy cut in. "We've been through this. When I'm not in uniform, you don't have to address me by rank. Dorothy is fine."

"Dorothy," Cheyanne said hesitantly. "I was just letting Nicole know that I'm taking Benton home."

"It's only day two of the festival."

"But–"

"You promised your son a week."

Dorothy had already taken hold of Mrs. Bertrand's arm. Talking while she moved made it easier for the RCMP officer to lure the woman away. Neither one of them said goodbye to Nicole as they disappeared into the crowd. *Distract and disarm.* It was a motto her mother said often, and no one could follow it through like she did. That was why the three of them had decided it was Dorothy's job to keep Benton's parents busy and out of the way. Nicole knew that she didn't have the time to dwell on what would happen if her mother failed in that task. She had already left Benton alone too long.

As much as she wanted to be there for him when he woke up, she was half hoping that he would be back to his normal, irritated self by the time she got back. No such luck. He was exactly where she had left him. Blocking the wind kept a small amount of warmth in the place. Her frozen feet melted slightly as she crossed the fur blankets. She sat down with only a few inches separating them. Still, he didn't look at her.

"Benton?" she whispered.

Careful not to spill, she placed a bowl down before him, hoping that the scent might draw him out. *Good luck.* Benton wasn't food driven at the best of times. *Might have a better shot with the water,* she thought. Shuffling until her hip pressed softly against his stomach, she cracked open one of the bottles and held it out to him.

"Come on, Benton. You're bound to be dehydrated. Can you take a sip? You don't have to talk."

He barely blinked.

"Please," she stressed. "You're really scaring me."

Benton's even breathing staggered for a second. Finally, his eyes flicked towards her. While he kept his silence, he did move, slowly extending a hand out the few inches needed to grasp the bottle.

"Here, I'll help you get your head up."

He didn't say a word as she awkwardly shuffled around until he could rest his head against her lap.

The small angle change made it easier for him to swallow down a few mouthfuls. Afterward, he just curled into her and wrapped his arms around her waist, clutching her close like a terrified child. She began to card her fingers through his hair, letting her nails scrape along his scalp. It was a gesture she had noticed him do to himself when he was looking for comfort.

Soft hair gave way to the long hard ridge of his old surgical scars. Curiosity burned inside her like embers. Using less than legal means, she had read all of the police files and medical reports on his attack. On the metal plate that now held his skull together. He never really talked about it, and she didn't press, but that didn't mean she didn't want to know. The problem was that he was always self-conscious about it. She was half sure that was the real reason behind his obsession with his hair.

It spoke volumes about his state of mind that he was letting her touch it at all. He didn't even seem to notice it.

"Do you think you can take one more mouthful?"

He did the bare minimum to make that happen. If she wasn't so relieved that he was finally getting some fluids, she would have found it funny. A little whimper passed his lips, and he resumed his position, melting under the constant motion of her fingers.

"Everything's going to be alright," she told him.

"You can't promise that."

*First words you say in hours, and it's to be snarky*, she thought with a slight smile.

"Have I ever broken a promise to you?"

Benton's voice sounded as if he had been screaming for years. "I'm going to die."

The air left her lungs in a sudden gasp. "What? No, you're not. I mean, one day, sure, we all do. But that's not going to be any time soon."

"There were bones in the earth," he said in a whisper. "It was a graveyard. That's what Mic was trying to tell me. I'm going to die."

"Is that what you're so worried about? Benton, you've always been connected with death."

He rolled his head on her thigh to look up at her.

"Don't think for a second that I'm not taking this seriously," she rushed. "I'm just saying that you might have misinterpreted it."

"Misinterpret?"

"Yeah. There's a lot of things that could mean."

He arched an eyebrow. "Like what?"

"Well, reaffirming your bond, maybe. Or maybe it's meant to draw your attention back to the barn. Or the pit."

"Huh?"

"The cursed fire in the basement. The police found the victims of the *Leanan Sidhe,* but no one else ever saw the fire that burnt you. And, we really haven't done anything about that. It's been bothering me since our trip into the forest. We saw what becomes of cursed ground. We can't just ignore it, right?"

Benton stared blankly up at her as he mulled it over. Finally, he rolled his face away.

"Right."

All she could do was continue to card her fingers through his hair, hoping that it would be some kind of comfort to him. She didn't trust herself to speak too much. Now wasn't the time to ask him about what his mother had confessed. She shoved it to the back of her mind but couldn't stop her brain from working on it. *Why wasn't there any mention of it in any of the police files? How far did it go?* Biting her lips, she forced herself to focus on the here and now. *Benton needs you.*

"We'll deal with it together, Benton. Just like always."

He was silent for a long moment. Long enough that she began to worry he had retreated back into his shell.

"You can't always protect me," he said in a whisper.

"Sure I can."

His arms tightened around her. A small smile crossed her face as she hugged him back as best she could.

"You still can't find out anything about Banshees, right?"

"That seems uncalled for," Nicole mumbled.

"Have you ever thought that's because we don't have a long lifespan?" Benton continued.

"You're just having a bad day," she said, making her voice as gentle as possible. "It'll all be better in the morning. So stop thinking like this, okay?"

He looked up at her again, a forced smile curling his lips. "Don't get killed because of me."

"Benton—"

"No, you're stubborn and stupid about these kinds of things. When it comes down to it, you need to save yourself."

"Stop with this—"

His eyes sharpened. "I will as soon as you promise."

She stammered.

"Promise me, Nicole!"

"I promise."

She regretted the words the instant they left her. It wasn't often that she lied to him, and it left a bitter taste in her mouth. But the fib calmed him. With a somewhat contented sigh, he burrowed closer to her and closed his eyes. *I'll correct him later*, she decided, rather proud of herself for getting him to relax a little more.

His breathing evened out and he steadily became heavier against her thighs. Suddenly, the walls of the teepee vibrated violently as hundreds of silent birds took flight. She looked up to the gap in the roof, watching as they crossed over the diming sky in a swarm. A sense of accomplishment rushed through her, strong enough to chase off her looming sense of dread.

*The elders will still be suspicious.* Right now, with Benton finally talking to her again, it would take a lot more than that to dampen her mood. *We'll deal with it in the morning.*

She reached over him to collect her own bowl of stew and took a large victory spoonful. Benton was alright. At least for now.

*We'll figure the rest out tomorrow.*

# Chapter 7

A solid whack across his face ripped Benton violently from sleep.

His heartbeat throbbed within his nose, making his eyes water as he struggled to understand where he was, what was going on, and who the hell was attacking him.

"Benton?"

Nicole's sleepy voice broke through his haze of panic. Reality snapped back into place, and he released an annoyed grumble. Grabbing her arm, which was currently still draped over his face, he gave her a shove. Hard enough to roll her over.

"What? What? What?" she asked in rapid succession.

Still blurry-eyed, she reared her upper body off the ground and looked down at him. This time, she got all the way through her intended sentence.

"What's going on?"

"You hit me in the face," he groaned.

"Huh?"

Rolling his eyes, he reached up and pulled one side of her noise-canceling headphones away from her ear.

"You hit me."

"Oh, sorry," she winced. "Does it hurt?"

He grumbled and rolled onto his side.

"Sorry," she said again, pressing against his spine and sweetly whispering in his ear, "don't be mad."

In her haste, her ice-cold feet ended up pressed against his calves. He jerked at the sudden onslaught.

"Get off," he said with a halfhearted shove. "You're freezing."

"Are you still mad at me?" she challenged, hugging him tightly.

"What the hell is wrong with you?"

"I'm remorseful!"

As much as he wanted to maintain his anger, he ended up chuckling. "Just go back to sleep, Nic."

"Are you sure?"

"I will forgive you right now if you stop talking and go back to sleep," he muttered, elbowing her in the ribs to both prove his point and make sure she didn't take too much offense. It was all about balance. "Limited time offer."

"Deal," she chirped.

Instantly, he was released from her icy grip. What followed was a lot of shuffling and a few stray bumps and nudges. He opened his mouth to demand that she return to her side of the 'fire.' The words didn't come out. His soul still felt raw and, while he wasn't excited about any actual interaction, he wasn't ready to be on his own.

After what felt like hours, Nicole finally settled, curling against his spine like a cat, but mercifully keeping her feet tucked away. A small smile curled one corner of his lips as he closed his eyes and tried to return to the sweet oblivion of sleep. There was a slim possibility that he might be able to get a few more hours before the nightmares dragged him under.

Just as he started to drift, he caught the first cries of a newborn baby. He groped blindly for a pillow to shove over his head. Nicole, on the other hand, bolted upright and started nudging his shoulder.

"Benton? Are you awake? Benton?"

He smacked at her hand and released an indignant groan.

"Do you hear that?"

Keeping his eyes firmly closed, he grunted.

"Benton," she whispered. "Hey, wake up."

"I'm awake."

"So?" she asked, puzzlement clear in her voice. "Why didn't you answer me?"

"The grunt was my answer. It's a baby. They're around."

"You don't feel anything strange about it?" she pressed.

"They're tiny irrational creatures that are always sticky," he mumbled. "Of course they're strange."

"Okay, I'm totally going to round back to your perception of children later. However, for now, can you wake up and focus, please?"

When he didn't get up, she shook him again.

"Benton," she whined.

"Oh my God, what?"

He jerked upright. His sudden motion ended with their shoulders colliding and both of them almost toppling over. It didn't make her miss a beat.

"Well? Concentrate."

He huffed. "It's a baby."

The moonlight was enough to see the annoyance scrunching up her face. *Does she have to do this the one night I'm actually getting a decent night's sleep?* Changing tactics, she gave him her sweetest smile. The one she always used when she wanted something.

"Please, Benton? Just try. I've got pretty good instincts for this sort of thing. And after last night–"

"What happened last night?" he cut in.

She stammered for a moment. "I'm not sure. But that doesn't mean I'm wrong."

"You're not going to let this go, are you?"

"Of course, I will. The second you do what I'm asking."

All the while, that smile remained locked on her face. Sensing defeat, he huffed a sigh and closed his eyes, making sure she knew just how annoyed he was.

He still wasn't sure what the hell it meant to open himself up to the cosmos or whatever it was he was supposed to do. For the most part, he tried to imitate the psychics he'd seen on T.V., just so it looked like he was doing something. He closed his eyes and took a deep breath, trying to focus on the sound alone. It was a shock when he actually felt the shift. Something inside him seemed to slide. A fluid motion that made him physically jolt.

"You sensed something, didn't you?" Nicole said swiftly. "The sound's wrong."

Benton couldn't pinpoint what it was about the constant whine that struck him as wrong, but he was certain that it existed.

"So," Nicole said softly. "I was right."

His eyes snapped open. "Really? Had to mention that one now?"

She shrugged innocently just as the wail began to move. They both turned around, shifting to track the noise as it circled their teepee. Soft but shrill, the longer he heard it, the deeper the sound cut into him. It approached the flaps of the teepee. They both threw themselves back, scrambling away without taking their eyes off the entrance. A passing breeze rippled the fabric, allowing the cry to enter. It curled against his skin like a frothing wave. A firm push that forced him back onto his elbow. Nicole whipped around to check on him but was unable to keep her eyes off of the tent for long.

As suddenly as it had started, it ended, leaving them to the steady chirp of the crickets. Nicole's hand gripped his shoulder tight.

"Come on," she whispered.

"Sorry?" he hissed back.

"We can't let it get away."

Benton tore his arm from her fingers. "Are you insane?"

"Just because it's something weird doesn't mean that it's evil."

"Besides me, name one supernatural creature we've met that hasn't tried to kill you."

"Just to be clear, I *can't* use you as an example?"

"Yeah. That's what the 'besides me' part meant."

Her silence spoke volumes. "I'm still going."

Benton watched her slip outside into the cold.

"Damn it," he muttered and hurried to follow her.

In his desperation to catch up, he completely forgot what he was wearing. The night air cut straight through his thin, and still damp, shirt. He wrapped his lithe arms around his stomach and hunched his shoulders. It didn't do much good. Shivering, he scanned his moonlit surroundings. A low murmur of life rolled to him from the main campsite. A nearby crunch of leaves made him turn. The crunch of dried grass made him twist around. Static electricity raced through his bones, a burst of energy that left him on edge and trembling.

"Nicole?" he asked the shadows that clung to the looming trees surrounding him. "Nic?"

"Over here."

*Yeah, Benton. Just follow a disembodied voice into the dark forest*, he thought bitterly. A rush of movement made him lurch back. Nicole emerged from the shadows with a frustrated sigh, grabbed his hand, and tugged him along behind her.

"Hurry up, you'll miss it."

"That's the idea," he snapped back.

Still, he didn't try to escape her grasp as they crashed their way into the forest. His longer legs made avoiding the smaller shrubbery a little easier, and he lobbed his way through, going wherever she dragged him. She weaved them around the trunks and somehow found a slender path. They had to run single file to fit. Her fingers tightened to a crushing grip as they ran deeper, a clear sign that she wasn't as carefree about the situation as she was trying to appear. The static feeling continued to grow, increasing until he was sure that she would feel the surge.

They burst past a low hanging tree limb and exploded out into a small meadow. It was barely bigger than a dining table, leaving their shoulders to bump together as they turned to search their surroundings. An opening in the canopy flooded the area with moonlight. It was a brilliant, almost blinding silver that danced upon the specks of dust that floated in the air. The ethereal beauty left Benton sure that it had to be some kind of illusion.

"Tell me you see this too," he whispered, his muscles twitching as the charge coursed through him.

"I do."

"Is this normal?"

She shook her head slowly, her mouth slightly open in astonishment. Another internal shift slammed into him, shaking him like an earthquake, leaving his muscles trembling with the aftershocks. Nicole managed to catch him just before he hit the forest floor. Taking his weight was a well-practiced maneuver by now. He draped an arm over her shoulder, let her grip him around his waist, and tried to lock his knees. It tended to keep him something close to upright. His legs trembled as if the world were shaking beneath him. Feet skittering, he struggled to regain his footing.

"Are you okay?" Nicole asked, still keeping her voice a low whisper, as if afraid that they might be overheard.

Slowly, the wave of dizziness receded. "Yeah, I think so."

"Do you see anything?"

Trying to calm his rampaging heartbeat, he tried to stretch his senses. Again, it was a task he wasn't sure how to complete. All he could do was relax as best he could and try to pay attention. The wind coursed through the leaves. Crickets continued to chirp and stray rodents scurried through the undergrowth. It was all normal. Nothing that would explain the sensation coursing through him.

Still, he felt it. A presence that stood within nature but remained removed.

He craned his neck. Winter wind stirred his hair, brushing it across his eyes. The moon hung low and swollen, blazing with a startling light as it filled the opening in the canopy. A strange sense of peace mixed with the bone-deep dread. A shadow drifted over the moon. He squinted into it, trying to discern some shape from the mist. The baby's cry returned, ringing in his ears as little more than a whisper. Fear cracked open his chest.

"Benton? Benton? Benton?"

"Sorry?" he gasped as he whipped around to face her.

Tearing his eyes off of the moon came with a physical ache.

"Benton, are you okay?"

"I'm slightly annoyed." The remark came out as a natural reflex. He started to pay more attention when he saw her face distort into concern. "What's going on?"

"I've been trying to get your attention for half an hour."

"Say that again?"

The squeeze of her fingers made him jump. *When did she take my hand again?* He stared down at the entwined hands, trying to unravel the mystery.

"Benton?"

Her voice was a sharp whisper that made him twist around. Confusion rolled over him in waves. She had been standing right next to him a split second ago, her hand gripping his tightly. Now she was before him, holding him by his shoulders as she shook him slightly.

"What?" It was all he could think to say.

Instead of answering straight away, she twisted around to stare up at the low hanging moon. Looking back to him, she whispered.

"What do you see?"

"Nothing."

The difficulty he had moving his tongue terrified him. He felt heavy all over. Like his muscles had turned to rock against his bones.

"You're going to leave, okay?" Nicole said.

Warm hands gripped the sides of his face and jerked his head around. Without his knowledge, he had started to stare at the moon again.

"Get me out of here," he whispered.

Nicole didn't hesitate. Never releasing her tight grip on him, she led them directly back to the campsite, never so much as glancing behind. Not even as the child's cry once more rose in pitch. Benton struggled to keep the pace.

In the end, he was the one who broke and sprinted the remaining distance back to the safety of the teepee.

# Chapter 8

*Benton stretched out a hand that wasn't his own. Skin fit over him like a glove, tight enough that it felt ready to split open if he moved too fast. As the dream continued, he settled into the flesh, melding with his host until the other man's mind overpowered his own. What remained of Benton's mind was merely a whisper, steadily growing softer until it vanished altogether.*

*Tender skin graced the palm of his outstretched hand. Instantly, he closed his fingers tight, trapping the small hand inside his grasp, remembering a moment later to take it slow. There were still too many people around for him to be sure that he had his prey.*

*"Thank you for your help," Benton said in his borrowed voice.*

*The little boy smiled up at him, his baby fat puffing up his cheeks all the more.*

*"Why couldn't you get the bag yourself?"*

*Sensing that the boy might run, Benton tightened his grip. Only releasing slightly when the boy hissed a pained breath.*

*"I'm too big. I can't get under the car far enough to reach it." Playfully, he wiggled the boy's arm, making him giggle. "You look about the right size."*

*"Hey, I'm big, too. I'm almost seven."*

*"Yes, but you're also like Spiderman. I'm sure you can scurry straight under."*

*Whatever hesitance the boy had vanished after the comparison to his hero. Side-by-side, they walked through the weakening night. Dawn wasn't far off now. He still couldn't believe his luck.*

*The dark-haired boy had caught his eye the moment he had arrived. Small for his age. Wide eyes. Slender, hairless limbs with just a hint of baby fat. Perfect. He had known from the start that he wasn't going to leave without the boy. But he had thought it would take more effort. Perhaps wait until he was playing with his friends and separated from his parents. To catch him coming back from a bathroom break unattended had almost seemed like a trap. He couldn't truly be so lucky.*

*They trudged down the small hill, and grass gave way to gravel as they entered the parking lot. Still, the boy made no attempt to leave. And no one moved to stop them. As they weaved their way through the first row of cars, it struck Benton that they* could be gone before anyone even noticed that the boy was missing.

"Which one's your car?"

"Over here. This way."

Heart slamming within his ribcage and body trembling with anticipation, he couldn't stop himself from quickening his step. The boy kept his silence until he was forced into a jog.

"What's wrong?"

Benton was too close now. His car was in sight, nestled in the back row against the beginnings of the tiny forest. Not a soul was there to stop him. This was going to happen. The boy was now his.

"Hey, Mister!"

Without responding, Benton scooped the boy up. His tiny frame made it easy. Chubby cheeks squished easily under his fingers as he clamped a hand over the boy's mouth, stifling his screams. He dug into his pocket for the keys to his car. Only a few more yards and it would be done.

The small box slipped between his fingers as he fumbled for the trunk release. The sudden flash of lights made his heart skip a beat. But no one came. The only noise around them was the crunch of the gravel and the muted sobs of the struggling boy. Far too low to draw anyone's attention. The truck swung open automatically, opening like the mouth of a cave of wonders, promising him his heart's desire if he could only reach it in time. Benton pushed himself faster, fighting to keep a grip on the now thrashing boy.

He threw the child in with a crushing force. It was never too soon to teach the boy who was in charge. The car bounced with the impact, the squeak of the suspension drowning out the boy's whimper. All it took was just one hand pressed against his sternum to keep the boy pinned. A rapid heartbeat fluttered against Benton's fingertips. The sign of fear fueling his own delight.

Reaching past the still struggling child, he grabbed the metallic tape he had put aside in anticipation for this moment. Long held fantasies flashed across his mind as he wrapped the thrashing limbs together. Not one of them held a candle to this moment. This reality. The boy was his now. A tool for him to act out everything he had been craving for so long. A rush of euphoric relief left him gasping for air.

Until now, fear and confusion had weakened the boy's cries into pathetic, gurgled grunts. Like a kicked dog. Without warning, he found his voice and screamed for the heavens. Benton could almost laugh when, once more, luck came to his aid.

*The boy's voice was lost under the blood-curdling wail that shattered the pre-dawn silence.*

*Chills trickled down his spine at the near inhuman sound. Like a death rattle mated with primal fury. Whatever it was, it didn't matter. The boy did. More specifically, not wasting this divine intervention and getting him out of here. Trembling with delight, he pulled the boy closer and violently pressed a strip of tape over his mouth. He didn't attempt to be gentle as he tossed his new toy inside the trunk and slammed the lid down.*

*Fumbling with the keys, he jogged to the driver's seat and was almost knocked over by a sweet scent. Not floral. Instead, something more akin to fruit. It came with such ferocity that he couldn't help but notice it. Before he could yank open his car door, the scent changed to the stench of rancid meat. Bile splashed the back of his throat. Pushing forward, he stopped to get inside. Motion drew his attention to the still dark canopy of trees. He looked up . . .*

Benton slammed back into his own flesh, reclaiming his body with enough force to jerk him upright. A scream shattered his chest as it surged towards freedom. He trembled with it, crushed under the blizzard that filled his frail human form. Then it was done. The sound ended abruptly and, without it, he flopped back like a puppet with severed strings.

Panting hard, he fought to reclaim command over his limbs. Everything felt alien. A shell too big for the creature it contained. *You have to remember!* The self-imposed order struck him as strange. There was no way he could ever forget. Each dream practically burned the victim's names into his brain. *Hurry up! He'll die!*

Nicole's voice wafted into his awareness. Whispered reassurances and sweet words that didn't change a thing. He was still trying to pull his mind from the memory of the killer's when she loomed over him, mobile phone in her hand.

"What's the name?" she asked.

The haze of his mind suddenly fell away. Shock made his exhausted body move. He gripped her shoulder tight and hurled himself to his feet.

"Benton, you need to rest. We can just call mom and tell her the name. Same as always."

He didn't look back as he threw himself out of the teepee. "Adam Auclair!"

Nicole was at his heels in barely a second. He didn't wait for her. Instead, he sprinted across the grass as fast as his body could carry him. It was rare for him to dream of someone he knew in his day to day life. Rarer still for them to survive.

Benton didn't bother to weave around the cars as he entered the parking lot. He knew where he was going. And he remembered the layout perfectly. Long legs let him leap onto the hood of the first car he arrived at; a family sedan that was parked too close to a smaller Volkswagen Beetle. It made the jump between the two easy. A Jeep with roof racks was parked on the far side, allowing him to swing his body up and keep his short cut, but more importantly, his element of surprise. All the commotion had made the man turn. He twisted towards Nicole's approaching footsteps, unwittingly giving Benton his back.

Even expecting it, the pain of impact took Benton's breath away. Unable to brace himself, he crashed down onto the gravel with the killer, his head cracking hard against the unforgiving earth. Instinct kicked in through the spike of pain, and he bellowed for Nicole. The man heaved, tossing Benton off of his back as he surged to his feet. A savage kick barreled towards Benton's head a second later. Bracing his feet, Benton rolled his body, narrowly missing the boot by inches. The man was quick to try again, this time aiming for Benton's legs. He rolled back, flipping his feet over his head to land in a crouch. A blur of movement made him tense, but the pain didn't come. Nicole ran at the man, twisting and ducking at the last moment to drive her shoulder into the tender flesh of the man's stomach. A gasped cry left the man as he doubled over. He groped for Nicole, but she swung first.

If Benton ever needed proof that Nicole was smarter than him, this was it. She had taken a second to retrieve the flashlight. It was the heavy-duty kind that could easily be used as a baton. Putting her entire strength behind it, she drove the long flashlight into the man's skull. Shattered glass scattered across the ground as the man staggered into the side of the car. In a flurry of precise movements, Nicole forced the man to the ground, pushed him onto his side, locked his arm against her chest, and pressed her knee into the back of his shoulder, just under the joint. What little fight was left in the older man quickly vanished in an agonized cry as she applied more pressure.

"I will break your shoulder," she snapped. "Don't try me."

Knowing he didn't have time to linger in his state of shock, Benton scrambled up and raced for the open car trunk, only pausing long enough to snatch up a shard of the broken flashlight glass.

He found Adam frozen in fear. Logic told him to be gentle as he pulled the curled boy up by from the depths of the trunk. But terror sharpened his movements. He tugged the small boy hard enough to jerk him out of his protective position.

"Adam, we don't have time for this," Benton said.

The tightly applied strip of tape muffled the boy's response. Tears carved paths down rounded cheeks. He gasped and choked on the snot that dripped from his nose. His narrow chest heaved with the desperate need to breathe. Benton ignored it all as he pulled the bound legs over the rim and hurriedly slashed at the tape. Adam whimpered, clawing at the tape on his mouth.

"You need to run," Benton commanded, his hard tone making the boy jump. "Faster than you ever have in your life. Don't look back. Don't stop. Do you understand?"

Adam nodded rapidly, his dark hair flopping over his forehead. With one last drag, the shard finally cut through the last of the tape. Instantly, Benton lifted Adam the rest of the way out and shoved him hard.

"Run!"

Adam's light-up sneakers flashed wildly in the dim light as he sprinted down the line of cars, the quickest route back up the incline to the campsite.

"Come on." Benton barely had the words out before he had latched onto Nicole's arm and pried her off the man.

"Benton, what are you doing? We can't let him go!"

Her words ended with a startled cry. Already the man was back on his feet and was lumbering towards them, injured arm cradled protectively to the soft padding of his stomach, a murderous snarl on his lips.

"He's not the one we have to worry about," Benton replied as he glanced behind.

The moment he spotted the figure, his legs turned to stone. Nicole noticed the change and whipped around to see what was coming. It was only after the man had his beefy hands clenched on her shoulders that he realized he wasn't the cause of the fear. Not releasing his grip, he twisted just enough to glance over his shoulder.

That seemed to be what the woman had been waiting for.

Benton had first spotted her hovering amongst the shadows, clinging to the higher tree branches. Her hair was a veil that blended into the darkness. The long gown that hung limply from her body didn't move within the wind. Nothing about her moved. She didn't breathe. Didn't blink. Stretched as wide as her flesh would allow, the floating woman's eyes were polished white pearls that reflected the slightest trace of light. Benton's stomach rolled as he saw the state of her skin. It was a milky, almost translucent film that neither dripped nor dried. Thin enough that he could see her veins swell and twitch with her heartbeat.

Benton pulled at Nicole's arm, never taking his eyes off of the floating woman. The motion caught the man's attention, and he snapped around to glare at them.

It was only a split second. Barely more than a blink of an eye. That was all it took for the woman to leave the trees.

Benton leaped back, heart hammering as he struggled to catch sight of her again. Rage slowly trickled from the man's face. Slowly, he turned back to look at the tree line. The slight shift of his shoulders brought the woman back into view. Barely a few inches separated her face from his back. She was still staring, her face expressionless. No one dared to move.

Suddenly, she pounced forward like a jungle cat, slamming against the man's spine with both hands and feet and driving him to the ground. Caught between the two men, Nicole staggered forward, barely able to keep her footing. She wrenched savagely, but couldn't break the man's hold. Not until the ghostly figure struck. Her fingers drove into the man's flesh like knives. The man's agonized scream crackled in his throat, allowing the wet bubbling of blood to be heard. A slick crack and the man's limbs dropped to the ground. Without the competition, Nicole and Benton fell back, landing in a pile a few feet away. Paralyzed, the man could only gasp uselessly while the ghost rose up, never releasing her grip on his broken spine. Watching the blood-slicked peaks of vertebrae poke out of the ravaged flesh jarred Benton back to his senses.

"Run," he whispered.

Nicole nodded rapidly. His body worked without his conscious mind, drawing him up onto his feet and forcing him into a sudden sprint. The cold air didn't quell the fire that ignited within his lungs. Sharp stones tore into the bare skin of his feet, the small spikes of pain it brought easily lost under a rush of adrenaline. Nicole was a long-distance runner. She'd outlast him without a problem but struggled to keep pace with him in short bursts. Unwilling to leave her behind, he fought against his survival instinct and slowed down.

Shadows lingered between the cars as they raced past, barely deep enough to hide anything. Still, he almost failed to see the small body crouched behind an SUV. *Adam.*

"Get help," he told Nicole on a panted breath.

Before she could argue, he suddenly switched directions, sliding across a sedan's hood before dropping out of sight. It was unnecessarily dramatic but kept her from following.

Without pause, he rounded the back of the sedan and cut a straight path to the trembling child. Claw marks lined his face, proof of his failed attempts to remove the tape. Gravel rash covered the front of his legs from thigh to shin and blood dripped from his shredded forearms. Benton didn't know if the apparent fall had really injured him too much to run, or if it was all in the boy's mind. There wasn't any point in trying to sort it all out now.

Benton swooped low and quickly ushered the boy under the SUV. Both of them were slender enough to slide under without much trouble. There wasn't much in the way of lingering shadows, but he hoped it would be enough. *It has its kill*, he reasoned. *It might not be interested in us.* He held tight to that thought as he tried to silence his heavy breathing.

Adam's whimpers were the only thing that broke the stillness. Catching the boy's eyes, Benton pressed a finger to his lips. *Quiet. You need to be quiet.* The wordless pleading didn't do anything. Benton clutched the boy's still bound hands, squeezing tight to offer some reassurance. Steadily, Adam stilled, more holding his breath than coming to his senses, and the world fell silent.

There was no crunch of gravel. No shadow to give a hint of movement. Nothing that Benton could point to as reasoning for his sudden conviction that it was still lurking nearby. But he could *feel* it. Like the weight of a boulder slowly being lowered onto his spine. A steadily increasing weight.

The breathless, gasping cry of an infant made them both flinch. As silently as possible, Benton scurried closer to Adam and pressed his free hand over the boy's mouth. It did little to keep the boy from falling back into terrified sobs, but muffled the sound. The wail drifted in the wind; everywhere at once before seeming to gather at some point far behind Benton's left shoulder.

While the sound remained barely audible over the distant rustling of long grass, the ghostly sensation against Benton's muscles continued to grow. A heavy pressure that bent his bones. Trusting in the sensation more than his hearing, he pressed closer still to Adam and desperately searched for an escape route. With Adam in tow, his already limited options dwindled even more. Even if he could still run, it wouldn't be possible to actually outpace the monster. Their only hope had hinged on the idea that she was distracted by the prey she had and wouldn't be seeking another. Perhaps they could move from car to car and slowly make their way back to the safety of the group.

*Nicole will think of something*, he told himself as the crying shifted, flittering along the side of the car like scattering leaves.

Adam's nostrils flared with each rapid breath. Caught between two survival instincts, flight and freeze, the little boy twitched randomly. The small motions were enough to rattle the gravel beneath him. Benton held his wide gaze and slowly shook his head. It wasn't any good. The whispered cry rolled around the front of the car and drifted down the opposite side. Benton's ribs groaned as the weight grounded him into the earth. He clenched his jaw, battling to keep his pained cries from working their way out.

Metal squealed as something collided with the side of the SUV. Dust billowed up to clog the air as the SUV slid across the ground and crunched into the neighboring car. Benton pushed at Adam's shoulder, shoving him to crawl the distance from one car to the next. Another blow made the SUV buck. Lodged as it was against the other car, the first attempt resulted in a little more than the scraping the two vehicles together. Another blow. Another. Each one growing with frustration and force.

Benton slipped under the next car. Lower to the ground, there was no way to move without losing bits of skin to the rocky earth. Reaching out, he grabbed Adam and dragged him closer. The tape and a loud crack covered Adam's pained cry. The SUV careened away from their new hiding place to crunch against the car on the opposite side. Dust stung Benton's eyes as he pressed the boy close to his side. His hands returned to their previous positions, one offering reassurance while the other clamped over the boy's jaw. Still and silent, he waited for his moment.

It came with a resounding thud. Glass rained down as the SUV rocked. The ghost battered the vehicle, trying to flip it, seemingly convinced that they were still underneath. Benton and Adam worked their way to the far side of the new car, using the sounds of twisting metal to hide their movements.

Benton made it out first. Reaching back under, he pulled Adam out after him. Bloodied and trembling, the boy was quick to follow. Grabbing him under his arm, Benton pulled Adam up onto his feet. The boy looked up. A sudden sharp tremor ran through his thin body, and the boy's dark eyes bulged wide. Benton whipped around, one arm shoving Adam tighter behind him.

The woman's face filled his vision.

Hardly an inch from his face, all he could see were the ashen eyes. No pupil or iris. Only a cobweb of slender veins that pulsed and flickered at random. Like a snake tasting the air for its prey. Benton's muscles calcified, locking him into place as the woman continued to rapidly sniff at the air. Each breath drew her a little closer. It moved with violent, bone cracking jerks, as if it didn't have full control over the whole of its body at once.

At last, it leveled its mouth to his ear and spoke in a throaty rasp, "What are you?"

Benton jerked back, the sudden motion cracking the internal casing that had held him captive. Instantly and without thought, he opened his mouth and released a Banshee wail.

No two of them were ever the same. This one was tainted with all of his fear and fury. A roar that belonged to some colossal, ancient beast. The earsplitting shriek of static. And somewhere, buried deep within the deafening scream, was something akin to human.

Driven back by the force of the inhuman sound, the ghost's body ripped apart, dispersing into the sky like crackling sparks. Bone deep terror pulsed though Benton when he saw that the damage didn't last. The severed specks of her body swirled in the air, constantly trying to combine once more.

*I can't kill it.*

Benton reached back, grabbed Adam's hand, and broke into a run. His voice echoed for a moment, leaving the dismembered spirit disorientated and thrashing. *It won't last.* The knowledge lodged in the depths of his mind and spread out like a poison. Adam stumbled and Benton almost dislodged the terrified boy's shoulder as he wrenched him up. Carrying the extra weight dragged Benton down, but a single, repeating voice kept him going. *She'll heal.*

He almost fell as they turned sharply, taking the single path that lead from the parking lot to the campsite. Despite everything that had happened only a few yards away, the campsite was still relatively quiet. The slight slope made his legs burn. Adam slipped his bound arms around Benton's neck and squeezed until the older boy choked.

*She'll heal.*

Seizing the last of his strength, he was barely able to keep his pace as the hill grew steeper and his muscles hardened. *She's coming.* He knew it before Adam began to squirm and sob.

Nicole came into view at the peak. She jumped and waved her arms, urging them on while never taking a step toward them. Instead, she threw rapid glances over her shoulder. He was vaguely aware of Wapun's presence. She held a bowl cupped between both hands, a thin trail of smoke snaking up from its depths. Every muscle of Benton's back clenched at once, suddenly feeling like stones grinding against each other as he moved. The air went rancid, making him gag. He could feel the woman close to his spine, knew that her hand was pulled back, ready to gouge out his spine. His skin prickled with anticipation.

"Benton!" Nicole screamed.

He flung himself forward at her cry, tucking himself as best as he could to take the impact and spare Adam. The first rays of dawn broke over the horizon and struck the wisps of smoke. Blinding color burst into existence. Benton hit the ground, his eyes burning and body rattling with a pulse of energy. Shielding Adam with his body, he risked a glance.

The blazing rainbow light snapped out like cracks forming in glass, jagged spikes that sought every insignificant speck of smoke. Each contact created another explosion until the air lit up like fireworks. Benton shielded Adam, refusing to look again until the sizzling air stilled and a greenish haze distorted his vision.

He jerked back as a snake of pure light coiled around his arm. It twisted around itself rapidly before slithering away. Another soon caught his eye. He instinctively retreated only to find that there was nowhere left to go. The living auroras moved across the earth, drifting through the air, covering the sky until they blocked out the sunlight. Vivid greens, scorching pinks, neon purples, and a shard of red that he had only ever seen in nebulas. They illuminated the world as they danced and swelled.

*Breathed,* Benton corrected himself. *They're all breathing. They're actually alive?*

His internal question was answered the moment the woman lunged towards him. In his state of shock, he had almost forgotten that she was there. The light hadn't. It swarmed to the woman in mass, knotting together to create an impenetrable wall and reducing her to little more than a shadow. Gradually, they loosened, only to rejoin forces when the woman attacked again.

"She can't get in," Benton mumbled aloud.

"Benton?"

He snapped around, finding Wapun looming over him. She wasn't alone. Nicole had pointed out every elder to him and, while he hadn't had contact with them, he recognized them instantly. The mix of fear and rage that burned within their eyes was also familiar. In his experience, it always came before acts of violence. As subtly as he could, he drew the still weeping boy closer to his side. The action only inflamed the elder's anger. Still, it was Wapun that spoke.

"I think there are a few things that we need to discuss, don't you?"

# Chapter 9

"What does it look like?" Adam asked as he clutched Benton's arm.

Nicole smiled, weary but relieved, as she watched Benton describe the newest band of light to the six-year-old. The color and shape and the way it twisted around his fingers. For once, she truly wished she could see what Benton did. It all sounded glorious.

A few shouts erupted from the RV behind them. All three of them turned, half expecting someone to emerge. No one did, and the voices returned to a murmur. She wondered if Adam knew that he had single-handedly saved Benton. The attempted kidnapping alone would have been enough for everyone to close ranks. Knowing that a murderous ghost was stalking around the edges of the blessed earth would have gotten everyone to battle stations. But add Benton to all of that and everyone was on edge.

Siksika knew well enough to fear ghosts, but there wasn't anything like Benton in the old stories. Or the new ones. Banshees were a completely foreign concept. *They were all ready to fight a coyote, she thought. They don't know what to do with a badger.* It was clear that they wanted him gone. Or, at worst, blamed him for everything that had happened. After all, he was physical and *there*. He was the one they could take it out on. No matter what she said, their anger and fear only fed one another until they looked to be seconds away from lynching Benton. She doubted she would ever get over seeing them like that.

It was Adam that had stopped them in their tracts. More precisely, it was his complete refusal to let Benton go. The second they had cut him free, he wrapped his limbs around Benton, sobbing wildly, screeching like a wounded beast when anyone tried to physically separate them. Even his parents weren't enough to tempt him away.

So the elders retreated to Wapun's RV and ordered the trio to sit on the log outside. That was where they stayed as the arguments drew on and the sun crept higher. They weren't left alone, of course. There was always one person standing by the door, staring at them in silence. Periodically, someone would come out and switch places with them. Nicole had a sneaking suspicion that this had turned into a tactic. Only Wapun had spent time with Benton. All of the rest had to be curious.

"Can you loosen your grip a bit?" Benton asked. "My fingers are going numb."

Adam's cheeks flushed as he begrudgingly shifted slightly.

"You know, Nic saved you, too. And she's way better at this comforting stuff." Benton winced as Adam returned to a crushing grip. "Guess that's a no."

The look Benton threw her way screamed for help, and she was quick to lean forward, peeking around him to see Adam's face.

"You were really brave," Nicole said sweetly. "It's okay that you were scared. We were all scared."

"Has anyone tried to take you before?"

She said 'no' in the same moment Benton laughed a 'yes.' Noticing the twin astonished looks, he shrugged.

"It happens. People are creeps."

"But that doesn't mean it will happen to you again," Nicole rushed to assure Adam.

"And if it does, Nicole will beat them up." Benton smiled. "Since when can you do that sort of stuff, anyway?"

"Well, after last time, Dad's gotten pretty insistent that I learn self-defense."

"Last time?" Adam asked.

"She'll explain it later," Benton cut in. "Right now, I want to know what she meant by *Dad*."

The obvious answer stammered over her tongue. "The man who raised me."

"I know what a father is. I meant, why does he know what happened?"

"Because I told mom."

"So?"

"So . . ." she drew the word out. "They're married. They have to tell each other everything. It's in their vows."

"I don't think it is."

"Well, it should be."

Benton's brow furrowed as he thought. "Everything. So he knows I'm . . ."

"A Banshee? Yep. And he's really excited about meeting you."

"What's a Banshee?" Adam asked.

"They're from Ireland," Nicole answered swiftly. "According to legend, they're beautiful women that scream or cry to warn people that something bad is going to happen."

Adam stared at Benton in wonder. "You're a girl?"

"Not to my knowledge."

"You were born in Ireland?"

"Vancouver."

"You cry?" he asked softly.

"All the time," Benton replied as dismissively as he had for any of the previous questions.

Adam studied him again. "Are you sure you're a boy? My brother says boys don't cry."

Benton barked a laugh. "Your brother also thinks that girls are incredibly impressed with his chest hair. He's an idiot."

"He also says you're a freak," Adam mumbled.

Before Nicole could but in, Benton laughed again and shrugged his free shoulder. "Even idiots can be right every once in a while. For the record, I saw your brother cry once."

"Really?"

Benton nodded. "The first night I met him. Did you hear about what happened at the diner with a guy called Victor?"

A torrent of emotions rose up inside Nicole at the mention of her childhood friend. It was the first time she had seen evil at work. It had latched only to him, and she hadn't been able to free him in time. He had been the first Fort Wayward victim of the *Leanan Sidhe*. And, thanks to Benton's help, he had been the last. She snapped out of her memories when Benton continued.

"I'd like to cry more," he was telling the child. "People cry when they really care about something. It just seems kind of sad if the only thing you give a shit about is not being murdered."

A moment of silence followed before both she and Adam said in unison, "You shouldn't say 'shit' in front of a kid."

He turned to Nicole but didn't get his snarky reply out before Rick came barreling up to the group.

"Adam," he gasped between panted breaths, "what the hell is going on? I got this weird text from mom and dad. Someone tried to kidnap you?"

"Benton and Nicole saved me."

Even though Rick was a year younger than Nicole, he was always trying to give the appearance of being far more mature. He wasn't. Right now, he was struggling to keep a calm air as he looked at everyone in turn.

"The freak?" he asked at last.

"He has a name," Nicole noted.

"You're a freak, too," Rick dismissed with a wave of his arm.

"Shut up," Adam's voice squeaked on the words. He jumped up, putting himself protectively between his older brother and Benton. "They saved my life!"

"Is that what they told you?" Rick said. "I'm sure you weren't in any real danger."

Shock crashed down on Nicole like a wave, leaving her dumbfounded and gaping. Color rushed up Benton's pale neck as he stood up and placed a hand on Adam's shoulder.

"This is a whole new level of stupid, Rick."

Anger flashed across Rick's eyes. He puffed out his chest and gripped his hips. Essentially reminding Benton that he had a good deal more muscle than he did.

"Stop warping my brother's brain. Stuff like this doesn't happen in Fort Wayward."

"What do you call Victor, then?" Benton challenged.

Rick stammered, suddenly looking like the young boy he was instead of the tower of masculinity he tried to be. "This stuff never happened until *you* rocked up! Everyone knows it! Do you know what we call you behind your back?"

"Maybe you could summon the courage to say it to my face one day," Benton cut in, his voice void of all emotion. He almost sounded bored. It enraged Rick all the more.

"You're a walking disease! Do us all a favor and stop infecting everyone else!"

The door to the RV slammed open as Adam began screeching at his brother. Benton, for his part, still seemed like he was barely paying attention to everything happening around him. Nicole suspected that he was doing it specifically to get a rise out of Rick. Stepping back slightly, she threw a pleading look over her shoulder, hoping that one of the emerging adults would put an end to this.

"What's going on?"

The brothers both fell silent at their father's question. Mr. Auclair's physical appearance leaned more to the French side of his Metis heritage than Siksika. His bright blue eyes made his tanned skin seem darker. He had a tendency to let stubble grow along his jawline while keeping his cheeks clean-shaven. Sometimes, she wondered if he was trying to grow mutton chops but just couldn't quite commit. The brothers took after their mother, inheriting her richer coloring, but not her dimples. The Auclair parents came closer while the elders stayed back, lingering by the door and whispering to themselves, simply watching it all unfold.

"Rick was being mean to Benton," Adam said at last, his voice turning into a whine.

Rick stammered under the sudden scrutiny of his parents. "I'm just saying that all we have is Benton's word on this, right?"

"Everyone saw the ghost," Nicole cut in sharply, gesturing at the group behind her and hoping that one of them would back her up.

"Ghost?" Rick asked. "What ghost?"

Nicole tensed, glanced at Benton, and blurted out. "Well, what the hell are you talking about?"

"The 'man' that tried to take Adam."

"Why did you use air quotations?"

"Because no one saw him, right? We just have Benton's word on it."

"And me," Nicole squealed, her frustration getting the better of her. "Not to mention Adam. You haven't even asked him what happened."

"Because the freak's had enough time to fill his head with lies," Rick replied.

"Are you actually insane?" Nicole screamed at him.

"Calm down, Nicole," Mr. Auclair said. "He's got a point."

Again, Nicole was rendered silent by shock. She turned first to the elders only to find them content with keeping out of it. Next, she turned to Benton. Meeting her gaze, he shook his head slowly. The resigned motion that spoke volumes. *How many times has he been through this?* Despite his silent request, she couldn't let the comment pass.

"Sir, with all due respect, what on Earth are you talking about?"

"It's too early to know what happened," Mr. Auclair said.

"There are three witnesses," she replied in desperation.

"You just saw a ghost, Nicole," he said with a roll of his eyes. "You're bound to remember things a little differently."

"It wasn't my first ghost." The words were out before she had time to consider if she should confess that or not. Quickly, she decided that it was better for the elders to know the truth rather than dance around the issue. Reaching blindly out, she found Benton's forearm and squeezed. He sighed heavily.

"And it wasn't my first experience with a child murderer, either," he muttered bitterly.

"What?" Rick asked.

Benton waved him off, not bothering to respond with words.

"You really are a freak."

"Yeah, pretty much."

Rick bristled at the dismissal. "Okay, if you're not lying, where is this guy? I want to see him. Is he at the station house?"

"He's dead," Benton said, returning to his bland, emotionless speech. "The ghost killed him."

"Killer ghost?" Rick said slowly.

"It's true," Adam chirped.

"See, this is what I'm talking about. Benton's obviously been lying to him."

"Perhaps," Mrs. Auclair said softly.

Benton's facade shattered like fine crystal. He turned onto the adults with a barely contained fury, absently shoving Adam behind him.

"He's not an idiot," Benton snarled. "Don't treat him like he is."

Mr. Aucliar bristled. "You want to watch what tone you use with me, boy."

"You might want to remember you're a goddamn parent and start acting like it," Benton retorted.

"Excuse me?" Mrs. Auclair said it as a challenge. "Our son has gone through a traumatic experience–"

"You don't help someone deal with trauma by belittling what they went through," Benton cut in. "Or by telling them it was all in their head."

"We're trying to help him."

"You're helping yourselves. Don't sacrifice his mental well-being to keep your denial."

Rage blazed in Mr. Auclair's eyes. He took a single rushed step toward Benton before remembering himself. Balling his hands at his sides, he spoke through clenched teeth.

"He's just a boy. We're trying to protect him."

"The time for that is so far gone that we can't even see it on the horizon anymore," Benton scoffed.

"We want what's best for him."

"Then give him the strength to face the truth!" Benton roared. "Life is a cesspool! It's terrifying, degrading, and disgusting. Just one long procession of misery. And then you die. And that can be just as messed up as life itself."

Mrs. Auclair glanced around Benton to her young son. "You're not going to die."

"Spoiler alert; everyone dies. You, me, her, that guy over there. Death ain't exactly picky."

"How can you say that to a scared child?" Mrs. Auclair hissed.

"Because it's the truth! Life is a constant battle to keep your head above the muck, and the only thing that makes it tolerable is knowing someone cares if your head goes under. Lying to him now isn't going to magically change what happened. Nothing ever will. All you're doing is leaving him to drown on his own!"

An uneasy silence suddenly claimed the small group. Benton could barely breathe through the tension that claimed his body. Fine tremors raced along his limbs, and the muscles in his jaw jumped and twitched. Nicole had thought she had seen Benton at his worst. But this was something different. A haunting, bone-deep ache shone in his eyes, and the sight left her breathless.

"Benton," she whispered.

Sucking in a deep breath almost shattered him. When the process was done, however, his mask of defiant indifference settled back onto his features. He turned to lock eyes with Wapun.

"I've had a bad morning, so let's not pretend; did you guys decide to kill me?"

Nicole instantly closed ranks with him. "Benton, no one's going to hurt you."

"That thing is pissed at me, and I can't hurt it," he said, his gaze never leaving. "Politely asking me to leave now is pretty much just socially appropriate execution."

A baffled laugh bubbled out of her throat. "No one's said anything about kicking you out."

Benton finally looked at her, and a small smile flickered across his face. "I know when people don't want me around." Turning back to Wapun, he continued, "I don't know the exact ratio, though. Who won the vote?"

"We agreed to hear from you before making a decision."

The answer left Nicole reeling, like the earth had just dropped out from under her.

"You can't be serious," she gasped, still trying to regain her footing.

"Nicole," Wapun warned.

"Are you insane? It shouldn't even be up for debate. Benton did nothing wrong."

"We have to think of everyone's safety," Wapun replied.

"Benton is included in that!"

It was impossible to tell who was more surprised by the outburst. Nicole had never raised her voice to an elder. Never even approached something that could be considered challenging. It had just come out, and she didn't know what to do now.

So she turned to her mother. Dorothy Rider was always cool under pressure. *Help,* she screamed with her eyes. Dorothy shot a quick glance to the elders before straightening her spine and taking a step closer to Benton.

"This is a private event and I can't force them to keep Benton here." Cupping her shoulder, she added, "But I can assure you that I won't let him leave alone."

"So can I," Nicole said.

Wapun's jaw dropped with shock, but it was another elder that asked, "Are you threatening us?"

Dorothy's sighed. "There's no point in trying to convince you to stay here no matter what, is there?"

"I'm kind of stubborn. Dad says that I get it from you."

"Has everyone lost their minds?" Rick snapped.

Dorothy threw her daughter a quick, reassuring smile, before turning to the Auclair family. "I will need to talk to all of you now. I am a police officer, after all."

"Right." Mr. Auclair sounded somewhat bewildered.

"I contacted Dr. Aspen," Dorothy continued. "I figured Adam might want to have a little chat."

"Why would I want to talk to Mr. Aspen?" Adam asked innocently.

While the parents struggled to find a delicate way to say it, Benton answered, "People talk to therapists when scary or sad things happen to them. It'll make you feel better."

"Does talking to him make you feel better?"

Having adjusted enough to small town living, Benton was not surprised that the boy knew he was in therapy.

"Yeah," he shrugged. "As much as any other therapist. He's a nice enough guy. Give him a chance."

Nicole gave Benton a swift, one armed hug. While it was true that he got along with Aspen better than most, he never hid the fact that he hated therapy. The fact that he would swallow his pride for Adam's sake made her grin.

"Shut up," he mumbled out of the corner of his mouth.

"Never," she whispered back, relishing the small moment of peace.

It was a skill that being friends with a Banshee helped her to perfect. Take the good when you could, because you never knew how long it would last.

"Well then." Dorothy crouched down in front of Adam. "Why don't we get some breakfast?"

Instantly, the child grabbed Benton's hand.

Benton knelt down, too. "Do you have a mobile phone?"

Adam's bottom lip stuck out as he shook his head.

"Bet Rick does, yeah?"

"Yeah," Adam whispered.

"Well, I'm sure he has Nicole's number, and she always picks up. If you need to talk to me, just get your brother to call her, okay?"

His little, podgy face scrunched up. "Why would I call her to talk to you?"

Benton shrugged one shoulder. "I'm always with her."

"That's weird."

"I am a weird little freak," Benton grinned. When that accomplished little more than a weak smile, he added, "We'll meet up later for lunch. Okay?"

Reluctantly, Adam nodded and released Benton's hand. Dorothy quickly took hold of it and offered Benton a thankful smile. Straightening up, he looked to Nicole, rolling his eyes when he found a grateful expression on her face, too.

"Let's just get this over with." Benton turned on his heel and stalked towards the RV, calling over his shoulder. "My parents are going to be up soon, and I'm not going to be the one to break it to them that the paranormal is real."

# Chapter 10

Benton reached out, grabbed Nicole's jumping knee, and pushed it down. She threw him a questioning look but kept her leg still. *You'd think she was the one facing the inquisition,* he thought.

It was both intimidating and infuriating that none of them seemed to know what they were doing. Their willingness to believe in the paranormal apparently didn't stem from actual experience. So they followed the path Nicole had carved months ago; blindly assuming that Benton had all the answers. It didn't do much to smooth over the mutual resentment that was brewing between them.

"You want us to believe that you have no idea what you are?"

Benton had only just met Daniel, but he already knew that the old man was going to be his biggest problem. There was pure hatred in the man's dark eyes. Where it came from, Benton wasn't sure, but it was clear Daniel's mind was set.

"You're not going to answer?" Daniel snapped.

"You've asked me the same question eight different ways," Benton said. "My answer hasn't changed."

Nicole squeezed Benton's hand and flashed her best 'beauty pageant' smile. "How can anyone know their history if they're never told it?"

"And his parents never told him?" Daniel challenged.

"They refuse to admit he's anything other than human," she insisted. "I've seen it myself. They're giving new meaning to the word 'denial'."

"What do they think his dreams are?"

"Meaningless," Benton answered.

Daniel looked to the other elders in frustration. "Who in their right mind can hear the sounds he makes and believe him human?"

"White people," Nicole shrugged. She quickly snuck a glance at him. "No offense."

"None taken," he whispered back.

It was clear by the grunted intake of breath that the conversation had gone full circle and Daniel was about to ask the same question again. Nicole cut in swiftly.

"With all due respect, I think we're not focusing on what's important. Whatever attacked us is still out there. It's clearly dangerous."

"It left at dawn," Daniel dismissed. "It obviously can't hunt during the day."

"And what are we going to do at sunset?" Nicole asked, her voice as sweet as honey.

Hesitating, Daniel looked to the others. They were just as clueless. *They don't know what it is, either,* Benton realized. Whatever satisfaction there could have been in that was lost to the knowledge that they had something else to deal with first. And, since no one had mentioned it yet, it seemed it was up to him.

"Has anyone taken care of the corpse?"

His question was met with tense, almost disgusted silence. Benton looked at them each in turn.

"Whatever she is, she killed that guy. Pretty soon, people are going to be getting up. Tourists will be coming and going. Seems like we should make sure he's out of sight." Benton shrugged. "You know, might be a bit problematic. I've been told children aren't supposed to see stuff like that."

Once more, a few people found it easier to lash out rather than deal with the grisly truth.

"Oh, that's something you've been told, is it?" Daniel snarked.

"I've been seeing stuff like this since I was younger than Adam."

"And it clearly hasn't affected you," Daniel replied as he surged to his feet.

He barked a few orders in a language Benton had heard snippets of before but didn't understand. Whatever he said was met with a lot of hesitation. Someone replied in the same native tongue, and it was Nicole's turn to lurch up.

"Mom isn't going by herself."

"Nicole, be reasonable," someone who had yet to introduce themselves to Benton said. "She's a police officer. Who would you send out?"

"I'll go with her."

"You don't know what you're dealing with," Daniel scoffed.

"I know about as much as you do," she snapped without thought. The following moment of regret was squashed under her determination. "I've faced these things before. Not exactly like this one, granted, but kind of similar."

"Really?" Benton smirked.

"They were all scary and attacked you first," she said. Suddenly, she paused. "Why didn't it?"

"Sorry?" Benton asked.

"Why didn't she attack you outright? You said she hesitated."

He shrugged. "She was confused."

"About what?"

"How would I know?"

"You know, you've repeated that sentence so many times that it's lost its charm," she said.

"Then stop asking me-"

He didn't get through the words before she waved him off and returned her attention to the elders. "I'll figure it out later. Making sure that man's out of sight is more important right now. I'll need some iron. Ghosts don't like iron."

Daniel heaved a sigh. "And you've tested that theory, I suppose?"

"Yes," Nicole answered simply.

That caused a lot more chatter that Benton couldn't understand. Tone and facial expressions filled in a lot of the blanks for him. Or, at the very least, confirmed what he had been expecting. *None of them have seen a ghost before.* He remembered a moment later not to think too bitterly about that. Before he had come to Fort Wayward, the monsters of his life had been more or less contained to his dreams. Every so often, a very human monstrosity would seep out into his waking life. But nothing like this. *When did I start seeing this as the norm?*

"Where?" Wapun finally asked.

"Mr. Ackerman still lingers in Benton's barn." Nicole's simple tone made it clear that this was her norm as well. Unlike him, she didn't seem bothered by it. Instead, it boosted her confidence. "Benton and I have also faced the ghosts in the forest along the Highway of the Lost. Did you know that there are tree demons in there? Oh, and we took down two Baykoks."

The mention of the Ojibwe legend gave them something to sink their teeth into. A way to ground themselves as she continued to ramble, counting off the monsters on her fingers.

"There was also a *Leanan Sidhe*. That's the one that had the murder museum in the basement. A *Dullahan,* oh, and let's not forget the swarm of *Sluaghs*."

"What?" Wapun asked.

"They're little flying demons that hide in storms." She shuttered. "They laugh as they snatch people up and drop them from a great height. That storm a few months ago, the one that almost wiped Fort Wayward off the map? That was the work of the *Sluaghs*. The whole town would have been wiped off of the map if it wasn't for us. We can handle this, too."

"Why do you keep jumping to 'we'?" Benton muttered under his breath.

Nicole threw him a dark look. As dark as she could manage at least. On the great scale of visual intimidation, it ranked somewhere around an angry kitten.

"You know I'm going to follow you," he begrudgingly huffed. "But I maintain the right to complain about it."

She thought about it. "Fair enough."

"Nicole," Wapun said sharply.

Benton flinched along with his friend. Nicole's antics made it easy to forget what was going on. The dread that he had managed to disperse while watching Nicole came surging back when he looked around at the sea of angry faces. *And there's my limit,* he thought as he got to his feet.

"Just remember to bring something to throw over the body," he told Nicole while stalking the short distance towards the RV's door. "He's not going to be a pleasant sight. No reason for you to see that."

She didn't hesitate to follow. "I can deal with it if you can."

A sudden slam made them both turn. Daniel's hand was flat against the small tabletop, and there was a fire in his eyes.

"We have given neither of you permission to leave."

"Hey, if you want to take care of the dead guy, go right ahead," Benton replied, sweeping one hand out to welcome the man to take the lead.

To Benton's surprise, Daniel actually squared his jaw and accepted the offer, shoving his way past Benton to fling the door open. It smacked against the metal siding hard enough to rattle the wall. Wapun huffed like a long-suffering mother and grabbed Benton's arm.

"Let's do this with some measure of intelligence, shall we? We know that the land blessing works to keep it at bay. Perhaps we could use this to our advantage."

"Sounds good to me," Benton said.

He let both her and Nicole out first. The others held their ground, watching him carefully and without expression. It might have been shy of messed-up priorities but, at that moment, he felt safer out there than in here with them. Jumping down the small flight of stairs, he raised one hand to shield his eyes from the brilliant green haze. Being inside, it had been easy to convince himself that the living serpents of light had been a temporary trick of his mind. The grotesque and the horrifying, he never doubted. Beautiful things, however, he was suspicious about.

*Like the lady in my vision,* he thought idly, extending a hand to let a thin strip of pink coil around his palm. *Why did Mic have to look like me? It's just creepy.*

The light weaved playfully around his fingers before taking flight again, rolling like an eel through a placid stream. Watching it go, he recalled just what a perilous situation he was in. It was still early enough that the campsite wasn't overrun with tourists. Locals and overnight visitors were just starting to get up and sleepily shuffle about. *Whatever Dorothy told them did the trick,* he thought. Search as he might, he couldn't find a single worried face. His parents weren't anywhere to be seen either.

Coming to stand beside Nicole, he whispered, "I'm starting to develop a deep fear of Rider women."

"You only need to be scared if you cross us," she giggled, careful to keep her voice down. "We're benevolent masters."

He snickered, quickly schooling his features when Daniel snapped around to glare at them.

"This is a joke to you?"

"Not a funny one," Benton shrugged, choking on his breath when Nicole rammed an elbow into his ribs.

"Sorry," Nicole said. "We don't mean to be disrespectful. It's important to keep up morale, after all."

Daniel looked like he had a lot to say in response to that. He kept it to himself when Wapun appeared at Nicole's other side. The two elders had a silent standoff that the older woman seemed to win. At least for now. A kind but cautious smile played on Wapun's lips as she looked the teens over.

"Are you sure you want to do this?"

"I have to," Nicole said. "I'm kind of the research branch of this partnership. And there was something familiar about that woman."

"Repeat that last part," Benton cut in.

"Something about her seemed familiar."

"And you didn't mention this earlier because?"

"There was a lot going on," she defended. "I'm not used to having so many people in on the secret. It's actually kind of exhausting getting it all in order."

"Do you want to take a nap?"

She tilted her head to the side. "Actually, I really do. We should probably get this over with first, though."

"Yeah, probably," Benton replied, barely able to hide his smile.

They were already heading back toward their teepee, which, incidentally, was at the furthest reaches of the protected land. The swirling mist followed them, a thousand different creatures swooping in to investigate them before moving on. In an odd way, Benton found their constant curiosity comforting. They almost seemed playful.

"So you've been through this before?" Wapun asked.

"Well, not this *exactly*," Nicole confessed. Rushing, she added, "But I'm sure we'll handle it just fine. We always do."

Benton felt the scars on his palms itch, along with the one just above his ribs.

*Yeah. All it takes is a little bit of flesh each time.*

Morning dew numbed his bare feet as they crossed the field, the chill almost as biting as the ice that was gathering along his veins.

*I wonder how much they'll take this time.*

The frost that clung to the trampled blades of grass encased her bare feet as they crossed the campsite. Her yoga pants offered little protection from the cold.

*At least they're cute.*

It was a small comfort as she shivered. The tribal owl print was meant as a bit of a joke. In a perfect example of delusional thinking, Benton still thought that she hadn't picked up on his new-found love for owls. Not because of their ties to death and Banshees, but because he just loved Bird. She hadn't been able to resist steadily incorporating the feathered creatures into her aesthetic. Right now, she was kicking herself for not bringing the fluffy sweatpants with a cartoon owl on the thigh.

A small gust of wind made her shiver violently. Benton kept his body focused straight ahead, even as his eyes snapped over to her. She nipped the tip of her tongue between her teeth, hoping that the small amount of pain would help her focus. Or, at the very least, keep her nerves from showing. *Don't let him see*, she ordered herself. This was new ground for both of them, and he was looking to her to see how he should react; if he should go along with this or try and drag them both out of the situation.

Everything had changed so swiftly. And none of it had been like she had envisioned. She had planned it all out in her head a thousand times, calculating how they could best keep control over the flow of information, sharing what they wanted at a pace that would keep Benton at ease. How she could act as the go-between, smoothing things over as they went and helping both sides navigate the other. Reality was just a jerk. Nothing had happened as it should have. The elders were suspicious, Benton was resentful, and she was left trying to figure out how to get back on track before one side just decided to burn the bridge and be done with it.

Meeting Benton's eyes, she smiled slightly at him, trying to be the picture-perfect example of calm composure. He didn't return the smile, a clear sign that he knew something was off.

*Deal with the ghost first*, she told herself. *Daniel won't let go of the idea that Benton's a threat until he sees him in action. So, we'll kill the ghost, Benton can strike a heroic pose, and we'll have a nice conversation over cookies.*

Agreeing with herself that this was an awesome idea, and utterly refusing to think further into how it could go wrong, she felt a boost of renewed confidence. It didn't take long for Benton to notice the subtle change and lift a questioning eyebrow. Her smile grew in response. It was a little insulting that this only made him more suspicious.

Crowding a little closer to her side, he whispered in her ear, "So, what's the plan here?"

"Walk quickly and wield the power of a positive attitude."

"Huh. So, this is how I die," he muttered. "I had a good run."

She huffed. "You're just a Negative-Nelly today, aren't you?"

His second eyebrow joined the first in migrating up to his hairline. "Negative-Nelly?"

"I stand by my statement."

"Congratulations. When did you become a grandmother?"

"Oh, shush," she dismissed. "It's a perfectly acceptable insult."

"For people in an older age bracket," he muttered.

He chuckled when confronted with her glare, filling her with a flush of victory. While tension still lingered around the corner of his eyes, his breathing evened out and his shoulders loosened. It was a beautiful sight.

"Can I trust these guys?" he asked abruptly.

The question caught her off guard. But it was her lack of instant response that made her stomach drop. Just a few hours before, she wouldn't have hesitated.

"Of course," she said at last.

His stormy eyes locked onto her. "Well, that was convincing."

Pulling herself up to full height, she lifted her chin. "I have full confidence in our combined awesomeness."

"You always say that."

"And we're still alive, right?"

Benton's response was lost under Daniel's clipped voice. "What are you two whispering about?"

"The weather," Benton shot back instantly.

An angry flush crept up the elder's neck, his mouth twisting down into a snarl.

"We're cold," Nicole said quickly, swiftly indicating their bare feet and lack of jumpers. "There wasn't time for us to get out of our pajamas. So, you know, we were chatting about the cold weather."

Daniel raked his eyes over Benton. Nicole couldn't stop herself from cringing back even though she wasn't on the receiving end of it.

"Your kind feels temperature, then?" he asked at last.

"Yeah," Benton said slowly. Cautiously.

"I thought you said you didn't know anything about your species."

"Obviously I know what *I* personally experience," Benton shot back.

Daniel bristled. "That's how you speak to your elders?"

"This is how you treat minorities?" Benton replied without missing a beat. He shrugged at Nicole. "What? I am. Name one other Banshee you know."

Her chuckle wasn't a good idea. She knew it the moment she saw the red flush work its way up Daniel's neck to splash out onto his face. Quickly, she looked down at her feet, knocking her elbow into Benton until he reluctantly did the same. Wapun used this moment of submission to swiftly swoop in and distract Daniel.

"Why must you provoke people?" Nicole whispered to Benton.

"It's part of my charm," he smirked.

She quickly decided that she wasn't going to push it any further. Benton had this strange sense of world order. If everyone liked him, and were generally nice to him, he would actually get paranoid. Like the cosmos was setting him up for some horrible, cruel twist. With Adam now seeing Benton as his personal hero, he was in desperate need to get things back to their normal state.

A thought hit her like an arctic wind. *He only feels safe when he's hated. He trusts more in rage than friendship. Is that because of his stalker?* The fact that he hadn't told her anything about this part of his past sunk into her brain like a branding iron. She had convinced herself that she knew everything there was to know about him. Now she was faced with the stark reality that there was still so much to him that he had refused to even let her glimpse. It made her stomach churn.

"Nic?" Benton's chilled hand wrapped around her wrist. He tugged a little to better get her attention. "Are you okay?"

She nodded hurriedly and grinned broadly. "Of course."

"I'm the one that tunes out, not you." His voice was laced with concern.

Trying to shrug it off, she noticed that they were already standing back at their teepee, right on the edge of the tree line, waiting for Wapun to finish her blessing. The other elders had gathered in a semi-circle around her, lending their voices to the chanted songs. Scented smoke and soft voices lingered on the morning stillness. Benton's fingers tightened around her wrist. Nowhere near hard enough to hurt, of course. Just a firm, constant pressure that allowed her warmth to seep from her skin into his.

"You're as cold as death."

By the time it occurred to her that it was a pretty callous thing to say, the words were already out. She stammered to form an apology as a small smile crossed his lips.

He rubbed his thumb back and forth over her pulse point, seemingly just savoring the small bit of warmth that was on offer to him. It spoke volumes that he hadn't complained about the cold once. *He's really trying,* she thought.

Always quick to pick isolation over irritation, Benton was swift to cut off contact with anyone that made him uneasy. The only reason he would stick it out with the elders was that he knew it was important to her. That was humbling. She leaned closer to him, positioning herself to break the creeping wind and hopefully keep him a little warmer.

"You're with me, right?" Benton whispered. "Don't leave me alone with these freaks."

Her automatic chastisement died on her tongue when her gaze skirted to Daniel. The elder stood a few feet away, simultaneously aiding Wapun with the blessing and glaring daggers at Benton. It was hard to take the man seriously when he was investing so much time staring down a teenager. She bit the inside of her cheek to keep from giggling. Momentarily ridiculous or not, he was still an elder and deserving of respect.

"Yeah, I've got you," she promised. "Oh, wait a second. I almost forgot."

Benton's jaw dropped as she ripped her arm free of his grip and bolted the limited distance back to their teepee.

"What the hell? You *just* said-"

"I'll be right back," Nicole cut in, keeping her voice to a harsh whisper.

It didn't take more than a few seconds for her to retrieve her newest gift for him and return. Still, he wasn't too happy about the whole situation. His face looked almost as dark and brooding as Daniel's. It made it impossible to hold back a small burst of laughter. The noise seemed all the louder since Wapun chose that moment to end the song and turn her attention back to the teenagers. Embarrassment flushed through her at the woman's questioning look. So she focused on pulling her present out of the thin drawstring bag.

Bone beads rattled together as she pulled the choker necklace free. She had never noticed how unnervingly similar that sound was to the clash of owl beaks. Ignoring the chill that ran down her spine, she quickly fixed the pale choker around Benton's neck. It was hard to tell which one of the witnesses was more confused. Either way, it was Benton that mumbled a 'thank-you' as if it were a question.

"It's held together with iron wire," she said. "It should keep the ghost from strangling you."

"That happens often?" Daniel asked.

"Yeah," Benton replied bitterly.

"And it's a real shame. You have such a pretty neck."

Benton's eyebrows shot up yet again.

"What was that?"

"You have a pretty neck," she repeated. Finally getting the latch to clasp, she stepped back. "I don't know why people find it so choke-able."

Benton stared at her for a long moment. "You're so weird."

"You're in no position to start throwing around those accusations," she said crisply.

He shrugged one shoulder. "You're still weird."

Puffing up her cheeks with a huff, she grabbed his hand and yanked him around to face the gathering elders. Her mother was still nowhere to be found, and that offered her a small amount of relief. None of this was going to be a pleasant experience for Adam. She couldn't imagine how much worse it would be to take his statement. *We can get this done before she even knows it*, Nicole reasoned to herself.

Carefully, she kept her mind from creeping towards the other reason why she didn't want her mother here.

Dorothy knew about what had happened on the highway; that they were attacked. That a serial killer had wrapped his hands around Benton's neck. And that, without hesitation, Nicole had put a bullet between his eyes. She didn't, however, know that her daughter didn't have the slightest slither of guilt over her actions. A part of her was still disgusted with herself. She knew she should care. That it should keep her up at night and churn her stomach until she could barely stand. As much as she knew it, the sensations never came.

And when that man came back as a Baykok to take another shot, she had gone after him again with just as much savage dedication. The guilt of not feeling any remorse had almost ripped her apart.

Then she talked to Benton. She heard how pleased he was that she could face these nightmares that clawed out of his head and not break. Nothing had ever made her as proud as knowing she made him feel safe. Protected. None of that meant that she was ready for her mother to know any of that. Dorothy was startlingly observant. Someday soon, she would see her daughter for exactly who she was.

*That doesn't have to be today*, Nicole told herself.

Out loud, she said, "Is everyone ready?"

The elders carefully arranged the items in the possession into a neat pile. They kept their solemn silence, though, each one cautious as to how to proceed even while they were determined to do so. Nicole didn't hesitate to fill the silence.

"She seems to like the trees," she said. "Kind of like a cougar. She keeps herself hidden until she's ready to kill."

"How could you possibly know that?" Daniel asked skeptically.

"Well," Nicole subconsciously began to pinch her thumbpad. "Either she's the one that's lured me out for two nights, or there's something else in there with her. I've got my fingers crossed for the first."

"Yeah, we don't want this to be our whole week," Benton said with a smirk.

"Exactly! I've had this trip planned out for months, and we're way off schedule." She noticed the expressions on the faces around her. "And, you know, other more socially appropriate reasoning."

"Wow, you can't even think of one example, huh?"

She shushed Benton and picked up the conversation where it had left off.

"She ambushed us from above, so I'm pretty sure she'd keep him in the treetops with her. If she hasn't already eaten him or something."

"Eaten him?" Rowtag Smoke asked quickly. The deep lines of his face became canyons as worry settled onto his features. "Are you actually suggesting that this spirit will devour the man?"

"Hopefully," Benton said before blowing hot air onto his fingertips. "Why is everyone looking at me like that? There's no non-disturbing reason to keep a corpse. Trust me, having him as a snack is probably the best option we're looking at."

"You don't sound at all disturbed by this," Daniel said.

Benton shrugged one shoulder and blew on his hands again.

Being so blatantly ignored enraged Daniel. He clenched his jaw, hissing his words out between his teeth. "I'm starting to question your mental health."

Benton put even less effort into his repeated shrug, more concerned with rubbing his hands together than with the enraged man standing a few feet from him. Nicole jabbed her elbow into Benton's ribs.

"Why am I in trouble?" he whined. Enduring her glare for a moment, he huffed loudly and turned to face Daniel fully. "I'm terribly sorry if you found me rude. There's obviously blame on both sides. You're not creative in your insults, and I'm not particularly excited by your existence."

Nicole pinched the bridge of her nose. "You suck at apologies."

"That's why I don't do them often," Benton replied, sounding all too pleased with himself.

Having seen this dance play out with numerous authority figures, Nicole knew that he wasn't about to let up. Trying to get him back in line now would only have him push back twice as hard. Daniel wasn't going to be any better at letting this go, either.

Clearing her throat loudly, Nicole regained everyone's attention. "Benton and I will use the trail to the parking lot."

'Trail' was a generous term to describe the narrow, overgrown path of least resistance. Summertime visitors eager to get to the shady riverbank had trudged through the clustered trees, trampling the undergrowth to sever the forest in two. Getting to the path would be the hardest part. Then it'd be a relatively clear shot to the parking lot.

Sophia, the youngest of the elders, toyed thoughtfully with the tips of her vivid pink hair. "Remember that, while the path will make it easier for you to move, it'll make things easier for her as well."

"We're talking about a ghost." Hurit's thick round glasses made her eyes seem unsettlingly large. Despite this, she could still barely see, and ended up glaring at everything with an edge of malice. "I don't think the trees cause it any problems."

"Then it could hide the body anywhere," Sophia argued.

"That's why we only have to make sure that the path is clear," Hurit shot back. "Right now, we only need to ensure that a random tourist isn't going to stumble upon a mangled corpse."

"Perhaps that's your goal, but I wish to have this thing removed from the land. And keep us safe while doing so."

"Which we will do *after* ensuring that there isn't going to be a panic," Hurit snapped.

"Ladies." Wapun's sharp tone made them all fall into silence. "There is no perfect scenario here. Let's focus instead on Nicole's assumption that she's going in alone."

"With Benton," Nicole blurted out like a child caught in a lie.

Benton waved. *Not exactly helpful*, Nicole sighed.

"We'll lose sight of you, and your mother has yet to arrive. I'm not comfortable with this," Wapun replied.

"Do you have your mobile, Auntie? We can video call. You'll be able to see everything."

"And offer no help."

"Well," Nicole pursed her lips and forced her brain to crack through an assortment of ideas. She couldn't give Wapun time to dwell on the idea of waiting for her mom. "Oh! Why don't we ask Mic to take a look first?" She turned to Benton and smiled as sweetly as possible. "Is she still around?"

"Who's Mic?" Daniel and Rowtag voiced the question in unison. The first as a demand, the second with curiosity.

"Mictecacihuatl is our friend," Nicole said. "She's been very helpful in the past."

"She's a Grim Reaper," Benton added.

*Really?* Nicole screamed at him with her eyes. He met her gaze with vague amusement. *You need to find a better coping mechanism.* She didn't think he'd catch on to the full meaning of the unspoken sentence. However, with just a tip of his head, she understood his reply with utter clarity. *Nah, I'm good with this.*

"And you can summon this creature?" Daniel asked.

Disgust crossed Benton's face. He quickly masked it with his usual state of disinterested disdain.

"I don't summon anyone. She's an independent embodiment of death with a will of her own."

"So why does she take such an interest in you?" Daniel challenged.

"Poor taste?" Benton replied.

"Benton." Nicole gripped his arm until he winced at the pressure. At least it worked to get his attention and stop the spiraling argument. "Can you ask her?"

There was a particular sound Benton made when he agreed to do something that he really didn't want to. A bitter, breathless scoff that somehow ended with a grunt. Hearing it now almost made her dance with relief. Pushing up onto his toes, Benton stretched out his neck and glanced around, trying to see over everyone's heads without having to move.

"I can't see her."

"Try calling her," Nicole whispered. "Be polite. She might be busy."

After sparing a moment to make that sound again, Benton's voice rose slightly. "Hey Mic. Are you around? Nicole wants to ask you for a favor."

Silence.

"Sorry," Benton got the word out right before releasing a startled scream. Cursing with creativity, he threw himself back, only maintaining his position because Nicole refused to release his arm. "Don't do that!"

Nicole couldn't help but smile, recalling how utterly terrified Benton had been when he had first spoken of the numerous Deaths that circled around him. Seeing him comfortable around Mic was an incredible leap forward.

"What did she do?" Sophia asked, fingers twisting rapidly around her neon hair.

"They're all big on jump scares," Benton replied before he ignored the living to explain the situation to the dead.

Nicole had never been able to catch sight of a Reaper. Still, she searched the air restlessly, trying to spot anything that was out of place.

"So, what do you think?" Benton asked awkwardly. "It was Nic's idea."

"Was that necessary to mention?"

"She likes Nic," Benton replied.

Throwing his arms out, Daniel looked at each elder in turn. "Are we really going to buy this? He's talking to thin air."

Rowtag rubbed a thumb over the lines of his forehead. "Perhaps he can see something we can't."

"Or he's playing us for fools." Whipping back around, he locked a dark glare onto Benton. "Prove it. Make her do something. Move a stone or make a sound."

For the first time, true rage welled in Benton's eyes, darkening the color to resemble a gathering monsoon.

"You delusional idiot," Benton growled. "How the hell do you think you have any right to order us to do anything?"

Daniel bristled. "Remember the position you're in, son. You need to keep on our good side."

Benton took a step towards the older man, only stopping when Nicole grabbed his arm with both hands. *Not good! Not good! Stop this!* For all her frantic orders, she couldn't get her brain to work.

"Finally, you're showing the monster you are. Go on, hit me. I'll have you banished," Daniel snarled.

The air suddenly plunged into darkness.

It happened so swiftly that everyone present instantly looked up to the sky. Everyone but Benton. He didn't move an inch as the sky filled once more with a flock of predatory birds. This time, they didn't land on the ground. They filled the nearby branches, looming over the small group, the ghastly cries shattering the silence. A silent figure swooped over Nicole's head. With a squeal, she ducked, still too late to prevent the light brush of talons. It was barely enough to be called actual contact, but more than enough to release pearls of hot blood. A stray drop trickled down her forehead as she looked up.

Bird had perched on Benton's shoulder. His massive wings were pulled back, his plumage bristled until he looked like a dark specter looming over Benton. Talons of polished onyx sliced easily into Benton's flesh. He didn't seem to notice. Didn't so much as flinch as blood began to stain the slashed material of his shirt. All of his attention was fixed onto Daniel alone.

"I live with demons." Benton's voice came out distorted. Softer, echoing within his chest before ever passing his lips. Lifting his chin, the world erupted in the wild cry of the ferocious birds. "Threaten him again, and I'll unleash them all upon you."

Heat cupped Benton's cheeks and he was jerked to the side, a sudden lurch that made his brain slosh around his skull. He staggered, barely able to keep himself upright. None of it felt like it belonged to him. Not his bones, not the blood rushing through his veins, not the pain pulsating from his shoulder. Bit by bit, he contorted his soul to fit the suffocating confines of his skin. It all felt terrifyingly similar to waking up.

Nicole's voice rolled in his ears. Just the tempo and volume. None of it made any sense.

"What's wrong?" he mumbled, his tongue feeling too big for his mouth.

The competing noise separated itself from her voice. He glanced up, shocked to find the flock that had crowded around them. The abrupt motion pulled the skin of his shoulder, the resulting spike of pain making him gasp. Jerking around jostled Bird, making him flap wildly to keep his balance. His talons scraped over Benton's collar bone, forcing a whimper from Benton's lips.

"What the hell, man? We talked about this," Benton grumbled through clenched teeth.

He held up three fingers. Trial and error had proven that was just thick enough for Bird to stand comfortably without his talons doing any damage. With a squawk, he fluttered over. The nails leaving his skin hurt just as much as they had going in. Benton almost doubled over before Bird had finished the transfer. Nicole appeared out of thin air, her delicate fingers peeling the blood-soaked material back from his slashed skin.

Enduring the touch, he glared at the owl. "If I need stitches, I'm going to be ticked."

Bird rotated his head around 180 degrees.

"I'm talking to you," Benton grumbled.

Nicole pressed a finger hard against his skin and he screamed, cringing away from the contact.

"It's already healing," Nicole whispered.

"So, by all means, open it up again," Benton snapped. The fear in her eyes shattered his anger. "Nic, what happened?"

"You don't remember?" Wapun asked.

Benton jumped. The jumbled mess of his mind had completely forgotten about the elders' existence. He was strangely repulsed to remember them now.

Shifting his shoulders to crowd closer to Nicole, he whispered, "What's going on? Did I fall asleep?"

The flock began to disperse as Nicole studied him closely, casting deep shadows through the brilliant green haze. A few of the light serpents coiled around them as he waited for her response.

"Does it feel like you fell asleep?"

He nodded shallowly. A dark look crossed Nicole's face. It was there only a moment before she covered it with a smile.

"Come on, I'll explain on the way."

"Explain it to us first!" Daniel roared.

Bird screeched and flung his wings wide, tipping forward as if preparing to attack. The ferocity of the gesture quickly had Daniel retreating. Benton could only stare in shock at Bird's barely contained fury.

*What happened?* The question raced around his head, unable to find anything that could possibly be considered an answer. It was as if he had blinked and the world had lurched forward without him.

"Would it be possible for you to calm it down?" Daniel reluctantly added after a heartbeat, "Please."

The utter lack of demand jarred Benton from his thoughts. He flicked his gaze from one face to the next, seeing a matching hint of fear upon each of their features.

"What the hell is going on?" Benton whispered.

Nicole swooped in once more, tentatively reaching out slightly to stroke the back of Bird's head. The owl crouched low and twisted his head around, flashing his beak threateningly at her approaching fingertips.

"It's okay," she cooed softly. "No-one's going to hurt Benton. It's okay."

Bird scooted along Benton's fingers, stopping just as one foot enclosed around his wrist. Pinpricks of pain sparked at the contact, racing up Benton's arm while remaining low enough to be easily ignored. Bird's head swiveled again. Large yellowed eyes locked onto Benton's. An odd sensation worked its way around his chest. Something almost foreign and yet undoubtedly familiar was emerging from within the depths of his soul. Suddenly, Bird settled back into his natural placid state, accepting Nicole's touch and even rubbing his head against her fingertips.

Never one to let an opening pass by unexploited, Nicole quickly grabbed Benton's elbow and dragged him towards the forest. With the elders caught between shock and dread, they were already past the first line of trees before they thought to intervene. She plowed a straight path to the thin, narrow opening he vaguely remembered from the night before. That was when he locked his knees and jerked her to a stop.

Nicole reeled and practically launched herself back onto his shoulder. Bird echoed his disgruntled protest. Not that it was enough to stop her. With rushed, careful fingers, she peeled the soaked material of his shirt from his skin.

"It's almost healed. How is that possible?" she mumbled over and over.

"Nic, I really need some answers. What happened?"

She swallowed thickly and stood still.

"How am I supposed to know?" she said, her attempt to make a joke falling flat when her fingertips brushed against his punctured skin. She winced at his sharp hiss. "Sorry. Is it still tender?"

Benton didn't reply. He only stood there and stared at her with an emotionless expression. She held out about as long as he thought she would. Barely twenty seconds or so.

"I don't know for sure," she whispered, avoiding his gaze. "All I can do is guess."

"So take a guess."

Biting her lips, she continued to fuss with the wound on his shoulder. But her motions were slower. More like a comforting caress than her sterile first aid training.

"You asked if you fell asleep. Why?"

"It felt like that," Benton said, not knowing how best to describe it. "Like someone else had pushed me out of my own skin."

Nicole swallowed again. "I think Mic jumped you."

"Jumped me?" he said carefully.

"It's a term I've heard on paranormal blogs. Basically, it just means that a ghost slips into your skin and takes over. I guess it's the same principle with a Grim Reaper."

His stomach opened up into a dark pit. "I was possessed?"

"That's a harsh way of looking at it," Nicole said.

"Mic took me for a joy ride. How would you word it?"

"Not like that either." It was clear that she was looking for a way to make this easier on him. She was failing. "Nothing bad happened."

"You opted for running into a haunted forest rather than try to explain this to your elders," he noted.

Nicole stammered. "You have me there."

"What did she make me do?"

"Nothing bad," she insisted quickly. "That's why I'm sure it was Mic."

Quickly running out of patience, and numb with fear, Benton growled her name.

"It's nothing. She more or less told Daniel to back off. She's very protective of you."

White static filled his head, drowning out the rest of her reassurances and promises that everything would be okay. The air was ripped from his lungs, forced out with his throbbing heartbeat. Gasping frantically, he couldn't stave off the numbness that settled into his bones, and dropped to his knees. Bird flapped around him. The beat of his wings intensifying the icy sweat that covered his skin.

"Benton? Benton? Just breathe, okay?"

*I can't!* he screamed within his head, unable to push the words past his lips. *I'm going to die.* The knowledge slammed into the forefront of his mind as his vision brightened and blurred. Nicole cupped his face and forced his head up to meet her gaze.

"You're having a panic attack," she said. "Everything will be okay. You're safe."

*There could be a killer ghost three feet away! The elders want me dead! Grim Reapers can use me as a meat puppet! What part of this is okay?*

Unable to scream the words, they were left to fill his head, an increasing power that threatened to break him apart. A piercing whine filled his ears, bringing with it a blinding pain.

"This will pass," Nicole assured. "Just take a deep breath for me, okay?"

He glared at her as his body began to shake violently. *Like it's that easy?*

Bird's screeching wail made it all the worse. He could feel the animals panic as if it was his own. It didn't feel real when Nicole grabbed his arm and tugged it off of the ground, like his muscles were water; sloshing about with no real form of their own. Scattering with the motion. Taking with it the rest of his flesh until he felt himself evaporate into the air.

A steady heartbeat rushed through him like a crashing wave. Frothing and churning, it gathered the broken parts of him, bringing them back together. The sensation didn't last. But, before he could break apart again, another pulse slammed into him. Bit by bit, he could feel his muscles and tendons regain their form. Panting hard, he barely had the strength to lift his head.

Nicole had his scarred palm pressed tight against her chest. Tight enough that he was able to feel her heartbeat through her ribcage. With her free hand, she brushed the hair off of his forehead, letting her nails scrape along his scalp. The tension in his chest began to relax. Blocking everything else out, he focused on the rise and fall of her chest, struggling to match his breathing to hers. It got easier with time. Bird calmed once more, and everything fell silent.

"You're doing so well," she encouraged. "Come on, one more big breath. That's it."

He relished the feeling of air swelling his lungs and forced a smirk. "You're going to be a great stage mom one day."

"Glad to see that you're feeling better," she replied.

Suddenly exhausted, he dipped forward to rest his forehead against her shoulder.

"I've never had a panic attack before."

"Well, today's been kind of stressful," she said.

He didn't have the words to describe how grateful he was that she kept carding her fingers through his hair. Somewhere in the back of his mind, he wondered when she had learned how calming that was for him. *Not the most obscure thing she's learned about me.*

Benton groaned and curled deeper into her warmth. "It's bad enough having them rip my mind apart every time I close my eyes. Now I have to put up with it while I'm awake, too?"

"We'll find a way to stop it."

"How?" A flash of anger sharpened his voice. Rearing back, he glared at her, her startled innocence stoking his anger. "You never listen! I told you not to mess around with this stuff!"

"I'm not messing around," she stammered in defense.

"You made me open myself up to the dead. What if I can't get them out again?"

For once, she didn't have a reply waiting on hand. No reassurances or assertions of approaching victory. She only sat there, staring at him, silent and defeated. *Good. Let her have a dose of reality,* he thought even as her expression gutted him. His shoulders slumped as the last of his fight left him.

"I'm sorry," he mumbled.

She sniffed. "No, it's okay. You're right."

"Yeah, I know," he squirmed, suddenly unsure what to do with any of his limbs. "But I should have worded it better. Maybe use a softer tone or something."

A weak smile twitched the corner of her mouth. "Yeah, maybe. I keep making things worse for you, don't I?"

"No," he replied instantly before shrugging one shoulder. "Well, yeah, you do sometimes. But you always drag me back out again."

Nicole wrapped her arms around her legs and rested her chin on her knees. It took a moment for him to realize that she was subconsciously mirroring him.

"Do you really think I'm going to get us killed one day?" she asked abruptly.

He shook his head. "No, just me. You promised, remember."

"Why do you put up with me?"

"Because you put up with me," he replied instantly. "Besides, who else have I got to hang around?"

Her smile reappeared, staying longer than it had before. "You always have yourself."

"That jerk?" he dismissed.

Nicole reached towards him. A peace offering. Forgiveness. The pain left his chest as he moved to take her hand.

An ebony stain rolled out from behind her, twisting like oil bleeding into water, blotting out everything it came into contact with. Benton latched onto Nicole's wrist and yanked her to his side. She tumbled down onto the undergrowth, giving him the second he needed to ensure he was between her and the gathering Death. The oblong smear that served as Mic's head tore itself free from the mass. She rose one bone-white hand, each joint locked to make the swift motion still distorted.

"Don't touch me." Benton's throat swelled with the promise of a scream, making his voice rumble.

Mic didn't retreat.

"I swear to God, I will find a way to hurt you."

The Grim Reaper locked into place, as still as stone even while the edges of its form wafted out like smoke. Benton refused to blink. Panic filled him like tidal waves. Of all the stupid, reckless things he had done in his life, challenging Death to her face was the worst.

Mic studied him carefully as she hovered in silence. He flinched back as her arm moved. Ebony shadows draped over the frail limb as she slowly swung it out to the side. The exposed bones of her fingers curled in, leaving only one to point the way into the depths of the forest, slightly left of where they had intended to go.

"What's going on?" Nicole whispered as she pressed against his spine.

"Mic's here to give us directions," he said.

Nicole squeezed his shoulder until the bones ached. "That's nice. Um, why?"

Without taking his eyes off of the Death before him, he turned his head slightly towards her.

"Not sure."

"Do we want to follow?"

"You make the call."

"Didn't we just agree that I suck at that?" Nicole instantly followed that up with, "Let's go."

Reaching blindly back, Benton grabbed her hand, clutching it tightly as they got up to their feet. All the while, Mic held her position with all the rigidity of rigor mortis. Cautiously, Benton edged around the figure, sneaking quick glances over his shoulder at the direction she indicated.

"She wants us to go to the river?" Nicole asked.

"Is the river over there?"

"Yes."

"Then I guess so," he replied.

Nicole tightened her grip on his hand a little more and gave him a slight tug. "Come on. We don't want to stay in here too long."

Not willing to give Mic his back, Benton walked backward, trusting Nicole to lead the way. Mic made no attempt to follow, remaining as a dark void against the rich colors of the forest.

Muffled noises drifted from the nearby campsite, the faintest rumbling sound that could barely be heard over the crunch of dried leaves. Morning light flashed through the canopy, striking his eyes with a blinding glare. Without the living aurora, all the colors were too bright. Pain pricked the back of his eyes as he searched the treetops for movement. It was easy to pick up on the sound of rustling leaves. Far harder to find the source.

The earth moistened under his bare feet as he followed Nicole's lead. Every step brought another ache to his legs. Not a throbbing pain. More like his muscles were hardening underneath his skin. The fingertips of his free hand began to toy with the thick beads of his choker, seeking out the thin iron wire that held them all together.

"We're getting close," he whispered.

"You see it?"

"Feel it," he replied.

She threw a questioning look over her shoulder, but he shook his head. *Now's not the time.* Reluctantly, she left all of her questions unspoken. The soft babbling of the stream emerged through the leaves. Flowing as it did around the bend had left it gently lapping at the muddy bank and gnarled roots. Ducking under a low branch, Nicole's foot found the soggy drop-off. Benton had barely enough time to grab onto the tree branch with his free hand before toppling down after her. Using their grip for leverage, she pulled herself back up.

"Watch your step over there," she whispered.

"No kidding."

There really wasn't anywhere they could have fallen that would have done much harm. The river pushed into the forest, depositing silt and claiming the fallen logs, creating a gradual transition from water to land. The steepest drop off was only a few feet at most, and the calm, clear water hid relatively little. None of that was enough to soften the ache forming in the back of Benton's throat.

"Where to now?" Nicole asked, still keeping her voice low.

Benton glanced around at the undisturbed beauty surrounding them. Sunlight glistened off of the water, making it shine like a shifting sea of jewels. The scents of fresh mud and pine lingered on every breath, and only the lapping water broke the silence.

"She's not here."

"Reassured or alarmed?" Nicole asked. "Which one should I be feeling right now?"

Instead of answering, Benton shifted his weight between his feet, feeling every muscle involved pull taut. Thick mud oozed between his toes, coating his feet and numbing them just a little bit more. Nicole began to squirm beside him, more out of impatience than trying to fight off the cold, although she would deny she felt either.

"Where is this guy?" she grumbled to herself.

Benton didn't know that he had moved until he noticed a pinched expression settle onto Nicole's face. He still had one hand holding tightly on to hers. The other now pointed to the branches that loomed above their heads.

# Chapter 13

Bark flaked away under Nicole's fingertips as she gripped the tree trunk. Benton was prepared for her to push off of his cupped hands and, without a word of warning, she began to climb. With his boost, she was able to reach the lowest branch and soon squirmed her way onto it. There hadn't been much of a debate over which one of them should actually go and check. Benton was the one who could see any lurking spirits. Nicole was the one who could actually get up the rope in gym class.

"Can't we just go?" Benton asked before she got too high to hear his harsh whisper. "No one's going to see him up there."

"*If* he's up here," she corrected.

For an instant, all of his concern was replaced with exhausted annoyance. "Which one of us keeps saying that I need to trust in my Banshee skills?"

She decided it was best to avoid answering. "We still need to check his wallet."

"Sorry?"

"I don't know how mom plans to deal with this, but it's bound to be a lot easier if she knows who he is."

"I get that part," he said, hurrying the last words as she continued to climb. "What I'm stuck on is; what kind of moron brings I.D. with them to kidnap someone?"

"Fair point."

"So let's just go and tell the people with guns where he is."

*Do guns hurt ghosts now?* Deciding that the question would only prolong the conversation, Nicole gripped the newest branch she was on and glanced down to him again. She had to raise her voice a little to ask, "Do you know this guy's name?"

Benton frowned. "I only get the victim's names. You know that."

"Then I'll be quick."

"Nic-"

"Traditionally, lookouts are silent."

He huffed something under his breath but didn't say more to her, instead opting to hug himself tightly and restlessly scan the area around him. She watched him for a moment, wondering if he knew that he shuddered every time he looked to the river. Then she put every ounce of her concentration into the climb.

Rough bark gouged her hands and feet as she forced herself higher. The branches became steadily shorter, forcing her to fight against clusters of pine needles for proper handholds. Squirming her way through a dense blanket of foliage, she smacked the top of her head into a hidden branch. Her foot slipped and her nails carved pathways through the bark as she worked her way around it. Heat hammering, she straddled the branch and hugged the tree tightly.

Buttery sunlight streamed in through the thinner canopy. Warm and welcoming, she relished the feel of it against her skin as she gulped down a few deep breaths. When her heart had slowed to a more acceptable pace, she opened her eyes. Her sight of what was below was broken up by the pine needles. What glimpse remained was enough to have her doubling her grip on the tree. Vertigo left her dizzy and her heart throbbed in double time. She had been so focused on going up that it hadn't occurred to her just how high she was. And the distance looked all the greater when there was nothing to break her fall but solid earth. To her right, she spotted another branch. Thinner than the one she sat upon now; it stretched out wide over the water. *The river's ten feet deep in places,* she told herself, only to recall a second later that a series of mud banks left it half an inch deep in others. Racking her brain, she tried to recall which parts were where.

Gathering her courage, she twisted the bare minimum necessary for her to sneak a quick peek around her. A rush of adrenaline brought pinpricks to her skin as she spotted him. Dying twigs and new saplings had woven together to create a nest a few feet back from where she was perched. The deep maroon of dried blood stained the tangled mess of rich greens and earthy browns. Small opens allowed her glimpses of fabric and flesh. Then, as if to chase any lingering doubt from her mind, the wind shifted and she was bombarded with a cocktail of various bodily fluids.

*At least it's only been a few hours,* she thought gratefully as she suppressed her gag reflex. Hunting with her father had taught her that it took about a day for larger mammals to really start to smell of death. That rank, pungent, sickly sweet stench that clung to everything around it. Compared to that, the aroma of a sewage system was easy to deal with.

Nicole put it all aside for a minute to wallow in self-pity, revulsion, and the desire to just climb right back down. The second that time was over, she pushed the thoughts aside and set herself to the task at hand. Twisting around without toppling over was harder than she had first anticipated. She just couldn't get her legs to move the right way.

A sudden shriek of noise made her jolt. Chunks of bark scraped her cheek as she flattened herself against the branch, hugging the hunk of wood with both arms and legs. Vibrations against her upper thigh made her squeal. She swatted at the spot, hissing again when her knuckles clashed against her hard phone case. Still gripping the tree with every part of her body that she could, she ripped her mobile free, answered it, and jammed it between her ear and shoulder.

"Hi," she squeaked.

"Are you alright?" Benton asked in a rush.

Nicole almost dropped the phone. Then almost fell as she tried to save it. "You have your mobile?"

"Duh." She could hear him rolling his eyes. "Now can you tell me if you're in a life-threatening situation?"

Nicole caught sight of the straight drop to the ground and squeezed her eyes shut. "I'm good. No sight of the ghost girl yet. Um, not that I don't love hearing from you, but why are you calling?"

"Deep concern," he replied. "Plus, a mix of fear, paranoia, and annoyance at your Auntie ringing me nonstop for the last fifteen minutes."

"Why would she ring you?"

"Because she's pushing 90 and doesn't know what Skype is." His frustrated sigh crackled along the line. "My best bet is that she put my number in her phone as 'Nicole's friend' and is too stressed out to read the contact title all the way through."

Keeping her eyes closed, she focused on Benton's voice, trying to convince herself that she wasn't a single flinch away from plummeting to her death. "Yeah, that does sound like something she'd do."

"Are you okay?" Benton repeated.

"Yes," she said. "I found him."

"And?"

"I haven't gotten close enough to check his pockets yet. She put him in a pretty far off branch. How are things down there?"

"Nic, you aren't trying to distract me from the fact that you're about to fall, are you?"

She paused. "No. I was just looking for a ghost update."

"I can feel her. I can't see her."

*Not comforting.* "I don't mean to be rude, but I kind of need my hands right now."

"Yeah, of course," he said hurriedly. "I don't like that I can't see you."

"I'll be right back down. Promise."

"Can you keep me connected?"

"Sure. Hold on."

She struggled to shove her phone back into the tight pocket of her yoga pants. Each shift and rattle left her convinced she was about to fall. *Stop it,* she told herself sharply. *Nothing gets done if all you do is freak out. Set a goal. Work towards it.* Her chest crushed against the unrelenting wood as she took in a sobering breath.

Opening her eyes, she focused her gaze on the nest. Carefully but determinedly, she braced her hands and pushed her torso up. Still feeling unstable, she remained like that, scooting forward inch by inch, her ears straining for the slightest hint that the wood was giving way. Violent trembles had wracked her body by the time she managed to get her hands on the edge of the tangled weeds.

Her arms gave out as she crawled her way over the rim, and she dropped hard over the man's legs. With a series of sharp snaps, the bottom of the nest fell out in patches. The man's right leg dropped, leaving Nicole's arm to follow it through the gap, the side of her head smacking against a harder patch. Her attempts to get back up widened the gap. Jolting and thrashing, she scrambled around until the sound stopped.

"Nic?" Benton's muffled voice whispered around her. "Nicole? God damn it, answer me!"

"I'm okay." She was barely able to get the words out through her heaved breaths. "I'm okay. Everything's fine."

Repeating the words until she could believe them, she braced herself to look down at the corpse. There wasn't anything she could pinpoint as to what had changed about him. Nothing more substantial than his drawn pallor and taut features. But he barely looked like the man she remembered. The cold weather had urged on rigor mortis, helping to lock his face into a distorted mask of pure terror. His eyes were fixed and lifeless, staring at her as she looked anywhere else. She screamed when she found her foot lodged in the man's open chest cavity. Throwing herself backward made the nest shiver and threaten to fall apart. She scrambled for purchase, bracing her feet and gripping the rim. Brittle twigs snapped under her fingers as the nest groaned. Holding her breath, she rattled with the heavy thumps of her heart, waiting to see if gravity would win or not.

Benton's voice crept from the phone's speaker, carefully soft so as not to startle her. "Nic?"

Refusing to move, she whimpered, "I kicked his kidneys."

"You kicked him? He's alive?"

"I've got bile between my toes."

"Oh, your foot was *inside* him." After a brief pause, he added, "Baking soda and vodka."

Surprise and curiosity crackled through her like a live wire, drawing her from her crippling fear. "Huh?"

"Mix them together to create a paste and use it as soap. It'll get rid of the smell."

*Disturbing that you know that,* she noted. Grasping onto that thought helped bring her back to her senses. She licked her lips slowly and leaned forward. It didn't take much of a stretch to reach the man's slack pocket. Searching them, in turn, produced a mobile phone and hotel room key. With a little organization, she was able to drop them both down to Benton.

"Are we robbing him now?" he asked, careful to whisper just loud enough to be heard through the covered phone. "Not opposed. Just wondering."

"Mom might need them."

"I don't think there's going to be a proper investigation," Benton said.

"Better to be prepared. I'm not making a second trip."

Trying her best not to look at the gaping wound of his stomach, she rolled the man up by the hip. Stiffening muscles made the motion strange, and she was half certain that she heard a strange pop and squelch. She slipped one hand into the narrow gap and searched for his back pockets.

Exposed spinal discs brushed across her fingertips and the coppery scent of blood assaulted her nose. If there had been anything in her stomach, it would have gushed out over the corpse. *Keep it together.* The demand didn't help much. She still had to squeeze her eyes shut in order to try again. This time, she managed to find a wallet. Tearing it free, she tossed it over the edge and retreated back, letting the body drop with another stomach-churning squelch.

Her stomach lurched. Bile burned the back of her throat as she shoved her face into a thick cluster of pine needles. The sharp, fresh scent masked the stench of blood enough for her stomach to settle a little.

"What grown man has a Velcro wallet?" Benton mumbled. "Oh, my God. He brought his driver's license along. Mason Costa. Huh, he's American. Good, no one will be looking for him."

"He came all the way to Canada for Adam?" Nicole croaked, still breathing the scent of pine deep into her lungs.

"The point was that they weren't local to him. Any kid would have done." His voice changed within a split second. Sharpening with urgency and bristling with fear. "Get down here now. I've got a bad feeling."

Nicole's body instantly responded. Tangling her fingers in the side of the nest, she dragged herself up and over. Loose bark flaked free under her hurried steps. More leaping than running, she slammed into the trunk, hugging it tightly to regain her balance. Arching her neck, she hunted for a foothold. Fear slithered along in the inside of her skull, an instinctual warning that she had caught the attention of a predator. Sweat prickled the back of her neck as she snapped her face up.

Feet hovered above her head. Mud sunk into the milky flesh, giving the appearance of rot. Seeing the heels nearest to her, she had a flicker of hope that she could slip away unnoticed. Lifting her gaze, she found glowing eyes locked onto her. They burned like dying embers in the shadows of her midnight hair. *Her feet are twisted the wrong way.* The thought barely had time to slip across Nicole's awareness before her primitive mind took over. *Run!*

Nicole broke to the side, scrambling onto the nearest branch and raced along its length. The air stirred and the stench of decay filled her lungs. Nicole didn't dare glance back. There wasn't a doubt that the ghostly woman was hunting her down. Bark shifted under her feet, tripping her with every step. In a few seconds, she reached the lengths of the branch, and there was nowhere left to go. Pine needles billowed around her as she threw herself out into the open air.

She plummeted, her vision consumed by the approaching river, her back suddenly on fire as the ghost reached for her. Nails shredded her thin shirt and sunk into her flesh. A pained scream ripped from her throat at the contact. There wasn't time to process it before she crashed into the frigid river.

Water clogged her throat as the cold squeezed her lungs. Amongst the froth and foam, hands drove down to grasp her. Blood seeped out into the water to further distort her vision. Her back hit the bottom of the stream, colliding with stones and sending clouds of mud coiling up around her. The water vibrated as an unearthly wail pulsated through it. The muffled noise sunk into her skull, liquifying her brain as her lungs ached for air.

In the murky depths, the ghost's eyes still burned with ethereal fury. They weren't focused on Nicole. Even as the specter held her down, forcing the life out of Nicole's lungs, it didn't have any interest in her. Instead, it looked to the surface.

*Benton.*

Nicole kicked and thrashed. The ghost's fingers tightened around her upper arms, nails cutting into flesh, holding her down without much effort. Still, she didn't bother to look at Nicole. Darkness slowly crept around the corners of her vision, steadily reducing the world down until all that remained were the ghost's blazing eyes.

The sudden pulse turned the lazy stream into rapids. Silt hit her like shrapnel as the water swirled around them, lashing at the ghost and vibrating its cells apart. The sides of its skull remained solid as they were shoved apart. Everything between became an elastic sludge slung between the two points.

Nicole seized the opportunity to make another attempt for freedom. Torn apart by the Banshee's wail, the ghost couldn't keep any real strength in its grip. The current took her instantly, battering her across the bottom of the river.

Desperate for air and numbed by the cold, Nicole gathered the last shreds of energy and pushed off the muddy bottom, surging up towards the surface. Sunlight glistened above her, glorious but always out of reach. Taunting her as she was carried away by the violent tide.

# Chapter 14

The tips of the grass smacked against Benton's waist as he sprinted to catch up to Nicole. She had still been spitting up water when she had started to run, choking out excited words that barely made any sense. He knew that energy, though.

*She knows what it is.*

Bursting through the wall of shifting color, he collided with Dorothy. The older woman wrapped an arm around Benton's waist and kept him up with a surprising amount of strength.

"What happened? Where is it?" The rapid succession of questions didn't come out like they would have if her daughter had asked them. Dorothy's voice remained solid. Controlled.

"I've figured it out." Nicole doubled over, braced her hands on her knees and sucked in deep breaths. All the while, she grinned with pure delight. "Oh, and the dead guy's Mason something or other."

"Costa," Benton supplied.

"You found him?" Wapun asked as she hurried over, the others close behind. She went straight for her great niece and placed a tender hand on her shoulder.

"We're alright, Auntie," Nicole said. Pausing to gulp down another breath, she gestured vaguely with one hand. "He's in one of the taller trees by the river. Pretty well hidden."

Benton used that time to pass the dead man's personal effects to Constable Rider. She studied them for a moment before glancing around and shoving them into her pocket.

"Why did you scream?" Sophia asked, once again fiddling with her pink hair.

*As far as nervous tells go, that one's pretty obvious*, Benton thought.

"What were you thinking?" Daniel cut in before either Nicole or Benton had enough air to reply. "We could hear you from here. How are we supposed to explain that to people? We have enough to deal with trying to keep everyone safe without you terrorizing them."

"Oh, my God. Deal with your issues," Benton hissed.

Daniel bristled, Nicole looked horrified, and Dorothy adopted a look of furious disapproval the depths of which only a mother could reach. Normally, it would have been more than enough to crush Benton into submission. But the horrors in his head fortified his will. Straightening his spine, he turned to the man, fists balling in rage.

"You never once considered the idea that the spirits beyond your understanding don't give a shit about what you want, have you? Always just assumed that the good ones held you in high regard and the bad ones feared your name. Must be one hell of a shock to learn that you're just as insignificant as everyone else. Well, get over it. Your inferiority complex is not my problem."

"How dare you speak to me like that," Daniel stammered.

"Yesterday, I was told that I'm going to die right there." He jabbed a finger towards the riverbank. "Today, I was possessed by death. Also, I don't like you. Pick any one of these as a reason for why I'm not going to hold your hand through this."

"Benton," Nicole beseeched.

Latching onto her forearm, he yanked his best friend roughly in the direction of the teepee.

"Hey," she protested.

"We're getting changed before we get hypothermia," Benton snapped.

Nicole didn't fight him. But she did look over her shoulder and request a laptop and breakfast before he managed to wrangle her inside. The moment the flap flopped back, severing them from the rest of the world, Benton broke. She squeaked a little when he engulfed her in a crushing hug.

"You scared the hell out of me," he muttered.

Tightening his arms made her gasp. He reeled back at the pained sound, catching sight of the blood that now smeared his forearms.

"You're hurt."

"It's just a scratch. Good news; we now know that this thing isn't poisonous."

*Idiot, you tell people about these things!* He barely managed to contain the words, switching them out with a gruff request to see. Turning around, she pulled her hair over one shoulder, allowing him to peel the back of her shirt up carefully. Blood stained water rained out of the soaked material to pool at their feet.

"No problem, right?" she pressed.

Thin claw marks started at the tips of her shoulder blades and worked their way up to the back of her neck. Starting shallow and growing deeper. Benton thumbed at the splinted beads of her choker chain.

"See? Not a problem, right?" she asked.

"Would have been if you weren't wearing your choker."

Barely contained energy made her squirm as he retrieved the First Aid kit from her bag. She was bouncing on the balls of her feet by the time he managed to smear the antiseptic cream over the cuts. They had mostly stopped bleeding by now.

"Don't tell mom," Nicole said. "She'll worry."

"Didn't you learn anything about the dangers of keeping things from her?"

"I'll tell her. Just not right now. She'll try and take over."

"Oh, yeah. Wouldn't want professionals calling the shots in emergency situations."

"Benton," Nicole whined.

"Fine." *I really hate that sound.* "There. All done."

She quickly turned around and brought him into another hug. "I'm sorry I made you worry. And that I brought you to the river. That was really insensitive."

He smiled. "You want to make it up to me?"

"Of course," she said.

"Let me be mean to Daniel. I really hate that guy."

Nicole giggled and gave him a playful shove. "Come on. We have work to do."

"I'm taking that as a yes," Benton noted.

He barely had time to pull on a clean pair of jeans before Nicole was already heading out again. Cussing under his breath, he threw his wet clothing onto the pile she had started, yanked on a hoodie, snatched up a towel, and barely remembered to grab some sneakers before following her out.

He found her at a picnic table set to the side of the R.Vs. Dorothy's laptop was nestled within an arrangement of half a dozen open Tupperware containers. He recognized the spread by smell before he was close enough to see inside them. Nicole's homemade breakfast feast was pretty familiar by now. Its presence made it all the more surprising that she had let him eat from the junk food vendors without complaint. Although, at the moment, he struggled to remember the last time he had eaten.

"I made Jalapeño Scramble," she said without looking up from up from the screen.

Deciding that his best course of action was to ignore anyone that didn't have the last name Rider, Benton straddled the bench seat beside Nicole. He had just enough time to bundle the saturated mass of her hip-length hair into the towel before his stomach began to grumble. The scent of his favorite breakfast was hard to deny, and she snatched up the whole container of scrambled eggs.

"You remembered the serrano sauce, right?"

"Of course. That's why the smell alone can burn your eyeballs."

The thick chili pepper sauce dripped from the mixture, giving enough heat to make him feel like he was eating fire. *Perfect,* he thought and hurriedly scoffed down two more mouthfuls. He stopped chewing when he noticed the screen.

"Are these your notes?"

"The binders were a little impractical to carry around," she said. "Besides, you'd be surprised how hard it is to find accurate information on this kind of stuff."

"No, I wouldn't be."

She nudged him with her elbow. May have done more if she wasn't more interested in a strip of bacon.

"There has to be a lot of other people who need help, just like us, so I created a website. ParanormalLibrary.com."

"And you didn't tell me this because?"

Her fingers paused. "It didn't come up?"

"You put stuff about me on there, didn't you?"

"All names and places have been changed to protect the innocent and the annoying," she chirped as she made a final click. "There it is!"

Benton took another bite of eggs and leaned closer to read over her shoulder.

"*Pontianak?*" he read aloud.

Everyone gathered closer. His frigid skin delighted in their body heat even as their proximity made it crawl.

"They're from Malaysia?" Sophia asked. "We're in Alberta."

"Banshees are Irish," Dorothy noted absently as she scanned the page.

Nicole instantly slipped into her 'museum guide' voice. One that she had picked up while working at the Buffalo Jump's gift shop and couldn't help using every time there was a chance to spit out random knowledge. "Actually, a lot of the beings we've come into contact with so far have been Irish."

"Perhaps they're following something," Daniel said.

Benton didn't have to turn around to know that the Elder's gaze was fixated on him.

"I don't care why it's here," Wapun cut in. "What does it want?"

"Mostly," Nicole dragged the word out, like extending it would distract people from the end of the sentence, "to kill people."

"Subtle," Benton grinned.

"That's all it wants?" Hurit adjusted her round glasses as she peered at the screen.

"Okay, according to my research," Nicole spared a moment to make sure that Benton didn't comment on what repetition had made her catchphrase. He shoveled some more food into his mouth and continued, "*Pontianaks* are the ghosts of women who died during childbirth. Or they were murdered."

"How are those two things alike?" Daniel asked.

"That's just how these things go," Nicole said. "Legends change over the years. You have to sift through a lot of possibilities to get to the core answers. Most of the stories agree that they're dangerous to everyone. Although, some state that they have a preference for men or pregnant women. I guess that explains why she went straight for Mason but hesitated with me." She fell silent for a moment before jumping in her seat. "Oh, and you."

Benton used the end of his fork to nudge her fingers out of his face. "I thought we agreed it was because I'm a Banshee."

"That's kind of what I mean. Look, when she was killing me, she wasn't all that into it. All of her attention was on you. I think you perplex her."

"Yeah. Alive, dead, place your bets."

"And also . . ." She waved a hand in his face again. "You know, the androgynous factor. If she's one of the *Pontianaks* that like killing men specifically, you might have thrown her."

"Oh, my God," Benton groaned. "You didn't even notice until I pointed it out."

Like falling dominos, one Elder after another figured out what they were talking about. There were a few mumbled comments about how he could make a 'pretty girl,' given the changes, but none of them bothered to bring it up to him.

"I'm just saying," Nicole continued. "She's eager to figure you out. I know that look."

"Awesome," Benton mumble. *Another person obsessed with me. That's just great.*

"I knew it!" Nicole almost squealed with victory. Tapping the screen, she continued. "She was the one luring us out. *Pontianaks* lure people away by imitating a baby's cry. Oh . . ."

"That's a comforting sound," Benton said.

Everything about Nicole screamed that she was expecting an outburst. "They use a trick. The closer they are, the softer the crying."

"So she was right near us last night? And you kept making us go further in."

Nicole smiled weakly. "Kinda."

There was a flood of words ready to burst out of Benton's chest. But they all died when it clicked into place. "The moon."

"What is that supposed to mean?" Dorothy cut in. Her eyes kept flicking to her daughter, each glance making Nicole's smile grow larger.

*They're going to have words later on,* Benton thought.

"When we went out looking for the child, I lost track of time."

"Completely tuned out," Nicole supplied in what she thought was a helpful manner. "Sorry, you talk."

"I sensed something. I think she hides in the moonlight. Is that in the legend?"

"No," Nicole said. "But now that I've seen her up close, I agree that her skin would really help her camouflage into it."

"You saw her up close?" Dorothy snapped. "When? How?"

"Can we get this out of the way first?" Nicole sweetened her voice. "Please?"

"You're grounded until you can dig yourself out of this hole."

"That sounds fair," Nicole replied.

"Does it say how we get rid of it?" Daniel asked.

Nicole and Benton shared a glance before both turned towards the man. He let her take the lead.

"Get rid of it?"

"What do you think we were trying to do?" Daniel snapped.

"Kill it," Benton and Nicole answered in unison.

Rowtag found his voice for the first time since they had gathered around the laptop. "Is that even possible?"

"Surprisingly, yeah," Benton said.

"If we just push it off our land, we're not solving the problem. Just passing it off onto someone else."

"We have children here," Wapun said.

Benton snorted. "And reproduction is something only local people can do."

"Again, I *really* want to get into what your issue is with kids, but right now, I've got to focus on this," Nicole told him in a flood of words. Shifting back to the group, she continued, "He has a point. We know what we're up against, so it's our responsibility to deal with it."

"You want to risk the lives of your family and friends for the sake of strangers?" Daniel asked.

"So, people only have worth if you know them personally?" Benton shot back. "And *I'm* the jerk."

Wapun placed a hand on Daniel's arm, carefully pulling him back slightly. Neither he nor Benton had noticed that they had been squaring off.

"Learn to respect your elders," Daniel said.

585

"Banshee," he reminded with a smirk. "We're so far removed that I could eat you, and it wouldn't even be considered cannibalism."

"Okay, I have a rule that once cannibalism is brought up in a conversation, we should move the topic along," Nicole said.

Wapun was quick to command the attention of all present. "Then let's consider all of our options before setting ourselves to a particular path. Nicole, what are a *Pontianak's* weaknesses?"

Unsure, she looked to Benton first. Whatever she was looking for, she found it quick enough and returned to her 'museum guide' persona.

"By legend, they like to hide in banana trees during the day. They say if you tie one end of a red string to the tree and secure the other to the end of a bed, anyone who sleeps on the bed will be able to control the *Pontianak*."

Benton blinked at her. "That's incredibly unhelpful."

"But we know what tree she likes," she protested.

"Yeah, it's still a hard no."

"Fine. Just know that was the easiest option," she snipped. "They're supposedly blind. Huh, I can change that to true now."

Rowtag's wrinkled brow furrowed as he watched Nicole type. "Who knows that to be true, exactly?"

Both Benton and Nicole lifted a hand.

"Right," he mumbled, still clearly not convinced.

"She sniffs around," Benton said. "I'm pretty sure she tastes the air like a snake. At least she did around me."

"And it also might be a contributing factor of why she didn't straight out attack me. There were a lot of smells in the corpse nest. She might not have been able to pinpoint me until I moved."

Sophia tugged on her pink hair. *Too stressed to just twirl it, huh?*

"There's an awful lot of maybe's in that reasoning."

*What absolutes do you think we'll find?* Since Nicole had only agreed to ignore him mouthing off to Daniel, Benton instead decided to say, "Personally, I have more of a problem with the term 'corpse nest'."

It worked. Nicole's competitive nature came out before Sophia would push her point, sparing them all a painful conversation about how this wasn't an exact science.

"What would you call it?" Nicole challenged.

"Carrion cloister."

"What is with you and alliteration?" Shaking her head, she turned back to her notes and continued to read. "Um, backward feet to trick people tracking her. Ah, here. If a nail is plunged into the hole at the nape of their neck, they'll revert back to a beautiful woman and good wife. However, if the nail is removed, the *Pontianak* will instantly return to its ghostly form."

"What do you think 'good wife' means?" Benton asked.

Daniel growled. "Do you think that's important right now?"

"Duh," he shot back. "If we're going to try and turn her into one, we should have some idea of what it means."

"This does seem like one of those 'be careful what you wish for' scenarios," Nicole agreed absently, scrolling through her notes again.

"What kind of nail do we need?" Rowtag asked.

Nicole sighed in bitter defeat. "I could never find a source that gave specifics."

Hurit adjusted her glasses again. By this point, she was practically bowed over Nicole and still hadn't had any luck reading the screen.

"Does it say how we're supposed to incapacitate her long enough to drive the nail in?"

"No," Nicole said. She suddenly perked up. "But we have Benton's screams. They seem to affect her on a molecular level."

Daniel scoffed and straightened, rubbing his forehead as if to stave off an impending headache.

"Explain to me how you came to that conclusion."

"She gets stretchy," Nicole said.

There was a long pause.

"Explain with more words," Dorothy prodded.

"Okay. But keep in mind that I haven't had time to really flesh out the idea." Sneaking another strip of bacon, Nicole chewed thoughtfully, basically doing whatever she could to buy herself more time. "In my research, a lot of sites refer to ghosts as energy. Some even say that it takes a lot more energy or concentration on the ghost's part to make themselves visible. That's why it gets cold when they're around. They draw in heat to power themselves up. Well, sound is energy, too. And they can clash. I think Benton's wail messes with her frequency; makes it harder for her to hold all her cells together. Yeah, it doesn't kill her, as much as you can kill a ghost, I mean. But she can't attack, either."

"So where does that leave us?" Sophia asked. "What does everyone think we should do?"

"She seems to be going to roost for the day," Daniel said. "She's far enough away from the parking lot that we have time to properly deal with it."

"And how do you classify 'dealing' with it?" Benton asked, using one knuckle to wipe some of the burning sauce from his lower lip.

Daniel's eyes narrowed as his nose scrunched up. While Benton knew it was petty to talk with his mouth full just to get a reaction out of the man, he couldn't deny that it felt good.

"Getting it away from here, of course."

"And sending it where?" Nicole pressed as respectfully as she could.

Hurit had to brace one hand on Nicole's shoulder to push herself upright again. "She's got a point. We can't risk sending her into town."

"To the open plains, then."

"That won't work," Rowtag cut in. "All we know about this damn thing is that it likes trees. It's not going to stay in the grasslands."

Daniel contemplated that for a moment. "The forest along Highway 43."

Benton's jaw dropped. He whipped around to find a look of pure horror etched into Nicole's face. Neither of them could speak a word for a moment, and the conversation went on without them.

"Lots of trees. And there's a good distance between here and Peace Springs, too," Rowtag thought aloud.

"And no one walks that stretch," Hurit agreed, cleaning her glasses as if that would make one bit of difference. "It's not likely she'll run into anyone that's not in a vehicle. Harder targets."

"You can't!" the words burst free of Nicole as she surged to her feet.

"Nicole," Daniel said softly, generally trying to sound kind. "You've been very helpful. We're all grateful-"

"It's already cursed land," Nicole pleaded.

Daniel's voice hardened. "In the end, this decision must be made by adults."

"Benton and I have been there! We've seen what's in that forest!"

"Nicole," Daniel said. "Sit down."

Hesitation ran through her when each Elder turned to her sharply. She balled a hand in Benton's hoodie as if he were a security blanket, physically struggling to hold onto her conviction in the face of such disapproval.

"There's a curse you don't know about. Its symbols are hiding out in the original site for Fort Wayward."

"The forest isn't anywhere near there, dear," Sophia placated.

"But it draws these kinds of things to it. I think that's what's been tainting the forest. Energy powering energy. And all the death on that road-"

"Nicole, you're babbling," Daniel said.

Nicole stammered as her conflicting emotions battered against the untested knowledge in her head. Without looking, Benton reached back and wrapped his hand around Nicole's wrist, offering what little encouragement he could without making the situation worse for her.

"The forest is absorbing the dead," she snapped, each word coming out sharper than a scalpel's edge. "They're melding together and mutating the spirits. There's nothing natural about what's happening. Go, and you'll feel it yourself. The land is sick, and the infection is spreading. The old settlement. The Bertrand property. It's getting closer to town. Sending the *Pontianak* there is like throwing gasoline on a fire."

"And that's your learned opinion?" Daniel asked after a long pause. "From, what, not even a year of contact with the other world?"

"Still more practical knowledge than you've ever had," Benton replied.

"It's easy to pass judgment when you don't have to offer suggestions."

"It's easy to make dumb plans when you're not the one that has to follow them through," Benton replied.

"No one has asked you to be a part of this!"

"That's because we've been the ones handling it! *You've* just been tagging along!"

"We'll put it to a vote, then," Wapun cut in, her voice leaving no room for argument. "All in favor of moving the *Pontianak* to Highway 43?"

The fabric of Benton's hood ripped under Nicole's tightening grip as, one by one, the Elders lifted their hands.

589

# Chapter 15

"We can't let them do this!" Nicole shrieked as she followed her mother.

The Elders had already dispersed, each returning to their own R.V. to collect whatever items might be necessary.

"Nicole, I don't have time for this," Dorothy dismissed as she stalked through the tents. "The Auclairs are struggling with what happened to Adam, and the Bertrands need constant supervision."

"Mom, will you listen to me, please," Nicole pleaded.

Dorothy stopped short and turned to her daughter. "The decision is out of my hands."

"Well, drag it back into your hands. You're the police. Surely you have some kind of authority."

Dorothy raked both hands through her hair. "For once, just this once, can you trust that other people know what they're doing and let it go? Can you do that for me? Let it go?"

"I have no idea what you're even saying right now," Nicole said, honestly perplexed.

"Okay, how's this? You're not having any part of this. You're benched."

"What?" Nicole squealed. "You can't do that!"

"It's done. You're out. Go back to your teepee and stay there until I say otherwise."

"They can't do this without us," Nicole said. "Well, Benton mostly. But he won't do it without me."

Both women looked at him, and he shrugged in agreement.

"Mom, we can't let them do this."

Dorothy took a step away then quickly jerked back. "Why are you like this?"

"Because dad taught me to fight for those who can't. And you taught me to do what's right no matter what the cost." Losing a bit of her fight, she squirmed slightly. "So, when you think about it, this is all your fault."

"She's got you there," Benton noted.

Both Rider women turned to him.

"What? It's a compliment."

"Aw, thanks," Nicole cooed.

Dorothy tried to walk away while her daughter was distracted. Nicole quickly grabbed her arm.

"What are we going to do?"

"You. Teepee. Now."

"Mom-"

"You're teenagers," she snapped. "Just kids. You shouldn't have to deal with any of this."

"Teenagers have been going to war since the beginning of time."

"None of them were my daughter!" Dorothy quickly got herself under control, remaining silent until everyone who had noticed the outburst had lost interest.

"I love you, mom."

"I love you, too."

Nicole hugged her mother tight. "Please don't make me go behind your back. It always makes me feel sick."

Resting her chin on the top of Nicole's head, she huffed, torn between frustration and amusement. Benton shoved his hands into his pockets and tried to blend into the background, wanting them to have this moment undisturbed. While he never intended to cause problems between them, his existence alone had strained their relationship.

"Are you certain of what you saw in the woods?" Dorothy asked.

"Yes."

"Go to the teepee, and I'll talk to the Elders," Dorothy said reluctantly.

"But-"

"Daniel's almost as spiteful as Benton," Dorothy cut in.

Benton huffed with indignation but didn't comment.

"Now that he's got his shackles up, he'd hold his ground just to prove a point. Let me take a run at him when you two aren't around. Just let me handle it, Nicole."

"Thanks, Dorothy," Benton said.

Feeling like a jerk, he reached out and tapped a knuckle against Nicole's arm. She still didn't let go of her mother.

"Come on. We need to let her get to work," he said.

"Right," she said while tightening her grip around her mother's waist.

Dorothy was torn between welcoming her daughter's embrace and doing her duty. She looked to Benton, and he sighed.

"Hey, Nic. My old dance academy's website still has pictures of me on it."

That got her attention. She perked, watching him carefully. Like she was a mongoose, and he a snake, and she wasn't quite sure she wanted to get into a fight.

"Dance Academy?" Dorothy asked.

"He was a ballerina."

Dorothy caught on instantly and grinned. "Find that photo."

"I know you're both just trying to distract me, and I'm not going to fall for it," she said. "The moment I find that website, I'm going to find you, mom. If Daniel's not on board, I'll take over. Love you!"

Benton twisted his shoulders to keep Nicole from barging into him as she sprinted back for the laptop. He watched her go for a moment.

"Obsessive tendencies are a double-edged sword," Dorothy noted wistfully. "Thanks."

"You owe me," Benton grumbled.

"Take care of my girl."

Shoving his hands deep into his pockets, he jumped his shoulders. "I always try to."

He had barely taken a step to follow Nicole when a scream cut through the relative calm. Jerking around, he spotted his parents barreling towards them.

"Oh no," he muttered.

Looking to Dorothy for help, he noticed her shoulders stiffen.

"Head's up," she said, motioning with her chin to Daniel.

The Elder must have noticed the Bertrands and was storming over with fury in his eyes. Nicole tried to cut him off, but the old man didn't hesitate for a second.

"Benton, we're going home," Cheyanne snapped.

"Are you his parents?" Daniel's snarl covered Benton's response.

Theodore and Cheyanne knew that tone. Instantly, they closed ranks and picked up their pace.

"Who are you?" Theodore asked.

"Daniel Long Fisher. I'm an Elder here. Is that your boy?"

"Back off," Benton said.

He would have been better off throwing a match on a keg of gunpowder. The older man didn't hesitate to start on his tirade, hurling out each word to try and inflict the maximum amount of pain possible. Theodore gripped Benton's arm, wrenching him back as the furious man closed the last of the distance. Cheyanne was quick to give as good as she got. As the argument grew louder, the conversation turned from complaints to insults and threats. Dorothy tried to keep the peace, but no one was hearing it.

"I don't even know who you are," Cheyanne hissed. "Stay away from my son!"

"Your monster! Were you the one that taught your boy to play with the dead? Or was it your husband?"

"What are you talking about?" Cheyanne snapped.

"Benton, get in the car," Theodore ordered.

"Which one of you did he get it from?"

Daniel repeated the demand as Nicole tried to edge him back.

"They brought all this death and madness into our town! Now they have to answer for it!"

"We don't owe you anything, you maniac!" Theodore roared.

"You raised him this way!"

"We've done nothing wrong," Cheyanne charged forward, only stopping when she struck Dorothy's outstretched hand.

"You're his mother! Who else is there to blame for this abomination? It's your genetics!"

"Not mine!"

Shock seized Benton's insides. It disemboweled him when he saw the panicked looks Cheyanne threw to her husband. Theodore stood aghast, unmoving, eyes accusing and sympathetic at the same time. Silence lingered over them. Crushed them. Chasing away any doubt that could have shrouded the meaning of Cheyanne's words.

Benton's mouth worked numbly around the question, "I'm adopted?"

"Benton," Cheyanne whispered helplessly.

Theodore softened his grip on Benton's arm even as he began to tug, "It's time to go home."

Benton locked his wide gaze onto his father. "Am I adopted?"

Both of his parents refused to answer.

"Oh, my God." Benton couldn't breathe. His vision blurred. "Oh, my God."

"It's complicated," Cheyanne said.

She took a step towards Benton, and he jerked back.

"Complicated? How is it *complicated*?"

"We didn't know," Theodore replied. "It was a mix-up. A huge mistake."

"I'm a mistake?"

"No, I didn't mean it like that," Theodore rushed.

"We didn't know, is what he means," Cheyanne said, once again attempting to close the distance between them.

Benton wrenched his arm free of Theodore to retreat a little further.

"You didn't know?"

"Not until after your accident. When you needed a blood transfusion," she rushed. "We always knew that you had a rare blood type. AB Negative." She said it almost wistfully. Swallowing thickly, she continued, "I'm A Positive. Theo's O Negative. We didn't know until that day that it was impossible for us to have had you."

"I was ten," Benton said. "You've known for *years* and haven't said anything?"

"We didn't know if you could handle it. It almost destroyed us," Cheyanne said, turning beseeching eyes onto Theodore.

"We can talk about this at home."

Benton flung himself away from Theodore's touch. "I'm not going anywhere with you!"

"Benton-," he tried again.

This time, Nicole stepped in-between them, protectively shielding Benton from the outstretched hand.

"This has nothing to do with you, Ms. Rider," Cheyanne snapped.

"All this time, you let me think that I was insane," Benton said, using Nicole as a human shield without a hint of shame. "How could you keep this from me? It could change everything!"

"What could it possibly change?"

"I could know why I am the way I am!" Benton shouted.

"You're the way you are because you have a brain injury," Cheyanne surged forward. "You were attacked. It damaged your brain. You now have nightmares. That's all there is to it, Benton."

"I'm a Banshee." He hadn't intended for the words to come out. They were just hovering between them before he knew his lips were moving.

"What?" Theodore gasped, his eyes closing in surprise. "Benton, no, you're not. And you need to come home now."

"I had my dreams before I was ever *attacked*." He stressed the word they always danced around. *Not an accident or a mishap or an incident. I was hunted and almost killed.* "I'm not human. I'm something else."

Cheyanne locked her eyes onto Nicole. "What have you been filling his head with?"

"This is enough. We're going." Theodore lunged once again for him.

Benton easily avoided his grasp. "No."

"Be reasonable," Theodore sighed wearily. "You have no money. No friends. No other relatives. No form of transportation. Benton, son, you have nowhere else to go."

The words didn't have time to hurt.

"He can stay with us," Nicole said.

Dorothy instantly stepped in to defuse Cheyanne's mounting rage. "Just for a few days. I think it'll be best for everyone."

Theodore's jaw dropped. "You're taking our son?"

"I'm offering him a safe place to stay until everyone calms down," Dorothy corrected.

"I don't need to calm down!" Cheyanne said.

"Look at what you've just said to your son."

Benton couldn't take another second. Snatching up Nicole's hand, he stalked away. A few cries followed him. Half angry, half wounded. He didn't look back.

"Benton?" Nicole asked.

He tightened his fingers and kept walking.

"Benton?" she repeated again a heartbeat later. "Benton?"

"You've got your jeep keys on you, right?"

"No, they're in the teepee."

Grumbling, he swung to the side, hurrying over. "We get them and the stuff Wapun used for the blessing. Then we get the hell out of here."

"Where are we going?"

"We're going to trap the *Pontianak* in my barn. Let's see them ignore that."

"Are you sure that's a good idea?"

"Hey, if you can think up a better way to get those two morons to see the truth, I'm all ears."

Picking up his pace forced Nicole into a jog. It drew a few odd looks, but he barely saw them. White hot static filled his head, burned along his nerves, stoked his rage and kept him just on the verge of a panic attack. He felt like a piano wire pulled tautly. A threat to himself and anyone else who got too close. Even knowing this, he couldn't let go of Nicole's hand.

"All I'm saying is that you might not want to make these kinds of decisions based on spite," she said.

"Since I'm constructed of equal parts spite, sarcasm, and caffeine, I don't really have much of a choice." Stopping abruptly, he finally met her gaze. The tender sympathy he found there made tears burn the back of his eyes. "This is an insane kneejerk reaction, isn't it?"

"Yep," she said. "It's basically elaborate suicide."

He deflated. "You don't have to come with me."

"Nah, I'm in," she chirped. "You get the keys from the front pocket of my backpack, I'll sneak Wapun's stuff, we'll meet back on the edge of the parking lot."

Without waiting for a response, she jogged off towards the rows of RVs, leaving Benton to stare after her in amazement.

*I'm not crazy. She might be, though.*

# Chapter 16

Nicole smiled gratefully up at Benton. It was a little insulting that she hadn't counted on him thinking far enough ahead to bring the bag itself. She dumped the assorted items into her backpack and zipped it up.

"For the record, I've never done the blessing myself," she told him. "I did manage to get her to write it down for me, though."

"How did you pull that one off?"

"Mostly playing on her guilt."

"And the other part consisted of being really annoying until she just wanted you to go away?"

She looked a little sheepish. "Maybe."

"That's my girl," he grinned.

Her mood brightened instantly. "So, have you thought up any more details for your plan?"

"It's baffled by me. We tick it off, run, and hope we get to the barn in time."

"Keeping it simple," she said. "I like it."

"No, you don't."

"I'm a little on edge, but we're all trying new things today." She flipped the keys around in her hand, toying one finger over the metal as if testing that it was real. "How do we tick it off?"

"Throw rocks at its nest?" he suggested.

She shook her head. "Then we have to run back through the undergrowth. She's too quick. I want to be in the jeep."

"Try and get some of the owls to attack her nest?"

"Better," she smiled. "Jeep first."

Having the few extra seconds to stretch out his legs was a luxury. One he took great advantage of. It was cut short soon enough when he heard the array of voices closing in around them. *The Elders can move quickly when they want to.*

Exchanging a quick glance at each other, they both burst forward, racing down the small trail back to the parking lot. Everything was different now. Down to the very core of his identity. He pushed the thoughts aside, focusing instead on the burn in his lungs and the mint green jeep in the distance. While they had replaced the windows, the bodywork had been left riddled with dents and scrapes. Gravel crunched under his sneakers, and the heavy thumps aggravated the dozens of cuts on the bottom of his feet.

He ignored it all.

Finally, they reached the jeep. Nicole opened the doors swiftly, allowing him to leap in, shoving the backpack down by his feet. They slammed the doors shut and hurriedly locked them again.

"Okay," Nicole panted. "So, now the birds."

Glancing over at Benton, she screamed. By the time he managed to twist around, the ghostly figure had already moved on, drifting up from his window and out of sight. Her journey was marked by the high-pitched whine of her nails across the metal roof.

"We have her attention," Nicole gasped, dumbfounded.

"Drive now," Benton said.

A heavy strike against the roof rocked the jeep. The scrape became a slash as the *Pontianak* tried to claw its way in. Before the engine had time to roar to life, she had already stomped down on the gas.

The jeep lurched forward, kicking up dust and gravel, the back wheels slipping slightly as she struggled to keep it under control. Weaving through the array of cars, Nicole shot for the entrance. The *Pontianak's* midnight hair seeped down from the top of the windshield, crawling like a living thing to cover the glass. Nicole yanked hard on the wheel. Barely an inch separated the side of the jeep from the van they passed. Benton wasn't prepared to hit the embankment. It sent them flying, sailing in an arch before crashing back down into the towering grass, the impact smacking Benton against the dashboard.

"Seatbelt," Nicole spoke on reflex.

Fear laced her voice. She tried to hide it, but it rung strong and true. With another lurch, she dragged the jeep from the depths and forced it up back onto the main road. Bracing himself against the door and dashboard, Benton tried to slow his breathing. Succeeding filled him with terror. Because it wasn't his success. The now familiar sensation of turning into stone started at his feet and worked its way up his body. Solidifying his legs and freezing his lungs. His breaths lightened into wheezes until they threatened to stop altogether.

"Benton?" Nicole asked.

"Keep going," he forced out sharply. *Breathe. Just breathe. Keep your voice.*

Steadily, the *Pontianak* seeped into the edges of his vision. She kept pace along the side of the jeep, her unblinking eyes restlessly searching for what they couldn't see. He sunk back just as Nicole swung the wheel again. This time not taking them away from the spirit but sideswiping it. Contact came with a squish of liquid and a crack of bone. The *Pontianak* scattered, releasing an electric charge into the air that sizzled along the hair on Benton's body. *It's coming into the car!*

"Do it," Nicole said, pressing one hand hard over the ear nearest him.

Gathering what air he could, he released a scream. It was shrill and weak. Still strong enough to make the windows rattle even if it couldn't shatter them. The static energy surged to an unbearable pitch before just as suddenly fading away. Benton flopped forward, pressing his head against his knees as he coughed and sputtered.

"Are you okay?" Nicole asked.

"Drive faster."

The engine strained as she forced it faster. Having studied the backroads in detail, Nicole weaved from one path to another, keeping to the little patrolled routes. Not that there was enough of a police force in town to actually monitor the roads during a festival. Pain inched into his jaw. Tightening each muscle and tendon until Benton was sure the bones would break if he tried to speak. His nails slipped over the plastic of the dashboard as he tried to straighten, still battling to breathe.

Something brushed over his knuckles. A soft, tender caress that made him snap his gaze up. Midnight hair slithered through the vents like snakes to twist around his wrist. He pulled his hand back, barely able to make it more than an inch before the hair drew him back. Milky slick fingertips worked their way through the dark strands. They wiggled against the tightly placed slates that covered the vents, making the plastic squeak and groan. Still fighting to free himself, he reached his free hand out to Nicole. With her focus locked on the roads, she hadn't noticed what was happening right beside her.

"What is it?" she asked, still unable to look at him while she took a short cut between two roads, crashing through the golden grass and bucking over the uneven earth.

Benton wheezed, unable to summon his voice. His lungs began to swell as they hardened. His elbow crystalized as he smacked his hand against Nicole's thigh. He was prepared for her startled scream. Not for the sudden slam of breaks. The seatbelt cut across his chest and gut. A sudden crushing blow that shattered the rock encasing his lungs. Nicole threw the jeep into reverse and stomped down, once more throwing him about. Air rushed deep into his lungs, and he gathered it within an instant. His scream still didn't have its usual power. Without warning, Nicole swung the jeep around, cutting across another field and throwing him about like a ball in a pinball machine.

"Is she gone? Can you see her?"

Benton heaved a few deep breaths before he was able to work up a response. Even then, it was still little more than a grunt. Nicole fell into a silence that neither of them was ready to disturb. Benton flattened himself against his seat and kept a constant, paranoid visual.

"You're with me?" Nicole asked.

He nodded.

"Good. Get the backpack for me? Start following what you can from the list. I don't think we're going to have much time when we get there."

The seatbelt locked into place a few times before he was able to reach it. Drawing it up into his lap, he rummaged through the array of items before he was able to find the list. Dizzy from lack of oxygen, he could barely focus his eyes enough to read the scribbled print. Beyond being all dried plant life, he couldn't put any link between the items. He knew the scents of the herbs but couldn't put a name to them. The plant cuttings looked somewhat familiar. He combined them in the bowl as best he could, adding the powders and hoping that he had the proportions right.

The loud cry of an infant made them both freeze.

"It's loud. So it's not too close," Nicole said.

As if in challenge, the cry steadily softened at her words. Benton twisted in his seat, searching out every window. All around them, the winter grass swayed like spun gold. His renovated farmhouse rose up from the gilded ocean. His barn a dark lump set nearby. Above, thick clouds hung low on a beautiful blue sky. A placid calm hung over the world, creating the illusion that nothing exciting could ever happen in such a sleepy town.

"Almost there," Nicole said. "Get ready."

The paper crumpled between his palm and the bowl. He vaguely remembered to check for a lighter in Nicole's bag before, with a final heave, they burst free of the towering grass and into the mowed field of his yard. The *Pontianak* materialized before them, eyes blazing behind the curtain of dark hair. Nicole revved the engine, urging the jeep on until it whined and strained. Crashing into the *Pontianak* scattered it like ash, the tiny specks flying in all directions and reveling the side of the barn. Nicole dropped her full weight onto the break. The wheels locked but the soft earth gave them no traction, forcing them into a slide. Red painted wood filled the windshield as they drove close still to the barn. Benton pulled on the emergency brake, forcing the jeep to fishtail. With one last gasp of the engine, the jeep finally came to a sudden stop. Benton shoved the bowl at Nicole and struggled with his seatbelt.

"I'll get it in the barn," he said.

Nicole gaped at him. "I haven't done this before."

"No time like the present," Benton said as he kicked open the door and threw himself out.

A quick sprint got him through the open barn doors. The moment he entered the shadows gathered within the large building. The world went silent. His panted breath turned to mist before him as the temperature plummeted. *Oliver.* Benton had found the old owners body buried in a shallow grave on his first night in Fort Wayward. He had lingered ever since, steadily devolving over the months into something not quite recognizable as human. Benton could feel the dead man's presence even as he remained unseen. The gloom that gathered around the rafters offered him a thousand hiding places. Somewhere, seemingly far in the distance, a baby began to cry.

His bones ached, and his muscles twitched as he worked his way deeper into the cavernous room. The dirt floor shifted under his cautious steps. For a moment, it seemed as if the soft whimpering came from all around him at once. Dust drifted down from above as something shifted in the darkness. He could feel the powers closing in around him even as they remained unseen. *Come on, Nicole,* he whispered in his head. *Come on. Come on. Come on.* Fine shivers shook him as he forced himself to linger. *Give her more time. This'll work. It has to work.* His reassurances weren't enough to keep the reality from creeping in. *I really screwed up.*

Soft cries grew weaker. The floorboards looming above him creaked and groaned, releasing constant waves of dust. Benton spun on his heel, coming face to face with the blazing, dead eyes of the *Pontianak*. Her nose flared as she sniffed the air before his face.

"What are you?"

Movement flashed overhead, bringing the sound of cracking twigs. Mr. Ackerman rushed down from the shadows on all fours. His joints pushed the wrong way as his limp hands and feet distorted into a cluster of gnarled roots. He landed before the *Pontianak*, his roots instantly twisted through the exposed earth. To move, he had to break the twisted vines, and he didn't hesitate to do so. It sounded like snapping bones. The *Pontianak* caught Mr. Ackerman's scent. Instantly, her hair reared up like a spider ready to strike. Her lips pulled back into a snarl that Ackerman mirrored.

The sudden burst of blistering air hit Benton like a steam grate. He reeled back, protecting his face as best he could, choking on the gathering heat. There was barely time to blink before the entire barn felt like a sauna. Two more breaths and the place became a sweat lodge. Hot enough to boil the flesh on his bones. Flames burst into existence. They sliced over the floor like in an intricate pattern, mapping out symbols he couldn't see from his position. Benton leaped away, careful not to let the lashing flames touch him. The scares on his palm throbbed as the heat climbed. Sweat dripped into his eyes, distorting his already light blurred vision.

The two ghosts clashed, and the fires exploded into an inferno. There wasn't any place left to run. Crackling flames, crunching bones, and an infant's squeal assaulted his ears. Bleeding into his mind to distort his thoughts further. He lost track of which way was out. All he knew was to keep moving. *Keep ahead of the ghosts. Don't let the flames touch you. Get out!* He repeated the commands over and over until they lost all meaning. The barn trembled around him as the fire spread. Embers spewed into the air, searing what parts of his flesh that they could find.

The scream and roar of flames rose to a deafening pace. He staggered under the weight of it, knees almost buckling to sprawl him across the inferno. Sure hands wrapped around his arm as the earth began to tremble. He struggled to break free, but the hand held strong, dragging him almost too quickly for his feet to keep up. *Nicole?*

The flames consumed his senses. Pain exploded in every cell. Each breath was agony.

Then suddenly it was gone.

The world rocked, and he fell, toppling onto Nicole as he drew in hurried breaths of the frigid night hair. The entire barn stood ravaged by flames, and still, the structure held. He watched until the pain grew too much, and he was forced to squeeze his eyelids shut.

"Benton?" Nicole asked. "Did it work? Can you see the aurora?"

"No."

Barely suppressed panic sizzled within her voice. "I'll try again. Tell me if you see her coming."

"You don't see the fire?"

Shielding his eyes and squinting made it bearable to look at her. Her brow furrowed. "Fire?"

It clicked for them both at the same moment. The flames of the pit. The ones only he could see.

"Oh, God," Nicole whimpered.

"We just created cursed earth."

\*\*\*

"We poisoned the earth near town," Nicole said numbly.

"Does repeating it help?" Benton asked.

"Nope."

"Then please stop."

Flopping her book down, she looked over her shoulder to glare at him. Two days had passed since they had set the barn alight. Periodically, they checked on it, just to see if it was still burning. It was. And while Benton could sense both spirits, he couldn't ever see them in the flames.

The hardest part was getting in and out without running into Benton's parents. They hadn't stopped calling, but after a stern warning from the Constable, they had kept away from the Rider residence. Benton refused to have anything to do with them. He wouldn't even let Nicole nudge the conversation in the direction. So it had been forty-eight hours of paranoia, guilt, and general anxiety.

Stretched out across the foot of her bed, she had been trying to read the same page for the last hour. Benton had taken to using her back as a pillow, letting his mind drift as he listened to his headphones.

"Do you want to talk about-"

"Nope," Benton chirped.

"You need to some time."

He pulled out one earplug. "What did you want to cover first? The whole impending death thing? The fact that I can be hijacked by spirits? Oh, I was also swapped out at birth. That could be a good conversation starter. Or how about the fact that my parents had decided sudden emotional distance with no explanation would be the better choice than telling me the truth? Your Elders hate me, I'm now homeless, I have no idea what to do with Adam, and I still haven't read *Dracula*. Find any of those topics interesting?"

"Yes. All of them," she said. "We should talk about all of them. In detail."

"Nah. I think I'm going to stick to 'suppress and deny.'"

"That sound healthy."

He snorted and settled down against her spine again. Nicole sighed. *Go at his pace. Don't push it. He'll tell you when he's ready.*

"For the record, you're not homeless. You always have us."

"Thanks," Benton mumbled sheepishly. "I'm sorry the powwow didn't work out. If you want to go back for a while, we could."

"I appreciate the offer, but no thank you."

"Oh, thank God. I need at least a year before I have to see Daniel again."

She chuckled. "Fine. Okay, I'm going to let it go. Just remember, I'm here when you want to talk about it."

"I know."

"You might want to take a nap," she said. "We're meeting the Auclairs for dinner in a few hours."

He groaned. "Yay."

"You like Adam."

"The little guy's alright," Benton admitted reluctantly. "I'm not too keen on the rest of the family."

"What a surprise," she replied.

This was the only way he would let her help him. Light teasing and mindless distractions. *Just be patient,* she told herself. It was a virtue that she'd have to learn quickly.

"I'm sorry I'm always a problem," he said abruptly.

"You're never more than you're worth."

"Like I believe that."

A small smile curled her lips. "Do you want to make it up to me?"

He popped out an earbud again and looked at her cautiously. "Yeah."

"What's the website for your dance academy?"

Benton broke the first real smile she had seen in far too long and put the earbud back.

"Benton?" she asked, only to be ignored. She smiled slightly. "Fine. I'll find it on my own. We both know I will."

* * *

# Death Veil
## Banshee Series Book 6

# Chapter 1

Soft leather and satin crackled as they stretched. The sound, smell, and sensation of the material melding to his foot opened a floodgate of memories. Not all of them were pleasant, but Benton found himself smiling as he was swept away within the nostalgic undertow. *Can something be nostalgic when it happened only a few years ago?* Benton decided that the answer wasn't worth the mental effort to figure it out. Preparing himself for the spike of pain, he drew in a deep breath and pushed up onto his toes, staggering a few steps before regaining his balance. Every joint groaned under the full weight of his body, bringing an ache that cleared his mind.

In the blissful haze, he rose into an *attitude,* with his right leg supporting his body while his left lifted back, coming to rest at a right angle with his hips. A slight bend in his raised leg brought enough momentum to slowly twirl him around. It was second nature for him to lift his arms over his head. *Pretty hands.* The thought wasn't in his own voice, but a perfect replica of Svetlana Maximova's Russian accent.

For almost four years, the Prima Ballerina had been the only person he had conversed with. At least, the only one with which he had actually wanted to.

*Pretty hands!*

This time, the thought came with the echoing memory of a swift crack. A crystal-clear recollection of the long, slender reed she never hesitated to turn into a weapon against imperfection. A lot of what people said about Russian ballerinas was complete nonsense. Svetlana's temper, however, surpassed all the stereotypes. She was the reason he was so good at dodging projectiles hurled at his head.

Smothering a chuckle, he lifted his leg higher, arching his spine until his delicately poised fingers found his ankle. With a slight pull, he managed to fold himself enough to rest the back of his head against his inner knee. *Inhumanly flexible.* That's what Nicole liked to call him. In that loving, teasing tone only best friends could muster. She wouldn't listen to reason. Thousands of people could do exactly what he did. Although, admittedly, he didn't have to try.

*If it's a side perk for being a Banshee, it's a weird one. And not worth the dreams.*

A fine tremor worked through his supporting leg, causing him to wobble. It would have been barely noticeable, but instantly caused his mind to reproduce that ruler's sharp crack. He readjusted his weight and quelled the tremor. Holding for a few moments longer, he switched his legs. Now on his right, he rested his left toes against his knee and used the momentum to twirl him around in a tight *pirouette*, his hands still above his head.

Spinning fast enough to turn the world into a blur allowed him only glimpses of the Rider family living room. Two walls were devoted to properly viewing the large backyard. The night had turned the glass doors into black mirrors. He used his reflection as his anchor point.

A sudden flash of light caught him off guard, burning his eyes and sending him toppling to the side. Muscle memory kicked in, allowing him to twist just in time to land on his butt. It still hurt, but he didn't injure anything. The back of his head collided with the padded edge of the sofa he had pushed back against the wall. Again, he was spared from injury. But the outside lights were kind enough to choose then to time out, returning the glass to its mirrored state, giving him a reflected view of his failure.

*Svetlana would kill me.*

His humored smile gave way to a frown of confusion. Nothing had changed that he could point to, but he felt the shift. Something deep within the pit of his stomach twisted. Not pulling tight, more slithering, like something living inside him was starting to stir. He slowly got to his feet, drawn closer to the blackened windows by invisible hands. The sensation in the pit of his stomach increased. Barely able to see past his own reflection, Benton inched closer still, his ballet shoes muffling his footsteps and leaving the entire house silent.

The winter chill reached through the glass to wash over the tip of his nose. He hadn't known that it could snow in the Alberta prairies. It didn't get nearly as cold as it did in other parts of Canada. Maybe a few feet in the places where it managed to gather in a snow drift. Other than that, it barely made an inch or so. It was still bitterly cold though. If the wind came from the right direction, the towering buffalo jumps could offer the town some protection. Every other direction only had a sea of towering grass. It allowed the wind to increase in speed, tainting it with the frost that clung to the tips of the swaying reeds.

Benton had lived in every major city in Canada and had never felt anything that could compete with the Fort Wayward winds. Even just hearing it sweep through the night was enough to freeze the blood in his veins. Benton shivered and flicked his eyes over the inky depths beyond the window.

The lights clicked on.

Benton jerked back, the sensation in his stomach thrashing wildly. *Something is out there.* It wasn't a question. Just a simple fact that he never thought to dispute. Blinking rapidly to adjust his vision, he snapped his eyes around, trying to search every window at once.

At the time, he was glad that he wasn't back home. His parents had deliberately picked the most isolated property they could possibly find. A farm home set in a vast field. Sometimes, it could take about an hour to get to the small cluster of buildings that served as the town. Their theory was that no one could be close enough to hear his nightly screams. They had seriously mistaken the capacity of his lungs.

Nicole's home, meanwhile, was far closer to town. She had neighbors and everything. There wasn't a house in Fort Wayward that didn't have a good-sized yard. Instead of a fence, the Rider household had a row of thick pine trees to mark out the property line. The glow of the floodlights reached far enough to illuminate the tips of the lowest branches, leaving the rest in shadows.

Between him and the trees was a flat stretch of grass. A dusting of snow covered the lawn in a thin carpet. Small flecks danced along the wind as it howled past the glass. Despite the serenity of the scene, Benton's stomach continued to knot. *Something's out there.*

The lights timed out. Unable to see anything, his hand slowly reached for the door's handle. His phone blared to life, making him jump and flinch away from the door. Swallowing thickly, he tried to get his now rapid heartbeat back to some kind of reasonable pace.

Utterly disappointed with himself, he muttered a few curse words and crossed back to the sofa where he had left his phone. He dumped himself onto it. And, since there wasn't anyone around to comment on his sitting habits, he flopped his back on the seat cushions; head dangling over the edge and legs stretching up along the wall. Finally, he reached blindly to grab his phone. He didn't bother to check the caller ID. There were only four people in the world that called him anyway, and he had personalized their ringtones. His parents both had organ music befitting Dracula's rise from the grave. Constable Dorothy Rider of the Royal Canadian Mounted Police had the theme music of the old *Dudley Do-Right* cartoon; all trumpets and galloping of horse hooves. She never admitted out loud that she found it amusing, but she had started 'accidentally' calling him more often. In keeping with the theme song trend, Nicole's was *Scooby Doo*. The best part was that, by refusing to tell her which character he thought she was like, she was slowly going insane. Which was kind of hilarious. With a flick of his thumb, he answered the call, cutting the person off as they asked, yet again, where Scooby was.

"Aren't you supposed to be hanging out with your parents?" he asked, lazily flexing and pointing his feet.

"They're having some time alone," Nicole replied.

"Already? Didn't your dad just get back a day ago?"

Benton had never met the soldier. Mr. Rider had been stationed at some distant post for the entire time he had been in Fort Wayward. It was a little intimidating to know that, come morning, he was going to be face-to-face with the man. Everyone else he had met in the Rider family was a force of nature, and he had no reason to doubt that Logan Rider would be any different.

"Yes," Nicole said slowly, as if she was trying to work the words out in her head first. "They've missed each other."

"Oh," Benton chuckled. "Gross."

"In a way, yes. But, I'm also happy for them. I read somewhere that continued physical affection can keep a marriage strong."

"What were you reading?"

"I can't remember. But I'm sure I can find it again if you're interested."

Benton rolled his eyes, unable to keep the smile off of his face.

"Nah, I'm good. Thanks, though."

Absentmindedly, he stretched out one foot until it was hovered over his head. They had been a gift from Svetlana. Black as onyx. Dancer or not, he went through an emo, punk, I-hate-the-world, set-everything-on-fire phase. A natural reaction to his friends refusing to believe him about his dreams. Savagely beating him and leaving him for dead in a dark alley had seemed like an overreaction. That kind of anger was exhausting to maintain, and he had more or less learned to swallow it down before coming to Fort Wayward. That time of his life, and the aesthetic he had been sporting at the time, was one of the few secrets he had managed to keep from Nicole.

"So," Nicole said slowly.

Benton glanced at the phone. He knew that tone. She was trying to be sneaky. Nicole was about as good at that as she was at lying.

"It's such a pretty night, huh?" she asked.

"What are you after?"

"What? Nothing? How could you even accuse me of –"

"Nic?"

"I'm checking up on you," she blurted out. The little hiss that followed was a tell-tale sign that she hadn't meant to admit that.

He chuckled. "I'm fine."

"Yeah, I'm going to need an in-depth analysis."

"Of course, you do," Benton scoffed. "What exactly are you looking for?"

"I don't know," she said. "Eating habits, homework update, general health. Maybe wax a little poetically about how much you miss me."

"You've been gone twelve hours," he chuckled.

"That's plenty of time to start missing me."

"Not really."

"Just so you know, I'm offended."

"Duly noted," he laughed.

There was really no point in admitting that he actually kind of did. They hadn't really spent all that much time apart since they had met. Since fleeing his parents' house to stay with the Riders, that time had dwindled to pretty much nothing, which was something he probably should have caught onto earlier.

"Seriously, though," she said, drawing him out of his thoughts. "How are you doing? Have you eaten your dinner? Did you remember to put on the security system?"

"Yes, and yes," Benton said.

"Did you lock all the doors?"

"Um."

"Benton," she sighed.

Fort Wayward didn't have much of a crime rate. The threat of supernatural attack, however, was ridiculously high. For him, at any rate.

"I'm getting up," he declared over her ramblings.

Flipping his legs over his head, he got up and started to move around the house.

"Is there any particular reason why you're being extra paranoid tonight?" he asked.

"You know how much evil things like to choke you. You're very choke-able."

"That's still not a word," he corrected, only to be ignored.

Completing the front and living room doors, he worked his way to the kitchen in the back of the house. There was a small side door that went out through the attached laundry area. In true Nicole fashion, she inexplicitly knew the instant his foot hit the tiles.

"You ate the dinner I left for you, right?"

"Yep."

"All of it?"

"Yes, Nic."

Benton closed his eyes and sighed. Only Svetlana had been this obsessed with his eating habits. He was just naturally lanky: broad in the shoulders but closer to a praying mantis than anything alluring. In ballet, his rather androgynous looks made it easier for him to simply take on the traditional female roles than trying to bulk up enough for the males'. Hitting the gym enough to be able to bench-press a human over his head sounded like torture. The struggle had always been trying to keep his bodyweight from slipping too low.

Nicole had almost instantly taken it upon herself to fatten him back up, delighted to have yet another person to fuss over. It was just her nature. Her perfectionist, compulsive, obsessive nature. The annoyance of having someone constantly nagging him to eat more was put off by the decreased hunger pains. Now, he was a few pounds over his ideal performance weight. Given his constant baggy sweaters, no one but her really noticed the change, but Nicole was brimming with quiet pride over it. *I'm gonna have to lose it again if I want to get back into training,* he thought. Svetlana had beat it into him that Ballet was a passion and a lifestyle, not a hobby. It was a hard mindset to break. Trying to get Nicole on board with this was just asking for an onslaught of hurt-puppy expressions. He wasn't getting into that anytime soon.

"How about the dessert?" she asked as he locked the laundry room door.

Shifting his phone to his other hand, he curled a finger around the lacy curtain that covered the window, peeling it back an inch. The set-up of the house meant that he now had a view of the shadowy edges of the yard. There wasn't much to see.

"Benton?"

"Sorry," he rushed, readjusting the phone against his ear. "I'm still here."

"What's wrong?"

"Okay, seriously now, why are you so paranoid tonight?"

Even as he asked, his eyes were drawn back to the darkened window. The gush of wind kicked up the snow, rolling it over the ground while the thick pine branches swayed. Steadily, his stomach began to roll again. What he wouldn't give for the ambient music of city traffic and aggravated neighbors. Something to break the serenity that covered Fort Wayward. Tonight, it felt smothering.

"Is it so wrong that your best friend takes an interest?" Nicole protested through the speaker.

"Nicole," he sighed, leaning slightly to the side to continue his search.

"It's the first time in years that you've been left alone."

He didn't bother to ask how she knew that. Nicole Rider was scarily good at finding out those sorts of things.

"I can handle my own company."

"Well, let's be honest, you're not that great at surviving without me," Nicole continued in a rush. "I was worried that you'd set the kitchen on fire, fall down the stairs, or get abducted by fairies. They haven't tried to kill you yet, so they'll probably turn out to be real and rudely aggressive soon enough."

The curtain slipped from Benton's fingers as he straightened. "Right."

"I just thought you might be a little on edge," Nicole said kindly.

"Well, I am now," he replied. "And that explains the strange lights I've been seeing in the back yard."

The choked sound came through the phone speaker promised that she had believed him for a second there.

"Don't joke like that," she scowled.

"If I can't laugh, I'd cry. Or become a bitter old man yelling at kids to get off the lawn."

"You are bitter," she said flatly. "Your hair is two shades of gray and I've seen you yell at kids."

"I didn't yell. I was authoritative."

"There was a definite increase in volume."

"They were being obnoxious," he defended. "And I didn't go anywhere near as loud as I could have."

Nicole tried her hardest not to sound amused and failed miserably. Smirking to himself, he returned his attention to the window. The rough lace brushed across his fingertips, his gut gave a sharp twist, and the motion-sensor light flooded the small room. Benton jerked back from the door, his shoulder colliding with a hanging shelf. Nothing fell, but the bottles clanked together. The noise instantly drew Nicole's attention.

"What was that?"

"Something tripped the outside lights," he mumbled.

Concern slipped from her voice as she shifted into 'problem-solving mode'. "Front or back?"

The Rider family home had been outfitted with motion sensing lights long before they had ever heard of him, and had been swiftly disconnected. The abundance of wildlife that called the prairies home worked their way into town during the night. Given that her daughter had come uncomfortably close to death recently, both figuratively and literally, Dorothy had reattached them.

"Back," Benton said.

Nicole started suggesting the most likely suspects. The birds nesting in the trees. A family of chipmunks. The neighbor's cat. The words kind of blended together as Benton stared at the back door. Yellowed light streamed through the tiny holes littering the hanging fabric. A stray gust of wind found the cracks around the doors, howling like a wounded beast. Nothing out of place happened, but he knew the sensation that scraped over his skin like icy nails. Repetition had taught him it well.

Despite everything that had happened to him in recent months, his brain lurched back to the events before he had come to Fort Wayward. To the dance academy and the one man that ruined the small bit of peace he had created there. Benton knew what it felt like to be watched. Stalked. And he felt it now.

"Benton?"

His breath caught in his throat. He had completely forgotten that he still had the phone to his ear.

"Benton?" Nicole repeated.

"I'm fine," he said.

"Are you trying to lie to me right now? That's just insulting to both of us."

A smirk twitched the corner of his mouth.

"Can you see any tracks in the snow?" Nicole asked. Adding quickly, "The doors are locked, right?"

"Yes, they're all locked," he said.

"And the windows, too?"

"It's freezing outside. I've had the windows closed for days."

Having Nicole's voice in his ear made it a little easier to take another step toward the door. Before his reaching hand could gather the curtain again, the timer ran out and the night swept back over the room like a flood. He had left the kitchen light on. Now it was the only thing that kept him from plummeting into complete darkness. Shrouded in shadows, he struggled to breathe against the pressure building within his stomach. His hand was still raised, poised to pull back the curtain. Benton was abruptly struck with the absolute certainty that he didn't want to see what was out there anymore.

Without taking his eyes from the small, concealed window, Benton backed out of the room, retreating to the warmth and safety of the kitchen. Once there, he closed the door dividing the two spaces and fumbled with the small hook latch that held it in place.

"Benton?"

It baffled him how she could repeat his name on end without ever becoming increasingly annoyed.

"Huh?"

"I'm calling Mr. Smoke to come over and check on you," Nicole declared.

The neighbor might have been pushing into 'elderly' territory, and his face showed it, but he still had the kind of fatty muscle that old boxers always seemed to have. Physically, he was far more intimidating than a scrawny seventeen-year-old.

"Don't do that," Benton sighed. "It's late. I'm sure he's asleep."

"If it's a coyote, you're going to want Mr. Smoke to drive it off."

Jamming the phone between his ear and shoulder, he got himself a glass of water. More to have something to do with his hands rather than any need for it.

"You think there's a coyote in your backyard?"

Nicole was silent for a moment before sighing. "You're such a city boy."

Before he could ask any follow-up questions, she continued, "If it's a badger, leave it alone. I repeat, don't tick off a badger."

"Even I know that one, Nic," he said.

Glass in hand, he decided to just call it a night and head to bed. With any luck, he might be able to get a few good hours sleep before the nightmares kicked in. It was still easier to think of them as nightmares. Knowing that he was drawn into a killer's flesh, forced to become them as they brutally murdered someone, was harder to take.

"Everything's fine," he assured Nicole as he flicked off the light. "I'm just feeling a little weird. You were right, yet again."

"Are you sure?"

He raked a hand over his face as he mulled over the question. It was easy enough to say the words. Far harder to believe them. The squirming sensation still lingered in the pit of his gut. Constant, but not strong enough that he could truly put his faith behind it.

"Yeah. I'm fine. I'm headed to bed."

He flicked the kitchen light off as he passed. A soft rattling made him pause. Snapping around, he glanced back at the latched door. He stared at it for a long moment, the sound replaying in his mind. It could have easily been the wind knocking something around. It also could have been someone rattling the laundry door handle. His eyes focused on the latch, as if it could be the deciding factor.

*Real or paranoid?*

Nothing more came.

*Paranoia.*

Still, he turned on every light he passed on his way to his upstairs bedroom.

# Chapter 2

"So," Logan Rider's voice was almost as deep and rumbling as the police cruiser's engine.

After a heartbeat, Nicole realized that her father was trying to pull her into the conversation. Her parents had been happily chatting amongst themselves since they had piled into the car, leaving Nicole alone to recheck her history essay. It was due in the morning.

Lifting her gaze, she found her father looking at her over the top of the front passenger seat. He looked like the *Incredible Hulk* trying to squeeze into a kiddy chair. With a lot of contortions, he had managed to slump enough to keep his head from smacking against the ceiling.

"His parents seriously never told him he was adopted?" Logan continued as if they were already in mid-conversation. For once, she actually knew what he was talking about. "I mean, I get how it might not come up in casual conversation. But when you suspect your kid's genetic history is why he's taking a leap off of the sanity bridge, ya mention it, right?"

"I guess not," Nicole said.

"You *guess*?" he taunted more than asked.

Nicole puffed out her cheeks in annoyance. "Mrs. Bertrand doesn't talk to me. She doesn't like me all that much."

Logan gasped, throwing one beefy hand dramatically over his mouth. "But you're adorable."

"I know," she squealed in frustration.

"Everyone loves you."

"Thank you!" Nicole flung her arms wide, making the beam of her flashlight wiggle around the car's interior.

"Nic," Dorothy warned from the driver's seat.

Nicole quickly brought her arms back down, smothering the light against the palm of her hand. A straight slab of asphalt connected the entrance of the reservation to Fort Wayward. While it took on patches of black ice, the deep grooves on either side kept the snow from building up. Essentially, it was the easiest road in the world to drive, but Dorothy always took it on as if it were a twisting mountain pass. Having light flashing around in the backseat was a big no-no. Especially tonight.

The elevation of the road kept them just above the sea of towering grass for the majority of the trip. Normally, the moonlight compensated for the lack of streetlights, drenching the world in silver, and highlighting the road. Tonight, thick clouds heavily smothered the sky. Everything beyond the reach of the headlights was a flawless wall of onyx, and the swirling flurries reduced their vision all the more. It had Dorothy on edge.

"There's still a question over whether he's *adopted* or not," Dorothy said, restlessly checking the side view mirrors as she tried to gain control over the conversation.

"How so, gorgeous?" Logan asked.

Dorothy huffed a long-suffering sigh at her husband's flirtatious tone but couldn't stop a smile playing at the corners of her mouth.

"They claim that they hadn't known he wasn't their blood until he was ten," Dorothy said.

"I recall someone mentioning that he got into a bad fight and they found out he wasn't theirs at the hospital. Something about his blood type," Logan cut in.

"It wasn't a fight," Nicole snapped. "The dirtbags he called his friends attacked him."

Logan twisted around enough to arch an eyebrow at her.

"Yeah, I said dirtbag. If there's a stronger insult I can use without getting grounded again, let me know."

Logan smiled but quickly returned to the topic at hand. "And they attacked him because," he drew the word out into a hiss as he thought, "he's a *Harpy*?"

"*Banshee*," Nicole corrected.

"There's a difference?"

"Banshees are omens of death," Nicole said. "He dreams through the eyes of a killer. And, when he wakes up, he knows the victim's name and how to get in contact with them."

"Right," Logan said slowly.

Dorothy checked the mirrors again, sneaking a quick glance at her husband.

"When he was ten, he started dreaming of one specific serial killer. A child murderer operating within a ten-block radius. All of the victims went to his primary school."

"So, he knew how these kids were going to die but lacked any real explanation of how he got that information?" Logan said. "Oh, yeah. That doesn't seem suspicious. They thought he was killing them?"

"Not for long," Dorothy said.

"He was tiny for his age. There was no way he had the upper body strength to pull off the causes of death," Nicole elaborated.

The car swerved slightly as Dorothy twisted to glare at the backseat.

"How do you know the causes of death?"

"Newspapers," Nicole replied quickly.

It wasn't a lie. Her research would have been incomplete without checking the media. Of course, the particulars came from using the station computers to access classified police records. Logan shared a knowing look with his daughter but didn't ruin her cover story.

Sighing wearily, Dorothy dropped that particular line of questioning. "The working theory is that Benton knows the identity of the perp and is actively protecting him."

"Actively?" Logan asked.

"Officially, the cases are still open," Dorothy said.

Logan hummed thoughtfully. "So, it wasn't really an attack?"

"How can they say that?" Nicole gasped. "He was a child."

Before she could say any more, he continued, "Well, they didn't want him, right? They wanted the killer. I bet you anything that they had asked him a question or two between punches. Call a spade a spade; they tortured that boy, or used 'enhanced interrogation techniques' if you want to sound all book-smart and fancy."

"Oh, God," Nicole whimpered. "How did I never think of that?"

It hadn't taken much for the police to piece together what had happened that day. All of the kids had been ready with an explanation as to why Mr. Bertrand had seen them when he had dropped Benton off. According to them, Benton had just left without a word of explanation, and they hadn't seen him since. The bowling alley's security cameras quickly revealed the lie. Not an hour after Benton had arrived, they had all snuck out of the fire doors that lead to the back alley he was found in. And not one of them could explain the blood on their clothes.

While the reports were kept professional, Nicole had clearly seen how frustrated the officers were that they couldn't press charges. The first hurdle had been public opinion. Everyone wanted to believe that Benton had been brutalized by the killer he was supposedly protecting. There was a sick kind of justice in that scenario. One that the traumatized public could take comfort in. They didn't have the man killing their children, but at least someone had been punished. It also spared them from having to confront the depths of depravity kids were capable of.

Mostly, however, it was Benton himself that had derailed the investigation. He was as horrible a liar as the rest of them. No one believed that he couldn't remember what had happened. But it didn't matter what they said. Benton kept the secret. And, without his cooperation, the case slowly died. Because of his 'friends', Benton had a metal plate holding his skull together. Because of him, they kept their freedom. Every time she thought about it, Nicole hoped that the contrast still tormented them. She wanted their guilt to eat them alive.

"I'm still confused as to how the Bertrands didn't know he was adopted," Logan said, snapping Nicole from her thoughts.

"There's no record that he was," Dorothy said.

Logan shuffled to get into a more comfortable position. "Don't people generally report if their babies are stolen?" He cast a quick glance into the back seat and grinned at Nicole. "I'd report it if someone took you."

"Aw, thanks, dad."

"You know, if they don't put me on hold or something. Because that's annoying." His wide goofy grin kept the words from getting anywhere near hurtful.

"What if they play 80's pop songs?" she asked.

"Well, daddy does have to get his groove on," he considered. Without warning, he once again switched back to being serious. "Are you thinking illegal adoption or black-market shenanigans?"

"They claim he must have been switched at birth," Dorothy said.

"And you believe them?"

"There's no record of any infants going missing around the time of Benton's birth. If they're not lying about where and when that happened."

"There had to have been an investigation," Logan said.

"It's sealed by court order," Nicole said.

Again, Dorothy shot her a dark, suspicious look.

"Or so I assume," Nicole back peddled. "Otherwise, you would have told him, right? And he would have told me."

"Okay, so, assuming that the Bertrands are telling the truth," Logan spoke slowly, like he was still testing the theory out in his head before he let it leave his mouth. "Somewhere out there, there's a Banshee family wondering why their son just can't scream right?"

"I guess so," Dorothy said.

"I've checked other sites to see if they're looking," Nicole added.

"There are sites for that?" Logan asked, turning to look at his daughter, stopping when Dorothy pushed him away from the gearshift.

"There are sites for everything, dad."

"What do you put on it? Lost Banshee found, please call for more details?" His eyes widened slightly. "Good Lord, that's exactly what you did, isn't it?"

"I added a brief description," Nicole protested.

"Of what? Teenaged white male. Formally a baby?"

"I think his birth parents will know."

"Right. Because Caucasian, blond males with light eyes are so rare these days."

"How do you know what he looks like?" Dorothy asked.

"Nicole has described him a few times," Logan muttered.

Dorothy chuckled. "Well, in her defense, it's just one of those things that can't be described. And you don't really notice it at first. But once you see it, it can't be unseen."

"Babe, you're incredible and look awesome in that top, but you make no sense."

Dorothy rolled her eyes at the praise and struggled to find the words. After starting a few times, she just huffed. "He's got an 'uncanny valley' aesthetic going on."

"What does that even mean?" Logan wailed, throwing his head back for added dramatics. He grunted when the back of his skull hit the car roof.

"It's a term used to describe the unease or revulsion people feel when viewing something that nearly looks human but not quite," Nicole offered. "You know, like dolls or robots or computer generated–"

"He looks like a doll?" Logan cut in.

"No," Nicole said.

"It's not that simple," Dorothy said. "Okay, he's a blond, but he hasn't got blond hair."

"What a brilliant example, love of my life and mother of my child."

"Honey, even after you throw that other stuff in, I still know you're insulting me," Dorothy said in a sickly-sweet tone.

Logan cringed. "No, you don't."

"Just wait until you see him," Dorothy dismissed.

Reaching back, Logan wiggled his fingers in Nicole's general direction. "You got any pics on your phone, Angel?"

"Oh, of course, hold on."

As he waited for her to organize herself, he asked Dorothy why no one had pushed the 'possible abduction' issue with Benton's parents yet.

"Benton's clearly not ready to hear it," Dorothy said. "That whole weekend was a nightmare. Benton's still got the tribal Elders on him about his connection to the spirit world. They keep asking him questions he doesn't know how to answer. You'd think they'd give up after hearing 'I don't know' for the hundredth time. And he's still convinced his sweat lodge vision was telling him he's going to die soon. I'm just giving him a moment to breathe."

"Oh, hey, look at that. I now understand why you refused to talk about him until we got in the car," he replied.

A metal mesh separated the back of the police cruiser from the front. It took a little effort to thread her phone through the gap and into her father's waiting palm. She made a slight noise of protest when he began to swipe through the gallery instead of studying the picture she had selected.

"Okay. Next question," he said, clearly distracted. "Why has no one had problems with him staying at our house for so long?"

"It hasn't been that long," Nicole protested.

"Approaching a month now," Logan noted, still swiping.

"I've had a few run-ins with the Bertrands," Dorothy said. "I've told them to stay away from Benton until he's ready."

Logan's thick finger paused midair. "Honey, stop me if I'm wrong, but this sounds awfully close to kidnapping."

"He wants to be with us," Nicole insisted, only to be ignored.

"They agreed it was for the best," Dorothy said. "Benton's first reaction is sarcasm, but he's loud when you get him going."

"Is that a Banshee joke?" Logan chuckled.

Dorothy bit down a smile. "No. Of course not."

"Right." After wiggling his eyebrows a bit, he held up the phone.

Nicole shuffled forward, curling her fingers around the bars as she peered at the screen. It was one of the few candid photos she had managed to sneak of Benton and probably didn't show him in the best light. Fort Wayward wasn't really large enough to offer many extra-curricular activities, and the ones they had weren't exactly that impressive.

"Okay, you have to know that Kimberly was being a real pain," Nicole rushed to say. "She's the only one that can do the splits and kept making fun of all the girls that didn't get into the cheer-squad, saying that they weren't of 'high enough quality' to share a stage with her. This was Benton's way of sticking up for them. And it was in free period, so he wasn't disrupting the class."

Logan looked at the screen again. It glowed in the darkness, showing Benton lying on his stomach, prompted up by his elbows. His feet were resting on the seats either side of him, pulling him into a deep split.

"He spent the whole period like that?"

"Yes."

"Just flipping her off?"

Nicole smiled nervously. "He might have also told her to 'choke on her own mediocrity' a few times."

"I'm in danger of liking this kid," Logan chuckled. "He's kind of a pretty boy, ain't he? But I get what you mean. There's something off about him. I just can't put my finger on what."

"It's worse when you see him in person," Dorothy whispered.

Nicole reached for her phone back, but her dad started skipping through the photos again.

"He's a scrawny little ball of bitterness, isn't he? Does he ever smile?"

"In a few of them," Nicole said.

Logan hummed.

"Don't judge him before you meet him, dad."

"I'm not judging. This is recon."

"Recon?" Nicole shot back. "Why?"

"Why would I want to know about the character of the paranormal creature currently living with my family, that has proven on numerous occasions to be dangerous?" Pausing to suck in a deep breath, he continued, "Gee, Angel, I don't know. We need the *Scooby Gang* to crack that mystery."

"So you do believe me that he's not human?" Dorothy asked.

"Of course."

"You just haven't asked me any follow-up questions about that."

"I'm still working through Nicole's 'monster file,' babe," Logan said, positioning Nicole's phone to cast some light across the binder on his lap. "I'll get around to it."

Shuffling as far forward as her seatbelt would allow, Nicole pressed her cheek against the metal mesh. All of her efforts didn't account for much. Her father's shoulder still blocked her view of her 'monster binder'.

"Are you finding everything okay?" she asked.

It was still strange to see people leafing through her binder. And, despite how much she told herself otherwise, really uncomfortable. Researching the paranormal hadn't been as easy as she had first thought it would be. Sure, there was a wealth of information out there. Most of it happened to be the same points constantly repeated without any further elaboration. And it was almost impossible to sort the reality from the fiction. She had worked her way through fan sites and horror shows. True believers and ghost hunters. It had surprised her how many people insisted they were supernatural creatures just to get a date.

"I marked the creatures we've actually encountered."

Logan held the binder up, wiggling it so all of the plastic tags wobbled slightly.

"You've marked every page, Angel."

"There's a color system in place," she said with a roll of her eyes.

"Okay."

"It would just be madness, otherwise," she said. "Encountered is yellow. Encountered and dangerous is sparkly yellow."

"I know that's the color that comes to my mind when I think about pure evil," Logan said. Turning to a new section, his brow furrowed, and he held the binder up again. "Demonic killer weasels?"

"*Kamaitachi*. They're from Japan. I'm both terrified of them and think that they might be kind of cute," Nicole said. "And they're marked with orange and lime green tags."

"Yes. That is meaningful to me," Logan said with complete seriousness.

Nicole sighed. "Orange means that it's only ever been reported in one country. And, as is clearly outlined in the key at the front of the binder, I've used lime green for ones that I haven't been able to find reliable corroboration on."

"Of course. I knew that." Logan was a brilliant liar.

"Logan, do you see that?"

Dorothy's question instantly grabbed both father and daughter's attention. Cautious of the gathering sleet, Dorothy was already traveling at a far slower pace than the speed limit dictated. Gradually, she brought them to a crawl. Gravel crunched under the tires as they inched to a stop. They idled there, staring beyond the reach of the headlights.

The night was dense and complete, like a sheet of black silk draped over the world. At first, Nicole couldn't see what had grabbed her mother's attention. She wasn't confused for long. A solitary patch of white disrupted the abyss. Nicole pressed herself against the bars. It was the like a living moonbeam, existing somewhere between solid mass and a trick of the light. The figure lurched closer to the car. Growing and morphing.

"Angel," Logan asked in a whisper, eyes fixed on the stark white that was steadily taking on a human form. "What does the glittery purple on the Hitchhiking Ghost mean?"

A burst of wind brought an onslaught of snow. A temporary whiteout that threatened to hide the creature from sight.

"Corroborated but not personally seen," Nicole whispered in return.

"And the penguin sticker?"

Pain spiked through Nicole's fingers as she clutched the mesh. "Known killer."

"That's comforting," Logan noted.

In one swift motion, he slammed the binder and silently slid it onto the dashboard. At the same time, he rocked forward as far as his body would allow, reaching behind him to retrieve a handgun from his waistband. Dorothy cast a quick, disapproving glare at her husband before refocusing her attention on the slip of ghostly ivory.

"That better be registered," she hissed.

"Can you not cop right now?"

Logan's deep voice rumbled like distant thunder. A stark contrast to the soft click of the safety being thumbed off. Silence descended upon them, made thick by anticipation. Nicole tried to be quiet, but there was no masking the sound of her seatbelt opening. Dorothy flinched at the sound. Her service weapon was in her hand a split second later. Nicole froze as her mother shot her a cold glare that said, *Don't you dare move.*

The wind lowered, revealing the creature once again. It was now just beyond the rim of light, close enough that they could hear its muffled, dragging steps through the closed windows. Out of the corner of her eyes, Nicole watched her parents quickly throw a few hand gestures at each other. Sharp little movements that allowed them to form a plan of counter-attack in moments. It infuriated her that she wasn't able to understand it. Her annoyance was short lived. It died as the creature took its final step from the shadows. Nicole hurled herself at the door, jiggling the useless handle and smacking the glass when she remembered she was in the back seat of a police car. The door couldn't be opened from the inside.

"Nicole!" Dorothy snarled.

"It's Benton!" She rushed. "Mom, please, get my door. It's Benton!"

The car rocked under her efforts to get out. Benton continued forward, his normally fair skin made pale as death by the cold. The part of him left with color was the deep blue of his lips. A mixture of mud and blood caked his feet, and his thin pajamas rattled in the wind.

"He's going to freeze. Mom! Let me out," Nicole beseeched.

"How the hell did he get all the way out here?" Logan asked.

Moving in unison, the married couple lunged for their doors. It was more of an afterthought for Dorothy as she reached back and finally opened the back door. Nicole threw her body against the door, shoving it open far faster than Dorothy had anticipated, and hit the ground in a flat-out sprint. She dodged her mother's grasping hand and ignored her father's demands to stay back. All that mattered was getting to Benton before frostbite took its toll.

Stripping her jacket off, she cut in front of Benton. He didn't seem to know that she was there, walking straight into her a few times before coming to the conclusion that he couldn't go any further. Then he just stood there, staring straight ahead with unseeing eyes, his facial features slack.

Nicole hurriedly wrapped her coat around his shoulders. A recent growth spurt had eliminated the difference in their heights. While she now matched his height, his broad shoulders still kept the jacket from being a perfect fit, forcing her to tug sharply in an attempt to get the zipper closed. The cold prickled her bare fingers. It didn't compete with the pure ice of his skin.

"Benton."

His eyelids hung over his dazed, unfocused grey eyes. They didn't see her. Didn't seem to see anything.

"Benton!"

After a moment, she tried again, putting the full force of her lungs into the shout. He didn't even flinch. Giving up on the zipper, she hurriedly rubbed his arms, trying to work some warmth back into him. He still wouldn't respond but began to tremble. Relief almost buckled Nicole's knees. *Shivering's good,* she reminded herself as the trembling turned violent. *Shivering means he's not hypothermic.* She called his name over and over. Statically, he came around on the eighth repetition. A burning lump of terror began to sizzle behind her ribs when she reached her twelve repeats and he still didn't show any signs of looking at her.

"Nicole, get back here," Logan ordered.

Nicole cupped Benton's frozen cheeks.

"Benton it's me."

"Now, Nicole!"

Ignoring her father, she jerked his head around until he was forced to look at her, hoping that the sharp motion would snap him out of his daze. It didn't work. *Get him warm!* Her brain screamed the command, and she hated herself for wasting time. He must have already been walking for hours.

"Come on. Let's get in the car."

He didn't move. Carefully curling an arm around his back, she urged him forward.

"It's nice and warm in there."

Benton rocked on his feet, making no attempt to catch himself as the motion threatened to tip him over. Finally, he moved, his jaw dropping as he sucked in a deep breath. Her stomach plummeted into her feet.

"Get down!" she screamed.

Finely honed reflexes had Logan leaping for one side of the road, tumbling down the incline and out of sight. Dorothy performed the same motion on the opposite side. Each one trusted their daughter to follow, but there wasn't time. Benton's lips pulled back from his teeth. He swelled and the muscles of his jaw drew taut. Nicole dropped. Pain shot through her ribs and down her stomach as she collided with the road. The sharp edges of gravel nicked her bare flesh. She had barely landed by the time the stones began to tremble.

A Banshee's wail cracked over her. Not just a sound, but a physical force. It crushed her down like a slab of steel, compressing the air from her lungs and squeezing her skull like a vice. Vibrations pulsated through the air and ground alike. Chunks of rock were ripped from the ground, some jumping where they were, while others were flung through the air. Somewhere within the ear-splitting scream was the crunch and squeal of metal. Droplets of blood trickled from her ears to curl along her jawline. Fire exploded behind her eyes. Her brain seemed to liquefy within her skull as the sound warped her bones. Gasping for air, she tried to drag herself to the side, knowing from experience that the screams were bearable beyond the line of fire. She could barely lift her fingers.

The high-pitched wail stopped as abruptly as it had begun. The damage remained. Nicole's vision pulsated and blurred, lurching from side to side as if she were upon a thrashing sea, bringing bile gushing up her throat. A sharp ringing filled her ears. The sound pushed her deeper into nausea. She blinked against the onslaught of sensations, trying to force her senses back under her control. The only reason she wasn't sick was that her body couldn't convulse enough to heave.

Tiny specks of snow landed upon her cheek, each one like a needle piercing her flesh. She relished the small spikes of pain. They were the only thing keeping her from passing out. Ice settled within her eyes as the sharp ringing dulled to a constant whine. Gathering tears blurred her vision all the more. It took the complete focus of her fractured mind to dig her fingernails into the earth. There was nothing left for her but to lift her head.

Beyond the road, hovering barely within the reach of the car's front lights, the wall of grass swayed and shivered. She blinked at the motion, aware that it meant something, but oblivious as to what.

Then something moved against the shadows. Nicole strained to push herself up. It was a small motion, but enough to slosh her brain against her skull. She whimpered and trembled, unable to keep the inch she had fought for, and dropped back down. Blinking hard, she strained to focus on the creature that stalked behind the first layer of reeds. A harsh gust of wind rushed over the world, parting the plant life, and she caught her first real glimpse.

Panic squeezed her heart like a vice. Even in her half-conscious state, she instantly recognized the textured skin of the bull snake. A speckled pattern of off-white, midnight black, and burnt wheat. It was the size that terrified her. The creature stood at least five feet tall as it moved along the edge of the road. But it wasn't slithering. Gaunt, boney limbs carried it with a heaving stride. She saw the back of it first. A quick flash, but it was burned into her mind all the same. It looked almost humanoid. As if an emaciated person had arched back and scurried around. A second later, she saw the front of the monster. This, too, looked almost like a crawling human, but twisted around to crawl on hands and knees. She didn't have time to work her shattered mind around the sight until the creature sunk back into the shadows.

The strength left her arms and she collapsed against the road, the stones digging into the tender skin of her cheek. Her head swirled, crashing and swaying, dragging her down into the dark oblivion of unconsciousness. Fighting to keep her eyes open, she watched as a face emerged from the reeds. The features hovered somewhere between human and snake, but belonged to neither. It smiled at her.

"Angel?" Logan's voice cracked through the ringing in her ears.

It sounded a million miles away. Still, she clung to it, trying to use it as a tether to keep herself awake. There wasn't enough strength left in her arms to point at the monster lurking at the edges of the minimal light. She couldn't work her voice out of her throat.

Her father crouched beside her and placed a large, warm hand against her back. "Angel. Are you okay, baby girl? Dorothy!"

*Mom*, Nicole thought with a spike of terror.

It was the last thought that chased her into the abyss – that the monster would find Dorothy first. That, before her father could intervene, it could drag her into the dark sea of endless prairie grass.

# Chapter 3

*Well, this is awkward,* Benton thought as he trudged down the dark, snow-dusted country road, the living mountain that had recently tried to strangle him barely a few inches from his side. His brain didn't feel clogged up or frazzled. He could clearly remember finishing his call with Nicole and getting ready for bed.

*That part's true,* he told himself, glancing down at his pajama pants. They were his proof. He had showered, changed, and laid down for the night. He recalled the chill of the air, the weight and warmth of the thick blankets piled up on top of him, the low howling wind that made him grateful to be indoors.

After that, he had to question himself. Sleep had started to pull at him, making his limbs heavy and thick. He remembered closing his eyes, feeling safe and warm. But when he opened his eyes again, everything had changed. He was freezing, thrashing, and terrified. Air had swelled within his lungs, useless as it failed to work past the mammoth hand squeezing his throat. The sudden shift had left his brain muddled and slow.

It had taken the chilled breeze against the soles of his feet for him to realize he wasn't standing. His toes clipped the ground as the giant pulled him off of his feet. Using one hand and showing no signs of strain, the man lifted him until their faces aligned. Light pulsated from somewhere out of Benton's sight, periodically illuminating the burning rage on the man's features.

"Scream again, and I'll snap your neck," he had hissed while Benton choked.

He remembered kicking and only finding air, carving his nails through the flesh of the man's arm only to have him squeeze harder. Choking tears had blurred the edges of his vision, but, as the light returned, he caught sight of Nicole's crumpled body. With the last of his strength, Benton had grabbed the man's arm with both hands and pulled his feet up. One swift roll of his body and he drove both heels into the man's face. The grip had finally weakened. Benton had dropped, hitting the ground as air flooded down his abused throat.

The giant had howled in fury and struck out. Loose-limbed and dizzy, Benton had barely been able to avoid each kick, inching ever closer to Nicole. His arms and legs had quivered as he branched himself between Nicole and the furious man. He desperately pulled for air, but hadn't been able to work in enough.

That was when Dorothy had intervened and made the introductions.

It had been weird at the beginning to know that the first words Logan Rider had ever said to him were a threat. Now that he had been randomly repeating it for going on two hours, the novelty was wearing off. Not that he blamed the man. Any resentment he might have felt had dissolved when he had caught sight of the police cruiser. Balancing on its roof, it had slowly spun, rhythmically bringing the crumpled front end into sight. The headlights had dangled from the wreckage but had somehow still worked. The combination transformed the broken vehicle into a makeshift lighthouse.

Shivering against both the cold and his memories, Benton snuck another glance at Nicole. Cradled in her father's arms, one arm danglingly limply, she looked small and fragile. *Two hours and she still hadn't regained consciousness. That can't be good.*

His stomach twisted tightly, trying to coax him back into the state of panic he had first felt at seeing her. He hoped Dorothy hadn't said anything too important when she had introduced him to Logan. It was around that time that he had managed to get close to Nicole, and he wasn't paying much attention to anything else. For one horrid moment, he had been convinced that the worst possible option had come true. His hands trembled at the memory of cupping her neck and finding no pulse. In his panic, he had pressed too close to the tendons. Dorothy had repositioned his fingers for him. He had never felt more relieved, or more stupid, when he felt Nicole's strong pulse surging under his fingertips.

Everything else had been a blur after that. A mesh of pointless words and motions. He couldn't remember anything beyond the steady rush of her pulse.

With the car completely totaled, walking back to town had been their only option. Their phones had worked enough for them to use the flashlight functions, but getting a signal would be impossible until they were closer to town.

Logan had carried his daughter the whole time. Even now, he didn't seem at all put out by the weight. While he was reluctant to admit it, Benton was pretty impressed. Although he wasn't sure if he should be. The man's biceps were thicker than Benton's head. He looked away when Logan shot him a dark look.

"I hadn't meant to hurt her," Benton mumbled.

"Well, that changes everything," Logan snorted.

"Logan," Dorothy sighed. "It was an accident."

"Did his Banshee yell hurt my baby?"

"*Our* baby."

Logan choked on his words before sputtering with force, "All the more reason for you to be alarmed and a little resentful."

"Darling, I am cold, sore, concerned, and frustrated. So, if you could do me a favor and remember one of the many conversations we've had over the past few months, I'd be very grateful."

"Any conversation in particular?" he shot back.

"Pick any of the ones where I mentioned how co-dependent these two are getting."

Benton hunched his shoulders. "We're not–"

"Oh, that sounds healthy," Logan said.

"But also proof that Benton would never do anything to hurt her. He wouldn't do that to himself."

Biting his lips, Benton fought down the urge to defend his honor. While he was far from a Prince Charming, he wasn't a psychopath, either. His reasoning for not hurting people didn't solely revolve around how it might affect himself. Dorothy pushed the issue for a few more moments, and, eventually, Logan came around to her way of thinking. There was no great change in the way he interacted with Benton. There was still suspicion and anger in his gaze. But he did let the Banshee check on his friend without death stares, so Benton supposed it was a win in his favor.

Another hour of walking, and Benton forgot what it was like to be warm. The Rider family traveled light. Benton had been given Nicole's overnight bag, and each parent had taken ownership of their own duffle bag. Unfortunately, no one had Benton's shoe size. Logan's oversized boots didn't fight off the chill, but they succeeded wonderfully in sparing his feet from the sharp gravel. Nicole's jacket was still draped over his shoulders. It didn't quite fit and barely helped keep in the minimal body heat he had left. Still, he couldn't bring himself to ask for another. It would just be too awkward. Right now, his goal was to get back home having spoken as few words as possible.

The night was as dark as it was cold, with only the glow from their phones' flashlight apps to break it up. Benton could barely see his own feet. It made it incredibly easy to avoid eye contact. Gravel crunched under their feet. The wind curled around them with a low howl. A feeling came creeping back before it slammed his spine like a physical blow. Benton stopped short and turned around. He had borrowed Nicole's phone. The 'accident', as he would continue to call it, had left her screen with a vicious crack. The light worked well enough. He cast the narrow beam from one side of the road to the other. Flurries swirled around them, casting shadows and creating the illusion of movement, like a thousand small beasts crawling through the undergrowth.

His arm jerked to the side, focusing the beam on the swaying wall of grass without any conscious input from him. Snow gathered along the sleeve of his jacket as he stood there, waiting, certain in the knowledge that he was being watched.

A shadow crept into his peripheral vision. Benton stifled a startled scream as he jerked away. With Nicole effortlessly cradled to his chest, Logan still managed not only to creep up on him, but to also crouch down to the same height.

"What ya looking at?" he asked in an almost sing-song tone.

"Don't creep up on me," Benton hissed.

"Nah, I think I will. You're kind of hilarious when you're scared," Logan replied. "Question; are you whispering because I whispered, or because you think something's out there?"

Benton had to think about that for a moment. "Because you whispered."

"Ah. That's less interesting. Pity, though."

Benton stammered. "That we're not being stalked by some unseen creature?"

"Yeah. I kind of want to shoot something paranormal. I don't know why. It's just a thought that's got stuck in my head."

Benton tried not to notice the way Logan's eyes slid over to study him closely.

"What are you classified as?"

"Your daughter's best friend," Benton said, still unable to work his voice any louder than a whisper.

"Are you done toying with him, Logan?" Dorothy snapped from a few feet away.

"Not yet, honey," Logan called cheerily over his shoulder.

Dorothy deadpanned. "You're an embarrassment."

"Okay, baby. Love you, too. You look so hot today." Logan's abundance of enthusiasm and childish glee disappeared the second he met Benton's gaze again. "You do anything to hurt my girls again, I'm going to make you suffer. A lot. Like, in really gross, disturbing ways. Then I'll shoot you. Do we understand each other?"

"Yes, sir," Benton said in a low breath.

"I'm really glad we've had this talk. I feel like we've grown closer. Don't you?"

Benton couldn't stop his eyes from dropping to Nicole, silently begging for her to wake up and tell him what to do. Logan walked a tightrope between playful and menacing. No matter how closely

Benton watched the man's twitches and mannerisms, he couldn't figure out how he was supposed to react.

It was unnerving. As discreetly as he could, Benton leaned away from the man. Logan moved with him, somehow still easily cradling Nicole's sleeping form in his arms.

"Logan," Dorothy snapped, rage bubbling on the edges of her voice.

"Coming, love of my life and woman who agreed to spend her life with me. No-take-backs. That's what the ring says."

Benton was convinced that the soldier was hovering somewhere between insanity and stupidity for half a second. That was all it took for Dorothy to take the bait. The impulse to educate her husband on the true meaning behind wedding rings overrode her original annoyance. Despite the miserable, painful cold, Benton found himself smiling. It wasn't often that Dorothy went 'full Nicole.' Although, even at her best, she could never rival Nicole's inner perfectionist. Right now, he'd love to be listening to her prattle on about all of this. He snuck a glance at her face. Carrying her more like a child than a teenager, her face was obstructed by the oversized bulge of Logan's bicep.

They resumed their trudge toward the town, but Benton could no longer keep himself from constantly looking around them. The sensation had become a constant pressure. There was no doubt left in his mind anymore.

Something was watching him.

"So, what do paranormal creatures have against cars?" Logan asked.

Benton didn't stop searching the darkness around them. If Logan noticed, it didn't stop him from continuing.

"Nicole's jeep. The police cruiser. Oh, and the Mac truck. Thanks for that one, by the way."

Most of the words had bled together into a meaningless rumble, but the Mac truck did ring a bell. Benton liked to believe that he was prepared for anything Nicole threw at him. However, even he hadn't seen her chasing a monster out into traffic. That was how they had realized his snap-fire screams could do some real physical damage.

"Sorry?"

"Thanks for saving my girl," Logan repeated. His brow furrowed as he studied Benton's face closely. "Don't be so obvious. Just keep walking."

"Sorry?" Benton repeated.

"I noticed it about a mile back."

"You did?"

"Yeah. But I'm not all that keen to fight a coyote or two while Nicole's passed out."

"Coyote?"

Now that it had been spoken out loud, Benton knew with absolute certainty that whatever was following them wasn't a natural part of the wildlife. There was nothing he could turn to as a reason for his thinking. Nothing he could grasp onto to try and explain. It was just a feeling. A whisper of absolute certainty that what stalked them wasn't anything he had experienced before. It just didn't *feel* natural.

"They like to stalk things for a while before they decide if they're going to try and take a bite," Logan said. "Just keep walking and it'll hopefully go away."

The soft breeze brought with it another rush of flurries and the tell-tale crunch of grass. Benton's hand trembled with the urge to whip the light around, to search for the lurking creature again, even though he knew that he wouldn't be able to see it.

"Don't," Logan said as he watched the flashlight beam tremble over the rocks.

Dorothy slowed her pace, falling back until she was on Logan's other side.

"Do you see it?"

"Heard it," Logan said. "Bit back to the left. A few yards in. Should I give Benton my gun?"

"No," Dorothy snapped quickly. Lowering her voice, she added, "He's a horrible shot."

"I'm not that bad," Benton protested.

Dorothy scoffed at that, and neither adult deemed it necessary to comment further. He tried not to take it personally. Knowing the Riders, all it would take was a loose sense of competition for them all to work their ways to sniper level perfection.

"Benny," Logan said. "If this coyote gets excitable, your job is to protect Nicole, okay? Just, scream at anything that comes near her."

"It's not a coyote," Benton whispered.

He hadn't really intended for anyone to hear it. So it was a little startling to be confronted by two laser-focused glares. He shrunk away slightly.

"What is it?" Dorothy asked in a clip, professional voice.

"I don't know."

"What does it look like?" Logan asked in a tone that was creepily similar to his wife's.

"I haven't seen it."

"Then how do you know?" The words were barely out of his mouth before they were followed with a gasp of barely contained excitement. "Are your Banshee senses tingling? Is that what this is? Do I finally get to see this in action? Honestly, I thought it would be more aesthetically impressive for some reason. Don't ask me why."

It went against all logic that the man could talk that fast without his words bleeding together. He left no room for any kind of reply. It was more like he was vocalizing a conscious stream rather than actually having a conversation.

"So that's where Nicole gets it from," Benton said, still not daring to raise his voice or glance behind him.

The longer the feeling remained nestled behind his ribs, the more it evolved. After another half mile, Benton could swear that he could feel the creature's body heat, almost hear the snow as it melted upon its skin. Logan tried to get general conversation going but was careful never to pick a topic that was too interesting. It was more about breaking the tension that threatened to consume the air, rather than serve as any kind of distraction.

Something in the air shifted and Benton whirled around. At his startled gasp, Dorothy had her weapon drawn and Logan had twisted his body, keeping the still slumbering Nicole behind his bulk, while freeing one hand to fend off an attack. Out of the corner of his eyes, Benton could see them cast a few unsteady looks at him. Neither of them saw the figure a fair distance down the road. As black as the night surrounding it, the Grim Reaper's form was noticeable only by the motion at the edges of its being. The way its body evaporated like smoke, curled like oil in water, while its central mass remained solid. The specter of death hovered a foot off the ground. Bone white smears served as its hands and face. They burned like hot coals within the darkness.

No matter how many times he saw the reaper, it still brought a slither of dread. He stopped walking, ignoring Logan's grunt of protest, and kept the beam of the flashlight lowered to the ground. The winter air swirled around them, never touching the figure even as it ravaged Benton's skin. Its presence pushed on his awareness. Ever since his vision at the sweat lodge, he knew that this was something close to communication. A language he couldn't understand.

Logan huffed, juggling Nicole in his arms and casting odd glances to the surrounding grass.

"What is it this time?" he grumbled.

"Mic is here."

"Mic?" Logan put an unnecessary amount of emphasis on the name. "Where have I heard that?"

"Mictecacihuatl," Dorothy said, already readjusting herself to hold the gun with both hands.

Logan's face was expressive enough that even muted light couldn't hide the realization dawning on his features.

"Isn't that what Nicole called Death?"

"One of them," Benton replied.

Logan clicked his tongue and cast a look towards his wife. "Yeah, this wasn't in my basic training. Love of my life, any suggestions?"

"Basically, mind the perimeter while she does whatever she came to do with Benton," Dorothy said.

Benton didn't need to look back to know that the idea of inaction didn't sit too well with the soldier. Still, he followed his wife's lead. He closed ranks with her, protecting Nicole between them, while remaining a few feet behind Benton.

"Hi," Benton said awkwardly. Conversations with the Grim Reaper never came easily. Anything he thought to say just seemed stupid. "You're not here for Nicole."

He said it as a statement, hoping that he wasn't about to be contradicted. Mic never moved. Never spoke a word. Still, its presence dominated his mind, consuming his thoughts until he almost forgot about the unseen creature lurking within the shadows.

"What was that about Nicole?" Logan snarled. "If it moves an inch towards my girl —"

Dorothy placed a steadying hand on his arm, instantly cutting off his words. Benton didn't look back at them. His focus was on Death alone.

"Is it trying to hurt me?"

"What's 'it'?" Logan snapped. A small hiss left his mouth before he whispered harshly to his wife, "I don't like being on the outside of this conversation."

"I know. I love you. Shut up."

Benton did his best to ignore the couple, a task made easier when the dry grass to his side rustled. His eyes snapped around to face it. Slowly, the smear of white that served as Mic's face did the same. Silver streaked across his vision. His throat swelled with a barely contained scream as he staggered back a step. Gravel shifted under his feet, loud enough to almost cover the rustle behind him. He snapped around to find the same silver glow.

*Eyes. They're eyes.*

"Communication skills, Benton."

Dorothy elbowed Logan in the ribs, turning the last of his snapped words into a pained grunt.

*Can't they see it?* He balled his hands tightly. Being the only one able to see these nightmares was quickly getting old. Drawing in a harsh breath, he turned to Mic, finding the Grim Reaper still tracking the unseen creature.

"Is it here to hurt me?" Benton asked.

The answer came without motion. Simply appearing in his mind as if it had always been there. *Yes.*

Benton turned on his heel. He knew that his time was coming. They had shown him as much in his fever visions. Of course, they had refrained from giving him any information that bordered on helpful.

He didn't know when it was coming, but it wouldn't be tonight.

"We need to get out of here," he ordered the pair.

"What was its answer?" Logan asked.

"They always want to kill me," Benton snapped.

Shoving past them, he skidded to a stop. Reapers stood as dark pillars along the stretch of dirt road. For some, only their faces were visible. Patches of white on an endless blanket of ebony. Dozens stood as silent witnesses for what was coming next.

"I'm not dying here!" he bellowed, his fists trembling as adrenaline pulsed through him.

In unison, the Grim Reapers morphed, each pale face drifting in an unearthly glide to face the right side of the road. Benton snapped his arm up, training the phone's beam onto the patch that had captured their attention. Dorothy and Logan followed suit. The combined force of their weak lights didn't break up much of the night but gleamed off of something small and silver that hovered several feet off the earth. It wasn't until it sunk back, emitting a low hissing growl as it faded into the darkness, that he confirmed they were eyes.

"That cannot be anything good," Dorothy whispered to herself.

"Okay gang–" Logan paused to take an audible gulp. "Who's up for a lovely jog into town while pretending that we're not terrified?"

Dorothy barely took a few fingers off of her gun handle to indicate that she was up for the idea. Benton shoved his hand straight up in the air, his eyes still locked onto the patch of night where the beast had disappeared. The constant pressure that had knotted his stomach slightly loosened, and he took a sobering breath.

Without a word, they broke into a sprint, keeping as close to each other as possible.

# Chapter 4

Nicole jerked awake, her breath like a rock in her throat, choking her as the Banshee's wail shattered the silence. The sound lingered somewhere between terror, rage, and disgust — human and something undeniably not. Her bulky noise-canceling headphones struggled to muffle the sound. But it was still painful to hear. The sound chilled her blood, filling it with shards of ice that scraped along her veins. Her heavy pulse slashed her brain into ribbons. Pain whited-out her vision as she bolted upright. She pressed the sides of her headphones harder over her ears, enduring the pain in an attempt to lessen the sound.

Blinking back tears, she tried to focus. The room hung around her like a mist; intangible and surreal, more of an illusion than reality. Benton was the only thing in sight. His eyes were open but unfocused, fixed on some unseen point while his whole body worked to purge the horrors from his mind. He screamed long beyond the capacity of his lungs, his face turning white instead of the splotchy red that would generally reveal oxygen deprivation.

Photo frames rattled against the wall. The small bulb of her nightlight flickered and hissed. Fine cracks snaked out across her window glass. Nicole couldn't hear the screech of them grinding together but she knew they were. Wrapping one arm around his shoulders, she clasped her free hand over his eyes, trying to shield him. On the few occasions Benton had actually blown out the glass, the larger shards had always been hurled outside. It was the smaller airborne ones that she was worried about. They cut deep and were impossible to remove.

Suddenly, the scream died. His muscles went lax. Without the tension to keep him upright, Benton slumped against her with all of the strength of a rag doll. Nicole was quick to bundle him into her arms, taking on his weight, cradling his head to make sure he didn't crack it against a bedpost. She had utterly failed to get the rust colored bloodstains out of the carpet from the last time.

Once she had his trembling body securely propped against her, she ripped off her headphones and tossed them to the side. Cold sweat dripped from Benton's skin. Oddly enough, that had been the hardest thing to get used to when she had started sharing a bed with Benton. Not the screaming, or the 2 am wakeup call, or the fact that he was an unrepentant pillow hog. She could take all that in stride. But waking up to find that her bed had transformed into a bog was unnerving and honestly a little gross. It made for a lot more laundry.

There was a startling amount of strength in his trembling arms as he looped them around her waist. Tightening like boa constrictors until she was sure something inside her was going to pop. Slick with sweat, his face slipped over the skin as he struggled to hide in the crook of her neck. Nicole grimaced. The spiderweb of cracks that now split her window into a thousand pieces was a bad omen on its own. But he only ever transformed into a strangling vine when his dreams sunk to a level of depravity that he wasn't used to. And that was a deep pit.

Holding him tight, she began to whisper the words that he needed to hear the most at these times; reassurances that he was safe, that he wasn't the person he had been in his dreams. He didn't do those things. She punctuated every sentence with a repetition of his name, reminding him of who he was. Each night shoved another person into his head and, sometimes, he lost himself in the crush.

"It's alright, Benton. I'm right here."

It terrified her that he still flinched at the sound of his name, like it was something he didn't recognize. Logically, she knew that it was Benton cradled against her. It didn't stop a voice in the back of her head from whispering that she held a stranger. One that had proved themselves to be a murderer. A sadistic one at that.

His nails scraped harshly against her spine as he balled his hands in her sweater. Still quaking, he squeezed her tighter, crushing the air from her lungs. It hurt, but she didn't try to squirm away.

"It's okay, Benton," Nicole said, fighting down the tremor in her voice. "I've got you."

He was still shaking when her bedroom door slammed open. Logan's massive bulk filled the doorway, sleep in his eyes and his handgun cupped between his hands. Benton threw himself hard against Nicole, seemingly trying to protect her and use her as a human shield at the same time. She rubbed his shoulders reassuringly.

"What's going on?" Logan snapped, blinking wide. "What should I shoot?"

"Nothing, dad," Nicole sighed. "Benton, calm down. It's pointed to the floor, his finger is off the trigger, and the safety is on. He's not going to hurt us."

Benton continued to squirm while a proud smile chased the sleep from Logan's face.

"Good observation skills, Angel. You got that from me, you know."

"Like hell she did," Dorothy's voice came a moment before Logan lurched forward. "Get out of the way, you giant dimwit."

Logan rocked his shoulders just enough to let his far smaller wife slip through.

"Love you, too, my gorgeous queen," he grumbled with a grin.

Despite her annoyance and iron will, the corner of Dorothy's mouth twitched with amusement. Logan smelled the blood in the water and smiled a shark-like grin.

"Can you be serious for five seconds?"

Logan started to fiddle with his watch as if to set the timer.

"You're an adult," Dorothy hissed.

Logan gasped, looking as mortified as possible while flattening his hand against his chest. The standard issue gun in his hand ruined the effect of a shocked old lady clutching her pearls. Nicole stifled a giggle just as a pained whimper escaped Benton. The sound snapped her back into the moment. Horrified to realize that she had let her attention wander, she quickly drew up her legs, creating just enough room for her mother to sit down. They had learned early on that it wasn't a good idea for the Constable to crowd Benton until he was ready.

"Okay, Benny-boy, you know the deal," Dorothy said, her tone professional but warm.

It was the kind of tone she used to get the most out of her witnesses. After a few attempts, Benton twisted his head, essentially turning to face her without releasing his grip on Nicole. Whatever words he was going to say were lost in a raw grunt of pain. His body convulsed, tightening around Nicole until she gasped. Logan jerked as if he wanted to rush forward. He was held off by his wife's raised hand.

"He starts to get crippling headaches if he doesn't give a name in a timely fashion," Dorothy explained. Shifting her attention to Benton, she softened her voice. "Come on, Benton. Just give me the name."

Grinding his teeth, he struggled to get his head up. Dorothy cupped his shoulder with one hand, keeping him stable, while Nicole slipped out from under him. His fingers clenched her sweater tight enough to make it rip, scrambling to draw her back.

"It's okay, Benton," she told him, stressing his name to give him another anchor. "I'm just going to make us some spiced hot chocolate. I'll be right back."

His hands trembled.

"If you need me, yell. I'll come running."

Her promise seemed to do the trick and, at last, Benton nodded. The moment her sweater slipped from his grip, he pressed his balled fists to his temples.

"I'll be back as quick as I can," Nicole assured.

She managed to suppress her need to check on them until she reached the door. The pain was clearly taking its toll on Benton. He had drawn up one knee, pressing his forehead against it while he clawed at the sides of his skull. But he had started to talk, softly mumbling his story while Dorothy took notes on her phone. Nicole forced herself to start moving again. They had their established routine, and she wasn't in any position to change it now. Constable Rider got the story. Nicole dealt with the aftermath.

Pushing past her father with a whispered apology, Nicole hurried down the stairs, setting herself to the task of getting back with the comforting drinks as fast as possible. It normally didn't take them that long. Everyone was careful not to say it out loud, but they all felt the seconds like lead weights upon their backs. All Benton knew with absolute certainty was the victim's name and how to contact them. He never had any idea when the murder would happen. They could have weeks to track the intended victim down. But it was just as likely that they only had seconds.

Dawn had already broken, filling the house with a muted light that did little more than her nightlight upstairs. Still, she flicked on the overhead lights before she began bustling around the kitchen. The neon glow did terrible things to her head. Pain welled behind her eyes, adding to her general nausea. For the first time, it occurred to her that she couldn't remember ever getting into the bed. Pausing, she thought back, trying to grasp the last thing she could remember. Vague notions of leaving the reservation floated across her mind. Any attempt to grasp the thought only made her head pound harder. She decided that there was enough time to deal with that kind of stuff later.

Setting a saucepan of milk to boil, she pulled out a tray and set out three mugs. *Oh, right. Dad.* She added one more to the set and rushed to the pantry. Checking off a mental list, she piled the ingredients into her arms.

"Cookies," she chimed out loud.

She almost lost the collection of items as she reached for the Tupperware container. It was another close call when Logan suddenly rounded the corner.

"So." He stretched the word out as he crossed to the kitchen table.

The metal framed chair groaned as he dumped himself into it, the legs skittering over the tiles with a sharp squeal.

"So," Nicole parroted back, admittedly showing more attention to the drinks than her father.

Logan looked at her expectantly. It became increasingly distracting.

"Do you want a hot chocolate?" she asked, lifting his mug to wiggle it invitingly.

Logan threw his arms out as if asking the universe at large if it were witnessing it.

"Are we really going to ignore this?"

Nicole's interest in the conversation had drifted somewhat when she had realized her dad wasn't eager for a drink. Focused on getting the measurements right, she hummed.

"Ignore what, Dad?"

Having a musclebound man thrashing his arms about over his head like a startled Muppet gained her attention instantly.

"What's going on?"

Logan's jaw dropped along with his arms. At a point Nicole couldn't recall, he had placed his handgun in the center of the table. He began to tap his index finger against the handle.

"Seriously? You too? I trusted you."

"I'm going to need more information," Nicole said.

"This is normal to you?"

That was when it clicked. "Okay, I admit that the nightly routine is a little hard to get used to at first, but you'll adjust soon enough."

Logan blinked at her. Long and shocked. "Yeah, okay, admittedly that is weird. But I feel that we should put that aside right now for a more pressing issue."

"Alright." She stopped everything and turned to face him fully. "What've you got for me?"

Logan pursed his lips in mock thoughtfulness. "Oh, here's a question. Does he normally sleep in your room?"

Nicole snorted. "You stopped me for that? You had me worried for a second."

Turning back to the counter, she resumed squishing a red chili pepper with the side of her knife, not stopping as her father spoke.

Logan leaned back in his chair, making it groan again. "It just seems that, as a father, I should raise the question. You know?"

Nicole shrugged. "I can see that."

"So?" Logan pressed. "Think you can throw an answer my way?"

Adding cinnamon sticks and the crushed chili to the simmering milk, she shrugged. "It's just easier to be in the same room."

"Yeah." Logan drummed his hands on the tabletop and clicked his tongue. "Can't cross a hallway. It's a whole three feet. How can anyone cross such a vast distance without proper supplies?"

Confusion slammed into Nicole, making her whip around to face her father. Her head was not grateful.

"What are you talking about?"

Her father hooked an arm over the back of a neighboring chair, the picture of nonchalance. "I remember what it's like to be a teenager. All hyped up on hormones and disco music."

A burst of laughter escaped her lips. Not at her father's poor attempt at a joke, though.

"What?" Logan asked.

She turned back to her milk, careful not to let it burn. "I don't exactly remember everything that happened tonight, but I'm guessing that you've actually had a conversation with Benton, right?"

"Yeah."

"Can you really see him making a pass? At anyone? Ever?"

"Oh, hell no." Logan made a sound between a snort and a laugh. "That boy's got way too many issues, and absolutely no game."

"Then what's the problem?"

He jumped one shoulder. "You're not exactly known for your impulse control, angel-girl."

Shock made the block of chocolate slip from her hand. It crashed into the saucepan, causing the contents to slosh to over the rim. The small flames of the burner hissed in protest at the liquid invasion. The scent of burning milk snapped her out of her daze. Caught between cleaning up the mess and stirring in the chocolate, she stammered.

"Dad, you're insane."

"Am I?"

She twisted around again, glaring at her father in challenge. One day, she'd be too old for him to make fun of. She looked forward to that day. Logan squished up one side of his mouth, clearly intent on driving her into madness.

"He's kind of a pretty boy, isn't he?"

"Dad," Nicole groaned. "You're not funny."

"I'm hilarious," he shot back.

"Can you do me a favor?" Nicole rushed to say before he could continue.

A broad smile stretched her father's lips, turning him a good few years younger. It didn't take the suspicion out of his eyes.

"Sure thing, Angel."

Nicole motioned to the kitchen door with her chin. "Go up and listen in on mom and Benton."

"Huh?"

"Just for a minute or two," she insisted with an innocent smile.

His eyes narrowed.

"Hey, I'm not going anywhere," she said, exaggerating the care it took to stir the contents of the saucepan. "Once you get back, we'll pick up this conversation again."

Logan hesitated, leaving only the soft bubbling of the chili hot chocolate and his tapping finger to break the silence of the room.

"Five minutes?" he clarified. "Then we start separating you two."

"Five minutes," Nicole agreed. Adding, once he was halfway out the door, "Then we'll discuss it."

Logan paused, turning to her with a raised finger and an open mouth. All that came out was a long-suffering sigh. Shaking his head, he left the handgun on the table as he silently disappeared into the murky depths of the house.

Nicole kept an eye on the now bubbling concoction as she set about cleaning things up. The innards of the chili peppers wafted into the air on the steam, making her eyes water. On Nicole's next trip to the pantry, she pushed up onto her toes, retrieving the bottle of scotch her parents kept on the top shelf. She was filling the mugs when her father came back into the room. He dropped hard into the chair, grinding the legs into the tiles. Nicole didn't say anything. She just offered a kind smile, a pat on his shoulder, and poured him a small cup of scotch. Logan drank it. All the while, his eyes stayed locked on the kitchen window, watching the morning light gathering its strength. Nicole waited intensely but was still surprised when Logan finally broke the silence.

"How old was he when he started having these dreams?"

Opening the Tupperware container full of homemade cookies, she selected a few.

"Full dreams? Around ten, I think. From what I can gather, he had little flashes before that," she said. "He doesn't like to talk about it, and I try not to push."

Logan took another mouthful of scotch, still staring absently at the window. The haunted look in his eyes made guilt bubble in the pit of her stomach. She could have given him a little more warning. Knowing there was nothing she could say that could help him, she delicately placed the open container before him and started returning everything to the pantry.

There wasn't enough time to push the bottle all the way back onto its high perch before she heard her father grunt and gag. Stifling a giggle, she gave the bottle one last push and hurriedly retrieved a glass of water. Choking and red in the face, he downed half of the glass in one large gulp, glaring at her the whole time. It was a relief to see some fire back in his eyes, so she didn't put much effort into hiding her smile.

"There's chili in the cookies," he said between heavy breaths.

"I know."

"*Why* is there chili in the chocolate cookies?" he demanded.

She shrugged. "They're Benton's favorite."

"They're an abomination," Logan grumbled.

It was hard for him not to laugh at a prank, no matter how bad or ill-timed. But his smile didn't last long. He gulped down the last of the water, dragged a hand through his hair, and braced a forearm against the table.

"He's just a kid," he whispered.

"I know," Nicole replied. "I guess that doesn't matter when you're a Banshee. Their visions don't really come with a child safety setting."

"He's *still* just a kid." The outburst made Nicole jump. Her father noticed. Squeezing his eyes shut, he scrubbed his hands over his face again, trying to gather himself. "I don't want you talking to him about this."

"Dad–"

"No, Nicole," he snarled. "I know you like to think you can take on anything, but I'm your father. And I say that you're too young to hear stuff like that."

"Really, it's okay. I can handle it–"

"It involves a baby." Logan spat the words out like he couldn't stand having them in his mouth.

Silence lingered between them before Nicole broke it with a heavy sigh. She deflated with it and solemnly clicked the lid back onto the Tupperware container.

"Not again."

"*Again?*" Logan snarled.

"Third time this month," Nicole said before she noticed her father's white-knuckled grip on his glass. "They always hit Benton the hardest, not that any of them are easy."

Her father watched her carefully. "Are they often about kids?"

"I wouldn't say often. But enough."

"One is enough," Logan mumbled under his breath, his lips barely moving as he resumed his staring contest with the window.

"Yeah, it is," Nicole agreed softly. "But you never really know which victims will stick with you. There was this one that kept me up for weeks. About an old man in a nursing home. They…" She let the sentence trail off into crushing silence.

*Dad doesn't need that in his head*, she decided. In truth, she wasn't sure she could force herself to say it all out loud.

Logan nursed his scotch, spinning the glass between his fingers. "How often does he dream?"

"He really doesn't like being examined. He calls me *Lady Frankenstein* every time I suggest it."

Her father stared at her over the rim of his glass. "How often?"

"On average, he can get about three hours of uninterrupted sleep before the first dream hits. It's a struggle to get him to sleep again after that. I can get him into a fitful doze but not much else. In that state, he'll statistically get about four or five hours of peace."

"Three hours of decent sleep a night?"

"Plus light, fitful sleep," she nodded.

Logan huffed and finally took the sip of his drink. "How the hell does he function?"

"Sarcasm and spite," Nicole said. "I asked him once."

Logan's brow furrowed as he started to crank the math in his head, trying to calculate just how many murders Benton's been forced to 'commit' in his lifetime.

"He's just a kid," he said at last. "Is there any way to keep him from dreaming?"

"Not that I know of. And he's not too keen to look." At her father's expression, she continued, "Banshees are only omens, Dad. They're supposed to give warnings, not save anyone. Sometimes we get lucky. Sometimes, it's enough. But if he doesn't dream, that's their one shot gone, and he knows it."

Chuckling sadly to herself, she fussed with the mugs on her tray. "I know he's, well, he's Benton."

Logan scoffed in understanding.

"But he's got a good heart. He'd never be able to live with the guilt of letting someone die if he could help it."

Logan nodded again, staring at the contents of his glass. "You have to do something. He can't go on like this forever."

"He's strong. Or stubborn, depending on how you look at it. Even when it was ruining his life, even though it takes a bit out of him each time, he keeps going."

"Explain that last bit?"

"He's not an observer when he dreams. He *becomes* the murderer. When he wakes up, he's a little disorientated and can easily forget who he is for a while."

"So he wakes up thinking he's a serial killer?" Logan's voice was like ice.

Nicole bristled. "Dad, I can handle Benton. Turns out, I'm pretty good at this kind of stuff."

"What kind of stuff?"

"Banshee care."

"That's not a thing."

Not wanting to dignify that with a response, she grabbed the tray. "Can we just agree that, with everything else he has to deal with, he shouldn't have to wake up alone?"

Logan pressed his lips into a thin line. It was something he did when he would rather gnaw his own foot off than admit defeat. Nicole took the win and headed back upstairs.

"Feel free to have more of those cookies," she called back.

Logan's voice followed her, "I'll see those cookies in hell!"

Dorothy took off like an Olympic sprinter the moment Nicole stepped back into her bedroom. It was the standard procedure. Until Benton had completely settled, he wasn't to be left alone. Sparing a quick smile, the Constable collected her mug and rushed from the room. She wouldn't be back for the rest of the night. Her job was to put Benton's warning into action. Nicole's was waiting for her in the exact place she had left him.

Setting the tray on the bedside table, she presented him with his hot chocolate and cookies. Now sitting against the headboard, knees pulled up to his chest, he munched mindlessly on the cookie. It was kind of astounding to watch him eat. She knew how much chili she put in those things. While he was distracted, she grabbed the blanket from the end of the bed, the one kept aside specifically for these moments. It was a massive feather down quilt; warm but light, perfect for one-handed maneuvering. In no time at all, they were cocooned within the fluffy comfort, cups clasped in hand, and Benton's head on her shoulder. Benton hadn't moved from his spot during the whole process. So it was a bit of a surprise when his hand slipped out just far enough for him to start on the second cookie.

"Benton burrito," she whispered with a slight chuckle.

Cookie clasped between his lips, he mumbled, "I've asked you to stop saying that."

"You asked, and I declined."

A grumble of protest left his throat even as he shifted closer. It was then that she noticed the thick, dark lines that circled his slender neck.

"What happened?" Instantly, she had one mug-warmed hand gently pressed against the marks.

"I don't think your dad likes me."

Caught off guard by confusion, she stammered, "What? When did this happen?"

"On the road." He looked at her from the corner of his eyes. "You were unconscious at the time."

"Right."

"I'm really sorry I hurt you. I don't remember doing it."

Nicole scoffed. "I'm fine. Really. A slight headache, that's all."

The mug rose up from under the blanket and Benton took a small sip. "I'll show you my memories if you show me yours."

She smiled but rolled her eyes. *Why can't anyone in my life tell a decent joke?* Between them, they swiftly worked out a basic timeline. Since she didn't have much to offer and he had been asleep for most of it, there were a few glaring holes. The mention of the unseen creature prickled something in the back of her mind. It infuriated her that she couldn't pinpoint why.

"At least it wasn't my jeep this time," she said cheerfully.

"That truly is the most important thing," Benton nodded.

She waited for him to take another sip.

"Do you normally sleepwalk?" she asked.

He shrugged one shoulder, the motion barely visible under the piled-up blanket. "If I do, no one's mentioned it."

"Where were you going?"

One eyebrow inched up towards his hairline. "Is that rhetorical, or do you think I have an answer to that?"

"Just thinking out loud," she noted. "Do you think the animal you saw has anything to do with it?"

His second eyebrow joined the first.

"You can have an *uninformed* opinion, Benton."

Taking a long sip, he spoke over the rim. "I don't think it's a coincidence."

She sighed dreamily. "Wouldn't it be fantastic if it were?"

"Life goals."

Fatigue dragged down his eyelids until he could barely keep them open. His head became a steadily increasing weight upon her shoulder, but she didn't try to take the still half-full mug from his hands. Benton was the only person she knew who could sleep without any risk of spilling a drop. The morning light strengthened as they sat there. In summer, it would paint her room in hues of pink. Winter clouds smothered it, transforming it into shades of gray, sharp yellow.

Only a few hours separated them from the school day. She was torn between sneaking in as much sleep as she could and trying to figure out what happened to the projects she had been checking in the car. Warm and comfortable, sleep won out. She, however, really needed to put her mug aside before sloshing it over herself.

Just as she tittered on the edge of sleep, her father came barreling into the room, crashing like a bull to the window. Jarred out of their doze, Benton and Nicole shared a look before turning their questioning gaze to Logan. At this point, he had wrenched the window open and squeezed his wide shoulders through the gap.

"Hey, dad," Nicole said softly. "What's going on?"

Logan pulled back, mouth slack and deep lines forming between his scrunched eyebrows. "Nicole, Angel, why are there hoof prints on the roof?"

# Chapter 5

Benton's breath turned into mist before him as he slowly collected his books. He was already the last person left inside of the makeshift 'demountable'. A pipe had snapped on the first really cold night. Luckily, it had only flooded one room.

Unfortunately, while Fort Wayward had a wealth of open space, there was a distinct lack of unused areas. Every room of the small building was taken for the whole stretch of the day. If someone hadn't thought of using the school bus, they probably would have been having class in the hallways. The aged heater struggled against the cold and frost clinging to the windows. But between their winter gear and the fur blankets supplied by the PTA, it wasn't all that unpliant. It actually worked better for Benton. The cold kept him awake and alert. The 68-ounce Thermos of his favorite coffee Nicole gave him every morning helped too.

Zipping up his backpack, Benton reluctantly headed down the bus stairs. The others had destroyed the snowdrift that had been steadily building up against the side of the vehicle, carving small pathways that kept him from being buried knee deep in the light powder.

*Free period.*

His pace slowed at the thought, and he took the long way around the yard. The gym class was already out, working together to set up large wooden targets at various distances. Half hidden under his hood, Benton watched them work. He doubted that any other school would decide archery was the perfect winter sport, and he was admittedly a little resentful. Nicole sucked at baseball, making gym the only subject where her grades were worse than his. Benton didn't include math. He was only good at it because he had dreamt of a cannibalistic accountant.

As petty as it was, he had enjoyed having some bragging rights. Then they had made the switch. As the only 'city boy' in the rural town, he had been unceremoniously cast down to the worst in class. To keep out of the way of the archers, and to buy himself a little more time, Benton rounded the building to enter through the front. The snow was thinner there, having nothing to block its path as it swept through the town. A thin layer of sleet crackled under his feet, and the chill was starting to bite.

He heard the squawk just as he reached for the door. A familiar, rough sound.

"Bird?" He glanced over his shoulder, expecting to find the great horned owl swooping for his shoulder.

The local owl population seemed to have accepted Benton as one of their own. Camaraderie amongst death omens and all that. Bird, in particular, took advantage of any opportunity to land on him. But the air remained empty. Sure that he had heard it, Benton scanned the small expanse of grass that separated the school from Main Street. A soft breeze rustled the flurries that had yet to settle. The street was empty. Everything was still.

A sudden thrashing made him jump. His head snapped around, tracing the sound only to find that a nearby tree obscured his view. Inching forward, he snaked one hand into his jacket pocket and grabbed his mobile phone. His first instinct was to call Nicole, or Dorothy, as he inched closer still to the building's edge. Bird's frustrated squawk coaxed him forward. With one hand clasping his phone, he braced the other against the brick wall and leaned forward, peeking around the corner while keeping his body protected.

Bird flopped and thrashed a few yards from his hiding place. His massive wings kicked up the snow, creating a shifting white haze around him as he struggled, his legs trapped by something unseen. Benton shifted his weight, stretching his body to try and get a better look. Then froze.

The skin at the back of his neck prickled as his gut twisted sharply. Breath stuck in his throat, Benton twisted around and searched every inch of space he could see for whatever was watching him. Low, fat clouds covered the sky, muting the light into a perpetual twilight. Still, there was nowhere dark enough for a monster to hide. Instead of bringing him comfort, the light left him feeling exposed.

*Grab Bird and run.* The thought slammed into Benton's mind with the force of a sledgehammer. The realization of how stupid that idea was came racing in its wake, but it was already too late. He stood a few feet away from his hiding place. Cool air swept around him, a shifting reminder that he had wandered from the safety of the herd.

The now frantic bird drew his eyes back. Loose feathers drifted down around the now still figure. Bird's head had twisted around as if severed from his body, his large, ebony eyes locking onto Benton with an unwavering intensity. The snow at Bird's talons shifted. It was a tiny movement. Something Benton wouldn't have noticed at all if it wasn't for the animal's sudden stillness. The small patch of ground rolled like the open ocean; undulating around the animal while never shifting him from his perch. With a sudden heave, Bird rose about a foot in the air.

Benton staggered back as an arm, as pale as the surrounding snow, broke free of the earth. It gouged the ground for purchase, crushing the thin layer of sleet while a rounded back heaved and bulged. A sudden, violent jerk allowed a second arm to join the first.

Benton ran.

Bird's feral shrieks followed him, mingling with a violent flapping of colossal wings and a rush of crackling snaps. The sound drew nearer and he chanced a glance behind. The humanoid creature slithered over the frozen grass on its stomach like a serpent, consuming the distance between them as its bird head stretched its massive wings.

His backpack smacked against his spine as he pushed himself faster, the weight dragging him down while the book edges gouged painfully into tender flesh. The harsh material of his snow jacket bunched under his fingers as he ripped at the straps of his backpack. He almost choked himself getting it off but it was worth it. Without it, he was able to gain back a few precious inches of separation.

Shielding his head with both arms, he threw himself at the school's glass front doors. They slammed open under his weight, and mercifully didn't break. Flailing his long limbs and groping blindly against the wall, Benton barely managed to catch himself before he fell against the floor. The rubber soles of his sneakers squeaked wildly in the empty hallway.

Lockers lined the long, straight corridor, separated only by a handful of closed classroom doors. A natural sprinter, Benton locked his gaze on the corner at the end of the hallway and barreled towards it. His legs barely protested, the distance too small to strain them. He didn't look back. He didn't slow down as he raced the monster behind him to the corner. The Fort Wayward high school didn't have a confusing layout. He just had to get around the corner before him and the internal double doors to the gym would be in sight. Sharp claws raked against the floor as the monstrosity closed in behind him. Grunted snarls tainted the air with rancid breath.

The end of the hallway came all too soon. Benton dropped, balancing on his right knee while straightening his left leg. The monster's body was too large and cumbersome to mimic the sudden slide. Momentum took it into the wall. The metallic groan of buckling locker doors rattled alongside the creature's furious scream. It swiped at his head, pale hand clawed and tipped with razors. At the same moment, Benton's foot hit the wall, allowing him to push off and lurch back onto his feet. The nails found the flesh at the back of his neck but couldn't sink deep enough to keep him back.

"Nicole!"

He screamed the name as loud as his lungs would allow. Scorching droplets of blood carved paths over his chilled skin. The lockers whined and thrashed, marking the creature's movements. Sparks spewed against the side of Benton's face as the beast lashed out again.

"Nicole!"

Classroom doors started to open around him, but Benton didn't care enough to focus on any of it. The only thing that mattered was the gym's double doors. They filled the end of the hallway, beckoning him, promising a slim chance at survival. She was never late to class. All he had to do was make it inside, and he wouldn't be alone. The doors loomed before him. Curling his spine and tucking his chin to his chest, he threw his shoulder into the door.

"Nicole!"

They opened easily. His feet knocked together, ruining his balance and tripping him. He barely had time to register the teacher standing in front of him before he was ripping the baseball bat from her hands. The fact that she had it was a small miracle that he wasn't going to question. The familiar sensation of dense wood made relief explode within him. Twisting his torso, he swung the bat with every ounce of strength his body could summon.

Unable to compensate for the movement, he fell. The unrelenting floor collided with his spine as the bat found something of flesh and bone. It was oddly satisfying. Even as pain jolted through his ribs and his head cracked against the floor. The pain brought tears to his eyes. Blinking past them, he stared in utter bewilderment at the stag that slumped beside him.

"Get up," the teacher stammered.

The stag's antlers scrammed against the ground, adding a heavy thud to its thrashing. A hand roughly grabbed the back of Benton's jacket, dragging him up. He stumbled to get his feet under him, all the while searching for the slithering monster. It was gone, replaced by a herd of bucks that bashed against each other as they surged in a stampede through the hallway.

"Everyone, get on the stage!"

The few students still frozen in fear snapped into action at the teacher's scream.

A raised platform at the far end of the cavernous room allowed the gym to double as the town's events hall. The scattering of students fled to it now, a living flood of panicked chaos. It grew worse as the stags barreled over the threshold. The floor vibrated and the wall rattled. Something crashed against his back, throwing him off of his feet and forcing him into a slide. The wall of the stage stopped him. Head spinning and vision blurring, he was only vaguely aware of the others scrambling up onto the stage, a few of them reaching down to help the others.

Instinct moved his body before he could make sense of the spikes driving down upon him. A heavy crack rattled along his arms and shoved him back against the low wall. Wood splinters burst out around him, cracking off of the wall as the longest antler spikes bore through the slats. Benton's brain finally caught on to what was happening when the snorting buck surged forward again. The baseball bat was clutched between his hands and lodged with a curve of the antlers. His elbows were locked but quickly gave way. The wall was holding it back, not him, and it was quickly giving way. He folded his legs up, twisting and shoving, narrowly keeping his feet out from under the stag's stomping hooves. A scream welled in his throat, and he clenched his teeth against it. He knew what happened when strangers saw what he could do.

A low whoosh rolled under the shrieks and thuds. Benton jerked as blood splashed across his face. The stag stammered and trembled before it fell. Its antlers gouged in the wood forced its neck onto a strange angle, creating a narrow space that Benton could hide in and not get crushed. An arrow protruded from its lifeless eye.

"Get out."

Nicole's cold voice thundered within the sudden silence. Gulping for air, Benton took his first look beyond the tangled mass of the stag's antlers. The other animals hadn't fled. Nor did they attack. Instead, the massive creatures lingered in a stunned state. They would have looked like statues if it weren't for the way their sides heaved with every snorted breath.

Startled gasps broke the uneven silence as one by one, the deer began to rise, drawing up onto their hind legs, their forelegs danglingly limply before them. They didn't wobble or waver or breathe. All signs of life fled from their bodies as they stood there. The world fell silent, broken only by a few shrieks when, in unison, the stags snapped their heads around to focus on a singular point.

The next arrow took out the closest deer, burrowing deep into its eye. It was dead before it hit the ground.

"Did I stutter?" Nicole bellowed. "I don't know what the hell you are, but Benton? He's mine. Get! Out!"

Stretching his torso, Benton caught sight of what she was talking to. The stags had ravaged the doors. What remained of the slats hung limply on the hinges, allowing small glimpses of the hallway and what lurked within it. Benton couldn't make out its lower body but could clearly see that it wasn't what had chased him. Its head shifted in and out of view. A buffalo skull hovering above a smear of black. Its eyes were holes and yet he could feel it staring at him. Terror worked through his veins like ice.

"Benton," Nicole said, her voice becoming tense with anger. "Are you okay?"

Gulping hard, he nodded, remembering only a second later that she probably couldn't see him. "Yeah."

"If it takes one step into this room, scream."

A crushing silence settled over them. The air grew as thick as tar, choking him as his chest swelled and tightened with the unleashed scream. It made him tremble. In the silence, the stags turned their attention onto him.

"Benton–"

Before she could finish the request, the buffalo creature sunk back and disappeared. It left without making a single sound. Seconds passed as everyone held their breath. A few startled shrieks shattered the silence as the stags lurched. They each fell forward, returning to all fours. Benton had never seen a confused deer before. Now he was faced with a dozen of them.

"Are you hurt? Don't move, okay?" Nicole almost beat her words as she scrambled down from the stage, one of the school's archery bows still clutched in her hand.

Life rushed back into the room at her sudden burst of movement. Screams, chatter, confusion, and demands filled the air. Nicole ignored it all as she grabbed the dead deer from behind and began to yank. Benton pushed at the same time. Between them, they were able to wiggle the antlers within the holes it had created but struggled to move it far enough to free him.

"I'm so sorry I took so long," Nicole rushed. "I heard you. And I was on my way out when Ms. Carter took my bat off of me. Can you believe that? I had to improvise. Are you hurt?"

"I'm alright," Benton mumbled, wide eyes flicking between her, the now empty doorway, and the dead creatures that littered the floor. "Good shot."

She paused in her efforts to yank the stag away. "Thank you. That's sweet."

"Please get the deer off of me."

"Right. Hey, Zack! Can I borrow you for a second? Please, and thank you!"

In the seconds it took for the towering teenager to work his way over, the reality of what had just happened settled within Benton's mind. *Everyone saw it. There's proof. They're not going to look the other way. Everyone saw!* The thoughts swirled within him until he was vibrating with the need to run. A pure, primal urge to flee from whatever was coming.

"Hey," Nicole soothed, her voice calm within the typhoon of panic surrounding them. "It's going to be okay."

He gulped past the lump in his throat and jumped at the chance for a distraction.

"Remember this morning? When I said we should skip school today and you insisted that we come in?"

"We both had tests, Benton," she said. "We can't let every little threat on our lives keep us from our education."

"I was almost impaled."

Her lips pulled into a tight, thin line, and curled at the edges to form more of a pout than a grimace.

"Yeah, I'm going to need you to say it," Benton said, dropping his voice a little lower when he noticed Zack jumping down from the stage.

"You were right," she grumbled.

# Chapter 6

Music blared through Benton's headphones, pouring the frantic, electronic beat into his skull. All of his thoughts drowned within the pulsating tide. His body moved out of pace with the song. Each shift and sway maintained the purposeful dignity that Svetlana would have demanded. Dancing was his only real escape from the mounting tension, both within the household and himself. At this point, they just kept the living room furniture pushed against the walls.

The two-week suspension had only caught Nicole by surprise. She had protested to the principle for hours that he couldn't do it. Challenged anyone who said otherwise to explain how Benton could be responsible for getting attacked by rabid deer on school property. Or how they could punish her for killing a few of the dangerous animals. Benton had offered support when she had asked but otherwise kept his silence. It wasn't about logic. Not really.

It was fear.

More than one teacher had opened their doors to investigate the noise and caught a glimpse of the snow-white monster. A classful of terrified students had seen the living buffalo skull staring him down. The stags had only come after him. No one knew *what* they had seen that day, but they knew exactly *who* it wanted. Serial killers, stalkers, monsters; there was really only one way people reacted to discovering Benton had a target on his back: they wanted him as far away from them as possible. *Paranormal quarantine*, Benton thought to himself. The thought was quickly lost again as some particularly difficult footwork demanded his focus.

Nicole was just collateral damage. He would have never asked for her to be, but he couldn't deny that, deep down, he was grateful. They were a packaged deal. Wherever one of them was, the other was sure to show up sooner or later. It was something he had come to rely on, and wasn't about to give it up. Especially when he didn't know how much time he had left.

Danny and Meg had taken to bringing over homework and assignments after school. Zack showed up more for gossip. They all knew from the beginning that Nicole was going to have rapidly dwindling interest in either. She had a mystery. And the school board had given her all the time she needed to climb down that rabbit hole.

They were almost a week in at this point as the vast majority of the living room wall was now devoted to her 'stalker wall'. Printouts of legends, historical photographs, urban legends, and a few crime scene photographs, that Dorothy herself had provided, were all pinned in neat disarray. They were connected by different colored threads of tinsel because Nicole still wanted it to be pretty.

Coming out of a spin, Benton arched his back, draping down until his fingertips grazed the floorboards. He had to admit; It didn't look that bad. Obsessive, strange, and creepy, but in an almost festive way. *She's getting way too good at this.* Drawing himself back up, he crossed the living room, his toes barely making a sound as they tapped the floor. He closed his eyes, trying to quiet his mind, to narrow his reality to nothing beyond the music in his ears and the air in his lungs.

Each day made it a little harder to pull off the feat. There was always something new to discover in the morning snow. Undefinable tracks circled the house, clustering at windows and pacing in front of the doors. The tree trunks had been slashed along with the car tires. A murder of crows had settled within the neighbor's fir tree, held off from the pines around the Rider home by the sudden increase in territorial great horned owls. And night never came without the yard being filled with glowing eyes.

In a town this small, everyone knew everyone. It didn't take long for Logan to be roped into helping animal control when the deer and coyote population had started to become a problem. It was now a near-constant battle to keep them outside of the town properly. An annoyance for many, a concern for few, and a curiosity that had the few tourists they got lingering a few days longer. For Benton, it was proof that he hadn't misinterpreted Mic's warning. He was going to die soon. And perhaps rise again as a reaper, just like her.

The thought invaded his mind, burning him inside like a branding iron. He pushed his body harder, trying to hide from the truth within the haze of muscle memory and blissful oblivion. While he could push it from the forefront of his mind, it was always there, lurking on the edges, ready to strike again. His exhausted body trembled as the music reduced to a single, lingering note, then cut off into silence. Without it, he almost dropped into a sweaty, terrified heap.

*I don't want to die.*

Nicole's enthusiastic clapping made him lurch back into reality. Panting hard and plucking his earphone out, Benton flopped down on his side of the sofa. A half-dozen items instantly dug into his back. Squirming, he struggled to retrieve the cluster of pens and highlighters from under the knitted blanket. Both of them were painfully aware of his stalker. Instead of mentioning it, Nicole had just decided to be his shadow. The sofa had become her 'neurotic-nest'. Used coffee mugs and bowls of snacks filled the few spaces not taken up by books, binders, and loose sheets of colorful paper.

"Hey, you're going to mess up my system," she protested as he continued to pull items out from under his back.

"This side of the sofa is mine," he retorted.

"I know."

"Then why is it covered with your stuff?" A collection of glitter pens served as his evidence.

She snatched them off of him. "It's not my fault that you're in their natural migration path."

In retaliation, he began a battle over his portion of the knitted blanket. She struggled to balance her laptop on her knees and fight him off at the same time.

"Stop it. You're all sweaty."

Deciding that he had annoyed her enough, he released the blanket and claimed her nearby glass of water.

"You're getting really good at that," she said, waving her hand to indicate the living room at large.

"I *am* really good at it," Benton scoffed, suddenly struck with the knowledge that he had something else to brag about. "I could have made a living out of it."

Dark eyes studied him carefully. She jerked. "You're not joking, are you?"

Everything about her screamed that she was about to start obsessing over this new bit of information. So, of course, he had to frustrate her to no end by changing the subject.

"Okay, I have to ask. The outfit. Is that an act of defiance or a sign of depression?"

Around the third day of their confinement, Nicole had started wearing a selection of footed pajamas instead of her regular outfits. She pressed a hand protectively over the pink fleece.

"I'm comfortable."

"But at what cost?"

"First of all, you have the wardrobe variety of a *Scooby Doo* character. Secondly, I look adorable in anything."

"Debatable," he shrugged.

She rolled her eyes and returned to whatever she was working on.

"My six-year reign as Little Miss Buffalo Princess begs to differ."

Benton blinked at her. "You're a beauty queen?"

That earned him a scowl. "It's not just a beauty contest. If you want to win, you also have to have talent, composure, intelligence, *and* display upstanding character throughout the entire rigorous competition. And yes, I won. A lot."

"Not surprised," he said. Watching her fingers fly over the keyboard, he asked, "You haven't got a title now?"

She refused to look up from her laptop. "I retired when I was seven."

A smile stretched his lips. "You got way too competitive and your parents pulled the plug, huh?"

"It was a *competition!*" she shrieked, her outraged voice carrying over his laughter. "If you're not playing to win, why even try?"

It felt good to laugh. He didn't try to hold back as she continued to protest her innocence, all frantic arm-waving and big doe eyes. By the time she gave up, his sides had begun to hurt.

"You are terrifying."

She huffed, and he nudged her with his foot.

"But adorably so."

That appeased her somewhat, and she went back to her work. Strengthened by his mirth, he gestured to the laptop and asked the question he had been avoiding all morning.

"So . . . any breakthroughs?"

"No," she said bitterly.

"Really?"

Her dark eyes narrowed on him. "Yeah."

"Sorry. It's just, well, you normally have something by now. The last one only took you a couple of hours."

"The other ones had a sense of decency!"

He didn't have time to backpedal before the flood gates opened and the tidal wave of her rant crushed down on him.

"They hid themselves, being all secretive and lurk-y. It makes sure that the few things you learn about them are significant. Important things that I can use to narrow down the suspect list. But this—" Not having anything to call it, she substituted it with a clench-jawed scream. "It doesn't care who sees it. So, what are the important parts? The defining features? How does it change physical form? Manipulate animals? The way it's become fixated on you, or how brazenly it attacks during the day? And in public, no less. Do you know how few creatures do that? Oh, and what about the fact that it has no problem chasing you around a public building, but apparently can't get through our front door? Can it come into a private residence without an invitation, or is it just oddly polite?" She paused. "Well?"

"Oh, I thought all of that was rhetorical."

The words had barely passed his lips before she had started up again.

"I have too much information, Benton! I need a memo, and he's buried me in paperwork!" She snatched up a fistful of the sheets, waving them in his face as if he had needed the proof. "He fits into too many categories! Is he a *Vampire? Witch? Wendigo? Gorgon? Ljiraq? Adlet? Bokkenrijders?*"

"I swear you made those last few up."

She waved the sheets with renewed fury. "How am I supposed to sift through all of this? I hate this guy!"

The following silence left his ears ringing. At some point, he had pressed his spine to the armrest, his hands coming up as if to fend her off.

"You've been holding that in for a while, huh?"

Her eyes were full of venom and rage. Unfortunately, the scrunch of her mouth gave the overall aesthetic of a petulant child.

"I hate him," she said on a grunt.

Benton fought back an amused smirk. "Me too. More because he tried to murder me, but this is also bad."

She didn't seem to hear him. "Why can't he just tell me how to kill him? I'm not asking for a lot."

"He's a jerk."

A frustrated sigh of annoyance deflated her, melting her against the sofa, as she muttered under her breath how much she hated this thing, and made vows of vengeance for her wounded pride.

"Didn't mean to hit a sore spot," Benton assured. "And I'm grateful that you're doing this. If there's any way I can help."

"Aw, Benton, that's sweet." She snatched up a book before he could reach it. "But please don't touch anything."

"I'm that bad at research?"

Her free hand found one of his. She held it with tender care and offered him the sweetest smile he had ever seen.

"Yeah, you are. Just watching you try makes me want to weep."

Benton's brow furrowed. "Ow. My feelings."

Squeezing his hand, she looked at him with complete serenity as she told him to 'walk it off'. With that, she began to gather her information nest protectively closer.

"Well, can I do anything at all?" he asked.

"You could have a shower," she said over the rim of a book. "You're still all sweaty. It's kind of gross."

"Wow. You're mean when you're mildly inconvenienced."

The good humor died in an instant. The intensity in her gaze let him know that he had messed up. He fed into yet another one of her obsessions.

"Being stalked is a minor inconvenience to you?" she asked.

He pulled his hands through his hair, the scars that marred one palm scraping against his forehead.

"You don't have to dance around it. Just ask."

"Who stalked you?"

A small smirk tugged at one side of his mouth. "You've accessed my police record. Doesn't it have a footnote?"

"A footnote sealed by court order."

"Ah. Well, there's not much to tell. After the..." He licked his lips and glanced down at his hands. "*Incident* at the bowling alley, I was in pretty bad shape. Doctors actually thought I wouldn't walk again. Through rehab, I was turned onto dance and met Svetlana. She took me into the dance academy."

"Okay," she said as he fell into silence.

Scratching at his scalp again, he blurted out the rest, trying to race his growing anger to the finish.

"Yeah, well, you've seen photos of what I looked like back then. Apparently, when I dance, I'm really pretty. Svetlana called it hypnotic. Hachiro used far more sexualized terms. After getting rejected by every girl at the academy, he decided that I was 'close enough.' It all went downhill after that."

"Did he hurt you?"

"Not intentionally. He just didn't think someone as small as me would fight so hard not to get pulled into a car."

"He tried to kidnap you?"

"And broke into my dorm room more than once."

"You went to the police, though?"

Benton nodded. "Stalking is a hell of a thing to try and prove. Really, it's just your word against theirs. You have to prove intent. Eventually, my parents caught word of it. Then they came back and decided that we had to move again. That's how they handle everything. Run. I mean, yeah, the other times didn't work out that great, but I was happy with Svetlana. I didn't do anything wrong, but–"

Anger had become a hard lump in his chest, so he left everything else unsaid.

"That wasn't the only time you were followed, was it?" Nicole asked softly.

"The only time it was for sexualized reasons. And, you know, proven in the court of law."

Nicole watched him carefully, studying his expression before venturing to ask.

"What happened to Hachiro?"

"We got a restraining order. Could have pushed for more, but my parents thought the court process would be too traumatizing for me. We came here instead." A bitter snort escaped him. "But I guess they're not really my parents, are they? Should I still be calling them that?"

"They did raise you."

"And they emotionally abandoned me that second they realized I wasn't theirs," he counted.

There was no need to disguise just how much that hurt him. Nicole would understand. She wouldn't judge.

"I don't want to overstep—"

"Hold up. Are you telling me that you've understood the concept of personal boundaries this whole time?"

He succeeded in getting her to smile despite herself.

"When you're ready, you really should talk to them."

"Why?" he asked.

"Because they might have an idea of what happened to your birth parents. And finding them would make it a lot easier to understand what you are."

"Any chance you can find them without Cheyanne and Theodore getting involved?"

She shrugged sheepishly.

"You've been trying this whole time, haven't you?"

"Just a little."

"What about the monster?"

"I can multitask."

Benton huffed a laugh and tipped his head to the side, letting it rest against the sofa's backrest.

"What have you found out?"

"You were a super chubby baby," she giggled.

"Anything more helpful?"

A sharp knock interrupted her response. Nicole checked her watch and hurriedly began to extract herself from her cozy nest of horrors.

"That would be Zack. He'll have the notes for our chemistry assignment."

Benton rolled his eyes but followed. "You remember that we were suspended, right?"

"Being suspended isn't a holiday."

It was a statement she had repeated so often that he could now mockingly mouth it along with her. It wasn't the most creative of insults, but worked well enough. She jabbed him with her elbow as they headed for the door. Ever cautious, Nicole checked the door's peephole before working on the locks.

"Now remember, Zack has been good to us and is still coming to terms with you being a Banshee."

"And killing flesh-eating ghosts in a haunted forest."

"Yes, and that." Swift fingers unfastened the chain lock. "Do you think you can be pleasant today?"

"I'm always pleasant. Don't look at me like that. It's not my fault that you have high standards. Lower them and I'm a dream."

Rolling her eyes, she pulled the door open.

"Hey, Zack. I baked some muffins today if you're hungry."

Benton's attention wasn't captured by Zack's response but by the lack of one. Zack towered over them, staring over their heads at the distant wall. Snowflakes clung to his long, ebony hair. The chill had forced a flush to his tawny skin and his arms hung loosely by his sides.

Benton's gut twisted sharply.

There wasn't time to back up before Zack charged past Nicole and wrapped his hands around Benton's neck.

# Chapter 7

Nicole hit the ground hard and slid until the foyer wall stopped her. The hard blow to her chest had knocked the air from her lungs. Gasping, she tried to force her lungs to work, clenching her teeth against the pain that sparked along her veins. White static filled her skull.

Her brain just couldn't make sense of what had happened. She had known Zack since birth. The last time he had raised a hand against her, they had both been in diapers. The first deep breath brought a new wave of pain and the fear that her sternum had cracked. *How is he this strong?* The slam of the front door snapped her out of her daze. She was alone.

"Benton." The name passed her lips with barely more strength than a whisper. "Benton!"

Dragging herself up onto her feet, she stumbled to the door, her legs refusing to work as her mind swirled. She wrenched the door open. Gripping the threshold to keep upright, she started, unable to believe what she was seeing. Zack had one hand around Benton's neck, squeezing tight enough to turn his pale face red. Benton's heels dug deep grooves through the snow as he struggled to break free. He clawed at Zack's hand and kicked wildly, but nothing he did slowed the taller boy down.

"Zack! Stop it!"

Nicole sprinted forward. In the same instant, Benton kicked out, driving his foot into Zack's leg with all of his strength and forcing his knees to buckle. The sudden jerk didn't bring Zack to the ground. It only loosened his grip enough for Benton to rip himself free. He didn't take more than a step before Zack grabbed hold of him again, this time throwing Benton hard against the side of the truck. It rocked under with the force of impact. Rage and pain flashed through Benton's eyes as his chest swelled. Zack's hands latched onto Benton's throat again. With both hands, he crushed the Banshee's wail before it could be released.

Nicole threw herself onto Zack's back. She didn't have the height to wrap her arms around his neck and was left grappling for a solid grip. All the while, she begged her childhood friend to stop. Pain exploded across her jaw, gathering behind her eyes and pulsating until she was sure they were about to burst like grapes. It was only when she hit her snow-covered yard that she realized he had hit her.

Blinking past the tears that lined her eyes, she watched, frozen in horror and disbelief as Zack shoved Benton toward the passenger door of the parked car. He only needed one hand to manipulate Benton's far smaller weight. It was the Banshee's wild ferocity that made him struggle to keep his grip. In rapid succession, Benton stomped his foot against Zack's stomach, his kidneys, his knees. Blood trickled from Zack's nose after Benton drove his fist against it. None of it was enough to bring life to Zack's dull, unblinking stare. He didn't even look at Benton as he tossed the smaller boy into the car.

"Zack!"

Both of Nicole's parents had made their daughter's safety a priority. They had taught her everything they knew, and that knowledge had carried Nicole with silent confidence. Now it all meant nothing. She knew where to strike. Knew exactly what she had to do to take down someone Zack's size. But the idea of doing any of it to Zack brought a foul taste in her mouth. Instead, she grabbed his arm, intending to drag him off of his feet, only to find his body as rigid as stone. *Snap him out of it. How do I snap him out of it? Think!*

Zack shook her off like she was a bug. But the moment of distraction had been enough. Benton had rolled up, not leaping from the truck bed but grabbing Zack's outstretched wrist. He yanked hard, toppling Zack forward as his other hand slammed the door shut. A scream ripped out of Zack's throat as the heavy door crunched down on his fingers. Benton smacked the lock down before the taller teen could reach for the handle. Life and pain filled Zack's wide eyes. He scraped at the doorjamb, clawed his fingers around the window, rattled the handle as if it had only just occurred to him. The truck rocked with his efforts, but he couldn't work his way free.

"Zack?" Nicole asked meekly.

His long hair swirled around him like a dark halo as he whipped around to face her.

"Nicole? What's going on?" His questions ended with an agonized gasp. Clenching his teeth, he tried not to sob. "My hand. Open the door. Open the door."

By this point, Benton had crawled over the driver's seat and, with one foot on the rim, was flipping Zack off over the hood of the truck. The bitter rage in his eyes screamed all the words he couldn't get out through his dry coughing fits.

"My hand!" Zack snarled, his fingertips squeaking against the window glass. "Just open it."

"Are you back?" Nicole asked.

"Back from what?"

She took a step forward but stopped herself just outside of his reach. "Is it really you?"

"What the hell are you talking about? Come on, Nicole. It hurts! Get the door!"

Nicole shifted her gaze to Benton. "Could you open it, please?"

His next set of choked wheezes sounded suspiciously close to a string of curse words.

"He obviously wasn't in control of himself," she insisted. "I think the pain snapped him out of it."

Benton held his ground until Nicole started forward, determined to do it herself. Then he waved her off and climbed back into the cab. While Benton took his time with the lock, Nicole tried to keep her old friend as calm as possible. Zack hissed through the pain, squeezing his eyes shut before forcing them open again. His brow furrowed as he stared down at her.

"Your lip," he said softly.

Nicole touched the tip of her tongue to the aching side of her mouth and flinched at the sudden copper taste.

"It's nothing. Let's just get you out."

The lock flicked open and she yanked the door instantly, trying to be fast and careful at the same time. Zack instantly reached inside. He dragged Benton out by the front of his shirt. Before he could fling the smaller teen onto the ground, Benton had coiled up like a snake, wrapping himself around Zack's arm and bracing his heels behind the taller teen's neck. Unable to shake off his weight, they both toppled. Snow exploded up against them as they landed hard. Refusing to release his grip, Benton pushed his hips up, trapping Zack in an armbar that threatened to snap his elbow. At the same time, Zack thumped Benton's back like a drum. Hard thuds that brought whimpers from the smaller boy's throat.

"Both of you, stop it right now!" Nicole snapped.

"I'm going to rip your throat out," Zack screamed.

Unable to get any words through his battered throat, Benton let a push of his hips respond. Zack clawed at Benton's spine, trying and failing to dislodge him, pain twisting up his face.

"Stop!" Nicole demanded.

"He hit you!" Zack's bellow grew stronger as Benton twisted to stare at him in surprise.

"You did this," Nicole said, pointing at her lip. "And you attacked Benton."

"Huh?"

Benton and Zack exchanged a confused glance before resuming their grappling, hissing out death threats and generally doing what they could to hurt the other. Tired, scared, and now nursing a quickly swelling lip, Nicole reached her limit when she saw her elderly neighbor poke her head outside.

"Mrs. Horn," she called out awkwardly between hissing at the boys to stop.

"Do you need me to call the cops."

Nicole jogged across the yard, smiling as sweetly as she could while she collected the hose mounted on the side of her house.

"No, I have everything under control."

"I will kill you!" Zack roared.

She closed her eyes as Benton howled a response. It included enough profanity to leave the retired chef, who had taught Nicole every swear word she knew, looking mortified.

"I'm going to call the cops."

"Oh, don't bother mom at work," Nicole assured. She turned the tap until water gushed from the end. "I've got this."

Striding back to the still struggling boys, she didn't hesitate to drench them both. Their yells turned into sharp, shrill screams. Snow melted under them. Hard tremors wracked their thrashing bodies as they lurched away from each other and searched for someplace safe from the onslaught.

"Nicole! Are you trying to give us hypothermia?"

"Do not use that tone with me, Zackary," Nicole snapped.

Directing the flow at the ground, she waited until both boys were staring at her, their teeth chattering too hard to yell at her.

"Are you going to listen to me now?"

Benton and Zack exchanged another look, but all the fight was out of them.

"Good. Now, get inside the house right this second. You're disturbing the neighbors."

She let them stagger in on their own as she replaced the hose.

"See?" She forced a smile for Mrs. Horn. "Everything's fine."

The gray-haired woman inched closer to their dividing fence, motioning with her head for Nicole to do the same.

"Is this about the Bertrand boy?" Mrs. Horn whispered. "Everyone knows he's a little off."

Nicole tightened her jaw, locking her smile in place while her protective instincts reared up inside her.

"He's a city boy. What do you expect?"

With a curt goodbye, she turned on her heel and hurried inside. Benton had left a trail of soggy clothes heading up the staircase. He jumped over the items on his way back down, now dressed in sweat pants and a shirt, an array of Logan's clothes bundled into his arms. She'd seen Benton's hair wet a few times now, but it still caught her by surprise. At first, it had been the surprising length. His carefully arranged fluffy spikes were oddly deceptive. Lately, though, it had been the color. Ever since the powwow, his light blonde hair had shone like liquid mercury when wet. He didn't see it.

Benton scrunched up his mouth and wiggled his arm, drawing her attention to the clothes he carried. Logan's larger size would hang loose on Zack but fit a lot better than Benton's ever could. It was his version of an apology, and it left her a little sheepish.

"Sorry I hit you with a hose. Are you alright? Can you breathe okay?"

"Yeah." It hurt just to hear the grating croak that served as his voice.

Benton winched, gripping the railing with one hand.

"Go sit by the fire. I'll take care of Zack's hand and bring in some hot drinks, okay?"

Careful not to startle him with any sudden movements, she pulled the clothes from his arm. The moment his arm was free, he brushed the pad of his thumb along her jaw, his brow furrowing in question.

"I'm okay. It doesn't hurt."

He frowned, lingering until she gently pulled his hand away. His skin was like ice.

"Really. I'm fine. Now go warm up. We'll be right in."

Reluctantly, he shuffled off, tenderly rubbing his throat with one hand. Guilt twisted up her insides as she watched him go. It had all happened so fast. But now that there was time to replay it in her mind, she could pick apart a thousand things she could have done differently. The variety of ways that she could have kept both of her friends safe.

*There isn't time for this,* she told herself sharply. *Make sure they're safe now.* With the idea implanted within her head, she hurried to the door, checking and rechecking that each lock was in place. The events played out in her mind's eye again, bringing with it a tendril of cold fear. She hadn't locked the door behind her when she had run out to stop them. In all the chaos, no one would have noticed anyone slipping inside. The idea that she had locked the monster inside with them bore into her mind. She couldn't let it go.

Taking the stairs two at a time, she started her search at the far end of the house. Quick but efficient, she checked under the beds and rifled through the wardrobes. Finding nothing out of the ordinary only fed her paranoia. Possibilities crammed her mind; images of the monster transforming to the size of a mouse and hiding itself away. She raked through drawers and scanned the bathroom cabinets, crawl spaces, and storage boxes in the attic. Frantic now, she bolted downstairs. Kitchen pantry, her mother's office, the fine china cabinets. The boys gave her a strange look as she ran through the living room again to rush down the basement stairs. She squeezed around the worn plastic containers filled with holiday decorations, sporting supplies, gardening tools, and memorabilia. Nothing. *The washing machine.* It seemed so certain until she was on her knees and staring into the empty barrel.

"Nicole?" Zack called from the living room.

She pushed back onto her knees. Suddenly, it was hard to breathe. A hot lump had formed in her throat, and she had to swallow a few times to sound anywhere near normal.

"Yeah."

"Is everything alright?"

Her hands trembled as she pushed her hip-length hair back from her face. "Yeah. Everything's fine. I'll be right in to help." Squeezing her eyes shut, she took a sobering breath and continued in a much cheerier tone. "I just had to check this one thing real quick first."

"Take your time," Zack replied, sounding awkward and worried.

Not wanting to cause either of them concern, she sat on the cold floor, trying to gather her senses. *That had been too close.* She held her breath, hoping it would dissolve the lump choking her, clenching her jaw until it ached. As much as she fought against it, the thought bubbled up from the darkest recesses of her mind. *Could I have killed Zack to save Benton? Or would I have let Benton go to save Zack?* Neither option was something she could live with.

"It's okay," she whispered to herself. "It's all okay now. I can figure out what this thing is. I can."

The assurances lost a little more meaning with every repetition. She was suddenly very aware that the feet of her pajamas were completely soaked through, allowing an icy chill to seep into her. *Just do what you have to do,* she told herself sharply. A second later, she burst into movement. She forced herself up onto her feet, found something in the hamper to wear, changed, and stalked out into the kitchen, only to find the first aid box missing from the pantry.

In her confused silence, she heard Zack's voice wafting in from the living room.

"Damn. I did that to you? God, I can't remember any of it. Are you sure it was me?"

Nicole had moved to the kitchen door without consciously meaning to. One hand held the doorframe as she watched her friends. They both sat by the fireplace, each looking less than their best, the first aid kit spread out between them. Benton had been in the process of applying antibacterial cream to Zack's torn knuckles, but the motion was paused as he stared at the taller boy. Zack had been using his good hand to probe lightly at the new bruises blossoming around Benton's neck. The others had just started to fade.

"Don't give me that look. I bet that you didn't even consider the idea that it wasn't me."

"You choked me." Even though Benton couldn't raise his voice above a whisper, it was clear that he was completely done with the entire situation.

"Are you sure?" Zack said, willing the fingers of his good hand. "It could all be an illusion."

"I want to stab you."

"Right. I guess it was me. God, that's, well–" He chuckled nervously. "It's terrifying, actually. What else did I do?"

"Call the twins."

"Huh? Oh, right. Because they can do a subtle headcount. Right." He pulled his phone from the pocket of his soggy jeans. A few flicks of his thumb and he just stared at the screen. Benton had lost interest and gone back to cleaning the dirt out of the wounds. "What do I even tell them?"

"What do you remember?"

Zack thought for a moment. "I was in the school parking lot. No one else was around. I got held up in the locker room."

"Don't want to know."

Zack snorted. "I was scrolling through Instagram."

Benton arched one eyebrow at him.

"Okay, I might have posted a few topless shots. And others. All tastefully done." A smug smile crossed his face. "You'd be surprised how many fans I have."

"Don't want to know." Benton still failed to increase his volume, but he was able to put force behind each word.

Zack's chuckle ended with a hiss when Benton pushed a little too hard.

"God, Benton. Nicole does it with love."

Benton just shook his head.

"I can take over," Nicole said.

Neither boy was surprised by her arrival, and she wondered if they had been aware she had been listening in all along. She reasoned that it didn't really matter either way. All things considered; it had been nice to see her friends getting along so well. Reassuring in a way. *Everyone's alright.* Settling down next to them, she took over Benton's duties, relieved to find that the damage wasn't too bad.

Carefully examining each finger, she mumbled, "I don't think anything's broken."

"Did you find what you were looking for?" Zack asked.

"Um, yeah. I did. I just wanted to make sure everything was locked up, that's all."

The boys looked at each other before rolling their eyes in unison.

"What was that?" she asked.

"You're a terrible liar," Zack laughed.

Benton gingerly pressed an ice pack to his throat. "The worst."

"Is this really what we should be focusing on right now? Hm? No? Okay. So, Zack, you were taking naked selfies in the school locker room."

"Everything was covered," he protested, his cheeks warming. "And you can't see my face."

Benton whimpered in pain.

"I know, I know." His impersonation of Benton was horrible. "You don't want to know."

"And then you went to your car," Nicole pressed, desperate to get the conversation back on track. Her eyes darted to Zack's pile of wet clothes as something occurred to her. "Where's your jacket? You weren't wearing it when you came to the door."

"I don't like to wear it while driving. The truck's heater is awesome."

"Do you wait for the truck to warm up before taking it off?"

"Yeah. Why?"

"Just establishing the timeline," she said.

"Oh," Zack said, confusion quickly chasing realization across his features. "Hey, yeah, I remember now. I was in the truck, listening to the radio. Nothing good was playing. I was there long enough to take my jacket off. So, five minutes."

"Were you posting?" Benton asked.

Zack blinked at him. "Right. Time of posting will narrow the window even more. I'm with ya."

Nicole made sure to avoid catching even a glimpse of the screen while he scrolled through his Instagram feed. Zack grunted as he checked between his phone and his wristwatch. He only actually spoke again when she started to wind a bandage around his ravaged knuckles.

"Fifteen minutes ago. How long was I whooping Benton's butt?"

"Hand in door," Benton croaked.

Zack wiggled a finger to indicate his throat. "Sorry, can't hear you, speak up a bit."

"Is this the way you two bond, or should I get the hose again?"

"Bond," Benton grumbled.

Zack just shrugged in agreement.

Rolling her eyes, she decided to leave that whole topic alone. It wasn't really her place and she had other things to worry about. As long as they didn't gang up on her, she'd deal with it.

"Okay, so, accounting for ice conditions, minimal traffic, and the little altercations," Nicole thought aloud. "It only took a couple of minutes, at most, for this thing to completely take over your mind."

"What was that?" Zack asked.

"Driving," Benton whispered.

"Right. He drove here."

It wasn't like Fort Wayward had a complicated setup, but there were a few one-way streets and intersections separating her house from the school. Given how many people were out for animal control, someone would have noticed if he had been driving erratically.

She switched from thought to speech as she continued, "And that truck's a stick shift. I haven't had much experience with this sort of thing, but that seems like an impressive amount of control."

"Someone controlled my mind?" Zack cut in, his eyes wide.

*How did this not occur to you already?* "I think so, yes."

"Like the deer?"

Nicole nodded. Zack quickly glanced between her and Benton.

"That creature that was in the hallway," he said in a meek, cautious voice. "The creature with the skull for a head. *That* thing was inside my head?"

"Sorry," Nicole said.

She wasn't sure what else to say in a situation like this. Zack's eyes roamed the room as he tried to come to terms with that theory. Nicole's skin went cold just thinking about it; that kind of violation from such a monstrosity. Having no control over it. No memory that it had ever happened. Somehow, that made it worse. *If things had played out differently, he could have killed Benton without ever knowing it.* She violently shoved the thought away.

"Going?" Benton asked.

Zack frowned, glanced at Nicole, and answered with a 'huh?'

"Where were you going?"

"Use more words," Zack teased.

Benton snatched the phone out of Zack's hands, winced at whatever he found displayed, and began typing furiously with his thumbs. Then he shoved it back.

"Zack, you unbelievable jerk," Zack read aloud. "You didn't just choke me out. You were trying to take me somewhere – alive. Do you have any idea where you were supposed to take me?"

"It's probably the same place that it's trying to lure you to in your sleep," Nicole said. Energy crackled restlessly under her skin, and she whirled back to Zack.

"Think really hard, Zack. It's important. Do you have any idea where you were supposed to go?"

"I don't even remember losing my mind to this thing."

"It doesn't have to be an actual location," Nicole insisted. "Maybe you have a strange feeling? A notion? Nothing solid but still there."

"Nope."

"Well, think about when you were first asked. Did anything come to mind? A smell or color or *anything*."

Zack strained himself with thought. It only left him looking more confused. "Grass."

"That's good," Nicole said with energy, getting the enthusiastic approval in before Benton could say anything. "You're doing great. Now elaborate. What about grass?"

Deep lines formed in his brow and gathered around his eyes. It actually looked painful to be thinking so hard. But whatever thought he was chasing remained just beyond his grasp.

"It's okay if it doesn't make sense right now. It could still be important."

"I just smelt grass."

"Only grass? No trees? Rotting leaves maybe?"

"Just grass."

Nicole was almost giddy with relief. "Awesome. Zack, you're the best."

"We live on a grass plain," Benton muttered.

"Yeah, as much as I like the praise, I'm going to have to side with the banshee. Grass is everywhere. It doesn't narrow anything down."

"But it does eliminate an option," she beamed.

Benton took Zack's phone again. Zack was just as confused as she was when Benton passed back the new message. Reading it quietly to himself, Zack snorted a laugh.

"You know, that describes her pretty succinctly."

"What did he write?" Nicole snapped a hand out for the phone only to have Zack pull it away. "Benton, what did you write?"

Benton smirked and kept his silence.

"You two are horrible," she sulked.

"How do you know it wasn't singing your praises?" Zack asked.

She rolled her eyes. "Anyway, back to the life and death situation." Accentuating the words didn't make either of them remorseful, so she plowed on. "Where in Fort Wayward wouldn't you smell grass?"

"At school?" Zack asked.

Benton pointed to the ground.

"Yes, in buildings, of course," she said. "But where else?"

"The same place as your point?" Before she could respond, Zack rushed to add. "My hand is sore. I'm not thinking straight."

She let her frustration leave her on a long breath. "The forest. At the very least, we know that whatever is after Benton isn't trying to take him back to the haunted forest. And, since the Highway of the Lost runs through it, we can safely assume that it's not going near there either."

"And that's important?" Zack said carefully.

"Did you want to deal with buffalo head, angry ghosts, and those tree-demons all at the same time? Not to mention whatever creep is roaming the highway looking for hitchhikers?"

"Hey," Zack grinned. "Look at that. We just found a silver lining."

"*We*," Nicole muttered under her breath, her eyes darting to stare bitterly at the phone and whatever comment lay there.

"What was that?" Zack asked.

"I was asking you to call the twins. The buffalo monster probably selected you because it saw you coming around here so often. You've failed, so it might go after them."

"There is no way your mumbling had that many words," Zack replied. He started dialing anyway.

Benton nudged her. "Call your mom."

"Why does everyone keep suggesting that? I can handle this."

His eyebrows inched towards his still damp hair. "She's a police officer."

"Oh. Right. Yeah, I should probably call mom."

Logically, Benton understood why people did it; he was a Banshee and all. It only made sense to ensure that he couldn't scream. But he was getting really sick of people using his throat like a stress ball. Zack's fingerprints now covered the faded damage Logan had left behind and, as the throbbing sensation faded, a deep ache rose up to replace it.

The innards of the ice pack Nicole had given him had long since melted into slush. Condensation drizzled down his battered skin. By this point, his shirt collar had completely soaked through. Every so often, a droplet would seep free and trail down his back or chest, making him shiver.

It had only taken two short calls for the Rider family to snap into action. Watching it all play out around him, Benton became convinced that, should they ever have the passing fancy, it wouldn't be hard for the three of them to take over a small country. Neither Benton nor Zack had been included in the Rider family's *Facetime*. Although, at Logan's request, Benton had been asked to display his new array of bruises. There were a few bad jokes about Zack hiding the evidence of Logan's previous assault before the soldier grew serious.

Rounding up the twins had fallen to him. Dorothy had taken damage control; interviewing the neighbors, making sure that they felt the issue was being properly dealt with without any further need of outside intervention. Benton wondered how she could convince people that everything was fine and stress that they shouldn't leave their home at the same time. Nicole's duty was to defend the home-front.

After making sure Zack and Benton were busy nursing their wounds and egos, she had begun fluttering around the house. At this point in their relationship, it didn't exactly surprise him to learn that Nicole was proficient at setting boobytraps. Zack had commented that she must have watched *Home Alone* a lot. Benton decided not to mention that a great deal of those traps would have been fatal in real life. Both of them had growing concerns as to why the Rider family had so many sledgehammers and bear traps on the premises.

Benton had decided it was best to stop watching once she brought out a large bottle of oil and a flare gun. People burning alive had a very distinctive, disgusting smell. He had experienced it in countless dreams, and even thinking about it made his stomach churn.

"Are you boys hungry?" Nicole asked with excessive sweetness. "I can get you something. Ice cream maybe?"

"You're busy, I can get it," Zack said.

Nicole's eyes widened, but her smile didn't fade. It was an unsettling combination.

"Maybe it's best if you don't move about too much," she said, hurrying off to the kitchen while spouting on about how it was her duty as their host.

Zack sunk back down onto the nest of blankets and pillows.

"We probably shouldn't touch anything," Zack whispered.

"Agreed."

A sharp rapping on the door came soon enough. After Nicole detached a tripwire that would have brought a large butcher knife swinging down, she opened the door and allowed her father to come inside. Meg and Danny were ushered into the living room and set down with the boys. The ice-cream Nicole brought them all didn't ease anyone's concern.

"This is a good set up, angel." Logan beamed with pride, jabbing a finger toward the dangling knife.

Nicole took the compliment with a blush and proceeded to answer a few follow up questions. There weren't many. Mostly, they switched between checking that Nicole was all right and asking if she had made any 'normal' cookies, whatever that meant. Meg and Danny were a lot more talkative. Zack was left to explain it all to them as Meg anxiously devoured her chocolate fudge sundae. Then her sister's.

"So why are we here? We didn't do anything." Danny winced in Benton's general direction as she added. "You look horrible."

"Thanks," Benton muttered, his voice guttural and raw.

"Oh, my God, you sound even worse," Meg chimed in. Putting down her spoon, she leaned over and prodded one finger against an exposed bruise, as if checking to make sure they weren't fake. Benton smacked her hand. "Zack did a hell of a job on you. How are you even talking?"

Like a bratty child at an aquarium petting pool, Meg tried to poke at him a few more times. Benton smacked her had away each time and tried not to be too insulted that she seemed to think just moving slowly would trick him. Zack eventually took mercy on him and cupped his hand over Meg's. She didn't try again after that.

"Did you really try and kill Benny?" Danny asked.

"I didn't mean to," he half snapped, half cringed. "I don't even remember doing it! I was at school and then suddenly my hand was locked in a door. And I apologized. Benton and I are cool now. Right, Benny-boy?"

Benton smirked. Nodding would hurt too much. And the way that slight bit of ambiguity drove Zack nuts was a bit of an extra bonus. It was another one of those situations where logic didn't quite cancel out his bitterness.

Danny cut off Zack's babblings. "Why does Nicole have so many bells?"

They all looked to see Nicole practically skip into the room, her long hair swinging, and an almost serene smile on her face. Benton was instantly on edge. She only ever smiled like that when she was sure she had just wrestled back control of a situation. That didn't always work out too well for him. Her wicker basket was hooked over her arm, filled to the brim with an array of shiny jiggling orbs. Without a word, she knelt down to join their circle and instantly set to work attaching long strings of bells around Meg's ankle, looping it a few times before fixing it with a tiny padlock. They were the kind that people attached to their suitcases for security.

"Hey, Nicole," Zack said with forced cheerfulness.

"Hey, Zack," she chirped back.

When she didn't offer anything more, the teenagers shot looks at each other. Benton often wondered how the trio managed to do this; if it was a talent learned from knowing each other since birth, or a survival skill developed specifically to deal with Nicole's more tenacious whims. Whatever the reason, they could actually conduct a game of *rock-paper-scissors* by glances alone. Zack lost.

"So, um, what ya doing?" Zack asked cautiously.

"Safety precaution," Nicole said as if this was the most normal thing in the world.

"To stop us from moving about?" Zack pressed.

Nicole giggled, swiftly finishing her work and moving onto Danny. "You make it sound like I've kidnapped you."

"Your father did bundle us into a car with minimal explanation," Danny said, subtly trying to pull her leg away.

Nicole had the padlock fastened before she got very far, then started on Zack.

"That won't hold up in court. Besides, it's for your safety, too. We don't fully understand what happened to Zack yet, and there's a risk it could happen to you guys as well. It's imperative we keep track of where you guys are for a little while." For a moment, her mask of sugar-sweet innocence slipped. "Don't try opening any of the doors without letting me know." She clicked the padlock shut. "Or the windows. Okie-dokie?"

Benton presented his ankle without prompting.

Zack chuckled in a failed attempt to hide his nerves. "But, if I black out again, wouldn't I just take it off?"

"Not without wire cutters," Benton croaked.

Nicole continued the thought. "I've woven the threads around a plaited strand copper wire. I mean, it won't stand up against the proper tools, but there's no way you'd be able to snap it by hand. Or scissors. I've checked. And the padlocks are small, but they work pretty well."

"Why do you even have these?" Meg asked.

"Some nights, I sleep heavy," she shrugged. "And with Benton sleepwalking now, I need to know if he gets up and moves around."

"Yeah, that's normal," Zack muttered.

Nicole bristled up slightly. "Hey, I thought this was a pretty good solution to the problem."

"So do I," Benton said.

Zack cocked an eyebrow at him.

"Her dad was suggesting to just hog tie me," Benton said. "Bells are better."

"And much more cheerful," Nicole said as she finished attaching the last one.

"But why do you have so many of them?" Danny asked.

"Hm?" Nicole both answered and dismissed at the same time.

"Don't ask," Benton grumbled. "Trust me. Don't ask."

"All right then." Nicole swiftly got to her feet.

"Wait," Meg snapped. "Why don't you get a bell?"

"Because I'm trustworthy."

"That's not fair," Danny protested.

"The monster has never used me to hurt Benton." The sentence ended with a far-off stare.

Suddenly, she ran for her binders, flipping through the pages as she grumbled to herself.

"Does no one else feel a little insulted?" Meg declared, twisting her outstretched foot to test her new ankle bracelet.

The bells might have been tiny, but they made a ruckus.

"I'm trying hard not to," Danny agreed.

Benton decided it was best not to comment and let the others continue their conversation in peace. Honestly, let them have their denial. It was easier than admitting that, if this creature was capable of overcoming the hurricane of Nicole's thoughts, bells wouldn't save them. Nicole was a force of nature that had proven she could kill a man. She hadn't even hesitated to put a bullet between the man's eyes. The fact that he was a serial killer who had almost led to all of their deaths had helped soften the blow for the group. In time, they had come to terms with what had happened as much as they could. They ignored the rest. Sometimes she still had nightmares over it. Everyone just assumed it was the guilt of taking a life. The only guilt she had was that she *didn't* feel guilty.

Only Benton knew that part. It was their little secret.

Carefully swallowing a mouthful of ice-cream, Benton pondered how much worse all of this would be if she had kept that last bit of information from him. Months had passed and he still couldn't figure out how to tell her how comforted he was knowing how far she'd go for him. He'd never had that before.

*Well, not since the Banshee genes kicked in.* That's when his parents had taken a giant emotional leap back and left him to deal with it on his own. *Not my parents,* a little voice whispered it in the back of his mind. He quickly shoved it away. He was too exhausted to think about that right now.

Benton's lack of interest had long since reduced the conversation around him to a bunch of sounds rather than words. It was the lack of noise that rekindled his interest. Following everyone's line of sight, he noticed Dorothy coming around the back of the house. The approaching dusk had just started to dim the winter sky. Clouds thickened with the promise of more snowfall, deepening the clustering shadows. None of them were dark enough to offer any real hiding places, but Dorothy still eyed each of them with suspicion, one hand resting upon her service weapon. Benton tried to warn her about the booby-traps, but all that came out was a pained grunt.

"I got it," Nicole called from the kitchen.

Benton must have missed the part where they discussed antipersonnel devices because Dorothy never made an attempt to open the door herself. She simply stood there, eyeing the back yard as she waited for her daughter. Logan beat her to it. *Oh, so he taught her,* Benton thought as he watched Logan dismantle the trap without hesitation. He still had deep concerns about her browser history.

"Have I ever told you how much I love a girl in uniform?" Logan asked.

"I'm armed."

"And you just got hotter." The soldier added a wink at the end for good measure.

"So," Dorothy said sharply, moving into the room while Nicole swiftly reset the trap. "Zack tried to kill Benton?"

"Abduct," Zack corrected. "What? Why is everyone looking at me like that? It's a very important detail."

Benton shrugged when the Constable threw him a questioning look, wincing with the movement of his neck.

"Do you need to go to the hospital?" she asked.

"No," he croaked.

Dorothy cringed in sympathy. "How about some ice cubes to suck on?"

He held up his dripping ice pack by way of response.

"All right." Dorothy nodded once and put her hands on her hips. "So, back to this whole attempted murder business."

"Abduction!" Zack protested.

She quickly met Benton's gaze again and they both hid a smirk. It was rare when their senses of humor lined up. Generally, it only happened when they were messing with Nicole.

"He wasn't in control of himself," Nicole defended.

Zack snapped his fingers a few times and pointed at her, "Yes! Also important. That makes me not legally responsible for my actions, right?"

Dorothy's whole body rocked with her disgruntled sigh. "Is there any good news today?"

"We're still alive," Nicole offered, with a smile that a Miss Universe contestant would be jealous of. "That's always one heck of a perk."

"And I didn't bludgeon a teenager," Logan declared with a grin. "Really, I should get more get more credit for that."

His wife whipped around to face him. "Sorry?"

He gestured loosely to Zack. "He hit my little angel. And I didn't break every bone in his body."

"I was possessed!" Zack squeaked.

Logan simply shrugged one beefy shoulder. A small movement that made it abundantly clear the details didn't matter to him, and drew attention to his muscle mass.

Dorothy rolled her eyes. "Well, thank you for not making me arrest you."

Flopping down into the armchair nearest his wife, Logan pouted and tapped his lips until he received a kiss as reward. Nicole released a sweet 'aw'.

*This is the Rider family,* Benton thought. *My last line of defense against the unknown.* Dorothy somehow managed to hold onto both her dignity and authority as her husband tugged her down to sit on the armrest. *It's probably the stab vest*, Benton decided.

It didn't take long for all traces of humor to seep from the room. Dorothy's gaze sharpened as she looked at each of the teens in turn.

"I've heard it from Nicole's point of view. Do either of you boys want to weigh in?"

Benton pointed to his throat and cocked an eyebrow.

"I don't remember anything," Zack insisted. "I swear."

"Can someone tell us what's going on?" Meg asked.

Nicole happily took the lead and started from the beginning. Benton watched her parents carefully, trying to pick up any trace of emotion that crossed their features. They were both as emotionless as stone. The only way he knew that Nicole was elaborating on things she hadn't been able to get into on the phone was when the couple cast quick glances at each other. The twins, however, made no attempt to hide their growing unease.

"Wait, you guys really think the Buffalo monster can do that to us, too?" Meg asked. "Take over our minds, I mean?"

"Perhaps," Dorothy said, clearly distracted by her thoughts.

Zack scrunched up his face. "Why would we lie about that?"

Mimicking Zack himself, Benton clicked his fingers and pointed to him. *Good point.* Both boys were ignored.

"My question is; why Zack?" Logan said.

Settling down next to Benton, Nicole piled the binders onto her lap and resumed flipping through them.

"We know that this creature has been stalking our house for a while," Dorothy said, her eyes scanning the curtained windows. "It would have seen Zack and the twins coming and going. Perhaps it reasoned that Nicole would open the door to a familiar face."

Nicole froze. Benton squeezed her knee. *You couldn't have known.* With a little smile, she bumped their shoulders and went back to what she was doing. Meanwhile, Dorothy had been sizing Zack up thoughtfully.

"He is also the most physically imposing," she continued.

"I'm not saying that he's not a good option," Logan said, waving a hand at the teenagers as if they couldn't hear or see him. "Clearly, he's the best out of the three."

Nicole opened her mouth, but Benton cut in first.

"Really, Nic? You're insulted you weren't chosen to kill me?"

She clamped her mouth shut.

"This is what gets me," Logan continued as if nothing had happened. "Why is everyone assuming that the other two were on the menu, to begin with?"

Dorothy licked her lips. "You're suggesting that it doesn't have the ability to take over anyone? That his victims must meet a set criterion? That's a good point."

"Wait." A huge smile stretched Logan's face. Leaning back, he balanced one ankle on his knee. "Did I just figure something out *before* you two?"

"Don't gloat," Dorothy said.

"Oh, no. I'm going to gloat."

"I'm thinking that it might have something to do with family lines," Nicole said, still skimming the pages.

Logan deflated. "Oh, come on."

"At least we know of two family lines that are safe." Nicole glanced up, seemingly becoming aware that she had everyone's attention. "It just seems like it could have saved itself a lot of trouble by picking one of us. You know, we already live here. Benton spends all his time with us. And I'm sure it's seen how easily we can lure him into a car. But it still picked Zack. His family has never married into either side of mine. Well, going back two-hundred-odd years. After that, the records get a little unreliable."

"You know everyone's family tree going back two-hundred years?" Meg asked.

"Oh, no." Nicole chuckled. "Just mine. Wait, did you forget about our third-grade family tree project?"

"I remember that we only had to go as far back as our grandparents," Zack muttered.

Benton smirked, repositioning the ice pack against his neck. "So, it can only possess annoying people?"

"Hey," Zack snapped.

Holding his gaze, Benton removed the ice pack, exposing the dark lines that now crisscrossed his neck.

"I withdraw my complaint," Zack replied.

"Aren't we assuming a lot here?" Danny asked.

Dorothy looked them all over in turn. "We know it can't be gender or age."

"It could be something he ingested," Logan offered.

"The whole town has the same food and water source. He wouldn't have had anything out of the normal." Dorothy hesitated to level a cold glare at the teen in question. "Isn't that right, Zack? You haven't been taking anything else?"

Zack paled as much as his tawny skin would allow. "No. I swear. I'm clean. Where would you even get anything illegal in this town? You do too good of a job, Constable."

Logan's laughter boomed around the room. "Yeah, buddy, flattery isn't going to get you anywhere with her. That only works when I do it."

"Logan," his wife growled under her breath.

"Hey, it's a good thing you're a sucker for my charms. We wouldn't have Nicole if you weren't."

Horror twisted up Nicole's features. "If it's hereditary, do you think it's possible that Zack's entire family be just as likely to fall victim to the Buffalo Monster?"

Ice trickled down Benton's spine. "How many people is that?"

He remembered her telling him on numerous occasions that there was barely a family in Fort Wayward not connected by blood or marriage. It was pure luck that they were as separated as is. He should have known that it wouldn't last.

"You know, it might not be *everyone* in his family," Nicole tried to soothe, seemingly forgetting that she was a terrible liar. And clearly didn't believe a word she said. "It might just be close relations. Like his parents and brothers."

"Don't bring my family into this," Zack whined defensively, clearly trying to defuse his growing concern with some humor.

"All of that is just guesswork at this point," Logan cut in. He hunched forward to rest his elbows on his knees as he continued, "What we do know for sure is that it has the ability to mess with people while they're awake. It hasn't done that before."

"It's either been holding back or growing stronger," Dorothy noted.

"I love you more than cheesecake, honey, but I'm trying to drag us away from speculation for just a hot second," Logan said. "It's showed us a little bit more of what it can do. So, can we finally figure out what it is?"

He gave every indication that this was a joint problem, and he intended them to brainstorm the answer together. That didn't stop the entire room from automatically turning to look at Nicole. Busy reading through her binder, it took her a few seconds to realize. She gaped for a moment, her dark eyes growing wide, before she balled her fists.

"Not really," she stammered at last, rushing to add, "it narrows it down a bit, though."

Logan's massive hand clutched at the free armrest, the leather crackling and the wood beneath groaning. "I'm getting really sick of this. It's right outside! Can we just try shooting it? Like, a lot. That has to do something!"

"Discharging a weapon in a residential neighborhood is dangerous *and* illegal," Dorothy said.

"I've never shot anything I didn't intend to kill," Logan growled, his fingers tightening until the chair was at the point of snapping.

Dorothy rolled her eyes. "That sounds a lot less badass when you take into account target practice."

"Hey, those paper targets can be dangerous," he shot back, unable to fight back the kneejerk reaction to tease his wife.

The distraction spared the chair from destruction. Still, he glared at the windows as if they had personally offended him. The muscles of his jaws jumped as he ground his teeth. At that moment, Benton was struck with the clear, burning knowledge that he was sick of being afraid.

"Can we capture it?" he croaked.

Logan slowly turned his head to face Benton, a smile stretching across his face. "I'm starting to like this boy."

"Is something like that even possible?" Dorothy asked. "It never seemed like an option with the other things we've encountered."

Benton swallowed, steeling himself for the pain a long explanation would bring. Nicole mercifully picked up on his train of thought and took the conversation over from there.

"Unlike the others, this one hasn't actually attacked Benton physically," she said.

"Um," Zack hummed, sheepishly lifting one hand.

Nicole waved him off. "You're just a proxy. Like the stags."

"A meat puppet, if you will," Logan cut in.

"What I mean is that it hasn't come after him as directly as the others have. The first time we saw it, on the road, it didn't physically come at us when we got in the way. Even now, it keeps trying to lure him out rather than come in and claim him. And at the school, it backed off when the stags didn't work."

"When you shot them in the eyes," Logan broke in, nudging his wife's hip with his elbow. "That's our girl."

Nicole preened under the praise before noticing the looks she was getting from the others.

Clearing her throat, she continued in a sober tone, "It still didn't come itself for the next attempt. Instead, it chose a proxy that it knew I wouldn't be quick enough to put down."

"What do you mean 'wouldn't be quick enough?'" Zack asked, his voice creeping up an octave.

Without discussion, the entire Rider family decided to ignore that question.

"All this time, it's been keeping a physical distance," Nicole continued. "And it's been careful never to let anyone get a full body look at it. I don't think it's shy. It's possible that it can't actually do physical damage on its own. We might be able to overpower it physically."

"Or, it's not corporeal," Dorothy argued.

"That means that it's not flesh and blood, right?" Logan's shock was short-lived. "I like coming home. It's full of new experiences."

"If it's not corporeal, then it can't hurt us," Nicole replied.

The Constable shook her head, absently hooking one thumb over the handle of her holstered weapon. "That's dangerous speculation."

"I saw it, mom."

"A whole gym full of people saw it," Meg added.

"Exactly. How often does that happen? Normally, only Benton can see them if they're not solid to some extent."

"The *Leanan Sidhe* was solid," she poised. "Benton almost killed both of you in a pit."

"And she's now in a shallow grave," Nicole countered.

Logan nudged his wife and Dorothy squirmed.

"The next time we're near the old Fort, I'll show you the corpse," Dorothy whispered.

"The old Fort?" He hummed dramatically as he thought aloud. "The grass would have claimed most of the place by now. Untended, it'll be at least hip high, easily hiding what you're doing. All that's probably left of the buildings would be a few basements and some hunks of wood and stone. No reason for anyone to go out there. Nothing else around for miles. Angel, you picked a good place to hide a body."

"Thanks, dad."

"The *Dullahan*," Dorothy continued, adding before her husband could ask, "A ghostly horseman. Invisible but capable of murder. And the *Slaughs* almost did more damage than the storm they flew in. The *Baykoks*. The *Pontianak*. They were all capable of doing a hell of a lot of damage."

"And we're still here," Nicole countered.

"Don't be so cocky," Dorothy said. "A lot of that was luck."

Danny whimpered, mumbling under her breath about the ghosts they had spotted in the woods. The monstrous beasts that looked as if the forest itself was swallowing them, deforming them into some hybrid of human and tree.

"Could those things touch us?" Danny looked to her twin and cringed. "Well, I won't be sleeping again for a while."

"You're just guessing that we'll be able to contain this thing," Dorothy said.

"And even if we could trap it, what would we do with it?" Logan asked.

"Put it in one of the basements at the ghost town," Nicole said. "It worked for the *Leanan Sidhe*. She stored all of her victims there."

Benton didn't mention the flinch that rattled Nicole's body, or the cold air that seemed to settle down upon the room. They had lost a life-long friend to the creature. Benton could sympathize with their grief but couldn't fully share in it.

"We can't just do nothing," Nicole said. "And we do have the upper hand. At the very least, we know that there are three people that it can't affect. Also, Benton, when he's awake. And we know it's wary of direct confrontation, for whatever reason. There has to be something to that. Let's use all of that to our advantage. Set a trap. Meet it on our terms."

Logan practically beamed at his daughter's suggestion but didn't say anything as Dorothy placed a hand on his shoulder.

"And if it doesn't work?" Dorothy pressed.

"Then at least I'll get a good look at it. I'll be able to tell what it is."

"You don't know that."

"There's a reason why it's hiding," Nicole insisted.

Dorothy released a long-suffering sigh. "Nicole."

"Okay, what about this. If we're right and it's getting stronger, how much longer will we be able to keep it out?"

"She's right, hon," Logan said softly. "Granted, it's not a great option, but at least it's one we can make on our own terms. So, let's do this before it takes the option away from us."

Dorothy absently rubbed a thumb across her bottom lip as she weighed their options. The room was left in a tense silence as they all waited to see what her decision would be.

"For argument's sake–" She paused, eyeing her husband and daughter as if waiting for confirmation that they agreed to this term. "What exactly are you two thinking? Whatever this thing is, it's smart. It's constantly following us and already knows our routine. Anything obvious will tip it off. It's not going to believe we just happened to let our guard down right after an attack."

"All good points, love. But I'll have you know that our plan is fantastic," Logan said.

"Which is?"

Logan met her challenging gaze. "I'm going to let Nicole explain it to you."

"Thanks, dad." Nicole stammered for a moment. "We could make it look like we're transporting Benton elsewhere. That's a logical reaction to its actions. Oh, we could take him to the hospital and lure the Buffalo Monster down to the morgue. That place worked well enough with the *Dullahan*. If we get the time right, no one will be hanging around. And, if we can't kill it, we might be able to lock it in one of the body drawers."

Logan raised both hands to display his child with pride. "See."

Dorothy cocked an eyebrow. "So that I'm clear, you two want to lure a creature that has proven it has mind-control abilities to a place full of people and sharp objects?"

"Right." Logan clicked his tongue. "Collateral damage. We need somewhere with no meat puppets." Logan clucked his tongue a few times. "Somewhere that will let us control the variables."

"The ghost town," Nicole suggested.

"Nah, too much tall grass. I want more visibility."

"Here," Benton croaked.

"And what? We just forgot to lock the door? We've been over this. It'll be pretty hard to make it believable." Logan put on a sweet voice one would use with a child to add, "But it's great that you're trying to help."

Benton stared at the man, deeply resentful that his throat hurt too much to put any of his annoyance into his voice. "Let Nicole sleep through the bells."

"Let it possess you?" Nicole clarified. "No. No way! That's crazy – hold on, that could work."

Benton rolled his eyes as Nicole's words picked up their pace.

"It wants Benton alive and is obviously trying to take him somewhere. And there's a decent chance that it watched me rig the door."

"You think that it needs to keep Benton in sight to control him," Logan took over. "To bypass a booby trap is a lot harder than opening a door. It might need a better line of sight. It could force it forward. If we close all the curtains, 'unfortunately' leaving a small gap, we'll be able to control where it goes."

"A camera and a flare and I'll at least have a chance to properly identify it," Nicole added with growing excitement.

Logan twisted around to eye the door in question. "I can rig that to be non-fatal. You know, in case it's not that great at manipulating finer motor functions."

Dorothy squeezed her husband's shoulder, silencing him for a moment to ask, "Benton, are you okay with this? The biggest risk will be on you."

"He suggested it," Logan declared.

Still, Dorothy waited until Benton nodded to agree.

"This isn't the best idea," she mulled. "But I suppose it's better than nothing."

"Aw, that's what you said at our wedding!" Logan clapped his hands with childish delight. "Now, let's go wrangle us a demonic spirit from beyond the grave!"

"We don't know that's what it is," Nicole said, barely getting the words out before her father demanded that she just let him have a moment.

# Chapter 9

The night had crept up slowly, only to fall upon them all at once – bitterly cold and impenetrably dark. The neighborhood had long since fallen silent, stirred only by the random chatter of a few owls.

Nicole was used to quiet nights. Fort Wayward wasn't known for its nightlife. But this one felt different; somehow empty. Before the sun had set, Dorothy had made sure to check in on the neighbors once more, softly suggesting that they might want to visit family or friends for the night, whoever was on the other side of town. Most of them had already had a bag packed before the Constable had even arrived. While the people of Fort Wayward weren't exactly superstitious, they knew better than to risk it. They had known that something was different about Benton for a while now. They didn't know what, but, after the last week, they knew to head for the hills. Nicole could almost feel their absence now.

A shiver went down her spine as she eyed the heavy curtains. There was only one thin slip that offered her a glimpse outside. It was a strip of pure onyx. Too deep for her to see anything lurking within it. Fighting to keep her growing anxiety under control, she curled up on her side, pushing a little closer to Benton. Every so often, she would hear the faintest trace of sound. A small crunch of snow, as if something were prowling around the edges of the building. There was every chance that it was the birds. Perhaps a rabbit. Her gut told her that it wasn't.

The idea had been to make it look like they were trying to avoid the Buffalo Monster's gaze; moving from her bedroom down to the living room to sleep. It was essentially a nest of blankets and pillows that was surprisingly comfortable. Nicole had made sure to stock the fire well before they settled down for 'sleep'. Perhaps too well.

Hours later, the room was still filled with an orange glow. Heat pulsated from the dancing flames. It was growing unbearably hot under the blankets, but she didn't make any attempt to remove them. The longer she waited, the more she wished that Zack and the twins had been able to stay. *Too risky,* she reminded herself. The situation was bad enough without Zack being taken over again. And there was no way to tell how the twins would react.

Anxiety simmered along her veins, making her heartbeat pick up. She took a deep breath, letting it out slowly as she pushed closer to Benton. He stirred slightly but didn't wake up, the slight motion marked by a tinkle of bells. Apparently, the looming threat of attack wasn't enough to overcome prolonged sleep deprivation. Which was a good thing. The plan only worked if he could sleep. Warm, comfortable, and exhausted, it hadn't taken long from him to nod off. Nicole watched him for a moment, hoping that he'd get a few decent hours before everything went down.

A part of her whispered that she should try and get some sleep too. There was no guarantee that she'd get another chance any time soon. It was a small, selfish voice that she quickly squashed. *Focus,* she told herself sharply. Unfortunately, to keep up appearances, she had to close her eyes. It took far less effort than she thought it would. What little adrenaline her body was still able to produce after days of being on edge wasn't enough to stand against the natural, unstoppable need for sleep. It was a fight she would have lost if she hadn't grown so used to sleeping with her headphones on.

Every little sound snapped her back to wakefulness. The push of the breeze, the crackle and pop of the fire, even the sharp little intakes of breath Benton made as his dreams started to take hold. Time stretched out as she waited. The little crunch of snow became more common. It pressed on her then, that all that separated them from the monster was a thin sheet of glass. *This will work. This has to work.*

The soft tinkle of a bell shattered her thoughts. She flinched, instantly hating herself for doing so. Clenching each muscle, she fought to keep herself still, to hold onto the illusion of sleep. Soft bells sounded again. A flinch of Benton's foot. A slight movement before he froze entirely. Nicole held her breath and waited. She counted her heartbeats because she needed something she could do. The blankets slipped from her torso as Benton sat upright. With her back to the doors, she felt secure enough to sneak a peek through her lashes.

There was something wrong about the way he sat. Some undefinable change that made him look as if he were held up rather than sitting with his own power. Like there was a string at the top of his head and some unseen hand was pulling it. His arms hung loose and limp. For the longest time, he hung like that; suspended within the moment. Still as stone. Then, in a sudden burst of movement, he was on his feet. A hailstorm of bells slowly tinkled into silence as he stood there. He wavered slightly. The firelight danced across his suddenly pale skin and glistened off his wide eyes.

Nicole tried not to move, clenched her hands until she ached to keep from reaching out and grabbing him. Every instinct she had screamed at her to end this. The sensation only got worse as he slowly began to stagger across the room. Unable to take the dread boiling inside her ribcage, Nicole squirmed. She wasn't much of an actor. All she could do was hope that it looked like the sound had simply stirred her in her sleep but failed to rouse her. Her stomach dropped more with every jingle. Soon enough, he was out of her line of sight, leaving her only the sound of the bells to track his progress across the room. He didn't go far. With a final, soft tinkle, the room fell silent.

Nicole's stomach churned restlessly. The longer she was forced to lie there, the quicker hear heartbeat became, until her blood roared in her ears with the ferocity of crashing waves. Energy crackled under her skin, making her tremble as she fought to keep herself still. Time passed. Biting the inside of her cheek, she strained to catch the slightest trace of bells. The only noise within the room was the soft crackle of the fireplace.

A sudden, sharp intake of breath made her stomach plummet. Instinct made her roll. The blankets tightened around her as she scrambled for the noise-canceling headphones hidden under the pillows.

Benton's scream shattered the tension of the night, driving into her ears like needles, causing her vision to blur. She strained against the blankets to shove the headphones over her head, succeeding at the same instant the windows exploded. Shrapnel rained down upon her back, the duvet sparing her from the jagged edges. Cool night air rushed through the broken windows; a cold rush that caught the fire and made it flare out with a guttural roar. Blistering heat rolled over her back, seeping through the slashes and heading the glass shards. It barely lasted a second but came with an intensity that made her gasp in pain.

She could only pray that the flames didn't catch hold of the material cocooning her. Benton's scream slowly tapered off into silence. Nicole took it as her sign to tear her way through the blankets, losing her headphones in her haste.

Frigid air struck her sweat-damp face. Each movement shook the glass fragments from her back. They tinkled as they toppled to the floorboards, clanking against each of the shards already scattered there. It was that sound that made her look to the window instead of trying to find Benton. Shock seized her. The core of her soul was consumed by an arctic wasteland. A rush of adrenaline left her dizzy and trembling.

The creature was already halfway through the gaping hole of the shattered window frame.

It walked on all fours. Slick skin rippled over its twisted bones, twitching each time its joints popped. It moved like a tarantula;

working each appendage independently, drawing the elongated limbs high above its low hanging humanoid torso. Blood and spit dripped from the curved fangs that pierced the flesh of its cheeks. The thrashing firelight glistened off of the polished onyx of its rounded, unblinking eyes. Bile seared the back of Nicole's throat as she looked at the mangled features of the otherwise human face.

Bulbous obsidian captured the room like a mirror, perfectly reflecting her horrified face back to her. Thick lips peeled back from rotted teeth as it invaded her home. It clung to the patch of wall below the window. It smiled at her and scuttled up the wall. Its body twisted around while its head remained riveted in place. A sickening snap made her jump and a lump of shattered bone bulged against the side of its neck. Still, it continued to move, smiling all the while. The monstrous sight made her ill. But it was the sensations it provoked that kept her rooted in place.

It wasn't like the others that had come before it. There wasn't hatred or hunger in its eyes. Nothing that made her survival instincts scream that she was in the presence of a predator. It wasn't driven by a primal, innate need to track down its prey. There was nothing natural about it. The being before her was removed from such things. It wasn't a living thing. Simply a sentient embodiment of sadistic glee. Pure, unbridled, malice given form.

The floodgates of her mind opened, unleashing a thousand campfire stories to crash down upon her. A lifetime of warnings from distant tribal elders. Tales her aunt once used to scare her into being good. The creature wasn't simply a monster. It was the boogieman that had hunted her people for centuries. Pure evil. A *Skinwalker*.

"You're a *Yee Naaldiooshii*." The words left her mouth in a whisper, crackling with unshed tears of terror.

Its smile widened, tearing the flesh around its fangs. A breath of wind flurried into the room and whipped the fire into a frenzy once more. The orange glow turned the *Yee Naaldiooshii's* flesh into molten lava. Nicole gasped, the sudden jerk shaking scorching tears of terror from her eyes. Desperate for air, her lungs strained against her ribs, the spike of pain the only tether she had left to her body. She longed to call her parents, to bring them out of their hiding places to force the monster back into the fevered nightmares of her childhood. Yet nothing but a broken sob worked its way through her frozen body. The *Yee Naaldiooshii* noticed. It delighted in it.

Benton's scream caught them both off guard. Nicole snapped toward the tormented, mournful sound. *He's dreaming,* she realized. *It didn't stop him from dreaming.* She had only taken her eyes off the *Yee Naaldiooshii* for a second. But when she looked back, it was gone. A flash of movement drew Nicole's attention to the shadows clustered around the front door's foyer. It clung to the ceiling, still staring at her as it sunk backward, shrouding itself into the darkness until only its eyes remained visible. Her father burst into her peripheral vision. She barely caught a glimpse of him but knew that he felt the same terror that she did.

"Angel?" he stammered, barely heard over the *Banshee's* wail.

She pointed a trembling finger to the glowing eyes. "There! There!"

Benton's scream cut off as abruptly as it had started, replaced by a tinkling of bells and the gasping hiss of an emergency flare catching light. Logan hurled the burning stick into the foyer, instantly destroying the shadows and exposing the *Yee Naaldiooshii* once more. Nicole choked, breaking her horrified scream into pitiful sputtering. Logan stood frozen in place, one trembling hand clutching his gun, his arm tensed by his side.

"Is that?" His question hovered between them, his tone clearly pleading for someone to tell him he was wrong.

Dorothy would be at the top of the stairs. She'd have a clear shot. And yet the booming sound didn't ring out. Somewhere under the storming sea of chaos her mind had become, Nicole knew it was because her mother had been caught off guard just as badly as the rest of them. A soft grunt echoed from beside her. It was barely more than a whisper, but she jumped, a startled scream finally escaping her lips. Benton flinched away, pushing himself up onto all fours as he cast quick glances around the room, trying to regain his bearings. Finally, his eyes fell upon the gruesome creature hanging from the ceiling.

"What the hell is that?" he asked. Before anyone could find their voice, his raw voice rose to a scream. "Shoot it!"

The *Yee Naaldiooshii* giggled with perverse joy and leaped forward. A click. A snap. Someone wrenched the door open and set the trap into motion. The slender, knife-tipped beam swung down, slashing into the *Yee Naaldiooshii*. Not dispersing it or shattering it. Merely passing through it as if it had never existed. The intruder shrieked.

Benton's eyes grew impossibly wider. "Mom!"

Benton was the first one to move, sprinting across the room before Nicole could stop him. So she followed, her father by her side, the staircase rattling as Dorothy thundered down to join the others. Benton rounded the corner, still a few steps before her. She only lost sight of him for a split-second, but it made her blood run cold. Hurling herself around the corner, she found Cheyanne Bertrand huddled in the doorway, kept from falling completely on her back by her husband. Theodore desperately gripped at his wife's shoulder, trying to slow the blood that flowed from the knife wound. Neither one cared about the people thundering towards them. Their attention was upon the creature that was darting across the lawn.

Benton had leaped over his mother to better position himself between them and the *Yee Naaldiooshii*. Time had caught up with him. The prophetic dream that had broken him out of the *Yee Naaldiooshii* hold was now taking its toll. His knees trembled and one hand pressed hard into his skull, as if trying to keep it together as his growing migraine threatened to crack it apart. Clutching the doorframe with his free hand, he clenched his teeth and glared at the monster sinking into the shadows.

As a single flock, the owls took flight. Their wings beat against the air without a sound, leaving only the sharp, bone snapping crack of their beaks. The *Yee Naaldiooshii* kept its sickening smile and turned to face them. Cheyanne and Theodore scurried further into the building, startled yelps and sputtered curses flowing endlessly from their lips. Nicole could feel the exact moment something shifted.

It can't control the owls, she realized. Great Horned Owls. Omens of death. They're Benton's. The birds swirled and swooped at the Skinwalker but couldn't touch it. Still, there was something different within the cold, dead gaze of the monster. Something she couldn't understand. It was only a feeling, but she found she wasn't surprised to see the creature slowly slink back into the deep shadows. Not fleeing, merely returning to wait and watch.

Benton held his composure until the glowing eyes disappeared. Then he doubled over with a pained cry.

"Mom, he dreamt," Nicole said as she crouched down next to Cheyanne, trying to pry Theodore's fingers away. "Dad, first aid kit."

"What was that thing?" Cheyanne asked over and over, leaving no pause to hear the answer.

"Mr. Bertrand, let me help your wife," Nicole insisted.

"Benton!" Theodore roared.

It seemed that neither one could see anything beyond their son. The boy that was currently ignoring them to detail his dream to the Constable.

"He needs to purge," Nicole said as her father returned. "Mom will take care of him. Mrs. Bertrand, let me take care of you."

"What was that?!" Cheyanne shrieked.

Nicole fought with Theodore's fingers, but he refused to release his grip. Every attempt only added to their panic. The passing seconds turned their frozen terror into a wild and thrashing panic. Blood slicked Nicole's fingers, glistening in the light of the flare, drizzling to the ground like liquid rubies. Pain suddenly exploded across the side of her jaw as a stray arm clashed against her. She staggered back with the blow as her father surged forward. It was a swift motion marked with a sharp crack and both of the adult Bertrand's fell abruptly silent. Blinking numbly, Nicole couldn't force her frazzled mind to explain what had just happened.

"Was knocking them out necessary?" Dorothy snapped, suddenly bringing everything into focus.

"They hit Nicole," Logan spat back, all of his normal humor gone, leaving his voice hollow and cold. "They're lucky I only drove their heads into the wall once."

Dorothy didn't bother to push the issue. Instead, she got to her feet, pulling Benton with her.

"We've got to get to the reservation before it catches up. Nicole, get the keys for your Jeep. Logan, we're taking those two with us."

"Mrs. Bertrand is still bleeding. I haven't had the chance to look at the wound," Nicole said.

"You can clean her up when we're on the road," Dorothy shot back.

"But, if it hit a vein, she could bleed out."

"Then she bleeds out!" Dorothy screamed. "That was a Skinwalker! We're not staying!"

Nicole flinched, having never heard her mother scream before. Never heard the panic that radiated from every word.

Spinning on her heel, she bolted for her keys.

# Chapter 10

A simple wooden sign barely rose above the towering grass. Benton had been desperately searching for that sign for hours, somehow sure that crossing that border would change everything. Now that it streaked by in a blur, he was crushed to find that the tension remained, like an iron ball sitting heavily within his chest.

"Okay, we're on the reservation now," Theodore snapped. "Someone explain to us what is going on."

"Shut up," Logan growled.

Benton watched as his father's face flushed red.

"You told us you would explain–"

"Be quiet, or I'll knock you out again," Logan cut in. "Your choice."

Theodore pressed his mouth into a thin line. It seemed to satisfy Logan, since the far larger man went back to scanning the jeep windows. The vehicle wasn't built to handle four grown adults and two teenagers. The way they were crammed into it didn't make things any more comfortable. Dorothy drove, keeping the headlights off as she sped across the dirt roads, the jeep bucking over potholes and skidding on random patches of ice.

Theodore and Cheyanne clutched each other with a desperation Benton had never seen in them. Since they had refused to let go, they had both scrambled into the backseat, with Nicole following to help tend to Cheyanne's wounds. Logan had leaped into the trunk to ensure that the *Yee Naaldiooshii* didn't attempt to follow them. The soldier hadn't given Benton the option of taking the empty front passenger seat and had dragged him into the back with him. Presumably, to keep him as far away from the driver as possible. Benton didn't know if there was any real concern of the *Yee Naaldiooshii* overtaking him again, or if Logan was more worried that, if attacked, Benton's attempts to help would do more damage than good.

After Dorothy made a call to the station house to report Benton's dream as an 'anonymous tip,' the Jeep had been forced into a tense silence. Benton wasn't sure if it was because the *Yee Naaldiooshii* would be attracted to human voices or if the Rider family couldn't stand his parents' screaming for a second longer.

Pushing himself into the corner, Benton took them all in again. Theodore was desperately trying to gain anything he could misconstrue as 'control.' Cheyanne sobbed in both terror and pain. His eyes moved to Nicole and lingered on his best friend's hands.

They were shaking. That, more than anything, fed the gnarled veins of fear that slithered through his bones. Nothing else they had been through had affected her like this.

Without a word, he slipped a hand over the seat backing that separated them. She didn't look at him but quickly snatched up his hand, fingers tightening until it hurt, her nails digging into his flesh. The dim light within the Jeep turned the blood along her nailbeds a tar black.

*Mom's blood,* Benton's mind acknowledged. It struck him then that she might want some kind of physical comfort as well. He flicked his eyes to the woman who had helped raise him. Curled up in the fetal position, she lay nestled in Theodore's arms. She bit her bottom lip, trying to stifle her whimpers as her husband smoothed a hand over her hair. The pair had shown more affection toward each other in the last few hours than they had for years. Benton didn't feel right imposing on that.

Dorothy didn't slow down to navigate the sharp twist in the road. The tires kicked up dirt and gravel, creating small clouds within the dark night. It jostled everyone. Nicole clutched Benton's hand, her nails digging into his flesh. The sea of grass parted before them, opening up to create a meadow that enclosed a large lake. Thin hunks of ice bobbed upon the surface, unable to attach to each other and create a complete layer.

A few houses came into view. The glow flooding out of their windows did more to illuminate the night than the moon was capable of. Suddenly amongst people again, Dorothy was forced to slow the Jeep. Benton took the opportunity to take it in as much as he could. Having never set foot on the reservation, he wasn't sure what he had been expecting. The houses were battered but still in good shape. Each one stood apart from the others, seemingly with no overall layout or uniform property borders. Smoke spiraled from the chimneys in thin snakes; proof that other people were present. They weren't alone. Benton wished that he could find more comfort in that.

Wapun had put the porch light on. The stark white illuminated a good portion of the carefully mowed yard but couldn't reach as far as the RV Benton remembered from the powwow. Snow clustered around the whitewashed pickets of the fence surrounding the porch and made the royal blue siding look even brighter. It was a one-story, shotgun home; narrow but long.

Dorothy brought the Jeep as close to the porch as she could. The front door opened before she killed the engine. Wapun emerged, a knitted blanket tightened around her shoulders like a shall, her graying hair drifting on the light breeze. Even seated within the dark Jeep, Benton could feel the old woman's penetrative gaze. She could skin someone alive with her eyes alone.

"Who's she?" Theodore asked.

"That's my aunt, Wapun," Logan said. "She'll keep us safe."

Theodore looked the frail woman over. "A soldier and a police officer, and we're going to a senior citizen for protection?"

"Careful, Theo." Logan grinned like a shark. "She's kin, and I'm not above hitting you out of anger."

"Auntie Wapun is an elder and very knowledgeable," Nicole cut in, her voice as sweet as sugar. "She's also able to bless the ground, which will keep the *Yee Naaldiooshii* at bay." She added 'hopefully' under her breath.

Theodore caught onto it instantly. "Hopefully? My wife needs a doctor. Surely there has to be one around here somewhere."

Nicole's diplomatic response was covered by Dorothy's razor-sharp voice.

"Get in the house." She spat out each word and growled the last. "Now."

Everyone evacuated the Jeep as if it were on fire. Benton's feet had barely touched the ground before Nicole rounded the end of the vehicle and grabbed his hand once more. Logan passed the gun to her free hand, a move that startled Benton's parents. Which was probably while Logan managed to scoop up Cheyanne with so little protest.

"Hi, Auntie," Nicole beamed as she sprinted for the stairs, Benton in tow. "We really need to get into the house right now. Love you."

Nicole pushed Benton toward the door but lingered on the porch, keeping watch as Logan ran up the stairs. There was a bloody woman in her nephew's arms and a trembling man a set behind him, yet she still motioned to Benton with her chin.

"Why did you bring *him* here?"

"Skinwalker," Logan said, as he slipped inside the house.

Instantly, Wapun's spine was replaced with a steel rod. "Where did you last see it?"

"Our house," Dorothy said.

Wapun nodded once and motioned to the door. "Get inside. Benton, be a dear and close the curtains. Lock everything."

Benton was slightly stunned to be invited inside. While there wasn't any bad blood between them, she wasn't exactly thrilled by his existence. Sometimes, it seemed like she saw him as a wild animal; fascinating but nothing she wanted too close.

"Go on," Nicole whispered in encouragement. "We'll be right behind you."

Benton slipped inside and found himself in a small box of a mud room. A door to his left opened up to a wood-paneled bedroom of around equal size. It could barely fit the queen bed nestled within. He had to climb over it to ensure that the high set window was locked. A folding door opened up to a shared bathroom. It only took three strides to cross the tiled floor and enter the next bedroom. It was almost identical to the first in size and shape. This one, however, had a narrow bunk bed, allowing for the addition of a sewing machine and miles of neatly rolled fabric. He closed the window and exited the main bedroom door, emerging onto the thin hallway that ran the length of the building. The master bedroom was slightly bigger. With its own bathroom and, surprisingly, a walk-in closet. The living room and kitchen were combined into one. Once more, it was perfectly square. It almost looked as if the house was a collection of blocks bolted together. In all, it barely took ten seconds to completely orientate himself and complete his assigned task.

His parents had been left to settle themselves on a low sofa pressed against the far living room wall. Logan had taken a sentry post by the back door. Floodlights illuminated the backyard. A small porch gave way to a sloping yard that was treated with the same amount of care as the front. That, in turn, transformed to a muddy bank. The lake gently lapped against the shoreline. It wouldn't have been visible at all if the minuscule waves hadn't kept some small clumps of ice in constant motion. The movement helped.

"Is the door locked?" Benton asked.

"Nah," Logan scoffed. "I've decided that it's about time that I died horribly. I've had a good run."

Benton bit back a smile, glad to have the man joking again. Even if it was at his expense.

"You are pretty old," Benton agreed in a deadpan tone.

Logan gasped audibly.

"I'm just saying, it's probably better for you to go out now before you start to deteriorate."

"Deteriorate?" He flexed one arm. "But my bicep is bigger than your self-esteem."

"That's not hard," Benton dismissed.

Logan made a sound of disgust before returning his attention back to the door. "Too sad, boy. You're sucking all the fun out of it."

Benton smiled slightly and shrugged in agreement. Leaning back slightly, he looked around Logan's bulk to check on his parents once more. Nicole was rechecking his mother's shoulder, taking full advantage of the better light and running water. Once more, she declared that it wouldn't need stitches. Apparently, it had just nicked the top of her shoulder. It was a good thing Nicole had set up the trap for a much larger target. Shuffling his weight from one to the other, he wrapped his arms around his chest and tried not to stare. He wanted to go over and check on them but forced himself to keep his distance.

Logan noticed and thankfully kept his voice low. "So, are they just horrible parents or something?"

"No," Benton said, adding with a scoff. "They're miles from perfect, though."

"They love you."

Benton shrugged one shoulder. "Maybe. They took me by accident."

"But they raised you."

"Give or take a few months," Benton said. He caught Logan's gaze and tightened his arms around his stomach. "Yeah, I know they love me. And I love them. But we've hurt each other a lot, and I don't know if we can get past that."

"Yeah, well, staring at them from across the room isn't going to get anything done. Your mom's hurt. They're both scared. This is the first time they've seen a monster in person, right?"

"Exactly." Benton looked Logan over, surprised that he hadn't caught on by now. *Nicole would get it.* "For close to a decade, I've been telling them about all of this stuff. They preferred to think I was insane, shove me through a revolving door of therapists, and drug me against my will. Now they know that it's all true. Any second now, it's going to click for them."

"That you're not human," Logan said.

"Not their son. Not human." Benton shrugged and stared out the window, hoping that the soldier wouldn't hear the quiver in his voice. "They're scared, in pain, and confused. Whatever conversation we have next isn't going to be pleasant. I'm not ready to hear that stuff right now."

Logan stared at him for a long moment. Just as the silence was becoming uncomfortable, he dumped a meaty hand on Benton's shoulder, gave it a reassuring squeeze, and said with all seriousness.

"Sucks to be you."

Benton barked out a laugh, loud and sharp, leaving his throat aching. Wincing sharply, he rubbed his burning throat with one hand and smacked Logan's arm away with the other.

"You're a jerk," Benton grumbled.

Trying to look stoic, Logan returned his hand to Benton's shoulder each time the lanky boy swatted it away, frustrating the *Banshee* until he could do little else but laugh. Then he shifted his hand to the crown of Benton's head and rubbed until his hair puffed up with static.

"Aw, there's a smile. Look at you. You're such a cute little harbinger of death."

Benton shoved at his hand, simultaneously trying to get his hair back under control and stifle his laughter.

"What the hell do you find so funny about this?" Theodore snapped from the couch. "Your mother is bleeding. There's that *thing* out there. And you're just mucking around with this colossal moron?"

"That's my father."

It was the first time Nicole had ever been anything but flowers and sunshine around Benton's parents. It caught Theodore off guard and he stammered for a moment before regaining his composure.

"I know you must feel very protective, Nicole, but I'm disciplining my son right now. It's not your place to interrupt."

The smile that settled upon Nicole's face was terrifying. Still, her voice remained sweet. "Mr. Bertrand, you're here under the protection of my family, including my father."

"Miss. Rider," Cheyanne said through clenched teeth, "just leave this conversation to the adults."

"Nicole," Wapun cut in before Nicole could do anything other than stare. "Would you be kind enough to gather some bedding for me? And perhaps put the kettle on?"

Apparently, her anger didn't outweigh her inclination to be helpful, and she begrudgingly got to her feet.

"Oh," Cheyanne said to regain Nicole's attention. "Stay away from my son."

Nicole gave her a dazzling smile. "Come and get him."

Her hair fanned out around her as she spun on her heel. Benton fell in step beside his best friend as they started down the hallway. His mother called for him but was quickly distracted by Wapun and the necessary introductions. The walk to the first bedroom was quick. Still, Nicole barely managed to get behind the closed door before lapsing into a toddler's temper tantrum – all foot stomping and arm flinging.

"Sorry," Benton said.

Nicole instantly latched onto him, encasing him in a bone-crushing hug and burying her face in his neck. Fine trembles rattled her body.

"Nic?" Benton asked.

"It's a *Skinwalker*," she said, suddenly sounding small and broken.

The word meant nothing to him. But, as he felt Nicole's fingers twist in the back of his shirt, he decided that it wasn't the right time to ask. They'd have to go through it all soon enough.

"It'll be okay," Benton told her, holding her back just as tightly.

Whimpering, she tightened her grip. *This is what Mic was warning me about.* The thought settled upon his mind, reminding him yet again that he wasn't ready. He didn't want to die.

"You're going to be okay," Benton whispered to her. *If nothing else, I'm going to make sure of that.*

Nicole squeezed the air from him before skirting across his shoulders to grip either side of his face. Almost holding him in place so she could rest her forehead against his.

"*We're* going to be okay," she promised. "You're not angry that I was mean to your mom, are you?"

"No."

"Are you okay?" she asked.

"Honestly, I have no idea what to try and process first." He gave it a second of thought. "You're not hurt, are you? It didn't make me do anything?"

"I'm fine. You?"

"I don't think I have any new injuries," he chuckled.

Seemingly channeling her father, she shook his shoulder.

"I guess we should go out there soon," she said at last. "Wapun will wait for us all to be together before explaining it all to your parents."

"Why are we getting bedding, anyway?"

"We're all going to have to bunker down in the same room," she said. "You don't go anywhere by yourself when a *Yee Naaldiooshii* is following you."

Pulling back, she cupped his shoulders and grinned. Bright and happy. Completely covering any trace of fear that had shattered her only moments ago.

"Ready?"

"Yeah, I suppose."

"Where's the enthusiasm?" she asked.

# Chapter 11

Benton sat at the small kitchen table, keeping a close eye on the back door as the others settled. It was hard to feel the same level of foreboding he had now that Wapun had blessed the ground. The night sky was lit up with dancing ribbons of flourescent green. Living auroras swam through the air like eels, drifting across the windows before disappearing out of sight. It was one of the few perks of being what he was; being able to see the display. It was hard to fear the dark when it was filled with the strange hybrid of an aquarium and a laser show.

"What is a *Yee Nandil?*" Cheyanne asked, her curt voice tugging his attention away from a neon pink light-serpent and its fascination with the windchime.

"*Yee Naaldiooshii,*" Wapun corrected.

Cheyanne's brow furrowed. "*Jee Keealdiookey?*"

"How did you even get that one?" Logan asked.

He had one of the kitchen table chairs flipped around so he could rest his arms along the backing, a glass of scotch dangling from his fingers.

"Seriously, you're not even close."

"Logan," Dorothy sighed.

"What? She's not even close! It's almost insulting."

"I'm in a great deal of pain," Cheyanne said.

"Oh, please," he scoffed. "Show of hands. Who here has been stabbed and was still able to form simple words?"

The ice in his glass tinkled as he shot his hand into the air. Dorothy rolled her eyes but humored her husband. Nicole, Wapun, and Benton all lifted their hands, each one having grown increasingly frustrated with Cheyanne over the few minutes they had all been sitting around the living room.

Both Cheyanne and Theodore glared at their son.

"When were you stabbed?" Cheyanne demanded.

"A *Leanan Sidhe* scratched me. If that doesn't count, I was also shot by a *Baykok*."

"What on earth are you talking about?" Theodore asked.

Benton shrugged, absently pulling at the neck of his hoodie. Since the excess material bunched around his shoulders, he had succeeded so far in keeping his bruises hidden. That was another conversation that he wasn't ready for.

"Don't worry about it," Benton mumbled. "It doesn't matter right now."

"So this," Cheyanne tripped over the name again.

Wapun rescued her. "What about the term *Skinwalker*? I've heard that's far more popular amongst you European types."

Cheyanne and Theodore shared a glance. Since both of them worked from home and had no real friends to speak of, they hadn't adjusted to small-town life at all yet. It still struck them both as weird to be reminded that they were the minorities here.

"I think we saw a horror movie about them once," Theodore said. He turned to his wife. "It was about werewolves, right?"

"Oh, yes, that's right." She turned to Wapun with a frown. "It didn't look much like a wolf."

It was the Rider family's turn to look at each other in disbelief.

"No. A *Skinwalker* is not a werewolf," Wapun said.

"Then what are they?" Cheyanne demanded.

"Mom," Benton sighed.

"I'm sorry, but I'm under a bit of pressure at the moment, and being treated like an idiot isn't helping. I just want some direct answers. What is that thing? What cut me? What is going on?"

Benton licked his lips and didn't try to argue. That was until his Cheyanne leveled a glare at Nicole and spat.

"What the hell have you dragged my son into?"

"I'm not exactly your son, am I?"

His parents flinched as if he had hit them.

"We've been trying to talk to you about that for weeks," Theodore said carefully.

"I've been busy," Benton replied, surprised by a surge of resentment. "But I had a whole heap of free time when I was ten and stuck in a hospital bed."

"You were a child–"

"Yeah. I get it," Benton cut him off. "You made a choice. You guys have made a lot of bad choices."

"We're trying the best we can," Theodore said.

"I know that!"

Benton's outburst startled him as much as it did everyone else. Everything he had been trying to ignore pushed at the corners of his mind. He couldn't breathe.

"I know," he said when he felt steadier. "We don't really have the time to talk about that right now. Just, be nice to Nicole."

Tension filled the room until just about everyone was squirming. Cheyanne cleared her throat and forced herself to meet Nicole's gaze.

"I apologize."

"It's okay," Nicole replied, quickly rushing to add, "I'm sorry, too. I know I get overly protective about Benton. He's just not that good at taking care of himself."

"Exactly," Cheyanne declared.

For the first time, the two women had found common ground. Benton wasn't exactly sure how to feel about it. Luckily, Wapun regained control of the conversation before he had to decide.

"Did you see this *Skinwalker*?"

Cheyanne and Theodore nodded, absently grasping each other's hand.

"It didn't look like a wolf," Theodore restated.

"They often don't," Wapun said. "Yes, they can transform themselves into almost any animal. But most eye-witnesses describe a monstrous combination. Something halfway between human and beast."

"But," Cheyanne stammered, as if her brain and mouth were battling for control, "what I saw. It's not possible. Something like that can't exist."

"Oh, it does," Wapun corrected. "Its kind has been amongst us for centuries. What perplexes me is what it's doing so far north." Seeing the confused expression leveled at her, she added, "*Skinwalkers* normally stay on Navajo land."

Nicole shrugged. "I don't think they really care about that sort of stuff anymore. After all, Benton's a *Banshee*. They're Irish."

Theodore released a choked scoff. "A *Banshee*? Now *Banshees* are real too?"

Logan perked up, shooting his wife a smirk. "So, *Banshee* is where you draw the line? *Skinwalker* is cool, but *Banshee* is crossing a line?"

"None of this is alright," Cheyanne shot back before catching herself. "I didn't mean anything by that, Benton."

"It's fine. I'm the first to admit that this is messed up."

Nicole poked up from behind her Aunt's laptop to chime in, "He really does."

"Really?" Benton asked.

She sheepishly went back to what she was doing.

"I suppose the most simplistic way to describe a *Skinwalker* is as a Shaman that turned to black magic."

"Learning some dark spells does *that* to you?" Theodore asked.

The Rider family smirked.

"It takes more than that," Wapun said. "Far more."

Cheyanne asked, "How much more?"

"To seal the deal with the dark forces, a Shaman must offer a sacrifice. One of a blood relative."

"So, this man was willing to kill a relative to have this power?" Cheyanne clarified slowly. "And it wants my son?"

"Yes, I believe it does," Wapun said.

"Why?"

"That's the question, Mrs. Bertrand."

During this time, Nicole had set herself up at the kitchen table with Wapun's laptop.

"I've been working on that," Nicole declared, bouncing in her seat like a child eager to show off something they had just learned.

Benton arched an eyebrow. This time, his reproach wasn't enough to dampen her enthusiasm.

"Let me just add this little disclaimer; my research makes it necessary for me to visit some sites of disrepute." She paused to grimace, then continued on with a smile. "Okay, so from what I've found, *Skinwalkers* have a kind of pecking order – a rank determined upon the power of the rituals they can complete."

"You found a *Skinwalker* chat room or something?" Logan asked.

"Of course not. They're way too secretive for something like that," she said. "But there are a few people that had relatives that became *Skinwalkers*. And a few others that run websites like mine."

"Paranomal.com," Benton offered before his parents could ask. "She's really good at this sort of stuff."

"I'm awesome at this sort of stuff," Nicole said sharply.

Theodore leaned forward, waving one arm while keeping a tight grip on his wife with the other. "I'm sorry, how does this help us? We fled from town. It's clear that you're all scared of it. We already know this thing is dangerous."

"Well..." A trace of self-doubt entered Nicole's voice. "From what I've seen, our *Skinwalker* is incapable of actually touching things."

"It threw a knife at me," Cheyanne snarled.

"Nah, that's on you," Logan said. "You opened a boobytrapped door. Go on, Angel. I want to know what you're thinking."

"*Skinwalkers* have always been physical in the stories. It got me thinking that something must have happened to this particular one. My guess? A ritual gone bad. I've seen it in enough forms by now, all of them twisted monstrosities, by the way, to know that it has to be strong in its own right. So, I researched the heavy hitters, focusing on the consequences. I found this." She paused only to turn her screen to her approaching Aunt. "Third off the bottom. When that one goes wrong, the Shaman can be trapped between reality and the ghost world."

"Ghosts?" Cheyanne mumbled to herself.

"Exactly." Flinging herself back in her chair, Nicole held her hand up for a high-five and waited expectantly for a response.

Benton gave her the requested high-five. "That's why it wants me."

"Does this make sense to anyone else in the room?" Theodore boomed.

"*Skinwalkers* take their power from the ghost world," Wapun said absently, squinting to read the laptop screen. "But they can only use it in ours. If he's stuck between worlds, he's essentially neutered. He needs to break through into either one or the other to regain his power."

"And that's why it wants Benton," Nicole declared. Again, she waited for accolades and was forced to elaborate. "Okay, how to explain. Ah. *Skinwalker* screwed up showing off and its demon friends shoved him in time out. They'll let him go if he offers them a big old apology. Something powerful and unique. Benton's a male *Banshee*. You don't get much rarer than that. And it's got to be an added bonus that he's Death's favorite. But that's just speculation."

"I can see it," Benton said. "I mean, both Death and demons claim souls. And demons are, you know, evil. There has to be some kind of rivalry going on there."

Wapun rested one hand on the tabletop to steady herself. "Benton is part of both worlds. Death with a heartbeat."

"Are you honestly suggesting that a creature of legend wants to perform a human sacrifice with my son?" Theodore asked.

Wapun nodded. "Yes, I'm afraid I am."

Closing his eyes, Benton tried to block out the flood of violent images trying to take over his brain. A single thought still emerged from the depths of his mind. *This is how I die.*

Cheyanne clenched her jaw. "How do we kill it?"

"Call it by name," the Rider family said in unison.

"Its human name," Wapun clarified.

Benton's parents shared a panicked glance.

"How do we do that?" Theodore asked.

"I'm not sure," Wapun said while Nicole snatched the laptop back and declared that she was working on it.

"I think Mr. Ackerman is the key."

"The ghost in my barn," Benton said before anyone could ask. "I found his body the first night we moved in."

"Don't forget the symbol on the wall." Nicole's bright smile became a resentful scowl. "I sure haven't. It's been driving me nuts for almost a year."

"You professor friend said it was from an ancient cult," Benton prompted.

"And the room of cursed land that we found in the *Leanan Sidhe* pit had the same markings." One hand continued to fly across the keyboard while Nicole flopped the other against his chest. "You didn't see it because you can see the cursed fire."

"That, and I was blinded with pain from getting burnt by it," Benton said, lifting his scarred palm as proof.

She ignored that bit.

"Where's this pit?" Logan asked, finishing the rest of his drink in one gulp and leaning over to see the screen.

"The ghost town," Dorothy said.

Nicole once again lifted a hand from the keyboard, this time to push her father out of her personal space. "And you get there by traveling down the road we found Benton sleepwalking on. That's where it wants him to go. That has to be where the ritual went wrong."

Benton tried to squash the prickling, fluttering sensation that had invaded his stomach. "*Has* to be?"

"You're the math boy. You work out the probability."

"So, we have a place of significance and a possible victim." Dorothy visibly winced as the thought hit her. "His family. Not one of them knew that Oliver had disappeared. They had no recollection of anything suspicious. Just a sudden, strong urge to leave Fort Wayward."

Logan whined. "No. You're thinking that the *Skinwalker* possessed them and forced them to sacrifice him, aren't you?"

"Daniel Long Fisher and Rowtag Smoke were good friends with Oliver, weren't they?" Wapun said. "I'm going to make a few calls. With any luck, they might recall someone acting weird towards him the days before his disappearance."

Dorothy shook her head. "I asked after we found the body. Nothing."

"They didn't know to look out for a *Skinwalker* before. There's a reason why it picked him."

"Ask if they ever went down the Highway of the Lost," Nicole added absently, engrossed in her work. "I'm thinking our first trip through there is where it caught Benton's scent."

Dorothy rushed toward the computer. "I'll log onto the police database. Check his record and coroner's report."

"Already got it up," Nicole chimed.

"Whoops," Benton whispered in his best friend's ear.

The fact that she had just admitted to stealing her mother's confidential password, again, hit Nicole like a brick. She snapped her head up, hands freezing in place.

Then the lights suddenly died.

Bathed in the glow of the laptop screen, Nicole rapidly took in the room around her.

"It's here," Dorothy said.

She moved as a shadow through the gloom of the room, retrieving her gun and moving swiftly to the doors.

"How did it get in?" Cheyanne asked. "The blessing."

"It's not alive. The dead can go where they please," Wapun said.

Logan placed his glass on the table and leaped over the chair, his firearm already in hand.

"Come on, Bert-ies," he said, ushering the Bertrand family closer together. "There's going to be some gratuitous violence. But, if you do what you're told and, you know, survive, I'll take you all out for ice cream."

Nicole stared at the computer before her. Her fingers twitched with the urge to do something, but her mind wasn't quick enough to tell her what. *There has to be a way,* a panicked voice screamed within her head. *We just need the name. Get the name!* The first crash made her jump. Startled cries sparked from the group as they searched the darkness around them. Sounds of movement circled the house. Thin curtains that did little to keep out the moonlight transformed everything to shifting shadows. There was only a single gap that allowed a glimpse of the outside world. Every glint of moonlight against the metal windchimes made everyone flinch.

Logan reached over his daughter's shoulder to grab the laptop. The screen became a makeshift flashlight. He scanned the room, snapping the beam from one point to another as unseen forces continued to beat the walls. Nicole lurched to her feet and grabbed Benton's arm. He didn't move. *It has him again!* The thought barreled across her mind and stole her breath. She tugged his arm sharply, drawing him closer. *Keep his mouth closed! Stifle the scream.*

"Over there." Benton's declaration made Nicole jump back in shock. "Kitchen window, upper left corner."

Dorothy whipped around and fired off a shot. The loud crack resounded through the room. Moonlight spilled through the new tiny hole in a solid beam.

"Did I get it?"

"Took down the largest stag," Benton replied. "Back door. Right near the handle."

Once more, Dorothy worked on reflex, puncturing the thick glass. Nicole couldn't tell if the animals retreated or if the gunshots just made everything else sound more distant. A few owl screeches rose over the remaining clatter.

"Are you seeing through the eyes of the owls? Are you mind-melding owls, young man?" Logan asked.

"No," Benton said. "The blessing creates a lot of light."

"I have a lot of follow up questions and expect answers later."

The thundering of hooves gave them a few seconds of warning before the glass back door shattered. A massive stag thrashed, antlers shredding the curtain and bloody hooves gouging at the floor. Steamed bellowed from its nostrils. The ground shook at each failed attempt to get up. With a series of soft pops, the curtain hangers snapped, allowing the material to drift to the ground. Revealing to them the next stag charging toward them.

"Okay, kids," Logan said as his wife opened fire. "Bathroom. Orderly file."

Nicole snatched up a handful of Benton's hoodie and forced him into motion, knowing that his parents would follow. The forgotten bells around his ankle jiggled almost jovially as they sprinted the small distance. He passed the master bedroom, instead leading the way to the shared bath.

"Not the best doors," Nicole noted as she locked the bedroom door.

"But two exits," Benton countered.

Birds slammed against the thin bedroom window, creating a series of cracks as they rushed past. Benton dragged the collapsible door closed behind them while Nicole hurried on to lock the adjoining bedroom door. A crow careened through the window, toppling onto the bed in a hailstorm of glass. Antlers stabbed blindly through the created gap. Crows flooded in around them, a flock of razor shape beaks and talons. Nicole screamed, shielding her head as she threw herself into what limited space remained unoccupied in the bathroom. Benton closed the door behind her. The small window didn't offer enough light to see. But she was bombarded with sound. Gunfire, screams, the thin doors rattling on frail hinges as claws ripped through the thin plastic. And, over it all, an inhuman voice calling for Benton by name.

Benton flinched. The sudden burst of motion ricocheted him off everyone else present. Squinting into the dense shadows, he managed to make out his silhouette. He wasn't looking at her or his parents. His focus was all on something in the slip of space behind him.

"Benton?" she asked.

He didn't seem to hear her. Instead, he turned to look at the door opposite the one he held and back to the corner.

"This is what you meant, isn't it? This moment."

"Benton?"

"Will they be safe?"

"Benton!"

He flinched more at her sudden touch than her shout. Theodore held the other door closed. Cheyanne searched for something to keep the slender window from shattering. None of it mattered. Dread had settled within Nicole's stomach and she tightened her grip on his arm.

"Is Death here?"

She longed to see his face but was left to stare at shadows and shapes.

"Mom? Dad?" Benton called.

"We're right here," Cheyanne assured.

"Just stay calm," Theodore said.

"I really do love you guys. You know that, right?"

Cheyanne pulled the towels off the rack and held them to the window, as if she could catch any flying shards. It dimmed the light even more.

"We love you, too," she said.

"Always have," Theodore grunted as a raging flock clawed and scraped at the door he held. "Always will."

Ice had replaced Nicole's blood. "Benton?"

"I'm really glad I moved here, Nic," Benton said abruptly. "All things considered; this was actually the best time of my life. And that was because of you."

Alarm bells blared in Nicole's head. She clenched her fist, her nails digging through soft material to find tender flesh.

"Thanks for everything, Nic."

"No," Nicole stammered. "You're not saying goodbye right now. I can fix this. I will. I promise."

"I was meant to die in that alley. All these years have been borrowed time."

"Just give me a second!"

His free arm looped around her shoulders and pulled her closer. "Death always wins. It's not your fault. Mic's promised that you'll be okay."

"I'm not letting you go."

She clutched onto him with both hands, burying her face in the crook of his neck. The trembling of his body made a mockery of his calm voice. One arm hooked around her, crushing her tight as hot tears fell onto her cheek.

"You don't have a choice."

Suddenly, he shoved her back. Her heels struck Cheyanne's feet and the two women stumbled against the rim of the bathtub. Theodore gasped in surprise and light burst into the room. Benton had flung open the door. Crows charged the gap like a swarm of bees. Before they could shred him with outstretched claws, he drew in a deep breath and screamed. The flock scattered, thrown back by the near physical pressure of the sound. The walls rattled, threatening to break the glass above the women's heads. Nicole snatched at the towel in Cheyanne's hands, yanking it up, hoping that it might do some measure of good. But the wail died before the window shattered. Numb with shock, Nicole gaped at the now empty door frame.

"Benton!"

She was up and out the door before the Bertrands could make sense of what had happened. They realized soon enough and followed at her heels, back through the bedroom, flopping birds crunching under their feet, and out into the living room.

"Benton! Stop!"

After the oppressive darkness of the bathroom, the moonlight seemed blinding. She spotted Benton just as he leaped over the dead stag and darted into the yard.

"What is he doing?" Logan roared.

"Mic told him to."

It was all she could think to reply. Ignoring her father's cry and narrowly avoiding his grasping hands, she scrambled over the stag. Winter wind encased her, ravaging her bare skin, seeping through the thin layers of her clothes, leaving her shivering and breathless. Massive deer rampaged past her, heads whipping back and forth to slash the air with their antlers. None of them spared a second for her. They were all racing toward the retreating sound of bells.

"Benton!"

She barely had the air in her lungs to call for him. A thin layer of snow crunched under her boots as she sprinted down the slope. Moonlight glistened off of the drifted patches of lake ice. There was barely enough light for her to see the long, narrow limb that stomped down beside her. The *Skinwalker* crawled on all fours, no longer spiderlike, but huge, towering over her with limbs like vines. Taller than the house behind her, it lumbered down to the water's edge, reaching out for Benton.

The frozen mud crackled as he ran over it. The water lay out before him, blocking his path. It didn't take long for the stags to fan out, cutting off all other exits, keeping him in place for the *Skinwalker's* grasping hand. Benton stopped. Shoulders back and chin lifted in defiance, he met the *Skinwalker's* gaze. He didn't scream. A gigantic but brittle hand swooped down upon him, drawing him up with a wild clatter of bells.

She pushed her legs faster, desperate to cover what distance still separated them. The sickening sound of crunching bones brought her to her knees.

No flames. No chanted words or religious artifacts. The *Skinwalker* needed nothing more for his sacrifice than simple death. *It can't touch him. It can't. It can't.* The words repeated rapidly through her mind as she watched the *Skinwalker's* fingers peel back. Benton's mangled corpse dropped like a stone. It was the splash that jarred her out of her shock. Something in the noise drove home the reality.

Tears blinded her as she shoved by the now placid stags. The deed was done. The *Skinwalker* had no more use for them. Gunfire and confused shouts followed her as she waded into the icy water. She barely heard it. Small chunks of ice bounced off of her shins. She latched onto Benton, cradling him to her chest as she fell back into the arctic slush.

"Benton."

A burning coal had lodged itself in her throat. It, and her tears, were the only points of warmth left in her body. A bitter cold consumed her, inside and out. With trembling fingers, she brushed some of his damp hair back from his face. His jaw dislodged at her touch. Something within her shattered. She cradled him close, his broken bones rattling within his skin.

"Nicole!" Her mother's cry barely pushed into her awareness. "Nicole! Get back here!"

Choking on her sobs, Nicole turned to her father's voice. Rage crashed through her grief to see the *Skinwalker* jerk and twist. There was nothing visible to note the difference. But she knew. His sacrifice had been accepted. He would live again.

*Burn him alive.* The thought emerged in the broken haze of her mind. She wanted blood. She wanted vengeance. *I'm going to rip him apart with my bare hands.*

The commotion had drawn the neighbors. Half a dozen stood beside Dorothy and Logan, hunting rifles trained upon the snarling monster. No one pulled the trigger, unsure of what it would do, unwilling to take the risk. Wapun stood slightly before the crowd, cradling a steaming bowl and softly singing a prayer. A few people had the presence of mind to keep the wailing Bertrands back, safely removed from the standoff. It wasn't a hard task. It seemed that neither one could even stand under the weight of their grief.

Nicole's eyes snapped back onto the *Skinwalker*. Bloodlust pumped through her, heating her chilled flesh, nurturing a hatred she had never thought herself capable of.

*Destroy it.*

Nicole shifted, the clicking of Benton's shattered bones tearing her apart, making her weep and growl. She couldn't get up without leaving Benton behind. Caught between fury and sorrow, she staggered onto her knees, glaring at the *Skinwalker*. One last thrash, and its skin peeled from its bones, falling in wet strips at its feet.

And he was a man now. Full and whole. Drenched in blood that gleamed back in the moonlight. He gasped like a man emerging from the ocean. Murmurs and shrieks washed through the crowd and they all shuffled back, guns still locked upon their target.

"Finally," the *Skinwalker* chuckled.

He sounded all too human. Nicole lurched up again, Benton's weight dragging her back down against the muddy bottom of the lake. The *Skinwalker* turned to her. It smiled.

"Hello, again."

Nicole's jaw clenched until her teeth threatened to snap. She bared her teeth in a snarl, unable to work a single word past her gut-wrenching sobs. The air stirred beside her. She snapped around to face it and realized that the comment hadn't been directed at her. A Grim Reaper hovered beside her, its body as black as the night around it. Hands and skull glowing like stars. It was the first time she had ever seen the ghostly specter of death, and she found herself completely numb to the presence.

The *Skinwalker's* grin grew feral. He spared the crowd a single, dismissive glance. "You're going to be busy tonight."

Death turned to look down at Benton's body. Slowly, it reached out, bare bones inching ever close to his corpse. Nicole tightened her grip, twisting slightly to protect him even as she knew there was nothing she could do. *Death wins in the end.*

The Grim Reaper's body fell apart like dispersing smoke. By the time its finger made contact with Benton's forehead, she looked as flesh and blood as any human. But still 'other.' Ethereal. A woman of toneless, milk-white flesh, flowing hair of the same color. And eyes that glowed like liquid silver. The features were alien, but the overall aesthetic undeniably familiar.

"Oh, my God," Nicole whispered. "Mic? Why did you do this? Why did you let him?"

The Grim Reaper smiled and carefully cupped Benton's mauled face. Instantly, his skin began to rot. Soggy hunks of flesh dropped into the lake with sickening plops. His crunched bones dislodged and followed.

"No, no, no," Nicole rambled. "Don't! Stop it!"

Her hands clutched and grabbed, but she couldn't keep him from falling apart. The *Skinwalker's* laugh drifted to her from the shoreline. It stopped abruptly when small patches of bleached alabaster emerged from the muck. Nicole's trembling fingers shifted from desperately trying to preserve the body in her arms to tearing at the rancid goop. Bit by bit, she revealed features that perfectly mirrored Mic's own.

"He died human," the *Skinwalker* snarled.

Mic slowly turned her unnervingly serene face toward the *Skinwalker*.

"Death can't interfere with the affairs of the living."

Nicole couldn't process it at first. It seemed too impossible to be true. Yet it was there. Clear in the anger that coated the *Skinwalker's* every word.

Fear.

*The boogieman's afraid.*

Startled cries rang through the small crowd as pillars darker than the night around them emerged from the water, each one hovering in place. One by one, the Grim Reapers shed their shrouds, revealing women that were almost carbon copies of Mic.

"He was alive!" The *Skinwalker* shrieked. "He wasn't yours! You can't touch me!"

Benton jerked against Nicole's chest. Her scream lodged in her throat as she looked down. It was clearly Benton. Yet undeniably not. A replica made out of frost. As pale as ivory. She couldn't place exactly what had changed. What line or curve of his face had been altered. But he now possessed the same macabre beauty as the Grim Reapers around her.

Benton's eyes snapped open.

"Take him and go." Bravado reentered the *Skinwalker's* voice as he repeated his claim. "He wasn't one of yours when he died. You can't touch me."

Mic rose, swift and silent. Her voice was the whisper of distant thunder.

"He's my son."

It was the *Skinwalker's* turn to be immobilized by the potent mixture of shock and fear.

In that split second, the women changed. Gone were their painfully beautiful shells, replaced by gnarled, grotesque crones. They moved like fog. Untouchable by man or any laws of nature. Swirling around the now frantic *Skinwalker.*

His body morphed, bones popping and flesh ripping as he transformed into something reptilian. The first *Banshee* scream ripped the scales from his skin. An agonized howl turned into a human scream. Nicole could only catch glimpses of the *Skinwalker* from within the swirling haze of *Banshees.* The earth trembled with their wails. Each brutal outburst carved another chunk from the *Skinwalker,* cleaving him to death one inch at a time. The *Skinwalker* made a desperate bid for freedom, darting out across the shoreline. There was no escape. The relentless attack ripped him apart and left him crawling through the mud.

The water stirred. A sudden, unexpected motion that left Nicole's mind reeling. Benton sat up, blinking around in confusion, his luminous eyes casting their own glow over his features.

"Nic?"

Nicole sobbed, shaking hard. He looked past her and got to his feet. There was a grace to his movements that had never been there before. A degree of fluidity that was impossible for something of bone or muscle.

"Get them inside," he said.

With that, he strode forward to join the others. Nicole shook herself from her stupor and scrambled to carry out his command. At first, the crowd refused to move. Their brains couldn't take in the sight before them and handle movement at the same time. It was a matter of getting the first person into motion. The others followed and they were soon fleeing from the otherworldly display before them. Logan flung Cheyanne over his shoulder, leaving his relatives to force the shell-shocked Theodore back into the house.

No two of Benton's wails were ever quite the same, but Nicole recognized it instantly. He joined his voice to the nightmarish choir. Each cell in the air vibrated with the force. Blocking the door with her body to keep the Bertrands inside, Nicole chanced a glance behind.

A geyser of blood erupted within the center of the *Banshees,* spewing a mile into the air, raining down with small chunks of flesh and bone.

Silence suddenly descended.

Forms emerged from the shapeless mist. Individual Grim Reapers that slowly glided out over the lake. Not one of them looked back. They had the soul they had come for. Nothing else held any consequence. Each randomly dropped into the dark depths without leaving a ripple. A soft thud made her turn to the muddy bank.

"Benton," she whispered.

Instinct alone took her back across the yard. Every bone in her body ached. Her body had long since run out of adrenaline. The combination had her fall behind him rather than crouch down. She scrambled forward and pressed her ear against his heart. *There! A heartbeat!* Ice swept down her spine. She looked up to find Mic kneeling on the opposite side of Benton's torso.

"He's got a heartbeat," she sobbed. "He's alive. Please don't take him."

A small smile curled the corners of Mic's mouth. "Of course. He has so much left to do."

Relief left her weak. Still, she couldn't help but babble, "Why? He died. I don't understand."

"He's a male *Banshee* born from a corpse. Death is complicated for ones like him."

*Like him?* "There are others?"

Something strong, ancient, and unrelenting flashed within the depths of her eyes. "He is Legion."

Nicole looked down to his sleeping form and back up to the ghostly woman, unable to sort her jumbled thoughts. "Will he stay like this? Why did you make him go through that?"

"Ahanu Adams," Mic pronounced the words carefully, a gift for Nicole to explore later, "has eluded us for centuries. Hiding between worlds where we could not reach. Benton needed to be reborn for us to end this. It was his part to play."

"And what will this do to him."

"Much."

"That's not an answer."

Mic lifted her serene face, training her gaze upon the moon that poked out from behind the drifting clouds.

"We are out of time. The veil between life and death is never lowered for long. Soon, you and I will once again be on opposite sides of it."

"The veil?" Nicole repeated, mind whirling. "That's why you told Benton to leave when you did. Why the *Skinwalker*, Ahanu, could touch him."

Mic's soft laughter interrupted her thoughts. Whatever crossed her mind, she kept it to herself, and took one last look at her unconscious son.

"I'll take care of him," Nicole assured.

"Of course, you will," Mic said, gliding back toward the lake without moving a muscle. "It's your part to play."

# Chapter 13

Benton absently gnawed on the homemade jerky, watching as the sun began to creep over the horizon. *Day two of my death.*

The first day had been filled with questions he couldn't answer, endless medical checkups, and disconcerting stares. He supposed it would take a while for that to change. An unexpected upside was that no one seemed all that afraid of him anymore. They still kept their distance. But now it was almost reverent. Helping to kill a *Skinwalker* had shifted him from 'freak' to 'celestial being.' Bird squawked, his talons scraping against the trunk floor. Benton retrieved a small chunk of jerky from the bag and passed it to his hungry pet.

"I don't know if owls can eat that," Nicole said.

"I'll look it up later."

Gulping down the dried meat, Bird silently took flight, sweeping out of the open trunk of the Jeep, dipping over the rim of the Buffalo Jump before soaring up into the endless sky. The crisp morning could have been bitterly cold if it weren't for the protection of the sleeping bag. They had been in it for a close to an hour, waiting for the gray sky to give way to the brilliance of dawn. Benton really didn't know why they had a sudden interest to watch the sunrise from this particular vantage point. But he didn't regret it. After everything that had happened, all that had changed, the moment of peace was exactly what he needed.

Out of the corner of his eyes, he noticed Nicole staring at him. "It's still creepy."

"You're just so pretty."

"That's what your father says," he grumbled. Nicole still stared. "Cut it out."

"Sorry. Sorry."

He knew she wasn't sorry at all.

"So, do you want to go first? Or should I?" she asked.

Benton thought it over, trying to decide which conversation he wanted to get over with quickest.

"You go."

She nodded. "There's not much to find on Ahanu Adams. The records were deliberately destroyed. Then it hit me. Fort Wayward can burn their files, but they couldn't control what neighboring settlements did."

"I'm ready to be impressed."

"It's all speculation and guesswork, but there's a record of Ahanu Adams working his way across the country when the white settlers first came through. People remembered him because he was trying to gather followers for a cult. He claimed that he could look through the veil and reconnect them with lost loved ones."

"He was really using them to boost his own power?"

Nicole swallowed thickly. "There's no actual record. However, I have basic math skills."

"I don't know what that means."

"Records show that a group of 600 settlers left Ottawa to create Fort Wayward, Ahanu Adams amongst them." Again she paused. "Fort Wayward's records say the number was closer to 200."

"400 people go missing, and no one says anything?"

"It's a Siksika tradition to move camp after a death to avoid any potential ghosts. And, if Ahanu had possessed them, none of them would have remembered what happened."

"Or they knew they were responsible and couldn't face it."

"Not something you'd want to tell your children, either."

"When I was your age, I joined a *Skinwalker's* cult and slaughtered a few hundred innocent people. Yeah, that's an awkward conversation." *And explains why only some bloodlines were still open to him. The sins of the father and all that.*

"When Oliver's sacrifice failed to bring him back, I think he stayed in the woods, feeding off the evil there to keep himself tethered to this world. Remember that theory – how the death of one paranormal creature would draw in others? I think it also created an energy that helped him. All this time, we were making him stronger."

"I wonder what his death will bring in," Benton mumbled around a new strip of jerky.

"Your turn," Nicole chirped.

Benton licked his lips and sighed. "There's not much to say."

She thumped his arm.

"Alright, alright," he muttered. "You know how they found out that we're related?"

"You were brutally attacked, needed a blood transfusion, and found out that two people with their blood types couldn't create a kid with yours," Nicole rattled off swiftly.

"Well, of course, the cops opened up an investigation. The leading theory was that I was abducted."

Nicole was clearly trying desperately not to hurry him but utterly failing in keeping a calm composure.

"There was a horrible storm the night I was born. A crash on the highway overwhelmed the hospital. Cheyanne gave birth to a child without a doctor present. Just a nurse. The child was stillborn." Benton took a sobering breath. It was still strange to think that he wasn't Benton. That name had been chosen for someone else. "In a weird twist of fate, the same nurse had been the only one in the room when a strange woman had died during childbirth. When the cops tracked her down, she admitted to switching us. By her thinking, she had spared everyone involved from painful truths."

"Why didn't the investigating officer tell you?"

He shrugged one shoulder. "I guess they decided I had been through enough."

"I'm sorry," Nicole whispered.

"They found them," Benton said absently. "The graves I mean. They had buried Jane Doe with little baby John Doe. That's why they left me with Svetlana. They went to pay their respects. I might have yelled at them a lot for that one. Guess what mom said in their defense? 'He was our son.'" He snorted. "She was my mother. I had something to mourn, too. But no, they just let me live some other kid's life for another few years."

"It's your life, Benton," Nicole insisted.

"Yeah."

The sky was filled with brilliant shades of gold and pink. They watched it for a moment before he had the courage to add.

"I kind of feel like a jerk now. I mean, I have a second chance to learn a bit more about my mom. Mic will be back once this all settles down. They're not going to see their son again." He groaned. "I should apologize, shouldn't I?"

"Maybe," she winced. "Although I think there's plenty of apologies that need to go around."

Benton smirked. "And I think we're finally in a place to say them. We, um, well, we came to an agreement. I get to keep living with you guys, but the Bertrands are going into family therapy. I also have to have three meals a week with them."

"That's great."

"They're still scared of me."

"But they're willing to put the work in, actually build a relationship with you. That's a good thing, Benton."

She beamed at him and he couldn't help but smile back.

"Yeah. It is, isn't it?"

"Of course, it is." Hugging one of his arms, she tipped her head against his shoulder. Apparently, being reborn as a *Banshee* didn't necessitate a growth spurt. They were still the same height. "And I'm always right."

He chuckled and they both let out an exhausted sigh. Sunlight had stretched out across the ground by this point, gilding the grass and making the snow shine.

"Fort Wayward really is a beautiful place," Benton said absently.

He felt Nicole's smile against this shoulder. "What did I tell you the first day we met? Huh?"

Benton rolled his eyes even as he smirked. "You're always right, Nic."

"I know. Stick with me, Benny-boy. It might rub off on you."

\* \* \*

If you enjoyed the book, please leave a review. Your reviews inspire us to continue writing about the world of spooky and untold horrors!

Check out these best-selling books from our talented authors

### Ron Ripley (Ghost Stories)
- Berkley Street Series Books 1 – 9
  www.scarestreet.com/berkleyfullseries
- Moving in Series Box Set Books 1 – 6
  www.scarestreet.com/movinginboxfull

### A. I. Nasser (Supernatural Suspense)
- Slaughter Series Books 1 – 3 Bonus Edition
  www.scarestreet.com/slaughterseries

### David Longhorn (Sci-Fi Horror)
- Nightmare Series: Books 1 – 3
  www.scarestreet.com/nightmarebox
- Nightmare Series: Books 4 – 6
  www.scarestreet.com/nightmare4-6

### Sara Clancy (Supernatural Suspense)
- Banshee Series Books 1 – 6
  www.scarestreet.com/banshee1-6

For a complete list of our new releases and best-selling horror books, visit www.scarestreet.com/books


See you in the shadows,
Team Scare Street